# THE
# ANCIENTS

# THE
# ANCIENTS

*A Novel of Time Travel*

Shand Stringham

# THE ANCIENTS
## A NOVEL OF TIME TRAVEL

*This is a work of fiction. All of the characters, names, incidents, organizations, and dialogue in this novel are either the products of the author's imagination or are used fictitiously.*

*iUniverse books may be ordered through booksellers or by contacting:*

*iUniverse*
*1663 Liberty Drive*
*Bloomington, IN 47403*
*www.iuniverse.com*
*1-800-Authors (1-800-288-4677)*

*ISBN: 978-1-4917-9221-6 (sc)*
*ISBN: 978-1-4917-9223-0 (hc)*
*ISBN: 978-1-4917-9222-3 (e)*

*Library of Congress Control Number: 2016904215*

*Print information available on the last page.*

*iUniverse rev. date: 03/24/2016*

# In Appreciation

*In preparing the manuscripts for this trilogy, Gettysburg Revisted, History Quest, and The Ancients, I have relied on a substantial group of highly talented people. These good friends assisted me with many writing tasks and challenges including chapter timeline chronology, storyline continuity, protocols for time travel, technical details of high security military environments, long-term archival storage, the wonders of theatre organs, and, of course, grammar, punctuation, and spelling.*

*Along with all the men and women of the Armed Forces I have worked with through the years culminating with my assignment at the U.S. Army War College, I particularly want to acknowledge and thank those who directly supported the writing and preparation of this trilogy: Brent and Lana Blackham, Karen Westergard Gill, Shellie Stringham Harris, Sandra and Robert Heinzman, Max and Janet Manwaring, John Oliver, Don and Nancy Schoeps, Lou Sheehan, Dwight Steinly, Corrie Stringham, Carson Stringham, Diane and Brent Thompson, Steve Trask, and Janine and Ron Weyers. I express my heartfelt gratitude and appreciation to all of them for being an important part of my life and contributing so much to my writing efforts.*

*And finally, I express my profound gratitude to my wife, Quin, who faithfully reads and edits everything I write and who provided patient support and understanding throughout the writing and preparation of this trilogy.*

*Shand Stringham*
*Carlisle Pennsylvania*
*March 2016*

# Prologue

*Air Canada Flight 2666, Final Approach into Ronald Reagan
Washington National Airport, June 4, 2013, 3:56 p.m.*

Samira Shadid sat restlessly in her seat between her mother and
father, anticipating the landing of the big jet following what seemed
to her was an interminably long flight from Beirut, Lebanon.
The passengers hadn't been allowed to deboard the plane at the
intermediate stopovers in London and Iceland and the nine-year old
had been cooped up on the plane for over fifteen hours now. The
plane was packed and Samira hadn't been able to lie down on an
empty row of seats like she had on the flight over. Her legs ached
from sitting so long and she was becoming fidgety and anxious to
get off the plane.

     The pilot had just announced that they were in the final
approach for landing, and the crew had turned the lights back up
in the cabin and asked everyone to fasten their seatbelts and return
their tray tables to an upright and locked position. Samira's ears kept
popping from the change in cabin pressure, and she realized belatedly
that she had to go to the bathroom. As a young flight attendant
passed their row hurrying down the aisle towards the rear of the
aircraft, Samira reached over her father and tapped her on the arm,
"Is there still time for me to use the bathroom again before we land?"

     The flight attendant was surprisingly abrupt and rude,
answering her at first in Lebanese Arabic between clenched teeth,
"Uskuti, mashgul shi," and then switching over to broken English,
"Be quiet, I'm busy. No time for that. Too much to do before we get
there. You must stay seated. It will not matter anyway."

     Samira was surprised by the attendant's brusque manner. She
shrugged and sat back in her seat, resigning herself to waiting until
she was in the airport terminal building. Her mother leaned over and
tried to comfort her. "We will be there soon, Samira, and we'll look
for a restroom as soon as we get off the plane."

\* \* \* \* \* \* \* \* \* \* \* \* \* \* \* \* \* \* \* \* \* \*

The flight attendant hurried on past them down the aisle toward the rear of the plane to the aft galley station and closed the curtains behind her. She reached down under the counter and lifted her flight bag up onto the galley counter. She unzipped the bag and withdrew a compact machine pistol with a long straight clip. She tucked it up under her arm with her finger wrapped tightly around the trigger. She glanced down at her wristwatch and tracked the motion of the second hand as it moved slowly back around the watch face. At precisely 4:00 p.m., she parted the curtains and stepped back down the aisle toward the front of the plane, her machine pistol gripped tightly in her hands. As she moved forward, she heard gunshots at the front of the plane on the other side of the curtain that divided the economy seats from first class. The flight attendant smiled as a man stood up in his seat towards the front of the economy class cabin and fired an automatic pistol into the chest of the passenger seated across the aisle from him. Another man further back in the plane also stood and began making threatening gestures with a weapon to the other passengers in his near vicinity.

* * * * * * * * * * * * * * * * * * * *

As the flight attendant made her way down the aisle with her weapon in hand, a large burly man seated in front of Samira and her family tried to stand up and attempted to disarm her as she passed by. She whirled around and fired directly at his face and the man collapsed back into his seat. The bullet passed through his head and the headrest behind him and struck Samira in the shoulder. Samira screamed out in pain as a dark red blood stain spread down across her dress. A second bullet hit Samira's mother in the neck and she slumped over off to the side, her head tilted at a sharp angle leaning the window. Samira's father attempted to disengage his seat belt to stand up and confront the attendant. The attendant fired another round into his abdomen and he was thrown back halfway out of his seat into the aisle.

Samira reached up desperately and touched the side of her mother's neck where she had been shot. As she brought back her hand, it was covered in thick, dark blood. In childlike panic, Samira wiped the blood off on her dress, trying to make the horror all go away. She let out another piercing scream and the terrorist turned back toward her and shot her again, this time in her other shoulder. Samira ceased screaming and thrashing about, wedged there between her dead mother and dying father, motionless, her eyes rapidly glazing over and petrified in terror.

\* \* \* \* \* \* \* \* \* \* \* \* \* \* \* \* \* \* \* \* \*

During the next few minutes, several other frantic passengers tried to get out of their seats to thwart the hijacking but to no avail. The hijackers killed them all as they attempted to stand and move into the aisle. Several of the bullets broke through the windows and side panels of the aircraft and the air rushed out of the cabin. The plane was at a sufficiently low altitude so that there wasn't an explosive, rapid decompression, but the emergency face masks deployed throughout the cabin, adding to the chaos of the situation.

Without warning, the aircraft banked sharply to the right, causing many of the passengers seated on the left side of the plane who had unfastened their seatbelts to spill out into the aisle. Gripping the nearest headrest with one hand to maintain her balance, the flight attendant fired into them at random, spattering blood everywhere.

\* \* \* \* \* \* \* \* \* \* \* \* \* \* \* \* \* \* \* \* \*

Samira sat terrified in her seat, searing pain emanating from the two shoulder wounds down through her body. She shuddered in fear as she saw the terrorist flight attendant turn around and start to make her way back towards them in the rear of the plane, stepping on bodies in the aisle as she went. As she came abreast of their row, Samira's father reached up and grabbed her leg as she attempted to step over him and he wrested the weapon from her grasp with his other hand. The attendant lost her balance and fell backwards against the seat behind her. Samira's father pulled the machine pistol around and pointed it directly into her face.

"You are too late," she shrieked at him. "It is all over now."

Samira watched in horror as her father stared motionless at the young flight attendant. He held the weapon in front of him, rigidly fixed on her head. The terrorist glared back at him, a look of disbelief and rage crossed her face. "Do it! Do it! she shouted. Kill me! Kill me! I want you to do it. We're running out of time."

As the terrorist screamed at her father, Samira painfully brought her hands up and covered her ears. The plane suddenly lurched to the left and then back to the right. Mr. Shadid struggled to stay seated upright in the aisle, bracing himself against the seat cushion behind him. The plane jerked again, this time even more violently than before, and Mr. Shadid's index finger clamped down on the trigger of the machine pistol. A short burst of the ammunition remaining in the clip sprayed the young flight attendant, knocking her backwards. Samira sat there open-mouthed as she watched the terrorist drop into the aisle on top of other dead passengers. When the firing at last stopped, her father dropped the weapon to his side and keeled over in death. Samira, struggled through her pain to unfasten her seatbelt to move to her father's side, but she didn't get far. A second later, the huge jet airliner flew into the side of the Washington Capitol Building and the interior of the cabin exploded in a wall of flames instantaneously incinerating everyone onboard.

# Chapter 1

Barton Stauffer and his wife, Gwen, walked slowly, hand-in-hand, down the ancient Inca Trail, picking their way carefully through the rocks and rubble that littered the path. The Stauffers were enjoying themselves immensely. Although they had their five children in tow, it was almost like a second honeymoon for them visiting Cuzco, and Machu Picchu again. The five Stauffer children ran ahead of them down the slope, playfully dodging in and out of the crumbling stone walls that framed each side of the path. The children came to the ruins of an Inca *tambo*, a stone building that served anciently as a way station where *chasqui* foot messengers could rest after a long run along the high Andean trail carrying *quipu*, or knotted cord messages, from one end of the Inca empire to the other. The children played tag, racing between the gaps in the walls of the *tambo*, and then continued on down the path toward the ruins of Machu Picchu.

Stauffer, had celebrated his sixtieth birthday a half year earlier, and his hair and beard were beginning to show streaks of gray. He wore a canvas floppy hat to shield the sun from his eyes. He stepped cautiously between the rocks in the path at a leisurely pace, taking in the sights as they descended down the trail into Machu Picchu. Gwen, several years his junior, had the look and vitality of youth about her. Her blonde hair and unlined face belied the many years the couple had been together. Looking down the trail, she tugged on Stauffer's arm, urging him to move faster.

"Barton, we really need to hurry more," Gwen said. "The kids are getting too far ahead of us."

Stauffer smiled contentedly. "Yeah, they're definitely having a good time. I wish that I still had their energy." Stauffer sat down on a large carved block of stone that stuck out from the end of the *tambo* wall and Gwen sat down beside him, snuggling up to him in the brisk, mountain air. He turned to his wife and playfully swatted a long blonde lock back from her eyes. "You know, Gwen," Stauffer said, "this has been a great family vacation. I'm really glad we finally decided to come back to Peru and see some of the sights again

1

now that the children have grown some." Looking back up the trail they had just descended, he added, "and I'm definitely glad we decided to make the climb up the Inca trail this morning. It's been a great experience for all of us." Looking back down the trail in the direction of the children, he suggested, "Gwen, you better go on ahead. I'm going to rest here for a minute and experiment with my camera and take some photos using my new telephoto lens." Stauffer leaned back and pulled the camera up to his eye and took a candid snapshot of his wife without warning. When she laughingly pulled on his arm in protest, he snapped a couple more.

Giggling, Gwen gave up. She stood up and took a step back. "Okay, you impossible man," she said looking back at the children. "Catch up as soon as you can. Remember that we've got a reservation for dinner at the hotel restaurant at six o'clock. That's only just a little over an hour away."

"I'll be there in plenty of time for dinner. Get the kids all cleaned up and I'll be along shortly."

Stauffer sat there on the wall watching the figure of his wife grow smaller and smaller in the distance as she hurried down the trail to catch up with the children. He leaned back against the wall, and took a deep breath. He was having a difficult time breathing in the thin air but he hadn't wanted to alarm Gwen. He sat there for a few minutes taking in measured, deep breaths until his light-headedness cleared. He pulled the lens cap off his new lens and attempted to frame Machu Picchu in the silhouette of the crumbling *tambo* in the foreground with the towering peak of Huayna Picchu rising up from the river valley floor into the sky high above the majestic ruins below.

A rustling sound behind him alerted him that he wasn't alone. He jerked around and found himself staring into the face of his old boss from Carlisle Barracks, General Cubby Goldwyn, who was standing there in the shimmering, iridescent outline of a time portal, set back against the ancient stone *tambo* doorway to his left.

General Goldwyn's sudden, unexpected appearance took him by surprise. The use of temporal technology out in the open like this violated the rules they had established long ago down in the Hole. "Sir, what are you doing here?" Stauffer asked. "Aren't you concerned about revealing the existence of temporal technology appearing out in the open like this in broad daylight? What if someone else were to come along right now?"

"Actually, Barton," General Goldwyn responded, "I chose my moment carefully. I've already scoped it out pretty thoroughly on the temporal observation monitor in my office. There won't be anyone else coming down the Inca trail for the rest of the evening, and the site guards set up a rope barricade across the entrance to the trail down below an hour ago so that no one would try to come up this way and get caught after dark. We're all alone. We can talk freely. Security is almost as good here as it would be if we were sequestered in my office down in the Hole back at the Barracks."

"Well then, sir, the obvious question is just what brings you here to Peru?"

"Barton....., I hate to interrupt your vacation time with your family. You know that I wouldn't do it if there were any way I could avoid it. There has been a terrorist attack on Washington, D.C. and I need your help back in the Hole to plan and implement a temporal interdiction strategy."

"A terrorist attack?.... On Washington, D.C.?"

"Yes, Barton. It's a matter of national security. We're working under the 12-hour limitation imposed by the Temporal Council. I'm going to need you for a day.... perhaps two at the most.... back at the Barracks. When we're through with you, I'll make sure to get you back here to Machu Picchu in time for dinner with your family at the hotel. Agreed?"

"Yes, sir. What's the situation in D.C. and back in the Hole?"

General Goldwyn's face immediately clouded over. "I was sitting in my office this afternoon when a breaking news story flashed across my unclassified Internet monitor. As soon as I saw the news flash, I got Garner Wilson and Bill Tipton focusing the efforts of Hole and Repository analysts to figure out the extent of what we are looking at. I had already been keeping tabs on you with your family vacation, and I came through the portal to retrieve you as soon as I had them moving to organize their teams. When we get back to my office, only thirty minutes or so will have elapsed real time from the 12-hour clock start time limitation. I'll brief you on what I know as soon as we get back to my office. Garner and Bill should be standing by with an update shortly after we arrive. Are you rested now sufficiently and ready to get back into the fray?"

"Yes, sir. I'll follow your lead."

"Good, then let's get moving."

General Goldwyn turned and walked back through the portal and disappeared. Stauffer followed closely behind him, leaving the Inca Trail deserted once again as darkness fell over the Urubamba Valley.

# Chapter 2

When Stauffer emerged on the other side, he found himself back in General Goldwyn's office in the Hole, a top-secret DOD research facility buried deep beneath Carlisle Barracks, Pennsylvania. Stauffer hadn't been there for over half a year, ever since he'd retired from active duty to stand down and spend more time with his family. He had kept very busy during the intervening months, and he hadn't really missed it all that much. But now, emerging into General Goldwyn's office, he began to experience the tingling excitement that he had always felt working on black project temporal issues that kept them busy down there in the Hole and the Repository.

General Goldwyn hurriedly glanced at the clock above the door and then turned and circled around his desk and began rummaging through papers on his desk. While Goldwyn was otherwise engaged, Stauffer took the opportunity to look around the office to see if anything had changed. Against the far wall, General Goldwyn still had books packed tightly together in floor-to-ceiling book shelves. Right in the middle of the bookcase wall, sitting on a broad, recessed shelf, was a bust of Louis Pasteur with a brass plaque tilted next to it on a mahogany pedestal, framing a quote by the French scientist himself,

**"Chance favors the prepared mind." Louis Pasteur**

Stauffer turned to face the opposite wall where General Goldwyn's conference table and chairs took up the greater portion of the room. Above the table, affixed to the wall, was an enormous 120-inch flat screen monitor, a new addition installed since he had last been there. On the end of the conference table, Goldwyn had positioned a laptop computer and wireless keyboard that Stauffer guessed were used to display temporal observation captures on the large wall monitor. In the center of the conference table, sat a bronzed adult oxford shoe. Smiling with recognition, Stauffer walked over and picked it up, turning it over and over in his hands. It was his own shoe that had been sliced through when he'd come back through a time portal during their first mission for Repository History Quest operations at the Barnum American Museum fire in New York City in 1865. He and his teammate were in a hurry to get back into the Repository to get out of the smoke that was filling the 4th floor of the museum, and Stauffer had called out, "Clear," while he was still coming through the portal. The recovery team leader, Bill Tipton, immediately shut down the portal to keep the smoke from filling up the temporal lab. As the portal closed, the back of Stauffer's shoe and heel had been sliced off cleanly, exposing the back portion of the interior of the shoe. Stauffer shuddered as he recalled that day. Had Tipton shut down the portal just a few micro-seconds earlier, it could have just as easily sliced off a piece of his heel or even his whole foot or leg. Stauffer looked over at General Goldwyn questioningly, without speaking.

"Yes, that's your shoe, Barton. I had it bronzed for you to keep out there in front of everyone in the Repository as a reminder of the dangers of the temporal technology and of not following our rules and protocols precisely. We kept it there on the conference table in your old office for six months after you left, and then it occurred to me to bring it over here to use as a training aid during my inprocessing briefings for all new personnel. It serves its purpose well. It seems to get everybody's attention right off. I ask everyone to pick it up and look it over. They fixate on the missing slice and start imagining the worst if they were to mess up. It's an effective way to get everyone focused on our temporal protocols right from the beginning of their assignment here."

Stauffer set the shoe back down in the middle of the conference table. As General Goldwyn returned to rifling through his papers, Stauffer continued eyeballing the room. On the wall above the entrance door to General Goldwyn's office hung a large, imposing digital clock with three readouts. This was also new. At the top of the clock, spelled out in a large raised Roman font, was the ancient adage, *"TEMPUS FUGIT,"* — *"Time flees"* —. Directly below it was a more contemporary rendition, *"Time's a-wastin."*

The top readout on the clock appeared to display the current time in military time: 16 hours, 43 minutes, 27 seconds. The middle readout appeared to be a stop watch of sorts with the digital numerals increasing in value. It read 0 hours, 28 minutes, 27 seconds.

The bottom readout appeared to be counting down the time. It read 11 hours, 31 minutes, 33 seconds. Motioning to the clock, Stauffer broke the silence again. "What's this, sir? I don't remember that clock being there when I was last here in your office. Pretty slick. Is this what you're using now to track mission time ?"

"That's right, Barton. I just had them installed a couple of months ago. There's one just like it in Bill Tipton's office in the Repository and in Garner Wilson's office here in the Hole. It's a countdown clock to help us keep track of the twelve-hour limitation imposed by the Temporal Council during emergency response temporal operations. As soon as we start the countdown, the three clocks are all synchronized; and we can monitor the time we have left from any of the three offices. As soon as I got wind of the disaster in D.C., I started the clock and got Garner and Bill on the horn to get their people started working on the issue. I told them to meet me here in my office at x+30 minutes real time. That's the second readout. They should be arriving momentarily."

"Pardon me, sir. Is that why you brought me here? You've got a catastrophe on your hands in Washington, and you want me to play in on it just like the old days before I retired?"

"Pretty much, Barton."

"But, sir, with Garner and Bill heading up their teams in the Hole and the Repository, just what is there left for me to do? Seems like I'm just going to be a supernumerary and get in everybody's way."

"Far from it, Barton. I brought you here to expand the brain trust. This one is big…. a really big problem…. and we're going to need to throw all the gray matter at it we can."

"Excuse me again, sir. But, before everyone else shows up here, maybe you'd like to fill me in on some of the details of what's gone down. You said you would brief me when we got here. What's this terrorist attack all about?"

"Right. A commercial airliner just flew in for a landing at Reagan National Airport about 35 minutes ago real time, but overshot the runway on the approach. It glided in low over the Tidal Basin and then banked sharply up the Mall and slammed into the Capitol Building and the whole place exploded in flames. The President was addressing a special joint session of Congress, and we don't know his fate at this point. Without his direction, I initiated an intervention to use temporal technology to eliminate this incident from our thread of history. That's what you're here for—to help us figure out how to do it. Have I piqued your interest yet?"

Stauffer just stood there dumbfounded at the enormity of the crisis, attempting to think through and process what General Goldwyn had just said. Finally he spoke, "Yes, sir. Anything I can do to help out."

# Chapter 3

As Stauffer was speaking, there was a buzzing sound from the direction of General Goldwyn's desk, and he reached up and pushed the door lock release button. As the door swung open, Colonel Garner Stuart Wilson IV and Colonel Bill Tipton burst into the room. Both had apparently been running and were out of breath. With them was Dr. Miriam Campbell, a research astrophysicist on loan from Jet Propulsion Laboratory in Pasadena. Dr. Campbell had joined the Hole staff a year ago when they had worked with NASA, Air Force Space Command, and JPL to avert a planetary disaster from a comet that had been discovered on a collision course with Earth. When the emergency had been dealt with, Dr. Campbell stayed on as a key member of the staff.

General Goldwyn greeted them, "Glad to see you, Garner.... Bill.... Miriam. Welcome Barton back. I brought him along to augment our team and to help keep us focused. We've got some serious work to do here, and not much time to do it."

"Actually, sir," Stauffer broke in, "you just demonstrated to me with your little side trip to pick me up in Peru that with the temporal compression capability of time travel, we pretty much have all the time in the world to plan and execute on this one. We just have to launch whatever intervention we decide upon and get it in under the real time limitation reflected on your countdown clock there on the wall. If there's something we need that is going to take a bunch of time, we can always compress it into our actual timeline using time travel."

Wilson, Tipton and Dr. Campbell all looked at each other, not entirely understanding what Stauffer meant by "little side trip," and then, realizing the beauty of what Stauffer was suggesting about time compression, all broke into big smiles. "As always, Barton," General Goldwyn acknowledged, "you're right on point. That's great thinking. Welcome back. I knew there was a good reason to invite you along to the party."

"Yeah, Bart," Tipton joined in, "it's about time you got back off that extended vacation of yours to put in some honest work. You've been missed." Tipton winked and smiled at his old artillery buddy. Wilson and Dr. Campbell chimed in as well, offering words of welcome.

General Goldwyn broke in on the pleasantries, "Let's get down to business, folks. Please, all gather around my conference table. Garner, let's hear first what you and your people in the Hole have come up with so far."

"Roger that, sir," Wilson responded. "As soon as you got us moving on the news, we did temporal scans on Capitol Hill to check out the actual crash and the extent of the destruction that followed. It was basically a 9-11 type terrorist attack, using a commercial jet airliner as a flying bomb. Both houses were meeting in a special joint session with the President, presenting an enormous target of opportunity for the terrorists to take out the greater portion of the U.S. seat of government with one violent act of terrorism. Due to security protocols, the Vice President was not present at the session but was sequestered in an unnamed location. It appears that the President did not survive the attack, and the Vice President has already been sworn in by a Federal Judge. Although there were some survivors, most members of the House and Senate perished in the flames or were crushed under the collapse of the Capitol building roof."

"Thanks, Garner. That's just about what I had surmised watching the initial news broadcast before I alerted you all.... It's an absolutely worst-case scenario. We're going to have to get this one right. The consequences are too dire for the survival of the nation otherwise."

Turning to Bill Tipton, General Goldwyn continued, "How about your team in the Repository, Bill? What have they turned up?"

"Sir, we focused on the terrorists and the situation on the plane. There appear to have been five terrorists, four thugs whose job it was to strong arm and subdue the crew and passengers, and one pilot-trained hijacker to take out the pilot and co-pilot and fly the plane after the takeover.... pretty much the same thing we saw for 9-11."

"Where did the plane originate?" Goldwyn asked.

"The flight started in Beirut. It was an Air Canada flight in conjunction with Middle East Airlines. None of the terrorists are on Interpol's Do-Not-Fly list. These are all new recruits who haven't been involved in terrorist operations prior to this attack. All of the terrorists apparently passed through the security check point without raising an alarm on anyone's scope."

Stauffer sat at the conference table digesting all of the information that Wilson and Tipton put out. Tipton started to continue his briefing on the background of the terrorists, but Stauffer interrupted impatiently, "Bill, we can cover the terrorists' backgrounds in detail later. For now, we need to know where the terrorists were located on the plane, and we need a schematic of the plane itself. Here's our first compression requirement. Bill, call your people in the Repository and have them produce a large chart-sized schematic of the plane mounted on cardstock of some kind. Have them indicate where each terrorist was located on the plane just prior to the hijacking takeover. It's going to take them an hour or two to produce the chart and that's okay, but when they've got it ready, have someone step through a time portal to deliver it here to General Goldwyn's office in...." Stauffer looked over at the mission status clock readout above General Goldwyn's door.... "15 seconds."

"I get you, Barton. Done." Turning to General Goldwyn, Tipton asked, "Sir, may I use your desk phone?"

General Goldwyn nodded, as he absorbed the flow of the conversation. "Sure thing, Bill. Get moving."

Tipton stepped over to the desk and phoned his people. He stood there for several seconds speaking in muffled tones and then hung up. "There. It should be here about now."

Tipton moved over to the door to General Goldwyn's office and opened it. Pete Pendleton barged through the door, carrying a large cardboard graphic. "Where do you want it, Bill?"

"Let's set it up on the flip chart easel, Pete, right over here at the far end of the table. Can you walk us through the schematic?"

"Sure thing. This is the seating layout for an Airbus A320, the airframe for Air Canada Flight 2666. It was configured with 138 seats, and the plane was near capacity with 127 passengers. It originated in Beirut, Lebanon, with two stopovers, one at London Heathrow, and a second in Iceland at Keflavik International, to drop off a large group of Icelandic tourists and pick up some additional passengers. While it was there at Keflavik, the plane topped off with fuel for the final run into Reagan International. The passengers already on the plane didn't deboard at either stop. With the flight originating in Beirut 15+ hours earlier, we're well outside the 12-hour limitation to pick the terrorists off before the flight initiated. We're going to have to deal with the terrorists on the plane."

"They refueled at Keflavik?" Stauffer asked. "Why?"

"That's right, Bart. Filled it right up for the continuing flight on to Chicago after the DC stopover. Makes for a faster turn-around transition at Reagan. They like to move them in and out of there fast. They also switched out the pilot and co-pilot but apparently kept the cabin crew on board."

"Well, that also means that as the plane approached Reagan," General Goldwyn observed, "it still had an appreciable amount of fuel in the wing tanks."

"Yes, sir. We think that the terrorists selected that flight precisely because of the flight plan to arrive in Washington airspace with enough fuel left on board to do significant damage flying into the Capitol building."

Stauffer acknowledged General Goldwyn's point and continued, "If we're going to intervene effectively to prevent a disaster, we need to get critical information out on the table up front to begin formulating a plan. First off, we need to know when the terrorists subdued the passengers and crew and took over the plane. And we need to know where each one of them was physically located on the plane immediately before the takeover."

"Actually, only three of the terrorists were onboard as passengers," Pete responded. "The other two were working as flight attendants. That's how they got the guns and ammunition aboard—in their airline flight bags. The security was lax at Beirut, and they just waved the attendants on through security without checking anything. We think that the airport security agents were in on it. We're using the temporal observation monitors to check them out now. Once the plane took off, the flight attendants distributed the guns and ammunition surreptitiously to the other three."

Stauffer was impatient and interrupted, "Okay, got that. But where were the three passenger terrorists sitting and where were the two flight attendants positioned when they took over the plane?"

"Ah, right." Turning back to the seating chart for the flight, Pendleton quickly pointed out their locations. "There was one terrorist seated in first class in seat 2D.... here. The two terrorists in coach were in seats 20C and 28D.... here and here. The male flight steward was up front in the first class galley.... here, and the female flight attendant was back in the rear of the plane.... here."

"Which one of the terrorists is pilot-trained?" Dr. Campbell asked.

"The flight steward in first class."

"Okay, that's good, Pete. We're making progress," Stauffer acknowledged. "But to help us keep track of these thugs, let's give them working names we can remember.... Um..... how about Muppet names.... Bert, Ernie, Kermit, Fozzie, and.... Uh.... Miss Piggy. Does that work for you? Those ought to be easy enough to remember." Stauffer stepped up to the chart and began labeling each of the terrorists in large block letters with a marker pen as he spoke. "Kermit is the flight steward in first class who is pilot-trained. Fozzie is sitting here in first class, seat 2D.... Bert is the guy sitting in coach seat 20C.... Ernie is sitting in coach seat 28D...., and Miss Piggy is the flight attendant at the rear of the plane. Now we have to figure out a plan that will take out all five of the Muppet gang without injuring any of the other passengers or damaging the plane. Any thoughts or ideas?"

General Goldwyn spoke up, "Pete, did your team assemble a video capture of the terrorists taking over the plane? Perhaps if we saw the whole thing from start to finish, it would give us some ideas."

"Yes, sir," Pete responded with a big grin. "I've got just the thing. Can I use your keyboard here to bring it up?"

"Go right ahead," Goldwyn answered, sliding the wireless keyboard toward him around the end of the table.

Using the temporal monitors, Pete's team had assembled a collage of video captures of the five terrorists so that those assembled around the table could see the actions of all five simultaneously throughout the hijacking on a five-way split screen. Pendleton briefed as the scene unfolded on the monitor. "It was obvious that the hijackers were working off a well-orchestrated, synchronized plan. They all looked at their watches and began the hijacking at precisely the same moment. Kermit, the steward in first class, knocked on the door to the pilot's cabin forward ostensibly to bring them some fresh coffee. When the door opened, he fired a handgun with a silencer at each of the crewmembers up front, killing them with one bullet apiece. Closing and locking the cabin door behind him, he pulled the dead pilot from his seat and heaped his body against the door. Then he climbed into the captain's seat and took over control of the plane. No one on the ground was any the wiser that the plane was now under terrorist control."

The scene on the monitor moved back to the terrorist in first class as Pendleton continued his narration. "Meanwhile, Fozzie, the terrorist in seat 2D stood and turned slightly, firing two bullets into the passenger in seat 3D behind him. Bert, the terrorist in 20C did the same, firing into the passenger across the aisle seated in 20D. "We think that those guys must have been the air marshals on the flight," Pete observed.

"While Kermit piloted the plane on the final approach into Washington, DC, airspace, the four other terrorists moved quickly through the two cabins making threatening gestures at all of the passengers with their handguns. One of the passengers towards the rear of the plane, made as if to stand up and confront Miss Piggy, the female flight attendant. She put a bullet right through his forehead, and he collapsed back into his seat in a pool of blood. The bullet passed through the seat headrest and struck the passenger, a little girl, in the seat behind him in the shoulder. Then she shot the passengers on each side of her." During the next ten minutes, the horrified observers around the table watched as the terrorists killed another dozen passengers that attempted to get out of their seats to intervene. Three of them were children caught in their field of fire. The temporal observation video capture continued on until Kermit flew the plane into the Capitol building and it exploded in flames.

Everyone in General Goldwyn's office sat there in their seats, unmoving in shock after the video ended, processing the gruesome scenes they had just witnessed. Finally, General Goldwyn spoke up. "Thank you, Pete. That was sobering and…. informative. Now, I want you to do one more thing. Switch the scene over to the joint session inside the Capitol building. We need to see the results of the crash on those inside. Run it in super-slow motion, please."

"Are you sure, sir? When we ran that in the lab, several of our people got sick and ran out of the room."

"At least run us a piece of it, Pete. We need everyone to understand what these terrorists brought about and what we are up against."

"Sure thing, sir." Pete typed another entry into the keyboard, and the scene changed. The President was standing at the rostrum speaking to the joint assembly. It looked very much like a scene from the President's annual State of the Union address. After just a few seconds elapsed time, the aircraft came crashing through the wall of the chamber in slow motion and the entire hall was filled with explosive flames. Even in super-slow motion, the effect in the room was almost instantaneous as the President and members of Congress were engulfed in the conflagration and incinerated.

"That's enough, Pete," General Goldwyn said with a wave of his hand. "Thank you. Does everyone have the picture here? These five terrorists are cold-blooded killers, and we need to exercise every capability in our grasp to rid the planet of them and their kind. The temporal technology provides a defensive capability and that is how the Temporal Council prescribed its use. But we're going to use it here in an offensive mode to terminate these guys with extreme prejudice. I hereby authorize the use of deadly force throughout the entire intervention operation. Do what is necessary to bring the terrorists under control and eliminate them. Do you all understand?"

There was silence in the room momentarily, and then Garner Wilson spoke up. "Sir, we've got at least a dozen experienced Special Forces guys on staff here in the Hole and Repository. We could open up time portals next to these guys and take them out by surprise."

"Yes, Garner," Stauffer responded. "I had been thinking the same thing, but there's a downside to that approach. It could easily devolve into hand-to-hand combat in the cabin with the terrorists firing off weapons all over the place, perhaps injuring passengers or knocking out windows with a subsequent high altitude rapid decompression problem. Furthermore, even if we were successful in subduing the terrorists, we are still left with the problem of a plane full of 130+ passengers and crew who would have witnessed the use of temporal technology. We can't have that. We've got to come up with a plan for taking out the terrorists without anyone on the plane seeing much of anything that would reveal the existence of temporal technology."

The room fell silent again. "Do you already have an idea of how we might do that, Barton?" General Goldwyn asked.

"Well…. yes, sir. I haven't thought it all the way through yet, but in principle, I think I know how we can use the technology to take out the terrorists and keep them from harming others on the plane."

General Goldwyn scowled impatiently, "Well, don't keep it to yourself, lad. What do you have in mind?"

"Well, sir, the idea occurred to me after I picked up my bronzed shoe," Stauffer responded, motioning to his shoe sitting in the middle of the conference table. "The shoe was sliced inadvertently when we accidentally turned off the portal while I was still coming through it. Had it happened a fraction of a second earlier, it might have severed my foot or even my whole leg."

"That's right. So how does that play into this situation?" General Goldwyn was anxious for Stauffer to get to the point.

"Well, sir, let me demonstrate with a simulation. Here, Bill…. Garner…. Pete…. All of you stand up. Bill, you be Fozzie, the terrorist in first class. Make a pistol with your fingers and point it toward the front of the plane at the door. Good. Now, Pete, you're going to be a team member in the Hole who opens up a time portal directly in front of the muzzle of the gun. That portal leads directly into an empty vault in the Repository. I'm another team member in the Hole, and I'm going to open up a time portal directly behind Fozzie. Now, we're going to do this in slow motion to see how it works. Garner, you come up behind Fozzie and reach through the portal and give him a good push forward. Fozzie, when you're pushed, it takes you by surprise. Allow the momentum to carry you forward. Pete, as Fozzie's gun hand passes through the portal that's been opened up in front of him, shut it down. Now, as Pete toggles the portal off, it creates a discontinuity between his gun hand and gun and the rest of Fozzie. The gun hand severs from Fozzie's body and drops to the floor in the safety vault, and Fozzie is left standing there on the plane disarmed…. literally. And there never was any danger of a loose bullet flying around the cabin of the plane."

"Bart," Tipton exclaimed, "that's brilliant. But, what if Fozzie stumbles and falls all the way through the portal and into the vault? What happens then?"

"Shouldn't be a problem. We keep the vault sealed shut and simply evacuate the air from the vault. Fozzie quickly keels over from lack of oxygen, and we have one less terrorist to deal with on the plane."

"Bart, I like it," Wilson offered. "But won't severing the guy's arm with the temporal technology cause massive arterial bleeding spurting blood all over the cabin?"

"Good question, Garner," Stauffer responded. "As I see it, there are two possibilities. First,.... what you describe..... massive bleeding, which would make it an unsatisfactory solution. The second possibility is that severing the guy's arm will cauterize the separation on both sides of the portal which makes it an ideal approach to the problem. We're going to need to run a quick test to see which is the case."

"I've got an idea, Barton," Pendleton spoke up. "On my way to work this morning, I watched the car in front of me run over a squirrel that darted into the roadway just down the street from my house. Squashed it flat. We could have the guys back in the Repository track the squirrel just before it darts into the road and initiate a time portal right in front of it as it steps down from the curb. We'll track it in slow motion, and when the squirrel is halfway through the portal, we'll shut it down and see what happens."

"Good, Pete. That will work. I'm generally against animal experimentation but the squirrel is dead no matter what we do. We're just going to learn something from it and maybe even give it a more humane death. Call the Repository and get it set up. Have them show up here at General Goldwyn's door in..... 30 seconds with the results."

"Roger that. General Goldwyn, can I use your phone?"

General Goldwyn nodded assent again, and Pete quickly called in instructions to the Repository. Almost as soon as he hung up the phone, the buzzer on General Goldwyn's door sounded.

Stauffer went to the door himself, and Maggie Martinez came in breathing hard. "Barton, good to see you again. I'll get right to the point. When we closed the portal on the squirrel, it cauterized the wound. There wasn't any blood on either side. It sealed up the two sides of the slice as if it had always been that way, and the squirrel died instantaneously, apparently without any pain."

"Thanks, Maggie. Take a seat here at the table." Stauffer turned back to the group at the table. "Well, it looks like this approach has great possibilities. No blood. We can keep it a clean, almost antiseptic operation."

General Goldwyn had watched the demonstration with great interest and quickly processed the new information concerning the cauterizing effect of cutting off the time portal with the terrorists part way through it. He sat back in his chair at the conference table considering the implications of the strategy and then finally spoke, "Barton, I think you've got a good strategy for taking out the terrorists, but there's five of them. What is your plan for coordinating our attack on them all? If we do it piecemeal, one of them might panic and start shooting there in the cabin."

"Good point, sir. I propose that we run the video Pete brought a few more times and identify the precise moment when we could engage all five terrorists at the same time. It will have to be before Kermit attempts to go into the captain's cabin and the other terrorists fire on anyone else on the plane. If we attack all five at the same time, no one gets spooked and everyone gets taken care of simultaneously."

"Sounds good," General Goldwyn acknowledged. "How do you propose that we proceed?"

"Well, sir, I think that we ought to form five separate operational teams working out of five different time labs in the Repository. Each team ought to have five or six team members. Each team needs to be well-rehearsed in what each team member is going to do to take out their assigned terrorist. We ought to be able to script a strategy for each individual terrorist in three or four hours at most. We could be ready to launch our intervention right after that. But time really isn't a factor here. If it turns out that we take too long in the planning phase, we'll have to back track using the time portals to run the intervention at an earlier time to stay within the 12-hour time limit. I think that will stay within the intent of the response time limit imposed by the Temporal Council."

"Done," General Goldwyn announced in a loud voice, slamming his fist on the conference table top. "Garner, you and Bill organize the five teams. Use the Special Forces guys as much as possible, but use our other experienced time travelers as well. When we're done with this, the President and Congress get to finish their joint session meeting, and the folks on Air Canada Flight 2666 won't be aware that anything much out of the ordinary has occurred. The air marshals will probably notice that the terrorist passengers are gone and the airline will probably initiate an investigation into their missing flight crew members. We'll let the FAA deal with that. But, when the plane sets down at Reagan the way it was supposed to, there won't be any terrorists left on the plane. They'll be gone. Disappeared. Oblivion. Do you understand my intent?"

Everyone in the room nodded understanding.

"Good, now get moving. Barton, you monitor what each of the teams is doing during the planning phase and offer any observations and suggestions as necessary. Keep me posted on how it's all going. Have a videographer film each of the team's planning activities and forward the video files to me over the classified intranet. I'll be sending a Minibago back minutes before mission launch so that we'll have a fairly detailed record of the entire event."

Everyone stood and quickly filed out the door. Dr. Campbell and Stauffer lingered behind to talk with General Goldwyn.

"Something wrong, Miriam?"

No, sir," Dr. Campbell answered. "Not at all. I was just wondering about this Minibago device. I've been here almost a year now and I still haven't got it entirely figured out. What's it all about? How does it guard against changes you might otherwise make in the past?"

"Good questions, Miriam," General Goldwyn responded. "I thought you had been read in on that. The Minibago was Barton's idea. Barton, would you please explain it all to Miriam?"

"Sure thing, sir.... Miriam, when we were first experimenting with temporal technology, we had no idea if we were affecting the past or creating significant changes that would carry over into the future.... our present. We reasoned that if we did make any changes in the past, it would send a temporal wave forward into the future to our present, rewriting history as it went, and we wouldn't have any idea that anything had been changed. It would seem to us that it had always been that way."

"I'm following you so far, Barton," Dr. Campbell acknowledged. "So how did you get around that temporal conundrum?"

"We knew that there was a possibility that a temporal wave could move from the past into the future into our present rewriting history in its wake, but we reasoned that it may not move backwards into the past. We came up with the idea of setting up an anchor station in the distant geological past.... 500 million years into the past, during the Ordovician era. The anchor station was a decommissioned nuclear submarine nicknamed the 'Winnebago' with a complement of almost a hundred crew members. At the time, we were being very careful with our temporal observation and time travel missions, and couldn't detect that we were making any changes in the past. But we didn't know for sure. We ran a couple of tests with the Winnebago crew to prove it out by running temporal observation and time travel interventions from the Hole onto the Gettysburg battlefield, and then sending CDs of a broad variety of history books back to the Winnebago anchor station. The historians onboard compared the CDs with the digital files of the same books they had recorded before we launched the Winnebago into the past. The theory was that if they detected differences between the histories recorded on the control files and the CD files we sent back, then that would be a sure sign that we were somehow changing the past and our own present."

"And what did you find," Dr. Campbell asked. "I would think that the mere act of observation could possibly exert some kind of influence in changing what you were observing."

"That's exactly what we found, Miriam," Stauffer admitted. "We didn't know we had been changing anything because we hadn't been able to detect it. But the initial Winnebago tests revealed that we were knocking huge holes in our historical past and creating a whole new present for us in the process. We discovered in horror that we were changing technology, society, and even language. We made the decision to stop all temporal operations and bring the Winnebago home, but before we could, we suffered a total temporal discontinuity and we lost contact with the Winnebago and its crew, including Hank Phillips, Max Manchester, and Mitch Monahan."

"That's awful, Barton. But you must have somehow managed to bring them back."

"Not exactly, Miriam. When we briefed the Temporal Council on the problem, they ultimately directed General Goldwyn to shut down all temporal operations. But before we did, I came up with the idea for a 'Minibago', a small, self-contained apparatus that could receive CDs of history we sent back and then forward it back to us after any type of a temporal intervention...., including shutting down all temporal operations. So that's how we salvaged it all. We knew that if we went back and shut down temporal operations before we had even begun, then we would lose all of the knowledge and expertise with the temporal technology we had accumulated thus far. So, just before General Goldwyn went back through a time portal and terminated the development of temporal technology before it even began, we launched a Minibago containing CD files about the whole program and everything we had learned down here in the Hole. Armed with that information that came back to him on that first Minibago, General Goldwyn restarted temporal operations in the Hole and we were able to side-step all of the developmental problems that we had the first go-around. In other words, we didn't actually bring Hank and Max and Mitch and the rest of the crew from the Winnebago back from being marooned in the geologic past.... they never went there in the first place on the timeline we're on now."

"I've got to think about that one, Barton," Dr. Campbell said. "It makes my head swim."

"That's okay, Miriam. None of us really entirely understand it. But we've perfected a practical methodology to monitor and ensure that we're not making significant changes in the past. On a weekly basis or any time we launch any kind of significant temporal operation into the past, General Goldwyn launches a Minibago mission to keep track of anything we might inadvertently change. For the most part, we've been doing a pretty good job. We've learned our lessons well and we're not changing much in the past at all. But every once in a while, we mess up and change the past a great deal and General Goldwyn sends the emergency response team into the past here in the Repository to abort that temporal operation before we run it and avoid the changes altogether."

"But, General Goldwyn, why are you going to launch a Minibago right before we launch our temporal intervention for Flight 2666? Don't we know that we're going to change history with our intervention?"

"That's right, Miriam," General Goldwyn countered. "But, if we didn't, we wouldn't have any memory or record of what has happened and what we averted by launching our intervention in the first place. In fact, we might not even be cognizant that we had launched an intervention. We need to document the terrorist attack and our own temporal intervention efforts."

"Miriam," Stauffer interjected, "with this operation to avert the disaster with Flight 2666, we're going to make a huge change in the past and it will move us off onto a very different timeline path than the one we're on right now. The historical record from the Minibago that General Goldwyn launches is going to seem almost like an almost impossible fairy tale that thankfully will now exist only on another timeline that never happened here."

"I'm beginning to understand it all better now. Just one more thing, General Goldwyn," Dr. Campbell said. "After all my time here, I've heard references to Minibagos hundreds of times but I've never actually seen one. What does it look like?"

"Perhaps I could show you, Miriam." General Goldwyn said. "Follow me."

General Goldwyn walked over to the far wall adjacent to the outside wall next to the hallway. He pressed a button on the wall which activated a locking mechanism and a door swung outward from the wall into the room. As the door opened a light came on in a room behind it, illuminating a large storage area packed with steel shelving. To the side of the door were several stainless steel roll carts, each loaded with an electronic apparatus about the size of a small microwave oven on top. General Goldwyn wheeled one of the carts out into his office and over to the side of his conference table.

"This, Miriam, is a Minibago,.... compact.... minimal footprint...., but just as effective as the Winnebago was at informing us about any changes in history we might chance to make. As soon as the teams report they are ready to launch the intervention, I will load up several CDs and DVDs with all the videos of our meetings and preparations, and the newscasts of the terrorist attack, and we'll have a complete record of everything that has transpired, even though it never will have happened on our own timeline following the intervention. It's a pretty slick system.... And now, I think you two better be hurrying down over to the Repository to ride herd on the plans and preparations for the temporal intervention. I think this is going to be really interesting."

Dr. Campbell turned and started to leave, but Stauffer lingered behind.

"Something else, Barton?" General Goldwyn asked.

"No, sir," Stauffer responded. "I just wanted to thank you for bringing me on board for this one. I haven't felt so energized in months. It feels real good to be back here."

"Barton, it's real good to have you back."

# Chapter 4

Barton Stauffer was in his element back in the Repository. Colonel Wilson and Colonel Tipton had the five teams organized and started on planning within 30 minutes of leaving General Goldwyn's office. They brought each of the selected team members up to speed quickly in a general group orientation meeting at the conference table in Tipton's office, showing them the video collage of the terrorist takeover so that they all knew what they were up against.

After they had viewed the videos, Stauffer stood and addressed the group solemnly. "You have all seen the videos and know what has gone down. It is our job now to plan and execute an interdiction mission that will put in place a new timeline in which the terrorists don't accomplish their mission objective. We have been told by General Goldwyn to attack the terrorists with extreme prejudice. I think that you all know what that means. We will give no quarter and take no prisoners. As we all know, the passengers on a commercial jet airliner are all packed in very close proximity to one another. We want each team to carefully consider your options and develop a strategy to take out your assigned terrorist, in concert with the other teams acting simultaneously, without detection by the other passengers. We will accomplish our mission if we can thwart the terrorist hijacking without any gunfire on the plane and remove the terrorists from Flight 2666 without anyone on the plane seeing anything that would reveal the existence of temporal technology. Now, that's a tall order."

Stauffer looked around the room and continued. "The first order of business is for all five teams to agree on the start time for the intervention on the plane. To accomplish that, I want you all to review the collage video of the entire terrorist hijacking of the plane several times. As you watch the replays, make careful note of the best windows of opportunity for your team to take out your assigned terrorist."

After watching the collage video three more times, they came up with two options that would work well for all five teams simultaneously. They ran the video one more time, running it in slow motion around the two time options to see if one option offered greater advantage over the other. The two options were only separated by 23 seconds actual running time on the plane, but they ultimately decided as a group that the first time frame provided the optimal opportunity to get the terrorists off the plane without bullets being fired and without the rest of the flight crew and passengers being aware of what was going on.

With the start point for the temporal interventions decided upon, the teams divided up and went to work developing plans to take out their individual assigned terrorist. Stauffer sent them off with one last word of encouragement. "Get to work now, and we'll gather again in several hours to see what you've come up with. The clock is running. We'll meet here at X+4 hours."

Pete Pendleton had a brainstorm and formed a logistics support team to locate and transport an entire movie set mockup of the interior of a similar airliner stored in a Hollywood studio warehouse to the Repository so that the teams could rehearse their plans in a realistic environment. The only location large enough to accommodate the mockup was right down the center of the Repository gallery. The gallery was an enormous quonset hut-shaped corridor that stretched several hundred meters down the entire length of the Repository. A continuous string of bright light fixtures were arrayed along the high arching gallery ceiling stretching off into the distance. Spaced along the curved walls at regular intervals were hundreds of massive steel doors on each side of the gallery leading into high security vaults where the Repository teams stockpiled immense quantities of recovered antiquities for future examination and long-range storage.

The teams took turns using the mockup to stage rehearsals to test out the assumptions that went with their interdiction plans. Stauffer spent the majority of his time watching the team rehearsals on the mockup and offering suggestions and advice based on what he saw on how the teams could fine-tune their activities to better ensure mission success.

Within three hours, all five teams felt that they had an effective plan that would get the job done. Wilson and Tipton sent General Goldwyn video captures of the five rehearsed plans and told him they were ready to launch and were standing by waiting for his go-ahead. General Goldwyn uploaded all of the files that documented the terrorist attack onto CDs and DVDs and launched the Minibago. Then, he personally went over to the Repository where a command center had been set up in Bill Tipton's office around his conference table. General Goldwyn joined Stauffer and Dr. Campbell there and gave the thumbs up to begin operations. Repository tech personnel had set up all the extra temporal monitors available in the command center so that General Goldwyn, Stauffer, and Dr. Campbell could observe what was happening in each of the time portal labs as it happened. The entire operation was rehearsed to be carried out with a minimum of verbal conversation. Most communication between team members would be accomplished with pre-arranged hand and arm signals. Stauffer glanced up at the mission clock on the wall. The countdown clock showed that they were well ahead of the 12-hour deadline with 7 hours, 47 minutes, 15 seconds remaining.

Team #1, led by Bill Tipton, was set up in Time Lab A. Their target was Kermit, the flight attendant, pilot-trained terrorist who was preparing to take out the entire flight crew in the captain's cabin. It turned out to be a relatively simple process to take him out unobtrusively. At launch time, Kermit was working in the forward galley with the curtain drawn about to take out his weapons and ammunition to begin the hijacking. The other flight attendant working first class was several rows back pushing a cart up the aisle picking up empty bottles and glasses from the beverage service in preparation for the plane's descent.

With the curtain drawn, no one in the first class cabin could see Kermit. Tipton's team simply initiated a time portal in front of him and then a small portal in back of him and gave him a hard push through the portal. As Kermit fell forward, they disengaged the portal as he was halfway through. Kermit's severed top half, cut at a diagonal above his waist, fell dead to the floor in the locked safety vault, the two weapons still clenched in his hands. Kermit's lower half dropped to the floor in the galley.

"Quick guys," Tipton urged his team, "Let's get the rest of Kermit out of here." They quickly reopened both portals and pushed Kermit's lower extremity and remaining weapons through the portal and shut down both portals again. When the legitimate flight attendant returned with the beverage cart to the front galley, Kermit was nowhere to be seen.

Team #2, led by Garner Stuart Wilson IV, was set up in Time Lab B. They were responsible for taking out Fozzie, the terrorist in seat 2D at the front of the first class cabin. The team had to take Fozzie out before he had the chance to turn and fire two bullets into the Air Marshal in seat 3D behind him. As Fozzie stood up with his gun drawn, Wilson signaled his team with the verbal command, "Now," to open a time portal directly in front of him in the aisle and another directly behind him. Wilson moved up behind the terrorist, and gave him a slight push through the portal. Fozzie's gun hand passed entirely through the portal as he fell forward. No one on the plane ever saw the gun. It went through the portal as soon as he turned. When Wilson saw that the gun was all the way through, he signaled for the team to shut down the portal, severing Fozzie's hand holding the gun, which dropped to the floor of the safety vault in the Repository. However, the nerves in the severed hand contracted the fingers on the pistol grip holding the gun tightly and the trigger finger slowly pulled the trigger of the gun back as it lay there on the floor. The gun fired and the bullet began ricocheting off the walls of the vault. On the fourth ricochet, the bullet passed back through the time portal they had reopened to push the terrorist's body through the rest of the way, and the wayward bullet hit the terrorist in the neck and passed on through the portal behind him into the Garner Wilson's chest, passing through his heart and lodging in his rib cage.

"Ughh," Wilson gasped as the bullet knocked the wind out of him. He stood there momentarily transfixed, surprised by the sudden turn of events, and then with one final physical exertion, he pushed Fozzie entirely through the portal in front of him. Wilson then collapsed backwards into Time Lab B into the arms of his teammates. His teammates quickly shut down both portals and tried to resuscitate Wilson, but it was a lost cause. He was already dead before they could lower him to the floor. When Dr. Gates came running into the time lab a moment later and checked for vital signs, he shook his head and had his teammates cover Wilson's body with a sheet. Surprisingly, no one, not even the Air Marshal, noticed that the passenger in seat 2D had disappeared. They were all engrossed in watching a movie on the seat back in front of them.

At the command post in Bill Tipton's office, when General Goldwyn, Dr. Campbell, and Stauffer saw Wilson get hit in the chest and keel over, Dr. Campbell let out a scream and Stauffer leaped to his feet to run to the aid of his friend in the next vault over. General Goldwyn stopped him in his tracks with a stern order, "AT EASE, soldier." And then more softly, "Please, Barton, sit back down again. There's nothing you can do for him now. We'll deal with this when the operation is over." "But, sir!" Stauffer started to argue, and then resignedly sat back down again.

Team #3, led by Colonel Jared Lincoln, operated out of Lab C. They were responsible for taking out Bert, the terrorist in coach seat 20C. They had a similar problem as Team #2. They had to take out Bert before he could fire across the aisle into the Air Marshal in seat 20D. Team #3 had developed a similar strategy and set up a portal in the aisle directly to the side of Bert's seat. As he stood to turn and fire on the Air Marshal, they simply gave Bert a hard shove from behind, and he fell through the portal into the vault. They allowed Bert's body to pass entirely through the portal before they shut it down, and so the terrorist arrived in the vault disoriented but whole and alive. He started firing his gun in the darkened vault as the team initiated the air evacuation system. A ricocheting bullet from his own gun caught him in the side of the head just before he lost consciousness from lack of oxygen. He was dead as he hit the floor of the vault. None of the passengers seemed to have noted Bert's disappearance.

Team #4, led by Maggie Martinez, was operating out of Lab D. They were responsible for taking out Ernie, seated in coach seat 28D. The two seats to the side of him, 28E and 28F, were unoccupied and the people sitting in row 29 directly behind him were asleep, and so the team came up with a novel strategy. Using the mockup seats set up in the Repository gallery to test their strategy, they developed a horizontal time portal set up on a vertical lifter. They opened the portal on the floor and moved it quickly up the three seats in row 28. As the portal passed upward through the seats, the entire row of seats was transported to a closed vault in the Repository with Ernie still belted into his seat.

As soon as they shut down the portal, Maggie hit the air evacuation button, and the air was rapidly sucked out of the vault. Ernie struggled to get his seat belt unbuckled but quickly lost consciousness. Looking through a temporal observation portal, Maggie watched as he passed out and slumped over. "Quick, she ordered, pump the air back into the vault and let's get him out of his seat and secured." As they pumped air back into the vault. Maggie directed two team members to enter and unfasten Ernie's seatbelt and pull the terrorist's inert body away from the airline seats over to a gurney where they disarmed him and duct taped his hands and feet together in case he regained consciousness. When Ernie was clear from the row of seats, Maggie gave the signal to energize the time portal once again and move the row of seats back into the plane so that only a micro-second passed in real time from the moment that the row of seats was removed from the plane and then reappeared back in place. For the passengers sleeping in row 29 directly behind it, they didn't even notice the switch out. Neither did anyone else sitting nearby. The operation went entirely unnoticed.

Team #5, led by Colonel Wynn Osterlund, was set up in Lab E and was responsible for taking out Miss Piggy, the female terrorist masquerading as a flight attendant, working in the coach galley at the rear of the plane. As she took out her weapon she had concealed in her flight bag and turned to move through the curtains into the passenger cabin, the team activated a time portal and she walked right through it into a vault which was quickly evacuated of all air. She was able to squeeze off several rounds as she fell to the floor but was unconscious within half a minute.

Each team had timed their temporal intervention for optimal efficiency. Each of the five interventions was pulled off real time on the airplane in less than 45 seconds. And so, when all five of the terrorists were subdued and removed from Flight 2666, General Goldwyn turned to Stauffer, who sat there at the conference table stiff-lipped and pale. "Barton, I need you to think this through calmly with me. It appears that our friend Garner Wilson has finally bought the farm, in the long-standing tradition of his forefathers. It is something that he has long anticipated and even hoped for and that places us in a bit of a dilemma. Do we use the temporal technology to intercede to prevent Garner's demise or do we permit the natural order of things to stand? What are your thoughts?"

Stauffer responded slowly, "Whew, sir. That places it in a whole new perspective. I hadn't thought of it that way. Yes, I remember well when I first went into Garner's office and he recited his genealogy of his noble ancestors and how they had all died on the field of battle. I could tell that he wanted to follow down that path."

General Goldwyn added, "I spoke with Garner several times on the matter myself, and each time, it was apparent that from his perspective, not having died on the battlefield haunted him as evidence of his failure to honor his ancestral lineage. And now, he has fulfilled that destiny, performing an act of noble military service that ultimately will save the lives of thousands today. However, we have the power in our hands to prevent his death. It wouldn't be difficult to make it happen. But do we have that right? I'm in a quandary on this one."

"Sir, I understand what you're saying, and it's a point well made. But I think that following the splashdown of the UARS satellite, he changed his thinking and recognized the importance of life and living. I think that he was finally at peace with his ancestors. I don't think he would object to our interceding on this one. Would you like me to do it, sir?"

"No, Barton. I need to do this myself. But I think you're right. It's just a simple fix. I'll be right back." General Goldwyn entered a few keystrokes into the computer keyboard in front of him on the conference table and the iridescent outline of a time portal appeared in back of him in front of Tipton's I-Love-Me wall. General Goldwyn strode over to the portal and disappeared as he passed through it.

Almost instantaneously, he reemerged and walked back over to the table. "I think we need to get over to Lab B and check on Garner. He took a bullet in the chest. That's got to hurt. General Goldwyn led Stauffer and Dr. Campbell on the trot out the door and over to Lab B where Wilson's team had set up for the operation. As they entered the lab, they found Dr. Gates there at the side of a gurney. Wilson was stretched out on the gurney with his Repository jumpsuit pulled back. A Kevlar body armor vest lay crumpled on the floor next to the gurney. General Goldwyn was ebullient. "How's our patient doing, Doc?"

"Well, his body has absorbed a lot of trauma. The Kevlar vest Garner was wearing stopped the bullet from penetration, but it did little to absorb the kinetic energy of the bullet itself. He's going to have a nasty bruise for quite some time and, as you can see, it's right above the area in his chest where his heart is located. I'm going to put him on a heart monitor for the next 48 hours to make sure that the impact of the bullet hasn't caused any arrhythmia."

Garner Wilson lifted his head from the gurney and looked up at General Goldwyn. "Sir, Doc Gates is being hyper-cautious and I'm grateful for that, but I need to get back to work. We still have the last phase of the operation to take care of, and I don't want to miss that."

General Goldwyn nodded, "I understand, Garner." Turning to Doctor Gates, he asked, "Do you think that we could keep Garner on the firing line, working out of a wheel chair for a few more minutes, Doc?"

"That shouldn't be a problem, but I do want to hook him up to a heart monitor. We can just wheel it around with him."

"That work okay for you, Garner?" General Goldwyn asked.

"Sure thing, sir. I can live with that. I'm just glad to be alive. Sir,.... could I speak with you privately a moment?"

"Yes, Garner. Would all of you folks please find something else to do for a minute or two so that Colonel Wilson and I can have a little privacy?"

Everyone quickly departed the lab, and General Goldwyn pulled up a chair close to the gurney where Wilson lay prostrate. "Sir," Wilson spoke up, "I've got a question for you. Just how is it that you gave me a Kevlar vest to wear just before mission launch and no one else seems to be wearing one? Is there something I should know about this operation? Is it just a matter of coincidence that the only member of the five teams to pick up a bullet in the chest just happens to be the only one wearing a Kevlar vest?"

"Pretty astute, Garner. Actually, I don't know what to tell you. I remember giving you the vest, but I don't remember anything out of the ordinary which prompted me to do it."

"Well, sir, the way I see it, I figure I must have picked up the bullet without a vest and cashed in the chips, and you intervened to take me on a different life path."

"Garner, I don't really know. Maybe it will show up on the Minibago DVD when it gets back to my office, and then again, maybe it won't."

"Sir.... General Goldwyn.... you need to know that I'm most grateful if you did intervene. I have a lot of living yet to do, and I think my ancestors can get along without me for awhile yet."

"Roger that, Garner. That's good. That's very good. I'm glad to hear it. Now, let's get Doc Gates to hook you up to that heart monitor so that we can launch the final phase of this operation."

* * * * * * * * * * * * * * * * * * * * * *

Toward the beginning of the planning effort, Stauffer took Pete Pendleton, Winston Greeley, Sandy Watson, Mitch Monahan, and several others aside and asked them to use the temporal observation monitors to backtrack the terrorists on Flight 2666 to their home source and identify a potential "drop zone" to send the terrorists back to once they had been safely removed from the plane. The team members each selected one of the terrorists from the plane and backtracked them through almost three months of seemingly unrelated activities, and then, quite suddenly, their paths all converged at an isolated compound on the outskirts of an Iraqi village twenty miles north of Baghdad.

When they all realized the trail for the terrorists on Flight 2666 started there from the same place, they used the technology to get a better feel for what went on inside the compound. It turned out to be a terrorist recruiting and training center, housing upwards of 150 people at a time. The team stayed glued to their monitors for hours making video captures of many of the scenes within the compound and meeting together to analyze their conclusions. They ultimately decided that this would be the ultimate "drop zone" for the terrorists on Flight 2666, kind of like a trip back home again, only this was going to be a trip back home.... with extreme prejudice.

* * * * * * * * * * * * * * * * * * * * * *

As each of the terrorists was removed from the plane, Pete Pendleton's team moved in quickly and transferred their bodies, alive and dead, on gurneys from the five time vaults where their bodies had been deposited across the gallery of the Repository to a larger time lab where they had positioned an oversized wooden pallet stacked high with boxes of C-4 plastic explosives. Pendleton was a highly-trained ordnance specialist and had wired the stack with a pair of detonators to trigger the whole load upon impact. They positioned the bodies of the terrorists on the outside perimeter of the pallet and duct taped them to the cases of C-4.

When all was ready, they positioned two time portal projectors focused on the pile, and then Pendleton invited Colonel Wilson to flip the toggle switch to engage the portals, transporting the whole array to a position approximately 1,500 feet in the air above the terrorist training compound. As the packed pallet loaded with explosives and the five terrorists materialized high in the air directly above the compound's main training and indoctrination building, it plummeted to earth. As it impacted the roof of the building, the detonators ignited the C-4 and the whole pile went up in a blast of explosive flame. As it happened, the terrorists had stockpiled a large inventory of stolen artillery and mortar shells, many of which were white phosphorous rounds, in an outbuilding adjacent to the training building. The shells were deconstructed to assemble various kinds of IED explosives for their terrorist attacks. As the explosion from the main building reached the explosive ordnance outbuilding, it went up in a massive secondary explosion, and the entire compound disappeared in fire and smoke.

\* \* \* \* \* \* \* \* \* \* \* \* \* \* \* \* \* \* \* \* \* \*

George Washington Black sat at his computer console analyzing satellite imagery piped into his CIA office work station at Langley, Virginia, from a spy satellite orbiting high above the Middle East. He was currently tracking movement of people in and out of a suspected terrorist camp in Iraq just north of Baghdad. Wide-eyed, he observed the sudden appearance of a large object, apparently stacked high with wooden boxes and human bodies as it materialized in his field of view directly over the terrorist camp he had been observing. From the shadows on the ground, he estimated that the object was at least a thousand feet in the air above the compound, but it quickly fell to earth, and the compound exploded in a blast of white light and flames.

Black called his supervisor over to examine the video tape of what had just happened. Neither of them had a clue what they were witnessing. The high resolution of the spy satellite camera was sufficient for them to read the stenciling on the side of some of the boxes, and they could see that they were labeled C-4 explosives.

What puzzled them the most were the five bodies strapped to the explosives. Some of them were missing arms and hands, which apparently were also strapped elsewhere onto the cases of explosives. One of the bodies appeared to have been sliced in two. The two analysts sat there at the computer work station trying to make sense of what had just transpired, and then a sense of dizziness and nausea overwhelmed them momentarily. When it had passed, they didn't remember what they had just witnessed of the falling pallet, but the chaotic scene of the terrorist camp ablaze on the computer monitor was stark evidence that a very significant event had just transpired.

* * * * * * * * * * * * * * * * * * * * * * * *

Stauffer, Garner Wilson, Bill Tipton, Bob Zazworsky, Pete Pendleton, General Goldwyn, and Miriam Campbell sat in Bill Tipton's office in the Repository around the conference table discussing the events of the day just past. Garner Wilson was sitting in his wheel chair still wired up to the portable heart monitor. Dr. Campbell was visibly shaken over the abrupt elimination of the terrorists from the plane and the subsequent destruction of the terrorist training camp.

"General Goldwyn," she said in a muffled voice, "it all seems so pointless and inhumane to kill women and children along with the terrorists at the camp. Couldn't there have been a better way of dealing with the situation?"

"I understand your concern, Miriam." Motioning to Pete Pendleton, General Goldwyn continued, "Pete, pull up the video file of you explaining preparations for the drop that just came back in the Minibago."

"Roger that, sir." Pendleton leaned over the laptop on the conference table and entered a few keystrokes. The oversized flat screen monitor that hung on the wall next to the table came to life. It was a video of General Goldwyn and Pendleton. Goldwyn was speaking. *"Pete, please lay out for me what you and your team encountered when you did the temporal observation scan on the terrorist camp and the people who were in the compound in preparation for the drop."*

*"Yes, sir. We counted a total of 136 people — 121 men, 10 women, and 5 children, apparent ages 10 to 16. There's some concern that we will be killing innocent bystanders as collateral damage when we take out the compound. Not so.*

*My team ran a scan on every individual in the compound, all 136 of them. It took quite a bit of doing, but we looked into their pasts and several potential futures for each one of them. All of the men, five of the women and two of the children already had blood on their hands from previous violence and terrorist activities."*

On the screen, Pendleton referred to his notes as he continued, *"The future scans reflected high probability of nine of the women all walking into open air markets, public buildings, hospitals, and mosques, strapped with explosives and detonators hidden under their burqas and blowing themselves up, killing hundreds of innocent bystanders. Three of the children were likewise all trained to make and deliver IED explosives along roadways near urban areas and would be responsible for the death or maiming of 67 American servicemen and women and 23 civilian international emergency relief workers. To summarize, from our future scans, only one woman and two of the children appeared to be clean. The rest all turned out to be assassins. We did a temporal snatch of the woman and the two children and relocated them about five kilometers outside a refugee camp in Kurdish territory. The remaining women and children in the compound have all been responsible for or would have been responsible for well over five hundred deaths and crippling injuries to our troops and innocent civilians in the area. All of them are drenched in blood. All are combatants and none of them are innocents."*

Dr. Campbell audibly gasped when she heard the gruesome statistics. Pendleton froze the computer vidcast on the screen and continued his report. "Everyone inside the compound died in the explosion. As directed, we eliminated them all with extreme prejudice. The blast radius of the explosive pallet and the secondary explosion of the terrorists' ammunition bunker were contained inside the high adobe compound walls. The compound itself was somewhat isolated from the adjacent village. Many people came running from the village to investigate the blast, but no villagers were injured that we can tell. That about sums up my report, sir."

"Thank you, Pete. I appreciate your team's thoroughness in setting up the final phase of the operation."

Pendleton shut off the video capture, and General Goldwyn turned to face everyone seated around the table, focusing on Dr. Campbell. "All human life is important, and it always bothers me when a life is taken. But this intervention doesn't bother me quite so much. I'm thinking about all our servicemen and women who won't be mortally wounded or crippled by those pint-sized, roadside bomber killers. I can see the faces of mothers and fathers and wives and children rushing out to greet their returning service members at the conclusion of their deployments.... all safe and whole."

General Goldwyn paused for a moment to collect his thoughts and then continued, "But I can also see the hundreds, maybe thousands of Iraqi worshippers in their mosques,.... and shoppers in the marketplace,....patients in their hospital beds,.... and government workers in their office buildings,..... who won't now perish at the hands of these angels of death. They will return to their homes and families, and life will go on for them. No, I am never comfortable with death. But I am most comfortable with what we have just done here in the preservation and protection of life."

General Goldwyn glanced down at his watch and commented, "It's getting late. Bill and Garner, I would like you to assemble everyone who works here in the Repository and the Hole in the theater for a briefing from me. Please have everyone seated by 2230 hours. I'll see you all there." General Goldwyn stood up and abruptly left the room. There was little more than an hour to assemble all the staff, and so they began the task of getting everyone together.

# Chapter 5

*Carlisle Barracks, Pennsylvania, Tuesday, June 4, 2013, 10:30 p.m.*

Bill Tipton stood on the stage as all of the staff gathered together in the Majestic Theater auditorium at the far end of the Repository gallery. When Tipton stepped forward to the edge of the stage platform, the noise from the crowd diminished to a hush as Tipton began to speak. "I'm glad that you were all able to make it this evening. I know that it's late. General Goldwyn wanted to meet with you all to acknowledge and thank you for your part in making the Flight 2666 interdiction operation all come together."

Tipton turned to the rear of the theater with a look of expectation on his face. Garner Wilson, posted at the rear entrance door in his wheel chair, turned and looked back down the Repository gallery. General Goldwyn was nowhere to be seen. Wilson turned back around to face Tipton up on the stage and raised his shoulders in a shrug.

Tipton nodded and continued to address the gathering, "General Goldwyn said that he would be here precisely at 2230, but apparently he has been delayed. If you would please be patient, he should be along momentarily."

As Tipton spoke, the shimmering outline of a time portal appeared at the right side of the stage. General Goldwyn emerged from the portal and walked briskly to center stage. "And indeed I am." Looking at his watch, he announced with a broad smile, "Precisely 2230. It pays to be punctual.... Ladies and gentlemen.... the President of the United States...."

Everyone in the audience looked around in surprise but quickly stood to their feet as newly-elected President Julian Holbrook emerged from the portal and joined General Goldwyn at center stage. He was followed through the portal by the other eleven members of the Temporal Council, several of them serving members of Congress, who formed a broad semicircle behind him on the stage. Waving his arm in a wide arc to take in everyone standing in the theater, President Holbrook turned to General Goldwyn and asked, "So these are the people we have to thank for saving our lives...., the lives of all the men and women serving in Congress...., and all the other good folks who work on the Hill...., and, of course, the men, women and children of Flight 2666?"

General Goldwyn nodded and replied, "Yes, sir. These are the heroes who changed the course of the nation today."

Acknowledging General Goldwyn's remark and turning back to face everyone in the audience, President Holbrook continued, "Heroes, indeed.... unsung heroes.... Ladies and gentlemen, I and the members of the Temporal Council standing behind me represent here this evening all of those people who would have otherwise perished, and we would like to give you a rousing round of applause for your courage, quick thinking and resourcefulness in saving the day, that we might live another." The members of the Temporal Council joined President Holbrook in clapping enthusiastically. They continued clapping as the President turned in a full arc to face every quarter of the room, a broad smile of satisfaction on his face. After fully 30 seconds, the President raised his hands and the enthusiastic applause slowly died out. President Holbrook continued, "Please, ladies and gentlemen.... everyone.... please be seated. I know that it's late in your time frame, and I'll try to make this brief. We have a few things we need to talk about here tonight."

General Goldwyn and Tipton moved off to the side of the stage where a couple of folding chairs had been set up. A team of Repository staff entered through the stage side door carrying folding chairs and quickly set them up for the members of the Temporal Council, and they took their seats in a broad arc behind the President center stage.

Satisfied that everyone had been accommodated, President Holbrook turned back to face the audience waiting expectantly in the Majestic. "We need to review here what happened.... earlier this afternoon. It was highly unusual and extremely unorthodox. In the absence of guidance from any members of the Temporal Council who were otherwise.... indisposed...., you performed your mission here with extraordinary resourcefulness and chutzpah. As soon as the mission was over and success guaranteed, General Goldwyn contacted us to convene the Temporal Council to inform us of what had transpired. We have come here to Carlisle Barracks on one pretext or another over the next three months, and General Goldwyn moved us all back in time to gather earlier this evening on the fifth floor of Collins Hall to brief us on the astounding events of June 4, 2013. We have seen the video captures of the alternate time line where most of us perished in the flames as Flight 2666 came crashing through the walls of the House chamber on Capitol Hill. We also viewed the video captures of your concerted efforts in subduing the terrorists on Flight 2666.... and taking them off the plane.... We also witnessed the extraordinary way in which you disposed of their bodies and substantially reduced the terrorist population in the world today."

President Holbrook cleared his throat and continued, "Some of you may be a little uncomfortable using the temporal technology as an offensive weapon. Now, to be sure, many of you seated here in the audience are experienced combat veterans who have served the nation well in many different theaters around the world, and you have witnessed death firsthand. This might just be old hat for you. But, many of you have not, and you probably have had little training to prepare you for your part in the events of the past day. For all of you, let me be clear on one thing. It is a terrible matter to take another person's life. I realize that some of you may be experiencing great discomfort and perhaps remorse for your participation in the mission.... this afternoon.... and wonder if there might have been another way to subdue the terrorists without the loss of human life. I suppose that that might have been the case. We members of the Temporal Council also asked the same questions during our briefing. In fact, we asked General Goldwyn to run the video captures several times so that we could absorb and consider all of the details and options that might have presented themselves to you in the heat of battle. We concluded, after some deliberation, that the course of action you chose and executed with such professionalism was extraordinary and entirely within the purview of the Temporal Council's rules for the use of temporal technology. You can be proud and comfortable with your service today as you responded so well to the call to action in the service and defense of your Nation."

President Holbrook started to choke up a little, and he paused briefly to wipe his eyes with his handkerchief. "We, the members of the Temporal Council, want to honor you all here today with a special recognition. We have directed General Goldwyn to set aside a vault dedicated to this great event.... an event that will go unnoticed by the people of the United States and the world, but that we will hold forever in our hearts. We have asked General Goldwyn that he prepare a memorial in that vault with enlarged photographs of the entire operation, the before and after pictures. We have asked him to direct the preparation of a large bronze plaque depicting the events of today so that, at least among us, the Temporal Council and the men and women who work so tirelessly down here in the Repository and the Hole, will never forget the momentous events that took place." Motioning to General Goldwyn, the President continued, "General Goldwyn, if you please...."

General Goldwyn stood and stepped forward to center stage to stand by the President, motioning for Bill Tipton to join them. As he reached the side of the President, Goldwyn took a folded 5X8 card out of his pocket and handed it to Tipton. "Here, Bill, would you please be so kind as to read this."

Surprised, Tipton took the card and began to read, "Attention to orders...."

He stopped abruptly as everyone in the auditorium stood and came to attention. In the back of the auditorium, Garner Wilson struggled to get to his feet with his heart monitor still attached. Doc Gates stood at his side and attempted to restrain him to remain seated in the chair, but he stood anyway. Tipton continued reading: "In recognition of their extraordinary contribution to the national security and welfare of the United States, June 4, 2013, the men and women of the Hole and Repository, Carlisle Barracks, Pennsylvania, are hereby recognized with a Department of Defense Unit Commendation Medal for their selfless service in eliminating a terrorist threat that might have brought the nation to its knees. Their quick response and actions in resolving and eliminating the threat reflects great credit upon themselves, their organization and the United States Department of Defense."

The President had been facing Colonel Tipton as he read the commendation. When he had finished, he turned to face the audience again. "I am new at this, but General Goldwyn assures me that we can follow this up after the fact with an appropriate certificate attesting to this commendation. I have asked him to have the certificate appropriately framed and hung in the memorial vault as a testament of your unfailing courage and commitment in our hour of peril..... General Goldwyn, please...."

General Goldwyn reached into his pocket and extracted another folded 5X8 card and handed it to Bill Tipton to read.

"Attention to orders. Colonel Garner Stuart Wilson IV, please come forward to be recognized."

Colonel Wilson was still standing. He collapsed back into his wheel chair at the rear of the auditorium as all eyes turned on him. Doctor Gates wheeled his patient down the red carpeted aisle and up the ramp to the side of the stairs to the stage. As he reached center stage, General Goldwyn asked Doctor Gates softly, "Doc, please turn your patient's chair around so that Garner is facing the audience."

Somewhat bewildered, Wilson sat there stone-faced in the wheelchair. Bill Tipton continued reading from the card, "In the heat of battle in subduing and removing terrorists from Flight 2666, Colonel Garner Stuart Wilson IV was killed in action, June 4, 2013, as a wayward bullet fired by the severed hand of one of the terrorists ricocheted off the walls of the Repository vault and traveled back through the time portal into the aircraft, passing through the body of the terrorist and striking Colonel Wilson in the chest. Although technically already dead, in one last magnificent effort, Colonel Wilson pushed the body of the terrorist through the time portal into the safety vault where he was terminated. Through a follow-up intervention, General Cubby Goldwyn time-leaped back to before mission launch and required Colonel Wilson to put on a Kevlar protective vest before the beginning of the operation. The vest ultimately stopped the bullet, saving his life, but giving Colonel Wilson's body what might have been a fatal traumatic blow to his heart and lungs. In recognition of his extraordinary heroism in securing mission accomplishment, and with no consideration for his own personal safety, and, in spite of his previous demise, Colonel Wilson is hereby awarded the Presidential Medal of Freedom, given under my hand this day, signed Julian S. Holbrook, President of the United States of America."

As Tipton finished reading the citation, President Holbrook stepped forward and pumped Wilson's hand. He turned to the audience and asked them once again to be seated. Then turning slightly so that the audience could hear his words, he addressed Colonel Wilson. "I have awarded several posthumous medals already in the short time since I took office, but this is the first time where the recipient lived to accept his award posthumously." President Holbrook paused as the audience erupted in laughter at his observation.

President Holbrook continued, "The Presidential Medal of Freedom is an award that is bestowed upon those who have made an exceptionally meritorious contribution to the national security interests of the United States. I want to point out that while it is typically awarded to civilians, it can also be awarded to military personnel and worn on the uniform."

Smiling broadly, President Holbrook continued, "Colonel Wilson, I understand you're sporting quite a bruise from the concussion of the bullet on your vest. I'm glad that it didn't turn out to be more serious than that. I'll get your medal to you shortly. Wear it with the honor and distinction that your service and sacrifice merit. A copy of the award will be filed in your official Military Personnel Jacket, but the citation will remain classified and will not appear on the award for obvious reasons.... Oh, and I suppose that there is another Purple Heart in it for you there. From what General Goldwyn tells me, you already have quite a collection of those as well."

Now, turning directly to face Wilson, the President pulled out a small card and referred to it as he went on. "Colonel Wilson, I have been informed by General Goldwyn that you come from a distinguished lineage of U.S. Army Officers, all of whom have died in the line of duty: your great-great-grandfather during the Civil War, your great-grandfather during the incursion into Mexico, your grandfather during World War II, your father during the Viet Nam war, and now you, in the ongoing War on Terrorism. I congratulate you sir, and thank you and your distinguished ancestors for your years of combined service in the defense of our country. I hasten to point out that you have now passed through that wicket yourself.... You have joined your distinguished forebears among the ranks of our honored dead who gave the last full measure of devotion in defense of our great nation. You can check that one off on your bucket list and move on with your life now for you indeed have much to live for. On behalf of a grateful nation, I thank you for your incredible service."

As the audience in the Majestic erupted in a standing ovation, President Holbrook pumped Wilson's hand again and then turned to

General Goldwyn. "Cubby, I believe that pretty well wraps it up. It's a little late in the evening for these folks but didn't you say something about refreshments?"

"Indeed I did, sir. Mr. President, members of the Temporal Council, and all Repository and Hole staff, please join us in the gallery for refreshments." As General Goldwyn walked passed Stauffer at the bottom of the stage ramp, he leaned over and said quietly to him in passing, "Barton, please meet me in my office after the festivities here are over, about 2400 hours."

General Goldwyn led the President and the members of the Temporal Council down the ramp from the stage and up the aisle to the theater doors. Everyone else in the theater filed out after them and joined them in the gallery, leaving Tipton and Stauffer standing and Wilson seated in his wheelchair at the bottom of the ramp by the stage. Stauffer shook Tipton's and Wilson's hands and remarked wistfully, "Well done, Bill! Well done Garner! It is a great pleasure to work alongside you both. I didn't realize just how much I've missed this place."

# Chapter 6

*Carlisle Barracks, Pennsylvania, Tuesday, June 4, 2013, 11:55 pm.*

Stauffer arrived a few minutes early and paused outside the imposing door to General Goldwyn's office. He looked up and down the hallway, recalling the frenetic activity of past years working there in the subterranean world of black temporal operations.

Stauffer had worked alongside many old friends earlier during the day as they put together the plan to interdict the terrorist attack on Washington. He had learned firsthand that the work in the Hole and the Repository was moving along rapidly and that they were making good progress in their areas of responsibility. The Hole team, led by Colonel Garner Stuart Wilson IV, was responsible for monitoring America's past and detecting any hostile threat tampering with temporal technology and potentially disturbing America's history that might weaken national security. The Repository team, led by Colonel Bill Tipton, had a very different mission. It was responsible for using the temporal technology for a History Quest, to examine the history of the world and correct distortions and fill in gaps that exist in the historical record and redact a more accurate depiction of the historical past, unvarnished and free of the conqueror's spin and the historian's whimsy.

Stauffer had, at one time or another, been in charge of both teams, and he was intimately familiar with their operations. He retired from active duty a half year ago to spend more time with his family. Although he hated to leave at the time, it was the right call. He enjoyed himself immensely getting reacquainted with his wife and children. At the same time, he also had to admit that he greatly missed the excitement of working down here deep beneath Carlisle Barracks.

General Goldwyn's voice, emanating from the small wall speaker at the side of the security hand pad on the side of the doorway, broke his reverie. "That you, Barton? Right on time. Please come in."

The locking mechanism on the massive door activated with a reverberating kerchunk, and the door slowly opened inward. Stauffer stepped through the doorway and closed the door behind him. General Goldwyn motioned to him from his desk. "Come over here, Barton, and sit down for a moment before we move you back to your dinner engagement with your family at Machu Picchu. I know you must be tired, but I have a few things I'd like to talk over with you."

Stauffer obliged and plopped down in the overstuffed chair facing General Goldwyn's desk. His eyes were slightly bloodshot, and his face looked a little haggard.

General Goldwyn eyed him with a grin on his face as he realized just how tired Stauffer must be. "Are you going to be able to stay awake during dinner or are you going to drop your head into your plate and fall asleep?"

Stauffer realized that General Goldwyn was teasing him and responded, "Oh, you know, sir, once I sink my teeth into some *lomo saltado* and down a bottle of Inca Kola or two, I'll be just fine."

Goldwyn chuckled, "I'm sure you will.... Barton,.... I need to ask you a direct question of sorts."

"Shoot, sir."

"How do you feel about all of the terrorists that died in the operation today? Do you feel any pangs of regret?"

"That's a tough one, sir. The President gave a good speech earlier this evening about that. I fall into the category of retired military officers who never were directly involved in combat. I was a Cold Warrior. I faced off against the East Germans and the Soviets in Germany in the early 1970s for four years and then against the North Koreans on the Korean peninsula in the 1990s for another two years. It was always a tense situation, especially in Korea where we have never signed a formal peace treaty with the North Koreans, and we occasionally exchanged shots at each other. I suppose that I had something to do with the terrorist's death on the Wolf Crossing Bridge here in Carlisle a couple of years ago, but that's on another timeline now and I don't have any memory of it. On this timeline, this is the first instance that decisions of mine have resulted in the loss of life. It's a little hard getting used to the idea. I know that it had to be done, but I'm not entirely comfortable with it."

"That's good, Barton," General Goldwyn responded with a big smile of relief. "That's what I hoped to hear from you. It wouldn't do to have someone who actually enjoys killing others working for me." General Goldwyn paused and then continued fixing Stauffer in

place with his eyes. "Listen, Barton, before I send you back, I want
to run a proposition by you. You have already seen that operations
here in the Hole and the Repository are moving along well. How
would you feel about coming back here to work for me, part time if
necessary, to still allow you the family time that you need?"

"Come back?" Stauffer questioned. "Everything seems to be
purring right along down here, sir. What would you need me for?"

"Actually, Barton, I have a whole new operational area I
would like to initiate, and I want to put you in charge of it."

"A whole new temporal project? What would that be, sir?"

"Well, Barton, without going into a lot of the detail
now, we've run into a bit of a challenge with monitoring ancient
history. You remember that Rule #1 set by the Temporal Council
proscribes against viewing any significant religious events or
spiritual activities. Faith-based religions are to remain just that....
faith-based. In response to that mandate, up until now, we've
avoided every historical incident or activity that smacked of religious
content or expression. The problem is that the further back in
history we explore, the more that history becomes intermingled
and indistinguishable from religion, ritual and belief systems. If we
were to hold absolutely true to Rule #1 as written, we wouldn't be
able to explore most of what constitutes ancient history.... Sumerian
legends and mythology.... Adam and Eve.... Enoch and Thoth.... the
Akkadians, the Babylonians, the Hittites.... the epic of Gilgamesh....
Noah and the Flood, the tower of Babel.... It leaves us with a lot of
gaps about the foundation of our history upon which all the rest is
based. I discussed the matter this morning with the President and the
other members of the Temporal Council, and they have given us the
nod to explore those areas as well, but they gave it one caveat. They
have authorized a very limited and very restricted temporal project
to explore these possibilities, but they want **you** to lead the team that
will do it. They want the results from such an historical investigation
to have very limited and restricted visibility. Only a handful of people
would ever see the reports you compile. Well, Barton, have I piqued
your curiosity yet?"

"Yes, sir.... very much so. I'll need to discuss the matter of
my coming back to work with Gwen. When do you need an answer?"

"I'm not in any particular hurry on this one yet. Take your
time and enjoy your Peruvian adventure with your family. When you

get back here to Carlisle, I'll contact you and we can get together again to discuss where we go from here."

"Roger that, sir. Is there anything else?"

"No, I think that covers it. Are you ready to transport back to Machu Picchu? We shouldn't keep your family waiting."

"Waiting, sir?" Stauffer looked over at the clock above General Goldwyn's door. "I've been gone almost seven hours. Right now, Gwen must be in a state of panic."

"Yes, I know, Barton. I've had a member of the Repository staff monitoring your family ever since you left to come here. Gwen became very worried when you didn't show up for dinner, and she reported your disappearance to the Machu Picchu site authorities within the hour. They immediately sent out several search parties with flashlights and lanterns up the trail where you should have come down, but, as you might expect, they came up empty. They're preparing right now to send out several major search parties at first light tomorrow morning. Gwen is beside herself with worry, and I'm sorry that we've put her through that. But it will all be erased as we send you back to finish your hike down the trail to the hotel to join your family for dinner. The missing evening and all the worry we've caused her and your kids will evaporate onto a different timeline, and they'll never realize that you've been gone."

General Goldwyn stood up and came around his desk picking up a photo from his desktop. "Here, Barton, stand up and let me take a look at you. Turn around please."

Stauffer stood to his feet as General Goldwyn compared him to the photo in his hand. "I took a screen shot of you as you came back here through the time portal so that we would have a graphical continuity aid of what you were wearing and what you looked like so that, as you go back, we can make sure that you look the same.... no detail out of place.... Hmmm.... You look good except you're missing your floppy hat and camera bag. Where did you leave them?"

"Oh, I forgot, sir. I think that they're over in Bill Tipton's office."

"I'll give him a call," General Goldwyn offered, "and have them brought over here ASAP. It won't do to keep Gwen and the kids worrying about you."

General Goldwyn walked back over to his desk and picked up his phone and spoke in low tones for a few minutes. As he set down the receiver and turned around to face Stauffer, there was a buzzing sound, and Goldwyn pushed the lock release button on his desk. Bill Tipton stepped into the office carrying Stauffer's hat and camera bag. "I did what you said, sir. I came through a time portal to get here with no delay. Pretty neat trick."

"Thanks, Bill. I appreciate you coming so quickly. We need to get Barton back to his family."

General Goldwyn took the hat from Tipton and set it on Stauffer's head and slung his camera bag over his shoulder. Tipton grinned at Stauffer and said, "Bye, Bart. See ya later." He faced about and hurriedly left the office. Then, leading Stauffer over to the wall to the side of his conference table, General Goldwyn pressed a few keys on the keyboard on the conference table and the outline of a time portal shimmered against the wall. "I preset the portal to take us back to Machu Picchu, but we don't have to rush getting back. We can fix our arrival to give us time to watch the sunset from there at Machu Picchu."

"What? Watch the sunset, sir?.... Well, okay. We won't have long to wait. There's not a bad view no matter where you are and which direction you face. It's all incredible."

"Yes, I know. That's why I arranged this little side trip for us."

"Sir? What do you have in mind?"

"Just follow me, Barton. This won't disappoint you." General Goldwyn's face revealed a wry smile as he turned and stepped through the time portal and disappeared from view.

Stauffer gripped his camera bag and scrambled to follow after him through the portal. As he cleared through on the other side, he found himself standing in a small deserted clearing strewn with boulders and cut stones. General Goldwyn was just a few steps ahead of him walking toward a low stone wall on an embankment. Stauffer hurried after him. As he caught up with him at the wall, he looked out over the wide open spaces before him and realized that General Goldwyn had transported them to the summit of Huayna Picchu. General Goldwyn had advanced to the edge of the precipice, looking down at the ruins of Machu Picchu below. The sun was just beginning to set, casting long shadows over the Urubamba River Valley.

General Goldwyn sat down on a squat stone wall. He turned to Stauffer. "You know, Barton, this isn't actually the same day you and your family were here at Machu Picchu. It was a bit foggy in places that day, and you couldn't see much from up here. I picked a better evening about four months earlier when visibility was excellent, and the sky and atmosphere combined with just the right placement of clouds for a perfect sunset. What do you think, Barton?"

"It's breathtaking, sir."

"Yes, and it's pretty much an exclusive view. They require all tourists who have climbed Huayna Picchu during the day to be on their way back down well before sundown to avoid getting caught up here in the dark. Not many folks ever get to see this view. Sorry that you can't take any pictures here."

"I can't?.... Why not?"

"Pictures of a sunset from Huayna Picchu would simply raise too many questions. Let your eyes and mind embed the picture in your memory."

Stauffer nodded understanding and sat down on the wall near General Goldwyn. They sat there in silence on the peak of Huayna Picchu without speaking, taking in the grandeur of the setting sun over the ruins of Machu Picchu and the Urubamba River Valley below. The setting sun illuminated the patchwork quilt mosaic of the terraced fields on the sides of the mountain ridge below Machu Picchu in the lower agricultural section marked by intermittent flashes of brilliant color and contrasting shadows. The magnificent architecture of the ancient structures of *La Ciudadela* in the upper residential area rose up from the summit of the ridge. It always excited Stauffer's imagination wondering how they had managed to build it all in such balanced architectural splendor. As the sun sank deeper below the horizon and the lively colors of the sunset started to fade, Stauffer at last broke the silence. "Thank you, sir.... I don't know what to say.... I would never in my lifetime have experienced this without you bringing me up here with the temporal technology.... I wouldn't have even been able to get up here on Huayna Picchu at all. My old knees wouldn't have allowed me to climb the steep path. It was hard enough when Gwen and I did it years ago when we were younger."

General Goldwyn stood and faced Stauffer holding out his hand. He took Stauffer's hand in his own and pumped it energetically. He steered Stauffer in the direction of the portal as he spoke, "Barton, I want you to know that I greatly appreciate your contribution in making the terrorist intervention go so smoothly. I explained it all to the President and the Temporal Council, and I believe that's why they want you to come back to take over the new project. Give it some thought, and I'll get with you when you get back to Carlisle. For now, it's still light, and if you head down the trail at a fast clip, you'll get to the hotel in good time. *Vaya con Dios, mi amigo.*"

General Goldwyn's valediction in Spanish surprised Stauffer, and he stopped momentarily at a loss for what to say. Finally he managed to get a few words out, "Thank you, sir, I…."

Still pumping Stauffer's hand, General Goldwyn turned him to face the outline of the portal and pushed him gently on through. "You talk too much, Barton," was the last thing he heard before he found himself standing right at the top of the Machu Picchu ruins at the end of the Inca Trail. The hotel was only a hundred yards away.

As he hurried along the path and approached the front entrance to the hotel, Gwen emerged and greeted him with a kiss. "You made it, Barton. Hurry and get washed up. The maitre d' is holding our table for us, and the kids are starving. Must be something about the altitude."

"Well, I'm a bit hungry myself. I think that I'll be able to put quite a bit of food away tonight."

"Did you enjoy your rest up at the *tambo*? I had to chase the kids full speed all the way down the trail here to the hotel. Turned out they all needed to use the restroom."

"Yes, I did. I had quite a relaxing time up on the trail at the *tambo*. I felt just like an Inca *chasqui* runner resting up for the final burst of speed down the hill into Machu Picchu. Nothing like a little relaxation on the Inca trail to close out a great day of exploring and adventure!"

# Chapter 7

Stauffer sat next to Gwen on the train travelling back to Cuzco from Machu Picchu. He was still tired from his involvement on the terrorist interdiction mission the day before and sat there drowsily in his seat trying to take in the breathtaking scenery as the train slowly wended its way along the valley floor next to the Urubamba River. With each passing mile, Stauffer's eyelids grew heavier, and he finally succumbed and nodded off, his head slumping forward.

Suddenly, something startled him to full wakefulness. He was a little dizzy and disoriented, and it took him a moment to catch his bearings. He looked around him, up and down the length of the train, but couldn't see anything amiss. Out the window, off in the distance across the valley floor, he could see the terraced fields of Pisac climbing up the steep slopes above the city. Gwen sat next to him quietly reading a travel brochure. The five C's were sitting across the aisle from them playing children's card games. Puzzled, Stauffer looked around him again. Nothing.

Finally, he lowered his head again to return to his nap and was surprised to find a long-stemmed rose laying across his legs. He hadn't brought it onto the train with him, and he could only guess where the rose might have come from. A long-stemmed rose was the entrée for personnel newly assigned to the Hole or the Repository. When they reported for duty, their escort officer led them to an office along a basement corridor of Collins Hall where they were coached into giving the long-stemmed rose to Mabel, General Goldwyn's topside secretary. Mabel received the rose and the sealed orders from the new arrival and gave them retina and handprint scans in return, entering their personal data into the organizational security system. The rose had become a long-standing tradition, sort of a rite of passage for all new personnel. Stauffer initially considered that the rose appearing on his lap was probably General Goldwyn's subtle way of welcoming him back on staff down in the Hole, but that didn't track with him. This seemed to be something different, far removed from the routine of Mabel's rose tradition. Hole and Repository personnel would never use temporal technology for personal purposes or to play practical jokes.

Stauffer looked up and down the length of the train car again, hoping to catch a glimpse of something that would explain the unexpected rose.

Gwen looked up from reading the travel brochure and immediately saw the rose. "Where did you get the rose, Barton? I didn't see you bring it on the train. Is it for me? You're so thoughtful remembering our anniversary like this." She gave Stauffer a hug and a kiss on the cheek. She took the rose and held the bloom up close to her nose to smell its fragrance.

Stauffer was at a loss for words. He had forgotten their anniversary and was grateful that she had interpreted the sudden appearance of the rose as a gift from a thoughtful husband. "Well, nothing too good for my bride," was all he could think of to say.

As Gwen picked up the rose, Stauffer saw a small slip of folded paper on his lap that had been positioned beneath it. He unfolded it as he brought it up close to his face to be able to read the handwritten message in small, precise, block printing. The note was short and to the point: *"I've got some good news and some bad news. First, the bad news. Sendero Luminoso is alive and well and blew up the train. The good news is that we went back and took them out first. We've got your back, compadre. See ya' soon, Ski."*

At first puzzled, Stauffer quickly connected the dots and realized the implications of Zazworsky's note. Apparently, a resurgent cell of the Peruvian Shining Path terrorist group had blown up the train and the whole Stauffer family with it. Stauffer guessed that once the news reached Carlisle Barracks, General Goldwyn had directed a temporal intervention to move into the past and interdict the Senderos and take them out before they could execute their work of destruction. He tried to imagine how they had pulled it off with the temporal technology.

Gwen interrupted his thoughts. "What's that you have there, Barton?"

"Oh…. nothing, Gwen. It's just a note from Bob Zazworsky. I saw him in Carlisle just as we were leaving on this trip, and he must have slipped this note into my jacket pocket. What a friend. I owe him one."

Stauffer slumped back in his seat, a big smile growing across his face. What a friend indeed. With his colleagues back in the Hole, armed with temporal technology, Stauffer felt practically invincible.

\* \* \* \* \* \* \* \* \* \* \* \* \* \* \* \* \* \* \* \* \* \* \*

When the Stauffers arrived back in Cuzco, they went to their hotel to drop off their luggage and then wandered around the city for the remainder of the day. They took a side trip up to the hill fortress of Sacsayhuaman above Cuzco, and the children spent the afternoon climbing around on the huge monolithic stones of the ancient fortress. When they finally got back to Cuzco late that afternoon, they had a light meal in the hotel restaurant, and then Gwen had everyone get their luggage together and get packed to be ready for the trip back to Lima the next morning. Stauffer wasn't tired, so when everyone else went down for the night early, he told Gwen he was going outside for some air. Leaving the room, he walked slowly down the ornate wooden staircase to the lobby, admiring the hand-carved pre-Columbian motifs on the side of the hand rail. Crossing over to the front door, Stauffer stepped out of the hotel into the brisk evening air. He would have enjoyed having Gwen join him for a stroll, but she was resting back in the room. She had taken in too much sun and had overheated.

The sun had gone down a little earlier, and gentle breezes wisped everywhere around the corners of the buildings, cooling the ancient city from the heat of the day. He walked slowly up the cobblestone street stepping back and forth from the occasionally broken-up sidewalk to the street, also in serious need of repair and realignment. About halfway up the street, he paused to reflect on the grandeur of the place. Although much of the city had been modernized with new hotels and ubiquitous Coca-Cola signs, Cuzco still managed to retain much of its aging colonial charm and even earlier Pre-Hispanic glory. Much of the old Inca stonework that survived provided the base foundations for the later Spanish colonial structures that had been erected above it. These foundations gave ample evidence of the industry and resourcefulness of an ancient people, laboring in communal groups, to carve out monolithic stones in impossible shapes and fit them together with a precision simply not attempted today.

The pungent smells of evening supper being prepared in countless simple kitchens wafted through the streets and invaded Stauffer's nostrils, exotic and somewhat strange, but entirely pleasurable. It encouraged Stauffer to want to visit each of the thousands of homes and sample whatever was on the stove or cooking fire that evening. Stauffer moved up the street another hundred paces and came upon an ancient-looking, dark-skinned woman, dressed in traditional Inca garb complete with a bright red shawl and derby hat and long black braids hanging down her back. She stood beside a street cart, tending the coals on a small homemade brazier. Arrayed on the wire grill were several skewers of *anticuchos*, cut up pieces of beef heart, which had been marinated in a rich seasoning of Peruvian *aji amarillo* hot chilies, vinegar, cilantro, garlic and oil. To the side on tin plates, the woman had already prepared small potatoes and *choclo* corn on the cob.

Stauffer greeted the woman in Spanish, and she nodded back with a faint smile, but continued tending the food on the grill. Stauffer looked on in fascination for a few minutes, torturing himself by the rich smells emanating from the meat, potatoes, and corn. Although he had just eaten a light meal in the hotel with his family, he finally gave in and purchased a skewer of *anticuchos*. Stauffer wasn't particularly concerned about the dangers of eating food prepared by street vendors. He had done it countless times in four overseas deployments during his earlier military career, and it had never bothered him. He brought the skewer up to his lips in great anticipation and pulled a rich piece of the *anticucho* beef heart off into his mouth and began to chew slowly, savoring with gusto the nuances of flavor in the marinade the old woman had used. She had apparently gone heavy on the *aji amarillo* because his mouth was soon on fire. He bought some potatoes and *choclo* to help quell the heat. The woman had been generous with the chili peppers in preparing the potatoes and *choclo* as well. Stauffer just stood there eating off the paper plate the woman had given him, trying not to be bothered too much by the burning in his mouth. Stauffer liked *picante* food, but this was close to going off the scale of heat that he found tolerable.

"*Le gusta, señor?*" the old woman asked, her mouth turned up in a crooked smile revealing a few missing teeth.

"*Si, señora, me gusta mucho. Buen sabor.…. delicioso. Un poco picante quizás, pero un sabor muy rico. Gracias.*"

Stauffer's Spanish was a little rusty, but he got along well enough with the people on the street. After all, most of them spoke Spanish as a second language also. In their own homes and villages, most spoke *Quechua* or *Aymara* as their first language, and Stauffer had never mastered more than just a few words of those native tongues of the ancient Peruvians.

In spite of the heat in his mouth, Stauffer was thoroughly enjoying his meal and purchased another two skewers of *anticuchos*. Stauffer had been assigned earlier in his military career to the Peruvian War College in Chorrillos on the outskirts of Lima for two and a half years, where he had learned to love Peruvian food. He reluctantly finished up the last bites of the *anticuchos*, scraping them around his plate to sop up the last remaining dregs of the marinade sauce, and then put the skewers and paper plate in the small trash can to the side of the old woman's cart.

Reaching into his pocket, he pulled out a couple of Peruvian bills and paid the woman. Before he moved on up the street, Stauffer offered up one last parting comment, *"Muchas gracias, señora. Una comida extraordinaria!"*

The old woman beamed, greatly pleased that the tall gringo had enjoyed her food so much. *"De nada señor. El placer es mío."*

Stauffer continued his stroll up the street in the direction of the Plaza de Armas, the central most part of the city. He stopped at a bakery shop door with its white flag extending from the wall above the sidewalk. The smell of freshly baked bread was overwhelming and Stauffer quickly gave in. He stepped into the shop and purchased a couple of *bolillo* rolls, an ideal conclusion to such a *picante* meal. The bread tends to soak up the heat from the hot chili peppers and cools down the mouth much faster than a cold beverage. He broke off small pieces of a *bolillo* and stuck them into his mouth as he continued his walk around the plaza.

He passed by several shops with red flags hanging out in front. These shops sold *chicha*, the pungent alcoholic beverage of the Andes, fermented from purple corn. Stauffer passed them by and stopped at a corner store where he bought an iced-down Inca Kola, the national soda pop. Inca Kola has a hyper-sweet flavor reminiscent of bananas, bubble gum and cream soda mixed together. It is an acquired taste. Stauffer nursed it slowly as he strolled around the plaza looking in the tourist shop windows built into the stone foundations of the ancient Inca ruins.

As he passed by one shop, something in the window caught his eye, and he turned around and went back to have a closer look. The window display was protected by a thick, slightly rusted, drop-down iron security gate. Sitting on a shelf amidst a grouping of wood carvings, stone statuary and ceramics, Stauffer saw a small geometric form, apparently made out of a shiny dark material, which very closely resembled the bronze dodecahedron that he had had on his desk back in the Repository before his retirement. His dodecahedron had apparently been discovered in a Roman ruin in central Europe back around 1100 AD and had eventually found its way to a marketplace in Venice where it was purchased by a Portuguese sailor who sold it to Barnum's American Museum when his ship was in port at New York City. Stauffer was very curious about such dodecahedrons because they were related somehow to Platonic solids and perhaps to what Plato called the *aether*. With recent astronomical discoveries, Stauffer equated *aether* to dark matter or dark energy today.

Curious, Stauffer opened the door and entered the shop. The shopkeeper immediately approached him and asked him in passably good English, "Can I help you with something, Señor?"

"Actually, I'd like to have a closer look at an item you have on display in the window.

"Ah, which one, Señor?"

Stauffer moved over to the accordion security bars that stretched across the inside opening to the window display and pointed to the small dodecahedron sitting on a velvet draped pedestal. "That one.... the dodecahedron."

The shopkeeper's face clouded over as he announced solemnly, "Ah, Señor, that one is very old and not for sale."

"I understand. Can you tell me where it came from and what it represents?" Stauffer asked.

The shopkeeper seemed perplexed and at a loss for words. "Well, sir.... it is very old.... it is a sacred relic from the days of Tahuantinsuyo, when the Incas ruled the four suyos from here in Cuzco."

"But.... do you know what it is? What is its purpose?"

"The Incas knew it as *chunka iskayniyuq uya*. Its purpose is sacred and not to be shared."

"Would you say that again, please.... chunka iska.... Uh.... Could you write it down for me please?"

Stauffer was nonplussed at the old man's resistance to answering his question. He looked at him expectantly until the old man finally responded, "My spelling isn't very good...., but I'll try. It is an ancient Quechua word...." As the old shopkeeper spoke, he carefully formed letters with a short pencil on a yellowing scratch pad. He stuck his tongue out between spaces in his teeth as he wrote and subvocalized the words, "*Chunka.... iskayniyuq.... uya.*"

When the shopkeeper finished printing, he tore the paper from the pad and handed it to Stauffer. Stauffer started to ask another question, but the shopkeeper waved him off with his hand. "Por favor, Señor, I've already told you more than I should. I can tell you no more."

Stauffer looked down at the paper, carefully folding it and placing it in his shirt pocket. Looking back at the shopkeeper, he exhibited a grateful smile and extended his hand. "Thank you very much, Señor. You have been very helpful. I appreciate your patience with me and my questions."

Stauffer turned and left the shop, walking slowly across the ancient plaza to return to the hotel. As he walked up the steps at the front entrance, he heard the haunting sound of Andean music emanating from the hotel restaurant where a group of young Cuzqueños were playing "El Condor Pasa" on traditional pan pipe wooden flutes. The loneliness of the high Andean altiplano tune touched Stauffer's soul with its doleful melody.

\* \* \* \* \* \* \* \* \* \* \* \* \* \* \* \* \* \* \* \*

The Stauffers checked out of the hotel the next morning and took an early afternoon flight back to Lima. They had an appointment for dinner in the evening with some friends whom they had met several years ago back at the Army War College in Carlisle. They had served as International Fellow sponsors for Colonel Jorge Armando Bustamante Goicochea and his family, and they had become good friends during the year. Upon returning to Peru following graduation from the War College course, General

Bustamante had quickly risen through the ranks and was now serving as the Chief of the General Staff of the Peruvian Army. General Bustamante had invited the Stauffers to join with them for dinner in their new home that they had just completed building on the eastern edge of Lima in the La Molina district. The home was palatial in size and spread out over a two-acre plot of land nestled up against the slope of a hill rising above the desert coastal plain.

As Gwen visited with Mrs. Bustamante in the house, General Bustamante led Stauffer on a tour around the grounds. As they walked past a large swimming pool where their children were playing and splashing around, General Bustamante related the story of the construction of the pool. "It was a very fortunate thing, Barton. When the workmen brought in a back hoe to excavate the hole for the pool, they unearthed an ancient burial tomb filled with ceramics and gold artifacts. I later sold all of the artifacts to the Museo de Oro over in the Surco District. It paid for the construction of the pool and the greater portion of the house and property. It has been a real windfall for us."

The two friends reached the far corner of the property where they came upon a small stone monument in the shade of a stately cypress tree. Nodding at the monument, Bustamante continued, "I had the remains of the man and the woman unearthed in the tomb reinterred in a small plot here in a quiet corner of the garden. There was no indication of who our benefactors might be, but the opulence of their clothing and burial implements suggested they must have been very high up in the ruling hierarchy of their day."

Stauffer was astounded, "What extraordinary luck you had to chance upon an ancient tomb."

General Bustamante's response took Stauffer by surprise, "Oh no, mi amigo, you can't dig a hole anywhere here on the Peruvian coast without unearthing a tomb of some sort or another. The ancient burial tombs are everywhere."

\* \* \* \* \* \* \* \* \* \* \* \* \* \* \* \* \* \* \* \*

Stauffer and Gwen and the children finally arrived at their hotel after dinner late that evening, exhausted from the long day's activities. They showered quickly and collapsed in bed. Gwen was asleep in a matter of minutes. Stauffer, however, lay there in bed mulling over the events of the day. He still felt a sense of exhilaration about surviving the terrorist attack on the train through some temporal intervention by Ski and his friends back in the Hole, and he kept running the thought through his mind.

Then, abruptly, he recalled the comment by General Bustamante about not being able to dig a hole anywhere on the Peruvian coast without unearthing a burial tomb. The hotel they were staying in was a large sprawling colonial style building, only one story tall, built of fired adobe brick constructed on a cement slab foundation. As he lay there in bed, he wondered if the people who had built the hotel had done much excavating before pouring the slab. If they hadn't, there was every possibility.... or probability.... that their bedroom lay directly on top of an ancient tomb or two buried four or five feet beneath the cement slab... one perhaps directly beneath their bed.

The thought was totally unsettling for Stauffer, and he tossed and turned the whole night long, unable to drift off to sleep. It had all the look, touch, and feel for him of camping out in a cemetery. When they arose the next morning, they took a minibus taxi to the Jorge Chavez International Airport to begin the long flight home. Stauffer finally fell asleep on the plane and didn't awaken until almost twelve hours later on the final approach into the BWI airport in Baltimore.

# Chapter 8

As Stauffer stepped out of his car in the Collins Hall parking lot later the following morning, Bob Zazworsky called out to him from across the lot. "Yo, Boss, how are ya doin'? When did you get back from Peru?"

Startled, Stauffer turned in the direction of Zazworsky's voice as the big man trotted toward him from across the parking lot. "Ski, I thought we agreed a year ago when you retired that the time had come to stop calling me 'Boss.'"

"Yeah, Boss," Zazworsky responded, "but that's all changed. I just signed on for a new gig, and General Goldwyn told me you're going to be the guy in charge. Just my kind of gig."

"A new gig in the Hole?" Stauffer turned around quickly to make sure that no one had overheard his slip. It was a Saturday morning and the parking lot was mostly empty with just a few cars parked here and there close to the front entrance. Knowledge of the underground top secret research facility was super "close-hold" and couldn't be discussed openly in public places. Turning back to face Zazworsky, he continued in a quieter voice. "Ski, I'm confused. I thought that when you retired, you had your sights set on traveling around the country in search of gold, and gems, and treasure. Why would you want to come back here to the grind?"

"Absolutely right, Boss. I was obsessed with treasure, especially the yellow stuff. But wherever we went...., everywhere I turned...., I found treasure.... emeralds in North Carolina, diamonds in Arkansas, opals in Nevada and Oregon, and gold in Alaska. I even hit the jackpot on a dollar slot machine in Vegas...., first pull of the handle. Heck, Boss, I just couldn't miss. I figure that Fran and I acquired more than three or four million dollars in a little less than fifteen months. It happened all so fast. It was simply too easy. It got so that it just wasn't as much fun anymore, and I was bored out of my mind. So Fran and I talked it over and decided to come home here to Carlisle for awhile. When we got here, we pulled our stuff out of storage and rented a nice house back up in North Middleton, and here we are. Two weeks ago, the day after we moved in, General Goldwyn came up behind me in the Commissary and invited me to come down to his office in the Hole to discuss a matter. Strangest thing. First time I've ever seen General Goldwyn topside on Carlisle Barracks. He told me to come and see him the next morning and to bring a rose for Mabel. That said it all. He wanted me back on the team. Well, I was up for the challenge, and Fran was in agreement, and here I am, just waiting for you to come onboard to tell me what you want me to do next. I gotta tell ya, from what I understand from General Goldwyn, this is going to be one exciting project."

"Whoa, slow down, Ski. First things first. I need to know what happened on the train from Machu Picchu to Cuzco. What was the rose and the note all about? What did you all do about the Sendero attack?"

"Boss, you know we can't talk about that topside. Let it rest for now, and I'll tell you everything I know when we get down in the Hole. But I'm betting that General Goldwyn will tell you more than I can. I suspect that he has the whole story. Hey, I see you have another rose in hand."

"Yes, it arrived by special messenger late last night after Gwen and the children had gone off to bed after we got home from the drive up from BWI. No note, just the rose with 'See me at 0845' written on the box lid."

"Well," Zazworsky said smugly, "it looks like you're good to go then. Let's go down to General Goldwyn's office. He'll lay it all out for you."

Zazworsky accompanied Stauffer up the steps to the front entrance to Collins Hall and escorted him through security and down the circular staircase directly to Mabel's office in the sub-basement. As they entered her office, even though he was carrying a rose in his hand, Stauffer was still somewhat surprised to find Mabel sitting at her desk working on the weekend. He observed that Mabel hadn't changed one bit in all the years he had known her. She was a prim, older woman of indeterminate age. A genuine, broad smile broke over her attractive face when she saw Stauffer.

"Colonel Stauffer! Good morning. How good to see you again! Are you back just for a visit or does General Goldwyn have something important for you to do that will keep you around for awhile?"

Stauffer chuckled at Mabel's astute observation. Nothing got by this lady. "It's good to see you too, Mabel," he said, as he handed her the rose. "Actually, it appears that the General does have something he'd like me to do. I may be around for a bit, but I'm not too sure for how long at this point. Could you enter me back into the security access system for now, please?"

"I would be happy to, Colonel Stauffer," Mabel replied as she accepted the rose and placed it in a tall crystal vase on the corner of her desk. Stauffer noted that it was already filled with water. "Actually," Colonel Stauffer, you are still in the system. I never deleted you. I just have to reactivate your personal data and identification information."

Not giving Stauffer a chance to respond, Mabel swiveled her chair around and entered a few keystrokes on her computer keyboard. Turning back to Stauffer, she said pleasantly, "There, you are, Colonel Stauffer. You are all set to go. Your hand print and retina scan are back in place and you have access to any of the high security, limited access points anywhere in the complex."

"Thank you very much," Stauffer said with a laugh. "As always, you demonstrate that you are the most efficient high security gatekeeper that any organization could ever hope for." And then as Stauffer turned to follow Zazworsky out the door, he added in parting, "Good to see you again, Mabel."

"And it is very good to see you again too, Colonel Stauffer."

Stauffer and Zazworsky walked down the corridor to an elevator and Zazworsky put his hand on the handpad to the side of the door. When the door opened, they entered and dropped down into the Hole deep beneath Carlisle Barracks. When they emerged, they went straight down the hallway to General Goldwyn's office.

Zazworsky went to put his hand on the hand pad to the side of General Goldwyn's door but Stauffer stopped him. Instead, Stauffer put his hand on the hand pad to confirm that he was indeed now in the security system. General Goldwyn's voice immediately sounded on the speaker to the side of the hand pad. "Welcome back, Barton. Come in. We have much to discuss."

General Goldwyn arose from his desk chair and greeted Stauffer and Zazworsky with an enthusiastic handshake and a slap on the back. "It's good to have you both back onboard. The rest of your team is waiting for you in your new work area. Bob, would you please give Barton and me a few minutes to talk one-on-one? Perhaps you could go down and make sure everyone is getting settled in okay. If you could come back here in about thirty minutes to escort Colonel Stauffer down to his new area, I would be much appreciative."

"Roger that, sir. I'll be back in thirty."

Zazworsky faced about and quickly exited the office. With his outstretched arm, General Goldwyn steered Stauffer over to his conference table and motioned for him to sit down. "Barton, I've already given you a teaser about this new operation. Are you up for it or do you still need more unobstructed family time?"

"Yes, sir. I think I'm ready to come back. We've had a lot of good times this past year together as a family, but when I explained to Gwen that I had been offered an exciting opportunity with a new DOD position, and we could stay right here in Carlisle, she readily agreed. Frankly, sir, I think she is tired of having me underfoot all the time. I think she welcomed the opportunity to get me out of the house."

"Well then, the job is yours. As I explained before, you're going to head up a small, elite team that will investigate ancient history in the distant past in areas that cross over the line into religious experience where I've had to set up blocks on the temporal observation scanners and time portals for the investigators in the Repository. In actuality, that covers practically everything before 2,000 BC, and a good deal of history since. What you uncover must be recorded, processed and written up, just like Repository protocols, but distribution of that dimension of the historical record you develop will generally be kept under wraps. You won't be able to share it even with most of the staff who work down in the Repository."

"Then what purpose will it serve, sir?"

"Ah, now that question cuts to the chase. The historians collaborating over in the Repository are processing all of the information and data provided by the temporal observation and ground repo teams over there, and they're putting together quite an account of world history.... a much different narrative from what you would find at the public library or even in the Library of Congress. And the Repository vaults are filling up fast with artifacts from the past that help to substantiate and complete the record."

"Excuse me for interrupting, but how close are we to reaching max capacity in the vaults here in the Repository?"

"Actually, Barton, we're about at 70% capacity, and we've already started transferring artifacts to some of the new auxiliary Repository vaults in the old super-collider facility at Waxahachie, Texas."

"Sir, that facility is in use already? It's only been a year since Ski and I scoped it out and provided recommendations and specs for the conversion of the facility over for Repository storage vaults."

"Well, yes, Barton," General Goldwyn responded. "We're moving fast. The construction engineers have installed about fifty vaults, and they're continuing working around the clock installing more."

"How many vaults are we going to install?"

"I haven't decided that yet, but at least another three or four hundred, possibly more. We'll just have to see how it pans out. That should serve our needs for at least the near term. We've already filled about five or ten of the vaults in the new facility. With all the missions they're running in the Repository, they're going to be filling up at a steady pace as we transfer more and more material down there."

"Whew, it is going fast," Stauffer observed. "Just how will this new project that you want me to head up mesh with all that's going on with Repository operations?"

"I think we can best describe it as close cooperation with a solid fire wall on the information and artifacts that your team may uncover, gather and develop. You will have full access to all of their files on the classified intranet while your team's output will be totally opaque to them."

"Understood." Stauffer paused and then continued, "Sir, before we go on,.... I need to know what that was all about on the train back to Cuzco from Machu Picchu."

"I knew that you might want to know more about that and so I prepared a short video file for you from the master DVD that came back from the Minibago mission that I launched just before I dispatched a team to go back in time and interdict the Sendero attack on the train. But the short answer to your question is that the Senderos blew up the train car where you and your family were riding, and you all perished in the blast and the train wreck that followed. As soon as I got word of the disaster, I scrambled Bill Tipton and Garner Wilson to get on it with their best people and undo the damage. They put the mission together in a little less than two hours. Because the Temporal Council had already tagged you to head up the new project, I didn't even consult with the President for permission to intervene."

General Goldwyn handed Stauffer a DVD. "Here, take this with you and review it in your office once you get set up. It's more than a little disquieting and extremely graphic, but I think you can handle it and you have a right to know. You've got an impressive family there, Barton. No one else has seen these files and so no one really remembers anything about it, except Bob Zazworsky. I briefed him on it as soon as the Minibago came back. At any rate, it's all history on another time line not our own now. I'll brief President Holbrook about it but I don't think anyone else needs to know. Come and see me later if you need to talk with me about it."

"Yes, sir." Stauffer sat back in his chair and looked at General Goldwyn intently. "We're not back here by accident, are we, sir." It was a statement, not a question. "The pieces all come together too tightly to be the result of mere coincidence. I just don't believe in coincidence."

"Well, you might be just a little right about that, Barton."

"I mean, when I saw Ski in the Collins Hall parking lot topside a moment ago, I asked him why he wasn't out on his retirement vacation quest for treasure.... more in jest than anything.... but his response surprised me. He told me that up until two weeks ago, he was absolutely bored out of his mind. He had discovered diamonds in Arkansas, opals and other precious gems around the country, discovered a whole new mother lode of gold in Alaska, and even hit the jackpot on the dollar slots in Vegas. In fact, he hit the jackpot on practically everything he had listed on his retirement bucket list. You wouldn't have had anything to do with that, would you, sir?"

"Well, that's a reasonable question, Barton, but you can't share the answer with anyone, especially not Bob. I might have had a little something to do with his extraordinary success. Bob has an incurable need for seeking out his fortune. He is fascinated by anything that glitters or sparkles. I had to help him get that out of his system so that he could come back focused and be your backup man on this new mission. My plan seems to have worked out nicely. The Zazworskys are back here in Carlisle and I think Bob has gotten his predilection for gold behind him."

"Understood, sir. By any chance, did you maneuver me and my family on our travels to work our way back here?"

"I might have finagled a minor intervention here and there, and I kept close tabs on you throughout your travels during the past eight months to make sure you were always safe, but you pretty much made your own decisions and set your own destiny. I wouldn't interfere with your need for family time if that's what you wanted to do."

A buzzing sound on General Goldwyn's desk signaled Zazworsky's return, and Stauffer took that as a cue to take his departure.

"Okay, sir. That sounds fair. Thank you," Stauffer said as he turned to move toward the door.

"Barton," General Goldwyn called after him, "please come back and see me Monday morning at 0900 hours. I need to fill in some details and my intent for this project and answer any questions you might have come up with by then."

Stauffer paused and looked back over his shoulder. "Yes, sir. I'll be here." Then he continued out the door to join Zazworsky standing in the hallway.

As Stauffer shut the door behind him, Zazworsky asked, pointing at the DVD in Stauffer's hand, "Whatcha got there, Boss?"

"Oh, something that General Goldwyn asked me to look over," Stauffer replied. "It's the Minibago file on the Sendero attack on our train. I'll get to it later." Zazworsky already knew part of the story, but General Goldwyn had asked him not to share the information with anyone. "By the way, Ski, keep a tight lid on the Sendero thing. No one else needs to know."

"Roger that, Boss."

Stauffer considered his new circumstances as he walked with Zazworsky to his new work area. That was going to be the hard part about this new job, not being able to share information, not even with old friends working in the Hole or the Repository.

# Chapter 9

Stauffer and Zazworsky descended two levels and walked down several corridors, making a number of turns until finally coming to an elevator door. Zazworsky put his hand on the hand pad mounted to the side, and the elevator doors parted and slid open. Stauffer looked at Zazworsky with a look of bewilderment. For him, this was exploring new territory in the Hole. "Where did all these new hallways and the elevator come from Ski?"

"General Goldwyn had them constructed two years ago while we were both still working over in the Repository. He just never told us about it.... close-hold, and we didn't have a need to know then."

As the doors closed, Stauffer looked around the interior of the elevator. There weren't any buttons on the elevator control panel, just a hand pad. Zazworsky placed his hand on the pad, and the elevator began a rapid descent.

Stauffer was startled by how deep the elevator seemed to be going. "Just how deep is our new area? This seems to be dropping pretty fast."

"Yeah, Boss. It's about ten stories below the Hole offices and temporal labs, and it's totally separate and compartmentalized from the rest of the Hole and Repository facilities."

"But why, Ski? Why the extreme measures? If it's not part of the Hole, what is it?"

"Well, we've taken to calling it 'The Crypt.' The name seems to fit. I guess that makes you the Crypt Keeper. With all the weight you've lost on your travels, you've got the right look for it. Zazworsky elbowed Stauffer in the ribs with a grin, much pleased with his joke, and Stauffer managed a slight smile.

Zazworsky continued, "General Goldwyn told me that whatever we research down here in the Crypt will probably never see the light of day in our time. It needs to be researched and written up, but it can't ever get out. Because we're pretty much self-contained here in the Crypt, we have more real estate down here than Garner's entire operation in the Hole and about a third of what they have over in the Repository."

The elevator came to a sudden stop and the doors opened onto a short corridor. The two walked down the hallway a dozen meters until Zazworsky stopped in front of an imposing door at the far end of the corridor. Zazworsky entered some key strokes on the key pad mounted to the side of the door and brought his eye close in to a retina scanner. A green light over the door illuminated, and the door began to swing open.

"Let me get this straight. In addition to all the security precautions just to get down here in the Hole, our work area has its own separate security code and retina scanner access?"

"Yeah, Boss. According to General Goldwyn, it's super-top-secret and absolutely controlled-access. We aren't going to be inviting many guests from the Repository or the Hole down here anytime soon. Most folks who work in the Hole don't even know of the existence of the Crypt. We have office space of various kinds for about 100 people here and a dozen temporal observation labs, eight time portal labs.... oh, and about nine dozen large vaults. They're for temporary storage until whatever artifacts we recover can be moved over to a special section of the auxiliary vaults at Waxahachie."

"Special section of auxiliary vaults?.... at Waxahachie?"

"Yes, Boss. General Goldwyn directed the construction of several hundred vaults for us over there entirely separate from the rest. The tunnel engineers actually tunneled out a new section of tunnels in the center of the super-collider ring. It's a small ring of vaults about another hundred meters deeper than the original collider tunnel. The tunnelers sealed the access tunnel they used to move tunneling equipment into the inner ring with 300 feet of gravel fill. In other words, the inner ring is entirely enclosed and sealed off from the outside world. There is no entrance and no connecting corridors to the rest of the facility. It's entirely isolated from the outside world."

"But Ski, General Goldwyn told me that the tunnel engineers are still building additional vaults for us down there in the outer ring. And you tell me they're also still working on additional vaults in an inner ring as well? If they've sealed up the entrance tunnel, how will the construction engineers get the cement and the metal fittings into the inner ring to build additional vaults and how will they evacuate dirt and rubble as they carve out the space for more vaults? And how will they get their tunnel boring equipment out when they're done? More importantly, how will we access the vaults? It doesn't track. It just doesn't make any sense."

"It's simple, Boss. The only way the inner ring can be accessed now is through time portals. The construction engineers get to the work site each day through a triple-wide time portal set up in a high security warehouse entrance on the surface at Waxahachie. They bring in vault construction materials and evacuate dirt and rubble through a similar system. When they're done building the vaults, they'll disassemble the tunnel boring machine and take it out piece by piece through the portal. After that, they'll disassemble the time portal and warehouse on the surface, and there won't be any access possible from anywhere on site at Waxahachie."

"That sounds pretty out-of-the box, Ski. General Goldwyn seems pretty intent on keeping our operation under wraps for a long time. Who's in charge of oversight for the outer and inner rings at Waxahachie and the ongoing construction efforts there?"

"That would be me, compadre. I was Repo Man in the Repository before," Zazworsky smirked, "but now I'm Lord of the Rings down there."

Stauffer laughed. He reflected that Zazworsky had a gift for always finding light-hearted humor in any situation, and his antics were infectious. Ski was a valuable man to have on the team. Out loud, Stauffer acknowledged, "Well, Frodo, it seems that we have pretty extensive facilities then."

Zazworsky grinned at the Frodo reference. Apparently the thought had occurred to him as well. "Yep, Boss, between the inner ring of new vaults at Waxahachie and the new Crypt facility here, I think that we have more than adequate infrastructure for whatever you might come up with for us to do."

Stauffer and Zazworsky were still standing in the hallway entrance. He paused a moment to digest all that Zazworsky had briefed him on and then changed the subject. "General Goldwyn mentioned that most of the team is already formed. Who do we have on the team? How did General Goldwyn select them?"

"Well, Boss, we've got a solid team of full-timers and a great back-up squad of part-timers who will have continuing responsibilities elsewhere in the Hole and the Repository. Why don't you go into your office and look around and I'll gather everyone up."

Zazworsky stopped in front of a door and placed his hand on the pad to the side of the door. The lock mechanism clicked and the door slowly swung open. Zazworsky stepped back and motioned for Stauffer to go on in ahead of him.

As Stauffer stepped through the doorway into his office, Zazworsky left him and disappeared down the hallway. Looking around the office, Stauffer was surprised to see a layout that was almost an exact replica of his old office over in the Repository. It was outfitted similar to General Goldwyn's office with a large conference table and chairs, a large flat screen monitor on the wall adjacent to the table, and a line of book shelves positioned against the far wall, already half-filled with an assortment of volumes. He walked over to the desk and sat down in the chair. It even felt like his old chair, comfortable as an old shoe. On the desktop, Zazworsky had placed an artifact from the Repository vaults, the small bronze dodecahedron that Stauffer had picked up during their first recovery mission at Barnum's American Museum. Next to it was a request form submitted by Zazworsky and signed by Bill Tipton authorizing its removal from the Repository vaults for storage in Stauffer's new office. Stauffer picked up the dodecahedron and turned it over and over in his hands. It still held the same fascination for him as it did when he first saw it. "Perhaps with this new assignment," he said wistfully to himself, "I'll be able to track it down and find out what's it's all about."

On the right side of the desk, there was a two-tiered inbox with papers already stacked up in the top box. Stauffer was leafing through the pile when a buzzing sound disturbed his concentration.

Stauffer pushed the lock release button on the corner of the desk and the door swung open. Zazworsky burst across the threshold followed by a parade of Stauffer's old teammates from his work at the Repository: Maggie Martinez, Miriam Campbell, Sanjay Singh, Sammy Woo, Ken Red Elk, Max Manchester, Mitch Monahan, Jared Lincoln, Winston Greeley, Ginny Nguyen, Sandy Watson, Hank Phillips, Pete Pendleton, and Bill Tipton. From Stauffer's perspective, this was indeed a great core team.

But Stauffer was puzzled by the presence of several of his new team members. They already held positions of responsibility elsewhere in the Repository and the Hole. He was surprised that General Goldwyn had reassigned them to work on the new project.

As he worked his way around the room greeting everyone, he drew Bill Tipton and Pete Pendleton aside to ask them what was going on. "Many of you are already team leaders in your own right in the Repository, and I don't understand why General Goldwyn has assigned you here to this team. It sounds like a demotion. Don't get me wrong. I'm delighted to have you here, but I'm a little confused."

"Well, get over it, Bart," Bill Tipton responded with a laugh. "Because of the sensitivity of the mission here, the old man needed to assign only experienced time travelers and historians. He asked if Pete and I would be interested in working on this new mission and we both signed up in a heartbeat. Once General Goldwyn had explained a little bit about what he had in mind, we couldn't pass up on it."

"But who's taking charge over at the Repository?" Stauffer asked, still incredulous at the unanticipated change.

"General Goldwyn had a bunch of great people to choose from," Tipton replied. "Alice Duerden is taking over for me, and Rick Bailey is taking over for Pete." They've got the rhythm of the place down to a science and they'll do just fine. We'll be on a short leash if they need any assistance from us if something comes up they can't handle."

Stauffer nodded understanding and invited everyone to join him around the conference table to discuss the new project. No one was totally read in on all of the details, but General Goldwyn had enticed each of them with a special inducement to encourage them individually to join the team. Acknowledging that, Stauffer suggested that they go around the room and have each team member sound off and explain what got them excited about the new project.

Bill Tipton led off. "It was sometimes discouraging working temporal surveys in the Repository only to find that General Goldwyn had placed a block on the temporal observation portals because the historical timeframe broached on religious or spiritual matters. The further back we went, it seems the more blocks we encountered. At a certain point, it simply becomes an impassable wall. I want to see what's on the other side of the wall." Several other members of the team chimed in voicing agreement.

"That sounds fair.... and more than a little intriguing." Stauffer stood and wrote on the white board:

## SEE WHAT'S ON THE OTHER SIDE OF THE WALL

Stauffer turned to Hank Phillips seated next to him. "Hank, you were responsible for overseeing all of the archival work in the Repository, and General Goldwyn had just given you the lead on the DNA archival project when I left. That's exciting stuff! What carrot could he possibly have dangled in front of you that could entice you to join the team here?"

"Oh, General Goldwyn really knows how to push the right buttons. He offered me the opportunity to chase down the ancient Hall of Records and other libraries and repositories of antiquity that up until now have been blocked from view. With the temporal blocks removed, it offers all kinds of new possibilities. I wouldn't have missed this opportunity for the world."

As Stauffer wrote

## FIND THE HALL OF RECORDS

he asked, "What's the Hall of Records, Hank? Sounds like an ancient repository."

"You're right on track, Barton. The legendary Hall of Records is a repository of ancient records reputed to be hidden away in a cavern deep in the ground under the paws of the Sphinx on the Giza Plateau in Egypt. I don't think that it's going to pan out exactly that way, but it will be exciting to see how it turns out."

"But who is going to take the lead on the DNA project?"

"Actually, if you're in agreement, I'll retain oversight there as well but work part time here on your team. Does that work for you?"

"Well, yes.... absolutely."

Stauffer smiled and nodded to Ken Red Elk. "Ken, what got you excited about this project?"

"That's easy Barton. I have always been a student of the history and mythology of my people, the Hopis and Navajos of today.... the Pueblo and Anasazi people of the ancient past. I just need to know what is fact and what is fiction in all of the stories and legends that have been handed down to us through the years. So much of it seems to be distorted or exaggerated or otherwise unbelievable. I just want to set the record straight."

Stauffer turned and wrote:

## UNCOVER THE TRUE HISTORY OF ANCIENT NATIVE AMERICANS

Stauffer turned back around and nodded to Max Manchester. "Max, how about you? What got your attention?"

Manchester smiled at Stauffer. "Well, you know, Barton, we've talked about this before. I'm curious about the stories of the Great Flood and the Tower of Babel. So much has come down to us from disparate sources that it just seems to be a mass of confusion. Like Ken, I'd like to get the straight story on the matter."

Stauffer laughed and added, "As would I, my friend." He wrote on the white board:

## LEARN THE FULL STORY ABOUT THE FLOOD AND THE TOWER OF BABEL

Dr. Sanjay Singh started talking even before Stauffer could finish writing the last entry on the white board. "Much of the history of India is shrouded in legend. The Sanskrit writings from antiquity are considered by most European and American scholars as mythology rather than historical fact. I've been blocked at every turn trying to get at the truth. With the temporal blocks now removed with this project, I think that I'll finally be able to lay out that discrepancy, and we will be able to see the worth of those records that have come down to us."

Stauffer wrote on the white board:

## DISCOVER THE REALITY OF THE HISTORY OF ANCIENT INDIA

Dr. Sammy Woo spoke up quickly as Stauffer turned back around and acknowledged him. "Me too. Much of ancient Chinese history is considered merely mythology by Western scholars. Part of the problem is our own fault. The Chinese government has buried ancient pyramids, denied the discovery of ancient Caucasian graves, and limited access to hundreds, maybe thousands, of ancient Chinese archaeological sites. They have totally politicized what should otherwise be an historical and archeological issue. I, for one, would like to get at the truth. Where does China fit into the history of mankind?"

Stauffer smiled and wrote:

# GAIN A TRUE UNDERSTANDING OF ANCIENT CHINESE HISTORY

Stauffer continued around the room getting input from each team member in turn about what had attracted them to this project. All of them added additional detail, but it all amounted to the same thing. All were insatiably curious about what lay on the other side of the wall in mankind's ancient history. What were the individual contributions of all the different ancient cultures? How did it all tie together to make us what we are today? Stauffer captured all the comments on the white board, and when everyone had expressed their perspective, he thanked them for coming and adjourned the meeting with a promise to meet with them again after he had had an opportunity to get back with General Goldwyn on Monday to discuss his intent and the general parameters of the mission.

As Zazworsky led the team back out of the office, Stauffer went back over to his desk and leaned back in his chair staring at the list on the white board and processing all of the ideas and hopes and aspirations that had been expressed in the meeting. His team obviously didn't need any additional motivation from him. They were all extremely excited about the possibilities of exploring whole chapters of mankind's past that up until now had been totally opaque to the present generation of historians and scholars and even to researchers down in the Repository.

His forehead wrinkled in a slight frown as he considered the risks in it all. They would be moving in and out among the roots of mankind's religious past and foundational belief systems, and there was every possibility that they would see and experience things that might alter or diminish the value of the historical and religious legacy in their own personal belief systems and traditions. He realized that the team would be thrown up against the stark reality of the ancient past. Stauffer wondered how they would fare.

# Chapter 10

*Carlisle Barracks, Pennsylvania, Saturday, June 8, 2013, 11:30 a.m.*

After Stauffer had worked his way through the papers in his inbox, he picked up the DVD disk that General Goldwyn had given him to review about the *Sendero Luminoso* attack on the train on their way back from Machu Picchu to Cuzco. He had put off looking at it, not sure if he really wanted to explore his and his family's violent death at the hands of the Senderos. Stauffer turned the disk over and over in his hands, pondering what the disk might reveal. Thinking back on General Goldwyn's cautionary advice that it was extremely graphic and more than a little disquieting, he considered once again that it might be better not to know. He reasoned that viewing his own death might not be the healthiest thing in the world for him to do. But curiosity finally overcame his reticence, and he slipped the DVD into the computer tray to view its contents.

The DVD contained only one file. It was a lengthy video file, and Stauffer soon found himself viewing a collage of video captures from that day on the train back to Cuzco from Machu Picchu. The first section of video displayed the scene of Stauffer, Gwen, and their children sitting on the Cuzco train. Gwen was reading and Stauffer was watching the scenery out the window and occasionally dozing, his head flopping back against the headrest. The children were sitting opposite them on the other side of the aisle engrossed in a game of UNO. There weren't many other passengers in the car, and the train compartment was almost deserted. A small group of tourists was huddled at the front of the car engrossed in reviewing the pictures they had taken on their digital cameras the day before exploring the Machu Picchu archeological site.

About five minutes out of the station, two men dressed in nondescript ponchos, with bandanas draped across their faces and brandishing Uzi submachine guns, burst through the door at the back of the car carrying a heavy suitcase between them. In their rush, the two men dropped the suitcase as they entered and started moving forward down the aisle, one following the other. The on-screen Stauffer heard the thud of the suitcase as it hit the floor of the car, and he drowsily craned his neck around to see what was all the ruckus. When he saw the terrorists and recognized the threat, he was instantly alert. As the men rushed down the car towards them, Stauffer leaped into the aisle and moved toward them, trying to intercept them before they could reach his family. One of the terrorists swung his weapon around in front of him and fired a short burst into Stauffer's chest. Stauffer was thrown backward by the impact of the bullets and fell off to the side, crumpling in a heap onto an empty row of seats, his body slowly sliding onto the floor in a pool of blood.

The terrorists moved past Stauffer's inert body and, ignoring the children for the moment, focused their attention on Gwen. One of them grabbed her arms and pulled her to her feet. The other pulled back on her hair in an attempt to immobilize her. By now, the children were fully aware of the attack. Showing no fear, Corbie grabbed ahold of the arm of the terrorist that was holding Gwen and started kicking him in the leg. Crystal and Carlee rushed toward him and started pummeling the man's back and neck with their fists. The unexpected counterattack by the children distracted him momentarily, and he lost his grip on Gwen's hair. Gwen straightened up and surprised him with a hard elbow to the solar plexus. The startled man gasped for breath. He lost his grip on the machine gun he held at his side, and it dropped to the floor.

Gwen and the children knew their way around firearms and were all trained marksman. Stauffer had taken them on many family outings to the rifle and pistol range to teach the children how to shoot, and they were all familiar with several kinds of guns. None of them had ever seen an Uzi up close, but Cameron jumped into the aisle and grabbed the submachine gun that the terrorist had dropped and turned it on him. He hesitated momentarily, but seeing his father lying dead in a pool of blood in the adjacent row of seats fortified him, and he pulled off a burst of half a dozen rounds at the terrorist, cutting a swath of bloody holes diagonally across his chest and shoulder. The impact knocked the man backwards and onto the floor between the row of seats on the other side of the aisle from where Stauffer had fallen. He was dead before he hit the floor. Gwen moved to try to get between the remaining terrorist and the children and took several rounds in the side and back. As she fell lifeless into the children's arms, they also took several hits apiece, and they all slumped down onto the floor in a heap.

Witnessing the attack on the Stauffers, the frightened group of tourists at the front of the car scrambled to open the forward compartment door and escape into the next car to get out of harm's way. The terrorist still standing turned and emptied the remaining rounds in his clip into them and they all went down. While the terrorist was engaged in shooting up the front of the car, Colin reached furtively for the submachine gun lying on the floor next to him and pulled it towards him. When he got his fingers around the pistol grip, he jerked it around and emptied the remaining bullets in the clip into the terrorist standing above him. The terrorist's body jerked violently as the hail of bullets literally cut him in two. As Colin squeezed off the last round, he finally succumbed as well, his head falling backwards and hitting the floor, his eyes wide open in death. The car was still for just a brief moment, and then the trigger mechanism in the heavy suitcase the terrorists had dropped at the back of the car detonated the explosives within and the back end of the compartment disappeared in a blast of fire and smoke, derailing the car and sending it careening down the steep slope into the river below.

As Stauffer watched the dreadful scene unfold on the monitor screen, he went into shock, unable to move, frozen in a kind of horrific fascination. As he saw the train car with his now dead family tumble down the slope, he reached forward and hit the pause button on the computer video playback. He sat back in his chair trembling. His heart palpitated, and he breathed erratically. The scene on the monitor had seemed so real that he experienced all of the feelings of anger and fear and terror vicariously as if he had just been there. He was anguished that he had been able to do so little to protect his family and yet, so proud of Gwen and the children and their response in the face of danger and the threat of imminent death.

Stauffer sat in his chair breathing heavily, staring at the frozen image on the screen of Gwen and the children lying there across each other in death on the floor of the train car. His breathing continued labored for almost half an hour as he struggled to get his emotions under control. He knew that everything he had seen was now on another time line, separate from the reality they now occupied. None of this had happened in their present reality. Finally, still breathing hard, Stauffer leaned forward and pushed the pause button to see what else General Goldwyn had recorded on the DVD. On the monitor screen, the train car continued sliding down the slope into the river and then the chaotic scene abruptly cut off. In its place was a different image. This time, it appeared to be a video capture of the passengers boarding the train at the Machu Picchu station earlier that morning. Stauffer watched himself and his family carry their handbags onto the train and deposit them in the rack above their seats and sit down.

Then, the other group of tourists boarded the train car and moved past them to the front of the car. The conductor stood on the platform checking tickets and observing the passengers loading. It didn't take long. There were only the two groups that were leaving to go back to Cuzco on the early run. Just as the conductor waved forward to the engineer to get started, two men came rushing forward from behind the station house carrying a heavy suitcase between them. They pulled scarves around their necks up and over their faces and pulled back their ponchos revealing the Uzi submachine guns they had concealed beneath.

As the train started to move, one of the terrorists came up behind the conductor and pistol whipped him with the barrel of his gun. The conductor started to go down, and the terrorists held him up by the arms and pushed him ahead of them into the last car of the train. They moved in behind him lugging the suitcase between them. The last car was empty, and so they threw the unconscious conductor's body off to the side on the last row of seats and began moving forward slowly, carrying the heavy suitcase between them. They reached the far end of the car and passed through the doorway into the next car. It was also deserted and the terrorists made their way down the aisle toward the door at the front of the car.

As they neared the forward door, Stauffer was startled to see two hands appear close to the floor on each side of the aisle in front of them, each grasping the end of a thin cord between them. As the terrorists reached that point in the aisle, the hands pulled back through the temporal openings and stretched the cord tight. As the terrorists' legs came in contact with the cord, a temporal portal opened up in back of them and Zaworsky stepped through into the aisle and gave the two terrorists a hard shove. The terrorists tried to keep their balance as they were pushed forward, but they tripped on the tightened cord and fell face first through another portal that had opened up in front of them.

As they disappeared through the portal, they dropped the heavy suitcase to the floor in the aisle behind them. One of the terrorists also dropped his submachine gun. Zazworsky moved forward quickly, picked up the heavy suitcase, and swung it on through the portal, and it too disappeared. Zazworsky leaned down, and, aware that the whole scene was being filmed with a temporal video capture, he turned in the direction of the temporal monitor that was recording the scene, picked up the Uzi and smiled. Holding the submachine gun in his left hand, he mugged the camera and gave a big thumbs-up sign with his right hand. Then he stepped back through the time portal behind him through which he had entered, and the scene on the monitor abruptly blacked out. After a brief pause, the picture came back into focus, this time on Stauffer and Gwen sitting in their seats on the next train car forward. Gwen was engrossed in reading some travel brochures, and Stauffer had nodded off and was fast asleep. Watching the monitor, Stauffer started to laugh as he watched a small portal opening appear directly in front of the sleeping Stauffer and a hand reaching through, depositing a small folded piece of paper and a long-stemmed red rose on his lap. The hand quickly withdrew just as Stauffer awoke and became aware of the rose. Once again, the scene faded out, and Stauffer was left there staring at a blank monitor screen.

Stauffer leaned back in his chair and put his hands behind his head to stretch. "I couldn't have pulled that one off any better myself. They're definitely good." Stauffer mused. "I wonder where they sent those two goons?"

"I'm glad you asked, Boss." Zazworsky had entered Stauffer's office through the open door and had caught the last bit of the video capture. "We talked about the possibilities for some time and finally decided that we ought to deposit them on Peruvian soil.... only, much higher up than Machu Picchu,.... way.... way higher up.... high in the clouds, where it's really brisk and invigorating. When I pushed them through the time portal, they landed on a small ledge in a crevasse in the ice on the summit of the Huascarán, the highest peak in the Peruvian Andes, about 22,000 plus feet up the mountain. The boys would have had a hard time breathing at that altitude, but it didn't really matter. When I threw their suitcase of explosives through the portal after them, it blew up and the explosion brought down an avalanche of ice and snow into the crevasse on top of them, and that will pretty much keep them on ice for millennia to come."

"Wouldn't the explosion and avalanche pose a danger to any climbers on the mountain or villages down below?"

"We thought of that, Boss, and we did a thorough survey of the mountain on all sides all the way down to populated areas. There weren't any climbing parties on the mountain the day we selected, and we chose the eastern face of the southern summit of the mountain, away from any villages below. The whole affair pretty much went unnoticed even by the villagers living closest to that part of the mountain below. It will be a long time before those two popsicles see the light of day again. Oh.... and, Boss, this is for you as a memento of that day." Zazworsky reached behind him and pulled out the Uzi submachine gun and handed it to Stauffer. "This isn't exactly an ancient artifact and I didn't even need to sign it out from the vaults. I think that you ought to have it as a memento of your adventure in Peru."

* * * * * * * * * * * * * * * * * * * *

That evening, when Stauffer returned home, he was extremely tired from the long day in the Crypt. But as he walked through the door, he encountered Colin and Cameron racing through the house playing with the toy wooden guns he had made for them, and Crystal, Carlee, and Corbie were arguing over the TV controller. He could hear Gwen in the kitchen moving pots around on the stove. As he stood there in the doorway, accosted by the cacophony of his noisy children, he was overcome by sheer joy just to see them all again. He was acutely aware that they had perished in other timelines before, but this was the first time that he carried with him the stark visual image of their deaths, and it became almost too much for him in the moment. The boys stopped racing long enough to acknowledge his arrival and as they tried to chase by, he grabbed them both and gave them a long, protracted hug despite their struggles to get away. Then, he walked over to the TV nook where the girls were fighting over the controller and gave them all hugs and kissed their cheeks as the boys shouted, "Danger, danger, Dad's in a hugging mood tonight."

Finally, Stauffer turned his attention to Gwen, who had just come back from the pantry carrying a bag of rice. He moved around the island cooking surface and grabbed her in his arms and gave her a long, loving embrace. "Well," she exclaimed, "to what do I owe this exceptional attention? Has it been that kind of a tough day?"

"Actually, Gwen," he responded, "you have no idea."

Turning in the direction of the children playing, he raised his voice and asked, "How would you all like to go for a family outing next week over to the pistol range to plunk a few targets? I have a friend who has an Uzi in his gun collection. It's a 9mm model with a 32-round magazine. How would you like to try your hand at firing a real submachine gun?"

"An Uzi?" Gwen questioned. "Isn't that just a little too much gun for the children at their age?"

"Oh, I don't know, Gwen. You never can tell when it might come in handy."

# Chapter 11

"So. Barton, how did it go watching the Machu Picchu train video captures?" General Goldwyn asked at the beginning of their meeting that Monday morning.

"Well, sir, that was a.... sobering.... experience. It really makes me appreciate what a great wife and family I have. It was hard to watch, but.... thank you for sharing it with me. It was important that I see it."

Stauffer had started to mist up just thinking about the video, and General Goldwyn changed the subject quickly, "I'm glad that it worked for you. You needed to see it. So, Barton, how did your first meeting with your new team down in the Crypt go on Saturday?"

"Extremely well, sir. Everyone is highly motivated and anxious to get moving to lay bare the mysteries of the ancient past."

"What did they seem most excited about, Barton?"

"Well, sir, they're all over the map. Here is a list of the things they mentioned as we went around the room."

Stauffer handed General Goldwyn a single sheet of paper of what he had copied from the white board following the team meeting. General Goldwyn quickly scanned down the page, stopping occasionally to smile. Finally, he looked up and commented, "You know, Barton, I could have predicted most of this list based on my initial interview with each of your team members. All of these things pretty much came up in our initial conversations. But Bob Zazworsky's list takes the cake.... King Solomon's mines.... the lost city of El Dorado.... the Oak Island Money Pit. I thought that I had cured Bob of his lust for gold and riches."

"You know, sir," Stauffer laughed, "I don't think we'll ever cure Ski of that. He has the heart of a lion and the curiosity of a child. But it's not the money nor the wealth. It's the adventure of finding and recovering lost treasure. I think we can leverage and focus that energy to advance our purposes on this project."

"Well, I hope you're right. Just keep him busy on the tasks at hand. Changing the subject, Barton, I like Hank Phillips' idea of trying to locate the Hall of Records. You know, Barton, in recent years, we have discovered a small handful of ancient libraries and caches of books and records.... the Dead Sea Scrolls, the Nag Hammadi library, the Ashurbanipal cuneiform library at ancient Nineveh, the Cairo Genizah library, the hidden libraries of Katmandu and Timbuktu.... the list goes on. But there are hundreds of other stashes of ancient records and artifacts that still lie buried and lost all over the world. Now that I'm removing the temporal blocks, it opens up the opportunity for Hank and the rest of your team to seek these out and perhaps add that knowledge to our collection of ancient records."

"Are all of the temporal blocks going to be removed so that we will have free access to all of our past? Most of the team are chomping at the bit to see what's on the other side of the wall."

"Other side of the wall?"

"That part of history that we haven't been able to examine because of the temporal blocks. They've been frustrated by the areas of history that have been denied to them up until now, and they're anxious to see what it's all about. Will we have free access without any temporal blocks?"

"Almost, but not entirely, Barton. I'm going to leave a few temporal blocks in place. You'll see the pattern as you explore the ancient past, and I think you'll see the wisdom in the blocks that remain."

"Like what, sir?"

"Well, although I'm removing most of the blocks for the Crypt Team, I'm keeping the temporal blocks on all areas of potential divine interaction with mankind. Some things simply must remain opaque to us. But you will be able to scope out pretty much everything else. I think that that will begin to satisfy the curiosity of your team members."

"Yes, sir. I can see the possibilities. Do you have a preference for where we get started?"

"From my perspective, Barton, the long pole in the tent is the Flood. It's the elephant in the room. Most authorities treat the historic mention of the Flood as myth or, at best, as fanciful oral traditions of limited, regional floods. This ignores the fact that practically every culture in the world has a flood story, even cultures that are land-locked far from the sea. There are literally thousands of flood myths and legends among the world's cultures, most of which associate the Biblical Flood with a complete cleansing of the earth from the wrong-doings of humankind by their god or gods and signaling a new beginning for their ancestors. Today, scholars sometimes use terminology like *antediluvian* and *deluge* in polite conversation, but most scientists are skeptical and do so tongue-in-cheek. But if there were such a flood, can you begin to imagine the artifacts, the libraries and the histories of the world that it might have eradicated?"

General Goldwyn was beginning to work up a head of steam. "The time period for the flood usually demarcates mankind's historical past from protohistory and prehistory since we have never discovered any written records from that time period or before. But, what if in fact, writing was already well-developed, and there were many collections of books and other kinds of records that were destroyed and lost in the flood waters that swept over the land?"

"That opens up all kinds of possibilities. Where are you at on this one, sir?" Stauffer asked. "Do you believe there was a universal flood like that described in the Bible?"

"Ah, Barton, it doesn't really matter what I believe. You and your team have to nail this one down yourselves. This is your baby. You will have to address a multitude of questions to gain a more precise and undistorted vision of antiquity. There's lots of questions that you will need to address. Was there a devastating flood anciently? Was there one great universal flood or were there many local, regional floods around the world recalled in myth today? Was there just one Ark or were there multiple boats and water craft used to escape the flood waters? Was there one Noah and family or were there many families and groups who escaped the devastation of a flood in boats? Lots of unknowns there. What do you think, Barton? Where are **you** at on this one?"

"Well, sir," Stauffer responded, "I understand scientific skepticism about the Flood traditions and the story of Noah's ark, but I've always wanted to believe the story unconditionally."

"But?" General Goldwyn asked, noting the hesitancy in Stauffer's voice.

"Well, sir. I have a hard time reconciling where all the water came from that would be required to inundate the entire planet all at the same time."

"Ah, now that may turn out to be the easiest part to document and prove out."

"What do you mean, sir?"

"Here, take this folder and look at the information it contains. It appears that old Mother Earth has a lot more water in reserve than we've given her credit for."

"Sir?"

"Just look it over, Barton, and then try to connect the dots. I'll be interested to see what you come up with."

Stauffer opened the folder and quickly scanned its contents. There was just one report, maybe six or seven pages, stapled together. The report paper was dog-eared and wrinkled at the staple. General Goldwyn had apparently read it through multiple times.

"What's this all about, sir?"

"I just received this report earlier last month. It's pretty heady stuff. It compiles the latest conclusions from scientific research that suggests that there is an enormous envelope of water buried deep beneath the earth's surface.... three or four hundred miles down and perhaps up to several hundred miles thick.... a veritable ocean that may contain up to three times as much water as we have in the earth's surface oceans. The surface ocean is on average only two and a half miles deep. At its deepest point in the Mariana Trench, it goes down to a depth of just 6.85 miles or so. This envelope of water they've postulated that lies deep in the earth's mantle may be **several hundred miles** thick. It's an enormous amount of water suspended in a massive layer of a crystalline mineral material called ringwoodite. Here, take a look at this."

General Goldwyn reached over to the conference table and handed Stauffer a large glass jar filled with small blue crystals.

"What's this, sir?"

"Ringwoodite crystals."

"Ringwoodite? What kind of name is that?" Stauffer asked.

"It's named after a scientist by the name of Ringwood who studied the kinds of phase transition minerals that might occur at great depths in the earth's mantle. Ringwood postulated the existence of this layer of crystals, and it came to be known as ringwoodite. According to scientists researching the matter, terrestrial ringwoodite rarely finds its way to the surface. To my understanding, there is only one known example in existence that was found in Brazil."

Stauffer turned the bottle over and over in his hands watching the light from the fluorescent lights overhead catch the tiny facets of the blue ringwoodite crystals. "But, sir, if it rarely comes to the surface, where did you get this sample?"

"That was tricky, Barton. When I learned about the potential existence of the ringwoodite layer and the subterranean ocean that it might hold, I had our techs rig a special time portal setup in a compact, super-pressurized chamber to extract a sample. This ringwoodite came through the portal with explosive force, powered by super-heated steam, and it took several hours for it to cool down sufficiently to extract it from the chamber and examine. Now, imagine an envelope of this stuff surrounding the earth hundreds of miles thick over four or five hundred miles down. Scientists have postulated that these crystals act like a gigantic sponge, holding massive amounts of oxygen and hydrogen.... water.... in suspension."

"I'm following you so far, sir. But so what?"

"Well, Barton, it appears that there's enough water deep beneath our feet to submerge the entire planet. The question is.... how would it get out to the surface to do the job?"

Stauffer immediately saw the implications of what General Goldwyn was getting at and his mind started racing.

"Okay, Barton, the ball is in your court. Start there and get to work on it. Is this ringwoodite layer the source for a universal flood and did it really happen?"

"Understand. I'll get right on it. Anything else for today, sir?"

"No, Barton, I think that is quite enough."

Stauffer started to face about with the file holder tightly gripped in his hand. "Wait, Barton," General Goldwyn interjected. "Don't forget this. You may need it." Goldwyn extended the jar of ringwoodite to Stauffer to take with him.

"Yes, sir. Thank you, sir."

* * * * * * * * * * * * * * * * * * * * * *

Later on, back in his office, Stauffer sat at his desk scribbling notes on a yellow pad of paper trying to get the big picture. On the desk beside him was the bottle of ringwoodite. From time to time, he would pick it up, turning it over and over in his hands as he watched the crystals cascade over themselves in a crystalline waterfall inside the jar. But he wasn't really getting anywhere. Frustrated, he got up from his desk, and, taking the pad and pencil with him, walked over to his conference table and sat down again. He scribbled a few more lines and then stood and started drawing rough conceptual images on the white board on the wall next to the table. After a few minutes, he sat down again and started scribbling more notes. He alternated between the chair and the white board a dozen times during the next several hours until he began to develop a germ of an idea about how the whole picture came together. Suddenly, it came to him, and he jumped to his feet and rushed out the door and down the hallway, bumping into Zazworsky by the elevator.

"Where ya goin' in such a hurry, Boss?"

"Oh, I'm going to take a long, late lunch hour and drive home. I need to pick up a couple of things. Could you arrange a team meeting in my office at about 1500 hours this afternoon? And make sure that everyone brings their impermeable lab coats and safety goggles. Oh, and could you please arrange to have a heavy-duty wooden lab table set up in my office? I'll need it when I get back. See you later."

The elevator door opened and Stauffer stepped inside. Turning back to face Zazworsky, he added, "1500 hours sharp, Ski. We're going to conduct a little science experiment."

The elevator door abruptly closed, leaving Zazworsky standing there in the hallway totally bewildered. "Yes, sir, Mr. Wizard," he saluted, and, totally puzzled by Stauffer's excitement, he walked back down the hallway to the team offices to set up for the afternoon meeting.

* * * * * * * * * * * * * * * * * * * *

At precisely 1500 hours, Zazworsky knocked on Stauffer's office door and ushered the team into the room. As requested, all were wearing their impermeable lab coats with their safety goggles perched back on their foreheads. As the team members entered, they had to walk around the wooden table that Zazworsky had set up in the middle of the office. On the table, Stauffer had positioned a small inflatable wading pool half filled with water with an enormous natural sponge that Stauffer used to wash the family cars sitting in the middle of the pool. Stauffer had been working at his desk pouring over some papers but stood up quickly and invited all to come into the room and take seats at his conference table. With puzzled looks on their faces, they all filed in, edging their way around the wading pool, and taking their seats at the table.

"Thank you all for coming on such short notice. We've got a lot of ground to cover. General Goldwyn gave me some significant guidance at our meeting this morning, and I need to pass it along to you."

"Sure thing, Bart, but why the slickers and goggles?" Tipton asked.

"That will become clear momentarily, Bill. First, I need to walk you through some of the ideas the Old Man passed on to me. He believes that the key to our mission here in exploring our ancient past is the Great Flood. It's kind of the line of demarcation between modern times and ancient times. If we can separate Flood fact from Flood fiction, he thinks that we will be able to mount an organized investigation of mankind's ancient past.... what scientists typically refer to as prehistory or protohistory."

"How does he propose that we do that, Barton?" Miriam Campbell asked.

"Okay, track with me on this," Stauffer responded. "Miriam, you're an astrophysicist. We just went through the '*what if*' scenarios last year as we confronted the meteoroid on a collision course with Earth. What would happen if a similar comet or meteoroid crashed directly into the earth travelling at high velocity in the earth's distant past?"

"Well, Barton, from what I understand of high energy impacts like that, and depending upon the actual size of the object, it would result in a massive explosion on the order of an ultra-high-yield atomic weapon that could throw us into nuclear winter or it might even be a planet killer."

"Yes, that's been the general consensus. But there's been some recent scientific discoveries that we need to factor into the equation. Ongoing research seems to suggest that there is an enormous volume of water buried deep beneath the earth's surface in a huge subterranean ocean. It's hundreds of miles down and several hundred miles thick. Estimates are that the volume of water it contains is three times that of the surface oceans. This envelope of water is suspended in a massive layer of a crystalline substance called ringwoodite. Here, this is what ringwoodite looks like." Stauffer passed the bottle of crystals around the table for all to examine.

Bob Zazworsky raised his hand and started to ask a question, but Stauffer cut him off. "It's named after a researcher by the name of Ringwood." Nodding to Bob Zazworsky, he observed, "If you had discovered it, Ski, it would be appropriately named 'Zazworskyite,' a totally improbable name." Everyone in the room laughed at Stauffer's observation. As Zazworsky turned the jar over and over in his hands fascinated by the sparkling crystals, Stauffer continued. "Now imagine a layer of the stuff, maybe three or four hundred miles thick, holding a huge basin of water in suspension like a giant sponge."

"Yes, Barton," Dr. Campbell interjected. "I've read recent journal articles about the ongoing research on the postulated ringwoodite layer. But isn't it all still somewhat speculative at this point?"

"Yes, I know, Miriam. Scientists are always cautious and slow to buy into a new paradigm like this. It will take years of further research and study before they've confirmed the existence of this subterranean ocean with absolute certainty, probably as long as it will take for the current generation of scientists who are dead set against the idea to die off. We don't have that kind of time. So, let's just accept the basic premise as fact for the moment. Now think, Miriam. As the explosive energy from the impact of an enormous comet or meteoroid started to spread fire and dust throughout the atmosphere, what if the kinetic energy of the impact punched down through the Earth's mantle to the ringwoodite layer, forcing enormous volumes of water to the surface, literally gushing out of every crater, crevice, cavity, hollow, and spring on the planet, effectively extinguishing the fires and inundating the planet with a great flood?"

Before Dr. Campbell could answer, Stauffer said, "Here, let's do a little demonstration of the concept. Would all of you please join me around the pool." Stauffer stood and motioned to everyone to come over to where he was standing by the wading pool on the table. As the team gathered around the pool, Stauffer continued, "The water in this wading pool represents the Earth's surface oceans. The sponge in the center of the pool is saturated with water and represents the water in the subterranean ocean buried deep beneath the earth in the ringwoodite layer. To be truly proportional for the experiment, the sponge would need to be about five feet in diameter, but this was the biggest sponge I had on hand at home and it will have to do. If the Earth was hit by a large comet or meteoroid in just the right place, I suspect that the water in the subterranean ocean would come spurting out like a soda bottle when you shake it up and then pop the cap. Everyone, pull your goggles down over your eyes." Handing Zazworsky Colin's Little League baseball bat, he continued, "Here, Ski, let's run the experiment. I want you to hit the sponge with the bat as hard as you can."

"Are you sure, Boss? I can hit pretty hard. I don't want to break anything."

"Go right ahead, Ski. Swing away. Give it your best shot."

Zazworsky reared back and brought the bat down hard on the sponge with all the force he could muster. The force of the impact cracked the bat on the wooden table top beneath the pool, but the impact of the bat on the soddened sponge sent water flying in all directions, soaking all of the team members standing in the tight circle around the pool."

As they stood there with water dripping down from their hair, goggles and lab coats, some began laughing uncontrollably among themselves.

"Can I be next, Barton," Max Manchester quipped. "I'd like to give that nasty old sponge a try."

Not to be outdone, Pete Pendleton spoke up, "If we had a bunch of sponges and Ski hadn't broken the bat, we could play Whack-a-Mole."

That cracked everybody up, and everyone started laughing and talking at once.

Dr. Campbell quieted them down, raising her voice in a more serious vein and asking, "Are you saying that's what happened, Barton? A comet or a meteoroid unleashed a massive volume of water from a subterranean ocean that caused the legendary Flood?"

"I don't know. I guess I'm only trying to suggest what we might look for as General Goldwyn removes the blocks on the temporal observation monitors for our team. Most scientists today are dubious of a universal flood, and argue instead for a number of much smaller, localized regional floods around the world at various times to account for the numerous flood myths in practically every culture in the world. I've been doing a little online research during the past two hours. Based on stratification studies done in the Middle East and a deep crater-like feature discovered on the ocean floor between Madagascar and the Indian subcontinent, some scientists have hypothesized that a comet or meteoroid traveling at very high velocity hit the earth around 3000 BC in the Indian Ocean just to the east of Madagascar. The impact from the object created a 30 kilometer-wide undersea depression in water over two miles deep that scientists today refer to as the Burckle Crater. They theorize that the impact of the object caused a tremendous tsunami that inundated all of the coastal lands surrounding the Indian Ocean. They suggest that that alone might explain all of the flood myths for that part of the world. But, think for a moment, Miriam, what would have happened if the kinetic energy from that collision impact punched all the way down through the earth's crust to the ringwoodite layer and opened up the way for the super-pressurized water to come rushing out?"

As Dr. Campbell stood there drenched and dripping water on the floor, her mind was racing, trying to calculate the parameters of the aftermath of such an event. "Let's see, Barton,.... such an impact might force enough water to the surface to cause a universal flood. The water would come to the surface not just in the vicinity of the asteroid strike but everywhere on the planet that sits on top of this subterranean ocean in the ringwoodite layer sponge. The water would be super-heated, and as it mixed with the surface ocean water, it would raise the temperature of the water appreciably, perhaps causing the extinction of some marine species. The impact would cause a massive amount of super-heated water and steam to flood over the land surfaces, cooking most living things.... effectively sterilizing the earth, much as Doctor Gates' autoclave he uses to sterilize his medical equipment."

"What would such an inundation of super-heated water do at the poles?"

"Well, I'm no climatologist, but it seems to me that if it happened during one of earth's ice ages, it would effectively melt a great deal of ice, perhaps abruptly ending the ice age as the glaciers and ice pack rapidly melted and retreated northward. Instead of taking thousands of years, an ice age might be reversed in a matter of a few years."

"What about all of the water that might escape into the atmosphere as steam?"

"Well, for certain there would be torrential rains for a considerable period of time."

"Okay, one last question.... what eventually would happen to all of the water?"

Dr. Campbell scratched her head and looked back at the water on the floor and the sponge in the wading pool on the conference table. She walked back over to the table and looked closely at the water remaining in the pool. "Barton, when Ski first hit the sponge and splashed water all over, it increased the depth of water in the pool an inch to two as the water in the sponge was released. Now, the water in the pool has receded back to almost nothing as the sponge has reabsorbed much of the water remaining in the pool."

"And what does that suggest to you?" Stauffer asked.

"Well," Dr. Campbell postulated, "in order for dry land to emerge again following a universal deluge as you describe, the water would have to sink down into the Earth and be reabsorbed back into the ringwoodite layer."

"Ah, now I think you may be on to something there. And why would the water eventually flow back into the ringwoodite layer, leaving the surface oceans at almost the same level, perhaps a little higher?"

"Maybe it has something to do with the way the earth's water system operates.... a certain volume of water has to be present in the subterranean layer to support a percentage of that volume on the surface. Maybe there's a natural required balance or ratio of subterranean water to surface water," Dr. Campbell suggested.

"Well said, Miriam." Stauffer applauded. "Now that you've already done most of the heavy-duty thinking for us on this one, we're going to need to work the temporal technology to see how it actually played out to answer the big questions."

Waving everyone back over to his conference table, he suggested, "Everyone leave your goggles and wet lab coats by the pool and come on back over here to my conference table. We need to get organized for our next steps. First, I'd like to ask Maggie and

Mitch to be responsible for organizing us into teams to divide up the earth's surface to explore the different geographical regions of the world. We're going to need to spread out and explore the distant past in the temporal vicinity of 3000 BC to see if we can pinpoint the comet or meteoroid strike in the Indian Ocean postulated by the scientists based on the crater on the sea floor there. As soon as anyone gets a hit in their observation area, we need to pass the word and everyone needs to focus in on that time window to see how the impact affected other geographical areas of the world. After we get some preliminary observations under our belt, we need to gather back here for a more extensive meeting and see what we have. Maggie and Mitch, as soon as you have divided up the Earth's land and sea surface into seven areas of responsibility and made assignments for all of us into two-person teams to each of those areas, we can get started. Bunch several of the teams closer together around the Indian Ocean area and spread the rest of the teams out across the remainder of the globe."

Maggie Martinez responded quickly, "Can do, Barton, we've already been discussing areas of interest among ourselves for the past two days. I think that we can divide up team areas of responsibility post haste and get the word out to everyone within the hour." Turning to face the group, Martinez rattled off guidance, "Okay, everyone, listen up. Once we get everyone divided into teams, be standing by at your temporal observation work stations. If we get lucky, we may have some results by the end of the afternoon."

# Chapter 12

The teams were up and running an hour later. Each team used a similar search protocol in looking for the comet/meteoroid impact or its potential effects. It was a simple bracketing technique that was used in most Repository operations. When they knew of an important event that they wanted to scope out but they weren't too sure of the exact time in history when it occurred, they bracketed it with best-guess earlier and later dates and then moved inward incrementally until they finally encountered the phenomenon. It was very much like the higher-lower card game. With the potential target date of 3000 BC for the comet/meteoroid impact as a start point, they began bracketing that date by going back 500 years earlier to 3500 BC and then moving forward 500 years to 2500 BC, then back again to 3400 BC and forward to 2600 BC and so on. Each of the scan windows took approximately 30 minutes as each of the teams had a lot of land and water area to look over during the scan. As time wore on, each of the team members grew more tense as they zeroed in on the targeted time frame.

But at the end of almost three hours' work at the temporal screens, they hadn't turned up anything promising. Finally, Stauffer called a time out and reconvened the teams back in his office. "Well," he said addressing the team, "either the comet or meteoroid never hit the earth, or we didn't go back far enough, or we went back too far. I think that tomorrow when we get started again, we may get some mileage out of reverse bracketing. We need to start at 3500 and work backward and at 2500 BC and work forward to see if our initial bracket missed the boat. For now, let's adjourn and go home and get some sleep. We're going to need all the energy we can muster for tomorrow."

\* \* \* \* \* \* \* \* \* \* \* \* \* \* \* \* \* \* \*

Maggie Martinez and Mitch Monahan got the teams working early the next morning, widening the bracket incrementally. They had only been at it for thirty minutes when all of the teams began registering some kind of unusual geological and meteorological activity between 2300 and 2400 BC. All of the teams switched over to bracketing by ten-year increments and quickly discovered a major earth upheaval at about 2350 BC. Max Manchester and Miriam Campbell were monitoring the coastline surrounding the Indian Ocean using a dual temporal monitor setup. Dr. Campbell adjusted the angle of vision on her monitor upward to view the sky over the Indian Ocean and was the first to spot the descent and impact of the meteoroid. It was apparently a large clump of rock and ice, about a kilometer across. As it entered the upper atmosphere, it exploded in a brilliant fireball and broke up into thousands of smaller pieces which rushed downward, impacting in the Indian Ocean in a highly dispersed array of icy debris.

When Dr. Campbell first spied the meteoroid, she shouted to Manchester, "Max, there's a super-bolide coming in."

Puzzled, Manchester turned from his monitor where he was observing the ocean surface further to the north. "What's a 'bolide,' Miriam?"

"It's a bright exploding fireball in the sky, and this one is off the magnitude scale. It's big.... real big.... and it just went from one massive object to several thousand smaller ones." While Dr. Campbell continued observing the impact of the meteoroid fragments, Manchester notified Martinez and Monahan, and the whole team gathered again in Stauffer's office to exchange information. Dr. Campbell gave everyone the exact time and location coordinates of the impact and projected on the large flat screen monitor on the wall the video capture she had made of the approaching meteoroid, its fiery entry into the earth's atmosphere and the impact of all the fragments.

As Dr. Campbell had predicted, the impact explosion looked much like an enormous, high-yield nuclear detonation with an ominous mushroom cloud climbing high into the stratosphere, its fiery cap extending for hundreds of miles outward over the afternoon sky. A fiery shock wave and several giant tsunami waves also sped outward over the water from the central points of impact from all of the meteoroid fragments until they overwhelmed the coastline surrounding the Indian Ocean and rushed relentlessly inland, destroying everything in their path.

Seeing the impact of the meteoroid fragments had an electrifying effect on the teams. Everyone rushed back to their temporal monitor work stations to input the time coordinates that Manchester had given them to be able to observe what happened in their own assigned geographical areas as a function of the meteoroid fragments' impact. They conducted those scans in real time and so they sat at their temporal monitors the remainder of the day observing the aftermath of the impact, moving the scans in broad sweeps across their assigned areas.

They all recorded similar observations. The sky quickly darkened around the world as dust and debris from the impact spread across the face of the planet. The meteoroid came close to being a planet killer as Dr. Campbell had suggested. The multiple impacts from the fragments sent shock waves through the Earth's crust around the world, totally disrupting normal plate tectonics. The impact caused massive earthquakes and volcanic eruptions in every part of the world. Continental and oceanic tectonic plates crashed against each other with enormous force and pressure causing some plates to push over others and rise into the air, forming new mountain ranges almost instantaneously, and forcing others to be buried back into the earth into the mantle in gigantic subduction zones. As Sanjay Singh observed in their next team meeting, "The whole face of the earth changed in a matter of a couple of days, not gradually over eons as most scientists theorize. It's not just a matter of the earth being submerged in the deluge. The whole relationship between land masses and seas seems to have undergone a monumental rearrangement."

Stauffer's prediction turned out to be correct that, in addition to the effects of the giant tsunami on the immediate coastline around the Indian Ocean, the comet's impact also must have sent a massive kinetic transfer wave down into the Earth's mantle because enormous fountains of water and geysers of steam started appearing all over the African, Asian and European land mass and in the surrounding oceans and seas. The energy behind the geysers was enormous. Some of them shot up 10-15 miles into the air. Zazworsky quipped, "It reminds me of seeing Old Faithful in Yellowstone last year, only these geysers are on steroids."

The air circulating around the Earth quickly filled up with a thick layer of dense steam and water vapor which climbed rapidly into the stratosphere. With so much moisture in suspension in the air, torrential rains began falling all over the planet, and, in combination with the effects of the tsunamis, the steam geysers, and the water fountains, the Earth was quickly inundated and rapidly began submerging in water. By the beginning of the second day, the teams were witnessing the beginnings of the Great Flood in all parts of the world. Although the surface of the seas was far from level amidst all of the turbulence, water managed to cover the Earth's entire landmass quickly, with the flood waters creeping up the steep slopes of even the highest mountain peaks, as the heavens unloosed a relentless downpour from above. Eventually, the torrential rains and thick layers of water vapor and steam made it difficult for the team to see much with their temporal observation monitors. By the time the teams called it a night, nothing could be seen on the monitors except roiling waters and pelting rainfall.

The next morning, the teams gathered around Stauffer's conference table to review what they had observed so far. Most significantly, they had confirmed that the earth had indeed experienced a universal flood which had affected the entire planet at the same time, and that, in this case, catastrophism trumped gradualism. Now, they had a whole set of additional tasks to check out.

Stauffer reviewed his notes and then spoke to the group. "With the destruction of living things as the deluge swept across the planet, there must have been survivors, otherwise, mankind and all of the species of plants and animals we see today would have been terminated then and there. However, the myths of the Great Flood that have come down to the present are sufficiently different in their details about the family or group of people that escaped the Flood that it warrants looking for a great multiplicity of boats and survivors rather than supposing merely one family, the family of Noah, escaped the flood." Several team members began to squirm in their chairs as Stauffer broached on what was probably a traditional and treasured narrative.

Stauffer looked around the room at his team, smiled, and continued in a conciliatory tone. "General Goldwyn suggested to me that we investigate to see if there was just one family that escaped the flood waters in an ark or were there perhaps many groups that managed to build boats or other watercraft to escape the flood. This

prescribes our next task. We're going to have to search for Noah....
and any others who might have somehow escaped the Flood. I think
this is going to prove a very challenging task to accomplish."

Stauffer stopped talking and sat back in his chair. There was
a palpable electrifying energy in the room, and everyone started
talking in side bars at once. Stauffer realized that they all needed to
weigh in on the matter, and he just sat there quietly letting them have
free rein. After about ten minutes, he stood and spoke with carefully
chosen words. "I think that we need to focus this next phase of our
investigation in a methodical and organized way. I think that it will
be prudent to begin with a search for Noah and then perhaps other
groups that might have been prepared for the Flood with a ship or
big boat that would provide sufficient room for provisions to support
them for an extended period of time. I'm going to ask Max and Hank
to head up this effort. We need to divide up the earth's pre-Flood
oceans and land mass and run comprehensive scans around the globe
from about five to ten years prior to the comet's impact forward
to see if we can discover the location of the construction of an ark
as reported in Genesis and any evidence of any similar projects as
described in the Epic of Gilgamesh and other cultural mythologies.
I don't think it's going to be particularly easy because we don't
really know where to look or precisely what to look for.... and it's
a big planet. Just because the people in the stories of these groups
are reported to have landed in certain parts of the world, it doesn't
necessarily indicate that that's where they launched from. Adrift at
sea for an extended period of time, they could have conceivably come
from anywhere on the planet. I think we've got our work cut out
for us."

Stauffer paused to give everyone time to consider and
process what he had just suggested. Then, turning to Manchester
and Phillips, he continued. "I'd like to get started on the search for
Noah as early as we can, tomorrow if at all possible. If you can get
us organized into teams as quickly as that, we can get started. Please
organize different teams from our asteroid-search teams to give
everyone an opportunity to work with different team members. I
think that we'll need to use two-person search teams again. I think
as we look for Noah, we're going to discover a lot of additional
information that we're going to need to capture, catalog, and share.
We need to set up some kind of information-sharing drop box on

our classified intranet so that each team will be able to access and benefit from what the other teams have found. Beyond that, we'll probably need to meet together a couple of times a week until we're on stronger footing on this period of prehistory about which we know so little. We've already had enticing glimpses of this era as we did our bracketing exercise to find the meteoroid. I know that many of you wanted to get right at the business of learning more about the Antediluvian societies that you observed in that search. Now, we're going to get that opportunity. I'm going to ask General Goldwyn to provide us an additional small team of historians to help us to begin organizing and cataloging these findings into a useful database. Hopefully, we'll have them on board quickly enough to be helpful as we get started on this next phase."

Stauffer smiled and scanned the room. "Well, that's it, folks. Let's get to work and get ready for the task ahead of us tomorrow. Get with Max and Hank for your team and geographical area assignments." Everyone stood and chatted excitedly as they departed Stauffer's office. Stauffer looked after them and remarked to Tipton who still stood by him at the conference table, "I hope we know what we're doing here, Bill. We may not like what we find."

\* \* \* \* \* \* \* \* \* \* \* \* \* \* \* \* \* \* \* \*

Finding Noah's ark under construction proved even more difficult than Stauffer had predicted. Although all the teams had been assigned geographical sectors all over the world, they initially began the search working together scanning all over the Middle East. But, although they found some very interesting villages, settlements, and cities, they didn't find any evidence of the ark.

Finally, Jared Lincoln had an epiphany and suggested that they look further to the north. During his team's meteoroid scans, they had discovered that prior to the flood, the area now occupied by the Black Sea was a wide, open, fertile plain dotted by thousands of small hamlets and a few large cities. Perhaps that was where Noah and his family had built the ark. But after several days of searching that plain, Stauffer finally conceded that it wasn't there either.

Then, quite by chance, while conducting a geological survey of the far eastern edge of Ireland toward the middle of the Atlantic Ocean, Sanjay Singh and Pete Pendleton discovered what they thought might have been the ark in dry dock construction on a small plateau located high above sea level then but which is totally submerged today at the bottom of the Atlantic in over 12,000 feet of water, five or six hundred miles off the coast from present-day Ireland. The area had sunk into the sea in a massive subduction shift of the tectonic plates on which it rested when the meteoroid impacted around on the other side of the earth in the Indian Ocean.

Stauffer immediately called a meeting and invited Pendleton and Singh to brief the rest of the teams. Singh projected images of the ark they had found on the monitor and began the briefing. "I know that many of us were initially skeptical about finding Noah and the Ark. Get over it. This boat.... er, ark.... looks very similar to many artist depictions based on the Biblical account. It appears that Noah and his family lived in an outlying area of a fairly substantial and sophisticated urban population center, and it was here that he and his sons built the ark on top of a flat hilltop near their home. Or rather, it appears that Noah and his sons supervised the construction of the ark by a large crew of workers. By our estimate, there were at least a hundred carpenters and other workers at the construction site at any given time. Apparently, this Noah was a man of considerable wealth and could afford to hire a substantial work force. We backtracked using the temporal monitor to the beginning of the construction and followed it through fast motion to the moment just before the meteorite strike. It was fortunate to have been built where it was. Had it been built on any land area surrounding the Indian Ocean, it is likely that the giant tsunami waves that immediately overwhelmed the coastal areas would have crushed the ark in its wake. As it happened, the ark just nestled down into the sea as the plateau on which it rested sank beneath it. It was fascinating watching the ark take shape. It appears to closely match the dimensions described in the biblical account, and it has the appearance of a long enclosed barge."

As Singh spoke, Pendleton cycled through an extensive series of video captures, and the other teams sat on the edge of their seats around the conference table looking on in amazement as the scenes unfolded. Toward the end of the video dump, depicting work on the ark as it neared completion, they observed that many of the workers turned their attention to building a large compound of animal stables and stalls. Soon, another team of workers began herding large groups of animals into the stalls. When the video captures finally ceased on the screen, everyone began talking among themselves about the significance of what they had just witnessed.

Stauffer nodded to Singh and Pendleton. "Thanks to Sanjay and Pete for sharing all this with us. Pretty impressive stuff. I think this is a fair indication that we have found Noah and his Ark. Pete, please make sure that the video captures you just put up on the screen are stored in the shared intranet files for future reference. And please ensure that they are cross-referenced with the time-location coordinates." Turning to the rest of the team, he continued, "Now, we have to fan out and search for evidence of other possible arks around the rest of the world. Let's get back to work."

\* \* \* \* \* \* \* \* \* \* \* \* \* \* \* \* \* \* \*

Stauffer and his new team mate, Miriam Campbell, sat at their work stations conducting scans across a broad expanse of turbulent water. They projected the scene onto a portable 60-inch screen that displayed in high definition the roiling waters on the face of the planet below their angle of vision. The picture kept going in and out of focus as the surface elevation of the water kept rising and dropping with the amplified wave action of the sea, still under great duress from the tsunamis set in motion by the asteroid. As Stauffer stared at the screen, he kept searching for some indication of the ark or one of the other boats they had documented before the comet's impact. As each hour passed, the motion of the ocean's surface on the screen began to get to him, and he finally became seasick and overcome with nausea. He barely got his head over the office trash can to the side of the work station before he started throwing up uncontrollably.

"Are you going to be alright, Barton?" Dr. Campbell asked. She seemed totally unaffected by motion sickness.

Stauffer looked up at her with a disheveled look on his face. "Why isn't this affecting you, Miriam? Don't you ever get seasick?"

"Practically never. When I was a little girl, I spent a lot of my childhood boating with my family off the coast from Martha's Vineyard. In fact.... and don't you go spreading this around.... when I was a young teenager, I actually worked as an extra in Spielberg's film, *Jaws*."

Stauffer tried to laugh but instead just nodded understanding and bent back down over the wastebasket again. He figured that he lost practically everything he had eaten during the past week.

At their team meeting the next morning, Stauffer acknowledged that monitoring the turbulent seascapes had gotten the best of him and that he was probably going to be permanently seasick. Most of the other team members chimed in that they were experiencing similar discomfort at their work stations, and several admitted to barfing into their trash receptacles as well. Hearing this, Stauffer turned to Zazworsky, "Ski, I think you're going to need to procure an inventory of hazardous waste containers with liners to position in all of the offices and at all temporal observation and time travel work sites."

"Another container, Boss? Let's see, that makes, a trash can, a classified waste container, a recycle container, and now a hazardous waste barf containment receptacle. That makes four. Do you think that's enough, Boss?" Zazworsky asked sarcastically with a big grin on his face.

Stauffer ignored the sarcasm and responded, "Yes, Ski, I think that's about right, and while you're at it, make sure that they're all color-coded so we don't get them confused."

\* \* \* \* \* \* \* \* \* \* \* \* \* \* \* \* \* \* \* \*

Stauffer sat in General Goldwyn's office providing an update on Crypt operations. "Yes, sir, after we discovered the location of Noah's ark in dry dock, we fanned out across the globe, searching land and sea for other potential large boat candidates for Flood survivors. We didn't find anything quite like the Ark. However, early on, when we were still bracketing around the world for evidence of the comet's impact, we observed a great number of ocean-going vessels of various sizes. Some of them were quite large and had a significant carrying capacity for hauling freight in maritime commerce. All of these ships were already launched and seaworthy. It's possible that some of them might have survived the turbulent seas and deluge following the comet's impact and possibly had sufficient provisions on board to sustain the crew until the land reappeared as the waters receded."

"Ok, that sounds about right, Barton. So what's the problem?"

"Well, sir, once the meteoroid had stirred up the atmosphere with torrential rains and a 50-mile thick layer of steam obscured our view, it became impossible for us to track the Ark or any of the other boats at sea that we had already located and documented. When the mists finally cleared sufficiently to see the water's surface, we found it impossible to scan for any length of time to relocate them. Many of us got seasick just watching the screen, and we never have located the Ark or any of the other vessels that were afloat as the comet touched down. We're going to need some kind of technological software solution to automatically search for and track such vessels in super-fast motion. Otherwise, we're all going to grow old and die just sitting at our temporal monitors trying to locate and track each individual vessel in real time. In part, it's simply a matter of size. As the Flood inundated the Earth, it became a water world with a surface area of almost 200 million square miles. It's simply a physical impossibility for a team as small as ours to try to scan the whole shebang manually. We're going to need a technological boost here."

"Ah, I see your point, Barton. Let's see if I understand what you're asking for.... This software fix would have to be able to rapidly scan the surface of the flood waters globally and lock onto any solid object adrift in the seas and track it over approximately a year's period of time. How many vessels in addition to the Ark have you documented thus far?"

"We are a victim of our own success on this one, sir. We initially located about 1375 vessels that we documented before the meteoroid impacted. It's simply way beyond our capability to track them across the turbulence of the ocean's surface to see if any of the boats and their crews made it back to dry land when the waters receded."

"Well, Barton," General Goldwyn responded with a smile, "you're in luck on this one. I've had the temporal technicians working on a special project for me that could easily be tweaked to meet your requirements. I'm not sure, but it might be possible to get the software fix to you by the end of the week."

\* \* \* \* \* \* \* \* \* \* \* \* \* \* \* \* \* \* \*

As Stauffer walked back down to the elevator to drop into the Crypt, once again he was amazed at how General Goldwyn managed to always keep one step ahead of him. Stauffer briefed the team and told them to switch from their endless sea monitoring work to checking out the antediluvian civilizations that predated the Flood for the five-year period leading up to the comet strike. Later, Thursday afternoon, Stauffer took a break from his team assignment to catch up on the administrivia in his inbox. As he sat at his desk working down through the pile of papers in front of him, the red phone on his desk sounded. He could see by the caller ID that it was General Goldwyn. He picked up the phone handset, curious as to what the Old Man might have for him.

"Hello, Barton," General Goldwyn began. "I've got good news for you. The techies just gave me a demo of the new software, and I think that it will do the job for you. I need you to scoot up here with a couple of your team members so that they can brief you, and you in turn can train up your full team on how to use it. Can you be here in about ten minutes?"

\* \* \* \* \* \* \* \* \* \* \* \* \* \* \* \* \* \* \* \* \*

Stauffer, Zazworsky, and Tipton hurried back down to the Crypt following their training session on the new software and had everyone oriented and trained in less than an hour. They programmed the software to run scans on every sector of the world ocean, dividing it up by assigned sectors. Once they activated it, the software very quickly began identifying solid objects afloat on the ocean's surface around the world. Each object was assigned a unique identification number that was displayed on the left side of the temporal monitor display. Within about two hours, the software had acquired and catalogued a little over 1100 objects afloat on the ocean's surface. The teams were able to divide up these objects into lists located in their assigned sectors. The display projected the object ID numbers on the side of the monitor screen with the object's location, using modern longitude and latitude coordinates. These coordinates were in a constant state of flux as the objects drifted rapidly across the ocean's surface driven by the winds, ocean currents and wave action. But the software locked onto the objects and kept track of them and their location updated despite their movement.

The teams were able to zoom in on the objects one at a time and monitor each one up close. Many of them were boats that appeared to be abandoned and adrift at sea. Some of them had already taken on considerable water and were about to capsize and sink. But they were able to detect crews still manning some of the vessels, and, more importantly, some of the people aboard those boats observed were women and children. There also appeared to be plants and animals on many of the vessels, probably as provisions for the journey; and so these craft might also qualify as contributors to the ancient flood mythologies.

Tracking the vessels real time was tiresome work, and so most of the teams did their initial surveys of each craft and then forwarded the software super-fast motion through the following weeks and months. The teams were surprised at the large number of vessels that simply disappeared off the grid as they eventually sank beneath the waves. The total number of vessels being tracked by the software was rapidly reduced from over 1100 to under 200 in just over three months' actual passage of time. Then, during the subsequent six months, another 185 vessels also disappeared from the grid. The teams backtracked all of these disappearances and found that most of them eventually became unseaworthy as they took on water and finally sank. A few of them apparently ran out of provisions, and the people onboard died off. And so, as the dry land began to reappear around the world, there were only 15 vessels still afloat. Including the Ark, 12 of them had human crews, most with plants and animals on board.

After all the boats afloat had been acquired and catalogued in the database, Stauffer and Miriam Campbell were tasked with tracking the progress of the Ark. During all of the preceding months, they hadn't been able to tell much about what was going on inside the Ark. It was completely enclosed. Although the Ark had window openings, they rarely were opened and most were sealed with pitch. Because of the great movement of the Ark upon the waves, it was practically impossible to get a temporal scan lock on the Ark's interior for more than a few seconds.

Then, approximately ten months into the Flood, the Ark began scraping bottom along the slope of a mountain mass rising up out of the sea as the waters receded. The Ark lurched and eventually came to rest, leaning slightly to one side. It remained there as the waters around it continued to recede. After several additional months, the Ark was completely isolated on the muddy slopes of the foothills of the mountain. The Ark was occasionally shaken as the sheer weight of the vessel pulled it down the slope as it settled. At one point, a huge mud slide further up the mountain peak broke away and slid down the mountain toward the Ark. It completely covered one end of the Ark with a thick layer of mud, and the impact of the muddy mass against the side and top of the Ark cracked some of the heavy timbers. Almost immediately, Dr. Campbell observed someone breaking the seal on one of the windows of the Ark from inside and releasing a flock of birds.

Shortly after that, Stauffer observed tools poking through the great side entrance door of the Ark, breaking away the pitch that sealed it shut. As the door was lowered to the ground, a somewhat disorderly procession of animals departed the Ark and started the long trek down the slope of the foothills to begin life anew on the rejuvenated planet. Last off the Ark was Noah and his family and their servants and boat crew. In all, about 25 people disembarked from the Ark. As he and Dr. Campbell tracked this new development, Stauffer wondered how the other teams were fairing tracking the surviving vessels in their geographic sectors.

\* \* \* \* \* \* \* \* \* \* \* \* \* \* \* \* \* \* \* \* \*

The team sat around Stauffer's conference table as he and Dr. Campbell briefed them on their screen captures from the landing of the Ark and the eventual debarkation of all of the animals and Noah's family. As two skunks waddled down the ramp, Zazworsky quipped, "Whew, I'll bet that was fun cuddling up to those two skunks for a year in a buttoned-up ark!"

Everyone laughed as Max Manchester added with a sly grin, "You know, Ski, my whole life, I've never ever stopped to consider the implications of skunks on the Ark. I'll bet that that was a.... poignant.... experience."

"What about the rest of you?" Stauffer inquired. What did you observe as the other fourteen boats made landfall.?"

Everyone started talking at once. Everyone had a story to tell. Stauffer laughed and put up his hands. "Alright, let's take this in an orderly fashion. Ginny and Ken, you go first."

Ginny Nguyen spoke rapidly, barely able to contain her excitement. "Well, Barton, Ken and I think we may have found the ship of Gilgamesh and his party. We haven't been able to account yet for its point of embarkation before the flood, but we picked it up and tracked it with the new software as the flood progressed. It was a very large boat, perhaps even larger than the Ark, but it was more square in shape. It was a very unusual looking boat. And, it was loaded with a cargo of animals and trade goods. The boat had a large rudder and was steerable, and, as the water receded, the seamen aboard steered the craft clear of mountain peaks as they appeared up out of the water. They eventually ended up landlocked in a small valley at the lower end of present-day Mesopotamia on the slope of a modest mountain peak that rose up out of the water. The boat came to rest leaning on its side, and as the water receded below it, the whole boat began to break up from the weight of the unsupported timbers."

"While it was afloat," Ken Red Elk continued, "we weren't able to observe much of what they had below decks, but once the water began to dry up around it, we were surprised to see the cargo of exotic and domesticated animals that escaped through the broken hull of the boat. The seamen tried to pull off an orderly evacuation, but something spooked the animals and they scrambled through the breaks in the hull to get off the boat. By the time the alarm was sounded and all of the seamen had assembled in the shallow water or on dry land to bring the animals under control, most of them had stampeded away heading off in all directions. The crew were only able to recover a small herd of sheep, goats, and cattle and a flock of assorted poultry. After everyone had disembarked, they abandoned the damaged craft where it had beached. We fast-forwarded into the future to see what later happened to it and found that it eventually sank under the waters of the Persian Gulf as the sea level rose substantially a hundred years later."

As they went around the room reporting their findings, several of the other teams reported observing similar behavior by the animals that people tried to disembark from the various kinds of water craft that had survived the flood. Once the animals got their footing on dry land again, they became unmanageable and stampeded away from the boats as fast as they could run. The survivors were typically able to restrain only small numbers of the animals they had on board. The net outcome from their observations was that small numbers of domesticated and wild animals escaped in various parts of the world as the fifteen boats made landfall. But the general consensus among all the Crypt team members was that the number and variety of animals that survived the flood would have been insufficient to repopulate the entire planet with wildlife. That was another issue that the team had to address.

# Chapter 13

*Carlisle Barracks, Pennsylvania, Thursday, June 20, 2013, 3:30 p.m.*

Stauffer called another staff meeting a few days later to allow everyone to brief what they had learned additionally from their temporal observation scans. Now that they had tracked and observed the landing of all the surviving watercraft from the Flood, he had directed that the Crypt staff divide up once again into new two-person teams to begin observing the antediluvian world leading up to the Flood and the postdiluvian world as the few human and animal survivors spread out over the face of the land from wherever their boats had landed.

Although the global land mass was configured considerably differently in antediluvian times, Bill Tipton and Pete Pendleton were assigned the geographical region corresponding to present-day Europe and North Africa, and Stauffer asked them to brief what they had learned first. Tipton stood beside the large flat screen monitor as Pendleton worked the controls on a laptop keyboard. "When we were doing the initial scans trying to ascertain the date of the Flood, we were fascinated by what we saw when we worked the earlier portion of the temporal bracket.... before the Flood. When we were given free rein to explore, we focused on antediluvian peoples and cultures."

Several people around the conference table nodded in agreement and voiced that that had been their approach as well.

Pendleton joined in, "We started our temporal scans in what is now southern Ireland and slowly worked our way eastward, scanning north and south as we attempted to get a feel for the lay of the land. We were surprised to find that the geography of the land was contiguous without a break all the way from Ireland to the European continent. Ireland and Great Britain and Europe were all part of the same landmass. And we discovered that Ireland extended much farther to the west than it does today as well. Apparently, a huge hunk of the landmass of Ireland simply broke off and sank into the sea with the shift of the tectonic plates when the asteroid struck." An aerial view of the North Atlantic region appeared on the screen depicting the geographic configuration Pendleton described.

Tipton continued, "As we were doing our initial survey scans in a haphazard kind of way, we observed an odd happening. A group of armed soldiers was marching along an open field in a double column. The soldiers were dressed in rough woolen tunics, leather body armor, metal shoulder plates and helmets, and carried heavy broadswords slung from a scabbard tied at the waist. Between the two columns of soldiers was a large wooden wagon the size of a Chevy Suburban. When we got a better angle on the temporal monitor, we were shocked to realize that there weren't any draft animals pulling the wagon and it didn't have any wheels. It just seemed to float in the air between them as they marched, and what we first thought was a wagon was really just a large, wooden crate with high, reinforced sides and open at the top. We could clearly see the contents of the crate on the monitor. It was full of scrolls, books, plaques, stacks of metal plates, and other like paraphernalia. The crate was almost full to the top and it must have been very heavy. But the soldiers weren't touching the box in any way. It just moved along between the columns, slightly above the ground, as they marched along the rough terrain. When they came to a village, the box settled to the ground, and the men started moving from house to house, plundering the villagers' homes."

"What were they looking for?" Zazworsky interrupted.

"At first we weren't sure, Ski." Tipton responded. "There didn't seem to be a pattern with the soldiers' search of the village. The houses weren't particularly elaborate. They were simple structures made of stone and brick faced with mud adobe. The villagers themselves displayed no great wealth. They were dressed simply in cotton tunics, wool robes, and leather sandals, wearing no jewelry or other ornamentation. The soldiers forced their way past the villagers into their homes and public buildings and occasionally emerged carrying scrolls, stacks of thick leather pages bound together on one edge like books, rectangular metal plates, and what appeared to be small cases of styluses of some kind or another and small earthen jars which we surmised might contain ink. Every once in awhile, the soldiers seized a sign or plaque from the village square or affixed to the front of a public building and threw it into the crate as well.

The squad of soldiers was followed by a crowd of angry villagers who were intent on trying to recover their property. They screamed and howled and some of them even beat on the backs of the soldiers with their fists, but to no avail. We dropped a microphone through a small round portal opening to get the drift what they were saying. But here's the corker.... Although it looked like the villagers were screaming and crying on the temporal monitors, we couldn't pick up much sound coming from them, mostly just muted grunts and groans. We could hear the clanking sound of some of the confiscated stuff as it was thrown into the crate. But although their mouths were open and their jaws flapping, the soldiers and the villagers made no appreciable vocal utterances of any kind that we could monitor. Nothing.... mostly just silence."

"Silence?" Stauffer asked. "They weren't making much of a vocal commotion at all?"

"Not that we could detect. We even retrieved our microphone and did a test in the lab to make sure it was functioning properly. It was working just fine."

"What happened then?" Stauffer urged them on.

"The soldiers simply ignored the villagers and unceremoniously dumped everything they gathered into the crate. When they finished their work in the village, they resumed their double column formation around the crate, and it again lifted off and floated between them as the soldiers moved out of the village across the field."

"They didn't march along roads?" Miriam Campbell asked.

"That's another funny thing, Dr. Campbell," Pendleton responded. "We didn't observe any roads at any time during a three-hour temporal scanning session.... and we covered a lot of ground. No roads. We fast-tracked the progress of the soldiers as they moved from village to village across the landscape, gathering up books and scrolls. Finally, when the box was full to overflowing, the column of soldiers moved southward along some very rocky terrain to the edge of a cliff overlooking the sea below. As they stood at attention, the soldier at the front of the formation, who appeared to be the squad leader, raised his hands in the air and then pointed out to sea. The crate floated past him through the air out over the edge of the cliff and slowly descended down to just above the level of the waves below, moving off away from the cliff across the water toward the horizon. After a few minutes, the box disappeared from view entirely. Then the squad leader faced the columns about, and the soldiers marched back the way they had come."

"Boy," Hank Phillips remarked. "I'd give a bundle to have a look at those books and scrolls and plaques and stuff. I can't imagine what the soldiers might have found so objectionable about them that they felt the compulsion to just toss them into the sea." As a professional librarian and archivist at heart, Phillips couldn't bear to watch the destruction of books or reading material of any kind.

"I share your curiosity, Hank." Stauffer smiled. "I think we ought to have a look at what was in that crate."

"I thought you might feel that way, Bart." Tipton replied excitedly. "We brought along some equipment to give a look. We can scope this all out together right here."

Before Stauffer could protest, Pendleton wheeled a portable temporal monitor over to the center of the room facing the conference table, and Sammy Woo started it up using another control laptop in front of him on the conference table. "We set the monitor controls on the last sighting location of the crate before it disappeared on the horizon. It should be coming up shortly."

As everyone in the room leaned forward in their chairs, the image on the monitor screen began to materialize into a scene of an endless expanse of ocean waves. As Pendleton operated the controls, he moved the scene slightly to the right and the crate came into view. It was still floating in the air about six feet above the waves. Although they didn't have a visual point of reference, from the location readout on the side of the monitor screen, they could tell that the crate was still moving relentlessly out to sea. They sat there watching for several minutes and then, without warning, the crate simply dropped into the water and disappeared below the waves as it sank out of sight.

"Whoa!" Phillips exclaimed. "Do you mean to say that they trashed the whole load of books, just like that?"

There was a shared gasp from everyone in the room as they watched the crate sink beneath the waves. "Wait a minute, guys," Zazworsky cried out. "This is low-hanging fruit. This represents the opportunity for an industrial-strength snatch. All we have to do is open up a time portal directly beneath the crate, and as it drops through, it will land right here in the Crypt. There must be hundreds, maybe thousands of artifacts in the crate. It's a virtual antediluvian library. It's got to be meaningful for us in our search for understanding of Antediluvian times!"

"Wait, not so fast. There's more at stake here. We're getting ahead of ourselves. General Goldwyn hasn't said anything to me about artifact recovery operations for the Crypt yet. As I understand it, this was supposed to be primarily just temporal observation missions. I'm going to need to consult with him and get his go-ahead. Furthermore, you're talking about bringing back a whole load of artifacts from a world that hasn't existed in many thousands of years. If we do the snatch, we're going to need to take all kinds of hazmat precautions to make sure that we don't bring back some nasty bug with the load. Ski, get Doc Gates on the horn over in the Repository and ask him to get over here ASAP. I want to talk with him about the possibilities first before I talk with General Goldwyn."

"Roger that, Boss." Ski moved over to Stauffer's desk and picked up the telephone handset and began a conversation in muffled tones. When he was finished, he put down the handset and turned back to Stauffer. "Good news, Boss. When I told him what we had, Doc Gates said he was already halfway here. He should be here in a couple of minutes. I'll go up to the elevator entrance in the Hole to escort him down into the Crypt."

* * * * * * * * * * * * * * * * * * * * * *

Zazworsky returned in ten minutes with a breathless Doctor Gates in tow. Gates was the Repository resident physician and epidemiologist. One of his primary roles was ensuring the medical integrity of all time travel interventions against any potential infectious disease contamination. He ensured that all time travelers underwent intensive decontamination prep before moving through the portals into the past, and he frequently placed Repository personnel into quarantine cells upon return from the past for observation to ensure that they didn't bring any unwanted contagion hitchhikers back with them.

After Stauffer had briefed him on what they had found and showed him the video capture of the soldiers loading the crate and sending it out to sea, Gates scratched his head and remarked, "I don't know Barton. This is new ground for us. We don't have any historical information about this particular time period. I can't give you any epidemiological projections because we simply don't know anything about it."

"I know, Doc. I anticipated that." Stauffer acknowledged. "But do you think that with the right decontamination and quarantine protocols, we could bring that crate back here and see what we have? I've got to tell the old man something before we make any recommendations about making the snatch."

"Well," Gates paused for half a minute as he considered the possibilities. "I think that we could pull it off, but we're going to need to have everyone suited up in hazmat suits and self-contained breathing equipment in an enclosed vault, sealed off from the rest of our facility here. We're going to need to put every artifact we pull out of the box through meticulous decontamination, and we need a methodology for removing it from the vault once it's clean."

"We can do all that, Doc," Zazworsky interrupted. "We've got a special vault with most of what you're asking for already built in."

Doc Gates and Stauffer smiled at each other and then looked back at Zazworsky. Stauffer spoke first with a slight shrug. "Let's give the good doctor a tour of the vault and show him what you have set up, Ski. With his go-ahead, I'll feel more comfortable going forward to General Goldwyn for his approval for the recovery mission."

\* \* \* \* \* \* \* \* \* \* \* \* \* \* \* \* \* \* \* \*

General Goldwyn gave the go-ahead for the intervention as soon as he saw the video capture of the soldiers with the crate and watched it floating out over the cliff and finally dropping into the sea. Stauffer had never seen him so excited.... or agitated. "We've got to recover that crate and all the records it contains," Goldwyn exclaimed, not concealing the excitement in his voice. "This may be the most important find we'll ever encounter out of the Crypt or the Repository. Work closely with Doctor Gates to ensure our decontamination protocols are in order. Set it up and brief me when you're ready for the recovery operation. I want to be there with you in the Crypt when you run the recovery mission."

\* \* \* \* \* \* \* \* \* \* \* \* \* \* \* \* \* \* \* \*

The following Monday morning, Stauffer, General Goldwyn, Bob Zazworsky, Bill Tipton, Pete Pendleton, Hank Phillips, Miriam Campbell, and Doc Gates were all suited up in special hazmat suits. Doc Gates went from person to person to make sure they had a good seal on the suits. When he gave the thumbs up, Zazworsky pulled the vault doors shut and confirmed the seal. The vault was divided into two sides, the dirty side and the clean side, which were separated by a heavy-duty drape curtain with a flap opening in the center. In the middle of the dirty side of the vault was an over-sized time portal array arranged to create a horizontal portal they would open up directly beneath the crate as it fell from the sky into the sea. But instead of going into the water, the crate would fall through the portal opening and impact on a pile of thick foam mattress pads stacked on a low platform set up in the middle of the vault. Zazworsky's crew had set up a series of long examination tables positioned end-to-end along the walls of the vault, and Dr. Gates had set up a decontamination assembly line system along the tables for the team to use to cleanse all artifacts recovered.

Once decontaminated, the artifact could be passed through the flap opening in the drape curtain into the clean side to Hank Phillips and Bill Tipton who would quickly examine the artifact and make a tentative catalog identification. Then they sealed the artifact in an oversized plastic zipper storage bag and placed it on a roll cart to move across the gallery to the inventory vault. They had projected that the entire operation to clear the crate and decontaminate all of the artifacts it contained would probably take at least six hours and they were all in it for the long haul. Max Manchester had wanted to participate on the operation as well, but he didn't think that he could stay on his feet for that long. The plan was that when they had emptied the crate, they would simply open up the time portal again, this time set up vertically alongside the platform, and just push the crate back through to drop harmlessly into the antediluvian sea.

General Goldwyn gave the command to begin, and Pete Pendleton opened up the portal. Moments later, the crate came dropping down through the portal and fell about four feet into the pile of foam mattresses. Team members standing around the platform quickly surrounded and steadied the crate to make sure that it didn't tip over on the wobbly mattress base.

"Whoa," Zazworsky exclaimed. "This crate is much bigger than it looked on the screen. If we had set the dimensional parameters on the time portal any less, we would have cut off the ends of the box."

Stauffer quickly surveyed the contents of the crate and yelled over to Hank Phillips in the clean room on the other side of the drape curtain, "Lots of books and scrolls here, Hank. Any preferences for what we do first?"

"Just get it moving, Barton," Phillips yelled back on the other side of the drape. "I haven't slept in two days just waiting for this moment. I'll see it all soon enough."

The team worked quickly according to their well-rehearsed protocol. Even General Goldwyn pitched in as one of the team members. He seemed to really enjoy getting into the thick of things. The team had been working at it for almost two hours and had cleared about three feet of artifacts from the top of the crate when Dr. Campbell let out a squeal, "There's a man down here under all this stuff!"

"What?" Dr. Gates retorted. "Clear everything off of him and help me get him over here to my emergency gurney. Can you tell if he's alive?"

The team worked together to lift the unconscious man carefully out of the crate. He was a large man, taller than anyone in the room, well over seven feet. When they laid him down on the gurney, his feet extended outstretched another twenty inches into the air. Dr. Gates wore a special hazmat suit set up with an internal stethoscope transmitter that he could hear without having to position earpieces. He held the sound drum diaphragm head of his stethoscope against the man's chest and listened tentatively. "He's alive! The guy's alive!"

The man was clean shaven and had scrapes and abrasions on his chin and cheeks. Gates examined the man's head carefully, pulling back his thick brown hair. Turning to General Goldwyn, he reported, "The man's got a goose egg on his noggin the size of a .... big goose egg. It looks like someone clubbed him and knocked him unconscious. What do you want to do, sir?"

General Goldwyn just smiled confidently and replied, "Well, it seems to me that we need to give him a good decon bath and make him as comfortable as possible until he regains consciousness."

Turning to Stauffer, he continued, "Meanwhile, Barton, use the intercom to send word out to the rest of the team to get to work using the temporal monitors to backtrack the soldiers gathering up these artifacts to see if we can discover how this man ended up in the crate with all this other material."

\* \* \* \* \* \* \* \* \* \* \* \* \* \* \* \* \* \* \* \* \*

While Stauffer and Zazworsky held up a sheet as a privacy shield, Dr. Gates cut off the man's linen tunic and homespun wool robe with scissors and went over his body with a decon soap solution and soft scrub brush and toweled him dry. Then they covered him with several layers of sheets and blankets and positioned him along the side of the vault still on the gurney with his feet supported on the end of one of the artifact examination tables. Gates pulled up a chair and sat there beside him, occasionally checking his pulse and his other vital signs. "Seven feet, six inches," he finally announced.

"What's that, Doc?" Stauffer asked from across the room.

"I just measured him. He's seven and a half feet tall. Pretty big guy."

Just then, Ginny Nguyen's voice crackled on the intercom. "Barton, can you hear me?"

"Sure thing, Ginny. What have you got?"

"We did a back-scan moving in fast-motion and found our stowaway getting bushwhacked by the goon squad when he tried to interfere with their taking a large scroll from his home. It wasn't a fair fight. The little guy was no match for those soldiers. They towered over him by a foot."

"Are you kidding me, Ginny? This guy is seven and a half feet tall. Are you suggesting that the soldiers were a foot taller than that?"

"I don't know what you have there, Barton, but on the temporal observation screen, some of the soldiers looked pretty big standing alongside the little guy."

As Stauffer and Nguyen conversed on the intercom, the giant man stretched out on the gurney started to stir. "He's coming around," Doc Gates shouted.

"Please stand back, everyone," General Goldwyn said calmly. "I'll try to help him understand what's going on here."

"How are you going to do that, sir?" Stauffer asked incredulously.

"Trust me. Just give me a few minutes. Would everyone please take a few steps back so that I can communicate with him alone."

Everyone did as General Goldwyn requested. Even Doctor Gates moved back a few feet, giving General Goldwyn breathing room. As the big man started to stir, he moved his arms to brace himself on the gurney to stand up. General Goldwyn reached out and placed his hands on the man's arm to gently restrain him. Through the visor on his hazmat suit, he looked deeply into the man's eyes but said nothing. Startled, the man looked back at Goldwyn, initially frightened, but he immediately calmed down as he stared back at Goldwyn through his visor. The man suddenly became agitated and started to struggle, but Goldwyn tightened his grip on the man's arm and said in a loud voice, "He's worried about a particular scroll that the soldiers took from his home. It's a large scroll as near as I can tell. Can any of you see it in the crate somewhere near where he was lying?"

The rest of the team surrounded the crate and started rummaging through the remainder of the artifacts where the large man had lain unconscious. Zazworsky shouted, "I think I found it!" He held a large scroll up in the air where the man could see it, and the look of immense relief that appeared on the man's face let them know that it was the right one. General Goldwyn began giving terse instructions. "Get that scroll through decon fast and let's get it back to its rightful owner. He's been through a lot to recover it." Yelling through the drape curtain, he asked, "Hank.... Bill.... do we have any extra large lab jump suits over there we can use to dress our oversized friend here?"

Phillips yelled back, "Yes, sir, we have a couple of 2XL lab suits that ought to do the trick. But if he's as tall as you say, it's going to be a tight fit. Maybe if we cut each of them in two, one high and the other low, we could put the two bigger pieces together to make a really big jump suit. We can secure it with safety pins for now."

"Thanks, Hank," General Goldwyn acknowledged. "Get working on it. We'll be sending Melek over to you in just a minute. He's already gone through decon. I've told him he can trust you and that you're going to help him get dressed."

126

"Melek, sir?"

"Trust me on that.... Melek.... his name is Melek." Turning to Doctor Gates, General Goldwyn continued, "Doc, you're going to have to help me out of this hazmat suit as I move through the drape with our friend."

"Yes, sir. I think we can safely do that."

Zazworsky came running around the crate where he had been working at the decon table carrying the large scroll with him. "Here it is, sir. I think we've done a fairly good job dusting it off with the decon powder. It should be clean."

"Thanks for cleaning it up so fast, Ski." Turning to the giant man, General Goldwyn held out the scroll to him, almost reverently. The man accepted it solemnly and clutched it tightly to his chest. The expression on his face needed no explanation. He was overjoyed to be reunited with his scroll. General Goldwyn assisted the big man in getting down off the gurney with the sheet wrapped around him, and they walked across the vault to the opening though the drape into the clean side. As the big man ducked and passed through the drape, Goldwyn quickly dropped his hazmat suit to the floor, assisted by Dr. Gates, and followed through after him. Phillips and Tipton were already helping the man into the makeshift jump suit as Goldwyn came through the drape. It would have gone much faster and easier but the man refused to put down the scroll, and so they had to do it slowly as he switched the scroll from hand to hand as he climbed awkwardly into the suit. When they finally had the two pieces of jump suit in place, they carefully safety pinned it all together.

"Well, that looks much better, my friend," General Goldwyn observed smiling. Turning to Phillips and Tipton, he nodded, "And thank you for taking such good care of my friend, Melek. He wants me to thank you for such a nice suit of clothes you've given him."

"Excuse me, sir," Phillips asked, "but how are you communicating with.... Melek?.... telepathically? How do you know all this?"

"Give it time, Hank. I'll bring you all up to speed shortly. But right now, I want to escort my oversized friend up to my office to rest and get him a bite to eat."

Doctor Gates came through the drape at just that moment and interrupted, "I understand your desire, sir, but I can't allow it just yet. I used the intercom a few minutes ago, and they're setting up a dispensary for me in the next vault. Zazworsky has them bringing over equipment from my dispensary in the Repository, and I should have a fully operational facility up and running in under an hour. I want to keep your friend under observation for at least a couple of days. Ski is requisitioning an oversized bed from a specialty mattress company and getting him some clothes that will fit him from a big and tall catalog. We should be able to make him perfectly comfortable for now. I understand that someone has already left to bring back some takeout, and we should have food for him momentarily. Would you please ask him what he would like to eat, sir?"

General Goldwyn nodded and looked up into the face of the young giant. He stared into his eyes just briefly and then turned back to Doctor Gates. "Melek tells me that he really likes fish. He eats lots of fish at home."

"Can do, sir. I'll make sure that Melek has a first class meal from Red Lobster within the hour. Please ask him to be patient."

While Melek was getting settled in the makeshift dispensary in the next vault, the team continued removing and decontaminating all of the artifacts as they pulled them out of the crate. When the crate was entirely empty and all of the artifacts had been decontaminated and sealed up in plastic bags on the trays on the clean carts, Stauffer directed everyone to wipe down all of the surfaces on the dirty side of the vault and put the wipes in large plastic bags. Then they fumigated the vault and the crate with decon dusting powder. All of the team members took off their suits and took down the decon drapes and loaded them all into the crate as well. When they had all of their expended equipment loaded into the crate, they filled it the rest of the way up with bricks they had prepositioned against the side of the vault for that purpose and nailed boards across the top of the crate. When they were finished, Pendleton opened up the time portal, and they pushed the crate off the platform and on through. Ginny Nguyen tracked the crate on a temporal monitor in one of the other vaults to ensure that it quickly sank into the depths of the sea as it emerged from the portal on the other side.

As the team members exited the vault, Zazworsky remarked to Stauffer, "Ya know, Boss, we've done some pretty strange stuff down here but this has got to be one of the strangest days I've ever had working for General Goldwyn."

# Chapter 14

All of the Crypt team members sat expectantly around Stauffer's conference table. Most of them were quietly discussing the books and scrolls and other artifacts recovered from the crate waiting for the team meeting to begin. A few were speculating about Melek and how General Goldwyn seemed to communicate so readily with him telepathically. At the side of the room next to the white board, Zazworsky had laid out a few of the artifacts from the recovery mission including scrolls, books, metal plates, stone disks, and a small collection of flat ellipsoidal crystals, joined together in pairs by wire and pieces of metal and wood.

As the last team members arrived and took their places around the table, Bob Zazworsky called the meeting to order. "Welcome everyone. Colonel Stauffer told me to get the meeting started if he didn't make it back in time. He said that he would be along shortly. It's been two days since we pulled off the recovery mission. All of the recovered artifacts have been photographed and inventoried, and the archivists are already making digital copies of all the scrolls and books. Most of it is already posted on the classified intranet. I've put out a bunch of the things we recovered over here on the table so that you can get a better look at the real deal up close. We were moving pretty fast when we pulled it all from the crate and put it through decon. Feel free to take a look at it at the end of the meeting. Since this was Bill and Pete's operation, Colonel Stauffer asked them to take the lead in the conversation and to provide a summary overview briefing on what we've found out thus far. Since the mission had so much to do with recovering written records, the Boss also asked Hank Phillips to stand in and help with the analysis."

Tipton stood and began distributing a stack of papers. "This is a tentative inventory list of all items recovered from the floating crate mission," he began. "Here's a quick summary — we recovered 208 scrolls, 433 books of various shapes, sizes and composition, 58 sets of inscribed metal plates, 53 small stone monuments and stelae of various shapes, 12 pairs of small ellipsoidal crystals joined together in pairs, and.... 1 very large stowaway by the name of Melek. At this point, we don't really have any meaningful analysis on any of the recovered items. We've made digital copies of all of the scrolls, books and metals plates available on a limited basis to the Repository translation and code decryption teams, but they've come up dry so far. What we do know is that the inhabitants of that part of the antediluvian world had a form of writing and in fact wrote on a number of different media."

"So what do our code breakers and translators think that it all says?" Zazworsky asked expectantly.

"Well, that's a problem, Ski.... According to the team that worked on it over in the Repository, all of these records appear to be written using unique written language forms and alphabets. In fact, they found very few points of commonality among any of the recovered records. We went back and carefully tracked which records came from which houses in which villages, and it appears that people living right next door to each other wrote in different language writing forms.... if you can call it a 'language' or 'writing.'"

"If it isn't a language, what is it then?"

"We're not quite sure at this point," Hank Phillips spoke up. "It might be merely graphical memory aids or mnemonic devices to help the writers remember the narrative of the message they were trying to record, similar to the *quipu* cords of the Incas or the *rongorongo* glyphs of Easter Island."

"So, have we hit a dead end?" Dr. Campbell asked.

"Not quite, Miriam," Phillips responded. "We do have one promising track that we haven't explored yet that could produce answers to all of these questions."

"What would that be, Hank?" Sandy Watson asked.

"Well, the elephant in the room is our very large stowaway friend now housed next door in the dispensary vault. He risked his life to recover and protect his scroll from the soldiers who took it from him, and I believe that he is the one who probably inscribed most of the material on the scroll."

"How does that help us?" Sanjay Singh asked. "He appears to be mute. How are we going to have him explain it all to us?"

"Well, Sanjay," Phillips responded, "I don't quite understand it all at this point, but it appears that General Goldwyn has the ability to communicate with him.... telepathically.... with his mind."

There was an immediate buzzing of conversations around the table as team members speculated on the rumors they had heard. Phillips waited for it to die down and then continued. "I've asked General Goldwyn to join us this morning to see if he could throw some light on these issues to help us move forward."

At that moment, Barton Stauffer opened the door to his office and stepped into the room, followed by Doctor Gates and Melek, who had to bend his head down to avoid hitting it on the door frame lintel. Stauffer and Gates were both six-footers but were dwarfed standing next to Melek. "Sorry, we're late ladies and gentlemen," Stauffer said. "General Goldwyn won't be able to be with us this morning, and he asked me to do the honors. I would like you all to meet Melek, our visitor from the antediluvian world."

Several members of the team hadn't yet seen the young giant and stood to their feet in amazement, mouths agape. Everyone else in the room also stood and offered friendly greetings of welcome across the table to him. "Welcome, Melek.... Howdy.... Welcome.... Glad to meet you...."

Melek stood there awkwardly, shifting back and forth from foot to foot. "I.... am.... very.... pleased.... to.... meet.... you.... all.... all of you."

Phillips blurted out the obvious question, "He speaks English?"

Stauffer responded. "General Goldwyn has given Melek a crash course in English and he's moving right along. Melek is not used to speaking out loud. In his society, they communicate mostly with their minds telepathically. But, it appears that he has an eidetic memory. He has total recall of everything he hears. With General Goldwyn prompting him telepathically as he speaks out loud, Melek has been able to learn English rather quickly."

"Read minds?" Zazworsky asked. "Can he read our minds right now?"

"Interesting question, Ski. I haven't discussed that with him yet." Turning to Melek, Stauffer asked, "How about that, Melek? Can you read our minds?"

Melek shook his head back and forth and responded slowly, "No.... not very well.... it's all.... jumbled.... not very organized.... I've learned to shut out the noise."

Max Manchester spoke up and quipped good naturedly, "You see, Ski, Melek has caught on to your brand of complex thinking already.... jumbled, disorganized noise."

Everyone laughed and it broke the tension in the room as several were already defensive about the possibility of someone intruding into their minds.

Melek was still clutching his scroll to his chest, and Hank Phillips ventured a query about it. "Melek, just what is on that scroll that you are holding? It must be very important for you to risk your life for it."

Melek looked at Stauffer and then back at Phillips. After a long pause, he finally spoke, "It is a.... record.... of my people.... from the beginning."

"I thought that it might be something like that, Melek. Why is it that none of our experts recognize the script? What language is it written in?"

"Language?.... I wrote in the language of Melek."

"Can we see it, Melek.... please?" Phillips persisted.

Melek nodded his head and Stauffer guided him to the edge of the conference table where he helped him spread out the first section of the scroll. Phillips came around the end of the table and looked down at the glyphs on the scroll. Pointing at the script, he asked, "Can you read these markings for us, Melek?"

"Read?"

"Yes, can you tell us what you have recorded here on your scroll?" Phillips extended his finger and pointed at a grouping of glyphs and symbols on the scroll.

Melek looked down at the scroll where Phillips pointed and then back at Stauffer. "I can't do it like that. I need my.... stones."

"Stones?" Stauffer questioned. And then, looking over at the artifacts on the display table against the wall, he walked over and retrieved a pair of small polished crystals fastened to a piece of curved metal. Returning to Melek, he handed him the crystals. "How about these, Melek? Will these do?"

Melek was apprehensive. "These are not mine, but maybe they will work for me too."

Melek slowly held the crystals up to his eyes and looked down through them at the scroll. As he scanned the glyphs looking

The

through the stones guided by his finger, he began to speak. "These are the generations of the fathers...."

"Wait, Melek," Phillips interrupted. "Do you mean to say that these crystals help you to read what's written here? How do they work?.... Where did you get them?.... Did you and your people make them?"

"Whoa, Hank," Stauffer interceded. "That's a lot of questions to throw at Melek all at once. Let's go at it more slowly."

"Yes, of course. I'm sorry, Melek." Phillips apologized. "That was clumsy of me. One question at a time.... Where did you get your stones?"

"My grandfather gave them to me just before he died. They were his stones."

Phillips continued his line of questioning. "Yes, and do you know where he got the stones?

"My grandfather told me he acquired them on the island city before it disappeared into the sky."

"Island city? Do you mean Atlantis?"

"Atlantis?.... Yes, sometimes people called it that."

"What do you mean, 'disappeared into the sky?'" Max Manchester asked.

"Our tradition is that the city was actually a big.... boat.... uh, er.... craft.... made of metal.... and that they made it fly up into the air. The craft lifted up into the sky and many other smaller craft followed after it. They kept going up like a flock of birds until they all were gone."

There was a long pause in the room as everyone considered that new information. Miriam Campbell finally broke the silence with a different line of questioning. "Melek, you are a big man. Much taller than any of us. Just how old are you?"

"Old?"

"Yes. How long have you lived?"

"I am 73 harvests."

"73 years old?" Campbell exclaimed! "You don't look a day over 25. Are you sure, Melek? 73 harvests?"

"Yes. I was one of the youngest in the village. I was due to be married at the end of the next harvest season. It was my time."

"Your bride? The woman you were to marry?" Dr. Campbell asked. "What happened to her?

133

"Ulla?.... She lived many villages away. She is the daughter of my father's distant cousin, Nehum. We don't know what happened to her. We received word that she and her whole family disappeared. Some say that they were taken by the people of.... Atlantis.... who came back to get them. I don't know what to believe. The people in her village are very.... unreliable.... I don't trust them.... They might have killed Ulla and her family." Melek's eyes filled with tears, and he wiped them with his sleeve. He hung his head down dejectedly.

Doctor Gates interjected, "Miriam.... Hank.... everyone.... I think that might be enough for now. Melek, why don't you come with me back to your room. You probably should get some rest. That concussion you got from the soldiers is serious business. I think you would benefit from a rest."

Melek stood slowly to his feet and turned to leave the room with Stauffer and Gates. Stauffer looked down at the crystals that Melek still held in his hands with the scroll cradled in his other arm. "Melek, would you like to keep those crystals for now?"

"Yes.... Barton Stauffer. Would that be.... acceptable?"

"Yes, Melek. That shouldn't be a problem." Stauffer motioned to Zazworsky. "Ski, sign out this set of crystals to Melek for now. We'll help him find his own set later on. He'll have his scroll and these crystals in the dispensary vault for now."

"Roger that, Boss," Zazworsky said. "What do you want to do about the staff meeting?"

"Why don't we just adjourn the formalities for now and let the team examine the artifacts over on the table. Some of you haven't seen any of it yet. Perhaps it will help us to organize our thinking as we reconvene this afternoon at 1300 hours."

\* \* \* \* \* \* \* \* \* \* \* \* \* \* \* \* \* \* \* \*

Stauffer and Doctor Gates accompanied Melek back to the dispensary vault. As they got to the vault door, Stauffer nodded to Doctor Gates. "Do you suppose, Doc, that if Melek were feeling up to it, I could ask him a couple more questions?"

Gates nodded cautiously. Turning to address Melek directly, Stauffer continued, "Would that be alright with you Melek? Are you up to it?"

"Yes, Barton Stauffer. What do you want to know?"

"Well, Melek, I've carefully gone back over the video tapes of the squad of soldiers that moved through your village and waylaid you and dumped you in the crate. I've watched it in super-slow motion and zoomed in close on some of the detail, and I've discovered a couple of things that I'm most curious about. The soldiers are wearing light armor and what appears to be heavy, metal-reinforced, leather gloves. But if I'm seeing right, the gloves have six fingers. Why? Can you throw some light on that?"

Melek's face clouded over. "The gloves had six fingers because the soldiers have six fingers on each hand." Melek spoke slowly, his face contorted in pain. "That's what caused the conflict among my people to begin with. Some of my people have five fingers and some have six.... even people from the same family. It didn't used to matter. But after the people gathered in the island city.... Atlantis.... had departed, things became complicated. In the last hundred years, some six-fingered people started making claims that six fingers were superior to people with only five, and they set themselves above five-fingered people. It happened little by little over the years, but the six-fingered men planted seeds of hate and distrust. There was much conflict and sometimes.... violence. Large numbers of six-fingered people gathered together and then went around in.... gangs.... trying to subject the people in their villages. Those soldiers that you saw in my village were one of the gangs."

"But why were they confiscating your scrolls and books and crystals and the like?"

"The leaders of the six-fingered people believed that if they could take away our family histories and records, they could more easily enslave us. I think.... they were probably right. Most people simply lost hope and gave up once their family history scrolls were taken. I have heard about these raids in other parts of the land for the past two years, and it was only a matter of time before the gangs reached our village."

"Why didn't you hide your scroll?" Stauffer asked.

Melek responded slowly. "I did. I hid my scroll and the scroll of my father under the floor boards of my house in a secret compartment. When I was a child, my cousin Neezrum and I used to hide in the compartment to avoid doing chores. When the gang of six-fingered soldiers came to our village, I quickly hid the scrolls out of sight in the compartment as they approached my house. When two soldiers entered my house, one held me while the other soldier went straight to the hiding place and lifted up the boards and took out the scrolls."

Melek started to choke up and the words came slowly. "When the soldier turned to leave, I realized that it was Neezrum, my cousin. I hadn't seen him in many years. Like most other six-fingered people, he had grown very tall. We were the same size when we were children. Now, he was almost a cubit taller than me. When I pleaded with him not to take my scroll, he laughed at me in scorn. He had changed. There was no love in his eyes anymore, and he refused to communicate with me with his mind. It was as if he didn't know me. The other soldier was going to club me with his sword, but Neezrum ordered him to leave me alone and left the house. The soldier pushed me to the ground and turned and followed Neezrum out the door. I got to my feet and rushed out after them. I reached Neezrum just as he threw my scroll into the crate. I tried to climb the side of the crate to recover my scroll. That's all that I remember. The other soldier must have hit me again in the back of my head with the hilt of his sword, and I passed out. That's all I remember until I woke up here."

Melek was obviously distressed remembering the events of his abduction, and Doctor Gates finally interceded. "Barton, I think we've probably tired Melek enough. Let's allow him to rest for now. You can continue this conversation later on if you like."

"Thanks, Doc," Stauffer replied. "You're right." Turning back to the Antediluvian, he said, "Melek, thank you for being patient with me and trying to answer my questions. I didn't realize it would be so painful for you. Rest for now and we'll get together later. There is so much that I need to learn from you."

Melek and Doctor Gates went through the vault door into the dispensary, and Stauffer turned to walk back to his office. He glanced at his watch. He just had time to grab some files and head up to General Goldwyn's office for a late morning meeting.

# Chapter 15

"Barton, you and your team seem to be making some good progress in.... exploring on the other side of the wall," General Goldwyn observed. "What do we have to talk about this morning?"

"Well, sir, I've been making a list of everything we have learned thus far, but the list generates far more questions than answers— answers that I think you may hold the key to." Stauffer paused, not quite knowing how to proceed, and then blurted out, "Sir, I've tried to be circumspect and avoid prying into your personal life, but I think the time has come that we have an open and candid conversation."

"You're wondering about how I can communicate with Melek telepathically?"

"Not just that, sir. There are a host of other questions that I'd like answers to. We discovered today that Melek looks through the crystal stones to read and write on his scroll."

"Yes, I know, Barton. They're a form of interpreter stones. I knew that as soon as I saw them all in the crate. Certain crystals have piezoelectric properties. In our own time today, we use crystals for tuning radios and keeping time on fine watches. Melek's people communicated primarily through telepathy, and the crystals that they used were attuned to their thought patterns and telepathic speech, which facilitated their understanding what they saw through the crystals written on scrolls. It's a little difficult to explain. We don't have anything like that technology developed and utilized today."

"Yes, but how did you know that about the crystals.... and how do you know how to speak ancient Greek.... and ancient Chinese? And where did you learn to like garum?" Stauffer was getting worked up. "There are just too many things that don't track about you, sir, and, I'm sorry, but I need a little clarification and enlightenment."

General Goldwyn paused for a moment, pondering Stauffer's outburst, and then responded thoughtfully. "You know, Barton, I think you're right. I've kept you in the dark this time around long enough. The time has probably come to reveal the whole story to you. But remember, what I'm going to tell you is privileged information. It's not for general consumption. You won't be able to share it with anyone else.... not even Bob Zazworsky or Bill Tipton. Understood?"

Stauffer was taken aback by General Goldwyn's bluntness. He hadn't expected quite that kind of response. "Yes, sir. I guess so."

"No, Barton. No guessing. I need your commitment on this."

"Yes, sir. I understand. What you tell me will have to remain just between us."

"Good. Now, first of all, you need to understand that we've had this conversation before on a different timeline. I answered all of the questions you just posed and many more, but then I set us on a different time line that's not part of this timeline's experience, and you don't remember any of it. Are you tracking with me so far?"

"Not precisely, sir."

"Well, it will become clear enough later on. For now, you need to understand that I am an Ancient. I was born over 5000 years ago.... many hundreds of years before Melek."

"5000 years ago! Just how old are you, sir?"

"Over 950 years now."

"How is that possible if you were born over 5000 years ago?"

"Well, I've been using Ancient temporal technology for a long time now, leapfrogging through time until I got here to the present day. I never spent very long in any one time or place until I got to this era. I lived in ancient China for awhile, India, ancient Greece, Mesoamerica, the high Andes, and a good many other places. Think of it as you would military deployments today. But I'm afraid I got my foot stuck in the door here and I haven't leapfrogged on. It's probably just as well."

Stauffer became more thoughtful as he processed Goldwyn's admission that he was an Ancient. "Sir, just what purpose does this whole operation down here actually serve then? What does DOD really get out of it all?"

"You don't buy the story about the Repository history quest or the Crypt research being useful?"

"Of course, it's useful to historians in general and perhaps to us in a limited, indirect kind of way. I just don't see how DOD gets any direct benefit from it all."

"Well, as usual Barton, you're a pretty astute observer, and you are right that the Repository and Crypt operations actually serve more of a secondary purpose for us. The primary purpose was to provide a temporal defense capability against another power acquiring a time travel capability and using it offensively against the United States. You are well familiar with that mission and how Garner Wilson's operations in the Hole are focused on just that. Perhaps, even more importantly, we've been using the temporal observation and time travel capabilities to keep tabs on all nuclear power plant operations and nuclear weapons capabilities everywhere in the world."

"What? This is all about nuclear deterrence?"

"Not just nuclear deterrence, Barton, but a nuclear fail-safe system to ensure that humankind doesn't blow itself up and destroy the planet with it."

"Who's doing all that down here?" Stauffer asked heatedly. "Certainly not Garner's team in the Hole or Alice Duerden's crew over in the Repository. And I know darn well that nuclear fail-safe isn't on our scope down in the Crypt."

"Right again, Barton. That isn't directly any of your missions. I have a separate team set up for nuclear weapons response operations. We've excavated a whole separate set of tunnels and vaults under the Barracks between the Hole levels and the Crypt levels just for that operation."

"But what do they do?"

"They monitor all nations in the world that have nuclear power plants or a nuclear weapons capability to make sure that all fissionable materials are safeguarded and used in proper ways. The bottom line mission for the team is to make sure that we don't have an unintended nuclear detonation or a nuclear holocaust if countries were to decide to duke it out with their arsenals of weapons of mass destruction."

"Well, in terms of nuclear power plants, with the disasters at Three Mile Island .... Chernobyl and.... Fukushima and.... and potential issues with Iran and North Korea...., it doesn't seem like your team is doing a particularly good job of keeping ahead of the nuclear threat."

"Actually, all those cases you cite are great examples of what exceptional work the team has been doing. Those are all success stories. All of those nuclear power sites were well on their way to becoming nuclear melt-down disasters of the first order. At Three Mile Island, Chernobyl, and Fukushima, the team intervened surreptitiously to avoid the inevitable melt down and ultimately runaway nuclear fission. In the case of Iran and North Korea, those nations aren't really much closer to a nuclear weapon and delivery system capability today than they were two dozen years ago. The team has been very effective in intervening in their technological development to ensure that they suffer frequent setbacks. But, you're leaving out my favorite, Barton, the Bad Kochsberg nuclear warhead detachment disaster."

"Sir, are you making fun of me? That was my first assignment in the Army as a young lieutenant, and we worked hard around the clock 24/7 to provide nuclear custody and security for all the tactical nuclear weapons we had stockpiled in war reserve for immediate deployment if the balloon went up."

"Yes you did. I can vouch for that. But the balloon never went up. The nuclear weapon response team had a great deal to do with that as well. But in the absence of an outright attack from the Soviet Bloc, what was the biggest threat you faced to your detachment's mission of protecting the nukes?"

"I suppose that it was the terrorist threat of the Baader Meinhof Gang. We were always getting security briefings on the threat they posed about their planning to take over one of our nuclear storage sites, and we were forever practicing emergency destruction exercises and retaking the site should a terrorist attack get that far."

"And were you successful in that endeavor?"

"Absolutely, sir. They were never able to penetrate any of our exclusion areas to gain entry to our nuclear weapons storage bunkers."

"That's true, but you don't know how close they came to doing just that."

"What do you mean, sir? We never had a problem.... never a glitch."

"Well, Barton, that's not exactly true. Late Tuesday evening, 13 May 1975, the Baader Meinhof gang had a well-orchestrated and well-rehearsed plan in place to take over your site and hold the world up for nuclear ransom. We didn't have the Hole operation in place then, and I had to act on my own. They were just about to execute their plan when I intervened with Ancient temporal technology and orchestrated a multiple vehicle collision on the Autobahn near your site involving all of the gang's vehicles it planned to use in the attack. Four of the terrorists were killed outright in the crash, and seven others were taken to the hospital seriously injured for treatment. They were later hauled off to prison when it was discovered who they really were. It ultimately set the gang back decades."

"Wait, I remember that night. I was on duty, and my driver had to slow way down to a crawl on our way to the site to get through the police barricades they had set up for traffic control. That was you?"

"Yes, Barton. That was me." General Goldwyn smiled. "You drove right by me. After I set the accident in motion, I was pulled off to the side and eventually parked near one of the emergency vehicles that had responded to the accident. All in all, between me and the nuclear response team, I would say that we've prevented nuclear disaster at least a dozen times in the past fifty years."

"Why all the interest in nuclear weapons by the Ancients?" Stauffer asked.

"Oh, that's pretty obvious, Barton. The human population of my generation almost destroyed the planet a couple of hundred years before the Flood with internecine nuclear war. Much earlier than that, my own people had previously migrated and centralized our society on an island out in the Atlantic, what you refer to today as Atlantis. When it was seen that humankind was bent on self-destruction, Enoch led the people of Atlantis off planet earth. But," General Goldwyn added, "several other cultures in the world had access to many of the same technologies that we had but they lacked the ethical or moral basis and restraint to use them wisely."

"What do you mean?"

"The people of these ancient cultures weren't primitives by any stretch of the imagination, Barton. Over a period of a thousand years, they developed fantastic, advanced technologies, some which we haven't even discovered and developed today in modern times. They used a form of computers but theirs were based more on crystal technology processing and memory storage. They knew about telekinesis and had a form of antigravity levitation."

"Is that how they moved that heavy crate around loaded with the scrolls?" Stauffer asked.

"Yes, you've already discovered that the Ancients weren't much into roads. They didn't need them. Although they had some forms of ground transportation, they also relied on small, efficient flying machines which they used predominantly for local travel and long distance aircraft to travel to distant points around the globe. They had a technology to project power through energy beams in various ways. My people used these energy beams to cut stone into enormous megalithic building blocks and built magnificent buildings and cities. During my day, they even developed temporal technology and were beginning to explore the past and the future."

General Goldwyn was beginning to get worked up in his reminiscing. "Barton, my people were a peaceful people, but others were not. As they acquired these technologies, they turned them to bellicose purposes. They manufactured sophisticated aircraft mounted with energy beam weapons and went to war against each other trying to establish hegemonic supremacy on the planet. The archeological remains of Mohenjo Daro in modern-day Pakistan provide sad evidence of that. In its day, that city was a thriving metropolis, densely populated with people living peacefully in beautiful buildings and lush gardens. It was attacked by air ships from a belligerent nation which used energy beams to reduce the city to ashes, and ultimately they deployed a thermonuclear device which totally obliterated the city and all of the surrounding land. Much that remained of the once magnificent city was a great vitrified lump of matter fused into glass. There are many vestiges of that atomic warfare all over the planet."

"That must have been horrific," Stauffer observed. "What did you and your people do?"

"About that time, these warring factions also developed temporal technology and began to experiment with how to use it as a weapon against their enemies. The situation on planet Earth was becoming precarious and dangerous, and my people made the decision to use the technology they had to evacuate the planet. They built a fleet of enormous space ships sufficient to evacuate the entire population gathered together on the island of Atlantis. When it came time to go, the leader of my people, the man you refer to today as Enoch, took me aside and assigned me to form a stay-behind team. Our mission was to use temporal technology to thwart the destructive forces of the warring nations and to try to keep them from blowing the whole planet apart. It was not to be a short-term mission. Enoch confided in me that we might be here for thousands of years. My team and I said our goodbyes to our wives and families and stood afar off when my people's mother ship lifted off from the island and moved upward into the sky. It was many miles across and made an eclipse in the sky for several minutes as it slowly moved between the sun and where my team was observing afar off.... And then they were gone."

"You were married? You had a wife and children?"

"Yes, I had just recently married, but we didn't have any children yet."

"And Enoch left you all alone here with your team to contend with all of the problems confronting Earth?"

"Not entirely. It turned out that we discovered that we could maintain telepathic communication with Enoch and my people, even across the vast distances of space. I was able to communicate with my wife frequently, and the separation over time wasn't quite so bad. She eventually rejoined me back here on Earth to support the stay-behind mission."

"How did that all work out?"

"Using temporal technology, we were successful for several hundred years in sabotaging the warring nations' use of advanced weaponry."

"And then?"

"They found ways to work around our interdiction efforts and once again, it looked bad for the planet. Wars of attrition were gradually reducing the planet to a cinder, and we had to find another way to stop it."

"What did you do?"

"Enoch and the people of Atlantis had established colonies on the moon, Mars, and on several of the larger asteroids in the asteroid belt. Enoch knew if they didn't do something about the growing threat on Earth, the people would soon destroy it entirely. He made the hard decision to take a good-sized asteroid made mostly of rock and ice out of orbit in the asteroid belt and start it moving in the direction of Earth's orbit. His scientists and engineers plotted the trajectory carefully, targeting a spot on Earth out in the middle of the Indian Ocean. If they could play it just right, they theorized that the impact of the asteroid would force great quantities of water from the Earth's inner oceans out over the face of the planet, flooding the land and destroying all of the people of the warring nations and their technologies of mass destruction with it."

"Are you suggesting that you and the people of Enoch.... the Atlanteans.... were responsible for the Flood?"

"Yes. Enoch confided in me that he had been inspired — and instructed — to do so." General Goldwyn shut his eyes, pausing briefly, and then, as he opened them again, continued, "I'm sorry, Barton,.... but I can't tell you more....right now.... I have been instructed not to share anything more about this with you at this time. I know you have many more questions for me but this will have to do. Have I told you enough to satisfy your most basic questions for now?"

Stauffer sat there incredulous. He didn't know what to think or what to say. General Goldwyn had indeed answered most of his immediate questions, but they only served to generate many more new questions. He responded slowly, carefully choosing his words. "Yes, sir. Thank you. I knew there was something most unusual about you but I had no idea.... Wait, you said that we had had this conversation before. Have you shared with me everything that you discussed in that conversation?"

"No, I haven't, Barton. Can we save that conversation for later? I think I've given you enough to think about for now, don't you?"

# Chapter 16

*Carlisle Barracks, Pennsylvania, Wednesday, June 26, 2013, 12:55 p.m.*

Stauffer ran into Zazworsky as he came back down the hallway from the elevator to the Hole returning from his late morning meeting with General Goldwyn. "Well, this has been an interesting morning," Stauffer observed, thinking back on his conversation with General Goldwyn about being an Ancient. "Ski, have we got everyone back now in the conference room for the staff meeting?"

"Yep, Boss, and everyone's chomping at the bit to get movin'."

"Good, well then, let's.... get movin'. I'm anxious to hear what everyone has to report thus far."

Stauffer and Zazworsky passed through the vault door to Stauffer's office and took their places around the conference table. Everyone else was already seated, talking excitedly among themselves.

"Thank you, everyone, for your patience." Stauffer began. "I'm sorry that we weren't able to finish our meeting earlier this morning, but I wanted to give you all an opportunity to meet Melek and gain a better understanding of his world. We've already learned a great deal from him. Here's a list I dashed off of the things I think we might have learned thus far."

Stauffer walked over to his desk and retrieved a sheaf of papers which he distributed around the table to the team. Let me walk you through my list, and I'm sure that it will prime the pump for the rest of you. First, let's see how many of the teams have made initial probes into antediluvian times immediately before the Flood."

Everyone's hand went up.

"Everyone?.... Well good. Then that makes this list a good place to get started for correlating our initial findings."

Stauffer held his list out in front of him. He adjusted his glasses on his nose and began reading:

"Item 1. Melek is 7 1/2 feet tall, yet he is apparently short in stature by antediluvian standards of his day. We've seen on the temporal observation monitors that the soldiers on the 'goon squad'

— as Ginny so aptly referred to them — are over a head taller than that. A couple of the real tall soldiers may be well over 9 feet tall."

"I'd hate to run into any of those guys in a dark alley," Zazworsky quipped.

Max Manchester spoke up. "What it tells me, Barton, is that we can't really judge magnitude or size of anything during antediluvian times on the temporal monitors without some standard unit of measure in the picture we're familiar with. We all thought the soldiers on the goon squad were normal-sized humans until we had Melek here for a size comparison. Size in the antediluvian world may well be all skewed. We're going to have to figure out a way to size stuff accurately using the monitors. I've been giving it a lot of thought but haven't come up with anything yet."

"Good point, Max," Stauffer observed as he captured Manchester's idea on the whiteboard.

"Item 2. Melek is 73 years old, yet it appears he is still a juvenile. Everyone else in Melek's community was older. Perhaps that may explain why he was shorter than the soldiers. Maybe Melek is still growing. Ancient records reflect seemingly impossible life spans for some of their rulers and patriarchs, some as old as 900-plus years, according to the Hebrew Bible. Sumerian cuneiform tablets assign life spans to some of Sumer's early rulers in the tens of thousands of years. Maybe they weren't exaggerating all that much." As he spoke, Stauffer's cheeks reddened slightly as he realized that he was telling a lie of omission by not revealing that General Goldwyn himself was an Ancient well over 900 years old.

"Item 3. Melek's normal mode of communication is by telepathy. Although he can speak out loud, it appears to be a new thing for him, and he prefers to communicate telepathically. When I asked him about it, Melek told me that it was only during his own father's generation that people started speaking out loud in a general way because telepathic communication was becoming harder for them. We're going to need to look at that much closer. Why would telepathic communication become more difficult for Melek's people? Could it be genetic degradation, or interference from the Earth's magnetic field, or maybe powerful solar flares. Sanjay, would you take the lead on investigating that question please."

"With pleasure Colonel Stauffer," Sanjay Singh responded with a big grin, jotting down a note on the pad in front of him. "Right up my alley."

Stauffer continued down his list. "Next, Item 4. Melek and his people have a writing system of sorts. They apparently have limited numbers of papyrus scrolls, leather books, metal plates, and stone tablets. But the writing systems appear to be unique to each individual. It's not precisely a standardized writing system that everyone has agreed upon. In order to read what Melek or anyone else has written, they need the assistance of crystals to look through. When I asked Melek again after our meeting this morning where the crystals came from, he told me that his grandfather had picked them up during a journey across the great waters to the west of his land to the great island city of Atlantis before it disappeared."

Stauffer smiled and looked around the room. "Max and I are going to look into that one. Ever since Plato wrote about it, we've always wanted to know more about the legendary Atlantis. Oh, and who has the landmass and coastal waters of North and South America on the other side of the Atlantic?"

"Ken Red Elk and I have North America," Maggie Martinez responded.

"And Ski and I have the Central and South American continents," Miriam Campbell said.

"Good. Your two teams need to approach the search for the island city of Atlantis working eastward from the coastal waters of the Americas."

"Can do, Barton," Martinez responded. "But Melek said that the island disappeared in his grandfather's day. Did he give a time hack for when that might have happened?"

"Only that it happened shortly after his grandfather's visit to the place when his father was yet a young man of 125. According to Melek, the island disappeared years later when his father was 330 years old. So I guess that puts it at least a couple of hundred years earlier, probably a lot more."

Martinez and Red Elk quickly jotted down the numbers and Stauffer continued. "Let me get back to my list."

"Item 5. I asked Melek again about his scroll and why it was so precious. He told me that recording family histories and genealogies on scrolls and books was a recent invention among his people and had begun when they started losing their facility for telepathic communication and their memories became faulty. I showed him the video of the soldiers confiscating scrolls and books and metal plates and throwing them into the crate, and he became overcome with grief. He told me that what the soldiers had taken probably represented the sum total of all written materials for his entire region. There probably wasn't much left that wasn't confiscated and dumped into the crate."

"If I track that logic," Sandy Watson offered, "then there probably aren't going to be any other significant targets of opportunity of large libraries of written materials for us to examine and perhaps retrieve from that time period in that area of the world."

"You may be right, Sandy," Phillips countered. "But I'm still holding out hope for a cache of books like the legendary Hall of Records elsewhere. I've got that search target high on my list."

"That's good, Hank," Stauffer responded. "We're all hoping that we can zero in on that soon. But, speaking of the crate...."

"Item 6. Melek's people appear able to levitate large objects and move them about telekinetically. And, although they walk around some of the time, they also seem to be able to levitate themselves. It's probably the reason we didn't see any evidence of roads outside of the villages."

"Levitate themselves? You mean they can fly?" Zazworksy exclaimed. "That's something I want to get in on. Do you think that Melek could teach us.... me.... to fly?" Zazworsky extended his arms and started flapping them comically.

"Sit down, big guy," Maggie Martinez elbowed him in the ribs, "before I sic Tinkerbell on you with her pixie dust and we throw you off the roof of Collins Hall to see if it really works."

Stauffer laughed at Zazworsky's antics and continued, "Actually, I think we're going to discover that the Ancients had access to a great many technologies, some of which we have only recently discovered today and some which we still don't have any knowledge of. We don't know what we don't know, and we need to pay special attention to those possibilities."

Max Manchester spoke up. "Barton, I like your short list of observations and I would like to hear everyone else's input. But, with your approval, I would prefer waiting until tomorrow so that each of the teams can put together a summarized 10 or 20-minute presentation on what we have discovered thus far. We haven't been at it very long, and we can frame those presentations in the context of your six points or any additional points that we might want to bring out. What say you?"

Stauffer nodded his head. "Max, I like your thinking on that. I know all of you are anxious to get started. But does everyone else support the proposal to wait until tomorrow to organize our thoughts and prepare what we have to share in an abbreviated format?"

Everyone in the room nodded. Some of the team members waved their hand in assent.

"Good," Stauffer responded. "Let's meet here in my office at 0800. I know that some of the teams have uncovered a lot of interesting material, but I'm going to ask you for this briefing to limit yourselves to a couple of key observations to add to our list. Everyone load your presentations and video captures on the classified intranet and we'll run them on the big flat screen here. The results of those presentations will probably frame our future research options as we move forward. Thanks, all. We'll see you tomorrow morning."

As everyone filed out of the room chattering excitedly about their various observation projects, Stauffer felt a consuming sense of uneasiness and guilt about not being able to share with his team what General Goldwyn had told him about being an Ancient. It put a new twist on their research mission. For Stauffer, it gave the whole project a certain feeling of artificiality. Whatever they discovered or uncovered about the antediluvian Ancients from their temporal observation monitor surveys, it was apparently all old news for General Goldwyn. And that took the edge of excitement of the venture out of it just a little bit for Stauffer.

# Chapter 17

*The Crypt, Carlisle Barracks, Pennsylvania, Thursday, 27 June, 2013, 8:00 a.m.*

The meeting began in Stauffer's office the next morning promptly at 0800 hours. Stauffer stood at the head of the conference table and referred to a flip chart easel. "Alright, everyone, good to see you all this morning. We have a lot to cover. Yesterday, Max suggested that each team take 10 minutes or so to provide a quick overview briefing to the rest of the teams on what you have turned up with your initial survey scans. That's not very much time, but I'm going to ask you to try to keep your remarks brief. We have seven teams. Pete and Bill already took some time last week talking about what they had discovered as they began their temporal survey of the area between Ireland and Europe. That resulted in our recovery of the floating crate of scrolls and Melek. I shared with you yesterday my short list of six specific things that I think we have learned from that experience. With Pete and Bill's briefing out of the way, that leaves six teams still left to brief. That ought to take a little over an hour. I'd like to lead off this morning with Max and pick up the thread of the conversation about Atlantis from what we learned from Melek. After that, we'll just go down each of the teams in the order I've indicated on the flip chart. If we adhere to the time limits, we can take some time after that to discuss whatever seems to you all to be most pertinent."

Max Manchester began speaking while Stauffer operated the presentation graphics and screen captures on the giant flat screen monitor mounted on the wall. "Melek suggested that Atlantis lay somewhere to the west of the land mass that made up Ireland, the Isle of Man, the United Kingdom, and Europe. Not knowing precisely when or where to look, we set up our temporal monitor for 1000 years earlier than Melek's time frame and started scanning due west from the coast of Ireland out into the Atlantic. We moved across the expanse of the entire Atlantic until we bumped into the coastline of Labrador and Newfoundland, and we realized we had gone too far. So we backed off half the distance to the middle of the

Atlantic and then started panning back and forth in broad sweeps as
we moved southward to see what we might find."

"That could have taken forever, Max," Maggie Martinez
spoke up.

"Yes, it could have, except that we did the scans super-fast
motion using the software for locating solid objects in the watery
ocean. We figured that if it located boats on the ocean so easily, it
would alert us if we passed over an island."

"Good idea," Martinez observed. "Did it work?"

"Yes. We were only at it a little longer than an hour when we
hit pay dirt.... literally.... We found Atlantis.... a great big island cluster
out in the middle of the lower Atlantic, between the present day
Azores and Bermuda."

"How do you know it was Atlantis, Max?" Sandy Watson
asked.

"We didn't at first. When we located the island, there were
only a few inhabitants on it. But we fast forwarded temporally
into the future to see what would develop. We observed a major
migration to the island that occurred over a period of a hundred
years or so, and the population on the island built up rapidly. People
flowed in from every direction in all kinds of boats and even some
flying craft levitating above the ocean surface. As the population
expanded, the island apparently became incapable of supporting
so many people, and they began levitating entire mountains from
the African and American mainland and brought them to Atlantis
to terraform the island outward from the ocean floor up. Several
of the smaller outlying islands in the cluster were simply absorbed
into the major island land mass in the process as Atlantis grew
and took shape before our eyes. After a while, we noticed that the
configuration of construction in the center of the island reflected the
concentric circles pattern described by Plato. We also observed that
they were using energy beam tools of some kind to cut and fashion
megalithic stone that had been brought in to build their city. Many of
the rocks were enormous.... hundreds of tons perhaps. After cutting
them into shape, they simply levitated them into place and fit them
tightly together."

Stauffer was forwarding through a series of screen captures
on the flat screen monitor for everyone to visually track Manchester's
narrative. "Barton," Dr. Campbell interrupted, "could you please

slow down as you move through those slides. I need more time to digest what I'm seeing."

"Sure thing, Miriam," Stauffer responded and then added, "but it turned out that they weren't constructing buildings. Look closely. Instead, it appears to be an enormous, circular, flat stone platform with smaller stone buildings and houses built way out on the periphery of the island. When the platform was completed, they started bringing in metal.... lots of metal..... steel, brass, copper, bronze and gold.... and some other metals we didn't recognize, aluminum and other alloys perhaps.... huge amounts of different kinds of finished metal sheets and girders and other construction materials. Rather quickly, an enormous metal structure took shape on the circular stone platform. It was big....very big. Although we can't be sure, we estimate that it was at least several miles across."

"For what purpose did they build it?" Dr. Campbell asked.

Manchester responded, "Good question, Miriam. At first we weren't certain at all of what we were seeing. The structure took on the same shape as the circular platform it rested on, including the concentric circles pattern indentations on the upper surface. We were moving fast using rapid temporal scanning, but we didn't observe stone being used anywhere in the construction. The structure appeared to be made entirely of metal and lighter materials. As we continued to fast-scan through, we realized that the structure began to look like an enormous flying saucer like you sometimes see in the science fiction movies. Work on the huge craft continued at a furious pace as the people moved about like ants on the superstructure. And then, the activity appeared to slow down as the craft neared completion, and construction work began on smaller stone platforms in the outlying areas. Some were circular and some were triangular in shape. On top of these platforms, they began building smaller metal aircraft. As soon as any of these smaller craft were completed, they levitated them away, vacating the platform, and construction on additional craft began immediately in its place."

"That's unbelievable organization!" Hank Phillips commented.

Manchester nodded and continued, pointing at the screen. "The Atlanteans soon had an enormous mother ship and a great fleet of smaller aircraft. We checked the time elapsed on the temporal monitor.... just two hundred years real time since they first started building up the island."

"I need a reality check here," Pete Pendleton interjected. "Let me make sure I understand this, Max. Are you saying that the fabled island of Atlantis, as recorded by Plato, was really an enormous space ship?"

"That's what we've concluded during our initial temporal survey. We need to go back now and check out the details, going much slower time motion. A lot can pass by unnoticed when you fast-track temporally through two hundred years of history in a couple of hours on the temporal monitor. We still need to find out more about writing and scrolls and crystals and telepathy and levitation and the like to confirm what we learned from Melek."

"What happened then, after they finished the mother ship, Max?" Ginny Nguyen urged. "Don't leave us hanging."

"You're right, Ginny," Manchester responded. "As we continued fast-scanning, something really remarkable happened. We observed a series of temblors that vibrated the image on our temporal monitors. At first we thought something was wrong with our own temporal equipment, but then we noticed that some of the taller buildings on the periphery of the island began to fall in on themselves, raising huge clouds of dust. Almost immediately, small aircraft began converging on the island, flying in over the ocean from all directions.... thousands of them. Most of them must have been built somewhere else because we hadn't observed that many being built on Atlantis. When the airships reached the island, they formed a huge fleet, a vast network of aircraft, hovering there in the sky above the outer perimeter of the island. Then, Atlantis, the mother ship, slowly lifted off its stone platform and levitated into the sky, slowly at first, but gathering speed as it ascended. All of the smaller craft still on the construction platforms on the island also lifted off and joined the rest of the fleet in the sky. Together, en masse, the fleet of ships moved upward through the clouds until they disappeared in the distance. We never did detect what kind of propulsion systems they might have been using. None of the craft exhibited any kind of exhaust flame or contrails like our own jet planes and rocket ships give off. We imagine that it had to be some kind of magnetic levitation or antigravity technology."

"They just lifted off and vanished into the sky?" Zazworsky asked. "Where did they go?"

"That's right, Ski," Stauffer answered, pointing at the visual image on the monitor. They just took off and departed. We gave up pursuit following them with the temporal monitors as they left Earth's upper atmosphere, and we turned our attention back to the island they had just left. And that's when a truly amazing thing happened. After the fleet had vanished, we saw no sign of any living thing on the now deserted island.... just the stone platforms. And then, suddenly, the island started to shake violently, and the stone platforms began to buckle and break up and fall apart. The vibrations from the earthquake grew stronger and more violent, and the ocean waters surrounding the island started to rush in over the land as the island began to sink into the sea. According to the time indicator on the side of the temporal monitor, it only took a matter of days for the entire island to disappear beneath the waves. There was nothing left. We searched the area for awhile, trying to see if there were any boats or signs of survivors in the sea.... Nothing.... except for a few small islands off to the east which we later discovered are the westernmost islands of the modern-day Azores chain, Corvo and Flores. But the islands of Atlantis were gone."

Everyone around the conference table sat there dumfounded, not saying anything. Finally, looking at his watch, Stauffer said, "There's a lot more, but that's it for now. Our ten minutes are up. I assume you all have a thousand questions, but I think we ought to hold them for now to see what the other teams have to brief. I have a feeling that a lot of the questions will be interrelated." Stauffer looked back over at the flip chart behind him and then turned to Martinez and Red Elk. "Let's keep moving west. Maggie and Ken, you had North America. What have you observed?"

Martinez began to speak as Stauffer passed the wireless keyboard down to Red Elk. As he keyed an entry, a new image appeared on the screen. "We did what Barton instructed us to do, looking for Atlantis off the coast of America, but we didn't turn up anything. And so, we turned our temporal survey inward. Our focus was on identifying population settlement patterns in the antediluvian Americas. We went back 800 years earlier than the Flood and started doing broad scans across the face of the North American continent. The topography of the land threw us at first. It was quite different from the geography of today. Like Bart and Max, we scanned fast-motion to cover the most ground in the shortest amount of time. We started in the north at the Arctic Circle and began making broad sweeps from coast to coast back and forth as we moved southward. In the north, we saw vast tracts of land buried under thick sheets of ice and snow many miles thick. As we moved south of the 40th parallel, the ice sheets began to disappear and we were surprised to find large groups of people gathered across the land from coast to coast. Most were scattered about in small agricultural communities, but there were many large population centers as well, with elaborate buildings made of wood, brick, mud adobe, and even some monolithic stone. We were surprised not to see many vast expanses of virgin forest. Much of the land was actually under cultivation. What surprised us most was the extensive open-pit copper mines in the area of present-day Michigan. There were copper smelters set up in hundreds of locations, and the refined copper was loaded into large boxes or barges and levitated away. I did some research after the fact, and, based upon archaeological evidence, there are scientists today who estimate that over half a billion pounds of copper were mined and removed from the area in ancient times. That's a lot of copper. There are some scholars today who suggest that the almost unlimited supply of copper promoted the early global transition from the Neolithic to the Bronze Age. Some attribute those mines in Michaigan as the source of the immense quantities of bronze and brass produced during the early Bronze Age. Ken and I think that we all ought to be looking for evidence of antediluvian writing on copper plates or scrolls or even copper monuments as we conduct our survey scans."

Martinez turned to Red Elk who continued the briefing, "We saw enormous ceremonial mounds everywhere, and we occasionally observed large gatherings of people in the precincts of these mounds, ostensibly in observance of some festival or significant community event. We saw many step pyramids and platform mounds, some faced with flat stones on top that served as construction sites and landing pads for flying craft. Some pyramids and platform mounds had elaborate stone buildings built on top. We assume that these had some religious or community significance. They might have been temple structures. We watched on several occasions when large aircraft flew in and focused energy beams of some kind on a mountain top in an isolated area and literally levitated the entire mountain into the air, guiding it off eastward towards the coast. After what we just heard from Bart and Max, now it all begins to come together and make sense. I guess those were some of the mountains of material which were used as fill to expand the island of Atlantis."

"What about the ancient Zuni and Pueblo peoples in the Southwest, Ken?" Max Manchester inquired. "I know you were interested in that. Have you had time to scope it out yet?"

"Not as much as I would like, Max. There were several large settlements there in the antediluvian American Southwest, but we weren't able to zoom in on them in any detail yet. We did observe quite a bit of aerial traffic in that area, some of which were flying barges filled with what appeared to be gold, copper and other precious metals. We tracked the flight of some of those barges to various destinations farther east where the metal was used to make elaborate ornamentation for temples and pyramidal platforms and for construction of aircraft."

Martinez continued. "We didn't have much time to explore such a vast land area in so short a time and so, for this initial survey, we typically observed everything from high up in the air at one or two thousand feet. We need to go back now and get down to ground level at a much slower scan speed and gather more detailed information about specific sites and peoples. We're hoping that the briefings today give us greater insight about what we ought to be looking for."

Stauffer spoke up as they finished their presentation. "Good overview, Maggie.... Ken.... Let's move on to what Bob and Miriam have to tell us about Central and South America."

As the wireless computer keyboard was passed to him, Zazworsky input a few keystrokes, and the scenes on the monitor changed again. Dr. Campbell began the briefing. "As we moved across the Central American land bridge to South America, we noted that it was much wider than it is today. Cuba, the Dominican Republic and Haiti, Puerto Rico, and the Antilles were all joined together with the coasts of the Yucatan in Mexico, Florida and the Florida Keys, and the northern coast of South America, forming two extensive inland lakes where the Gulf of Mexico and the Caribbean Sea are today."

Zazworsky input a few more keystrokes, and the image on the screen panned out to reveal the greatly modified geography. "Wow," Pete Pendleton whistled and remarked. "That's different. That would really put a crimp in the cruise ship industry today."

Dr. Campbell laughed and continued. "We also tried to focus in on settlement patterns as we began this survey. As we panned southward over the South American continent, we noted that there were extensive built-up areas in what is today the Amazonian tropical rain forests of Brazil and Bolivia. The people living there were concentrated in great numbers across a broad grassy savannah plain. Settlements were marked by extensive round earthen mounds and broad plazas joined together by elaborate roadway systems, causeways and bridges. They were all connected by intricately-engineered canal systems which seemed to support a system of intensive agriculture, using what appeared to be *terra preta*, enriched black earth soil. At one location, we even saw what appeared to be an astronomical observatory tower made of monolithic cut stones. Nearby were large flat stone platforms which seemed to serve as landing places for aircraft."

"You saw all this out in the middle of the Amazonian rain forest?" Mitch Monahan asked.

"Yeah, Mitch," Zazworsky answered, "but much of it wasn't an impenetrable jungle then like it is today. It was a broad open plain.... a grassland.... similar in many ways to parts of the great American Midwest. Today, all of the mounds and structures and causeways and canals lie buried under millennia of silt and decayed matter and jungle canopy, and it isn't until the jungle is cleared away nowadays that the mounds and causeways are detected. It would take a major archaeological excavation effort to really understand the antediluvian settlement patterns of the area."

"Let's move on," Dr. Campbell interjected. "We scanned westward from there and ascended the eastern slopes of the Andes to do a quick survey of the Bolivian and Peruvian *altiplano*. Everywhere we turned, we observed antediluvian cities constructed of great monolithic stones precisely cut, shaped and fitted together."

Scenes of great structures built of enormous monolithic stone work appeared on the screen. Dr. Campbell pointed at the monitor as Zazworsky brought up screen captures of antediluvian cities. "There were large settlements at Tiahuanaco and Cuzco, both sharing the same architecture of monstrously-large stones cut in irregular shapes at odd angles and fitted tightly together. We slowed down the scan briefly and observed a group of stone masons working on one of the buildings, and we saw that they used some sort of device employing an energy beam to slice the stones at precise angles. After the stones were levitated and assembled in place together, they used a broadened beam on the completed wall and the stones seemed to flow together, eliminating all spaces and air pockets between them, almost like soap bubbles."

"What about Puma Punku?" Sandy Watson asked. "That site has always fascinated me."

"The ruins at Puma Punku were something quite different," Zazworsky spoke up. "They seemed to be much older than the newer construction at Tiahuanaco, although Puma Punku is only a kilometer or so north west from the major plaza at Tiahuanaco. Some of the Puma Punku structures were already in ruins as we began our survey scans. We realized that the site must have been built at a much earlier time. We scanned backward on the temporal monitor to see if we could determine when it was built and possibly what had led to its decay. We bracketed in and by luck encountered the construction of the place more than 1000 years before the Flood."

Zazworsky put several screen captures up on the monitor as Dr. Campbell continued. "Puma Punku was a terraced earthen mound faced with gigantic stone blocks. It was put together literally overnight with prefabricated stones cut into intricate shapes with precise interior and exterior right angles. Aerial barges arrived at the site and offloaded the prefabricated stones. Workers at the site levitated the stones into place, and construction of the major elements of Puma Punku was completed in less than three days. We followed the barges back to the quarry source near Lake Titicaca, roughly ten kilometers away. At the quarry, workers cut out the blocks using automatic energy beam equipment that produced blocks of identical uniformity according to some pre-planned design. The construction of Puma Punko resembled the assembling of huge Lego blocks or Lincoln logs more than anything else."

"Were you able to determine what destroyed the Puma Punku site?" Phillips asked.

"Yes," Zazworsky responded excitedly. "Once we had bracketed in on the construction of Puma Punko, we set the temporal monitor to move into the future in super-fast time. The site apparently went through several periods of construction additions and renovations through the years. And then, approximately six hundred years before the Flood, a fleet of aircraft swooped in over the Bolivian altiplano in attack formation and fired energy weapons at the settlements at Puma Punku and Tiahuanaco. Puma Punku suffered the greatest damage, with most of the site blown to smithereens and reducing it to a pile of rubble. The Tiahuanaco structures and plazas fared much better with little actual destruction of the stone walls themselves. When the attacking force had finished their work of destruction at Puma Punku and Tiahuanaco, the fleet moved off to the northwest in the direction of Cuzco. We followed them on the temporal monitors and watched them reduce many of the antediluvian buildings in the valley of Cuzco to rubble as well. They were about to turn their weapons on the fortress of Sacsayhuaman when another group of aircraft flew in from the east, and an air battle took place over the valley of Cuzco. Several of the aircraft in the first fleet were hit by energy beams and stayed aloft apparently only with great difficulty. As they began to falter in the sky, the entire fleet retreated, taking off vertically.... practically straight up.... and disappeared, saving Sacsayhuaman from further damage. We are anxious to go back and observe in much greater detail, but that's about it for now. We've got a lot of work ahead of us trying to make sense of everything we've seen in this initial survey."

Zazworsky pushed the wireless keyboard on around the table to Winston Greeley as Jared Lincoln stood to speak gesturing towards the new visuals that appeared on the flat screen.

"We were tasked to survey the landmass of Africa south of the Mediterranean coast," Lincoln began. "Today, we refer to that area as Sub-Saharan Africa, but, for a period of time before the Flood, much of the area of today's Sahara Desert was actually a fertile savannah supporting large populations of people and animals. In certain areas, such as southern Sudan, we saw large rivers, thick vegetation, dense forests, and numerous freshwater lakes. Following the Flood, after the waters had receded, the monsoonal rains that had watered the region diminished and the natural processes of desiccation began. Over a period of hundreds of years, the whole area was swallowed up by encroaching desert sands.

We initially focused in on the time frame during antediluvian times when the Sahara Region was essentially green and populated. We counted well over a thousand human settlements. Due to the scarcity of rocks in many places, the cities were generally constructed of adobe mud, and they cultivated grain crops and herded domesticated livestock such as cattle, sheep and goats. In the open areas away from the human settlements, we saw herds of wildlife everywhere, including giraffes, elephants, rhinos, crocodiles, hippopotamuses, and crocodiles."

"Hippopotami, Jared," Zazworsky corrected.

"What?" Lincoln looking askance at Zazworsky.

"The preferred plural for hippopotamus is hippopotami, not hippopotamuses. I learned that a long time ago in Mrs. Demetrious' fourth grade class."

Zazworsky's observation caught Lincoln off guard, and he started to laugh. "Why don't we just compromise on 'hippos,' Ski," he suggested.

"That works for me," Zazworsky responded solemnly, a mischievous smile creeping across his face.

Lincoln continued, sporting a big grin himself. "Like most of you, our initial survey involved scanning broad swaths across the continent, beginning in the Sahara region and moving south. Remember that the African continent is actually three times the size of the continental United States, and we had a lot of ground to cover, so we're going to be brief here.

"On the northern edge of the Sahara in what is today southern Egypt, we discovered an extensive complex of large, uncut stone slabs arranged in a massive array on the savanna floor. If we have our temporal dating correct, the complex predates Stonehenge by at least a thousand years. The layout of the stones isn't circular like at Stonehenge, but spread out over an area of almost two square miles. Some of the stones in the complex are big. At least a dozen of them appear to be at least eight or nine feet high. There are at least seventy or eighty other large stones, many of which appear to weigh upwards of several hundred pounds apiece. Many of the stones are arranged in five radiating lines, one of them oriented exactly east-west. There's also what appears to be a small calendar circle with alignments perhaps on the summer solstice. The Ancients in this area certainly had a good working knowledge of astronomical alignments.

Dr. Greeley jumped in. "As we panned across the Sahara, moving forward and backward in time, we also discovered massive areas covered by desert glass, where the sand had been vitrified by intense heat. We scanned backwards temporally to see if we could discover what had caused it. We didn't have far to go. Approximately two hundred years before the Flood, there was an aerial battle fought in the skies above the desert in that area. Both combatant sides had energy beams mounted on their aircraft, and as they focused the beams on each other in the conflict, they frequently beamed down on the desert floor, melting the sand under extreme temperatures into glass. We understand that such expanses of desert glass and vitrification of stone occur on all of the continents, and we believe that this requires further investigation by all of our teams."

"That's a good point, Winston," Stauffer acknowledged. "Everyone, please make it a point to follow up on that and investigate any vitrification situations you might discover in your areas during your survey scans. This appears to be a strong indicator for energy weaponry and perhaps even nuclear detonations."

Stauffer nodded back at Lincoln and he continued, "This leads us to a very interesting discovery. As we panned further south, we discovered a uranium mining operation in present day Gabon, West Africa, operated by the Ancients."

"They appeared to process the uranium on site and then loaded it on huge barges which they levitated into the sky and flew off. We followed one of the barges for several thousand miles before we dropped off and returned to Africa. The barge was set on a course heading for the Indian subcontinent. We suspect that the processed uranium was being utilized in some way there."

"Roger that." Sanjay Singh spoke up while taking notes. "I'll be on the lookout for it. Have you posted the time-location coordinates so that I can pick up the trail?"

Lincoln nodded in the affirmative and gave Singh a thumbs-up sign. "As we returned southward to the mining operation, when we were still at quite a distance, there was a blinding glare in the sky and a mushroom cloud rose up ominously over the horizon. Apparently, someone had attacked the mining operation or the uranium ore had reached critical mass during processing and detonated of its own accord. We moved temporally into the future a hundred years and scanned the area where the mine had been. Everything was pretty much obliterated, and any evidence of previous mining was gone."

Stauffer interrupted at this point, "Everyone, Jared and Winston's presentation raises a serious issue, one that I don't know at this point how to confront. What happens if we're conducting temporal scans into antediluvian times and we end up looking directly into a nuclear blast? Can we be blinded by the intense light coming through the temporal monitors?" Stauffer paused for a moment considering the implications and then proceeded speaking slowly. "Ski, would you please look into the possibility of having the techs install some kind of a cut-out system that automatically shuts down the temporal monitors instantaneously should we find ourselves in such a situation. We know that at least some groups of Ancients were messing around with nuclear weaponry. I'd hate to have to conduct all of our temporal scans wearing welders' goggles to protect our vision."

Zazworsky scribbled a note to himself, and Greeley picked up the thread of the briefing. "As we scanned further south, we saw extensive antediluvian settlements spread out across the land. We followed up with some quick scans following the flood and noted that, although some occupied ships made landfall on the African continent, it took a long time for the population to build back up anywhere close to what it had been before the Flood. And they never achieved the level of technology that had been in use there before.... Barton, that about sums up our observations at this point."

Greeley passed the wireless keyboard on around the table to Sandy Watson and Hank Phillips. Watson put a new set of graphics up on the screen, but these graphics weren't screen captures from their temporal monitors. The screen was divided into eight partitions showing examples of writing. Phillips stood and walked over to the screen pointing at each of the sections as he spoke. "These are examples of the writing patterns taken from the scrolls and plates recovered from the floating crate mission. The script here in the upper left corner is taken from Melek's scroll. I wanted you to see this so that you could get a better understanding of the analysis given me by the translators and cryptologists. They initially couldn't see any form or similarity between any of the scripts recovered. But when they separated out these eight and compared them side-by-side, they think that these might hold the key to some form of proto-Sumerian cuneiform. They haven't the tools to translate any of it, but it does seem to point in that direction."

"What about the crystals, Hank?" Dr. Campbell asked. "Can't we use the crystals to read the scrolls like Melek does?"

"We've tried but it doesn't seem to work for us like it does for Melek. We've tried a number of different combinations of crystal sets with different scrolls and.... nothing. It hasn't produced anything at all yet. What we do know is that the Antediluvians had a form of writing. Modern researchers refer to that period of time as 'prehistory' or 'protohistory' only because we have never had examples of writing from that period before. We have broken through that barrier now, and we are on the brink of redefining human history and pushing back prehistory thousands of years. The issue of writing defined the thrust of our initial scans across Mesopotamia and North Africa. Scientists have always used written language as an indicator of the emergence of civilization. We used to believe that it started with the Sumerians somewhere around 3000 BC. The earliest Egyptian hieroglyphics also date to about that time. But evidence of earlier writing in China and the Indus Valley has been pushing that estimate back."

"What do you mean, Hank?" Stauffer asked. "What have you been looking at?"

"Well, Sandy and I are both librarians, and we've been looking for anything that resembles memorial plaques, books or libraries. We've scanned across the area of the Mesopotamia, Asia Minor, and the Fertile Crescent, moving south into Egypt and parts of North Africa. We operated two separate temporal monitors to cover twice the ground. Every time we encountered a community or group of people of any size, we zoomed in to see if we could detect any writing activity or evidence of writing like scrolls, plates, stone tablets.... anything."

"Did you find anything?" Max Manchester asked.

"Actually, we did. Once again, we saw a few people writing on scrolls or metal plates looking through crystals to guide their efforts. And then we saw an extraordinary example of writing. It was at the site we call Baalbek, situated today in modern Lebanon. The Ancients used focused energy beams to cut out enormously large stone blocks from quarries to construct a huge flat platform. Some of the stones weighed upwards of a thousand tons. Once they had cut out several of these stones, several workers stood on top of the stones and began to engrave a lengthy message into the stone face using a small hand-operated, energy beam tool. When it was finished, they levitated the stone and moved it the distance from the quarry to where they were constructing the platform. As they got it to the construction site, the stone rose up into the air and then slowly rolled completely over so that the inscribed side was now facing down. And then they fit the stone into place."

"Do you mean, evidence of antediluvian writing is right there at Baalbek on the underside of one of the foundation blocks?" Zazworsky asked.

"That's right, Ski," Phillips answered. "Only the inscription is sandwiched between two stones weighing almost 2,000 tons between them. But we did get a couple of screen captures of what the workers engraved before they hid them in the stone sandwich." Sandy Watson projected the image of the inscription up on the screen as Phillips spoke. "We have the translators and cryptologists looking over it now. So far, they don't know what to make of it."

"What about the Hall of Records, Hank?" Dr. Campbell asked. "Isn't that your primary focus and concern?"

"Yes, certainly, Miriam. But we wanted to do an initial broad scan across the region to observe what we could about the progress of writing. The legendary Hall of Records is rumored to be located in a cavern buried deep under the paws of the Sphinx at Giza. As we were scanning for the evidence of writing in Egypt and North Africa, I took time to examine the Sphinx. It was in place there in Egypt long before the Giza pyramids, which were all built after the Flood. When I located the Sphinx on the broad Giza plateau, it was a solitary construction sitting there all by itself, in its recessed enclave cut into the plateau. I did a quick backtrack in time and observed its construction. Most of the upper portion of the Sphinx was carved out of a spur of solid bedrock limestone that jutted out of the plateau. Here, let's show you what it looked like before they started carving on it."

A picture of a broad, flat plain opened up on the screen. In the foreground a rocky outcropping protruded up from the desert floor. "What's that?" Zazworsky asked.

"It's technically called a yardang, Ski. It's formed by wind erosion as the wind wears away softer material leaving the harder rock in place. As we fast-forwarded through time focusing on the yardang, we observed teams of Ancients who flew into the area on aircraft. They used energy beam tools to cut out limestone blocks which they carefully removed and stacked neatly on top of the plateau. The excavation soon left a long solid block of limestone in the center of a large hollowed-out enclosure which was eventually carved to form the body of the Sphinx. The yardang, which protruded out of the east end of the block, was ultimately carved into the head of the Sphinx."

As Phillips talked them through the construction of the Sphinx, Sandy Watson projected a stop-action video of the Sphinx as it took shape. "Hank.... Sandy.... the Sphinx isn't on the Giza Plateau," Ken Red Elk observed. "It appears to be below the plane of the plateau. I always thought that it was right out there on the plateau at the same level with the Giza pyramids."

"That's a common misconception," Watson responded. "The Sphinx is actually almost concealed in the enclosure cut out of the limestone strata of the plateau. The camera angles that are used to show both the Sphinx and the pyramids in the same frame create an optical illusion that they're level with each other. The Sphinx today measures approximately 70 meters long by 19 meters wide by 20 meters tall. The top portion of the head of the Sphinx barely extends above the plane of the Giza Plateau where the yardang used to stick up."

As they spoke, the screen captures of the carving on the Sphinx progressed to completion. Phillips pointed at the screen and then turned to the group assembled around the table. "Anyone have any idea whose face this is which was originally carved onto the Sphinx's head?"

"Well, I know that that isn't the face or head that's there now. The current one is much smaller and looks very different," Dr. Campbell observed. "But I can't place whose face that is."

"We couldn't either at first, but I think that Colonel Stauffer or Dr. Manchester might be able to make the connection. What do you think? Do you recognize the face?"

Stauffer looked long and hard at the face of the Sphinx, and then it suddenly dawned on him. "If I'm not mistaken, it's the face of the leader of the people of Atlantis, the man whom we refer to as Enoch. We saw him interacting with the people during the construction of Atlantis on several occasions.... Yes, I'm fairly certain. I think that that's a likeness of Enoch."

"That's what we were thinking, and after we saw your presentation earlier, we became convinced."

"But why doesn't the Sphinx look that way today?" Ginny Nguyen asked.

"We asked the same question. Once the Sphinx was completed, we fast forwarded temporally to see when it was recarved. It happened long after the Flood. The Sphinx didn't fare well being underwater for almost a year, and when the flood waters finally receded, the body of the Sphinx was badly weathered in places but the face and head were eroded almost beyond recognition. When people began repopulating the area in the vicinity of Giza many years after the Flood, they recarved the head and face and parts of the body to portray an early pharaoh of Egypt. That's why the head of the Sphinx is smaller and out of proportion with the rest of the body today."

"All very interesting, Hank and Sandy," Stauffer interjected. "But what about the Hall of Records? Did you find the Hall of Records buried under the Sphinx?"

"We haven't had time to pursue that possibility yet," Phillips responded. "But, as you see in the video capture, back when it was first carved, the Sphinx faced the edge of a limestone cliff that dropped off out in front of the paws. The builders of the Sphinx took the limestone blocks they excavated to carve out the enclosure that surrounds the Sphinx and built a small temple right at the feet of the Sphinx on the edge of the cliff. During the Flood and over the thousands of years since, the area at the base of the cliff gradually filled in until it's at the same level as the plane of the Sphinx. In the process, we think that it might have covered up a tunnel opening in the face of the cliff. That's the next thing we're going to investigate. If there was originally a natural opening in the face of the cliff, that's where we'll find it."

"Thank you Hank and Sandy," Stauffer acknowledged. "That was most informative. I hope that you find that opening. I can't begin to imagine what records and artifacts the legendary Hall of Records might contain." Stauffer paused and looked over his shoulder at the flip chart. "Meanwhile, we still need to take a look further east. Sammy and Sanjay, what have you found in your initial surveys?"

Watson passed the wireless keyboard to Singh and new images appeared on the screen as Woo began to speak. "We were tasked with the Pacific Rim, China, Mongolia, the Himalayas, and India. That's a lot of ground to cover, and we only have a few anecdotal observations to report at this point. We were surprised to discover how heavily populated all of the areas we observed were during antediluvian times. On the coast of present-day Japan, we saw huge monolithic structures carved right out of the stone cliffs that rose up out of the sea. Many of these same structures exist today, although they are now underwater off the coast of the southern Japanese islands at Yonaguni. Moving farther inland into China, we saw numerous groups of people spread out across the land. There were cities and ceremonial centers everywhere. Some areas were blanketed by dozens of pyramids that were strangely reminiscent of the later pyramids of Egypt, while others looked more like the step pyramids of Mesoamerica. We were scanning fast-time and so much of what we saw went by in a blur. At one point, we slowed down and observed a group of scholars or scribes sitting at long low tables outdoors in a large patio adjacent to one of the pyramids writing on parchment scrolls and engraving metal plates. We zoomed in and took some screen shots, and we're working with the translators to analyze those now."

"Would you mind sharing those screen shots with me?" Hank Phillips requested. "I'd like to start a collection of samples of scrolls and metal plates and the like from all areas of the world so that we can track the evolution of writing."

"Not a problem, Hank," Sammy responded. "We've already posted them on the classified intranet. Sanjay, why don't you take it from here?"

"Thanks," Singh acknowledged. "As we moved across southern China and up the highland slopes toward the Himalayas, we continued to see large populations of people. Even as we moved across the Himalayas themselves, we observed settlements of people established in high mountain valleys. What we were specifically focused on confirming were the ancient legends of the *vimanas*, the flying chariots or cars described in the Vedas and other Sanskrit texts."

"And did you find them, Sanjay?" Bill Tipton asked.

"Yes, sir, we did. The people of that era had developed extraordinary advanced technologies, and although much of it was turned toward constructive purposes, some of it was used to promote war among the various competing population centers. As we scanned back and forth across the Indian subcontinent, we moved backward and forward in time. By chance, we witnessed a great aerial battle fought by two opposing forces high in the sky over the western edge of present-day India. The aircraft in the battle came in all shapes and sizes. Some were triangular, some were spherical, and some were tubular in shape. Both sides in the conflict were armed with various kinds of automatic guns and energy beam weapons, and some of the energy bursts that traveled across the skies between the combatants had the appearance of small bursts of light in the shape of stars, almost like modern fireworks. Apparently they were also employing temporal technology because their maneuvering in the sky defied physical laws, making abrupt right-angle turns at high speed or reversing direction altogether. At one point, one of the warring sides in an aerial dogfight disappeared entirely, and their opponents disappeared after them, apparently giving chase."

Sammy picked up the thread of the briefing. "At first, we didn't know what had happened, and then Sanjay remembered having seen a woodcut from 14th century Germany from the OOPARTS files last year depicting a similar battle in the sky over Nuremburg. That event was witnessed by many people and is well-recorded, and the woodcut made at the time appeared in the local broadsheet shortly thereafter. We looked up the details on the OOPARTS file to locate the date. The battle in the sky over Nuremburg occurred on April 14, 1561. We quickly reset the parameters on the temporal monitor and picked up the battle as the combatants emerged temporally into the sky over Nuremburg early that morning. One of the large black triangular craft received a direct hit from one of the enemy's energy beam weapons and plummeted to the ground outside the city. As it crashed, there was a great secondary explosion, and the aircraft disappeared in smoke and flames as bits and pieces of the craft flew in every direction. Some of the other aircraft on both sides were also shot down out of the sky. The surviving aircraft eventually used their temporal capability to escape and evade, and the entire battle disappeared from the skies over Nuremberg."

"Well, that clears up a number of UFO mysteries that we've been tracking in the OOPARTS investigation," Mitch Monahan blurted out.

"Yes, Mitch," Sammy responded. "I suspect so, but it illustrates a much more important learning point.... Mixing temporal technology with high tech warfare greatly increases conditions where the natural limits of war can get totally out of control."

Stauffer nodded affirmatively to Woo's comment. "Thanks Sammy and Sanjay. That last piece about Nuremburg provides a good segue into Mitch and Ginny's briefing on the OOPARTS files. All of you are well familiar with the DOD classified OOPARTS site that parallels a similar unclassified site on the Internet. As a reminder, OOPARTS is an acronym that stands for Out Of Place Artifacts — objects of historical, archaeological, or paleontological interest, found in improbable contexts, usually meaning that the objects were far too technologically advanced for the time frame when they were supposed to have come into existence. There are thousands of objects that have been discovered in the past several hundred years that don't fit well into the framework of history described by mainstream scientists. Ginny's and Mitch's final assignment in the Repository before they joined us over here was to investigate each one of the OOPARTS files and check them all out for scientific validity or to reveal them as frauds or misinterpretation of history."

Stauffer smiled at Nguyen and Monahan and continued. "Ginny and Mitch haven't been assigned a geographical area here in the Crypt yet. Back in the Repository, they investigated the front end of many OOPARTS cases but generally couldn't go back far enough to find the source because of the temporal blocks that were in place. And so now, they get to continue their ongoing OOPARTS investigation. Nodding to Nguyen and Monahan, he continued, "Ginny.... Mitch.... where did you get started once you could look on the other side of the wall?"

Nguyen responded, "Thanks Barton. While we were still working over in the Repository, we investigated upwards of 150 OOPARTS cases, confirming most of them and exposing a few as frauds. But over half of our case investigations were open and still in progress because of the temporal blocks that prevented us from going back far enough to get the full story. And so, we've started out here in the Crypt trying to wrap up those cases we were still working on."

"Have you been able to confirm any of those cases thus far?" Stauffer asked.

"Actually, Barton, we've been able to confirm quite a few. Almost all of the OOPARTS cases concerning early flying vehicles appear to be confirmed. We still have more specific detail work to accomplish, but the evidence clearly points in that direction. The Palenque astronaut sarcophagus, the Quimbaya airplane, the Saqqara bird, and the relief carvings of airplanes and helicopters on the temple walls at Abydos all appear likely, and it shouldn't take too much additional investigation to confirm them. Sammy and Sanjay have just confirmed the aerial battle over Nuremburg. And we suspect that the existence of flight among the Ancients also confirms the purpose and placement of the Nazca lines, the Candelabra at Paracas, the Serpent Mound in Ohio, and even the Piri Reis map depicting Antarctica long before it was discovered in modern days. Those phenomena only make sense if the Ancients were able to view the Earth from the air at a considerable altitude. However, there's still a long list of items on our list that we need to check out, but the existence of advanced technologies that the teams have witnessed during their initial scans would seem to indicate that many of the remaining OOPARTS cases will probably pan out as confirmed as well."

Stauffer leaned forward in his chair and addressed the team. "Thanks to all of you for your observations this morning. I think we have a great many observations to add to my initial list about antediluvian times, including...." Stauffer glanced down at his yellow pad he was using to take notes.... "advanced avionics and flight technologies, antigravity propulsion systems, energy projection tools and weaponry, advanced metallurgy, temporal technology, human civilization settlement patterns, catastrophic encounters with celestial bodies impacting the planet, rapid climate change, and tectonic and geological reshaping of the geology of Earth. I'll update the list and post it on the intranet and pass it along to General Goldwyn. I was going to allow additional time for conversation about our observations thus far, but, unless you have something significant that you still have a burning need to talk about right now, I'd like to suggest that we all get back to our temporal monitors and see what else we can discover as we hone in on specific events or places or people. Let's agree to make this meeting a weekly event with each team summarizing new discoveries and observations. Meanwhile, please post everything new that you turn up on the classified intranet, and if you find something truly fantastic that can't wait and everyone needs to know immediately, send out an email to let us know what to look for. We've been at it just a little over an hour and a half now. If there are no other comments or discussion, let's get back to work."

# Chapter 18

*Carlisle Barracks, Pennsylvania, Thursday, July 18, 2013, 10:40 a.m.*

When Stauffer arrived down in the Crypt after a meeting with General Goldwyn, instead of going directly to his office, he walked down the corridor to the dispensary vault where Dr. Gates was attending to Melek. The doorway to the vault was partially open. Stauffer knocked lightly on the door frame and Dr. Gates came to the door and stepped out.

"Good morning, Barton. Good to see you."

"Good to see you, Doc," Stauffer responded. "I dropped by to see how Melek is doing."

"Melek seems to be doing very well," Dr. Gates answered. "There doesn't seem to be any residual ill effects from his concussion. Several of the members of the Crypt team are having him help them on their temporal scan surveys and he's keeping busy at it."

"Helping them on their temporal scans?.... How?"

"Well, it appears that whenever they observe something in their antediluvian survey scans that they don't quite understand, they bring in Melek as a consultant to see if he can explain to them what they're seeing. Sometimes Melek draws a blank and it's as much a mystery to him as it is to them. But Melek is surprisingly very well informed, and most of the time, he is able to go into some detail explaining whatever it might be."

"That isn't too tiring for him, is it, Doc?" Stauffer asked.

"It doesn't appear to be. In fact, it seems to energize him. He's glad to be doing something useful. In the evenings, he comes back here to the dispensary and sits at the desk and records on his scroll. I think that it is good for him to be able to record what he is seeing on the temporal monitors and how he has been able to help out here."

"Well, go figure.....," Stauffer said. "I'll bet that's a big help to the teams in understanding the parts of the world they're exploring. I'll bet our next team meetings are going to be pretty interesting. You're invited to come, Doc. I'll bet that you would enjoy it. Say, has

Melek been able to tell you much about antediluvian medical science and technology?"

"Actually, Barton...., not much at all. It appears that people didn't get sick in Melek's community."

"Didn't get sick? What about when they got injured?" Stauffer asked.

"Well, that's the part I'm having a difficult time understanding, Barton," Dr. Gates responded. "Melek tells me that whenever anyone got hurt or injured, it healed quickly and didn't really require any medical attention. Melek told me that they didn't have a doctor in his village. Apparently, they simply didn't need one."

"Well, that's one way to get put out of a job," Stauffer laughed. "Say, Doc, where is Melek now? What's he up to this morning?"

"He's over across the way in the time lab working with Dr. Campbell and Ski. They're still scanning the settlements that later got swallowed up by the Brazilian rain forest. Turns out that Melek once took a trip with his father in a flying craft of some sort to that part of the world when he was younger and he is well familiar with the place. He's been invaluable in helping them decipher some of the puzzling things they've encountered. Ski told me that Melek even showed them where there was a modest cache of small stelae and stone tablets hidden. They're trying to decide now whether to recommend a plan to recover all of the tablets or leave them in place for future generations of archeologists to discover when they get around to clearing the triple canopy and excavating the jungle floor."

"That sounds fascinating. I'll be interested to hear what they recommend."

"Say, Barton, it's about time for me to go and take Melek away from his consulting work and get him back here to the infirmary for a break. Want to go with me to check out what they're doing?"

"Thanks, Doc, but I'm going to pass. I'm way behind on the paperwork and I've got a couple of reports to write up on what we've learned about Atlantis so far."

\* \* \* \* \* \* \* \* \* \* \* \* \* \* \* \* \* \* \*

Zazworsky showed up at the dispensary at the end of the morning with a couple of pizzas and quart of ice cream. Dr. Gates met him at the door to the vault. "Hi, Doc," Zazworsky greeted him. "How's it going today?"

"Hello, Ski," Dr. Gates responded. "What have you got there?"

"Oh, I brought you and Melek some pizza and ice cream. I thought that we might sit down and have a working lunch. There are a couple of things I'd like to pick Melek's brain about."

As Zazworsky was talking with Dr. Gates, Melek came up behind him, drawn by the irresistible smell of the pizza. "Hello, Bob Zazworsky," Melek said with a large smile breaking across his face at the sight of the pizza boxes. "Have you brought food for us?"

"That I have, Melek. I thought that we might break bread together and maybe talk about a few things that I'm trying to connect the dots on."

"Connect the dots?"

"Yeah, Melek," Zazworsky grinned. "It's an expression that means 'complete the picture'.... get a solid understanding of something.... like that."

"What do you want to know?"

"Well, let's sit down and get started on the pizza and we can talk about it," Zazworsky urged. "Doc, would you like to join us?"

"Thanks, Ski," Dr. Gates chuckled. "Don't mind if I do."

As Zazworsky and Dr. Gates pulled up chairs to the table in the middle of the vault, Melek was already halfway through his first slice of pizza. Zazworsky had always considered himself a big pizza eater but he couldn't keep up as Melek wolfed down the first pizza followed quickly by the second. Zazworsky and Dr. Gates each managed to get just two small slices apiece. As Melek got down to the last slice in the second box, Zazworsky opened up the container of ice cream and handed Melek a spoon."

Melek eagerly started on the ice cream. "This is very good ice cream, Bob Zazworsky. What kind is it?"

"It's one of my favorites, Melek," Zazworsky responded. "It's called 'Moose Tracks.' It's vanilla ice cream with lots of fudge and peanut butter cup chips mixed in."

Melek nodded acknowledgement without responding and continued happily spooning the ice cream into his mouth. When he had emptied the container, he looked back over at Zazworsky. "I think that I like Moose Tracks ice cream the best of all, Bob Zazworsky." Melek took one last swipe of the spoon through the container to get at the dregs and then set it down on the table. "That was all very good. I am filled. Now, what is it that you want to know for our working lunch?"

Zazworsky smiled at Dr. Gates as he got around to his ulterior motive for bringing them lunch. "Well, Melek, it's like this. I've been reviewing the original video captures of when the soldiers came to your village and stole everyone's scrolls and books. I don't understand how those thugs levitated the crate. How did they do it? Did they just move that crate around with their minds?"

"Yes, Bob Zazworsky. It is like what you call telepathy, the way we communicate with our minds rather than talking with our voices. We can move objects around by just thinking about it and directing them where to go."

"Wow, can you do that? Could you give me a little demonstration?" Zazworsky was getting visibly excited.

"Yes, I've already shown Dr. Gates how it is done." Melek turned his head around the dispensary vault and eyed a book sitting on a shelf. "Look, do you see that book over there. All I have to do is think the book up into the air and direct it towards me and it will come."

As Melek spoke, the book lifted off from the shelf and floated across the room until Melek reached out to grab it.

"And that's how the soldiers moved that heavy crate around the countryside?" Zazworsky asked. "Is there any limit to the size of an object you can levitate like that?"

"I have known some people with well-developed power who can move very big things.... even large cut stones with their minds. But for most real big objects, we use special antigravity machines to lift them into the air."

Totally intrigued, Zazworsky finally worked his way around to his real purpose with this line of questioning. "How about people, Melek. Can you levitate yourself into the air?"

"Yes, Bob Zazworsky.... for short distances."

"Could you show me how it's done?"

Melek nodded and stood up. Dr. Gates went to stop him but Melek said, "It will be alright, Dr. Gates. I will be careful." Melek paused and stopped speaking. His face contorted slightly as if he were concentrating a great deal. Slowly his feet left the floor and he levitated upwards into the air until he reached up with his hands and pushed back on the curved ceiling of the vault.

As Melek slowly floated back to the floor, Zazworsky said excitedly, "That was terrific Melek! Can you teach me to do that?"

"Well, I don't know Bob Zazworsky, Melek said solemnly. Maybe you can do it. Let me try something first."

Melek's face contorted slightly again in deep concentration and all of a sudden, Zazworsky heard Melek's voice in his head, *"Can you understand this Bob Zazworsky?"*

Zazworsky practically shouted back, "I can hear you loud and clear, Melek!"

Melek raised his finger to his lips and cautioned, "Not with your voice out loud, Bob Zazworsky. Answer back only with your mind."

Zazworsky concentrated on the words, *"I can hear you loud and clear, Melek."*

A big smile broke across Melek's face. "I heard that.... very faintly, but I heard that. You have a limited ability to speak with your mind. Maybe you have the power to move things with your mind as well."

"What do I do now, Melek?" Zazworsky asked.

"Why don't you try levitating the spoon into the air?"

Zazworsky focused on the spoon sitting on the table next to the ice cream carton, imagining it lifting up into the air, as Melek and Dr. Gates looked on. The spoon started wobbling at first, and then slowly raised off the table into the air. It held in place about a foot off the table for a brief moment and then came crashing back down on the table top with a clatter.

"What happened Bob Zazworsky? Why did you let it fall?" Melek asked.

"I think I must have lost my concentration," Zazworsky answered back. "Can I try levitating myself?"

Dr. Gates interceded at this point. "I'm not too sure that's a good idea, Ski. You could hurt yourself."

"Maybe Dr. Gates is right," Melek cautioned. "It took children in my era many years to learn to levitate correctly."

"Well, let's give it a try. It can't hurt," Zazworsky said determinedly.

Zazworsky concentrated on the picture in his mind of him raising off the ground and focused on the words in his mind.... *"Raise my feet off the ground.... Raise my feet off the ground.... Raise my feet off the ground."*

Slowly, in a subtle jerking motion, Zazworsky began to lift ever so slightly off the floor into the air. As Zazworsky was concentrating on his self-levitating experiment, Maggie Martinez and Ken Red Elk came walking into the vault. "Howdy Melek...., Howdy Ski...., Howdy Doc. How's it going?"

As Martinez greeted them in her loud, chipper voice, Zazworsky's feet were about an inch off the ground, and at the sound of Martinez' voice, he suddenly flipped over and his feet shot up into the air. It took Zazworsky by surprise and, as he flipped, his head banged onto the side of the table and then smashed against the cement floor of the vault. As his head came in contact with the table, Zazworsky totally lost concentration and his feet followed his body down onto the floor in a heap.

Martinez convulsed in laughter. "Well, that wasn't exactly the response I was looking for, Ski,.... but it was interesting.... very interesting." And then Martinez saw the blood. "Are you hurt, Ski? Can you get up? Do you need help?"

Martinez, and Red Elk rushed around to the other side of the table and assisted Dr. Gates and Melek in helping Zazworsky get back up to his feet and then to sit down in his chair. Zazworsky was still slightly dazed from hitting his head. A small wound on his hairline dripped blood down his forehead and into his right eye. Dr. Gates retrieved a towel and basin of water from the dispensary table and gingerly washed Zazworsky's wound and wiped the blood from his eye. It apparently was only a superficial scratch and it had already stopped bleeding.

"That was incredible!" Zazworsky exclaimed.

"What was incredible?.... Turning upside down and smashing your head on the table and the floor?" Martinez asked

"No, Maggie. I flew. I actually levitated off the ground just as you came in. Melek taught me how."

Martinez and Red Elk looked over at Melek and Dr. Gates in surprise. Melek managed a weak smile and Dr. Gates only shrugged.

"No.... really...., everyone. My feet actually lifted off the ground," Zazworsky contended. "Melek, you saw me. Tell them it happened."

"Well it looked like he was starting to levitate but then he flipped over too fast to really tell," Melek said. "What were you concentrating on Bob Zazworsky?"

"Just like you said, Melek," Zazworsky retorted. "I kept saying over and over again in my mind, "Raise my feet off the ground."

"Raise your feet off the ground!" Melek asked. "Why didn't you visualize your whole body raising off the ground. Why only your feet? No wonder you flipped over. Your feet were only obeying what you asked for."

"Tell me, Doc," Martinez said. "What did you see? Did Ski really start to levitate?"

"Well, it all happened so fast and I was on the other side of the table. Ski stood up and he started to extend his head upward just as you walked in. I couldn't see from where I was sitting if Ski's feet actually left the ground or not. He might have been levitating and he might not."

"Bob Zazworsky," Melek said, "clear your mind. I'm going to try to talk with you telepathically."

Zazworsky scratched his head and smiled. "Sure thing, Melek. Go for it."

Zazworsky sat there patiently waiting for several seconds and then said, "Go ahead, Melek. Give it your best shot."

"I have been trying, Bob Zazworsky," Melek responded. "That bump on the head appears to have clouded your telepathic ability and you may have lost your ability to levitate as well."

"Looks like you're grounded for awhile, Ski," Martinez consoled him. "You're just going to have to walk around like the rest of us. But next time you want to try that stunt, let's do it in a padded vault and I want to be there with a camera."

\* \* \* \* \* \* \* \* \* \* \* \* \* \* \* \* \* \* \* \*

Stauffer was sitting at his desk in his office when Hank Phillips knocked on the open door. Stauffer looked up and smiled. "Come on in, Hank."

"Thanks, Barton. Am I interrupting something important?"

"No, not at all. I'm just working on some stuff in the inbox. It can wait for now."

"Can you spare 20 or 30 minutes?" Phillips asked. "There's a couple of things I need to talk with you about."

"I've been meaning to get with you to catch up on all you've been working on," Stauffer responded. "General Goldwyn had just put you in charge of the DNA archival project as I retired last year. How's that research coming along?"

Phillips grinned and replied, "That's precisely why I'm here. The old man assigned me here to the Ancients project, but he didn't release me from my responsibilities heading up the DNA project. I'm splitting my time about 70 and 30. I'm spending more time there and not nearly as much time here as I would like to chase down the Hall of Records."

"I understand, Hank," Stauffer responded. "By the way, who took over oversight for all of the archival work ongoing in the Repository?"

"Colonel Wynn Osterlund stepped up to the plate and volunteered to head up that project. He has significant previous experience with archival long-range storage, and he was kind of excited to move that part of the project along."

"How's the DNA project and crystal data storage research coming along over here in the Hole? You've got your own operation going separate from the Hole, the Repository, and the Crypt. You've established quite an important piece of turf for yourself. Are you getting any closer to developing the technology and techniques for recording archival data on DNA or crystals?"

"Actually, Barton, we're well beyond that. The technical team has successfully recorded test data on DNA material, and we have the technology in place to recover and read the data. Not exactly a perfect science yet. The recovered data is only about 98% accurate from what we recorded originally. But, we're getting close and the tech team is pursuing a new line of research that looks very promising."

"That's terrific, Hank. I'd...."

"Excuse me, Barton," Phillips interrupted. "I need to get to point of why I'm here. Do you remember what Ski once said in a meeting we had a couple of years ago about DNA archival storage when he joked about reading a book recorded on a cockroach? Well, for a variety of reasons, we decided to begin our work on recording DNA there. Cockroaches are one of the most successful animals in nature. They're pervasive around the world, and they've been around, basically unchanged, for millions of years. In developing the technology to retrieve and read data stored on the DNA, the techs experimented with cockroach DNA to see what could be recorded. But when they pulled a DNA sample to get started on, they found a pattern in the noncoding DNA sequences they didn't expect.... it appears to be some kind of code."

"Code?" Stauffer asked.

"Yes, Barton.... code. It appears that the cockroach noncoding DNA sequences are not entirely random."

"Wait, Hank, hold on a minute.... noncoding DNA sequences? What are you talking about?"

"You're right.... I'm going too fast. I'll try to slow it down some. It took me a long time to wrap my head around it.... Noncoding DNA sequences used to be referred to as junk DNA— sequences that initially appeared to have no apparent biological function. We've discovered more recently that that isn't entirely true. Some apparent noncoding DNA may actually have some unknown biological functions. There's much to be learned yet in that arena."

"Go on," Stauffer urged.

"Well, the cryptographers have been trying to decipher the code for about two months now and they think they're on to something. There appears to be some kind of a message hidden in the cockroach noncoding DNA sequences."

"A message.... in cockroach junk DNA?" Stauffer was almost speechless.

"Yes, Barton.... a message. Without telling them where it came from, I took a copy of the potential coded data on the junk DNA over to the Repository and gave it to the ancient language translation and cryptologist teams and asked them to have a try at it. They immediately came back at me and told me that it appeared to be some form of early Sumerian, a linguistic variety they had never seen before, but it has all the earmarks of early Sumerian."

"You've got to be kidding me, Hank. Were they able to break the code on any of it?"

"Not in any intelligible form yet. But they've got a few words here and there, and they think that they'll have something shortly. When I reported the matter to General Goldwyn, he gave the teams top priority on pursuing the translation of the data set, and they're hard at work on it."

"Well, that really gives me something to think about, Hank."

"Wait, there's more, Barton," Phillips added.

"More?"

"Yes, as I was leaving the translation team work area, I walked by a vault where they're inventorying some materials recently recovered from ancient Egypt. Out of idle curiosity, I went into the vault to see what they were working on. There were a couple of artifact archivists at work inventorying and describing each of the items for the data base. One of the archivists was holding a jar in his hands with a scarab beetle inside that had been interred with a pharaoh from one of the earliest Egyptian dynasties. The Egyptians worshiped the scarab beetle as part of their pantheon and equated it to ideas of resurrection and immortality. They frequently used the scarab motif for charms and document seals, and there are scarab motifs carved into the walls of Egyptian temples everywhere. Only this wasn't a charm or seal, it was a real scarab that had been interred in a sealed clay jar that they had only recently been opened under controlled conditions in one of the labs. They immediately placed the beetle in a sealed jar, replacing the oxygen in the jar with an inert gas to protect the beetle from decomposing. The archival techs weren't quite sure what to do with the beetle jar. I made sure that they had captured its description on the data base, signed it out, and took the jar with me for further examination in our DNA labs. Since the beetle had been snatched not too long after it was originally interred, I thought there might be a possibility of finding viable DNA for further examination."

"What did they find?" Stauffer asked anxiously.

"Stand by, Barton," Phillips responded. "They're still working on it, but there's more. All this gave me an interesting idea for follow-up. I have a friend assigned with the U.S. Embassy in Cairo, and I sent him a confidential cable asking him to round up a few live scarab beetles there in the near vicinity of the Giza Plateau and seal them up in a steel thermos bottle and ship them to me in the embassy pouch. I drove down to D.C. to the State Department last week and picked up the thermos. My guys in the DNA project

182

lab extracted DNA from the ancient scarab and the modern scarabs for comparison. They just called me to report what they found. It appears that the ancient scarab and the modern scarab junk DNA both reflect patterns that might be encrypted data. I gave the new data sets to the cryptologists to see what they could turn up. It didn't look like any form of recorded text to them. I was puzzled at first and then I had a epiphany. The ancient Egyptians didn't write with a structured alphabet. They wrote with a form of hieroglyphics. I gave the code back to the encryption team and told them to look for some form of graphical pattern. That was it! They came back to me the next day. They're still working on it to refine the image, but it looks like a very early form of ancient Egyptian hieroglyphs."

"The ancient scarab DNA?" Stauffer asked.

"Both. The ancient and the modern scarab DNA seem to share a very similar structure. It looks almost like they might reflect the same hieroglyphic message."

Stauffer fell silent briefly to process all of the information that Phillips had shared. Then he asked the obvious question. "Hank, by any chance, has your team run an analysis on human non-coding DNA to see if it also exhibits similar patterns?"

"Human non-coding DNA is very different from other species. Comparatively, there's a lot more of it. About 95% of the human genome appears to be noncoding DNA. In other species, it is much less.... a whole lot less. In humans, it represents tremendous possibilities for recording archival information. Computer memory works with a binary system composed of zeros and ones. Since DNA is made up of four base pairs, it has four states. A DNA sequence has the capacity to store much more information than a similar length of computer memory."

Stauffer worked to get Phillips back on topic and answer his question. "Got it, Hank, but have you run a coding analysis on human DNA?"

"Yes, Barton, we ran a few tentative experiments. There's so much non-coding human DNA that it makes the problem incomparably more complex and difficult."

"But what have you found, Hank?"

"Well, our initial analysis suggests that there's some kind of coded message there as well. Our translation and cryptologist teams just don't know how to break the code and read it.... yet. Perhaps it's gibberish, but, on the other hand, maybe it's not."

"I see. Well, Hank, that gives me a lot more to think about. Compared to my 2 terabyte hard drive on my desktop computer, what would be the storage capacity of non-coding human DNA if it were all freely available?"

"I've already asked that question of my DNA research team. DNA is an incredibly dense data storage material. They tell me that you could record all of the information from all of the books in the Library of Congress and have room left over. Nature has created an incredibly efficient data storage medium with the human DNA structure. Who knows what we will find if we're able to break the code?"

Stauffer paused to absorb that new information, then continued, "Okay, thanks, Hank. You have anything else for me today?"

"Not right now, Barton. I'll get back with you later when I have something new to report."

"Thanks, Hank. Keep me in the loop."

Phillips turned and exited Stauffer's office, leaving him highly perplexed. His analytical mind was racing, trying to tie together all of the loose ends this new information suggested.

\* \* \* \* \* \* \* \* \* \* \* \* \* \* \* \* \* \* \* \*

Later that morning, Stauffer made it a point to get up from his desk and make the trek over to the Repository. He went by Alice Duerden's office to say hello and get an update from her, and then the two of them walked down the Repository gallery to the vault where the artifact inventory technicians were still working on the material recovered from the ancient Egyptian tomb. As they entered the vault, Stauffer was amazed by all of the artifacts they had recovered. There were at least 15 or 16 examination tables, all loaded with material awaiting examination, classification, and recording on the Repository inventory data base.

As Stauffer and Duerden walked around the room looking over all of the artifacts, Stauffer spied three ornamental scarab beetles, carved out of green Libyan desert glass, one of which was much larger than the other two. The workmanship of the glass scarab was superb, and, although somewhat oversized from nature, it looked almost lifelike. Stauffer picked it up and turned it over in his hands. Although the beetle looked delicate and fragile, it had been carefully crafted and was quite substantial.

"Pretty impressive stuff, huh Barton?" Duerden asked. "This was all recovered from a minor Egyptian pharaoh's tomb we discovered during our temporal observation scans. It was all covered over with a great deal of sand by his brother after he had the older pharaoh assassinated so he could ascend the throne. The dead pharaoh hadn't been in the ground a week when his brother wiped his memory from history, literally. Apparently, obliterating the tomb was a way that he could legitimize his own ascension to the throne. We fast forwarded through history and found that the tomb had never been discovered and had never been raided. Well, this presented an extraordinary opportunity for us. We moved in through time portals and evacuated the entire inventory of artifacts and implements that had been buried with the dead pharaoh, even as the new pharaoh's army of workers were covering over the tomb with a mountain of sand above on the surface. I believe we recovered over twenty-five hundred separate items including several scrolls and copper plaques. That's why it's taking so long for the techs to conduct an inventory and move the stuff on to permanent vault storage. There's just so much of it. Some of our Egyptologist historians are chomping at the bit to get their hands on these things. It apparently brings a whole host of new information to bear on a rather obscure period of an early Egyptian dynasty."

Stauffer was only half listening as he turned the scarab over and over in his hands. "Listen, Alice, has this scarab been scanned, inventoried, and entered into the data base yet?"

"I don't know, Barton. Let me check."

Duerden took the beetle in her hands and turned to converse with the inventory technicians. Turning back to Stauffer, she reported, "Yes, they tell me they've inventoried everything on this examination table. Why? Are you interested in checking it out?"

"Yes, Alice, if it's alright with you. I'd like to examine it further in my office. It could help me out on a problem I'm working on."

"Sure thing. Come on over to my office and I'll sign the appropriate forms."

\* \* \* \* \* \* \* \* \* \* \* \* \* \* \* \* \* \* \* \*

Stauffer was soon on his way back on the moving walkway to the Hole and dropped back down on the elevator into the Crypt. As he entered his office, he walked over to his desk and carefully laid the glass scarab down on his desk top. He reached into his drawer and pulled out a large magnifying glass and began examining the scarab in minute detail. The detail work was astonishing, and he marveled at how the artisan that made it had been able to work the glass material in such detail. Then, as he brought the lens in close on the scarab's back, he noticed some minute scratches across the breadth of the wing casement. He strained his eyes to focus in on the scratches. There appeared to be something there, but he couldn't quite make it out. Puzzled, he got up and carried the scarab down the hallway to one of the lab vaults where there was a large microscope set up. He placed the scarab on the microscope imaging slide tray and had to bring the focusing body much higher up to accommodate the scarab's thick body in the focal plane. When he finally brought the scratch marks into focus, he was dumbfounded to realize that he was looking at microscopic, laser-etched Egyptian hieroglyphics. The microscope was hooked up to a computer, and Stauffer projected the image onto a large flat screen monitor. It was definitely Egyptian hieroglyphs, of that he was certain. Stauffer made a screen capture of the image and emailed it over to Duerden with a request to have the Repository Egyptologists give it a quick look to see if they could decipher the hieroglyphics.

Duerden responded back in less than ten minutes. "What have you got there, Barton? My expert on Egyptian dynasties tells me that it's written in a very rare hieroglyphic style, one that they rarely see. But, loosely translated, the hieroglyphs read, 'Here lies the Hall of Records.' What do you make of it, Bart?"

Stauffer answered back, "I don't know yet, Alice. I'll get back with you when I know something."

Stauffer rushed off another email, this time to Hank Phillips, with the screen capture of the microscopic hieroglyphic text and the potential translation. Later, after a short staff meeting in his office with Tipton, Pendleton, and Zazworsky, he picked up the beetle from his desk and took the elevator up to the Hole and went to Phillips' office in the work area designated for DNA research. Phillips' office door was standing open and so Stauffer knocked quietly and stepped over the threshold. Phillips was hunched over his desk as he entered the office. He was so engrossed in what he was doing, he didn't notice Stauffer's presence. Stauffer turned and knocked again on the inside of the door frame, this time a little louder. "Hank, is it okay to come in? Looks like you're pretty busy."

Phillips looked up, startled. "Barton, I'm glad you're here. Where did you get this screen capture of the scarab?"

Before Stauffer could answer, Phillips spied the scarab Stauffer was carrying in his hands and jumped up from behind his desk and rushed across the room. "Is this it, Barton? May I see it please?"

Stauffer carefully transferred the scarab into his anxious hands, and Phillips hurried with it back to his desk. He pulled a large magnifying glass out of his desk drawer and began examining the hieroglyphic inscription on its back. After a few minutes, he looked up excitedly. "Barton, do you know what this suggests?"

"Well, Hank, I have my own thoughts on the matter, but I would like to hear yours."

"It suggests to me that the ancient Egyptians had access to technologies far beyond anything which we have supposed. These microscopic etchings are solid evidence that they had access to lasers, computers, and nanotechnologies. When we add to that the apparent encrypted message recorded on the scarab DNA, it suggests a comprehensive knowledge of microbiology. Somehow, they had the knowledge and technology to record their history on DNA, and the scarab beetle apparently served as their storage medium. We've got to put on a full-court press to break the code and translate the DNA samples we have from the ancient and modern scarabs. Who knows what we might find?"

"That's about what I had concluded," Stauffer nodded. "Do you think that the scarab junk DNA has much storage capacity?.... If we can decode it, will it provide a complete, unabridged history of ancient Egypt up to that dynasty or will it be only an abridged snapshot of the era for the rule of a particular pharaoh?"

Phillips responded quickly, "I've got one of my DNA researchers who specializes in data storage capacity making that calculation right now. Because we're looking at graphical images of hieroglyphs, it's a much different calculation than if it were recorded using some kind of alphabetic structure. But her initial thoughts were that a significant amount of hieroglyphic material could be recorded there."

"Well, keep me informed," Stauffer replied as he turned to leave the office. "And for sure, keep me up to speed on what you find out about the coded human junk DNA. I feel like we're on the brink of discovering hidden knowledge of tremendous import to the project, and I haven't yet figured out what to do with it once we find it. Oh, and be careful with the glass scarab. I signed it out from Alice Duerden in my name. If you like, I'll call her and switch it over to your signature card."

"Roger that, Barton. Thanks, that would be much appreciated," Phillips deadpanned with a casual salute. "I'll keep you in my classified Rolodex."

Stauffer returned a mock salute and turned and left the office, leaving Phillips still examining the glass scarab.

# Chapter 19

*Carlisle Barracks, Pennsylvania, Monday, September 9, 2013, 8:30 a.m.*

Zazworsky sat at his temporal monitor exploring the surface of the antediluvian sea, pursuing an idea that had come to him over the weekend. He had realized early on during the search for Noah and other Flood survivors that the software that General Goldwyn had provided for tracking boats afloat in the aftermath of the Flood could be tweaked slightly to also provide them with a powerful tool in the search for artifacts and valuables. As delivered, the software scanned the watery planet during the Flood looking for anything solid afloat, and then logged it in and continued monitoring it until it sank or made dry land. Using the software, they had been successful in identifying and tracking a large number of ships as they grappled with staying afloat during the Flood.

Only fifteen vessels had ultimately survived the Flood. Several of the Crypt teams were hard at work investigating what happened to them after they made landfall as the water receded. But over the weekend, Zazworsky started wondering about all of the vessels afloat sometime during the Flood that didn't make it. He came into work early Monday morning and started compiling a list from the software database. Most of the boats that eventually sank were deserted. Their crews had abandoned ship or were thrown overboard during the extreme ocean turbulence from the comet's impact. Later on, as the floodwaters began to recede, the majority of the boats lay foundering in the ocean, slowing taking on water until they finally sank beneath the waves.

Zazworsky reasoned that this was a target-rich environment for recovering the cargoes of the abandoned, sinking ships. He started exploring each ship one by one with the temporal observation monitors. He did a couple of experimental temporal observation scans of the holds of several ships and was delighted to find that his assumption was correct. The first several ships he surveyed were all heavily laden with various kinds of trade goods that could possibly add to their understanding of the antediluvian world. And it didn't hurt that he observed a considerable amount of artifacts made of gold, silver and other precious metals.

Zazworsky was elated. He quickly prepared a formal request through Stauffer to General Goldwyn with the details of his plan to recover those ships' cargoes. Stauffer was initially dubious, but General Goldwyn was delighted with the simplicity of the plan and quickly gave his approval. His only caveat in approving the plan was that each ship targeted to be salvaged had to be thoroughly studied first to establish its point of origin, if possible, and to gain a preliminary idea of the ship's cargo before any recovery mission could be launched.

\* \* \* \* \* \* \* \* \* \* \* \* \* \* \* \* \* \* \* \*

Zazworsky's heart was palpitating wildly and he was breathing heavily. He had just located a ship in the antediluvian Atlantic off the coast of southern Spain that had been hit broadside by a rogue wave. It ended up lying on its side with its sail lying flat on the undulating waves, as the ship slowly took on water. The sailors onboard all abandoned ship and swam toward the distant shore, clinging to pieces of wooden debris as flotation devices. Zazworsky engaged the chronograph on the side of the temporal monitor and measured the actual time it took for the ship to completely submerge from the moment the sailors all abandoned ship.... 23 minutes, 25 seconds. In his estimation, that was plenty of time to make a snatch of any precious cargo that the ship might be carrying.

He and his team did a temporal observation scan to get a feel for the ship's cargo. It was a relatively small ship, and there wasn't much cargo in the hold.... a small shipment of large earthenware jars sealed with pitch, an assortment of farming equipment — plows, hoes, and shovels — and several wooden cases of assorted weaponry — swords, maces, knives, short spears, body armor, and helmets — and a half dozen bundles of textiles wrapped tightly together with thick twine. Zazworsky moved the temporal monitor view to the captain's cabin to see what treasures it might hold. "Bingo!" Zazworsky exclaimed out loud with unabashed enthusiasm. The cabin was stacked with gold and silver artifacts of curious manufacture, several pieces of sophisticated nautical instruments, and two large wooden chests secured with heavy locking devices.

Zazworsky couldn't wait for the actual repo mission to begin so that he could get his hands on the chests and see what treasures might be inside.

Zazworsky quickly assembled a five-person recovery team with Sanjay Singh to act as the operational team chief, and Ken Red Elk and Sammy Woo for recovery team #1 to work the cargo hold, and Jared Lincoln to work with him on recovery team #2 to work the captain's cabin. The salvage operation plan was quickly approved by Stauffer and General Goldwyn, and Zazworsky and his team suited up in hazmat gear and self-contained breathing equipment for the repo mission. They had set up two time portals in one of the larger vaults and decked it out with a dirty side/clean side hazmat decon station and curtain array. After Dr. Gates had double-checked their hazmat suits, Zazworsky and Lincoln stepped through their portal and into the cabin, while Woo and Red Elk passed through their portal into the hold. A small logistics team composed of Pete Pendleton, Maggie Martinez, Sandy Watson, and Mitch Monahan stood by in the vault with Singh to assist with putting the recovered materiel through decon and then moving it on over to the inventory and classification vault.

As Zazworsky emerged from the portal into the captain's cabin, he turned around to take it all in. It was awkward moving around the cabin with everything jumbled around from the ship having tipped over on its side, but he was surprised at how big and spacious the cabin appeared to be, even on its side. He moved through the toppled furniture over to the hatchway leading out to the main deck and was surprised to see by measuring it with outstretched arms that it was over eight feet high. When he had been using the temporal observation monitor in prepping for the mission, he had watched the captain bend down and duck his head each time he came through the hatchway door. Zazworsky held his arms with fingers extended again to take the measure of the captain's bunk against the outer bulkhead. Zazworsky did a quick mental calculation and guessed that the captain must have been at least nine feet tall, and he was reminded that, like Melek, this antediluvian crew was of much greater stature than modern humans.

Turning around to survey the interior of the cabin, he quickly realized that all of its contents were oversized as well. The desk, table and bunk were all sized appropriately for an individual of extraordinary height. While Lincoln received the empty cardboard boxes being pushed through the portal toward him by the logistics team, Zazworsky made his way over to the wooden chests. Based on appearances from examining them through the temporal observation monitor, he had assumed that they were about the size of a microwave oven, and he thought that he and Lincoln could easily manhandle them back through the portal. As he drew near them, he could see they were much larger, about the size of a typical Army one-pedestal steel desk. He tried to move the one closest to him but it wouldn't budge. It was clearly much heavier than he and Lincoln could move without mechanical assistance, and Zazworsky made his way back over to the time portal and stuck his head back through into the lab. "Sanjay, we're going to need some heavy-duty lifting equipment to get some of this stuff out of here," Zazworsky reported. "The chests are much bigger and heavier than I thought. Get me the biggest two-wheeler you can find, the kind that furniture movers use."

Singh had already seen Zazworsky standing by the two massive chests through the temporal observation monitor he was using to track mission progress and realized there was going to be an issue. He had immediately dispatched Pendleton and Tipton through a time portal in a different vault to pick up a fork lift on the sly from one of the warehouses on the Miracle Mile over on Carlisle Pike. The team arrived back at the vault just as Zazworsky stuck his head through the portal. Pointing at the fork lift that they had just positioned next to the portal, Singh asked with a smirk, "How about this, Ski? Do you think you can move it with this?"

Zazworsky grinned and responded, "Can do, my friend. That will do nicely. I'll get out of the way, and I need you to move the portal opening right over adjacent to the chests. Throw me some heavy duty straps through the portal, and I'll wrap them around the chests and hook them on the lift. Then it should be a fairly straightforward operation to just raise them up and back the forklift with the chests suspended in air back through the portal."

As Zazworsky moved over to the side, he watched the shimmering outline of the portal inch forward over to the chests and the two long forks of the lift emerge through the portal. He quickly wrapped the straps they threw through the portal around the first chest, and when he had it secured to the forks, he twirled his index finger in an upward motion to signal to Singh back in the lab who was observing his progress through the temporal observation portal. The lift slowly raised the chest off the side of the ship and maneuvered it back through the portal. When they had the first chest secured in the time lab, they brought the forks of the fork lift back through the portal and recovered the second chest.

While Zazworsky was working on the chests, Lincoln was filling cardboard boxes with artifacts strewn around the room that had been sitting on the desk, table and shelves along one of the walls before the ship had rolled over on its side. With the chests secured back in the lab, Zazworsky turned his attention to assisting Lincoln in snatching the artifacts they had identified in the pre-mission survey. Zazworsky's plan was just to strip the cabin of its entire contents and sort it all out later in the Crypt inventory and classification vault. As they filled each box, they pushed it through the portal and another empty box was pushed back through at them.

Zazworsky glanced down at his mission watch and saw that they had just eight minutes left to finish recovery operations before the ship would take on water and sink. They were right on time, plenty to spare in fact, but Zazworsky was fascinated by the huge captain's table, desk and chair. The table, which had been set with the captain's dinner, was almost four feet high, over a foot taller than most modern tables. He rushed to maneuver the fork lift to bring the furniture back through the portal as well. He reasoned that they would work well in the vault they had set up for displaying antediluvian life. He signaled Lincoln to help him wrap straps around the desk, and Singh, back in the lab, obliged by sending the arms of the fork lift back through the portal into the cabin. They quickly evacuated the heavy desk and the captain's table and chair through the portal and then rushed through after it. As they cleared the portal, they heard Singh count down the time remaining on the mission clock. As Lincoln yelled "clear" and Zazworsky yelled "check," Singh toggled the portal shut. Zazworsky checked his mission watch again.... Five minutes to spare.

Meanwhile, down in the cargo hold, Red Elk and Woo were having an equally challenging time moving the oversized cargo back through their portal into the hazmat vault. They managed to manhandle the large earthenware jars over to the portal by rolling them on the rounded bottom and sides of the craft. They had to move the plows, hoes and shovels one implement at a time, handing them back through the portal to the waiting logistics team. The metal swords and spears and other weaponry were extremely heavy, and they decided to move them piece by piece through the portal, working together using a two-person carry. When they finally got to the bundles of textiles, their mission time was almost gone. They hurriedly started pulling the bundles toward the portal and pushing them on through.

As Red Elk pulled the last bundle away from the side of the ship, it revealed a large rat's nest and a very large mother rat and a litter of babies. The mother rat was huge, about the size of a beagle. She rushed forward towards him with teeth bared. Red Elk raised the textile bundle up and tried to keep it between him and the excited rodent as he made his way back to the portal. But the rat came right over the top of the bundle and bit him on the arm of his hazmat suit. Although the suit was built of extra heavy-duty rip-stop nylon, the rat's teeth cut right through the suit, and into his arm, slicing a deep gouge almost down to the bone. The hazmat suit started to turn red around the wound, and Red Elk tripped and fell to the floor just short of the portal.

Zazworsky, who had been standing by Singh and watching the scene on the temporal observation monitor, came rushing back through the portal carrying one of the large swords they had just evacuated from the hold and thrust the point of the sword toward the rat's head as it hovered above Red Elk's prostrate body ready to take another bite. The sword's blade gave the rat a glancing blow on the side of its head, and she thrashed about for a moment on the floor and then made her way back towards her nest. Zazworsky helped Woo pull Red Elk back through the portal and over to the decon table where the team used the decon solution to clean off his suit and breathing equipment. Then they stripped the hazmat suit off him and carried him over to the decon curtain where they loaded him on a gurney and pushed him out the door of the vault. Singh had alerted Dr. Gates and he met them on the run and steered the gurney over to another empty vault. He barked orders as they ran. "This vault is now a temporary dispensary and is now under quarantine. I'm going to need two or three beds and a complete set of medical gear for intravenous antibiotic drips and a complete blood workup. I'm going to need a microscope and glass slides too. Get one of my nurses moving on it fast. Tell him he's going to be here for the duration."

"Why a couple of beds, Doc?" Singh asked.

"We're going to have to stay with Ken throughout the medical exam and treatment follow-up. It may take days or even weeks. It will be better if we all just hunker down in the vault and stay quarantined until we're sure we don't have a virulent strain of something from that rat bite on our hands."

\* \* \* \* \* \* \* \* \* \* \* \* \* \* \* \* \* \* \*

While Doctor Gates attended to Ken Red Elk, Zazworsky and the logistics team worked feverishly on the decon table, processing all of the recovered items. They moved all of the loose artifacts and the captain's table, chair, and desk through the decon line and then pushed them on transportation carts over to the inventory and classification vault.

Then, all that remained were the two massive chests. They were much too heavy to try to move to the table, and so Zazworsky got down on his knees to examine the locking devices. They appeared to be simple mechanisms, about the size of hockey pucks, with five metal knobs protruding out from the face of each. Zazworsky studied the devices for several minutes, and then it occurred to him that these were similar to modern locks where you spin dials to certain numbers for the combination. He went back over to the temporal observation monitor and dialed up the captain's cabin before the crew abandoned ship. He moved the monitor view over to where the two chests sat on the floor and moved the time gradient slowly backwards in time, hoping to catch a glimpse of the captain unlocking the mechanisms.

He was in luck. Earlier that morning, the ship's captain had gone over to the chests and bent over to unlock them. Zazworsky watched the process closely over his shoulder as the captain pushed on the knobs on the face of the dial. Zazworsky memorized exactly what the captain did and then rushed over to the chests sitting on the floor of the decon vault to see if he could duplicate the action. As he pushed the last knob on the first chest, the mechanism made an audible click, and the curved locking bar disengaged from the body of the mechanism and swung open. Zazworsky looked up in triumph as Tipton, Pendleton, and Watson looked on in fascination. Zazworsky quickly moved to the other chest and repeated his success. He pulled both locks from the hasps on the chest and lifted the lid on the chest farthest from the decon table. Inside were stacks of gold-colored metal bars. Zazworsky let out a whoop, "Eureka.... Gold!"

His team members started slapping him on the back through his decon suit. "Ski," Tipton remarked, "you've done it again. You've discovered another treasure chest full of gold. You've got the gift, pal! You're a gold magnet!"

Zazworsky picked up one of the gold bars and hefted it in his hands. It was very heavy. He estimated that it must have weighed at least fifty pounds. He sat back on his haunches, a look of extreme satisfaction swept across his face. And then, as his eyes moved to the other chest, he said jubilantly to the crowd around him, "Let's see what the other chest has in it."

Zazworsky carefully replaced the gold bar back into the first chest and sidled over to the other chest and slowly raised the lid. Zazworsky was immediately disappointed. No more gold bars. Inside were dozens of wooden boxes of various sizes, some with intricately carved lids. Zazworsky lifted one of the boxes from the chest and placed it on the decon table and attempted to open the box. The lid was wedged tight and he had difficulty in working it free. Finally, after a little effort using a knife blade, he was able to loosen the lid from the box casing, revealing a bronze-colored mechanism of some sort that looked quite a bit like an elaborate clock with a multitude of gears. He placed the mechanism on the decon table to the side of the box and turned to the decon team. "Why don't you get to work on this stuff so that they can be moved over to the inventory and classification vault."

Zazworsky started to lift another wooden box from the chest when Mitch Monahan let out a yelp and pushed past him to pick up the mechanism. "Do you know what I think this is, Ski? It looks a lot like the Antikythera mechanism.... only it's in pristine, perfect working condition. We've only been able to guess at the purpose of the one that was recovered from the bottom of the Mediterranean off the coast of Greece. It was badly corroded and fell apart into several pieces when it was pulled from the sea and examined. Scientists ultimately had to use X-rays to get a look at its inner working. It's full of intricate gear works. Most researchers think that it was some sort of early analog device for computing planetary orbits and other astronomical data. We can put our engineers and scientists to work on this one, and we'll finally get to know for certain."

"Antikythera mechanism?" Zazworsky asked. "Isn't that one of the items from the OOPARTS list that General Goldwyn has a personal interest in? We better get word to him fast."

Realizing that the carved wooden boxes might contain other devices and technology worth far more than the gold in the other chest, Zazworsky removed another box from the chest and gingerly placed it on the decon table. The lid on this box swung open easily. Zazworsky stared at its contents in disbelief. Turning his head, he yelled over his shoulder, "Someone get word to Colonel Stauffer to get here on the double. He's gonna want to see this."

Zazworsky turned his head back and stared down into the box at the delicately-fabricated, golden dodecahedron.

\* \* \* \* \* \* \* \* \* \* \* \* \* \* \* \* \* \* \* \*

The repo team worked quickly with the decon-logistics team, unpacking each of the boxes and placing their contents on individual trays after they were thoroughly decontaminated. Then, they put all of the trays on wheeled carts and carefully transported them over to the inventory and classification vault. General Goldwyn and Stauffer arrived together at the vault just as the last cart of trays was offloaded onto the inventory tables. They had been engaged in a meeting up in the Hole in General Goldwyn's office. Both arrived slightly out of breath from hurrying along the corridors after getting off the elevator down into the crypt.

"Where is it?" both said simultaneously.

Monahan held up the tray with the Antikythera-like mechanism at the near table. Goldwyn moved quickly over to examine the bronze clockwork mechanism. "I haven't see one of these in a very long time," he said appreciatively. He held the device out in front of him, turning it over and over in his hands, inspecting every surface.

"You've seen one of these before, sir?" Stauffer asked.

"Yes, Barton, a long time ago when I was a much younger man."

Only Stauffer realized the significance of what General Goldwyn meant by that.

"Would you like to take this one with you back to your office?" Zazworsky asked.

General Goldwyn looked puzzled. "That would be nice, Ski, but I would think that you'll want your engineers and technicians to examine it to figure out what it does and how it works."

"That's right, sir." Zazworsky responded. "But we found three more of the same devices packed in the chest. That gives us a total of four. They all appear to be the same. Looks like someone shipped a small consignment of the darned things. No reason why you can't keep one in your office for now. I'll prepare the paperwork. You can take it with you now if you would like."

"A small consignment? There were four of them?" General Goldwyn looked perplexed. He paused to consider this new information and then turned back to address Zazworsky. "Yes, Bob, I would very much like to keep this one in my office."

As Zazworsky and General Goldwyn were talking, Stauffer was anxiously eyeballing the room, checking out all of the recovered items laid out on the tables. And then something caught his eye on the far table set against the back of the vault. Stauffer quickly made his way around the other tables and moved toward it, his eyes fastened on the object. When he got there, he just stood there looking downward. Like the mechanism General Goldwyn was discussing with Zazworsky, this item was also packed in its own individual wooden box. Stauffer stood there unmoving for just a moment staring at it and then reached down and carefully lifted the object from its case.

General Goldwyn came up behind Stauffer and asked, "What do you have there, Barton?"

Stauffer held up the golden dodecahedron and showed it to Goldwyn. "Sir, it's a dodecahedron similar to the one made of bronze I recovered from the Barnum American Museum fire, but it appears that this one is made of gold.... pure gold."

"Pure gold, huh? That would make it kind of special. Is it exactly like your other dodecahedron otherwise?"

"It appears to be the same, sir. I'm going to need to sign it out and take it back with me to my office and run a side-by-side comparison."

"What do you think you'll find?"

"Well, I don't know for sure. At first blush, it looks to me like they're pretty much an exact match.... same size, same knobs at the vertices, same hole sizes and alignments in the pentagonal sides."

"If they're exactly the same except for what they're made of, what do you think that tells you?" Goldwyn asked.

Stauffer thought for a minute and then responded, "I suppose that it would mean they might have come from the same source, or that the Roman bronze version may be a copy of the original gold version. If they were made at a similar time, that would throw the dating of all similar dodecahedrons that have been discovered in Roman ruins back by a couple of millennia. But it still doesn't help me know their purpose. Why were they made and what was their purpose?"

"Barton, I suspect if you think about it long enough, you'll come up with a solution."

"Do you know, sir? It's one of the big mysteries of antiquity. No one seems to know what purpose the dodecahedrons served."

"I think we can talk more about that later in my office once you've had an opportunity to think more about it." General Goldwyn abruptly changed the topic. "Barton, did you look at any of the other recovered items yet?"

"No, sir. I was distracted by this."

"Well then, let's take a look."

Goldwyn and Stauffer began walking along the rows of inventory tables looking at all the artifacts recovered. Zazworsky followed closely behind. Most of the items were not yet inventoried or classified. On one of the tables were a number of small boxes of different kinds of mechanisms and artifacts. "Were these down in the hold of the ship, Ski?" Stauffer asked.

"No, Boss," Zazworsky replied. "These are all the boxed items that came out of the second chest from the captain's cabin."

"Second chest?"

"Yes, there were two large wooden chests in the captain's cabin. One of them was full of gold bars. The other contained all of these boxes with the devices inside."

Goldwyn spoke up. "Let's take a look at those chests, Bob. I'd like to see the gold bars."

"Sure thing, sir."

Zazworsky led them down the row of tables to the far end where the two oversized chests were sitting on wheeled carts with the lids propped open. General Goldwyn reached into the first chest and pulled out one of the gold bars. He turned it around in his hands. "Bob, I think you might be mistaken about these gold bars. I think what you might have here instead is orichalcum."

"Orichalcum? Never heard of it." Zazworsky was genuinely crestfallen. "Are you sure these aren't gold bars, sir? They look and feel like gold."

"Pretty sure, Bob. According to Plato, the ancients used a natural occurring amalgam of gold, silver and copper he identified as *orichalcum*, which he recorded was used to decorate Poseidon's temple and was considered of lesser value to gold. The Romans called it *aurichalcum*, which some think meant gold-copper. Orichalcum itself has been lost to history, and scientists have long argued what it was made from. Most agree today that it was a gold-colored alloy composed of some mixture of gold, copper, tin and perhaps zinc. Because we don't have any examples of it today, this shipment of orichalcum bars may be almost as valuable as gold itself because of its rarity. We'll have to run some tests on them to figure out their composition. Meanwhile, congratulations on your recovery mission."

"Yes, thank you, sir," Zazworsky responded and then continued slowly, "General Goldwyn, we did run into a big problem with the mission. Just as we were finishing up, Ken Red Elk was bitten by a very large rat. Doc Gates has him isolated in the lab across the way, running tests and administering some antibiotics."

"Is Ken alright?"

"He seems to be just fine. He's going to be sore for quite awhile where the rat bit him. The doc is playing it safe to make sure that he hasn't picked up any infections."

"Well, let's go over there and check it out."

Zazworsky led General Goldwyn and Stauffer out of the vault and across the broad corridor to the vault door which Dr. Gates had secured and posted a large hand-written QUARANTINE sign. Zazworsky pushed the push-to-talk button on the side of the vault door frame. "Hey Doc. I've got General Goldwyn and Bart Stauffer here with me. How are things going in there?"

"Glad you're here, sir.... Ken seems to be doing just fine. I cleaned out the bite wound with a disinfectant bath, and I've started him on a series of intravenous antibiotics. But I'm not sure that there isn't something else involved here like an ancient form of rabies or something similar. I really need to examine that rat.... alive."

General Goldwyn spoke up. "Yes, Doctor Gates. I understand. We'll send a team to recover the rat right now." Goldwyn turned his head and nodded to Stauffer, who stepped aside and dispatched a team to get the rat. General Goldwyn continued, "What do you want us to do with the rat when we bring it back?"

"Put it into a decent-sized cage with bars close together so that it can't escape and spray it down with hazmat decon solution. Put the cage on a wheeled cart and put a couple of sets of heavy-duty leather handling gloves and a set of syringes and veterinarian anesthesia ampoules on the lower shelf. Also, I'm going to need a microscope and some testing equipment. My nurse will know what I need. Then position the cart outside the vault door. Buzz me when you have it all there and then leave the area so that I can open the door and pull the cart in. I don't think there's any real danger from contamination at this point, but it won't hurt to play it safe until we know."

"Roger that, Doc," General Goldwyn replied. "Look, you both need to know that we recovered some very important material from the mission. But you are much more important than that. If either of you takes a turn for the worse, I'm going to activate the emergency response team to go back in time and scrub the mission before it launched. Keep me posted if either of you exhibits problems that have you concerned. Understand, Doctor Gates?"

"Understand, sir. I'll get word to you quickly if either of us starts to display symptoms of something more serious."

\* \* \* \* \* \* \* \* \* \* \* \* \* \* \* \* \* \* \*

Stauffer escorted General Goldwyn cradling the wooden box with the Antikythera-like mechanism in his hands to the elevator up to the Hole and then walked back down the hallway to his office. In his own hands, he carried the small box with the golden dodecahedron within. He sat down at his desk and opened the wooden lid to the box. He carefully lifted the dodecahedron out of the box and positioned it on the desk in front of him. Then he reached across the desk to the far corner and retrieved the bronze dodecahedron and set it down side-by-side with its golden counterpart. He rotated and turned the bronze dodecahedron until it was oriented in exactly the same way as the golden one. Then he started turning them both together to check them out to see if they were identical. After about ten minutes, he concluded that they appeared to be. He pulled a micrometer from his desk drawer and measured them both from knob to knob and side to side. Identical. Absolutely identical. Stauffer set them both back on the desk, pondering what might be their purpose. He sat there for another half hour just staring off into space and then finally gave up and left his office to check out how Dr. Gates was doing with the tests on Ken Red Elk.

\* \* \* \* \* \* \* \* \* \* \* \* \* \* \* \* \* \* \* \*

General Goldwyn went back up to his office and sat down at his desk. He took the device that he had brought back with him out of its wooden protective case and set it carefully on the desk in front of him. Then, as he began pushing buttons, maneuvering bezel rings, and turning the small hand crank on the side, the indicator needles on the device's front face moved and changed position as the device activated and began to perform complex astronomical calculations. Goldwyn sat back in his chair and closed his eyes, a look of great satisfaction crept across his face.

# Chapter 20

*Carlisle Barracks, PA, Monday, October 14, 2013, 1:45 p.m.*

Stauffer got a call on the red telephone from General Goldwyn to come up to his office early that afternoon, and Goldwyn asked him to bring Bob Zazworsky with him. When the two friends arrived at General Goldwyn's office, Stauffer was surprised to find a large group already gathered around the conference table.

"Glad you could make it Barton.... Bob.... Please be seated. I have a special briefing update for you all on the results of the investigation into 'the man in the ill-fitting suit'.... the one who appears to be responsible for acquiring the remains of giant humanoids and other ancient artifacts discovered in the United States during the past hundred and fifty years or so. I've had Colonel Smathers following up on Max Manchester's initial investigative work, and I've asked him to brief you all here this afternoon.... Colonel Smathers.... the time is yours."

Smathers stepped up to the side of the conference table and pushed a key on the wireless keyboard. A still image of the man in the ill-fitting suit immediately flashed on the screen. Gesturing to the image on the monitor, Colonel Smathers began his briefing somewhat stiffly and methodically. "Good afternoon. All of you have some connectivity in your research and recovery work to this man. That's why General Goldwyn asked you all here today.... to provide an update to you on where we are at in understanding who he is and what he is about."

Stauffer knew about his own early encounter with the man, but he was unsure of how all of the other people seated around the table tied in. Smathers continued, "Dr. Manchester initially ID'd this man as the individual who travelled around buying up the remains and skeletons of giant humanoids discovered during the past century, boxed them up, and squirreled them away in the basement of the Smithsonian Museum of Natural History and other warehouses spread out around the Beltway. None of these remains and related artifacts were ever given a satisfactory scientific examination and remain boxed up in wooden crates to this day."

Smathers touched the keyboard and the image changed. This time, it was a still screen capture of apparently the same man being forcibly escorted from the American Museum by two of Barnum's house detectives. "Dr. Manchester was also instrumental in making the connection between this man with the ruffian who was ejected by the house detectives from Barnum's American Museum the evening of July 13, 1865. In the scuffle that ensued, the man dropped a lit cigar into a trash pail filled with crumpled-up paper and later in the evening, after the museum had closed, the smoldering cigar finally caught the paper on fire, quickly moving to adjacent exhibits and ultimately spreading to the entire building, burning it to the ground."

Smathers pointed to some screen captures of the burning museum on the monitor and continued, "General Goldwyn asked me to use the temporal observation monitors to look into the activities of this man to see if I could ascertain what he was up to and determine what his agenda was. I reexamined all the observed activities of this man that Dr. Manchester, Dr. Nguyen, Dr. Monahan, Colonel Stauffer and others had reported. But it really got interesting when I backtracked his activities from his ejection from the American Museum. I followed him in reverse-motion back in time, day by day, for over two and a half months and discovered that the man had recently travelled through the Midwest."

`Smathers pointed to a screen capture of a small traveling circus on the monitor. "At one point in time, he visited the National Circus, a small regional traveling circus, where he tried to buy from its owners what was advertised as the 'Real Mermaid,' the supposed body of a mermaid suspended in a tank on display in its sideshow. But, he was disappointed in that endeavor. The owners had already sold the Real Mermaid to an agent for P.T. Barnum for an exorbitant price, and our guy stood there and watched as the mermaid tank was crated up for shipment to New York City. Barnum had long had the FeeJee Mermaid on display at the American Museum but that was patently a hoax created by Barnum by sewing the tail of a large fish to the torso of an ape. Barnum appeared convinced that this was the real deal and paid the circus owners quite a substantial sum. I tracked the crated mermaid's journey from Saint Louis to New York City, where it went directly from the train station platform under armed guard to the American Museum, where it was carefully lowered into a basement workroom. I captured a video of Barnum as the mermaid tank was uncrated, and his face displayed absolute childlike excitement and fascination. He clearly thought that he had a real biological specimen, not a fabrication or a hoax."

Smathers touched the keyboard again and a portion of a poster advertising Barnum's American Museum appeared on the screen. Smathers motioned to the still and continued, "Anticipating the ending of the war, he circulated flyers all over New York City announcing the new exhibits that would be displayed at the American Museum with the Real Mermaid as the centerpiece."

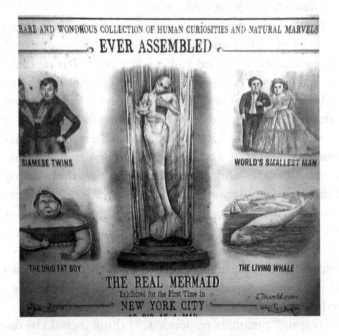

Stauffer blurted out, "I remember seeing those posters on the walls of the fourth floor of the museum during the night of the fire."

General Goldwyn waved his hand at Smathers. "Hold that picture there for just a minute, Colonel."

Goldwyn stood and walked around the table to face the monitor from the front and stared at the poster silently for a few minutes. Then he turned and walked back around the table to his seat and waved to Smathers to continue.

"That's right, Colonel Stauffer," Smathers responded to Stauffer's observation about the poster. "With Lee's surrender at Appomattox, April 9, 1865, Barnum put on a full-court press, building up public anticipation for the opening of the new exhibits, as the nation turned its attention from the war to more peaceful pursuits. Note the date for the grand opening at the bottom of the flyer, July 15, 1865. Two days before that, our man in the ill-fitting suit showed up in the museum, tossed his cigar into the waste basket and burned the place to the ground. From my perspective, I believe it was deliberate arson to keep the Real Mermaid from going on display."

"But, what happened to the mermaid in the tank in the basement workshop?" Zazworsky asked.

"I scoped out the basement of the museum throughout the entire evening of 13 July and all of the next day. Most of the objects stored in the basement burned and at some point, during the night, all five floors above it collapsed, creating a superheated inferno that destroyed everything down there. Barnum and his recovery crew began sifting through the ruins of his building over the next few days, but when they pulled back the burnt timbers and assorted tangled metal pieces in the basement, they didn't find anything recognizable from the workshop. There wasn't anything left of the tank or the mermaid. Barnum was devastated. The Real Mermaid exhibit apparently was going to be his breakthrough into the realm of legitimate science, and now that opportunity was gone forever."

General Goldwyn spoke up abruptly, "Does the degree of destruction to the mermaid and tank warrant our going into the workshop and recovering it from the flames before it was destroyed?"

"Yes, sir," Smathers responded. "I think it could be done. But I recommend replacing it with a substitute tank and some kind of a large fish to provide the rubble and burnt animal matter that would provide reasonably good evidence that the exhibit had been destroyed in the fire."

"Done." General Goldwyn responded enthusiastically. "Alice, I'd like your people to get to work on that immediately. Please let me know when you have the mermaid secured in the Repository in its own small private vault."

\* \* \* \* \* \* \* \* \* \* \* \* \* \* \* \* \* \* \*

As everyone filed out of the room, General Goldwyn asked Stauffer and Colonel Smathers to stay behind. As the door closed behind the last to depart, Goldwyn asked Stauffer and Smathers to sit back down with him at the end of the conference table. He turned to Colonel Smathers. "That was a good briefing there and an excellent piece of detective work, but I don't believe you were quite finished yet. What more do you have to tell us Colonel Smathers?"

The otherwise self-assured Smathers squirmed slightly in his seat and answered, "Yes, you are correct, sir. There is more." Glancing to the side at Stauffer, he added, "but I'm not too sure that this is the right forum to share that information."

"Yes, Smathers. I understand your hesitancy, but I assure you that it will be alright. Barton already knows that I am an Ancient. I don't think it will cause any harm for him to know that you are an Ancient as well." Turning to Stauffer, Goldwyn continued, "Barton, Smathers is a trusted member of my stay-behind team. He has been with me from the beginning. I think we need to hear what he has to say about our friend in the ill-fitting suit."

Stauffer nodded numbly, not knowing quite how to respond to this new information. Turning back to Smathers, Goldwyn urged, "Go ahead, Smathers, please continue your report."

Colonel Smathers scowled at the revelation of his true nature to Stauffer but continued as Goldwyn had instructed, "Yes sir, I conducted a thorough temporal survey into the background of the man in the ill-fitting suit, and I think I have discovered who he is. He is one of us.... He is an Ancient. At your suggestion, I integrated the facial recognition software you provided me into the temporal monitor station I am using and began checking out the construction site where Noah and his sons supervised the building of the Ark. I began when they first broke ground and set up the support framework for the Ark in dry dock and worked my way forward in time. The construction of the ark took a long time.... over two hundred years. During that time, Noah had well over a hundred workers at any given time working at the site. I calculate that during the duration of the construction, there were at least fifteen hundred to two thousand different men who worked on the ark. I set up the facial recognition software to automatically scan the faces of everyone who came to the work site, whether they were construction workers or not. About a hundred years into the construction, I got a hit."

"You got a hit? The man in the ill-fitting suit showed up at Noah's construction site?" Goldwyn was ebullient and the excitement showed on his face.

"Yes, sir. A man with a face identical to the man in the ill-fitting suit showed up about the time the workers were finishing up the inner skeleton of support beams and beginning to fasten planking for the inner and outer skin of the Ark. The man was sporting a light beard, but when I did a side-by-side comparison of his face with that of the man in the ill-fitting suit, I could tell that it was him. On the temporal monitor, he appeared to be a relatively small man, at least a head shorter than most of the other workers on the site. He was dressed as a laborer, but he was out of place. He wasn't muscular at all, and when I zoomed in on his hands, I saw that they were smooth and uncalloused. The man had obviously never worked with his hands a day in his life. He initially went through the motions of working on a team moving heavy planking timbers into place. But the man clearly knew nothing about construction. He moved around the construction site from work area to work area, taking it all in but accomplishing very little work. At one point, he moved away from the Ark construction and tried to enter an outbuilding where Noah frequently withdrew to work.

Noah saw him trying to enter his building and confronted him. There was an argument and Noah motioned to his sons to escort the man from the site. They grabbed hold of his arms and dragged the struggling man down the hill for several hundred meters before they finally let go of him and he fell to the ground. As he scrambled to his feet, he shook his fists at Noah's sons and then turned and continued moving down the hill. As Noah's sons turned to return to the work site, a strange thing happened. The man turned and saw that Noah's sons were walking back to the Ark construction site with their backs to him. He walked a few more steps down the hill and then simply vanished. It was as though he had walked through a time portal, but I didn't detect the outline of a portal anywhere. He just vanished."

"He just vanished?" General Goldwyn questioned. "He has temporal power to move through time without the assistance of portal technology?.... Interesting.... Smathers, would you please put a close-up of the man's face here on my monitor. I want to get a better look at him."

"Yes, sir." Smathers took the wireless keyboard that General Goldwyn pushed his way and entered a few keystrokes. The image of the man in the ill-fitting suit, dressed in laborer's clothes and sporting a short beard, appeared on the screen. Smathers pushed another key and the monitor zoomed in on the man's face until it almost filled the screen.

"That's good, Smathers. Would you back it up just a little bit. Give me a shot of his face with upper torso, please."

Smathers made the adjustment, and General Goldwyn stood and walked around the conference table to look at the man's picture straight on. He stared at the man's face for several minutes and then, with a look of recognition on his face, he turned to Colonel Smathers and said, "I think I have seen this man before."

"Where, sir?" Colonel Smathers inquired.

"At the construction site for the Atlantis ship. If I remember correctly, his name was Garash. He showed up one day and asked me if he could join our community and help work on the ship. I welcomed him into our number and he began to work alongside us. He was a loner, a very private individual, and kept pretty much to himself. As I recall, he was much shorter than the average man in our community and perhaps he felt like he didn't mix in. But when he did try to associate with others, trouble generally erupted shortly thereafter. In groups of our people, he was argumentative and disruptive and began to cause a great deal of unhappiness and discontentment. I counseled with him on several occasions but finally had to ask him to depart.... leave the island and not come back. He mounted one of the small aircraft on a nearby platform and flew off in a huff. That was the last I ever saw of him. I was always on the lookout to see if he ever showed up again but, he never returned."

"Sounds like we might have discovered what motivates this guy," Stauffer observed. "General Goldwyn, you threw him off the Atlantis construction site, and Noah threw him off the Ark construction site. After Atlantis departed without him, and seeing Noah getting ready to depart as well, he must have been harboring one gargantuan grudge against the world."

"That's a very interesting observation, Barton. I think you just might be onto something there. Colonel Smathers, here's what I would like you to do. Use your temporal monitor with the facial recognition software to find our man at the Atlantis work site. It shouldn't be too difficult. Garash was there for several months before I finally banished him. Then, I want you to follow him from Atlantis to see where he went and perhaps you can also use the temporal monitor to backtrack in time to see where he came from. Find out all you can about him and get back with me. We can't have an Ancient wandering around through time causing havoc. It violates our prime directive." Goldwyn turned his head from Smathers to Stauffer and back again, "We will all meet back here in my office when you have something more to report.

\* \* \* \* \* \* \* \* \* \* \* \* \* \* \* \* \* \* \*

Stauffer was sitting at his desk in the Crypt several days later when his classified red telephone rang. It was Alice Duerden. "Barton, I just called General Goldwyn, and he's on his way over to the Repository. We have the mermaid. And it does appear to be the real deal."

Stauffer grabbed Zazworsky and they went on the run up and over to the Repository. They got there just as Alice Duerden was escorting General Goldwyn and a small group of staff from the Repository and the Hole into a vault. They joined the group and surrounded the glass tank where the mermaid hung suspended in eternal death.

General Goldwyn stood there quietly staring at the tank and then slowly approached it, placing his hand on the tank opposite the webbed hand of the mermaid. He stood there quietly for a few minutes with his head bowed. The rest of the group realized that General Goldwyn was having a significant moment and stood their quietly, puzzled, in a circle surrounding the tank. Finally, Goldwyn turned and, with a tear moving across his cheek, questioned Duerden. "Alice, have you done a forensic examination of the body yet?"

"No, sir. We did just what you said. We just made the snatch a few minutes ago and I called you immediately. But I have a couple of forensic scientists on call to take measurements and see if we can pull a DNA sample to figure out what it really is."

"That won't be necessary. I can tell you what he really is, Alice, without running all of those tests. He's a sentient being, a being whose habitat happens to be the world ocean rather than some land mass, but a being, with a family and a community, who chanced to be hauled up out of the depths in a fisherman's net and placed on display in a travelling circus. This might sound odd and totally unscientific to you all but here's what I would like you to do right now. Have the techs bring in a portable time portal projector. Our friend here deserves to have a proper burial at sea."

Puzzled, Duerden turned and spoke quietly with Rick Bailey, who quickly faced about and left the vault on the run. Noting his departure, General Goldwyn continued. "I would have you transfer the body to a coffin of some kind but I don't think that will be necessary. We just need to get him to the right place at the right time."

As he was speaking, Bailey rushed back into the room, followed by two temporal technicians pushing a time portal projector. He had them set up the projector focused on the tank and positioned the laptop controls next to General Goldwyn. Goldwyn nodded thanks to Bailey and the technicians and addressed the rest of the group. "If you would excuse me just a moment." He turned and started entering data on the control keyboard for the time portal projector. He paused a few minutes as he seemed to be searching in his mind for some piece of information and then continued typing.

After a few minutes, apparently satisfied with the set up, he turned back to face the group. "Ladies and gentlemen, this may be a first in human history, one that you will never be able to share with anyone outside this vault, not with anyone else in the Repository or the Hole, nor with anyone outside the entire facility.... ever. This must remain a matter of absolute confidentiality." General Goldwyn scanned the faces of all gathered in the vault for understanding and commitment. Then satisfied that they understood his intent, he went on. "If you would please join me in a brief moment of silence."

Goldwyn faced about and looked at the mermaid suspended in the tank. His face betrayed an intense look of sadness. He bowed his head again and stood there quietly for almost a full minute. When he raised his head, he said softly. "Goodbye, old friend."

As Goldwyn turned once again to face the group, he spoke softly, "I appreciate your solemnity at this time. It is important for the human race to recognize the dignity and worth of all sentient beings."

Goldwyn turned and announced, "Stand clear." He touched the keyboard and the projector hummed briefly as the tank holding the Real Mermaid disappeared from view, leaving the group surrounding General Goldwyn alone there in the vault. Turning to face the group again, Goldwyn said quietly, "Thank you all for being here to share this moment. Now, as you leave the vault, there are going to be a bunch of staff members out there in the Repository and the Hole who will be curious about our mermaid friend. Remember, you can't tell them anything. This is a small vault. I am going to direct that Colonel Duerden have this vault sealed, never to be opened again. As far as anyone else is concerned, the mermaid is still here with us in the vault."

Colonel Duerden replied quickly, "Yes, sir. I'll take care of that right now as soon as everyone is out of here."

"Thank you, Alice," General Goldwyn replied. "Tell your people involved in the recovery operation that they did good work and that I greatly appreciate it."

General Goldwyn turned abruptly and left the vault, and the rest of the group followed out after him, leaving Duerden and Stauffer standing there alone. "That was interesting in a strange kind of way," Stauffer acknowledged. "I don't know what to make of all that. Where and when did General Goldwyn send the mermaid?"

Duerden walked over to the control laptop screen and read off the monitor, "January 15, 1865, about a hundred miles north of Puerto Rico out in the Atlantic Ocean. My guess is from the settings, that the tank would have materialized right at ocean level and then sunk immediately into the depths of the sea."

Stauffer responded, "General Goldwyn has his reasons for all this and perhaps one day he'll share them with us. We never could have displayed the mermaid anywhere except down here in the Repository anyway, and I'm good with General Goldwyn's solution. It makes sense in an out-of-the-box kind of way. There appears to be a lot more to this old Earth that we don't know about yet."

Stauffer turned and left the vault as Duerden followed him out, shutting the massive vault door and changing the settings on the dial access code so that the vault would remain permanently sealed.

Stauffer exited the Repository gallery and found Zazworsky waiting for him by the moving walkway back to the Hole. "Okay, my strangeness meter is pegged," Zazworsky quipped. "The good news is that our aquatic friend is back on his way home to his final resting place in the depths of the sea. The bad news is that I will never be able to tell the story to anyone about the big one that got away."

Stauffer laughed and slapped Zazworsky on the back, and the two friends mounted the moving walkway to make their way back to the Hole and their work area down in the Crypt.

# Chapter 21

*Carlisle Barracks, Pennsylvania, Thursday, November 21, 2013, 1:30 p.m.*

"How is Ken Red Elk doing?" General Goldwyn asked. "Has he fully recovered from the rat bite yet?"

"Yes, sir. He made a rapid recovery and Dr. Gates released him to return to duty early last week. Ken seems to be doing just fine and he is hard at it running temporal monitor surveys on his antediluvian sector.

"That's good, Barton, General Goldwyn affirmed. "Tell Ken that I'm glad that he's okay and please extend my appreciation to Dr. Gates for taking such good care of Ken."

"Yes, sir," Stauffer responded making a note on a 3X5 card.

"What do you have Bob Zazworsky working on these days, Barton?" General Goldwyn asked.

"Actually, pretty calm stuff, sir. Since that last recovery mission, I've had him working with Sammy Woo and Hank Phillips on exploring ancient China for lost records and libraries. Right now, they're working on the mystery of the Longyou Grotto cave system to see if it doesn't yield some examples of early Chinese writing.

"Actually, that sounds pretty exciting to me. But I agree. For Bob, that's probably a pretty tame endeavor. How would you like to suggest to Bob an opportunity to explore something more to his liking and taste?"

"What did you have in mind, sir? Is there some long lost stash of gold or diamonds that he could seek out?"

"Even better. Do you recall hearing about the legend of Manco Capac and Mama Ocllo when you were assigned to the Peruvian War College?"

"Yes, sir." Stauffer smiled as he remembered those earlier days in his career. "One of my classmates told me the story one day on a lunch break. As I recall, Manco Capac and his sister wife, Mama Ocllo, rose up out of the waters of Lake Titicaca where Inti, their father, the Sun God, gave them a golden shaft and told them to search the area for a place to establish a city and a temple dedicated to him. The father Sun God told them that where the shaft would sink into the earth, that would be the place where they should build their city. The couple wandered northwest from Lake Titicaca and eventually entered the Valley of Cuzco, where Manco Capac drove the golden shaft into the ground and it sank out of sight. And so that's where they built Cuzco, which would become the capital city of Tahuantinsuyo, the Inca center point of the four corners of the earth, the navel of the world." Stauffer nodded back to General Goldwyn, somewhat pleased with himself for remembering the legend's details so clearly after such a long time.

"That's about how I heard it too when the legend was related to me by an aging Quechua *curandero*. He even had a set of *quipu* knotted cords that he used to remember all of the details. What do you make of the story?"

"Well, it's a powerful explanation for the origin of the Inca empire, and it established legitimacy for the Sapa Incas, the royal line of Inca emperors. When I first heard the legend, I was so impressed that I even bought a golden brooch pin for Gwen that depicts Manco Capac and Mama Ocllo sinking the golden shaft into the earth to found the city of Cuzco."

"I'd really like to see that brooch, Barton. Do you think that Gwen would mind if you borrowed it?"

"I don't think she would mind at all. I don't think she would even miss it if I borrowed it without asking. The brooch is fairly large and made of 21 carat gold. It's quite heavy and she doesn't wear it very often because it tears her blouses where it pins on."

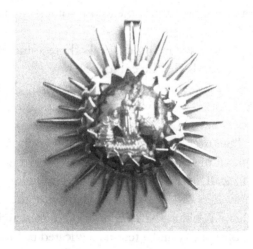

General Goldwyn laughed. "There is irony in that, Barton. But getting back to my point. The Manco Capac and Mama Ocllo legend is patently fiction, but it is based on a certain amount of underlying historical fact. Many years after the Flood waters subsided, a group of people established several small communities on the Andean Altiplano near the ruins of ancient Tiahuanaco and Puma Punko. Tiahuanaco had survived the Flood fairly well, but the ruins of Puma Punko were almost totally buried under a layer of silt, sand and rock carried in by the Flood. One day, a meteoroid came flaming out of the sky from the south directly overhead and continued in a northwesterly direction. It wasn't moving particularly fast, but as it passed overhead, it broke up into two large pieces and continued northward. The two pieces eventually impacted in the Valley of Cuzco burying themselves deep into the earth. When the people of Tiahuanaco traveled the distance from Lake Titicaca to the Valley of Cuzco and found the small elongated crater from the impact of the two meteoroid fragments, they dug down to see what they might find at the bottom of the crater. Well, the two meteoroid pieces were made up almost entirely of pure gold.... over a hundred tons of it. The people were astounded by what they found. The *cacique* tribal chieftain of the Tiahuanacan people that came over from Titicaca named the two meteoroid fragments Manco Capac and Mama Ocllo, the children of the Sun, and reestablished a city right on top of the impact crater in the middle of the ancient antediluvian ruins. Over the years, he built up his kingdom into an empire and established himself as the first Sapa Inca. The Incas mined a small amount of the gold to decorate their temples, but the bulk of the two meteor fragments still lies buried deep beneath the ancient city of Cuzco."

"Are you telling me that Cuzco lies on top of a bonanza of a hundred tons of gold?"

"That's what I was told by the old Quechua *curandero*."

"How have they managed to keep it secret all these years?"

"Oh, there's a small group of descendants of the Inca nobility who work very hard to preserve their history while maintaining the secrecy about Manco Capac and Mama Ocllo and all of the golden treasure they hid away during the Spanish conquest. Do you think that Zazworsky might like to check the story out? It probably wouldn't prove too hard to bracket the meteoroid impact and then check out the migration of the people of Tiahuanuco to Cuzco to found the Inca empire."

"Sir, that sounds fantastic. When I tell Ski about the tasking, he'll be so excited, he may stop breathing. I'll have to be careful how I break the news to him and have a defibrillator standing by," Stauffer laughed.

"That's about what I thought. Bob has been doing great work and I think that he deserves a little excitement since I brought him back out of retirement. Oh, but there's a catch. Bob can only scope it out using the temporal monitors. There won't be any recovery missions using the time portals. Manco Capac and Mama Occlo are the sacred property of the surviving Incas."

"Well, Ski may be disappointed to hear that, but I think he's going to enjoy the adventure of checking it all out," Stauffer said.

"I'm counting on it," General Goldwyn replied.

* * * * * * * * * * * * * * * * * * * *

As soon as Stauffer alerted Zazworsky to the tasking, he wasted no time in putting together a team to assist him on the project. He asked Ken Red Elk to be his partner, and Maggie Martinez, Miriam Campbell, and Pete Pendleton to serve as the rest of a five-person team just in case the opportunity should present itself for some on-the-ground operations. Then he initiated a temporal observation monitor scan to see if they could bracket the actual impact by time and location. They hit it lucky. In less than an hour, they zeroed in on the impact of the meteoroid in the valley. The whole team reviewed the video capture of the impact several times, the last in extremely slow motion. They were surprised to see that it touched down in two large pieces just twenty meters apart. The team backed off the time gradient and raised the angle of vision to watch the meteoroid earlier in its trajectory.

It first appeared as just a dim disk of light in the late afternoon sky, about 30 degrees above the horizon. Ever so slowly, it grew larger as it moved from the southeast towards them, almost in slow motion. Stauffer had alerted Zazworsky that the meteoroid was probably almost pure gold and he stood there with his mouth agape, marveling at the majesty of so much gold simply dropping down out of the sky. Out loud, he muttered to Red Elk, "It gives a whole new spin on the Chicken Little story, doesn't it, Ken."

The team was surprised that the meteoroid impact hadn't resulted in a high energy detonation as the two huge hunks of gold simply buried themselves deep into the earth upon touching down, sending an enormous plume of rocks, dirt and dust high into the atmosphere and spewing droplets of molten gold over the entire area. No expert on extraterrestrial dynamics, Zazworsky reasoned that it might have something to do with what appeared to be an extremely slow entry speed into the Earth's atmosphere. Dr. Campbell concurred that that was probably a correct assumption.

The impact craters were right in the middle of the ruins of a fair-sized city that had been long deserted, the vestige of an ancient antediluvian metropolis. On the slope of a hill above the city, the monolithic ruins of the Sacsayhuaman fortress stood in silent, majestic watch over the whole valley. The asteroid fragments had obliterated the ruins of several large buildings as they impacted, creating a broad, shallow, concave bowl hollowed out in the center part of the city.

Zazworsky's team set their temporal monitors on fast-forward to check out the response of the Tiahuanacans as they arrived a week later from their journey from Lake Titicaca to the Valley of Cuzco. It didn't take them very long to begin excavating in the bottom of the craters to discover the immense quantity of gold that had been deposited by the two fragments. The *cacique*, the tribal chieftain of the new arrivals, quickly took charge and got the people organized in collecting all of the gold that had broken off and splattered around the craters. Then, in super-fast-motion, the team watched the new city of Cuzco grow out of the ancient antediluvian ruins. The cacique directed his people to bury the craters and begin construction on immense walls made up of monolithic stones surrounding the leveled-off plaza where the craters had been. After ten years elapsed time, the major buildings of the budding Inca empire had been erected and the outlines of the growing city of Cuzco were clearly evident. After fifty years, Cuzco had fully emerged as the capital of the empire that would dominate the whole Pacific coast from the sea to the eastern slopes of the high Andes and from present-day Colombia in the north to present-day Chile in the south. Many of the sacred precincts of the renewed city were lavishly decorated with golden ornamentation that glistened in the sun and gave Cusco a surreal appearance.

Having scoped out the impact of the asteroid fragments from the visual vantage point of the Valley of Cuzco, Zasworsky had the team turn their attention to Tiahuanaco, about 370 miles to the southeast. According to Stauffer's initial project guidance, the trajectory of the meteoroid had passed almost directly overhead at Tiahuanaco, and had been observed by the people who lived in small villages on the shores of Lake Titicaca. They set up the temporal monitors to track the asteroid when it first appeared in the evening sky and passed overhead and moved on to the Valley of Cuzco. It was enlightening, but Zazworsky wasn't satisfied with the artificial view the monitors provided. He wanted to get out on the ground to see it in the same way the people of Tiahuanaco and Titicaca had experienced it. The idea was strongly supported by Dr. Campbell, who wanted to get some high resolution video of the comet during its entire trajectory for scientific study. Zazworsky put in the request to Stauffer, who conferred with General Goldwyn. Goldwyn reluctantly gave his approval, based on Dr. Campbell's scientific support for the project, cautioning the team to avoid intermixing with any of the local inhabitants of the area.

Encouraged by the opportunity to do some on-the-ground observation, Zazworsky and Red Elk suited up in costumes resembling the clothing worn by the native inhabitants of that era. The native peoples of the region around Lake Titicaca and Tiahuanaco were generally short in stature. Because of his bronzed complexion and slight build, Ken Red Elk would blend right in with the locals. Zazworsky, on the other hand, was a large man, well over six feet tall with very fair skin and sporting a close-cropped beard. It would be more difficult for Zazworsky's presence at Tiahuanaco to go undetected.

Zazworsky asked Dr. Campbell to act as team chief and operate the time portal controls during on-the-ground operations, and had Maggie Martinez and Pete Pendleton suit up in period-appropriate costumes to be ready to move through the portal as a back-up team should the need arise. To take the high resolution videos, Zazworsky and Pendleton mounted some miniaturized video cameras to the ends of five foot wooden staffs made from thick, straight limbs of a tree that had recently fallen on the installation grounds next to Collins Hall. The staffs would serve as one-legged platforms to give them greater stability for taking the videos. To disguise the cameras, they covered them with a rough burlap material with a hole exposing the lenses. It was an ingenious setup, but Zazworsky and Red Elk had to practice working the camera controls through the burlap cloth to take steady video.

When they were finally ready for the ground operation, Red Elk stepped through the portal with Zazworsky following, carrying the two staffs. They had carefully selected the spot where they would emerge at Tiahuanaco using temporal observation monitors. Over the centuries since the Flood, the area around Tiahuanaco had been partially recolonized by small groups of people. These were mostly engaged in subsistence farming, tilling the soil on nearby plots of land. To avoid their sudden appearance out in the open where they might be observed, Zazworsky selected a spot adjacent to an immense stone door set in the ancient stone wall surrounding a large patio enclosure. The doorway to the enclosure was massive, a remnant from the antediluvian occupation, and appeared to be carved from a single monolithic rock. The plan was for Red Elk to emerge against the side of the portal where he wouldn't be observed. If he determined that everything was clear, he would stick his hand back through the portal to give Zazworsky the thumbs up and Zazworsky would pass through the portal as well.

The operation was planned extremely well, with each element of the plan carefully timed, coordinated, and rehearsed. They timed their emergence onto the enclosed patio with just one minute to spare to set up the video cameras before the asteroid would appear and pass overhead. But as plans sometimes go awry, this one was no different. As Zazworsky stepped through the portal, Red Elk was standing beside the right supporting column of the massive doorway. Zazworsky had to step to the left of Red Elk which framed him right in the center of the doorway. Some Tiahuanacan peasants happened to look up from their field work precisely at that moment and saw him appear in the doorway as if by magic, and they gave a shout to others nearby to come running. Zazworsky didn't know what to do. As a crowd gathered on the patio on the far side of the doorway, he just stood there holding the two camera staffs, unable to move to set them up to film the asteroid.

At that precise moment, the asteroid burst into view along its trajectory, backlighting Zazworsky as it passed slowly overhead. To the crowds gathering on the plaza in front of the portal, it looked like Zazworsky was holding two large snakes in his outstretched hands and his head, hair and beard glowed from the brilliant light of the fiery asteroid above him. The asteroid exploded and divided into two pieces, raining small pellets of molten gold all over the plaza. All of the Indians dropped prostrate to the ground, bowing low and paying obeisance to Zazworsky. Clearly, their behavior reflected that they thought Zazworsky must be a god.

Zazworsky turned to Red Elk who was hunkered down in back of the stone doorway out of sight. "What do I do Ken? I think they're worshipping me."

"Well, Ski," Red Elk responded with a grin on his face, "I suggest you do something godlike.... See if you can get them to go away so that we can go back through the portal and get back to the Crypt."

Taking Red Elk's cue, Zazworsky stepped forward through the stone gateway, and, holding his arms stretched outward, a camera staff in each hand, he began pointing and gesticulating wildly with the staff in his left hand in the direction that the asteroid had gone. The peasants remained prostrate for several minutes, but finally got to their feet and, leaving their farming implements behind, moved off in the direction of Lake Titicaca following the trail of smoke left by the asteroid. Off in the distance, Zazworsky could see that the crowd was growing as the peasant farmers excitedly talked among themselves and pointed at the trail of smoke in the sky. The group of peasants eventually skirted around the southern shore of the lake and then moved en masse north along the western edge of Titicaca.

Zazworsky and Red Elk soon found themselves on a deserted plaza. Zazworsky reached down and picked up a couple of small globules of gold that had congealed on the plaza stone work, using his sandals as tongs to avoid burning himself, and then stepped through the monolithic doorway following Red Elk back through the time portal. Back in the time lab, Maggie Martinez and Pete Pendleton were laughing uncontrollably. They had observed the operation on the temporal monitor with Dr. Campbell and had seen how the peasant farmers had responded to Zazworsky's sudden appearance in the monolithic doorway.

"Well," Pendleton quipped sarcastically, "I think that went well considering. It could have been better, of course, but it went quite well, I think."

"Ski," Martinez laughed, "could I have your autograph? I've got rock singers and movie stars and politicians and all kinds of famous people..... but no gods yet. This will be the showpiece of my collection."

And then Pendleton and Martinez convulsed again in raucous laughter.

Dr. Campbell was smiling but not laughing. "Wait a moment guys. This is serious. We didn't get the videos we wanted, and Ski definitely departed from General Goldwyn's directive not to intermix with the locals. I suspect he'll direct the emergency response team to intercede and scrub the whole mission before we even get started."

"Well, Dr. Campbell," Zazworsky asked sheepishly, "What do you recommend we do at this point?"

"Well, if General Goldwyn decides to scrub the mission anyway, we might as well try to get the videos we went after in the first place. Since you and Ken and are already decisively engaged at the monolithic gateway, my suggestion would be to have Maggie and Pete go back through the time portal but emerge in the far corner of the enclosure. They may be seen by the peasants gathered on the other side of the gateway, but at this point, I don't think it really matters. Their attention is focused on Ski. They can take the camera staffs back through with them and try to capture the flight of the asteroid along its trajectory. One can start shooting southward and bring it up to directly overhead as the asteroid approaches and the other can be facing in the opposite direction and pick it up from directly overhead and track it down its trajectory in the direction of Cuzco. It seems to me when we splice the video clips together, we'll have a continuous view of the whole over-flight."

"What do you think Ken and I should do?" Zazworsky asked.

"Well, at this point," Dr. Campbell observed, "since you will already be standing there by the gateway to the enclosure, you probably shouldn't go back through the portal. Why don't you stay here by me and just look over my shoulder at the temporal monitor tracking scan."

"That makes good sense," Zazworsky agreed. "Let's do it."

As Zazworsky released the two small round golden droplets from the comet wedged between his sandals onto the corner of the table, Ken Red Elk asked, "What have you got there, Ski?"

Dr. Campbell answered before Zazworsky could reply, "If I'm not mistaken, Ken, Ski has brought back two nugget samples of the 'Sweat of the Sun God.'"

\* \* \* \* \* \* \* \* \* \* \* \* \* \* \* \* \* \* \*

Later that afternoon, Stauffer, Zazworsky, Campbell, Red Elk, Pendleton, and Martinez sat silently around the conference table in General Goldwyn's office. "Perhaps I can explain what happened, sir," Zazworsky offered.

"No explanation required, Bob," General Goldwyn responded. "It was just one of those operations that didn't pan out as planned. We've had a couple of them, but I think this one takes the cake." Goldwyn was trying to keep a straight face but finally gave up as a broad grin swept across his face. "I just got back the Minibago DVDs, and my tech team has reviewed them to see what we've changed. I was prepared to dispatch the emergency response team through a time portal to scrub the mission before it could launch. I thought that your little highly visible intervention would have thrown history totally out of whack, but my analysts say that it didn't. In fact, they could only find one major change in history that resulted from this mission hiccup.... and frankly, I find it most amusing."

Goldwyn leaned forward and pushed the return on the keyboard in front of him and the flat screen monitor came to life. "This is what the monolithic gateway at Tiahuanaco looked like before your little operation. I pulled this screen capture from the DVD that came back with the Minibago. The Ancients had cut out a gigantic stone portal with their energy tools, almost three feet thick, thirteen feet wide, and ten feet tall.... and totally flat and unadorned. The Ancients didn't go much for decorating edifices with images of people.... animals, yes.... people, not so much."

"And this is what the gateway eventually was changed to look like by the Tiahuanacan people after Bob's remarkable appearance framed there in the gateway with the asteroid flaming past high above him in the sky." Goldwyn leaned forward and pushed another key. The image of the original gateway faded out and a new image of the present gateway appeared in its place. Everyone in the room gasped. Several broke out into laughter.

The new gateway was covered with relief carvings across the entire upper facade of the gateway above the level of the door. Centered directly above the door opening was a large carving of the figure of a man with rays of light seemingly coming out of his head with his arms outstretched holding a staff or a snake in each hand. "I think it's a pretty good likeness, Bob. You've been immortalized in stone for posterity. I think, my friend, you have become the model for the Andean deity, Viracocha. The likenesses we see today of Manco Capac and Mama Occlo are all made up.... pure fiction. But Viracocha, no.... this is something entirely new and different. Had you been better prepared, you might have said something more profound to those peasants, something that would have ennobled their spirit and eventually their culture, instead of just waving your arms and pointing in the direction of Cuzco with your staff." General Goldwyn was clearly enjoying himself by this point.

"Do you mean that you're not going to send the team back to abort the mission, sir?" Zazworsky asked sheepishly.

"That's right, Bob. After a few hiccups, you accomplished the purpose of your mission just fine. We now have some excellent high definition video shots of the asteroid coming in and breaking up and eventually impacting in the center of the deserted city of the Ancients in the Valley of Cuzco. You even have some great fast motion video of the new Cuzco being built up over the craters of Manco Capac and Mama Ocllo in the center of the city.... Oh, and by the way, Dr. Campbell is correct. The legends of the Andean peoples have long referred to gold as the 'Sweat of the Sun.' Now we know where that comes from and we even have a couple of beads of golden sweat that Ski brought back with him to remind us. Nice work, all."

Everyone seated around the table looked at each other in surprise and disbelief. They had all anticipated a butt-chewing from the Old Man but instead he actually seemed to be enjoying the outcome from the failed mission. As everyone got to their feet to leave, General Goldwyn added one additional point. "Oh, and Barton, I want you to know that I'm going to dispatch a special team to Bolivia to negotiate with the powers that be there to make a casting of the Puerta del Sol gateway. I'm going to have a full scale copy made that we can transport to a vault in the Repository. We may even be able to set it up against the wall between two of the vault doors in the gallery as a reminder of the seriousness.... and humor.... of our circumstances down here."

As everyone filed out of the office, General Goldwyn asked Stauffer to stay behind for a moment. After everyone was gone, Stauffer asked, "Yes, sir, what do you want to talk with me about?"

"I just wanted to thank you for doing such a good job in organizing efforts down there in the Crypt. Your teams are assembling a great deal of information .... and artifacts.... that will enlighten our understanding today of antediluvian times. We need to get together soon to discuss my role in that."

"Yes, sir. I would like that very much." Stauffer turned and departed Goldwyn's office. On his way back down to the Crypt, Stauffer thought out loud, "We've got to think of some clever ways to ensure that Ski never lives this down."

# Chapter 22

General Goldwyn sat at his desk. He had just pushed the lock release button for his office door and Stauffer rushed into the room.

"I got here as soon as I could, sir. What's happening? What's it all about?"

"No emergency, Barton. I just wanted to talk with you about a couple of things that are on my mind. Can you spare me an hour or so?"

"Sure thing, sir. What do you want to talk about?"

"Well, I just talked with Alice Duerden and she tells me that Ken Red Elk is doing fine with no lingering ill effects from the rat bite. When Doctor Gates tested the rat, he found that it didn't harbor rabies or any other vectors like that. He had Bob Zazworsky's team return the mother rat to her babies on the sinking ship. Of the fourteen sailors that jumped ship to try to swim the distance to shore, only eight actually made it, the captain and seven seamen, but the mother rat managed to get there."

"That doesn't sound promising," Stauffer observed.

"You're right, Barton. Even worse, the sailors were almost dead within two weeks. Nothing much to eat.... If it hadn't been for the mother rat, which dragged herself up on shore, the sailors would all have died of starvation after all those months at sea."

"They ate the rat?"

"That's right. They made a feast of her, and it saved their lives while they figured out how to get fish from the sea. Yes, although it doesn't seem like much, returning that mother rat to the ship turned out to be a significant event in history."

"How so, General Goldwyn?" Stauffer asked.

"Well, two of the seamen were actually seawomen, and that small group of survivors eventually founded a great nation."

"Which one, sir?"

"Ah, now I'm going to have to leave that to you and your team to sort out."

"Sir, there is an issue that the team has been concerned about. After running survey scans on all of the fifteen surviving boats that made it through the Flood, the team has concluded that not nearly enough diversity in animals or plants was brought forward on the boats to account for the biodiversity we have in the world today. We're having a hard time understanding it."

"Well, Barton, I understand your concern, but the answer is quite simple. You just haven't yet chanced to see any of Enoch's scout ships that returned to Earth right before the Flood and collected huge quantities of plants and animals from around the globe that they later dispersed across the new world after the waters of the Flood receded. These scout ships were large vessels, almost a mile across, and the men and women who made up the crews were all expert biologists, highly skilled in their various fields. They carefully screened and selected all of the animals and plants that they took on board for the purity and consistency of their species. According to what Enoch told me, one of the main purposes of the Flood was to eradicate all of the bio-engineered and genetically modified plants and animals.... and humans.... They were trying to rid the Earth of all the unholy cross-breeds that were never meant to be."

"Like what, sir?"

"Well, Barton, in ancient mythology you can read about all kinds of fantastic creatures that once roamed the earth, creatures that were part man and part beast in a whole variety of hybrid combinations — minotaurs, centaurs, satyrs, harpies, dagons, sirens, and gorgons. Many of them weren't just mythical lore, Barton, they were part of our reality before the Flood. There was a secretive movement around the world by microbiologists and genetic engineers who set about creating all kinds of absurd combinations through gene splicing. The Flood was, in part, a strategy for eliminating those hybrids altogether. For the most part, it was successful.

"Were the mermaid people hybrids, sir?"

"No, Barton. They are a legitimate species reproducing after their own kind. They are not hybrids at all."

"Tell me about the Real Mermaid, sir. It seemed to me that you knew him personally."

"Yes, Barton, I did. I had made his acquaintance a long time ago. The people of the sea — the merpeople — live for a very long time. There was a time long ago when humans of the family of Adam and the merpeople communicated freely, even cooperated on some issues. The race mostly survived the great Flood without a problem, but their numbers have been greatly diminished in recent years by over-fishing, off-shore drilling, and more recently today, by the sonar testing conducted by the navies of the world. Sonar waves completely disorient the merpeople and many of them, particularly the young ones, don't fare very well. In Atrol's case, Barnum's 'Real Mermaid' was simply in the wrong place at the wrong time and got tangled up in a fisherman's net. He died an excruciating death when he was hauled up out of the depths onboard a fishing trawler and left to die on the deck. His body was put on ice and eventually sold to the circus. I really appreciate everyone's help in returning him to his home.... the sea."

"I'm glad it worked out, sir." Stauffer responded. "We just didn't understand what it was all about." Spying the mechanism sitting on General Goldwyn's desk that he had brought back from the Crypt, Stauffer asked, "Excuse me, sir, but can you tell me about the Antikythera mechanism?"

"Yes, Barton. I can tell you, but it will have to remain confidential between you and me for now. Before Enoch assigned me to the stay-behind team, I worked as an astrophysicist and research scientist. Dr. Campbell and I actually have a lot in common, but you can't tell her that. My last major project before I was reassigned was developing the *Star Box*, what modern archaeologists have been referring to as the Antikythera mechanism. I was very proud of that invention. It was a totally mechanical, analog computer.... the first of its kind in the world. It was designed to calculate the moon phases, the orbits of the planets, and the movement of the Zodiac star constellations. It was designed to be used as a navigational tool for ships at sea and for astronomers to predict the seasons for planting and harvesting."

"All that?" Stauffer whistled.

"Yes, I had just completed work on the design and it was going into production when everything was disrupted. I didn't know that they had actually produced any until I saw the Antikythera mechanism in the Archaeological Museum in Athens many years ago and realized what it was. Because it was later found among artifacts from a Roman shipwreck off the coast of Greece near the village of Antikythera, they labeled it the 'Antikythera mechanism' and assumed it was a product of Greek manufacture. I couldn't tell from the crusted relic in the museum if it was one of the original prototype mechanisms I worked on or if it was merely a copy made by Greek metal artisans many years afterward. If it was a copy, they did a pretty good job on it. And now, with Bob's team having recovered four more of the original final design pieces, I'm overwhelmed."

"It's an impressive piece of work, sir. You have every right to be proud."

"Thank you, Barton. I am. On another note, I've been doing a little research of my own on the temporal observation monitor, and I have confirmed that Ulla, Melek's bride-to-be, and her family were picked up by one of Enoch's scout ships that was gathering up stragglers from the original exodus of the Atlanteans. Both Ulla and Melek's families were scheduled for pick up, but Melek got bushwhacked before the team could get to him."

"Yes, sir. I've conversed with Melek on several occasions. Although he's trying to make the best of his situation, he clearly is unhappy here and would prefer returning to his home, even knowing that it was about to be destroyed in the Flood."

"I understand, Barton," General Goldwyn remarked. "But I think we can offer him a better deal than that."

"How's that, sir?"

"I've communicated with the Atlantean command and they've agreed to pick him up."

"How are we going to pull that off, sir?"

"They gave me the time-place coordinates to send him back and they'll take the hand-off from there. Ulla is excited to see him again. She's preparing her wedding trousseau."

Stauffer's head was spinning. No matter how well he intellectually understood temporal technology and time travel, he still found it difficult to wrap his arms entirely around the idea of Melek rejoining his bride.

"I get what you are saying, sir, although I don't entirely understand it. Just what do you want me to do?"

"I'll come down to the Crypt tomorrow to say goodbye to Melek. You don't need to say anything to him yet. I'd like to be the one to break the news to him. If you could arrange to have a portable time portal wheeled into the vault where Melek is staying, I'll be there about 1000 hours. I think that it would be alright for you to gather the entire Crypt team together to say goodbye. I'll bring the coordinates and set the portal to send him off. Does that all work for you?"

"Yes sir. It sounds like an ideal solution. But I wish that Melek could stay. There is so much we could still learn from him down in the Crypt."

"I know, Barton," General Goldwyn agreed, "but I think the young man has suffered enough. It's time for him to rejoin his people."

Stauffer rapidly thought through the details of what he would need to do to prepare his staff for Melek's departure tomorrow, but then that thought was sidelined by a more significant matter — significant at least to him.— the golden dodecahedron. "Sir, what can you tell me about the dodecahedrons? What were they used for and what do they represent?"

"Barton, you have been associating the dodecahedron with the fifth of the Platonic solids, and that's moving a step in the right direction. But that idea wasn't original with Plato. Like Socrates, Plato was an inveterate borrower of other's ideas. He had access to ancient records that had survived the Flood that never received a public viewing, and he studied them thoroughly, popularizing many of the ideas he found there in his own works. That isn't bad in and of itself. It's just that he never identified the source. Today we would call it plagiarism. Some of the scrolls we've retrieved through Repository recovery missions were part of Plato's personal library. Some were copies of ancient documents that go all the way back to the Flood and even earlier. Repository translators tried their hand and failed at translation of these scrolls. They were written in languages unknown to them. When Bill Tipton advised me of the problem, I had him sign out five of the mysterious scrolls and bring them to my office for me to look over. After Bill left my office, I opened the first scroll and found references to Antediluvian astronomy and astrophysics."

"How do you know that, sir?"

"Because I wrote it originally."

"Ouch," Stauffer uttered. "You mean that Plato lifted some of your ideas?"

"Not just mine but a host of Antediluvians and a great many writers who came after the Flood. The scrolls were copied and recopied over the years and were kept secret from the world in general. At an early age, Plato joined the secret society of Eleusis, and he admits in his writings how, after proving himself, he was given the secrets of the mysteries of the past. These ancient writings were considered secret knowledge, privy only to a small coterie of mystics and philosophers. The scrolls even provided a history of the departure of the people of Enoch into the sky in their aerial vehicles. That was much too fantastic and unbelievable for Plato to share publicly, and so he concocted the story of Atlantis sinking into the sea in a deluge. But that was a big distortion. The departure of Atlantis and the advent of the Flood occurred over six hundred years apart."

"Excuse me, sir," Stauffer interrupted. "I know it must make perfect sense to you, but I'm not making the connection here with the dodecahedron. How does it fit in?"

"I'll get to the point, Barton. When Plato received a copy of the secret scrolls and he deciphered their meaning concerning the true nature of the universe, he shared a slim portion of that knowledge in his identification of the five regular geometric polyhedrons that came to be known as Platonic solids. To shroud this revelation in mystery, he related the first four of these solids with earth, air, water, and fire. He concluded his exposition remarking that the dodecahedron....," General Goldwyn paused and then began to recite from Plato's *Timaeus*, "'the god used for arranging the constellations of the whole heaven.' Countless philosophers have since tried to deconstruct Plato's meaning here. Plato was merely trying to convey, in a cloudy sort of way, the arrangement of our universe in a larger system of a greater multiverse."

"Are you telling me that Bertrand Russell got it right, the universe is in the shape of a dodecahedron?"

"Well, Barton," Goldwyn observed, "that appears to be at least a partial truth. There's more to it than that, but it gives you the basic idea of the purpose of the dodecahedrons. They represent the cosmos in its most holistic sense."

"Did the dodecahedrons have a more practical use or were they just fancy paperweights to remind the owners of fundamental cosmological truths?"

"Once again, Barton, you demonstrate the ability to zero in and ask the right questions. Yes, the dodecahedrons served a most practical purpose. They are keys."

"Keys?.... Keys to what?"

"They serve as keys to certain gateways to other dimensionalities."

"Gateways?" Stauffer uttered. "To other dimensionalities?.... Do you mean wormholes, sir?.... stargates?"

"Yes, Barton.... gateways to other dimensionalities. Portals to other universes in the multiverse. The term *wormhole* is greatly overworked and vague, and it slightly distorts the reality. The Ancients set up cosmic gateways leading to other dimensionalities at various sites around the Earth. Most of these gateways were obliterated during the Flood, but several survived and are still functional today."

"Some gateways are still around today?....Where are they located?"

"Well, let's see.... Tiahuanaco in Bolivia.... Hayu Marca in Peru.... Teotihuacan in Mexico.... Giza in Egypt.... Stonehenge in England.... Xian in China.... Padmanabhaswarmy in India.... and Easter Island in the Pacific, off the coast from Chile. There was once a portal in a repository cave in the Grand Canyon, but I relocated that one."

"Is that all of them?"

"Oh no, there are another dozen or so, but I have identified here just the ones you would most likely be familiar with."

"You say the dodecahedron acts as a key? How? How does it work?"

"It's quite simple. You just place the dodecahedron on the locking mechanism of the portal, and the energy field detects its presence and opens the gate. The placement and orientation of the dodecahedron determines the destination through the gateway. It's really quite simple."

Stauffer was really getting excited at this point and started to ask another question, but Goldwyn interrupted him. "Barton, our time is drawing short and we really need to discuss another issue."

"Another issue?" Stauffer asked.

"Yes, historians in the Repository have been hard at work for over three years now, focusing mostly on the past four thousand years of human history, and they're beginning to piece together a more complete and accurate record of man's past. It's time to begin assembling that revised history for permanent storage here in the

Repository and Crypt. We've got the whole thing recorded on an electronic database. It is constantly being updated and we can call it up and print it out whenever we want. But that digital archival approach is decidedly ephemeral. It simply won't last very long. We need a much more permanent archival means. Hank Phillips tells me that we aren't where we need to be yet in storing the record on DNA or crystals. For now, I would like to engrave what our historians have assembled as a revised history on gold leaves and bind them into a comprehensive set of historical volumes. The approach is decidedly low tech but it is long-lasting."

"That's got to be a lot of history, sir. Do we have enough gold bullion on hand to do the job?"

"Actually, Barton, we have access to all the gold we could ever possibly want."

"How is that, sir? I know that we've accumulated a large quantity of gold down here in the Repository, but it's by no means unlimited."

"It would probably be easier for me to show you rather than just try to tell you about it. Hungry?"

"Sir?"

"Are you hungry?"

"Well, I suppose so. I was going to take Gwen and the kids out for burgers later this evening, but since I skipped lunch to get over here, I suppose that I could snack on something right now without spoiling my appetite."

"Excellent. I'm hungry too. Let's go get something to eat."

"Do you want to go to someplace here in Carlisle?"

"No, I had something else in mind. Follow me."

General Goldwyn stood up and walked over to the computer console on his desk and typed an entry on the keyboard. Suddenly, a portion of the wall between two bookshelves on the far wall began to shimmer slightly."

"What's that, sir?"

"Oh, it's a little innovation I had the temporal technicians install for me. It's a private time portal disguised to look like the framing between the two bookcases. You would never know its true purpose unless the portal is activated."

General Goldwyn walked toward the shimmering portal and motioned to Stauffer to follow him.

"Where are we going, sir?"

"To get something to eat."

"But where, sir?"

"Ah, Barton, I think you'll figure that out soon enough."

As Stauffer followed Goldwyn through the portal, he found himself standing in a dark alleyway sandwiched between two massive stone walls. As they moved along the alleyway and emerged out onto the street, Stauffer was surprised to find himself back in Cuzco, on the same street as the hotel where he and his family had stayed during their trip to Peru.

Without pausing, Goldwyn turned left and started walking up the street at a brisk pace with Stauffer scurrying along behind him trying to keep up. At the end of the block, they came upon the same aged woman tending the coals on her brazier on a street cart set up on the corner. As they came up abreast of the woman, Goldwyn acknowledged her with a nod and a greeting as he walked by, "*Napaykuykin*, Chaska."

"*Hola*, Goldwyn," she responded with a wide smile.

Stauffer nodded to the old woman as he hurried by trying to catch up with General Goldwyn. He half wanted to stop and sample the *anticuchos* again, but Goldwyn was moving at a fast clip up the street. After half running for ten or fifteen steps, Stauffer succeeded in coming up abreast of him. General Goldwyn was walking on the sidewalk and Stauffer was reduced to walking on the broken pavement in the street to the side. "Sir, do you know that woman?"

"Certainly, Chaska makes some of the best *anticuchos* in town. I know that you like them. You ate enough of them last time you were here."

"You watched all that? How do you find time to keep such close tabs on everyone?"

"I don't. I just keep aware of what some of the folks on my important-people list are up to."

"I'm on your important-people list?"

"Yes, Barton, right at the top of the list."

Barton stopped talking to process this new information. He wondered how closely General Goldwyn monitored his activities and whether he really had any privacy at all.

General Goldwyn came to an abrupt halt on the sidewalk and turned to Stauffer, who had stopped on the street beside him. "Here we are…. Best food in the whole city. I think you're going to like it."

An aged, nondescript sign which extended out over the sidewalk above the doorway said simply, *Comida Típica Peruana*, Typical Peruvian Food. Back home in the United States, Stauffer would have classified this eatery as a greasy spoon, one that he probably would have passed by in favor of something a little more upscale. As Goldwyn opened the door and entered the humble establishment, the smell of charcoal-grilled meat hit him in the face, and Stauffer knew immediately that he was going to like eating here. As he followed General Goldwyn into the dingily-lit room, they found a small table in the corner and sat down. A dark-skinned waiter with long braided hair hanging down his back was immediately at their table.

The man spoke in broken English, clearly not his preferred language. "Good evening, Goldwyn. Long time. What do you want to eat tonight?"

"Good evening, Maicu, good to see you again. I'm kind of hungry my friend. I think that I'd like a nice *cuey*…. *comida completa con papas y choclo*. Maybe even a small glass of *chicha*. My friend would like the same only he'll drink Inca Kola, no ice. Maybe you could bring us a couple of *chorizos* and some *bolillos* to get us started. That sound okay?"

"Yes sir, Goldwyn, can do. Be right back with the *chorizos*."

"That guy knows you," Stauffer said almost accusingly. "Do you come here that often?"

"Yes, I suppose I do…. maybe once or twice a month. There's a lot of advantages with having your own private portal in your office. You can eat anywhere in the world you want."

"Is that how you get around…. using the time portal I mean? When I was working down in the Repository, no one ever seemed to see you coming and going. Most folks assumed that you just bunked down in your office."

"Well, not quite. I'm working in my office most of the time, but I slip out occasionally to take a break and get a good meal now and again. It's one of the perks that goes with this assignment."

"Why did you bring me here, sir? Just to eat?"

"Well, no actually. But I thought that while we were here, we could get some really good down-home cooking."

"Charcoal-grilled *cuey* and *chorizo* sausages are down-home cooking for you? Not many folks put guinea pig at the top of their favorite foods list."

"I've always enjoyed *cuey*. Some folks think it tastes like chicken but greasier and stronger, but I've always thought about it the other way around.... chicken tastes just like *cuey*.... only drier and blander."

Stauffer laughed. "Well, I have to agree with you on that one, sir. I sampled c*uey* many times during my assignment down in Lima when I was at the Peruvian War College, and I really like it. I just don't get to try it very often anymore. I haven't been using the time portals for lunch dates."

"Nor should you," General Goldwyn laughed. "In this case, rank does have its privileges."

At that moment, they were interrupted by their waiter, who had returned with a tray stacked with plates of steaming hot chorizo sausages and bolillo rolls. "*Servidos, señores.*"

"*Gracias*, Maicu," General Goldwyn responded. "As always, five-star service and great food."

The waiter's smile revealed a set of broad white teeth. "*Gracias*, Goldwyn," he replied, and disappeared back into the kitchen.

General Goldwyn turned back to Stauffer and said, "*Buen provecho*," the traditional Peruvian salutation for the beginning of a meal, and began to devour chorizo sandwiches. Stauffer followed his lead and their conversation devolved down into small talk discussing the merits of the strong Peruvian mustard that was favored here in Cuzco. The waiter soon returned with a large platter containing two *cuey* which had been roasted on a rotisserie over a charcoal fire, and a large plate of roasted potatoes and *choclo* corn on the cob. Stauffer was impressed. As he ate his way through his portion of the food, he fully supported General Goldwyn's assessment that this might indeed be the best restaurant food in all of Cuzco.

After half an hour, they had made a serious dent in all of the food and Stauffer was beginning to get full. General Goldwyn was still going strong, using pieces of bread to sop up the juices from the *cuey* on the plate. Finally, he too, pushed his chair back slightly from the table. "No room for dessert after a meal like that," General Goldwyn observed.

Stauffer laughed, "If you did have room, sir, just what would you ask for?"

"Oh, that's easy, Barton.... *Mazamorra morada, manjar blanco,* or *suspiro a la Limeña.* I like them all. Maicu's wife makes a real good *mazamorra morada.*"

As General Goldwyn named off his favorite desserts, Stauffer was surprised to find that it was his same short list of Peruvian dessert favorites. He ventured a suggestion, half in jest, "Perhaps if we wait long enough, we'll get hungry again and we could try one or two of those possibilities."

"Oh, that we could, Barton, but we've got more important things to attend to. We need to get a move on."

As General Goldwyn stood up, Maicu appeared out of the kitchen and Goldwyn handed him two crisp twenties. *"Muchas gracias, mi amigo. Mis saludos a la señora y a los hijos.* Until next time."

*"Muchas gracias,* Goldwyn. *Un placer."*

General Goldwyn moved quickly to the door and exited out onto the street with Stauffer following closely behind him. As Maicu closed the door, Stauffer looked at General Goldwyn inquisitively. "Where do we go from here, sir?"

"Oh, I think that after a meal like that, a walk around the Plaza de Armas would do us good."

General Goldwyn continued on up the street to the plaza, walking across the open expanse in the direction of the little shop where Stauffer had seen the curious looking dodecahedron in the window when he was here in Cuzco with his family. When they arrived at the door of the shop, Stauffer asked, "You want to go in here, sir?"

"Well, yes," General Goldwyn responded. "I think that you will find answers to some of your questions here, lad."

As Goldwyn opened the shop door and motioned Stauffer to move on into the shop in front of him, Stauffer was greeted by the shop owner he had spoken with during his earlier trip to Cuzco. As Goldwyn entered the shop behind Stauffer, the owner's face lit up. "Ah, welcome, Goldwyn. Good to see you again."

"Always good to see you, Capac. How have you been doing?"

"Fair, Goldwyn. Many tourists. Business is good."

"That's good, Capac. I have a special request for you."

"What's that, Goldwyn? You have only to ask."

"I would like you to let my friend see your dodecahedron that you have displayed in the window. I know that it is not for sale, but he would really like to look at it up close. Would you mind?"

"For you, Goldwyn, anything."

The shop owner pulled out a large ring of keys and opened the grate that provided access to the window display. He reached in and carefully lifted the dodecahedron from its perch on the velvet stand and handed it to Stauffer. "Please be careful with it, my friend. It is very old."

Stauffer took the proffered object in his hands, almost reverently, and turned it over and over, comparing it mentally with the dodecahedrons he had back on his desk in the Crypt. This one was about the same size as the others, but it seemed to weigh much more. "Excuse me, sir. This is very heavy for its size. What is it made from?"

The man shrugged and General Goldwyn reached over and took the object from Stauffer, hefting it up and down a couple of times. "I'd say that it's possibly made of solid gold, or perhaps some combination of gold and lead, but more likely it's made of depleted uranium."

"Depleted uranium, sir? With all due respect, sir, are you crazy? He just said that it was very old.... an antique. How could it possibly be made of depleted uranium?"

General Goldwyn just turned to Stauffer and smiled. "That, Barton, is precisely what you and your team are going to need to find out as you explore the technologies of our prehistoric past."

Goldwyn handed the dodecahedron carefully back to Capac, the shopkeeper, and bowed. Then he turned and led Stauffer through a door at the back of the shop and down a long stairway leading into a sub-basement. At the far wall of the sub-basement, he used a key on his key ring to unlock another, much heavier door. As he swung the door open, he turned to Stauffer and said, "Watch your step going down. It is fairly steep and the steps are narrow."

General Goldwyn reached over to a small table to the side of the doorway and retrieved two large flashlights and handed one to Stauffer. As Stauffer followed him through the doorway, he found himself on a stone landing, with a steep stairwell carved into the living rock, burrowing down into the earth. Goldwyn pushed a switch on the wall to his left, and a set of light bulbs suspended to the side of the stairwell came on, dimly illuminating the passageway downward. They descended slowly, approximately forty or fifty feet into the earth, before they finally arrived at the bottom where the stairwell opened up onto a long, passageway carved into the rock. General Goldwyn turned back to Stauffer and cautioned, "It is a little rough going from here, but it's not far, maybe a half hour or so. Bear with me. It will all become clear in just a few minutes."

General Goldwyn started moving down the incline of the passageway, his large frame silhouetted against the narrow, dimly-lit tunnel ahead. The passageway wasn't straight but twisted to the right and left at intervals until Stauffer was no longer sure where they were beneath the streets of Cuzco on the surface. With each additional step downward, his latent claustrophobia excited greater panic, but he forced himself to follow closely behind Goldwyn, his curiosity trumping his natural fear of enclosed places. They walked down the inclined passageway for what seemed to Stauffer like thirty or forty minutes. Every so often, they came to a lateral passageway that branched off to the right or left, which appeared to connect to other stairways carved into the rock going upward.

Finally, as Stauffer was finding it increasingly difficult to breathe, the narrow passageway opened up into a large chamber cut into the rock. General Stauffer turned his flashlight to its highest power setting and motioned to Stauffer to do the same. Sensing Stauffer's claustrophobic distress, he said, "We have arrived, Barton. Take deep breaths and you will get over your claustrophobia soon enough. It was overwhelming for me also the first couple of times I came down here."

"I can understand that," Stauffer acknowledged, still breathing hard. "Why didn't you just bring us down here through a portal? It would have been so much easier."

"Well, Barton, I needed you to get a feel for where all this is located under Cuzco and the history it represents. This tunnel and these chambers are the key to understanding some of the deep mysteries of the conquest of ancient Peru."

As General Goldwyn was speaking, Stauffer panned the beam of his flashlight around the large chamber. "Just what is this, sir?". "After that walk down the incline of the tunnel, we must be several hundred feet below the surface."

"Actually, Barton, we are just short of five hundred feet underground. These are the tunnels where the Incas in Cuzco hid their gold after the debacle at Cajamarca when Pizarro and his soldiers ambushed the Inca nobility and slaughtered them. The Spaniards made off with most of the gold and silver that the Incas brought to Cajamarca to fill the room to the level of Pizarro's upstretched hand on the wall to pay the ransom for Atahualpa. But the rest of the gold that was used to decorate the walls of the ancient city of Cuzco abruptly vanished as the Incas escaped with it through these passages to hide it in safekeeping until the danger from the Spanish conquistadores was past. Well, that time never happened, and the Spaniards were successful in killing or subduing the Inca nobility and reducing the common people to slavery. And so, the golden ornamentation stripped from the city to protect it from the Spaniards lies secured here deep beneath the city hidden away to this day."

As Stauffer listened to General Goldwyn's narrative, he continued to sweep the room with his flashlight. The chamber was large, perhaps 100 feet across, cut out of the living rock. Around the circumference of the chamber were many doorways cut into the rock. Between the doorways set against the walls were what appeared to be small stone platforms on which rested mummified human remains seated upon ornately carved wooden thrones.

"What are those bodies between the doors. They look like mummies dressed up in golden finery and feathers."

"That's precisely what they are, Barton. These are the remains of the Inca royalty, from Manco Capac, the first cacique and founder of the Inca empire down to Atahualpa, the last Inca emperor who was executed by Pizarro and his conquistadores.

"Before the Spaniards arrived, these mummified remains of deceased emperors were brought out of the Inca temple during festivals and holidays where they were displayed on litters and paraded around the streets of Cuzco. Sometimes, the remains were carried with the Inca armies as they sallied forth from Cuzco on wars of conquest against neighboring tribes."

Stauffer had wandered over to one of the mummies which appeared to be in terrible condition. "Which one was this? It looks like he's suffered some serious damage."

"That is Atahualpa. He was the Inca who assassinated his half-brother, Huascar, and assumed the throne just as Pizarro and his small army of conquistadores arrived on the northern coast of Peru. Atahualpa was holed up at Cajamarca, an Inca city in the tops of the Andes, and he actually sent word to Pizarro inviting him and his conquistadores to make the difficult journey up to Cajamarca to meet with him. Atahualpa had a plan to kill the Spaniards once they arrived, but Pizarro ambushed Atahualpa's retinue before he could put his plan into effect. Pizarro held Atahualpa for ransom, requiring the Incas to fill a room full of gold and twice full of silver. After a sham trial at which the Spaniards found Atahualpa guilty of several trumped-up charges, he was sentenced to be executed. In order to avoid being burned alive by the Spaniards and risk losing a safe journey to the afterlife, Atahualpa consented to be baptized just before his execution. After which, they strangled him with a rope garrote. Then the Spaniards stripped him and burned his clothing along with some of his skin and his body was then given a Christian burial. Later on, his remains were secretly exhumed by some of the surviving Inca courtiers and transported back here to Cuzco to be stored and displayed alongside the other Inca rulers.

"Sounds like a pretty ghastly custom."

"Well, it was part of their religious observance and it worked for them." General Goldwyn sounded a little testy.

Stauffer decided to change the subject. "What's behind the doors?"

"Well, here, take a look." Goldwyn walked over to the door to the left of Atahualpa and pulled out his key ring once again. Separating out an old-fashioned skeleton key on the ring, he pushed it carefully into the hole and slowly turned it. The locking mechanism groaned and the door slowly swung inward. Goldwyn and Stauffer stepped into another large chamber, three times as deep as it was wide. As the two moved the beams of their flashlights around the room, they saw gold and silver artifacts stacked to the ceiling, glistening in the light.

Stauffer was overwhelmed. He did a quick mental calculation and realized that this room held more gold treasure than all of the gold they had accumulated in the vaults at the Repository by the time he retired. "Are all of these rooms the same? Do they all contain such a quantity of gold and silver?"

"Yes, they do, although this one may be a little smaller than some of the rest."

"How many of these rooms are there in all?"

"Twenty-four.... Quite an extraordinary amount of gold."

"So this is all the gold that the Incas hid from the Spaniards?"

"Actually, no. There are several large workshops on a lower level with many additional storage vaults where the Incas stored large quantities of refined gold brought from throughout the empire to be used in fabricating more golden artifacts to adorn the Inca and the sacred precincts of Cuzco. I estimate that they may have accumulated upwards of fifty to a hundred tons of the precious metal in those holding vaults. Also, there are other repositories of gold where the Ecuadorian Inca nobility hid the gold they were carrying south from Quito to Cajamarca when Atahualpa was assassinated."

"Where is that all hidden?" Stauffer asked.

"In an almost inaccessible region of the Ecuadorian highland rain forests in an area called Llanganatis," Goldwyn responded. "After they deposited the treasure deep in ancient mine tunnels, the Inca nobility concocted a myth about how it had all been dumped in a nearby lake. But it was all a fabrication and diversion to keep the voracious Spaniards from finding the true hiding place."

"How much gold is stored there, sir?" Stauffer asked.

"I am told that there is about half again as much gold hidden away there as there is here. It is a lot of gold, Barton."

"Sir, that amount of gold would be of inestimable value today. How have they managed to keep these tunnels and vaults hidden for so long?"

"Here in Peru, Capac, the owner of the shop on the Plaza de Armas, is part of a group of Inca custodians descended from Atoc, an Inca prince who served as chief courtier to Huascar. After Atahuallpa was executed, Atoc ordered the temples of Cuzco stripped, and all of the golden ornamentation and the mummified remains of the Incas were brought down here for safe keeping. There have been sporadic initiatives by Spanish colonial authorities through the centuries to find the rumored tunnels where the Inca gold is hidden, but this close-knit group of descendents of Atoc has managed to keep the location of the tunnels secret and protected. There is a similar group of Ecuadorian Inca nobility providing the same custodial oversight over the treasure buried at Llanganatis."

"Is the entrance through the shop we came through the only entrance to the tunnels here in Cuzco?"

"Actually, no. I am aware of at least five or six others. One entrance is located at quite a distance in a bakery shop way over in Pisac, down in the Sacred Valley of the Incas. It is quite a walk to get here from there. The bakery shop is built on the ruins of an ancient Inca temple and disguises the entrance to the tunnel system. Like Capac, the baker is also a descendent of Atoc and part of the Inca custodial team which guards the tunnels."

"And so," Stauffer postulated, "are you saying that we have access to as much gold as we might need to fabricate books with golden pages on which to inscribe the histories our historians have fabricated?"

"Pretty much, Barton. I have negotiated with the elders of the Inca custodians, and, although the gold ornamentation and artifacts stored in these vaults are strictly off limits, they have offered me access to as much of the unworked gold stored in the workshops in the lower levels as we might need. They have even offered to fabricate the gold into thin sheets and bind them together into books with large golden clasp rings. All we need is a technology to print the histories we are developing onto the gold sheets.... something similar to the old dot matrix impact printers perhaps or even laser-etching technology of some kind. I have a technical team experimenting with laser engraving right now. At any rate, we are going to be ready to go to press on the Repository histories within about two or three years. I would like you to have a good start on the Crypt histories that go much further back into prehistory in the same time period. Do you think that you will have a lick up on it by then?"

Stauffer just followed the beam of his flashlight around the gold-filled vault with his eyes as he responded, slightly bewildered, "We'll give it our best shot, sir."

General Goldwyn turned and faced Stauffer. "It is about time for us to be getting back. But before we go, would you like to take a look at Manco Capac and Mama Occlo?"

"Sir?"

"The golden asteroid fragments that got this all started."

"Are they down here too?"

"Oh yes, Barton. I just found where they are located on my last visit down here two weeks ago. When they came here from Tiahuanaco and settled here near the crater, the Incas took small amounts of gold from the top of the two asteroid fragments, but they left the bulk of the gold in place, buried deep beneath the Plaza de Armas. Here, follow me."

Goldwyn closed the door to the vault they had just emerged from and secured the lock on the door with his key. Then, he turned and continued on around the circumference of the chamber until he came to a large passageway situated between two of the mummified Incas. Goldwyn led Stauffer down the passageway several hundred feet until they came to another massive door. Once again, Goldwyn pulled out his key ring and unlocked the door, allowing it to swing inward. As Goldwyn stepped into the room within, he reached for a torch from a fixture on the wall. He pulled a lighter from his pocket and lit it. As the flame leaped up from the torch's head, it illuminated the chamber and Stauffer could see that it stretched on for forty or fifty meters into the distance. But what amazed him was the ceiling to the chamber. It appeared to be made of solid rough-worked gold.

"What's this, sir?" Stauffer asked incredulously.

"Barton, you are looking at a portion of the underside of Manco Capac. Over there, off in the distance, is the underside of Mama Ocllo. They're pretty much just as the original founders of Cuzco found them. Oh, they used some of the gold taken from the top side to decorate their temples initially. But they later discovered that the Andes Mountains are rich with gold ore and they began mining that gold in earnest. That is where all of the gold down in the workshops came from. It is the surplus from their mining operations."

"But why would they keep all of this gold here untouched?" Stauffer inquired.

"Barton, you miss the point. For them, this is sacred ground. This is Manco Capac and Mama Occlo, the children of the Sun God...., sent from Titicaca here to help them establish Tahuantinsuyo, the navel of the world at the center of the four *suyos*. You have been granted a great privilege by the remaining Inca custodians to come down here and view their holy precincts."

Goldwyn turned and, holding the torch high over his head, led Stauffer a few steps to his right toward a large enclave carved into the stone walls of the chamber. The enclave was perhaps ten feet across and ten feet deep into the wall and was filled up with small pellets of gold, much like the two that Zazworsky had recovered from the plaza at Tiahuanaco. General Goldwyn scooped up a handful of the golden pellets with his hand and let them fall gently back into the bin. "These are the beads of gold that the early Incas collected from all over the *altiplano* from Cuzco all the way back to Tiahuanaco. There's probably fifteen or twenty tons of the gold pellets collected here. All of it dripped off the two pieces of the asteroid as it broke up and eventually impacted here. They believe that these pellets are indeed the 'Sweat of the Sun,' because their forefathers saw it happen. It literally rained droplets of gold from the asteroids as they passed overhead."

"That's incredible, sir." Stauffer observed. Wasn't anyone hurt by the downpour of molten golden rain?"

"Oh, yes, quite a few were hit by some of the pellets and some were severely burned. Those who were wounded by the falling pellets never had the gold removed from their wounds and just left it in place to coalesce. The wounds soon healed over, attesting to their having been witnesses and participants in the downpour of golden sweat. They were revered by the rest of the people as being singled out and blessed by Inti, the Sun God."

"I feel bad, sir, at this juncture, that Ski picked up two of these pellets and we have them back in the Crypt. Perhaps we should bring them here to be reunited with the rest of the pellets."

"No, Barton," General Goldwyn responded. "That's a nice thought, but I've already cleared it with Capac for you to keep the two pellets there in the Crypt for safe keeping. I promised that you would protect them in a reverent fashion and that you would explain to all of your team members about their sacred nature to the Inca people."

"Yes, sir. I'll do that at first opportunity and set up a special display case in my office for all to see and appreciate."

"That will be a good thing, Barton. And now, we need to get back to Carlisle. We both have a lot of work to do."

\* \* \* \* \* \* \* \* \* \* \* \* \* \* \* \* \* \* \*

When Stauffer got back to his office, he became engrossed in catching up on the paperwork in his inbox. Finally, after many hours, he sat back in his chair and stretched. He had failed to note the passage of time. He glanced over at the clock on the wall and realized that it was already 11:00 pm. He was over five hours late getting home to his family. He knew that Gwen must be beside herself with worry. She had gotten used to Stauffer keeping regular hours and having him return home not later than six o'clock most days.

Stauffer quickly cleared the clutter on his desktop and organized his inbox for the next day and went into the first time lab down the hallway. Setting the controls on the console, he passed through the portal to travel back six hours. As he emerged on the other side, he hurried out the lab door and down the hallway in the direction of the elevator. As the door opened, Zazworsky met him coming out. "How's it going boss? Had a good day?"

"Yes, I think you might say that, Ski. A pretty good day." Stauffer stepped into the elevator, and as the door closed behind him, he said softly, "Yes, Ski, a very good day at that."

# Chapter 23

*Carlisle Barracks, Pennsylvania, Tuesday, March 4, 2014, 8:35 a.m.*

Stauffer and Bob Zazworsky sat at the conference table in Stauffer's office, hashing out the details for the acquisition and installation of additional high-density storage shelving for some of the vaults in the Crypt. Just as they were finalizing the purchase request, the red telephone on Stauffer's desk rang. Startled, Stauffer sprang to his feet and moved over to his desk. The caller ID indicated it was General Goldwyn. Stauffer answered quickly, "Yes, sir. Stauffer here."

"Barton, I'm glad I caught you in. If it is convenient, could you and Bob Zazworsky come up to the my office right away for a quick meeting.... Something has come up."

"Yes, sir. Be right there."

Turning to face Zazworsky, Stauffer said, "Come on, Bob. We just got a come-hither to the Old Man's office."

"Did he say what it's about?"

"No," Stauffer responded as he moved toward the door with Zazworsky following close behind. "He just asked that we come up on the double."

Stauffer and Zazworsky hurried down the hallway to the Crypt elevator and were shortly standing outside General Goldwyn's door. Before Stauffer could put his hand on the hand pad to signal their arrival, Goldwyn's voice came booming over the intercom speaker to the side of the door. "You made good time. Glad you are here. Come in. The meeting is just beginning to get interesting."

The door locking mechanism activated and the door swung open into the office. Stauffer and Zazworsky rushed in, finding Bill Tipton, Alice Duerden, Pete Pendleton, and Rick Bailey already sitting with General Goldwyn at the head of his conference table. "Come over here and please take a seat around the table," General Goldwyn requested. "We have something intriguing happening over in the Repository that I would like Bob to get involved in."

Turning to Duerden, Goldwyn continued, "Perhaps, Alice, you could give Barton and Bob a quick review of what you just told me to bring them up to speed."

Stauffer shifted his attention from General Goldwyn to
Duerden. She had been leading the Repository team since Bill Tipton
left to join Stauffer in the Crypt. She spoke matter-of-factly with a
slight smile on her face. "Good seeing you again, Barton.... Ski....
It's been awhile. You guys need to get out more. I'm going to cut to
the chase. One of my Repository teams has discovered a series of
caverns and tunnels in Victorio Peak, a small, mountain mass out
in the middle of a dry lakebed in the southern New Mexico desert.
Legend has it that hidden deep within the mountain there is a rich
treasure of gold bars, artifacts and antiquities, and other treasure. We
are just beginning to investigate using temporal monitors, and we
have reason to believe that the legends are probably true."

"Why?" Stauffer countered. "What have you found?"

"This, Barton," Duerden responded reaching around behind
her and sliding a wheeled cart up next to the conference table.
Centered on top of the cart was a large canvas bag. She grasped
hold of it to transfer it over to the conference table, but it was so
heavy that she and Rick Bailey were only able to lift it from the cart
and deposit it on the conference table with major exertion. Bailey
unbuckled the bag at the top and pulled the sides down, revealing a
very large bar of what appeared to be solid gold.

"What's that?" Zazworsky exclaimed leaning forward over
the conference table, staring at the sparkling bar of metal. "It looks
like gold, but it's bigger than any bar of gold bullion I've ever seen."

"You're right, Ski," Duerden responded. "It's atypical
of anything we have today. It's way too heavy. It weighs over 85
pounds.... Makes it almost totally unmanageable for one person to
lift and carry."

"If it's solid gold," Zazworsky responded, "it must be worth
a fortune. At today's prices, 85 pounds of gold would go for....,"
he paused to run the calculation in his head...., "over a million five
hundred thousand dollars."

"That's what we figured, Ski. The good news is that there are
several more where this came from. In fact, we believe there may be
as many as two or three thousand of the things."

"Two or three thousand!" Ski exclaimed, his eyes growing
wider as he calculated in his head the value of such a find. "That
would be worth almost five billion dollars!" Zazworsky was clearly
getting worked up over the possibilities. He jumped up and moved

around the conference table, and with great effort, picked up the bar from the cart and hefted it in his hands. "Wow, who would make a gold bar this heavy? It would be almost impossible to move about much."

"That's what we thought, Ski. Maybe that's why it's so big.... It makes it really difficult to steal."

"Be careful with that, Bob," General Goldwyn cautioned. "I'd hate to have you drop it on my conference table.... or on my lap. Someone help him lower it back down again."

Bailey complied and assisted Ski in lowering the gold bar back down onto the tray top of the cart. Zazworsky turned the cart around, examining the bar from all sides. He noticed a small slice was missing from one of the corners. "Looks like someone has taken a sample off the corner here. Did you run assay tests on it? What did it test out as?"

"It's almost 100% pure gold, Ski, just a very small trace amount of copper. Someone went through a lot of trouble with a very sophisticated process to make this bar that pure."

Zazworsky was getting more excited by the minute. "Boy, I'd like to have a piece of this action. Just what is it you want me to do?"

"And that, Barton," Duerden spoke up, "brings us to the issue of why we asked General Goldwyn to invite you both here to this meeting. There isn't anyone down in the Repository who has Ski's level of expertise on recovering large quantities of gold. We've asked General Goldwyn if we can have Ski on loan for a couple of weeks to head up the team for this recovery mission."

General Goldwyn turned to Stauffer. "That's right, Barton. I knew we wouldn't have to work very hard to get Bob excited about the offer once he saw the gold bar, but I needed to get your clearance to break him away from whatever you have him working on for a couple of weeks. How about it? Can you spare Bob for that long?"

"Sir, you know that this will seriously cripple my whole operation," Stauffer responded with a sardonic grin, "but.... I think we can make the sacrifice and give it a try. I don't know though....," Stauffer said feigning doubt. "Maybe Ski isn't really all that interested."

"Are you woofin' me, Boss? I'd give anything to be on that recovery team."

"Ski," Duerden interjected, "to be clear, we're not asking you to be **on** the recovery team. We're asking you to **lead** it. Are you up for the challenge?"

"Well, I think I can clear my social calendar for a couple of weeks if Colonel Stauffer gives the nod.... Count me in!"

As everyone departed General Goldwyn's office, he asked Stauffer to hang back for a minute. "Barton, we keep postponing Melek's departure for one reason or another, and now we are going to have to postpone it one more day. There is too much going on right now. And besides, that will give your people additional time to pump Melek for all the information they can get out of him before he leaves. Better get them moving."

\* \* \* \* \* \* \* \* \* \* \* \* \* \* \* \* \* \* \* \* \*

Later that afternoon, Bob Zazworsky, Alice Duerden, Rick Bailey, Wynn Osterlund, Nathan Burgess, Neal Tandy, and Brandon Smith sat around the conference table in Duerden's office in the Repository discussing the gold bar recovery mission at Victorio Peak.

"Hey, you all know that I would just as soon rush in and start packing out gold bars as fast as we could get them uploaded," Zazworsky acknowledged, "but I think that it would be prudent to have someone update me on what your research team has uncovered so far. I assume you've been doing a thorough site survey with the temporal observation monitors."

"That's right, Ski," Duerden responded. "But it hasn't been as easy as you might think."

"What do you mean?"

"Well, we became aware of the potential existence of a treasure trove of gold ingots when Colonel Osterlund was reviewing a history book about the American West and came across a chapter about the Lost Dutchman Mine in Arizona and the Victorio Peak Treasure in New Mexico. He asked his teammate, Winston Greeley, to focus in on the Dutchman Mine and he elected to research the Victorio Peak treasure. Here's where the complexity comes in.... There isn't just one legend of Victorio Peak. There are a half dozen legends that seek to explain the origin of the gold and other treasure that have been discovered there. One legend points at Don Juan de Onate, founder of New Mexico as a Spanish colony. Another story suggests that the treasure belonged to Emperor Maximilian, who moved his fortune out of Mexico City when he heard rumors that enemy forces were planning to assassinate him. Another legend describes the sojourn of a Catholic missionary, Felipe La Rue, who led a group of monks and Indian peons from a large hacienda in the state of Chihuahua in Northern Mexico into the area to escape famine. When they arrived in the vicinity of the Hembrillo Basin, they discovered rich veins of gold in Victorio Peak, and La Rue directed his followers to begin mining and smelting operations. According to the stories, immense amounts of gold were mined, cast into gold bars and stored in neat piles in the caverns in the peak. Another legend suggests that Chief Victorio, an Apache war chief, led raids throughout the southwest desert region on wagon trains, stage coaches, villages and churches, making off with whatever gold and riches they could find and hiding it in the Victorio Peak caverns."

"And which legend panned out as the true version?" Zazworsky asked.

"Actually, Ski, that's the difficulty. There appears to be elements of truth in all of the legends. The Victorio Peak caverns may hold treasure from all of those sources."

"You've got to be kidding me."

"No, it appears that after one group deposited their riches in the caverns, another group would come along and hide their own treasure."

"How was the treasure discovered?"

"In 1937, a man named Doc Noss apparently was out hunting in the area and stumbled upon an entrance tunnel into the caverns high on the peak during a rainstorm. He later filed several mining claims with the New Mexico government on the Victorio Peak area and removed, according to his own account, at least 200 bars of gold and a large number of gold coins and other artifacts. But, there was a problem. Congress had passed the Gold Act just a few years earlier in 1934, and it was now illegal for citizens to own gold except in the form of jewelry. That made it impossible for Noss to legally sell any gold and profit from his discovery. Although Noss was apparently successful in selling some of the gold bars on the black market in Arizona, it's rumored that Noss hid most of the treasure he removed from the caverns, burying it in the desert sand so that no one else could find it. He also attempted to enlarge the tunnels leading down into the caverns with a large charge of dynamite. His effort failed miserably and instead filled the tunnel with tons of debris totally blocking access to the caverns.

"That must have been slightly disappointing for him." Zazworsky scoffed.

"Oh no, Ski." Colonel Duerden responded. "It just keeps getting better. There followed a whole series of intrigues between Doc Noss, his wife and associates. Noss was eventually shot and killed by one of his partners in a dispute. Then, to add a whole new twist to the story, the US Army took control of the whole area in an expansion of the White Sands Missile Range and put it all off limits, preventing Noss' widow from attempting to excavate the tunnels and regain access to the caverns. It was rumored that soldiers stationed at the missile range installations heard about the treasure hidden in the peak and started explorations of their own. Some folks say that they found another entrance to the caverns, and the Army was successful in surreptitiously removing the remainder of the gold and treasure from the caverns. When Noss' wife was finally successful in gaining legal access to her claim in the caverns, there wasn't anything left of the treasure that she and Noss had discovered. She brought in a scientist from the Stanford Research Institute, who used sonar to try to find hidden tunnels or chambers that still might be buried in the rubble in the cavern. He detected another cavern another 300 or 400 feet deeper in the peak, but they couldn't find an access tunnel and they finally had to give it up."

"So, does that summarize pretty much what we know at this point?" Ski asked.

"Not quite, Ski. Wynn used the sonar data from the Stanford Research Institute guy and searched the deeper portions of the peak with a temporal monitor sweep. The cavern was right where the SRI data said it would be. The cavern is huge and totally shut off from the outside world. With the military still keeping tight control of the area as part of the White Sands Missile Range, there is little possibility that anyone will access the cavern anytime soon. And so, Wynn opened a time portal into the cavern to see what it might contain. He led a small recovery team in exploring the cavern, and it opened up a whole new spin on the mystery surrounding the peak."

"What do you mean, Alice?" Ski asked.

"Well, all of the gold bars that Doc Noss and the US Army removed from the Victorio Peak caverns were normal-sized bars, each weighing about 30 pounds or so each. We believe those came from sources in the last five hundred years. The cavern that Colonel Osterlunds' team explored was filled with gold bars stacked high, but these bars were enormous, weighing over 85 pounds apiece. This bar here is one of them that they brought back for further inspection and analysis. The problem that it creates is that it doesn't coincide with any of the known legends of Victorio Peak. It appears that the cavern has been sealed off from the outside world for a very long time. We haven't yet a clue where the gold bars came from or who left them there."

"Haven't you been able to track backwards using the temporal monitors to figure that out?"

"We tried, Ski, but we got back as far as 2200 BC and then we ran into a temporal block and we couldn't go any further."

Zazworsky immediately understood the implications of the temporal block and made a mental note to get with Stauffer to have a Crypt team check it out. With any luck, they would be able to go beyond the temporal block that hindered the Repository team's investigation. He turned back to Colonel Duerden and offered, "Okay, Alice, we'll come back to that later. For now, we know that the gold bars and other treasures that were stored in the upper caverns have mostly been removed. We can perhaps recover some of that by having Repository teams use temporal monitors to track where Noss buried his cache in the desert. It's probably still right where he left it and we ought to be able to recover that pretty easily. We can also track the removal of any treasure from the caverns by US Army personnel and find out what happened to it. My guess is that it was all packed up in storage crates and moved to a DOD secure warehouse somewhere. We need to figure out just what was removed and where it is now located."

"What about all of the gold bars in the lower cavern?"

"Ah," Zazworsky responded with increased enthusiasm, "now that is where this operation gets exciting. We're going to need to mount a recovery mission to bring all of that gold back here to the Repository. We're going to need some specialized handling equipment to move it. It's way too heavy for us to try to manhandle two or three thousand 85 pound bars of gold. What we need are a couple of those heavy duty field forklifts like we used in the Gulf War to load up the bars on pallets and move them back through double-wide portals."

"I can take care of that one, Ski," Rick Bailey said. "I know just where I can lay my hands on two or three of those puppies."

"Thanks, Rick," Ski responded, "but we're going to need to mount a comprehensive survey of the cavern first to inventory what we have there before we can get started on any on-the-ground recovery missions. And, we're going to have to run it by General Goldwyn before we take anything out of the cavern. By the way, how's the air in the cavern?"

"We went in the first time wearing self-contained breathing units, Ski." Osterlund responded. "Recommend that we continue that practice. No telling if we're going to run into pockets of bad air in the far reaches of the cavern. It's been sealed off from the outside world for a long time."

"Agreed, Wynn. We're also going to need to bring Doc Gates on board for a epidemiological and contagion scan. Since we don't know who put the bars there in the first place, we better make sure that we're not bringing back an uninvited hazmat contagion with the treasure."

"Just so you'll know Ski, we dusted off this bar from the cavern with some disinfectant before we brought it back through the portal, and we put it immediately through a thorough hazmat bath in the time lab before we did anything else with it."

"Good work. We're going to have to set up some kind of a similar hazmat assembly line for everything else we bring out of the cavern. Rick, can you take care of setting that up in one of the time lab vaults? We're also going to need several vaults for storage, and we'll need a group of historians standing by to catalog and describe all of the artifacts that we might recover from the cavern. Perhaps we'll even be able to sort out all of the different contributors to the loot in the caverns."

Zazworsky paused to think through the tentative plan that was taking shape in his mind. "Alice, if you can get all of these initial things up and running, I have to go back to the Crypt to finish up a couple of issues that I left hanging to come down here. Can we agree to meet back here in your office at 0800 hours tomorrow morning to continue the planning phase?"

"Roger that, Ski," Duerden responded. "I think we can have most of the initial elements of the plan in place by then, and we can work on fine tuning whatever you want us to do."

\* \* \* \* \* \* \* \* \* \* \* \* \* \* \* \* \* \* \* \* \* \* \* \*

With Melek's departure postponed for the moment, Stauffer advised the Crypt teams to work with Melek as intensely as possible to grill him for whatever information he might be able to reveal about the antediluvian world. It had proven impossible to directly translate any of the scrolls and books and other written materials recovered from Melek's crate using the crystal sets. And so, whatever they were able to glean from Melek as he read aloud while viewing the scrolls though his crystals was a big plus.

In addition to the historical narrative recorded on the scrolls, Melek was able to provide them with much detailed material well beyond an understanding of his own little village. He had listened carefully to the stories of his ancestors related by the elders of his village at gatherings around communal fires, and he had a broad understanding of the history of mankind well back before the days of Enoch. They worked Melek for hours at a time, and when he tired, they plied him with pizza and ice cream, his favorite modern foods, to give him energy to keep on going. Dr. Gates stood by patiently observing the interviews, and occasionally, he called a time-out to give Melek a break and a good rest period.

While the teams were interviewing Melek, they had a custom-fit jump suit made for Melek. It was designed after the same pattern as the jump suits that everyone in the Repository and Crypt wore, only his was very large to accommodate his gigantic frame. When they presented Melek with the jump suit, he was overjoyed and rushed back behind a privacy screen in his vault where he quickly changed clothes. When he emerged minutes later wearing the jump suit, he had a broad smile on his face and he was obviously delighted with his new outfit. Zazworsky had been able to break away for the presentation ceremony, and as he presented Melek with a couple of additional jumpsuits gift-wrapped for the occasion, he quipped, "Melek Alikimaka, my Antediluvian friend."

A blank, puzzled look crossed Melek's face revealing that he didn't understand what Zazworsky had just said. Some of the members of the team didn't either. But a few members of the team that had been around Zazworsky for a long time immediately got the joke and realized that he had dropped the most awful pun imaginable and Martinez began pummeling him on the arm. "That was bad, Ski.".... "Clear the air!".... "They could lock you up for that!"

Zazworsky just smiled and responded, "It was the least I could do to show my appreciation for Melek. You all just wish that you had thought of it first."

\* \* \* \* \* \* \* \* \* \* \* \* \* \* \* \* \* \* \* \*

Later that day, as Zazworsky returned from a planning meeting down in the Repository, he hurried along the moving walkway back to the Hole and then dropped down into the Crypt on the elevator. As he emerged into the hallway leading into the Crypt, he went directly to Stauffer's office. As he stuck his head in the door, Stauffer looked up and saw him enter. "Come in, Ski. How's it going on the gold bar recovery mission? Pretty straightforward operation?"

"Not at all, Boss. In fact, it's turned out to be pretty complex. There's a lot of moving parts on this one. And to top it off, I think that it involves the Ancients as well. It may be that we're going to have to get the Crypt teams involved."

"Why is that, Ski? What do you mean?"

"Well, the Repository teams were hindered in their search for who deposited the cache of oversized gold bars in a sealed-off cavern buried deep under Victorio Peak."

"What hindered them?"

"Hindered by a temporal block. They encountered the block at approximately 2200 BC. Whoever deposited those over-sized gold bars did it before then. That means that the Ancients are involved, I think."

Stauffer sat back in his chair processing the new information. "I think you're probably right, Ski. I'm going to need to get with General Goldwyn ASAP to see how he wants us to proceed. I think he's going to direct that a Crypt team research who deposited the gold bars in the first place. What else is complicating the issue?"

"The whole area became part of the White Sands Missile Range some while back, and it appears that a U.S. Army team accessed the tunnels and caverns at the upper levels back in the 1940s or 50s and made off with all of the remaining smaller gold bars and artifacts from other sources. I've got a Repository team chasing that one down to see where it all went. I'm betting on one of those secret warehouses inside the Beltway."

"You're probably right. I'll have to ask General Goldwyn about that as well. Anything else, Ski?"

"Not for now. When are you going to see General Goldwyn?"

"Stand by, Ski." Stauffer picked up the phone handset and dialed Goldwyn's number. He spoke in low tones briefly and then put the handset back.

"General Goldwyn is waiting for us now. Come on. Let's get moving."

\* \* \* \* \* \* \* \* \* \* \* \* \* \* \* \* \* \* \* \* \* \*

General Goldwyn leaned forward in his chair as Stauffer and Zazworsky updated him on the details of the Victorio Peak treasure they had developed thus far. "Let me get this straight, guys, the 85 pound gold bars were discovered in a sealed cavern deep down inside Victorio Peak. When the Repository team used the Temporal Observation monitors to go back in time to check out who deposited the gold there, they got all the way to 2200 BC before they encountered a temporal block and couldn't go any further. Is that about right?"

"Yes, sir," Zazworsky responded. "I think that that's a pretty good indication that the Ancients are involved somehow."

"You are right, Bob," Goldwyn responded. "The Ancients are directly involved. Victorio Peak sits directly atop an enormous deposit of gold. The peak has been mined by many different cultures going all the way back to antediluvian times." Turning to Stauffer, Goldwyn continued, "Barton, I want you to have a Crypt team get the specific coordinates for the cavern from the Repository team that did the initial temporal scanning and have them pick up the trail on the other side of the temporal block and see what they turn up." Turning back to Zazworsky, he said, "I don't see any reason why the Repository team you are leading can't do the recovery mission from the cavern once we get a read on who deposited them there. Work up a plan but wait to execute it for now. Since some of the artifacts they pull from the cavern will probably be antediluvian, we may need to bring them under special control. You two keep me posted as the situation unfolds."

General Goldwyn sat back in his chair and put his hands behind his head. He stared at the ceiling thoughtfully and then turned back to Zasworsky. "Bob, you say that US Army personnel stationed at White Sands might have policed up all of the later gold bullion and artifacts from the upper caverns in the Peak?"

"I believe so, sir. I'm not sure why they would do that. It clearly wasn't the Army's property and removing it from the cavern constitutes theft and fraud."

"Well, Bob, let's not jump to conclusions too early on that one. Have one of your teams observe what actually happened with everything the Army removed from the cavern and see if you can determine where it all ended up. I need to know that. Meanwhile, I am going to conduct a little investigation of my own. Let's get together here in my office tomorrow afternoon at 1300 to compare notes and see what we have found out."

"Yes, sir," Stauffer and Zazworsky said simultaneously. They came to attention, faced about, and quickly left General Goldwyn's office. As they walked down the hallway, Stauffer suggested, "Ski, you better get back over to the Repository and make sure your team is working on what General Goldwyn asked you to find out and get to work on the recovery mission. I'll drop down into the Crypt and get a couple of folks working on figuring out how the Ancients came to deposit that huge cache of gold bars in the cavern. I may even get involved on that one myself. Send me a copy of the coordinates so that we can pick it up on the other side of the temporal block."

\* \* \* \* \* \* \* \* \* \* \* \* \* \* \* \* \* \* \* \* \*

Neal Tandy and Brandon Smith formed the team in the Repository that investigated where Doc Noss buried the gold bars and artifacts out in the Hembrillo Basin desert. It was a relatively easy investigation. They just bracketed in on Doc Noss as he removed large numbers of gold bars two at a time up the tunnels to the cave entrance on Victorio Peak, and then tracked him forward to where he started burying the loot in the desert. It turned out that he didn't bury it all in just one spot. He actually buried the gold bars in ten different locations. He marked the desert floor where he buried them with a pattern of rocks and he carefully recorded the spot on a map of the Hembrillo Basin so that he wouldn't forget. They witnessed that later, when Noss' partner turned on him and started stalking him with a gun. Noss took out his map and set it on fire to protect the secret of the locations where he had hidden his treasure. With Doc Noss dead and the map destroyed, no one had any idea where he had hidden the gold in the desert. This was clearly a target of opportunity for Repository recovery teams to retrieve the gold caches.

\* \* \* \* \* \* \* \* \* \* \* \* \* \* \* \* \* \* \* \* \* \*

Stauffer tasked Mitch Monahan and Ginny Nguyen to start running temporal scans on the other side of the block to investigate how the oversized gold bars ended up being stored there. Using the bracketing technique, they observed that a group of Ancients discovered rich veins of gold that were abundant in the peak and surrounding area and set up an intensive mining operation at a very early time. Monahan and Nguyen noted a curious thing. As the Ancients mined and smelted the gold and poured it into molds to form bars, the bars didn't look particularly large and the Ancients lifted them with little effort. They concluded that was the real reason that the bars seemed so heavy for them today.... If these miners were as tall as Melek.... or taller...., then the gold bars would be proportionately about the right size.

Building on Max Manchester's earlier observation about the difficulty in gauging size on the temporal monitors, they decided to set up some kind of surreptitious measuring device to determine the stature of the Ancients working the mine. During a sleep period when the mine shafts were unattended, they opened a time portal into the tunnel and quickly scratched marks on the mine wall beginning at six feet and moving up the wall in one foot increments, just like height strips you see marked off on the door frame of a convenience store. The tunnel wall itself was almost ten feet in height, and they had to bring through a ladder to scratch the upper marks on the rock wall. Then, they exited back through the portal and fast forwarded to the next work period as the Ancient miners returned to the mine. As the miners walked past the marks scratched on the tunnel wall, they realized that the average height of the miners was about 8½ to 9 feet. These were very large men.

Monahan and Nguyen were surprised to see that during Antediluvian times, the Hembrillo Basin wasn't a desert at all but an expansive shallow lake surrounded by a broad grassy plain. In the center of the lake was a modest-sized island dotted with trees, shrubs and flowers with the Victorio Peak rising up in the center of the island.

Using temporal observation fast forwarding, the team observed that much of the output of gold bars from the smelting operation was loaded onto metal barges which were levitated into the air and moved away from the island across the lake and disappeared in the distance. But much of the gold was stacked onto heavy wooden pallets which were levitated and moved back into the mountain down through the tunnels and stacked in side vaults off the main cavern. When a side vault was filled to capacity, the workers stacked cut stones in the tunnel opening to the vault until it was sealed shut. Then, they focused an energy beam on the wall which seemed to melt the cut stones together to form a natural continuous rock wall. Surprised, they bracketed backward in time to determine when the Ancients first started storing gold in the cavern and then fast forwarded through time to see how many of these side caverns had been loaded up and then sealed shut with energy beams. They documented 27 sealed, side vaults in the cavern, after which the Ancients just started stacking the gold bars on the cavern floor itself. Nguyen and Monahan estimated that the cavern and side vaults held a total of approximately 200,000 gold bars, considerably more than the original 3,000 estimate.

As the team fast forwarded through time, they found the mining and smelting operation suddenly deserted. They started bracketing backwards until they found when the Ancients left off work and abandoned the site. It wasn't easy to understand what was happening, but it appeared that the site came under fire by a small group of aircraft firing high energy beams at the smelting operation facility. The energy beams caused it to explode in a fiery blast, raining droplets of molten gold around the edge of the island and rippling out into the lake. The miners tried to defend themselves with the limited firepower of their own weapons but they were clearly outgunned. Finally, after most of the miners had retreated into the mine, a lone remaining miner turned his own energy beam on the mine shaft opening and a landslide sealed it shut with tons of falling rock. He continued firing the energy beam, and it melted the rock into a solid rock face, effectively shutting off the tunnel entrance and the cavern deep in the peak below.

* * * * * * * * * * * * * * * * * * * * * *

General Goldwyn sat at his computer using the temporal observation monitor to look into the report of the US Army making off with gold bars and artifacts from the upper caverns at Victorio Peak. He was doing a temporal scan in super-fast motion. He started the scan from the date that the Army had extended the White Sands Missile Range into the Hembrillo Basin area and moved forward from there. When he observed soldiers exploring the Victorio Peak area, he slowed down the scan on the monitor to observe real time exactly what was going on. He observed a jeep-load of soldiers circling the peak and zoomed in on them. With a start, he realized that one of the soldiers was Garash, the man in the ill-fitting suit. He appeared to be the ring leader of the young soldiers who showed them where the back entrance to the upper caverns was located. He had them stop the jeep and led the soldiers up the slope of the peak and into the caverns. They emerged a short time later carrying gold bars in their arms. They loaded them into the jeep and drove off.

Goldwyn fast-forwarded and shortly thereafter, a long line of 5-ton ammunition trucks pulled up to the tunnel entrance and a company of soldiers started packing out all of the remaining treasure from the upper caverns. It required 35 trucks to load it all out. When the last truck was loaded and the tailgate secured in place, the convoy moved away from the site across the desert to the railhead in the White Sands cantonment area where it was loaded into boxcars and shipped east. The shipment was routed to Washington, DC, where it was offloaded and trucked across the Potomac to the Pentagon building. It was offloaded there and lowered in small increments on freight elevators deep into the building's sub-basement and ultimately stored in top secret, restricted-access vaults. General Goldwyn fast-forwarded all the way to the present day and it appeared that the gold and treasure was never examined or removed and was still stored there in the sub-basement vaults deep beneath the Pentagon.

* * * * * * * * * * * * * * * * * * * * * *

The next morning at 1000 hours, General Goldwyn showed up in the Crypt to participate in the sendoff for Melek as he returned to his homeland. As Stauffer escorted Goldwyn to Melek's dispensary vault, members of the Crypt staff fell into line behind them. Stauffer had told them that Melek would be leaving and they all wanted to pay their respects. Just inside the vault door, Doctor Gates waited with Melek standing beside him. As General Goldwyn entered, Melek grabbed his hands and shook them both. Then he embraced General Goldwyn and, with tears in his eyes, said, "Thank you Goldwyn. You have been most.... kind and.... hospitable to me."

General Goldwyn smiled and returned Melek's embrace in a hearty *abrazo*. "Well, my friend, it is the least we could do after we snatched you from your own world. I hope that you have been comfortable here during your stay with us."

"Oh yes, Goldwyn," Melek answered. "I have learned so many things from you here. And I have learned to like new foods. I am going to miss ice cream and pizza. Perhaps I will be able to teach my own people how to prepare these delicacies."

"That is good, Melek. Now, I know that Colonel Stauffer has briefed you on my intention to send you home, but I don't believe he has told you the whole story. When you cross over through the time portal, you will find yourself out on a grassy plain near your home. It will just be getting dark and there won't be anyone near where you emerge. After the outline of the portal disappears, I want you to just stand there for a few minutes. Someone will be along in a flying craft to pick you up and take you to Ulla. I think it's long overdue for you to be married and raise a family of your own."

A look of astonishment came over Melek's face. "Ulla? I'm going to see Ulla again? Goldwyn, you are a great man, and I am your humble servant. You are the best great-great-great-great uncle thrice removed that a man could ask for. We will name our first child after you, Kubal Golden One. It is a proud name and I will be proud for him to bear it."

"Well, thank you for that honor, Melek. Please extend my best wishes to Ulla, your bride, for a long life and much happiness. Perhaps we will meet again sometime."

The members of the Crypt team stood on the periphery of the room listening to the exchange between General Goldwyn and Melek. As Melek referred to him as a distant uncle and called him

"Kubal Golden One," the staff members gave each other puzzled looks, clearly not tracking or understanding the conversation. Then General Goldwyn turned to all assembled raising his hands and invited everyone present to step forward to say their goodbyes. One by one, each member of the Crypt team stepped forward. Finally, Doctor Gates grasped Melek's hands and said, "Melek, thank you for being such a good patient. I have enjoyed our long conversations. You have taught me much and I will long remember our association." Gates reached around on the table behind him and picked up Melek's scroll and his crystal stones that they had finally found during the inventory and classification process. He reached out and solemnly handed them to the Antediluvian.

Melek nodded with tears forming in the corners of his eyes as he accepted the scroll and crystals and he clutched them to his chest. "You are a good and just man, Doctor Gates, and I appreciate your nursing me through my illness when I arrived here. I too will long remember you."

General Goldwyn had been standing to the side setting the controls on the time portal keyboard. He now stepped back toward Melek and, placing a hand up on his shoulder, gently turned him to face the portal. "Melek, you will need to be very careful passing through the portal. It is a double-wide but you will still need to duck your head when you are passing through. We will wait a brief moment after you have gone through before we shut down the portal. Please move away from the portal and make no attempt to come back through. Be on the lookout for the aircraft that will come to pick you up to take you to Ulla."

"I will do exactly as you say, Goldwyn," Melek replied. "May your footsteps always be guided through the darkness."

Melek turned back to face the portal, and, as General Goldwyn, pressed a key on the keyboard, the shimmering outline of the portal appeared. "Now, Melek, it is time for you to go," General Goldwyn said in parting. "May your future be bright and may you have many children and a rich posterity."

Melek moved forward resolutely and, lowering his head, disappeared as he passed through the portal. General Goldwyn counted to five under his breath and then shut the portal down.

Turning to the Crypt team members assembled, Goldwyn spoke with a big smile on his face. "Ladies and gentlemen, I greatly appreciate all of you being here to give Melek a good sendoff. But please remember.... anything you heard or think you heard here this morning must stay in this room. You cannot discuss anything with other personnel here in the Hole or the Repository. And no discussion even among each other, please. This episode with Melek is now a closed chapter in the annals of the Crypt. It's been a great morning. I hope to be able to get together with you all again soon."

General Goldwyn smiled and abruptly turned about. He left the startled Crypt team standing there as he departed the vault and headed down the hallway in the direction of the elevator up to the Hole.

* * * * * * * * * * * * * * * * * * * * * *

As previously arranged the afternoon before, Stauffer and Zazworsky met with General Goldwyn at 1300 hours that afternoon to discuss what they had uncovered in their investigations. Zazworsky began the meeting with his report on the gold bars that Noss had hidden in the desert. "Looks like the legend is true about Doc Noss hiding away most of the treasure he removed from the peak out in the desert. We've documented ten separate burial sites where he stashed the loot. The inventory we conducted using the temporal monitors indicate that there are 238 gold bars and several golden statues and other artifacts and an assortment of gold coins buried out there. With your approval, sir, we'll set up recovery missions to bring all of the treasure under control back in the Repository vaults."

"Approved, Bob," General Goldwyn said. "Please post inventories of all recovered items with some screen captures on the intranet so that I can monitor mission progress."

"How about you, Barton? What have you and your team in the Crypt turned up about the origin of the large gold bars buried deep under Victorio Peak?"

"Well, sir," Stauffer responded, "the short story is that the rich veins of gold ore in the peak were mined over a period of several hundred years by the Ancients. It was all smelted and processed into gold bars right there on site. Much of the gold was transferred to other locations using large metal bins that were levitated into the air once they were filled with the bars and then steered away from the island across the lake that surrounded the peak and continued off into the distance. We haven't had time to check out all the different possible destinations where it all might have gone."

"That might be good enough as is," General Goldwyn observed. "I'm not sure that that information would do us any particular good at this point. Chasing gold is probably not as important to us as chasing history. We're going to have to keep our priorities in order."

"Yes, but there's something else, sir, that I need to brief you on."

"What's that, Barton?"

"Well, like I said, the mining operation apparently went on for over two hundred years. Although the Ancients shipped a great deal of the gold they produced elsewhere, they stored even more of it in vaults they carved out of the sides of the great cavern buried deep under the peak."

"Vaults, how many vaults, Boss?" Zazworsky interrupted.

Stauffer smiled back at Zazworsky as he broke the unexpected news. "Twenty-seven vaults, Ski.... really large vaults loaded with a total of least two hundred thousand gold bars.... It's just a SWAG at this point, but it's a great many more than the two to three thousand bars that we originally estimated."

Zazworsky paused to do a quick mental calculation. "At approximately 85 pounds a bar, that's more gold than we have stored at Fort Knox, the Denver Mint, and the Federal Reserve Bank of New York combined. That's a lot of gold, Boss." Turning to General Goldwyn, he exclaimed, "What are we going to do with it all, sir? Do we attempt to recover it and store it in vaults down at Waxahachie, or do we just leave it in place? That represents a major work effort to move that much gold."

"Good question, Bob. I'm going to have to think about that one. I think we have sufficient vault space completed in the inner ring at Waxahachie to accommodate that much gold, but I would have to organize a separate team to do the transfer. Very difficult but doable. I'll have to think about that one."

"Sir, there's one more thing," Stauffer interjected.

"Yes, Barton. What is it?"

"At the end of two hundred years or so of mining the peak, the miners and foundry workers were attacked by aerial vehicles firing some form of energy weapons. The gold smelting operation went up in flames with a violent explosion. Most of the miners ran back into the mine, but one stayed behind and turned an energy weapon of his own on the mouth of the tunnel blowing it up and causing an immense cave-in and landslide, which totally closed off the tunnel leading into the cavern. Then he adjusted a dial on his weapon and hit the fallen rock with the energy weapons again, and it fused into a solid rock face, leaving no trace of the mine entrance at all."

"What happened to the miners who ran back into the mine?" Goldwyn asked.

"I had my team go back and check it out. They reported that the miners used their energy drills to cut out another large side cavern and most of them went inside and sat down. A small team started gathering large stone blocks and built up a thick wall covering the tunnel leading into the vault. As they neared the top, most of that team shimmied up and dropped down on the other side of the wall and sat down with the rest of the miners gathered there. The two miners who remained outside in the cavern finished piling stone blocks on the wall until it completely covered the tunnel entrance. Then, one of them turned the energy beam on the block wall and fused it into a solid stone mass like the other vaults holding the gold bars. Then, the two remaining miners each turned an energy beam on the other and they were instantly incinerated, leaving no outward evidence in the large outer cavern of their ever having been there. With the exception of the gold bars stacked around on the floor of the cavern, we would never have known there was anything there."

General Goldwyn thought for a minute on what Stauffer had said and then spoke to Zazworsky. "Bob, would you please get back with your team in the Repository now and give them the word to proceed with the recovery of the gold hidden in the desert. Keep me posted on your progress. There are a couple of matters I need to discuss with Colonel Stauffer alone. I'll let you know shortly what I decide to do about recovering the gold bars from the deep cavern."

"Sure thing, sir," Zazworsky said with a big smile on his face. "The team will be excited to get on with the desert recovery operation."

"Oh, and Bob, for now.... keep a lid on all the gold concealed in the walls of the cavern. No one need know about it for now. The fewer who are aware of that, the better."

"Roger that, sir," Zazworsky replied. He turned about and left the room quickly, in a hurry to get back with his team and get started on the desert gold recovery mission.

Turning to Stauffer, he continued, "Barton, I really appreciate the thoroughness of your report. I need to have you tell whatever team members down in the Crypt, who assisted you with discovering all that transpired there with the Ancients in the mining and smelting operation, that they need to keep a close hold on that information. No one else need know for now. Okay?"

"Yes, sir," Stauffer answered. "Sir.... I'm sensing that you are closer to this incident than you're letting on."

"Once again, Barton, you've demonstrated your keen powers of observation. When Alice Duerden first came to me to tell me about the Victorio Peak treasure, I began to suspect that it was all tied in somehow to the Ancients' gold mine operation in that region. Your report confirmed that to me. I lost two distant cousins in that raid. A total of two dozen good men were lost. It was one of the last raids on my people by hostile forces before Enoch made the decision to evacuate the planet. I need you to send me the temporal coordinates so that I can view it here in my office. I would like to pay my last respects."

"Yes, sir. I'll do that ASAP."

Stauffer sat there in his chair not speaking as General Goldwyn was obviously caught up in a consideration of memories long forgotten. After a few minutes had passed, Stauffer ventured an interruption, "Sir, will that be all?"

Stauffer had startled Goldwyn from his introspection and looking back at him, replied, "No, Barton, there is one more thing. I used the temporal monitors to track the gold and artifacts that the US Army removed from the upper caverns of the peak all the way back to vaults buried deep under the Pentagon. Garash was the ring leader that led the operation."

"Garash, sir?"

"Garash, Barton.... the man in the ill-fitting suit. He struck again. He showed the Army personnel where the back entrance to the upper caverns was located and they moved in and gathered it all up and locked it away in vaults under the Pentagon without so much as a look at what they had."

"Do you want to stage some kind of recovery operation to get that treasure under our control here in our vaults in the Repository or Waxahachie?"

"I haven't decided yet on that one either, Barton. I'll get back with you later as soon as I've thought through everything that you and Bob have shared with me today. Thank you."

Stauffer recognized General Goldwyn's subtle dismissal and excused himself. "Okay sir, I need to get back to the Crypt and brief up any team members who are privy to the temporal survey of the lower cavern and commit them to silence on the matter. See you later, sir."

Stauffer faced about and left the office, pausing in the hallway outside General Goldwyn's door to consider all of the implications of everything he had learned that day. Trying to pull together a meaningful narrative about antediluvian times just kept getting more and more complicated. He and his Crypt team had their work cut out for them.

# Chapter 24

Stauffer asked his teammate, Max Manchester, to continue the survey research on Atlantis while he moved to the period of time immediately before the Flood to conduct an observation monitor survey on Noah. Stauffer was obsessed with Noah. For Stauffer, the episode of Noah and the Ark and the Great Flood was perhaps the most important and exciting event in the prehistory of humankind.

During earlier temporal observation surveys as he watched the construction of the Ark, Stauffer saw that Noah frequently moved off to a building adjacent to the Ark construction site and shut the door after him. Curious, he followed him in on the temporal observation monitor and found Noah seated at a heavy wooden table. A large pile of vellum animal skins stitched together as a binding lay closed on the table before him. The vellum pages were wrinkled and worn and had the look of great age about them. Noah opened the book to a page that was only partially filled and began writing slowly using a quill pen and making awkward strokes with the plume dipped in dark ink in characters of an unknown language.

Curious about the origin of the leather book he had seen, Stauffer decided to use the temporal observation monitor with the new tracking software to trace the book back through time to its source. Once he had locked onto the book and set the software moving backward through time in fast motion as video images raced across the screen, Stauffer just sat back in his chair and watched with fascination. It was a little unsettling watching the scenes unfold in reverse but Stauffer discovered that Noah didn't make the book. It was given to him by an older man, who in turn received it from another man who in turn received it from still another. This last man bore a strong resemblance to Enoch, whom Stauffer had observed supervising the construction of the Atlantis mother ship. An electric shock jolted through Stauffer's system when he realized that a second man standing behind Enoch looked a lot like a young General Goldwyn. Stauffer paused the program freezing the face of the General Goldwyn lookalike on the screen. It was an uncanny resemblance. Stauffer took a screen capture and then restarted the software, journeying back through time tracking the book.

Enoch received the book from another and he from another and he from another and so on. The date and place coordinates on the side of the screen recorded the movement back in time until it finally stopped at 4002 BC, and the picture on the screen froze as if it had been paused. Stauffer pushed the pause button to release the pause and continue but it wouldn't budge. There was a temporal block in place that wouldn't allow him to go any further back in time.

Stauffer leaned back in his chair to think it through logically. He stared at the man on the screen where the screen had frozen. He was a muscular young man and he walked hand in hand with a lithe young woman. They were both dressed in animal skins and the man carried the vellum leather book under his arm. It had the appearance of being almost new. The pages weren't wrinkled at all and lay flat between the covers.

Unable to go back any further, Stauffer moved forward in time, fast-motion tracking the movements of the man and woman. As he tracked them, he monitored the date on the side of the screen. The years clicked off relentlessly, and the scenes on the monitor passed by so quickly that Stauffer couldn't really discern what was happening. After almost 900 years had passed on the monitor, he paused the picture on the screen to reassess the situation. The young man had aged appreciably in those 900 years. He was now bent over with age. His hair was white and his face was lined with deep wrinkles. The woman stood near him, and she too had aged greatly and showed the years. The old man still carried the vellum book tightly under his arm. As he approached the next man in line to receive the book, he looked into his eyes for several minutes saying nothing.

And then, as he moved forward to hand him the book, a puzzled expression crept across the old man's face and he began looking around as if searching for something. Finding nothing, he turned around to face the man to whom he had just given the book and they stood there looking at each other unspeaking for several more minutes before the old man and the woman turned and slowly walked away, hand in hand.

Stauffer was puzzled by what he had just witnessed. Finally, the blinding glimpse of the obvious occurred to Stauffer that this just might be Adam and Eve, the first parents of the human race according to the Biblical tradition, and that the program had stopped when it did because General Goldwyn had placed a temporal block around that period of time. It didn't look like he was going to get a glimpse of the fabled home of mankind's origin, the legendary Garden of Eden.

Stauffer stared at the screen, frozen on the image of the backs of the elderly couple retreating into the distance having turned over their precious book to the next in line to receive it. Stauffer realized that the passage of the book from person to person that he had just observed in reverse motion was a lineup of the Biblical patriarchal order, from Adam to his son, Seth, and so on down to Enoch, Methuselah, and then finally, to Noah. Enoch was indeed the man who gave the book to Methuselah with the General Goldwyn lookalike standing behind him. Stauffer couldn't conjecture what that was all about.

\* \* \* \* \* \* \* \* \* \* \* \* \* \* \* \* \* \* \* \* \* \* \*

Suddenly, it occurred to Stauffer that he didn't know what happened to the book during the Flood. He quickly reset the time-location parameters on his temporal monitor, and he found himself back inside the building with Noah sitting at his table looking through his crystals, slowly coaxing words out onto the leather pages. Stauffer looked more closely at the book itself. After the passage of so much time, it was now well worn and dog-eared. The edges of some of the pages had started to disintegrate and crumble off. Stauffer rechecked the temporal coordinates on the side of the screen.... 2340 BC. Almost 1660 years had elapsed since he first saw the young Adam walking with Eve with the book tightly grasped under his arm. With good reason, the book was starting to show its age. Stauffer touched the controls and started the scene moving forward. He saw Noah set down his quill and then slowly close the book. He leaned over and reverently kissed it, and then carefully wrapped it in a thin, brightly colored shawl. He placed the package in a sturdy wooden chest that was daubed with what appeared to be pitch inside and out. Then he lay the crystals alongside the book and

closed the lid. Noah stood slowly and went outside. He returned a
short time later with a small bucket, and he carefully sealed the seam
between the body of the box and its lid with more pitch.

When Noah appeared satisfied that he had a good seal on
the box, he went outside and returned with a servant whom he
directed to pick up the box and follow him up the ramp and into
the Ark. They traversed a series of ramps inside the Ark that led to
the uppermost level of the interior of the Ark where the family's
quarters appeared to be located, and Noah had the servant deposit
the chest on a table in his cabin. Once the servant had left the
room, Noah crossed over to the far side of the cabin and opened a
large cabinet with a heavy door. He returned and picked up the box
from the table and deposited it in the cabinet. Shutting the door, he
dropped a heavy metal cross bar into place and secured the cabinet
with what appeared to be an elaborate mechanical lock. Stauffer saw
that there was another large cabinet to the side of the first. The door
was standing open and Stauffer was startled to see that it appeared
to be full of golden artifacts, gems, and other treasures. Stauffer
remembered that the Crypt team had discussed at an earlier staff
meeting that Noah appeared to be a very wealthy man. This must
have been his repository of material wealth that he had prepositioned
to take with him on the Ark. Noah shut the door to that cabinet
and secured it also with a heavy lock as well. Then, the old man
moved over to his bed on the other side of the room and knelt down.
Stauffer got a glimpse of his face. It was weathered and slightly
wrinkled and tears streamed down his cheeks. Noah lowered his
head and clasped his hands in front of him as Stauffer quickly exited
the scene. He shut down his temporal monitor, leaving Noah to his
private veneration and supplication to his God.

* * * * * * * * * * * * * * * * * * * * * *

Intrigued about the future disposition of the book, Stauffer
reset the time parameters on his monitor and observed Noah and his
family departing the Ark after the Flood. The servants had assisted
Noah's sons in letting all of the animals out of their stalls and the
animals were slowly making their way down the slope of the mountain,
mostly still walking in pairs. As the last animal departed the Ark,
there was a trembling in the earth and a massive mudslide high on

the mountain above the Ark started to make its way down the slope. The Ark was directly in its path. By the time it reached the Ark, the avalanche of mud had slowed but it was still moving at an appreciable speed, and it pushed the Ark several meters down the slope in front of it. Some of the mud came up and over the top of the front end of the Ark, and Noah and his family had to scramble to get out of the way.

Realizing the danger in remaining there, Noah's sons urged their father to get into the large hand cart loaded with bags and luggage that they had pulled from the Ark down the ramp. But Noah appeared to be in a state of panic. He rushed past them back up the ramp and disappeared into the Ark with his sons following close behind him. Stauffer followed them up the system of ramps with the temporal monitor to Noah's sleeping quarters and observed as Noah rushed across the room to where the cabinets were positioned. Noah pulled a key on a leather thong from beneath his robes and quickly unlocked the cabinet door and withdrew the heavy chest with the leather book inside. Noah handed the box to one of his sons who had followed him into the Ark. Noah looked anxiously at the other cabinet, but the Ark began to shake again with more mud slides threatening their safety. The other two sons helped guide their father back down the ramp and out of the Ark. They loaded him into the cart and handed the chest to him, which he clutched tightly on his lap. Then, they quickly made their way down the mountain to the new world that awaited them below.

They were about five miles down the slope when another avalanche came crashing down from the mountain peak above and almost completely buried the Ark in a thick covering of mud. Only the pointed bow end stuck out of the mud as a marker where the Ark was located. Noah just shook his head and directed his sons to continue the journey down the mountain. The family fortune remained in the other cabinet back on the Ark, buried under such a tremendous volume of mud, Stauffer reasoned, that it would be all but impossible for Noah's family to ever recover it. Stauffer sighed and made a note of the date-location coordinates for Noah's family as they trekked down the mountain and determined that he would return on another day to track the location of the leather book to its final destination.

\* \* \* \* \* \* \* \* \* \* \* \* \* \* \* \* \* \* \* \* \* \*

Stauffer observed that Noah and the members of his family never spoke aloud directly to each other, although earlier, they spoke aloud frequently with the workers on the Ark. One day, Stauffer was observing Noah and one of his sons facing each other but without speaking. Stauffer zoomed in with the temporal monitor and sensed a telepathic communication. Noah's face clouded over and Stauffer heard these words in his head, *"Who are you? Why are you spying on us?"*

Stauffer immediately shut down the temporal connection and contemplated what just happened. Later, the next day, at his weekly meeting with General Goldwyn, Stauffer explained what had occurred when he was observing Noah. "Sir, I clearly heard a voice in my head and I think it was Noah. I believe he was communicating with me telepathically. I could hear him in my head and he could at least sense me. And if that's the case, then I've violated our protocols against direct contact with religious figures and political leaders in the past. This could have created all kinds of problems with distorting or changing the past and our present."

"When did you say this happened, Barton?" General Goldwyn inquired.

"Yesterday afternoon, sir," Stauffer responded with a note of despondency in his voice.

"Well then," General Goldwyn observed, "I think you can rest assured that the interaction didn't result in any changes. I sent out a routine Minibago mission the day before yesterday and it came back early this morning. The technicians just completed a comparison analysis and reported no significant differences noted. You don't need to worry about that one."

"Well, that's a relief, sir."

"However, Barton," General Goldwyn's face clouded over as he spoke, "we need to have that talk I promised you before. There's more to the story of my being an Ancient that you still need to know, and I think that it might explain why it is that Noah can communicate with you telepathically."

"How is that, sir?"

"A year and a half ago when you were feeling despondent over the deaths of George Smedley and Kassiopeia when they abruptly returned to Pompeii and their lives were snuffed out by Vesuvius, I had a long conversation with you about your family growing up and the relationship with your own family today. And....

I revealed to you an important element about who you really are....
After your mother and father were first married at the onset of
World War II, they tried for six years to have children but it didn't
happen. Finally, they started working with a fertility doctor who gave
them some hope. I had a professional working relationship with your
Mother's doctor and I intervened in the process. You were finally
born nine months later, November 1, 1947."

Stauffer was startled at where the conversation was going.
"Yes, sir. That's my birth date."

"Well, Barton," General Goldwyn continued, "you already
know that I am here on assignment from the Ancients. I was kept
very busy during World War II tracking the state of human affairs as
each side created and deployed more terrible weapons of destruction.
When the war finally ended, I was given the short-term assignment
to assess just how much the human race had changed or evolved
physically since the people of Atlantis departed almost five thousand
years earlier. The key question was — could Ancients still intermingle
and mate with modern humans and produce viable offspring? To
run that assessment, I became involved with working with several
fertility doctors, including your own mother's physician, Doctor
Gerstenmeier, to assist with your conception, using one of your
mother's eggs and sperm donated by an Ancient who somewhat
resembled your father."

"What?" Stauffer exploded. "Are you trying to tell me that
I'm not my father's son?" Stauffer was highly excited and raised his
voice in anger. Then, as he regained composure, he asked slowly,
"Just who is my father then?"

"Barton, your reaction is understandable and it's practically
identical to your response when I told you all this the first time.
And I'm going to tell you once again what I told you then.... You
are your father's son in practically everything that matters.... But, to
answer your question, I was the one who donated the sperm. Once
your mother became pregnant through an artificial insemination
procedure, I worked with Dr. Gerstenmeier to monitor your prenatal
growth pretty carefully...."

"You are my.... father?" Stauffer interrupted, trying to make
sense of all the implications of this new information and its impact
and meaning on his life. Finally, he eked out another question,

almost in a whisper, "How many more of us are there.... or was I the only one.... in your experiment?"

General Goldwyn responded quickly, trying to keep the conversation upbeat in spite of Stauffer's increasingly black mood that was overwhelming him. "I worked with several fertility doctors that year and we had five or six dozen assisted-conception births. We had almost a 100% success rate, which demonstrates that there is no appreciable difference genetically between the Ancients and modern man."

Stauffer was still scowling and Goldwyn attempted to placate him with additional details to get his analytical mind engaged. "After our teams were finished with their work, we loaded up our equipment and records in our scout ships and started the journey back to our home base. But along the way, as I flew over New Mexico, my ship lost power and we crash-landed outside Roswell. Another of our scout ships attempted a rescue mission but it also went down a hundred miles away in the desert. We still don't know what caused the avionics problems, but it appears that there was some kind of magnetic anomaly in the area that somehow affected our flight instrumentation."

"You are behind the Roswell UFO incident?" Stauffer stammered. "Wasn't that all about the recovery of little gray alien bodies with big heads and bug eyes?"

"That was the story that eventually came into being. After the public didn't buy into the weather balloon cover story that the Army clumsily issued, the supposed existence of little gray aliens became the core of the Army's systematic program of disinformation. But it was all pure fabrication. It never happened. My copilot and I survived the crash and when the Army deployed a team out to investigate the crash site, they found us and evacuated us to a medical facility where they nursed us back to health. When our own command center became aware of our plight, I was instructed telepathically by Enoch to work with the Americans from the inside rather than only observe from the outside. We negotiated a deal with the U.S. Army to provide them certain advanced technologies if the Army would keep the presence of the Ancients secret. They policed up all of the wreckage of our aircraft and shipped it off to Wright Field in Ohio. When we were sufficiently recovered, we worked with the Army engineers to explain how the technology worked. With us working alongside them, they were able to reverse engineer a great number of technologies that ultimately put them well ahead in the space race and the Cold War."

"How did they allow you to be so involved in all that and you aren't even a citizen of the United States?"

"Oh, but I am. My copilot and I were both sworn in as naturalized citizens in a very private ceremony within a few months of the Roswell crash, and after that, people seemed to lose track of the fact that we were Ancients. The whole program was kept very hush-hush, and today, there isn't anyone left alive on active duty that remembers anything about our origins."

Stauffer was having trouble keeping up with processing all of this new information and its implications, and he stifled his anger and confusion at the surprise revelation of his actual parenthood. Finally he took the conversation back in the direction of where it had started. "And so, sir, just what does this all have to do with why I am getting telepathic interference from Noah?"

"It's really quite simple, Barton." Goldwyn responded. "You have certain telepathic capabilities because you are my biological son. Oh, and there's another reason.... that I think you might find slightly amusing.... Noah is your half-brother."

"What?" Stauffer had just begun to calm down and get adjusted to the idea that Goldwyn was his biological father, and the revelation that Noah was his half-brother got his hair on fire again. "What are you talking about, sir? That doesn't make a lick of sense."

"Actually," Goldwyn beamed, "it makes a great deal of sense. Enoch's son was Methuselah. At the age of 187, Methuselah begat Lamech, and then just another 56 years or so later, Adam, the first patriarch, passed on. After Enoch later departed with the people of Atlantis, his father Jared, his grandfather, Mahalaleel, his great-grandfather, Cainan, and his great-great-grandfather, Enos, who all stayed behind, eventually died, leaving only two living patriarchs, Enoch's son Methuselah and his grandson Lamech, to carry on the patriarchal lineage on the Earth."

"Okay, I think I understand all that so far. So what?" Stauffer was growing impatient with General Goldwyn's roundabout way of laying out all of the details of his story.

"Well, to carry on the patriarchal order, Lamech needed a male heir and, although he and his wife initially produced several daughters early on, they had no sons. And then the couple became infertile and didn't produce any children at all for quite a time. Methuselah began to become concerned about the time that Lamech turned 180 and had still not produced a male heir, and he came to me for counsel. When Atlantis departed, Enoch left me and my stay-behind team in an overwatch position. At the direction of Enoch, and following yet another year of infertility, I stepped in with an assisted conception intervention using my sperm and Lamech's wife's egg and Noah was born just short of a year after that. Noah matured into a bright young man and became an astute merchant. He acquired a great deal of wealth which he used, as instructed, to build an ark. Lamech died just five years before the Flood as the Ark was nearing completion. It was Methuselah's death five years later which actually signaled that the time had arrived for the great Flood intervention. When the rains started, with Lamech and Methuselah now departed, Noah, with his three sons, was the sole surviving patriarch in the lineage down from Adam."

Stauffer didn't quite know how to respond. His mind was working overtime trying to make the connections in how all this new information fit into what he thought he knew about antediluvian times and what his team had learned during the past several months. "But, how does that satisfy the lineage of the patriarchal order. You're not in that lineage."

"Well, Barton, in fact I am.... kind of.... I am Enoch's identical twin brother. He was born five minutes before me, but because he came out first, he had the blessings of primogeniture in the patriarchal order, and I remained in the background supporting him in his work."

"You are the brother of Enoch?" Stauffer sputtered. "This gets more and more complicated each minute."

"Not at all, Barton," General Stauffer replied. "It all fits tightly together once you have all the facts."

Stauffer had a thousand thoughts and ideas swirling around in his head. He ventured yet another question. "If Noah can sense my presence telepathically when I look in on him with my temporal monitor, then I probably shouldn't make the connection anymore."

"Not necessarily, Barton. Nothing happened as a result of your last telepathic connection. Perhaps this is a low-risk situation. But I recognize that it could pose difficulties. So be careful and let me know when you plan to look in on Noah the next time. I'll launch a Minibago in advance of your monitoring, and if we get back feedback after the fact that it has dramatically altered history, I can always launch the emergency response team to scrub your mission beforehand. Is that fair? Are you comfortable with that strategy?"

"Yes, sir," Stauffer responded. "That sounds like it would work.... Uh, sir. Is there anything else you can tell me about our relationship? It raises a ton of questions. I already know that I'm slightly telepathic, at least with Noah. Why can't I hear your thoughts telepathically? And.... am I going to live to be nine hundred years old as well?"

"Those are reasonable questions, Barton," General Goldwyn responded. "We haven't communicated telepathically because I have set a mental block in place that prevents that from happening. As for how long you're going to live, I don't think so. Shortly after you were born, we drew some blood and I ran a series of DNA tests. The tests were inconclusive at the time. Although you have the genes for longevity, they don't appear to be activated."

Stauffer paused and then broached a question that had been troubling him ever since General Goldwyn had revealed that he was an Ancient. "There's one other thing that's been troubling me that doesn't fit in with this whole story."

"What would that be, Barton?" General Goldwyn asked.

"Well, we've seen on the temporal monitors, and experienced firsthand with Melek, that the Ancients were of exceptionally large stature. And although you are a tall man, you aren't a giant like Melek. Why? Why aren't you exceptionally tall like all the other Antediluvians?"

"That's another good question," General Goldwyn chuckled. "When we realized that after the Flood the human race was growing shorter in stature with each successive generation, we realized that our scout teams that had been left in place would soon stick out like a sore thumb and we wouldn't be able to blend into a crowd of people. And so, one of our scientists hit upon the stratagem of using the temporal technology for passing through temporal portals in a series of interdimensionalities which had the net result of compressing our physical stature down considerably. I'm literally not the man I used to be. I'm about two feet shorter than I was when I began this mission. We even had to reconfigure the control panels on some of our aircraft considerably to accommodate our new, diminished size."

"Do you know why the human race started to get shorter in stature and lose their capability for telepathic communication?" Stauffer asked.

"No, Barton, we never did discover that, but we think it had something to do with the minor degradation of our DNA genetic code. About that time, mankind also lost the genes for longevity as well, and the life span of men became greatly reduced from 900+ years to 100+ years."

"Sir, you said something about 'interdimensionalities.' What does that mean? What's that all about?"

General Goldwyn chuckled again and responded, "I don't really understand it myself. It's not my field. One of the scientists on our stay-behind team came up with the idea and put us all through the process. We all went through portals back and forth between certain interdimensionalities and each time we emerged, we were a little shorter. It worked and we were able to continue our mission without being detected due to unnaturally large stature. I'm sorry that I can't explain it any better than that."

"Yes, sir. Thank you.... One more thing, sir. You mentioned that we have had this conversation before. Do you by any chance have a video capture of that so that I can fill in the blanks and better understand all of what's going on here?"

"As a matter of fact," General Goldwyn responded, "I've had a DVD sitting here on my desk for the last several weeks to give to you to review. I was just waiting for the right moment. I guess that moment is now. Here, look it over and if it generates any additional questions, come and see me again. Fair?"

"Yes, sir," Stauffer responded. "Fair. You've given me a lot to think about. I'm certain that I'll be back to talk with you more about it." Stauffer faced about and departed General Goldwyn's office, a dual sense of exhilaration and foreboding titillated his senses sending shivers up his spine.

# Chapter 25

Stauffer and a few of the Crypt team gathered with members of the Repository team in Alice Duerden's office. At Duerden's request, Stauffer stood to address the group. "Thank you all for being here. I need to talk with you concerning a matter that I think is pretty important and significant for our work here. Alice, Hank, and I have been discussing the topic for some time now, and we believe that we need to bring you in on the conversation.... In our Repository and Crypt operations, we have been collecting numerous documents of various kinds.... books, cunabula, scrolls, cuneiform clay and stone tablets, stelae, et cetera. They collectively represent the sum total of all the world's written languages down through the history of mankind. We are making some progress capturing all of these texts digitally, and we have engaged a very capable team of linguists, philologists, etymologists, ethnologists, cryptologists, and historians to translate the texts to put them into a common context. But, I fear that we aren't doing enough."

Stauffer cleared his voice and went on, "We have all these various examples of original source material stored here in the vaults, and Alice tells me that we have accumulated almost two million documents here in the Repository alone. That means that our translation capability is being far outpaced by our ability to accumulate original source material. The work of translation will be on going for years to come as our historian teams try to make sense of all the new material and integrate it into a history that accurately portrays our past."

"The truth of the matter is," Stauffer went on, "that we have a significant amount of material written in languages that we simply don't yet understand. They are, for all intents and purposes, dead languages and we don't know how to decode or translate them. Now, here's my point. Along with our primary mission of filling in the blanks and correcting the distortions of history, we're going to need to provide a resource book of some kind relating all of the world's languages down through time to each other or at least to some core language, so that whoever one day accesses this trove of material we're accumulating will be able to translate and understand it. In short, we need a rather sophisticated 'Rosetta Stone' to facilitate access to and understanding of all the documents we accumulate."

"What do you have in mind, Bart?" Pete Pendelton asked.

"Well, Pete, I'm not quite sure. But let me illustrate why I'm concerned. It happened to me last night when I was chatting with the kids at dinner. Colin was playing with his cell phone and I got annoyed and asked him to hand it to me. When he passed it over to me, I glanced at the screen. This is what I saw." Stauffer walked over to the white board, picked up a dry erase pen and began writing:

## HAD A GR8 TIME LOL. THX 4 UR HELP. CU 2MRW.

As he returned the pen to the tray, Stauffer turned to the group and asked, "Does that make sense to everyone?"

A few hands went up in the air but most of the group clearly didn't understand the text message.

"See, that makes my case. We are in the midst of a great linguistic paradigm shift and social upheaval. The English language is evolving at an accelerating pace away from the language you and I were taught in school. The same thing appears to be happening to all languages around the globe. This text message would make sense to almost anyone under the age of 15 or so, but it was almost totally opaque to me, and apparently to most of you. I asked Colin what LOL meant. He said that it was a short cut for saying "laughing out loud." Curious, I asked him just how many texting shortcuts there were like that. He told me there were probably four or five hundred, maybe more. He showed me where to find a list on the Internet of commonly understood texting abbreviations and shortcuts. I was astounded. It's a whole new language and way of communicating."

Stauffer picked up a stack of folders and passed them around the table to each member of the group. Inside was a stack of papers. Zazworsky immediately started leafing through the papers in his folder, but Stauffer quietly asked everyone to refrain from opening the folders just yet.

"The evolution of language isn't anything new. Language is a living thing, it grows.... adapts.... changes over time. But the language of computers and information technology has greatly accelerated the evolution of our language in just the past thirty years. We have a whole new vocabulary that we use today that a time traveler from the past century simply wouldn't understand. Now, open your folders. On each sheet of paper is an example of written work from earlier times. With Exhibit 1, you have Lincoln's Gettysburg Address, delivered in 1865, about a hundred and fifty years ago. It's pretty understandable, but you need to know what a 'score' is to really understand it. For Exhibit 2, I've included an excerpt from George Washington's Farewell Address, delivered in 1796. You and I can probably follow the address with a fair degree of understanding, but I daresay that the average young person today wouldn't understand the gist of what Washington was trying to convey. Exhibit 3 is an excerpt from Shakespeare's *Hamlet*, written circa 1600. Most of us need a Cliff Notes Study Guide to really understand today anything written by Shakespeare. Exhibit 4 is an excerpt from Chaucer's *The Canterbury Tales*, circa 1400. It is pretty much incomprehensible to anyone today without relying on a full translation into modern English. The same thing goes for Exhibit 5, *Sir Gawain and the Green Knight*, circa 1300. It's totally incomprehensible to the average English reader today. Likewise, Exhibit 6, *The Owl and the Nightingale*, circa 1190 or Exhibit 7, *Beowulf*, circa 1000, written in Old English, the language of the Anglo-Saxons."

Stauffer closed his folder and continued, "Or, take the example of Latin, the universal language of the Roman empire. It didn't take long after the empire's demise before Latin had devolved down into a whole host of Romance languages including modern Spanish, Portuguese, French, Italian, Romanian, and a host of other languages that didn't survive into common usage today, such as Galician, Aragonese, Catalan, Occitan, Friulian, Provençal, and Dalmatian."

"So, where are you going with all this, Bart?" Hank Phillips asked.

"Well, I think that we need a team of very smart individuals, probably a linguist, a philologist, and a paleographer as a minimum, to begin work on compiling our own Rosetta Stone documentation. The original Rosetta Stone was written in three languages from top to bottom on a stone stela: ancient Egyptian hieroglyphics, Demotic script, and Greek script. The stone provided the key to translating those languages from one to another. Without it, scholars wouldn't have been able to translate ancient Egyptian hieroglyphics. The 'Rosetta Stone' I am suggesting would provide a key for translating back and forth between perhaps thousands of languages over thousands of years of time through all the permutations and combinations of evolution that they have undergone. I believe that such a translation aid is important enough to imprint on gold sheets and keep here in a special vault so that the key to translating all of the world's languages as they have evolved is never lost."

Stauffer closed his folder and looked expectantly around the room. He had anticipated a great deal of conversation and input on his suggestion but everyone just sat there in quiet contemplation. Finally, Zazworsky spoke up. "You know, Boss, everyone here in the room speaks several languages because of their academic credentials and professional experience. I may be the dummy in the room on languages. I only speak two, English and treasure. But I see your point. My grandparents were immigrants from Poland and they spoke Polish between themselves in their home until their dying day. I never learned to speak Polish and they had to switch over to broken English to communicate with me. It would be a tragedy to lose that ability to translate any language. But, Boss, that's going to be one thick Rosetta Stone book.... You're going to need a whole bunch of gold to pull it off.... I need to get to work on getting us some more gold right away."

Everyone in the room erupted in laughter as Zazworsky adroitly laid out an unexpected rationale for another treasure hunt. Stauffer laughed and acknowledged, "You just may be right on that one, Ski."

With the ice broken, everyone in the room started exchanging thoughts and ideas and Stauffer let the energy flow without trying to direct or control it. Thirty minutes later, as everyone began to file out of the room, Stauffer walked over to the white board and wrote:

^5

"What does that mean, Boss?" Zazworsky asked.

Stauffer walked back over to Zazworsky and held up the flat of his hand, "High five, Ski. High five."

\* \* \* \* \* \* \* \* \* \* \* \* \* \* \* \* \* \* \* \*

Stauffer sat in his office fingering the DVD General Goldwyn had given him during their last meeting. Goldwyn had indicated that the DVD had a video file of a meeting that they had had a year and a half earlier that was now on another timeline, just before Stauffer had made the decision to retire to spend more time with his family. Stauffer turned the DVD over and over in his hands, wondering whether he should view it or not. He was still very uncomfortable with the notion that General Goldwyn had been the sperm donor that had resulted in his own birth.

After sitting there pondering what to do for over an hour, he finally decided to view the DVD to see what additional information it might hold beyond what General Goldwyn had just told him. He slipped the DVD into the tray on his computer and initiated the video. He was surprised to see that it was a scene recorded in his old office down in the Repository. General Goldwyn had walked in on him as he was using the temporal observation monitor to look at a scene from his boyhood when Stauffer and his family were gathered in his backyard for an evening barbeque. That led to a long conversation about Stauffer's family, and eventually reinforced his own decision to retire.

But the video revealed two important pieces of information that Stauffer hadn't known before. First, there were two additional staff members working down in the Hole, the Repository, or the Crypt, who were assisted-birth hybrids like himself. Goldwyn didn't reveal who they were. Stauffer tried to imagine who they might be.

But the second piece of information was even more startling. On the video, Stauffer had asked General Goldwyn about his family. Stauffer and Gwen had adopted all five of their children. Stauffer asked General Goldwyn if he had interceded with their adoptions. Goldwyn allowed that he had but didn't go into any details. The Stauffers had adopted their children during military assignments in Mexico, Peru, and South Korea. The adoption process had never been easy and Stauffer wondered how Goldwyn might have interceded and why. Those were all questions that Stauffer planned to address to General Goldwyn during their next meeting.

# Chapter 26

*Carlisle Barracks, Pennsylvania, The Crypt, July 23, 2014, 2:30 p.m.*

Stauffer was sitting at his desk working his way down through his in-box when Max Manchester stepped through the open door threshold and entered Stauffer's office. "Am I interrupting, Barton? Do you have a minute to talk?"

Stauffer looked up and grinned. "I always have time for you Max."

"Well, it's not precisely just me," Manchester corrected. "Most of the team is gathered outside and I'd like for them all to come in and stage an impromptu team meeting on the fly. Is that okay with you?"

Stauffer glanced down at his in-box, sighed, and stood up. "Sure, Max. Invite everyone in. I can give you about an hour. Will that be enough?"

"I think so, Barton." As he spoke, Manchester extended his arm out the door and waved the rest of the team on in. They quickly entered and gathered around Stauffer's conference table. As Manchester took his place at the table, he continued, "Most of you don't have any idea why I've asked for this meeting, and I appreciate you all coming on such short notice. But I've discovered an important dynamic in my survey of Atlantis that may have an important bearing on everyone else's survey research work."

"What's it all about, Max?" Stauffer inquired leaning forward in his chair.

"Yeah, Max, did you find an enormous stash of gold and treasure?" Zazworsky spoke up.

"Actually, Ski," Manchester responded. "you're not far off in a round-about kind of way."

Now Manchester had everyone's attention. "Barton, can I pull up a screen capture from our initial short briefing on Atlantis?"

"Sure, Max," Stauffer responded. "Did we miss something important in that first survey?"

289

"Actually, we chanced upon a very important element of the antediluvian narrative that has far-reaching consequences. We just didn't connect the dots at the time."

As an image of Atlantis appeared on the flat screen monitor, Manchester pointed in its direction and continued, "Here's what we saw in that initial survey. When the Atlanteans outgrew the real estate of their island, they simply imported more land by levitating entire mountains of rock and dirt from other continents, moving it long distances through the air, and dumping it around the island to extend it further outward into the sea. They did that quite a few times, and the island was ultimately several times larger than its original configuration when it finally sank beneath the waves."

"Yes, we saw that in the initial scan," Stauffer said. "What did we miss?"

"Well, we missed the blinding glimpse of the obvious. The Ancients had harnessed the technology giving them the ability to levitate and move entire mountains. And they used that ability to enlarge Atlantis. What we missed was how else that ability was later put to use."

Manchester began working through a set of screen captures to illustrate his point as he moved on through his explanation. "The Atlanteans used that capability at times to sheer off mountain tops, leaving a perfectly flat plateau in place on which to build cities, or ceremonial centers, or even aircraft landing pads." Gesturing at the screen, he pointed at a flattened mountaintop in Peru. "Here on the Nazca desert, they sheared off several mountains leaving perfectly flat platforms in place. Modern scientists have long recognized the problem and questioned what happened to all the dirt and rock that was removed. It wasn't just heaped off to the side of the mountain.... It simply isn't anywhere to be found.... It's gone. It's disappeared entirely. The same technique was used at Monte Alban in Mexico and a dozen other sites around the world. The Ancients were simply master earth movers."

"I get your point Max," Stauffer interjected. "But I think we already intuitively understood most of that. What's the new information that's so earth shattering?"

"I'm getting to that right now. As I was conducting follow-up scans to our initial survey, the thought struck me to back track all of the aircraft that converged on Atlantis just before the mother ship lifted off leading the entire fleet into the sky. I back-scanned using the temporal monitors to see where all the smaller ships had flown in from. Clearly, the Atlantean civilization wasn't confined to just the island. In fact, I had suspicions that it extended much more throughout other parts of the world."

"That idea is provocative, Max," Dr. Campbell said. "What did you find?"

"That's precisely why I've asked you all to gather here for this meeting. I found that there were isolated colonies of the Atlantis culture, some of them quite extensive, scattered all over the world. They were generally located in remote areas where they didn't intermix with other population centers. They displayed all of the advanced technologies which we saw in our initial scans of Atlantis, but here's the surprise. As these dispersed colonies prepared to evacuate their community centers and join Atlantis as it departed, they went through a systematic process of destroying everything before they left. They executed a scorched-earth policy. They apparently didn't want to leave anything behind as evidence of their having been there. And so they simply destroyed it all using energy weapons or buried it under massive amounts of rubble, dirt and rock."

As Manchester spoke, the video capture on the monitor showed several Atlantean airships maneuvering a very large mountain through the air until it hovered directly above a great city. Then, almost in slow motion, the mountain slowly settled to the ground, covering up the city and its environs under many hundreds of feet of rock and dirt. Once the mountain had settled, the airships flew the perimeter inspecting the effectiveness of their efforts. There was one small pyramidal platform sticking up out of the pile, and one of the airships flew off and returned with another small mountain of dirt and covered up the exposed structures the rest of the way.

Manchester continued, "Now, doing back-scans, I did a brief survey of all of the sites that the Atlanteans destroyed or hid. I counted a total of 135 advanced population centers. All of them were characterized by elaborate community networks and groupings of step pyramids and pyramidal platforms. All of them were destroyed or hidden as the colonies loaded up in their airships and joined the Atlantis mother ship out in the Atlantic as it lifted off."

"Are you saying, Max, that there are numerous archaeological remnants of colonies of Atlantis spread out across the world today buried under mountains of rubble that the Atlanteans dumped on them to hide their existence?" Maggie Martinez asked.

"That's precisely what I'm saying. I've posted the coordinates of all of the sites I surveyed on the classified intranet to let you know what sites there are in each of your sectors of responsibility. No one is left out. There's a little bit here for everyone and I suspect that it represents low-hanging fruit for us to mount on-the-ground artifact recovery missions before everything is buried. Actually, it may even be possible to recover material even after it is buried. I haven't run any tests using the time portals on sites buried deep underground, but I think that it deserves some kind of a field test to prove out the concept."

Everyone around the table was fidgeting, clearly excited to get back to their own labs to check out the sites Manchester had identified for their areas. Stauffer recognized the excitement and brought the meeting to a hasty conclusion. "Okay, folks, here's how we're going to approach this one. I'd like all of you to survey the sites that Max has identified for us and perhaps even develop snatch lists of significant artifacts you think we might be able to recover. Meanwhile, I'll run this by General Goldwyn to get his guidance on what he wants us to do. If he gives his go-ahead for on-the-ground recovery missions, we can begin preparing operations plans to pull it off. We'll need to organize five-person recovery teams to do that, so be thinking of how we might most effectively organize. Let's meet back here in my office tomorrow morning at 0900 to discuss where we're at. Everyone come prepared to input what you've discovered so far."

Everyone jumped to their feet and practically raced out the door to get back to their labs, leaving Stauffer and Manchester standing there by the conference table.

"Max," Stauffer acknowledged, "That was some mighty fine detective work. Thanks for sharing all of that information with us. It's bound to have an important impact on our work from here on out."

"Thanks, Barton, but actually, I wasn't quite finished with my presentation. There's more."

"More?"

"Yes, can you spare another fifteen minutes or so?"

"Sure thing, Max. What else do you have?"

"Well, I think I just better show you."

Manchester hit another key on the control keyboard and a new scene appeared on the flat screen monitor. It was a view of an extensive Atlantean settlement dotted with numerous pyramidal platforms, and an enormous step pyramid in the center of the array with an imposing cube-shaped structure on its summit.

"What's this, Max?"

"It's a ceremonial center here in the northeastern part of the present-day United States. It's somewhat smaller than most of the other Atlantean colony settlements, but it appears that it held a high significance for the culture. The step pyramid is mostly solid but there are passageways and vaulted rooms honeycombed throughout. That boxy-looking structure on top of the pyramid appears to be a repository of sorts, housing all kinds of advanced technology artifacts as well as a large collection of scrolls and metal plate books. There's also a large ceramic urn in the center of the enclosure set upright on a stone pedestal. Although I'm still no expert on estimating size for antediluvian objects through the temporal monitors, I estimate the size of the urn to be at least three or four feet in diameter and about five feet tall. It's a really big urn."

"Do you know what's inside it?" Stauffer asked.

"No, I was planning to do a back-scan to see when the urn was installed in the enclosure but I haven't got to that yet. I've decided that it would be best to leave that task up to you."

"Why, Max? What's so special about the site or the urn for me?"

"Here, let me show you." Manchester started inputting data on the keyboard and the view of the pyramid and cubical enclosure on top grew smaller as the perspective from the temporal monitor soared into the sky. "Here, let's leave it at one thousand feet so that you can see the whole area at the same time. Now let me start moving forward through time." As Manchester spoke Atlantean aircraft moved in from several different directions and dumped several mountains of rock and dirt on the site. Manchester pointed at the screen and continued, "I'm going to leap over the Flood years. On the other side, the site looks somewhat different now that the floodwaters have smoothed out the contours and sharp edges of the rubble dumped on the site."

"Yes," Stauffer acknowledged, "And I can see that there's no observable trace of the Atlantean colony left at all. They did their job well hiding the place."

"That's right, Barton," Manchester agreed. "The whole area is buried under at least two or three hundred feet of dirt and rock. All you can see is the trace of the pyramidal structures as high points on the new, modified landscape. Now, I'm going to put the temporal scan into high gear and rapidly move into the future so you can see how the appearance of the site evolved through the years."

Manchester pressed a couple more keys and the image of the site began to change and evolve as grasses, and brush, and forests grew in rapid succession. Rivers and streams cut through the valleys and ridges, changing the shape of the landscape as they went. On the side of the screen, Stauffer tracked the date as the scene changed and moved forward into the future. As the scan approached the modern era, the site took on a vague sense of familiarity for Stauffer. Manchester sensed the recognition and slowed down the progression of time on the monitor as it moved through the last hundred years into their own day.

"Is it beginning to look familiar to you yet, Barton?" Manchester prodded with a sardonic grin on his face.

All of a sudden, it hit Stauffer. It was Kendor Summit, the residential area built on a ridgeline in North Middleton overlooking Carlisle and the Cumberland Valley where his house was located.

"Stop, Max." Stauffer blurted out as he stared at the screen. "Are you telling me that my house is built on top of an antediluvian city?"

"That's it, Barton. I've checked and double-checked the coordinates. Your house is built precisely on top of the blockhouse on the summit of the tallest step pyramid. It's about 200 feet below you today, but.... there it is."

As he considered this new information, Stauffer had a flashback to his conversation with General Bustamante in Peru and his comment that you can't dig a hole anywhere along the Peruvian coast without encountering a tomb of some kind. "Tell me, Max," Stauffer probed, "you didn't by any chance encounter any tombs or burial chambers on the pyramid as you conducted your survey, did you?"

"As a matter of fact, Barton, I did. There's a large stone sarcophagus situated just a few feet below the floor of the stone blockhouse."

"Any idea of who might be buried in the sarcophagus?" Barton asked.

"Not a clue Barton. But it kind of gives you food for thought, doesn't it."

"You have no idea, Max."

\* \* \* \* \* \* \* \* \* \* \* \* \* \* \* \* \* \* \* \*

"Sir," Stauffer said at their next weekly meeting, "I reviewed that DVD you gave me and it raises several questions I'd like to run by you."

"Shoot, Barton," General Goldwyn responded, obviously in a very good mood. "What have you got?"

"Well, sir, on the video you said that there were three assisted-birth hybrids on the staff down in the Hole or Repository. I'm one of the them. Do you mind telling me who the other two are?"

"No, Barton. I don't mind at all. But you can't tell them. They don't know and I don't think it will do them any good if they were to find out."

"Well then, sir, who are they?"

"Bob Zazworsky and Bill Tipton."

"Ski and Bill?" How is it that both of them ended up assigned down here in the Hole?"

"Well, Barton, much like I did for you, I intervened in their military careers along the way to ensure that they eventually would be in a position to work for me when we finally put together this temporal research facility down here below Carlisle Barracks. Bob was the first one I hired. He has been working for me for a long time now. You came along later.... twice. After working a variety of black assignments inside the Beltway, I was finally able to get Bill up here to the Hole."

"And they don't know that they're hybrids with the Ancients?"

"No, Barton, they don't, and please help me keep it that way."

"Yes sir. Close hold on that. But there's another thing. On the video, you alluded to the fact that you had assisted Gwen and me with the adoption of the Five Cs. Just what was that all about? Are our kids assisted-birth hybrids too?"

"Actually, Barton, some of the them are. Two of them are assisted-birth hybrids, two are normal modern humans, but one of them is an Ancient, the child of two of my advanced party team members who were killed in an aviation accident. I needed adoptive parents and a good home and family to raise the child. You and Gwen were the natural choice. I pulled strings on the others to get them all moving your way."

"Which is which?" Stauffer asked.

"I'm not going to answer that one, Barton. It will be better that you don't know that for now. I want you to be able to continue thinking about the children all in the same way.... Do you have any other issues we need to talk about?"

General Goldwyn's abrupt change of subject signaled to Stauffer that the conversation on that topic was closed for now. Stauffer took the cue and continued, "Well, sir, I've just had a most disturbing conversation with Max Manchester. He described to me how the Atlanteans destroyed or buried all vestiges of their civilization before they departed."

"Yes, that's right, Barton," General Goldwyn responded. "We did. We wanted to make sure that none of our advanced technology would fall into the wrong hands and be used for destructive purposes."

"Yes, I understand that. But Max showed me how one of the Atlantean colony sites was buried under mountains of rubble and broken shale, covering over even the centerpiece pyramid that rose up from the main plaza of the site...."

"Yes, that happened at quite a few sites...."

"Sir, please hear me out," Stauffer interrupted. "The site I'm referring to is apparently buried deep beneath Kendor Summit today in North Middleton, and my house is situated directly over the pinnacle of the pyramid. Did you know about all that? More importantly, did you have anything to do with this?" Stauffer was clearly perturbed.

General Goldwyn started to respond and then abruptly changed his mind. He paused for a moment apparently not quite sure what to say next. After a few moments, he finally continued, choosing his words carefully. "Barton, perhaps we ought to have a candid conversation about all this. Yes, I was aware of the Atlantean site buried deep beneath your subdivision. In fact, I had something to do with burying it in ancient days in the first place. More recently, in modern days, I also had something to do with the initial surveying and subdividing the lots for the whole development when it was originally laid out some fifty years ago. I knew exactly where the pyramid was buried deep beneath the development, and I ensured a special organization for the lots, with the lot for your house situated directly above it."

"But with what purpose, sir?" Stauffer asked querulously.

"The pyramid not only provided the final resting place for one of the great noblemen of our society, but the block house enclosure on top of the pyramid is a small repository, housing some of the most important technological artifacts of antediluvian times. It also houses a modest library of antediluvian books and scrolls and a fairly substantial collection of gold and silver artifacts that would make even Bob Zazworsky drool."

"Max Manchester mentioned something about an enormous urn on a carved stone pedestal in the center of the repository," Stauffer added. "What's that all about."

"I'm glad you asked, Barton," General Goldwyn responded. "That would be what's referred to in history and mythology today as 'Pandora's Box.'"

"Box, sir?" Stauffer asked.

"Yes, what we call Pandora's Box was actually a large urn or jar."

"What's in it, sir?"

"It's a very large urn, almost five feet in diameter. Inside is a large inner golden framework which houses tens of thousands of crystal shards that were used for recording data and information. It represents the very technology that Hank Phillips' team is working on for solid state crystal data storage today."

"It sounds a lot like the Superman movie where Superman goes to his Fortress of Solitude and becomes acquainted with his father, Jor-El, when he activates one of the crystals in the technology console."

"Did you like that movie? One of my team members worked on the script and the special effects to get mankind thinking today about crystal storage. The whole project had very salutary effects."

Stauffer paused for a moment, but passed that by quickly, continuing his line of questioning. "Are you telling me that buried deep beneath my house is Pandora's Box.... er, Jar.... with the history of the Ancients and all your technology stored on the crystals inside?"

"That's it, Barton."

"But why would you engineer it so that my house would eventually be built right on top of it?"

"The fundamental reason for ensuring that your house lot was directly over the pyramid was that on top of the cube at the apex of the four sides of the stepped pyramid on which it rests was a power generator, an emitter of enormous energy. We disabled it for the most part before the pyramid was covered over. But even today, it emits a certain limited amount of energy."

Stauffer was beginning to become uneasy and concerned about this new revelation.

General Goldwyn sensed his discomfort and asked, "Do you remember the numerous inspections you had to go through when you first bought the house from the Zazworskys? One of those tests was the standard test for the presence of radon in the basement. Remember? The meter readings were high and they had to install a special radon mitigation system to bring the levels down. That was most likely a function of the energy emitter on top of the pyramid buried deep beneath the house. It wasn't actually radon but an energy source that registers a similar reading."

"But isn't the radiation harmful to people? Will it hurt my family?" Stauffer protested. "Why didn't you shut down the power source all the way before you buried it?"

"To answer your first question, no.... it won't hurt you or your family. In fact, we believe it could prove beneficial and salutary to you all. Because the emitter was part of a universal power distribution network of similar emitters situated on pyramids scattered around the world in precise locations," Goldwyn explained, "the emitter needed to remain at least partially active, if only temporarily, to complete the network. My stay-behind team relies on the network power grid for power and navigation as we move around the world in our aircraft monitoring mankind's activities today."

"Why hasn't the pyramid ever been discovered before?"

"Well, it is buried pretty deep underground. Wells in the area only go down a hundred and fifty feet or so, still well above the level of the step pyramid and pyramidal platforms in the complex buried deep below. To be fair, Bob Zazworsky almost caught onto its existence when he and his wife lived there in the house."

"He did? What happened?"

"Bob was out working in his vegetable garden one morning when he came across a hole dug in the lower end of the garden by a ground hog. The ground hog had excavated quite a pile of broken shale hidden under a canopy of horseradish leaves, and when Bob discovered the hole, he started clearing away the debris to see if he could get at the ground hog. As he was scraping back the broken shale, he discovered a small golden pendant from the step pyramid's blockhouse repository. Apparently, the groundhog's system of tunnels went much deeper than I would have ever imagined and went all the way down to the blockhouse."

"What did Ski do with the pendant?"

"Well, that's the good part. Ski brought it to me the following Monday morning to report it and suggested that we do some excavating there on the hill in your back yard."

"As soon as Bob left my office, I did a little temporal intervention on my own and went out earlier that morning while it was still dark and retrieved the pendant before Bob could discover it. Then I used my temporal monitor to explore the labyrinth of tunnels that the groundhogs had dug through the years and, using time portals, I filled up all the lower tunnels with quick-setting cement."

"That took care of the issue for the moment but now, here you are, asking me pretty much the same questions as Bob did."

"Are you going to go back in time and work another intervention to wipe the memory of all this from my mind?"

"No, Barton. I don't think so. In fact, I'm going to suggest that you mount an on-the-ground recovery mission into the repository blockhouse to retrieve the urn and all of the other artifacts and get them safely stored in a vault in the lower Waxahachie ring."

"Will my historians have opportunity to examine the artifacts or do I need to keep this from the rest of the team?"

"What do you want to do, Barton?" Goldwyn asked.

Barton was surprised that General Goldwyn would even ask the question and he didn't have an immediate response. "Whew, sir, could you give me a little time to think about that one and I'll get back with you?"

"Take all the time you need, Barton."

# Chapter 27

*Carlisle, Pennsylvania, July 23, 2014, 8:35 p.m.*

Stauffer sat at his desk in his home office, leaning over his computer keyboard and staring fixedly at the monitor in front of him as he worked on personal emails. As he finished up the last one, he went back to the desktop and activated the icon for Google Earth. As the sphere of the earth came into view, he typed in the street address for his house and he was quickly looking at a satellite view of his housing area. From 10,000 feet, he could see how the Kendor Summit residential area today was nestled in an oxbow of the Conodoguinet Creek as it meanders across that portion of the Cumberland Valley.

Zooming in on the property itself down to 1,000 feet, Stauffer was amused once again that Ski's vegetable garden was so plainly visible from space. Before they had bought the place from the Zazworskys, Ski and Fran put in long hours in the garden, raising vegetables and herbs for their summer and fall table. Stauffer always knew when the harvest had begun because Ski would show up in his office with a big bag of zucchini, which the Stauffer family always appreciated. Barton loved zucchini bread and Gwen made stir fry with it several times a week. The children liked it all. One of the major selling points in buying the Zazworsky's house was that they could continue the tradition of raising zucchini and other vegetables right there on Ski's garden plot.

Zazworsky had related to him that he had labored hard for an entire month hauling in rocks to build an above-ground vegetable garden plot when they first moved in. When he was laying out the plot, he used a rope tied to a center stake to mark off a perfectly round outline on the ground. But as he started digging into the ground to place and anchor the rocks, the shape of the garden took on a life of its own, and it ended up looking more like something else entirely, certainly not a perfect circle. Stauffer zoomed in to examine more closely the odd shape of the garden. It wasn't round. It looked very much like the actual shape of a real human heart. Stauffer switched over to Google and checked out a couple of graphic images of hearts.... almost exactly same outline. "Odd," Stauffer muttered. After they had bought the home, Stauffer himself had spent quite a bit of time working in the yard planting additional trees and shrubs, and he knew full well what lay below the thin surface dressing of topsoil.... a mountain of broken shale. But Stauffer knew he needed to go back to the office in the Crypt to use a temporal monitor to examine what lay buried under that.

Before he left Google Earth, Stauffer zoomed back in so that he could just see the circle of houses in the neighborhood that surrounded their house. It looked like the other homes in the neighborhood had circled the wagons leaving his home in the exact center. He zoomed back out again to see if there were any repetitions of that pattern elsewhere in the development. There weren't. He zoomed out more and navigated over to nearby developments for a few minutes to see if there were any other houses arranged in that peculiar stand-off position. Again, nothing. Stauffer zoomed back in on the house, just so that he could see the two lots that comprised his property. As he moved around the yard, the elevation indicator registered the changes and he got a feel for the slope down the hill from the back porch. He couldn't really get a visual three-dimensional feel for elevation from the two-dimensional image that Google projected, and it absolutely flattened out the house so that you couldn't really see it in context of the setting on the top of the ridge. In his mind, Stauffer tried to visualize the slope of the steep steps leading up the front face of the step pyramid that lay buried deep beneath the mountain of broken shale.

Later that day, Stauffer made his decision to mount a comprehensive recovery mission of the site and informed General Goldwyn. The next morning in the Crypt, Stauffer briefed Zazworsky on what lay beneath the mountain of shale under Kendor Summit and asked him to take charge of a team to run survey scans scoping underground with the temporal monitors to see what they could discover. When he told him that it potentially involved Pandora's Box, and that there was probably a cache of golden artifacts and treasure involved, Zazworsky practically ran out of his office to form a team and get started. Within two days, he had a detailed recovery plan already elaborated and the team was ready to go. General Goldwyn quickly gave his approval and the mission went ahead as planned.

* * * * * * * * * * * * * * * * * * * * * *

Two months later, Stauffer assembled the entire Crypt team in his office around his conference table. General Goldwyn sat at the head of the table with Stauffer seated on one side and Zazworsky on the other. Stauffer began the presentation. "Sir, two months ago, Max Manchester alerted us to the phenomenon of the Atlanteans burying their cities and pyramids and technology before they departed with Atlantis. This is the first recovery mission we've mounted based upon that information. There are several hundred similar sites around the world that were buried by the departing Atlanteans. This first recovery mission was designed to help us understand the extent of our possibilities here and to fine tune our temporal technology to recover whatever artifacts that presented themselves. I assigned Bob Zazworsky to work with a small team to explore and recover artifacts from an ancient Atlantean site right here in our own neighborhood. I'll let Ski continue from here."

Zazworsky motioned to the flat screen monitor as Maggie Martinez worked the computer keyboard. A picture of the antediluvian site appeared on the screen. "General Goldwyn, Colonel Stauffer alerted me to the possibility of a rich recovery mission of an Atlantean site right here in the North Middleton area buried deep beneath a thick layer of broken shale under the house that I used to live in that I sold to the Stauffers a while back. That made it all the more exciting and personal that we do a good job on this first Atlantean recovery mission. I formed a five-person team with Bill Tipton, Pete Pendleton, Ken Red Elk and Maggie Martinez. We started our survey scans going back to the time before the site was buried by the Atlanteans. It turned out to be a tremendously important site with targets of opportunity everywhere. There were hundreds of pyramidal platforms and several prominent step pyramids surrounding an enormous step pyramid positioned in the middle of the central plaza. Surrounding the whole ceremonial site was a large community of public buildings and private residences. In all, there were approximately 1,500 structures in the city that we needed to survey and discover what the Atlanteans buried and perhaps see what they were so anxious to hide."

As Zazworsky delivered his briefing, Martinez maneuvered the scene on the monitor showing a panoramic view of all of the extensive site from a high altitude perspective and then zoomed in on the individual structures almost at ground level.

Zazworsky continued, "We divided it all up between the five of us so each of us had about 300 buildings to check out initially. We were quickly overwhelmed with the task. We discovered that literally every structure had intriguing artifacts and technology that we believed to be important enough for separate recovery missions. Although they took a lot with them when they departed, the Atlanteans left a lot of stuff behind as well. We quickly realized that this operation was going to require everyone in the Crypt to get involved. We divided up the site into sectors and everyone in the Crypt worked with us surveying each structure individually and making lists of likely recovery targets. The block building on the big step pyramid in the center of the plaza took the longest to survey. It was much larger than it looked on our temporal monitors, and it was filled with artifacts that we ultimately targeted for recovery. We observed a substantial library of scrolls and metal books made of copper, silver, and gold, numerous technological devices for which we haven't yet figured out their purpose, numerous chests of jewels and golden artifacts positioned on display around the room, and a large earthen jar in the center of the structure that Colonel Stauffer suggested may be the fabled Pandora's Box."

Zazworsky paused and looked over expectantly at General Goldwyn, anticipating that he would ask about why Pandora's Box was really a large earthen jar. General Goldwyn just sat there smiling and when he realized that Zazworsky was waiting for some response from him, he simply motioned with his hand to continue the briefing.

"Once we completed our initial survey scans and developed lists of prime recovery targets, we divided up into our standard five-person recovery team configurations with backup logistics teams for decon and recovery support in the time labs. Everyone in the Crypt rotated through the teams, and everyone had an opportunity for on-the-ground experience and providing logistics support in the labs and moving recovered artifacts to our inventory and classification vaults."

Zazworsky paused as Martinez cycled through a number of stills showing examples of some of the artifacts that had been recovered. When Martinez nodded back to him, Zazworsky continued the briefing. "When the Atlanteans who occupied this city were preparing to depart, they completely evacuated everyone from the site about four hours before several enormous mountains of rock and dirt were floated in to bury the place. The people had previously loaded up in flying craft and had flown off eastward in the direction of Atlantis before it was buried, and the site was essentially left unobserved and unsecured. We had to do the recovery operations entirely inside the site structures during that four-hour time window to ensure that any Ancients who might be hovering in the air didn't detect what we were doing as they were preparing to bury the place."

"And your entire operation went unobserved and undetected?" General Goldwyn asked.

"Yes, sir." Zazworsky responded. "As near as we can tell, no one ever suspected that we were stripping the inside of the buildings before they could bury them. The hardest part of the overall operation was evacuating artifacts from the block building on top of the great step pyramid in just four hours. One team couldn't pull it off alone and so we set up four separate teams operating simultaneously out of four separate time labs. Each team worked one side of the block building removing artifacts, moving toward the center of the enclosure as they went. When at last all of the smaller artifacts had been removed, all that remained was the enormous urn in the center of the room. We had one of the teams open up a double-wide portal and we brought in a big fork lift with a modified solid metal plate that we slid under the urn as team members tilted it slightly. Once we had it on the lift, we positioned team members to steady the jar on all sides to ensure that it stayed upright on the lift as it moved slowly back across the room and through the double-wide."

"And was it indeed Pandora's Box?" General Goldwyn interrupted. "What was in it?"

"We didn't know what to expect and so, after decontaminating the outside of the urn, we moved it to a solitary vault and had two team members suit up in heavy duty hazmat suits to remove the lid. It was sealed with pitch and it took some effort to get the lid off. But our efforts turned out to be overkill. There wasn't anything sinister inside at all. What they found was a metal frame housing thousands of elongated crystals. When we had determined that there wasn't a hazmat or physical threat, we brought in Hank Phillips to look over the array. He thinks it's a crystal library, a collection of records which the Ancients recorded in some way on crystal shards. At his request, we moved the entire jar up to his crystal research lab for further study."

Hank Phillips spoke up from where he sat. "From their initial examination, my people believe that this is indeed an ancient library recorded on crystal shards. There was a small device in the center of the array that we believe may be a reader-player of some kind that was used to access and extract information, but we haven't figured out yet how it works. We haven't even figured out how to turn it on."

"Sounds like you're on the right track though," General Goldwyn observed. Turning back to Zazworsky, he asked, "So where are we at now, Bob?"

Zazworsky responded quickly, referring to his notes. "Sir, the overall recovery mission took seven weeks and two days, during which time we recovered over thirty thousand planned targets and another five hundred or so targets of opportunity. Most of the artifacts are small household items, but there is also a large quantity of tools, weaponry, manufacturing implements, and what we think is a storehouse of mechanical and electrical spare parts. The tedious part of the operation was moving everything through decon as we brought it back through the portals. Our inventory and classification vaults are totally packed, and it will take our inventory technologists months to examine and classify everything. Meanwhile, the Crypt historians are trying to make sense out of all the artifacts that have passed through inventory and classification thus far. Most of the historian vaults are stacked high with artifacts and they've been checking them out trying to figure out what purpose they might have served. We have a special team of technicians and engineers working on the technological items. There's a whole passel of devices that we don't have a clue of what they might have been used for. Figuring that out just by examining the artifacts could take quite a long time so I've got some of our team members going back using the temporal monitors and trying to observe the people who lived there in the complex using these things in practical applications. Watching and recording how the items were used should give us a better idea of what they were all about."

"Good thinking!" General Goldwyn commented enthusiastically. "Bob, you and your team.... everyone here in the Crypt.... has done an incredible job on this recovery mission. I've been tracking its progress as you recorded your inventories of recovered items on the classified intranet." General Goldwyn paused and then continued slowly with a twinkle in his eye, "Bob, there is one particular item which I would like to see. Do you think you could bring it in here for me to examine more closely?"

"Sure thing, sir." Zazworsky responded. "Which one?"

"It's listed as item 43C-554 on the intranet inventory list. It was one of the items removed from the block building on the step pyramid in the center of the main plaza."

"Yes, sir. That would be one of the artifacts that Sammy Woo's Charlie Team brought back on Day 43."

Woo was already on his feet and moving toward the door. "I'm on it, sir. Be right back."

Everyone in the room began chatting quietly as they waited for Woo to return. Five minutes passed.... Ten.... Finally, twelve minutes later, Woo came running breathlessly back into the room. "Sorry it took me so long, sir. The inventory and classification specialists are knee deep in artifacts and it took them a few minutes to locate it."

Woo held out a shiny bronze object and handed it to General Goldwyn. Goldwyn took it in his hands and held it up close to his face to examine. A smile crept across his weathered face as he turned it over in his hands. After a few minutes, he announced, "I think that I would like to examine this a little while longer in my office. Would you please sign it out to me for now. I'll get it back to you later."

Stauffer went over to his desk and quickly filled out a form and signed it. Turning back to General Goldwyn, he said, "You're all set, sir. Let me know when you are finished examining the artifact and I'll come up to get it and bring it back to the vaults."

General Goldwyn stood and nodded to Stauffer. "Thank you, Barton. I'll do that. Turning to Zazworsky, he said, "Bob, again, great work on this project. Thanks to all of you for a very nicely executed piece of work."

General Goldwyn abruptly turned, cradling the bronze artifact in his hands, and moved quickly to the door and left the office vault. Everyone in the room was puzzled by his unexpected departure.

Zazworsky looked at Stauffer and whined, "But I wasn't quite finished with my briefing yet."

\* \* \* \* \* \* \* \* \* \* \* \* \* \* \* \* \* \* \* \* \*

Several days later, Stauffer reported to General Goldwyn's office for his weekly meeting. As he entered the office, he saw the bronze artifact sitting on General Goldwyn's desk.

Stauffer walked over to the desk and motioned to the artifact. "Do you mind if I pick it up, sir?"

"Not at all, Barton," General Goldwyn responded. "Go right ahead."

Stauffer picked it up and turned it over in his hands. It appeared to be a brass sphere, about the size of a softball. Around the circumference of the sphere, there was a series of crystal surfaces that looked like they might have been readout screens. There was also a line of indented buttons and dials set above and below the circle of screens. On each pole there was a circular indentation with floating needles under transparent covers. Stauffer turned it over and over in his hands, trying to get a feel for the device's purpose. Finally he looked up and shrugged.

"Did you figure out yet what your artifact is, sir?" Stauffer inquired.

"Oh I know precisely what it is, Barton. I should know.... I invented it."

"You what?" This revelation took Stauffer by surprise and he struggled to process its implications. "You invented it?.... Well.... good.... then, just what is it, sir?"

"Good question, Barton, but difficult to answer. It's many things. It's a multipurpose device. I guess it corresponds most closely to the modern smart phone with communication, auto-location, photography, computation, memory storage, and chronograph functionalities. This device was also capable of energy transmission, levitation, precious metal detection, telepathic encryption, and a number of other functionalities that are difficult to explain. All in all, it was a pretty handy piece of technology. Once it was introduced in the marketplace, it became a runaway best seller. This is one of the original beta versions and was on display in the museum."

"Museum, sir?"

"Yes, Barton. The block building on top of the step pyramid was a cross between a museum, a library, and a research center."

Stauffer processed that new information and stored it for future reference. "Does the device still work?"

"Yes, it should. It's practically brand new, but it only works in a limited way. The antediluvian energy transmission systems that it depended on simply don't exist today. It's drawing power right now from the energy transmission apparatus on the pyramid buried beneath your house in North Middleton."

"You had energy transmission and reception capabilities to run your technologies?"

"That we did, Barton. One of our scouts.... you know him as Nikola Tesla.... tried to introduce energy transmission technology at the beginning of the last century, but he couldn't generate sufficient interest to get it moving."

"Tesla was an Ancient?"

"Yes, Barton. He was one of the members of my stay-behind team. He was a brilliant scientist in his own right, and I put him on special assignment during the last century as modern researchers began to develop and exploit the generation of electricity. He was very successful in some endeavors. He was able to steer electrical transmission away from the direct current approach favored by

Edison to alternating current applications, a much better solution for long distance wire transmission."

Stauffer sat down hard in the easy chair in front of General Goldwyn's desk, a feeling of despondency rapidly overwhelming him. "Sir, I get the idea that we are not responsible for most of the new technologies introduced in the past century."

"Oh no, Barton. Your generation has demonstrated extraordinary creativity and inventiveness during the past two hundred years. My team has only attempted to steer you on a couple of matters."

"Like what, sir?"

"The atomic bomb is a good example."

"The atomic bomb?.... Nuclear weapons?"

"That's right. Your own scientists developed the technology for generating nuclear energy and its subsequent specialized application for nuclear weapons. My team just tried to steer development and implementation efforts to keep you from destroying yourselves in the process like the people of my generation were about to do when Atlantis fled and my team was left behind to attempt to minimize the destructive power of the warring nations. But our mandate was very limited."

"Limited?" Stauffer asked.

"Yes, we are prohibited from meddling in the affairs of people as they develop into cultures and civilizations. It's kind of like the Prime Directive on the Star Trek series. In fact, it was one of my team members who worked that idea with Gene Roddenberry into the first season's writer's guide, and it became a fixed part of the founding rules for the Star Trek franchise universe. Essentially, it espouses the guiding principle of self-determination.... that man has the right of free will to live as he will, free from any outside interference or intervention."

"How well has your team done at exercising restraint in interfering in the affairs of us mere mortals?" Stauffer asked somewhat sarcastically.

Goldwyn ignored the sarcasm and answered straightforwardly, "Actually, not too badly, Barton. Throughout the ages, we've allowed mankind to do some pretty stupid and horrendous things that we could have easily intervened in and hindered or stopped altogether. You can't imagine how difficult it was to stand by and watch Vlad the Impaler hoist thousands of people on the points of sharpened stakes, or ritual human sacrifice on Mesoamerican pyramids, or the Nazis' slaughter of millions in the Holocaust death camp ovens." Goldwyn paused as he recalled all of the horrors he had experienced first-hand during his lifetime. Turning to address Stauffer directly, he lowered his voice and responded quietly, "No, I think we've done quite well in keeping out of your affairs along the way. Oh, we did get involved during World War II when mankind began to develop weapons of mass destruction capable of destroying the world. That **was** part of our mandate. Many Nazi super weapons on the drawing boards were never finished because my team members interfered in some way or the other with the project development. We managed to sabotage a couple of particularly heinous weapons of mass destruction they were working on."

"But you allowed the US to develop and drop atomic bombs on Hiroshima and Nagasaki," Stauffer pointed out. "Why?"

"Yes we did," General Goldwyn responded. "It wasn't my call. I would have tried to hinder the American development of nuclear weapons as well, but I was overruled by Enoch. He felt that modern man needed to see the horror that such weapons can cause to serve as a warning to not go down that road."

"That approach hasn't seemed to work out very well in retrospect," Stauffer observed solemnly.

"No, Barton, it hasn't.... not very well at all. These days, it's a full-time job for us to monitor all of the rogue nations and terrorist groups that are trying to acquire nuclear weapons and delivery systems technology. Humankind has come close a couple of times in the last fifty years to crossing over the line and we just barely held it all in check."

Stauffer considered Goldwyn's last comment and related it to his own participation as a custodial officer during the Cold War, overseeing several bunkers of tactical nuclear weapons and how uncomfortable he had been during the four years he was on that assignment that things could quickly get out of control. He pushed that thought back into the remote recesses of his mind and changed the subject. "But, sir, what about all of the UFO reports of alien abductions and animal mutilations and such? Doesn't that constitute interference with our development and violating your Prime Directive?"

"Yes, it does, Barton. But that isn't us. In fact, it's part of my stay-behind team's mission to provide a protective buffer force against alien intergalactic ships crossing the cosmos and coming here to Earth to work their mischief among the human race. Earth is essentially a quarantined planet. All of those reports of sightings of strange looking alien beings and abductions and human experimentation..... that's part of what we're here to try to prevent. Unfortunately, it's hard to sustain a completely effective quarantine shield on Earth against all potential intergalactic interlopers. And unfortunately, a couple of alien races have evaded our defenses and have struck secret agreements with certain unscrupulous government officials here in the United States and other nations around the world, exchanging rights to human experimentation and mineral exploitation for advanced weaponry technology. My stay-behind team knows where and when it's taking place, but it's extremely difficult to eliminate the embedded threat surreptitiously.... It's a never-ending challenge and we continue to work at it."

Stauffer thought about what General Goldwyn had just said but he didn't entirely track the logic. "Sir, if reinforcing the quarantine of Earth against the encroachment of alien beings from other worlds is one of your stay-behind team's primary missions, it raises a serious question. I know that there are billions of galaxies out there in the universe, each one with perhaps billions of stars, and many of which may have inhabitable planets in orbit around them. It stands to reason that many of them may have spawned intelligent life forms, some of which may have advanced technologies sufficient to allow them to travel around the cosmos. But just why would any alien race out there take an interest in planet Earth? With so many potential planets in the cosmos to exploit, just what is there about Earth that might attract aliens across the vastness of space?"

"Once again, Barton, you've nailed the right question. The answer is quite simple. The earth is rather unique in two very special ways. First, it is a water world. Over 70 percent of the earth's surface area is covered by liquid water. It turns out that liquid water is a rare commodity in the cosmos. Some alien ships just show up here to lay on a store of water."

Stauffer considered that revelation and then continued his line of questioning. "Okay, General Goldwyn. Got that. But that doesn't seem to be reason enough. What's the other draw for wayward aliens?"

"Gold, Barton. There's lots of gold at the earth's core. Some scientists today suggest that there is enough gold at the Earth's core to cover the entire planet in a blanket of gold over ten feet thick."

"Is that the source for all the gold we've acquired from mining operations here on the surface?"

"Actually, Barton, no. The gold at the Earth's core dates back to the beginning formation of the planet when heavier elements like iron, gold, and platinum, gravitated together forming the core and the lighter elements coalesced around it eventually forming the mantle and crust. Most theories about the Earth's core center around its solid and molten iron cores. But some scientists suggest that there may be more gold at the Earth's core than there is iron."

"But where did the gold that's been mined on the surface come from?"

"Meteorites, Barton. As the Earth's crust coalesced into a solid mass, meteorites carried in a significant quantity of gold and other metals and minerals in small lots and deposited it around the globe.... nothing quite as dramatic as Manco Capac and Mama Ocllo, but a lot of gold fell from the sky and impacted on Mother Earth during its early formative years. We've only managed to exploit the gold that was deposited relatively close to the surface of Earth's crust. There's a lot more of it down there deeper in the crust. And that's the primary reason alien races are so interested in Planet Earth. Like liquid water, gold is also a rare commodity in the cosmos, and they need it for their electronics and other technological gadgets."

"Are the aliens setting up surface mining operations deep in the crust?"

"Yes, Barton.... in part. But some alien races have technologies available to them to draw off molten gold directly from the Earth's core."

"Is that a problem for us?" Stauffer asked. "It seems to me from what you just said that we have a pretty much unlimited supply."

"Well, Barton, there is a lot of gold at the Earth's core, but it isn't unlimited. And in fact, as the aliens draw off water from the surface oceans and gold from the Earth's core, it upsets the delicate electrical and magnetic fields that holds all of Earth's systems in balance. If enough gold is taken, it could totally upset that balance and ultimately destroy the Earth and all of its inhabitants."

"And your job is trying to stop that....? Your stay-behind team tries to keep the aliens in check to prevent them from messing with humankind and from taking Earth's water and gold....? Well, what's the box score....? How well are you doing? Stauffer was becoming excited and raised his voice.

General Goldwyn answered patiently, keeping his voice even and measured, "Actually, Barton, we are doing pretty well.... better than you might think."

Stauffer pondered what General Goldwyn had just revealed and responded venting his frustration and self-doubt. "You know, sir, sometimes I feel like a double agent when I'm sitting in a briefing or meeting with my team...., like Ski's briefing the other day as he talked us through the recovery mission for the Ancient site buried deep beneath my house. He was excited about all of the unknowns we had encountered...., but they're not unknowns to you at all. For you, it's like old home week. Here you are telling me about saving the world from aliens...." Stauffer started to sputter as he blurted out his words, "and I am more than a little concerned about this Pandora's jar of crystals thing. If it is really a library of Ancient knowledge, just what information is stored on all those crystals? Is it the kind of technology that could be used to make super weapons and maybe even lead to our own self-destruction? Maybe we don't even want to try to learn how to read them. We may not have the maturity or self-restraint to use that knowledge wisely."

"Actually, Barton, you're not far off. Those crystals contain information concerning a broad range of discoveries that we acquired over a period of hundreds of years, much of which was kept secret and hidden from common knowledge even in our own day."

"Then why are you being so blasé about the whole matter?" Stauffer was getting excited and raised his voice. "Shouldn't we be keeping the whole thing under tight wraps?"

"Actually, Barton, it was your call to mount a recovery mission for the site. What do you recommend we do with the crystals now?"

Stauffer paused to consider what Goldwyn was suggesting. "Maybe Hank's team will be able to learn something from examining those crystals about how the technology works to store information. Once we've learned all that we can learn about that, perhaps we ought to store the urn and all the crystals in a small out-of-the-way vault in the inner ring at Waxahachie. I would hate any of that information to ever get out. We're having a hard-enough time with all of the horrors scientists have managed to figure out for themselves in our own day."

"That's probably a wise decision, Barton. How long are you going to give Hank's team to examine the crystal technology before you put it into storage?"

Again, Stauffer had to pause to process the implications of the situation before answering. "I think, sir, that I need to talk with Hank to discuss that question. But I don't think it will take too long before we need to tuck it all away."

"Well, keep me posted, Barton, on what you decide."

Stauffer turned toward the door and started to leave but paused and turned his head back towards General Goldwyn, somewhat perplexed. "Just why are you leaving decisions like this up to me, sir? You're the one in charge."

"Only nominally, Barton. This isn't my era, it's yours.... And our 'Prime Directive' requires me to back off when I can...., and I think that time is close at hand."

# Chapter 28

By this time in their temporal investigations, Crypt team members had all staked out a claim on specific areas of the world and eras of time to survey and had begun to fill in the historical gaps. Several of the team members focused on tracking the postdiluvian activities of the Flood survivors from wherever they made landfall as they spread out over the land to repopulate the Earth. What was more difficult was backtracking the watercraft to their port of origin before the Flood.

They remained working together in teams of two, each team working out of a separate temporal observation lab, although the individual team members frequently worked on different projects of discovery at the same time. Stauffer had modified their weekly staff briefings so that only two teams, four individuals in all, briefed their progress from week to week. The challenging part of these briefings for Stauffer was figuring out how all of the various findings reported by the individual team members were interconnected into one holistic narrative of the antediluvian history of mankind.

On this particular morning, Sammy Woo was the first to brief his initial research scans on the early Chinese emperors and the development of the proto-dynasties. Sammy's face was flush with excitement as he related his most recent findings. "Following our experience with Melek and his scroll, I became very curious about evidence for early Chinese writing systems. Symbols and inscriptions of various kinds have been discovered on pottery shards in many locations in China, some of them dating well back into antiquity and prehistory. But there has been much discussion and disagreement among modern scholars about whether or not they constitute actual writing systems or were merely non-writing mnemonic symbols for purposes of remembering oral histories and branding property for ownership identification."

Woo worked the keyboard on the conference table in front of him and a screen-capture appeared on the wall-mounted flat screen monitor. He pointed at the symbols on the screen and continued, "These are examples of Banpo and Jiangzhai pottery symbols. Although most scholars are convinced that these are merely ownership or clan symbols, there are some scholars today who believe that these early glyphs show evidence of an embryonic writing system that eventually matured into a more sophisticated Chinese writing protocol. Our experience with Melek has helped me to understand that these symbols could in fact be part of a writing system, but limited to the individual who inscribed the symbols and read them through some system of interpreter crystals."

Woo forwarded through several more screen stills. "I've also been attempting to document the immigration of non-Chinese people into the area based on initial landing sites following the Flood, and assessing their influence on the development of early Chinese technology, culture and language. A prime example of such influence might be the construction of pyramids near the ancient city of Xi'an, on the Qin Chuan Plains in Shaanxi Province. In modern times, the Chinese government has placed investigation of the ruins of these pyramids strictly off-limits and little direct information is known about them today. Chinese authorities have gone so far as to bury many of them under blankets of dirt and plant them over with thickets of shrubbery. However, using the temporal monitors, I've discovered that when these pyramids were first built, they originally resembled the step pyramids of Mesoamerica and the Pyramid of Djoser at Saqqara, the oldest pyramid in Egypt. The similarities between the step pyramids in these areas and the tiered ziggurats of Mesopotamia strongly suggest some form of global intercommunication or cultural exchange. There's something about step pyramids that seems to tie together the history and culture of the Ancients throughout the world, both before and after the Flood. I think we need to tie that one down."

All of the team members gathered around the table started talking at once voicing agreement and several of them were taking notes to follow up on Sammy's suggestion. They had all discovered step pyramids in their respective geographic areas, many of which had been covered over by the Atlanteans before their departure or were later destroyed by the Flood. Stauffer allowed the team members to interact with each other for a few minutes before calling the room back to order. "Thanks, Sammy. That was informative and

I imagine that it generates some ideas for our other teams to explore in their respective areas."

Nodding to Sanjay Singh, Woo's research teammate, Stauffer prompted him to brief his findings. "Sanjay, what do you have to report today?"

Woo pushed the keyboard in Singh's direction, who quickly set up his graphic presentation on the monitor and immediately launched into his briefing. "I've been bouncing around in time checking out the early pre-Upanishad scholars and philosophers on the Indian subcontinent. The Sanskrit term *Upanishad* is a very ancient word and is translated by modern scholars variously as 'secret doctrine,' 'mystic meaning,' or 'hidden connections.' All of these possibilities strongly suggest pieces of history that have been lost or concealed over time. I'm convinced that the Upanishad tradition reaches back much further in time than modern scholarship suggests, and it could be that perhaps it dates back to the passing down of sacred oral and possibly written histories from the original survivors of the Flood."

"Now that would be a find," Hank Phillips spoke up.

"Yes, Hank," Sanjay responded, "but finding that connectivity is the hard part. So far, it has eluded me. I think that in my assigned geographic area, the answer might lie in a grouping of antediluvian cities along the western coast of present-day India. Today, they're referred to collectively as the Gulf of Khambat Cultural Complex, which now lies several miles off the coast in the Indian Ocean under 130 feet of water. I've been using the temporal monitor to scan the public buildings in those cities during antediluvian times before the sea level rose to see if I can turn up any evidence of writing or books."

"Have you discovered any libraries or repositories yet, Sanjay?" Stauffer asked.

"No, nothing quite like that, although I did find something that still has me puzzled. I chanced upon what appeared to be an open air factory where the Ancients were fabricating aircraft of various kinds. One of the workers was walking around the stone platforms where the airframes were being assembled, carrying a small device in the palm of his hand. It appeared to have a brass casing and some kind of crystal readout screen inset in the surface. From the way he was using it, it appeared he was inputting information, pushing buttons with his index finger. It reminded me for all the world of a modern iPad but it didn't look anything like one."

"What did it look like then, Sanjay?" Dr. Campbell inquired.

"This," Singh responded, pointing at the screen as he pushed a key on the keyboard in front of him. A new image appeared on the conference room monitor. It looked like the man in the image was holding a large metal discus-shaped object. They could clearly see a glass or crystalline screen inset into the body of the object.

"Were you able to zoom in on the readout display to see what he was looking at on the screen?" Phillips asked.

"As a matter of fact, Hank, I did. Here's an enlarged screen capture of the readout."

The screen capture of the readout appeared, showing a blueprint schematic for the aircraft. "This is just one of three dozen schematics that I was able to record using a video screen capture. It appears to be the blueprints for aircraft the Ancients were constructing on the stone platforms."

The room fell silent as the team members considered the magnitude of what Sanjay had found. Dr. Campbell was the first to speak up and break the silence. "Sanjay, with our former experience working at Jet Propulsion Laboratory, you and I are perhaps the best equipped on the team to review those schematics to see what technologies they might reveal. We still haven't figured out how the Ancients powered their aircraft. This might hold the key for their anti-gravity or magnetic-levitation technologies."

Turning to Stauffer, Dr. Campbell continued, "Barton, with your permission, I think it would be prudent for Sanjay and me to lay our current research efforts aside for the moment and see if we can learn what information these schematics might hold."

"I agree, Miriam. I'll get with General Goldwyn immediately after this meeting to see how he wants us to proceed."

Stauffer turned to Hank Phillips and continued, "Hank, you're next. Hard act to follow. What do you have to report? Are you any closer to finding the Hall of Records?"

Phillips smiled and shrugged. "Well, I wish that I did have something extraordinary to report like Sammy and Sanjay, but for now, I'm going to be brief. Since I last briefed, I've been side-tracked by the ongoing work on the development of DNA data storage. But in the time I've had for research, I've continued a careful survey of ancient Egypt in the vicinity of the Giza plateau. I am still certain that there must be some element of truth and fact in the legends of the Hall of Records, and that, if I could only find it, it would open up much greater clarity and understanding on the early history of the world. But, I'm making only slow progress as I eliminate false leads one by one. My research efforts are greatly limited by the need for me to split my time between here and the DNA and crystal data storage research teams. Hopefully I'll have something more to report next time."

"Thanks, Hank," Stauffer responded. "Keep at it." Turning to Bob Zazworsky, Stauffer observed, "Bob, you have the final report for this morning's meeting. What do you have to tell us?"

A cheesy smile spread across Zazworsky's face. "I've been spending most of my time coordinating construction requirements for the vaults at Waxahachie and I haven't had much time for research. What time I have had, I spent chasing down the legends of El Dorado and the Seven Cities of Gold in the Americas. I theorize that, if true, the existence of large caches of gold signify elements of history and culture of great significance for the Ancients. Like Hank, I'm convinced that the legends are based on an ancient reality and that hidden somewhere in the deserts of the American Southwest, and on the high slopes of the Andes, and deep in the jungles of Central and South America, are archeological ruins hiding untold riches and important knowledge just waiting to be discovered. **And I wanna be the guy who finds them.**" Nodding to everyone seated around the table, most of whom were laughing by now, he concluded, "If any of you guys find something that points in that direction, please shoot it my way. I need all the help I can get on this one."

Amidst all the laughter, Dr. Campbell raised her hand. "Barton, I have a quick observation I need to share that may be of great help to everyone. It goes right along with Sanjay's comment about ancient ruins off the coast of India now buried in over a hundred feet of water."

"What are you getting at, Miriam?" Stauffer asked.

"It's this, Barton. After your little demonstration here in your office playing whack-a-mole with the baseball bat and the sponge, I became very interested in the whole concept of water balance between Earth's surface oceans and the subterranean ocean in the ringwoodite crystal layer. When I saw that the islands of the

Caribbean and the landmass of North, Central, and South America were all conjoined together as one land mass during antediluvian times, I became curious about how long it took for Cuba and the other Caribbean islands to become isolated from the mainland and so much of the Central American coastline to sink beneath the sea in the postdiluvian era."

"Didn't that happen with the Flood, Miriam?" Max Manchester asked.

"No, as a matter of fact, Max, it didn't. Initially, I thought so too, but when I did a careful survey with my temporal observation monitor, I found that the flood waters, at least in the Americas, eventually receded to a point slightly below the level of the sea before the Flood as the waters on the surface and the subterranean ocean sought a new balance. But that all began to change, slowly at first, and then much more rapidly as time went on. The super-heated subterranean water that covered the earth temporarily during the Flood apparently accelerated the melting and retreat of the two-mile thick ice sheet in North America and brought the Ice Age to a rapid conclusion. As ice melted back after the flood waters subsided, it added considerably to the volume of the surface ocean, and, over the next two hundred years, sea levels around the world began to rise, as much as 100 to 200 feet in some locations. Fast forwarding with my temporal observation monitor, I watched countless coastal cities and settlements gradually sink beneath the waves in the Caribbean area. When I realized what was happening in my area of responsibility, I did a quick check on the Indian subcontinent and the land mass in South Asia and along the Pacific Rim down through Malaysia and Indonesia. It was the same everywhere. It was most remarkable in the area of the Gulf of Arabia. Before the Flood and even a little after the floodwaters had receded, the area of the Persian Gulf was a broad fertile plain. As the sea level rose, waters washed in from the Indian Ocean and flooded the whole area forming new coastline along the modern day United Arab Emirates, Qatar, Bahrain and all the way up to Kuwait. I think that there must be at least a hundred or more cities and settlements that were flooded out and are now buried beneath the shallow waters of the Persian Gulf. A similar thing happened with the broad plain that was flooded over by the waters of the Mediterranean as the sea level rose and rushed in to form the Black Sea."

"And so, Miriam, what are you suggesting?" Stauffer asked.

"Well, Barton, since people tend to settle and live close to water and particularly sea coasts, it stands to reason that during those two hundred years or so following the Flood, most of the early antediluvian and postdiluvian settlements probably ended up under the encroaching sea and much of that piece of the history of mankind went with it. I think this ought to become a focal point of our surveys to see what we lost and possibly what can be recovered. Without it, we're going to have a gaping two-hundred year hole in the historical narrative at the beginning of the postdiluvian era."

"I have another potential observation," Max Manchester offered. "I don't claim to be a Biblical scholar but I think that the time period that Miriam is signaling here falls within the lifetime of Peleg, one of the descendants of Noah. If I'm not mistaken, I believe that the Hebrew Bible announces that in the days of Peleg, the earth was divided. Based upon what Miriam has observed, that might refer to all of the landmasses that sunk beneath the rising sea, leaving mountains, hills, and higher elevations as separate island groups and archipelagos around the world. What do you think?"

"Whew, Max and Miriam.... there's a lot of food for thought there," Stauffer observed. "I think we need to follow up and make this an integral part of our research effort. I know that some of you have already started looking at sunken cities and ceremonial sites off the coast of Japan, and India, and Cuba, but perhaps there's a lot more that we ought to be looking at in other parts of the world as well. Let's spend at least a portion of our time on it during the week ahead and be prepared to report back initial findings next week."

\* \* \* \* \* \* \* \* \* \* \* \* \* \* \* \* \* \* \* \* \* \*

"Well, Barton," General Goldwyn asked, "what did the Crypt team have to report this week?"

"Sammy is making good progress on his investigation of ancient China, and he noted that there seems to be a structural element that ties all of the ancient cultures together."

"And what would that be?" Goldwyn asked.

"Step pyramids, sir. Everywhere we look in the antediluvian world and in many places in the world after the Flood, we see evidence of step pyramids, many of them looking remarkably similar in spite of the great distances that separate them. Sammy has suggested that we look harder to find the connection."

"Sammy is very perceptive.... and correct. There is a connection. There was a great deal of communication between the various cultures of the ancient world, much more than modern science will acknowledge. There was a vast global trade network. The Ancients shared numerous trade goods, but also ideas about technology, art, architecture, and philosophy. It didn't take long for an idea that originated in one part of the world to travel to the far reaches of the planet. The step pyramids that were constructed after the Flood were an attempt to reestablish a global energy grid network again like the one the Ancients had before the Flood. It didn't work out very well and was only partially effective. What else came up in the meeting?"

"Miriam Campbell briefed us on the research she has done monitoring sea levels from antediluvian times to the postdiluvian era after the floodwaters receded. She suggested that sea levels returned to about the same place they were at before the Flood, but that within a two-hundred-year span, with the melting of the Polar ice cap, sea levels around the world rose from 100 to 200 feet and submerged countless cities and settlements that had just gotten started again in postdiluvian times. Max Manchester tied the idea in with the story of Peleg and the division of the Earth reported in the Biblical record."

"Well, Barton, Miriam, as usual, is absolutely right. There's a lot of postdiluvian history that was flooded over along the world's coastlines and buried in the shallow waters. And Max doesn't know how right he is. As the descendants of Noah spread out over the land following the Flood, Peleg originally settled with his family on the southern coast of the Arabian Peninsula. When the sea level started rising and flooding the land, he spent the majority of his life picking up stakes and moving to higher ground.... not once, but literally a dozen times. Finally, in disgust, he and his family moved all the way back to the high ground on the western end of Mesopotamia and settled in the vicinity of Noah's tents far distant from the encroaching sea."

# Chapter 29

Since his earlier telepathic connection with Noah, Stauffer had avoided going back and observing Noah with the temporal monitor. He wanted to avoid any intervention that might change history and he didn't feel entirely comfortable with telepathic connectivity. But he was obsessed with learning more about Noah. After several months of devoting himself to investigating other areas of history, he finally determined to go back and visit Noah in his later years.

According to the Bible, Noah lived to be 950 years old, more than 340 years beyond the time they disembarked from the Ark. Stauffer decided to look in on Noah towards the end of his life span. During one of their weekly meetings, Stauffer advised General Goldwyn of his intention and Goldwyn immediately launched a Minibago to check for historical distortions that Stauffer's contact with Noah might cause.

Stauffer returned to his office and turned on the temporal observation monitor on his desk. He wasn't quite sure where to begin, and so he input the time-location coordinates on the keyboard for the last location where he had left Noah and his family moving down the mountain slope from the Ark.

As the monitor came to life, Noah's family reappeared and Stauffer sat back and watched their slow progress through the foothills of Ararat. They were a long way from where they had originally built and launched the Ark, and all of this terrain they were exploring was new ground to them. Stauffer watched their progress in fast motion as they continued down from the mountain heights into the rolling valleys below. The family finally settled in the western reaches of the fertile valley between the Tigris and Euphrates rivers. When they at last stopped from their journey down the slopes of the mountains of Ararat, Noah directed his sons in the building of an altar made up of large stones gathered from around the site where they set up their tents. Then, Noah gathered his family around the altar and they offered up sacrifices and prayers of thanksgiving.

Stauffer observed that Noah set up a wooden table in his tent and from time to time, he would take out the ancient leather book and his crystals and would write in his slow careful script. Occasionally, one or another of his sons would come to visit and join him in his tent as he wrote, looking over Noah's shoulder as he painstakingly formed the characters on the page. Stauffer noted that the book was beginning to fill up and that there were only a few unused pages left. From time to time, Noah would gather his three sons together in the tent and open the book and look at them silently as he leafed through the pages. The men sat there in silence looking at their father, apparently intent on the telepathic instruction he was sharing with them. Through the years, Stauffer noted another singular occurrence. As time passed, Noah and his sons began speaking openly to each other, depending less and less on telepathic communication, until finally, they spoke aloud to each other whenever they came together.

As Stauffer fast-forwarded through time, he saw that Noah's extended family initially lived a pastoral life, herding animals and raising crops occasionally. But over time, Noah's descendents began moving away and gathering together in settlements, some of which grew into substantial urban centers.

In one of the biggest cities that sprang up, he noted that large bodies of people gathered together and began to erect a great building out of fired bricks. Because he was viewing the passage of time in very fast motion, the construction work took on the appearance of a colony of ants, scurrying around the construction site. The structure quickly began to look like a massive, steep-sided ziggurat, perhaps a half mile on each side. As the people continued to gather clay and fire more and more bricks, the structure climbed rapidly into the sky. And then, suddenly, construction abruptly stopped, and all of the workers separated into groups and moved away from the city in large migrations spreading out in all directions. Stauffer realized that, once again, he was observing one of the great stories recorded in Genesis, the building of the Tower of Babel and the dispersion of the descendents of Noah before the tower reached completion.

As construction on the Tower ceased, Stauffer slowed the pace of the passage of time on the temporal monitor down to real time so that he could observe the details of the event with greater clarity and understanding. As migrating peoples began passing by the vicinity of where Noah and his family lived, he gathered his sons together around him standing in a tight circle and they stood there once again without speaking, apparently returning to telepathic communication. Occasionally, they would turn their heads, almost in unison, looking from one brother to the other. Finally, Noah nodded to each of them in turn and pointed in three different directions. Each of his sons nodded his head in understanding, and, after a brief moment standing there together in silence with their heads bowed, they each embraced their father and their brothers and turned and walked away. The three brothers gathered together their wives and servants and flocks and began moving off in the direction that Noah had pointed for them. Japeth and Ham and their family groups quickly disappeared in the distance, but before Shem, the middle son, could get very far, Noah started after him and called for him to return. He led Shem back into his tent where he wrapped up the ancient vellum leather book in its protective shawl covering and placed it in the wooden chest with the crystals. Closing the lid, he handed it solemnly to his son, thus designating his middle son, Shem, as his heir in the patriarchal order. Then, placing his hand on his shoulder, he guided him to the opening of his tent and watched him rejoin his family and move off to the southeast. Noah turned and reentered his tent and sat down on a wooden bench. His eyes misted up in tears and he wept openly.

\* \* \* \* \* \* \* \* \* \* \* \* \* \* \* \* \* \* \* \*

Stauffer was intent on tracking the disposition of the book and followed Shem and his family and flocks moving to the south. Scanning fast time, he saw that after traversing hundreds of miles, they eventually came to a gigantic stone platform that had been erected by the Ancients in antediluvian times. He established his family there in the vicinity of the platform and through the years built up a city. Stauffer noted that Shem continued the custom of his father, withdrawing to the privacy of his inner chamber from time to time and recording in the leather book.

After much time had passed, a small group of marauding soldiers attacked the settlement, moving through the streets of Shem's peaceful city, plundering as they went. But the leader of the band appeared to be looking for something. As he entered buildings, he pulled open boxes and chests and emptied their contents on the ground. When he finally encountered the building where the ancient book was stored, he went to take it, but was restrained by Shem, the now-aged keeper of the record. The warrior grabbed the old man by his arm and shook free. The old man tripped and fell backward, hitting his head on the stone floor. The soldier set the book back on the table and assisted the old man over to a cot on the far side of the room and helped him lie down. He tore a strip of cloth from his own garment to place over the old man's bleeding forehead and then returned to the table where the book lay. The soldier wrapped the book in the shawl and placed it in the wooden chest. He retrieved the crystals from the far end of the table and put them in the box with the book and closed the lid. He turned and looked back at Shem just before he left the room carrying the box protectively under his arm. Shem was still lying prostrate on the cot holding the cloth to his head. The soldier rushed out into the street. Calling his forces together, they quickly departed the city and began a long march over rough terrain moving in a southwesterly direction. Stauffer followed the movement of the band with the temporal monitor as they went. He didn't want to lose track of the disposition of the book.

As the band reached their apparent destination on the banks of the Nile in Egypt, they were met by another elderly man who Stauffer observed bore a strong resemblance to Noah's oldest son, Ham, and Stauffer assumed that was who it was. The old man led the soldier carrying the box into a palace to a small room on one of the upper floors of the building. He had the soldier deposit the box on a table in the center of the room and pointed at the door. As the soldier departed, the old man turned and faced the box, his mouth drawn up in a tense, grim smile. He lifted the lid of the box and opened it. He gingerly extracted the parcel inside and laid it on the table. Slowly, he unwrapped the shawl and exposed the leather book. Looking back into the box, he extracted the crystals and laid them beside the book on the table. Then, he pulled up a heavy chair and sat down. Holding the crystals before his eyes, he began scanning the pages, his lips moving as his finger traced a path across the characters on the page. As he read, he paused every so often, a look of sheer pleasure on his face. The old man sat there at the table for many hours, slowly turning the pages as he examined the record of his forefathers. When at last he tired, he closed the book and returned it and the crystals to the box. As he left the room, he secured the door with a heavy lock.

Ham returned to the room where the book was stored many times after that, always leaving guards posted at the entrance to the room, while he studied the book by himself. As he worked his way through to the last page in the book, Stauffer observed that Ham would sometimes weep openly as his finger traced the words on the page. Finally, when he reached the end of the script characters on the last page, Ham got up and left the room. He came back shortly with a small bowl of ink and a feather quill and began recording characters on a portion of the remaining space on the last page. When he was done writing, he sat back in his chair. A look of satisfaction and relief swept across his face.

After that, Ham didn't return to the room for many days and Stauffer fast-forwarded the temporal monitor to track the disposition of the book. Stauffer noted there was always a guard posted at the entrance to the room day and night. Noting the passage of time on the temporal readout on the side of the screen, Stauffer observed that after the passage of several years, Ham finally returned to the room and directed a servant to pick up the box and follow him. They left the palace and stepped up into a large four-wheeled chariot with driver waiting outside. They left the city and continued out into the desert where Stauffer observed that there was a small group of people gathered around the front end of the ancient statue of the Sphinx.

The Sphinx looked quite different from how it had looked before the Flood. The stone had seriously deteriorated from having been underwater for almost a year during the Flood, and Ham had apparently directed stone artisans to repair the damage. The workers had carved away much of the damaged surface of the head of the Sphinx, and when it was finished, the head and face were much smaller. Most significantly, the face of Enoch was gone, and it now sported the face of Ham.

As the old man approached, a group of soldiers standing at the top of the cliff in front of the Sphinx came to attention. The old man moved past them and made his way to the edge of the cliff at the front of the plateau on which the Sphinx rested. Holding tightly to a rope anchored near his chariot up on the plateau, he carefully made his way down a series of steps that had been cut into the face of the cliff. Several dozen meters down at the base of the cliff, he came to an opening about the height of a man cut into the face of the rock and entered. The servant carrying the box dutifully followed behind him through the opening. Stauffer followed after them, manipulating the controls on the temporal observation monitor into the confining space of the passageway. There were steps cut into the rock leading downward into a long tunnel, and a guard posted at the top of the steps led the two men downward carrying a torch in each hand to light the way.

At the bottom of the steps, they advanced another dozen steps and came to a large hinged wooden door. While the old man stood to the side, the guards pulled the massive door open. As the guards stepped back out of the way, Ham entered a large cavern, perhaps 30 or 40 feet across. The cavern was filled with golden artifacts, uncut gems, ornate jewelry, elaborate statuary, and a large pile of scrolls, wrapped around heavy wooden rollers. Stauffer was shocked when he realized that some of the treasures appeared to be the same ones that he had observed earlier in Noah's other cabinet on the Ark. Ham must have mounted an expedition sometime back up the mountain at Ararat and dug down through the thick deposit of mud to the Ark to recover them. The old man looked around the assemblage of wealth with a look of great satisfaction and motioned to the servant carrying the chest to approach. The man took the chest and carefully set it down on a stone table positioned in the middle of the cavern. Ham waved his hand again signaling for the guards to leave and he stood there alone in the cavern looking at the box with the Book of the Fathers within for some time. Then, he slowly turned and departed. The guards gathered outside closed the heavy wooden door behind him as he left. As the old man slowly climbed the steps to the mouth of the tunnel, the guards below began sealing up the door with multiple layers of heavy stone blocks. When they were finished with their work, they repeated the process at the mouth of the tunnel entrance on the cliff, sealing it up with multiple layers of stone. When their work was completed, the workers packed up their equipment and climbed back up the steps cut in the face of the cliff and left.

\* \* \* \* \* \* \* \* \* \* \* \* \* \* \* \* \* \* \*

Stauffer decided to return to look in on Noah's tents but jumped ahead another hundred years. As the temporal monitor cleared, Stauffer found Noah and his wife still residing in a grouping of tents in the same area where they had settled two centuries earlier. Stauffer was surprised. He had imagined that Noah and his wife would have moved into more comfortable, permanent quarters in one of the cities which were springing up around Mesopotamia as his descendents spread out over the land. Noah looked somewhat older on the monitor screen but his face still reflected the exuberance of youth. Noah was sitting on a carpet spread out over the sand, his back leaning against a pile of large cushions. Noah was munching on a plate of grapes and figs. As Stauffer observed the scene, Noah slowly raised a hand and motioned in the air, *"You are back.... Yes, I spoke to you, Barton Stauffer. I am Noah, son of Lamech, I want to communicate with you before I pass over to the other side."*

Totally at a loss for words, Stauffer began to stammer--he didn't know what to do or say.

*"I know this may be uncomfortable for you. You don't need to speak out loud. I can't hear you anyway.... just like you can't hear me. Just form the thoughts in your mind and I will sense that."*

Stauffer thought about that for a moment and then started forming sentences in his head without speaking. *"How is it that I can hear you in my mind telepathically? I have been monitoring you for quite a long time now and, although I realized you were communicating with your wife and sons that way, I never heard anything before."*

*"I know. I'm afraid I owe you an apology, Barton Stauffer. I was blocking you out. I sensed your presence the first time you looked in on me back when we were building the Ark, and I blocked you out. Even worse, I'm afraid that I frequently eavesdropped on what you were thinking as you looked in on us. It was an unequal and unfair exchange for which I am sorry. But, I came to realize through the early years of eavesdropping that you are a good man, a very good man, and genuinely interested in and concerned for the people of my day. You have been a sensitive visitor, not an insensitive voyeur."*

Stauffer tried to think of what he might say to the old man. *"I believe that I owe you an apology as well, sir.... er, Noah. I was observing you to learn more about you and your people, but the rules and protocols I work under forbid me from making direct contact, and so I couldn't approach you openly to ask permission."*

"*Yes, I know. I learned that early on. I was always fascinated by your conclusions from what you were observing. It was a little disconcerting when you would throw in thoughts of future events.... for me at least.... that hadn't yet happened and I tried not to let it affect my actions. But it was.... challenging.*"

"*I'm very sorry, sir. I'm afraid that I have placed you in a very uncomfortable position.*"

"*Not at all, my friend. Over time, I learned to look forward to your looking in on me. It was a most welcome.... intrusion. I particularly enjoyed searching your random thoughts and memories. Many of them don't make much sense to me. I don't have the context for understanding. And now I am an old man and nearing the time to die.*"

"*I hope not yet, sir,*" Stauffer countered.

"*Oh, I know that the end for me is near. I can't communicate with my mind to anyone but my wife anymore.... not even with my own sons. I've lost that facility. But I can sense your thoughts clearly. That is most puzzling. Can you sense my thoughts clearly, Barton Stauffer?*"

Stauffer formulated his response in his mind. "*Yes, I can hear you loud and clear.... Excuse me, but why does your speech sound so modern in my mind. I would have expected you to speak much more formally and using words of an ancient language that we don't use any more.*"

"*That is an interesting question, Barton Stauffer. I was told by my father that we don't really think in words most of the time. We usually think in pictures and ideas. When we communicate — 'telepathically' is the word you seem to use — we generally translate the thoughts and pictures that come to us back into words that we might hear if spoken aloud. It is certain, however, that this form of communication is much faster. In some circumstances, it is almost instantaneous. And, it is almost impossible to lie.*"

Stauffer quickly considered the implications of Noah's statement about the difficulty of lying while communicating telepathically. It would create a wholly different dynamic in human interaction.

"*I have missed your company, Barton Stauffer. It has been a very long time for me. Where have you been? Have you stopped looking in on my people?*"

"*Not at all, sir,*" Stauffer acknowledged. "*My team and I are continuing to monitor the days before and after the Flood to try to put together a more accurate record and history of mankind.*"

"*And what have you found, my friend?*" Noah asked.

"*Well, that's an interesting question,*" Stauffer acknowledged. "*It's pretty much a mixed bag.*"

*"A mixed bag?"*

*"Yes. Sorry, sir. That's an expression we use in my time. It means that we've seen a broad variety of activities as your descendents spread across the world since the Ark settled on the slopes of Ararat."*

*"Like what, Barton Stauffer?"*

*"Well, like you and your wife, and some of your descendents are still dwelling in tents and living the simple nomadic life while many others of your descendents have gravitated to towns and cities. Some of them have built enormous urban centers with elaborate temples and public buildings."*

*"Yes,"* Noah responded. *"I have been told that. I am worried. I have warned them against that many times. Large cities are generally not good for a people to inhabit. It places strains on family relationships and some people almost always set themselves above others. They adopt strange gods and strange practices and soon the people are living in misery."*

Stauffer replied hesitantly, *"I'm sorry to have to confirm that, but we have observed many of your descendents placing others in slavery to do the work of building their cities and palaces while they lie around doing little for their own welfare. We've also observed the establishment of armies with soldiers beginning to do battle with one another. There has already been much blood spilled."*

*"Yes, and some of my children and my children's children are falling into barbaric and idolatrous practices as well. One of my descendents ten generations removed came through here several months ago with his family and flocks. He had fled for his life from the city of Ur. He was on his way to Haran when he passed by here. I invited him and his company to rest here from their journey.*

*"Who was it, sir?"* Stauffer inquired.

*"His name is Abram and he brought me news of the southern extent of the valley, news which greatly distresses me to learn that my descendents are so quickly falling back into their old idolatrous ways that brought on the Flood in the first place. Abram is of the patriarchal order, removed some ten generations from me. He showed me that he was the great-great-great grandson of Peleg. We spent many long nights discussing the immensity of creation and I shared with him some of the history of mankind from the Book of the Fathers."*

Stauffer was thoroughly intrigued at this point. *"Would you mind if I went back and looked in on that visit. I would very much like to know more about this man, Abram. We know him today by a longer version of his name — Abraham. He is considered the father of many nations."*

*"Please do so, Barton Stauffer,"* Noah responded.*" "I think you will find it enlightening. But, if you do not mind, I am getting tired and need to rest. Will you come back and visit me again?"*

"Yes, sir. I'll be back."

✳ ✳ ✳ ✳ ✳ ✳ ✳ ✳ ✳ ✳ ✳ ✳ ✳ ✳ ✳ ✳ ✳ ✳ ✳ ✳ ✳

Stauffer squirmed in his chair in excitement as he recounted his visit with Noah to General Goldwyn.

"What happened then, Barton?"

"Well, sir," Stauffer responded, "I reset the controls on my temporal observation monitor, and, using an abbreviated bracketing technique, quickly zeroed in on Abraham's sojourn with Noah. Abraham passed many weeks encamped near Noah's tents. I observed that during their conversations, Noah frequently grew frustrated and impatient as they talked and used his walking stick to draw pictures in the sand to illustrate the ideas he was trying to explain."

"And what was he teaching young Abraham?"

"I was astounded when I realized that he was giving Abraham a lesson in mathematics and basic astronomy, as Noah outlined the orbits of the planets around the sun and drew circular objects on the orbital lines representing each of the planets. What was most amazing to me was that Noah drew the circles proportional to the actual size of the planets themselves. Then, Noah erased that schematic with his stick and began to sketch the structure of what looked like a spiral galaxy, ostensibly the Milky Way, and he pointed to a spot on one of the spiral arms he had drawn. Sir, I'm no expert in astronomy and I had Miriam Campbell review the video captures of the scene. She confirmed that the schematic was a fairly accurate representation of the Milky Way galaxy and where Noah was pointing was precisely where our solar system is located in the galaxy itself on one of its spiral arms."

"Very interesting, Barton," General Goldwyn interjected. "What happened then?"

"Abraham spent several weeks with Noah receiving instruction from the old patriarch before he took his leave and continued his journey into the land southward."

Goldwyn interrupted again, "The land of Canaan, named after one of the sons of Ham who settled that area."

"Yes, sir," Stauffer responded. "I lost track of Abraham briefly when I encountered a temporal block, but I picked him up shortly thereafter as he and his family and herds moved further south along the highland ridgeline. Abraham and his family wandered around Canaan for some time, moving from place to place, and then, in the midst of a drought and famine, they continued their journey southward into Egypt. He was received there by Noah's son, Ham, who had set himself up as Pharaoh and absolute monarch of the land. Abraham apparently shared with Ham news of his father which was well received by the old Pharaoh."

"And," Goldwyn observed, "I can imagine that Ham pumped Abraham for the astronomical and mathematical knowledge he had received from Noah. What else did you observe, Barton?"

"Abraham was in Egypt for quite some time and then he departed to return to Canaan, accompanied by a very large party of family members, servants, herdsmen, and flocks. I put the temporal monitor on fast-forward to track his travels. They eventually settled in an area just north of modern-day Jerusalem. In those days, the Bible narrative refers to the walled city that was built up where Shem had settled earlier simply as Salem. After a while, Abraham's nephew Lot separated his group from Abraham's and led them northeast and settled on the broad, open plains near the River Jordan and the Dead Sea. Since I was focused on Abraham, I asked Ski to pick up the scan on Lot's family. I thought it would be important to learn about the destruction of the cities of the plain including Sodom and Gomorrah."

"Be sure to tell Ski to exercise caution. The cities of the plain were destroyed by a small asteroid that impacted near the city of Sodom, causing a high energy burst on the order of a ten-kiloton nuclear blast. The temporal monitor will filter out the bright light but it wouldn't do to have Ski looking directly into the blast."

"Yes, sir, I'll give him a heads up to be careful."

"What else did you observe about Abraham, Barton?"

"Well, sir, he settled just a dozen miles north of ancient Salem. That place interests me very much. It was a fortress city, built on the ruins of an enormous stone platform that had been erected by the Ancients during antediluvian times. They used it for the construction of aircraft and later as an airport of sorts before Atlantis lifted off. Many of the stones used in the construction of the platform weigh upwards of five hundred to a thousand tons. I set my temporal monitor to antediluvian times and watched the Ancients construct it. The quarry was nearby and they cut the stones with energy beam tools, and then they simply levitated them into place without the use of mortar. With the technology at their disposal, the Ancients made short work of the construction."

A huge smile broke out over General Goldwyn's face and Stauffer paused from his report. "Have I said something humorous, sir?"

"Not at all, Barton. You have merely reminded me of one of my finer moments. I think if you go back and look more closely at the construction of that platform, you may see me there as a much younger man directing the construction efforts. Aviation platforms were one of my specialties in my earlier days."

"You were responsible for building the great platform that the Jerusalem Temple Mount sits on today?"

"Yes, Barton, and I was also responsible for the construction of a similar platform just to the north at modern-day Baalbek in Lebanon. Those are two of the stone platforms we built that have survived into the present day. We destroyed many of the others as we prepared for Atlantis to depart and the rest are pretty much buried deep under water today." General Goldwyn paused to reflect on earlier days, and then abruptly turned back to Stauffer. "But I'm interrupting your report. Please continue."

"Well, sir, I observed that Abraham made frequent trips to Salem and met often with Noah's other son, Shem, who had settled there. According to the Biblical writ, Shem was sometimes referred to as Melchizedek, Prince of Peace. During their conversations in Shem's private quarters, he would sometimes take out Noah's leather book and discuss passages with Abraham as he turned the fragile pages.

Stauffer paused, a little choked up.

"What is wrong Barton?" General Goldwyn asked seeing Stauffer's distress.

"Well, sir, while I was previously tracking the disposition of the book that Noah had bequeathed to Shem, I watched a marauding squad of Egyptian soldiers attack Salem and take the book from Shem's custody and carry it back with them to Egypt to turn over to Ham. Shem was injured in the encounter and the soldier that took the book from him left him bloodied in his room."

"Yes, I know, Barton," General Goldwyn responded. But don't fret too much about Shem. He recovered from his injuries and lived to a ripe old age. In fact, as an antediluvian Ancient, with the exception of Eber, Shem actually outlived all of his next nine descendents in the patriarchal order, including Abraham."

"Shem outlived Abraham?"

"That's right, Barton. Shem lived to the ripe old age of 610. Abraham only lived to 175. Shem actually outlived Abraham by five years."

"But what about the book? Noah gave it to Shem for safe keeping."

"That's right. But when Ham found out about it, he was greatly perturbed. He aspired to the rights of primogeniture in the patriarchal order and to become the custodian of the book. And so he sent a squad of soldiers to Salem to retrieve the book, but he gave the soldiers strict instructions not to harm Shem." General Goldwyn paused and then continued thoughtfully. "It was a regrettable incident,.... but it had a most fortuitous outcome in the long run."

"A fortuitous outcome, sir? How is that possible?"

"Hundreds of years after Ham caused the book to be hidden in the cavern hollowed out deep beneath the Sphinx, a young Hebrew prince, a descendant of Abraham, by the name of Moses, was being raised in the household of Pharaoh. He used his royal position to excavate the cavern and access the book. Using the crystals, he spent months carefully copying the text from the pages of the book onto papyrus scrolls. When he was finished, he had the opening to the cavern and the tunnel entrance again sealed up, and the entire depression in front of the cliff filled in with rubble up to the level of the plateau. He kept the scrolls with him when he later fled Egypt to the land of Midian. During his long exile in Midian, he studied the scrolls night after night by candlelight until he had them almost memorized verbatim. That turned out to be very useful later on after the Exodus when Moses set his mind to recording the history of mankind in what we know today as the book of Genesis, the first Book of Moses in the Old Testament."

"If Moses had access to the Book of the Fathers," Stauffer excitedly exclaimed. "then Genesis isn't just a recompilation of the Epic of Gilgamesh and other ancient Sumerian legends like so many modern scholars and academics contend today?"

"No, Barton," General Goldwyn responded. "Moses had access to primary source materials, just like we strive for here in the Repository and the Crypt to improve the quality of the historical narratives we record."

"What happened to the scrolls that Moses copied from the Book of the Fathers?" Stauffer asked.

"Moses stored them in the Ark of the Covenant along with the crystals and the stone tablets engraved with the Ten Commandments."

"But what happened to the Ark of the Covenant?" Stauffer pressed.

Goldwyn laughed a deep throaty laugh, "Now that, lad, is a story for another day."

# Chapter 30

*Carlisle Barracks, Pennsylvania, Friday, February 6, 2015, 6:30 a.m.*

Because Stauffer's conversations with Noah didn't seem to have any significant impact on changing the past, General Goldwyn had given him the go-ahead to continue his temporal monitor interactions. Stauffer dutifully went back to observe the construction of the Ark. It was an enormous project carried out over a very long period of time, and Stauffer was amazed at how the work was carried on in such a focused and well-organized manner.

During his next visit with Noah, Stauffer asked him how he had managed the project so well.

Noah threw back his head and laughed. *"Ah, Barton Stauffer, it didn't go as smoothly as you seem to think. In fact, we had quite a few construction problems and setbacks we had to resolve."*

"Like what, sir?"

*"Well, you know that our standard unit of measurement was the cubit. I was instructed to build the Ark 300 cubits by 50 cubits by 30 cubits."*

"Yes, sir. What was the challenge with that?"

*"Well, those measurements made for a very big vessel. The problem lay in the notion of the cubit. The cubit is simply the distance from the tip of the middle finger to the end of the elbow."*

"Yes, sir. I understand, but I still don't see the problem."

*"Barton Stauffer, you are missing the obvious point. The cubit measurement worked just fine for most applications that didn't require precision. However, everyone has different physical characteristics and everyone was cutting timbers and laying them in place according to their own personal cubit. It was a mess. Nothing fit right and the framework superstructure for the Ark was shaky and insubstantial. The construction project was doomed to failure from the beginning."*

"So, what did you do, sir?"

*"I had to standardize everyone on the same system of measurement. I had my sons bring me a stack of wooden rods and I marked off the cubit length on each of them according to my own measure. Then, we had to go back and redo some of the construction. But after that, from then on, everyone working on the*

*construction site used the Noah cubit rods to measure off cutting timbers for the Ark construction.*"

Noah finished his story and laughed again. He obviously remembered those days of construction on the Ark with great satisfaction in accomplishing a Herculean task.

* * * * * * * * * * * * * * * * * * * *

After Stauffer had broken the temporal monitor connection with Noah, he sat there pondering the conversation they had just had. Noah shared the same kind of humor as Stauffer, and he enjoyed communicating with him. He was fascinated by Noah's story of the Noah cubit. He ran the idea through his mind several times and turned his chair back to his temporal monitor controls and set the time/location parameters for the area near the Ark, just as Noah and his family were closing the door. All of the movies and dramatizations that Stauffer had ever seen depicted a crowd gathered outside around the Ark as the door was closed. The crowd was always clamoring to get in, but that was patently a Hollywood fabrication.

After loading all of the animals, they closed the door to the Ark late at night when no one was around and the work site was deserted. There wasn't anyone to be seen. Stauffer used the opportunity to look around to see if he could spy a Noah cubit rod. He didn't have to look long. Over by a work bench stacked high with tools, he found a bronze bucket filled with Noah cubit rods. He figured that since Noah and his family had closed up the Ark and would soon be departing, it wouldn't change anything temporally if he were to make off with the bucket of the rods.

Although it was a relatively simple mission, Stauffer quickly assembled a five-person repo team according to established temporal protocols. They gathered in an adjacent time lab and suited up in hazmat suits. Stauffer set up a small time portal next to the bucket of rods and reached through and pulled the bucket back through the portal. The other team members followed up reaching through the portal and recovering a collection of tools laying on the workbench that had been used to build the Ark. Then, they quickly toggled the portal shut.

After his team had put the bucket of rods and the other tools through a thorough hazmat decon bath, Stauffer took the bronze bucket of rods with him back to his office and set the bucket to the side of his desk. He pulled one of the Noah cubit rods out of the bucket to examine it further. The ancient cubit was typically divided into smaller measurements of palms, hands, and fingers. Stauffer examined one of the rods closely and found that it indeed had been subdivided into these smaller units of measure. Stauffer became curious. The Noah cubit rod seemed longer than he had imagined it would be. As Noah had explained, a cubit was typically measured from the tip of the middle finger along the forearm to the bended elbow. According to most textbooks on the matter, the average ancient cubit was just 18 inches long. Stauffer stood the Noah cubit rod on its end vertically from his desk top and placed his elbow beside it. Extending his fingers straight up, he measured them against the rod. Noah's rod continued another 4-5 inches beyond the end of Stauffer's extended fingertips.

Stauffer was a tall man by modern standards, six foot four inches, much taller than the national average. He was reminded that Noah must have been much taller than that, probably greater than seven feet. If that were the case, then, like Melek, everyone living in the days of Noah was much taller than people are today because, proportionately on the temporal monitor, they had all seemed normal-sized; no one was excessively taller than anyone else they had studied on the monitors. Stauffer had lost sight of the probable size difference and just assumed that they were the same size as we are today. Stauffer realized that if he were to stand in a crowd of Antediluvian people in Noah's neighborhood, he would have seemed like the runt of the litter by comparison.

Suddenly, another out-of-the-box idea occurred to Stauffer. He searched around the Crypt for a yard stick and brought it back to his office. He set it upright on his desktop and measured his own forearm from fingertip to elbow.... about 20½ inches, about two and a half inches longer than the ancient cubit recorded in history. Then he placed the Noah rod alongside the yard stick.... just over 24 inches long and fully six inches longer than the ancient cubit. Since the length of the Ark has always been typically calculated by multiplying 300 cubits times 18 inches, Biblical researchers have usually calculated the length of the Ark to be about 450 feet long.

But if the Noah cubit was really 24 inches, then the real length of the Ark was 600 feet long, the length of two football fields. Stauffer was somewhat familiar with modern naval vessel statistics and displacements, and he projected that the Ark probably displaced in the neighborhood of 20,000 tons, comparable with a modern, modest-sized aircraft carrier today.

And it was built entirely by hand out of gopher wood.

# Chapter 31

Another year passed and the Crypt team was making great progress in surveying Earth's antediluvian past. Research activity in the Repository was also moving forward and all of the staff working in the labs under Carlisle Barracks were making great strides in their individual work areas.

Stauffer was just getting off the elevator coming into the Crypt when Bob Zazworsky and Bill Tipton came running at him down the hallway from one of the labs. "Boss," Zazworsky blurted out as he rushed past Stauffer into the elevator, holding the door open, "Garner Wilson just called and asked that we come to his office on the double. He thinks that they've just detected their first act of temporal terrorism."

"What?" Stauffer stammered.

"That's what he said, Boss," Zazworsky replied. "Garner asked that you, Bill, and I get up to his office on the fly. He's got Alice Duerden and Rick Bailey on their way coming over from the Repository."

"Sounds big. Did he give you any idea of what was going on?"

Zazworsky and Tipton both shrugged. "Not a thing, Boss," Zazworsky countered. "I guess we'll find out when we get there."

The three friends met Duerden and Bailey coming from the other direction as they reached Colonel Wilson's door. Wilson was standing in the doorway and rushed them all into his office.

"General Goldwyn told me he would be attending a meeting down in Washington, DC, this afternoon and so he's not readily available," Wilson explained. "Since this issue has to do with detecting a hostile organization potentially using temporal energy against us, I guess that puts me in charge of our response. I wanted to include all of you around the table to help me think through all of the issues at stake and how it affects everything else we're working on."

"Roger that, Garner," Stauffer acknowledged. "Just what have you detected?"

"Well, with the new software the techies worked up for us, it gave us the capability of detecting whenever anyone uses temporal energy. Although we can't backtrack to the source, we can pinpoint whenever a time portal is opened in the areas we're monitoring. Alice is aware that we've been testing out the software trying to detect on-the-ground time travel missions any of the Repository teams have mounted during the past several weeks. At first, the results were spotty and inconclusive, but as we've used the software, we've gotten better at it.... much better. Checking against the actual Repository mission files, we've been able to track temporal energy usage with almost 99% accuracy. Only a couple of missions escaped our detection during the past week. We're getting very good at it."

"Okay, Garner," Stauffer acknowledged, "but what's the problem? Why have you called us all here?"

"We detected a temporal incident an hour ago. It happened at a fairly recent date in 1349, just south of Paris. The software detected a temporal burst and focused in on a scene where peasants were evacuating bodies of people who had succumbed to the Black Death to the outskirts of Paris, where they dumped the bodies in large pits they had excavated and then burned them. The Black Death years are one of those time periods which Doc Gates has pretty much nixed for any time travel activity because of the epidemiological risks, and so when we checked it against the Repository's mission files, we knew immediately that it wasn't any of us. Someone else is mucking around in the past."

"Have you been able to figure out who it is?" Tipton asked.

"Nope, not yet. But we detected at least two dozen other similar temporal hits within the next twenty minutes. This wasn't an isolated event. It appears to be some sort of orchestrated pattern."

"What's your plan for now?" Stauffer asked.

"I'm not sure yet, Bart. I've contacted the old man, and he's on his way back to Carlisle, but he won't be here for another hour. I have a sense of urgency about this that we don't have an hour to play with. I've got to do something now and fast."

"What has been the observed temporal activity for each of the other incidents?" Duerden asked.

"Well now, that's what has me worried. It appears to be some kind of collection activity. At the site south of Paris, as the peasants were dumping the bodies off their carts into the pit to be burned, a horizontal temporal portal opened up directly beneath one of the bodies and it disappeared through the portal as it fell into the hole."

"I know you can't tell where the body went when it dropped through the rogue portal," Stauffer observed, "but does the software tell you precisely how long the portal was open from start to finish?"

"Yes, it does. In each case, the portal was open for just a brief moment.... no more than ten seconds. We assumed that it was open only long enough to snatch the body and still escape detection in case anyone was monitoring."

"What were the other temporal hits you detected?"

"Now, that's what has me really concerned. Each of the hits seemed to be part of a massive collection effort to gather up samples of dead bodies from epidemics and pandemics that have afflicted mankind during the past five hundred years or so." Wilson referred to the list in his hands and continued, "— the measles and smallpox epidemics that Europeans brought with them to the Americas in the late 1400s,.... the black death plagues of the 1600s,.... the global cholera pandemic of the 1850s,.... the influenza pandemic of 1918,.... the polio epidemic of the 1940s and 50s,.... the 1942 British anthrax bioweapons trials on Gruinard Island during World War II,.... the Hong Kong flu outbreak in 1968-69, the HIV/AIDS epidemics that began in the early 1980s,.... the dengue fever outbreaks in 2008,.... the influenza pandemic of 2009,.... the Asian bird flu outbreaks in the early 2000s,.... the Ebola outbreaks in 2013 and 2015,.... the yellow fever outbreak in 2012,.... the swine flu outbreak in 2015, and the recent SARS and MERS outbreaks. There's more, but you get the idea."

"That doesn't sound good," Stauffer acknowledged. "Whoever is using the temporal technology, they seem intent on collecting all of the virulent, infectious diseases that have recently taken their toll on mankind. Worst-casing it, they possibly might be preparing some kind of biological attack combining all of these vectors laced into one super-contagion package."

Everyone around the table started speaking at the same time, all coming to a similar conclusion. Dr. Campbell observed, "All of the evidence points in the direction of this worst-case scenario. The fact that they gathered all of the vectors at precisely the same time within minutes of each other suggests that this is a highly organized threat and that a biological attack is imminent. We probably don't have much time to respond before they unleash death on the world."

"Yes, I agree," Stauffer chimed in. "How can you deal with that, Garner?"

"Well, General Goldwyn and I have been discussing various aggressor scenarios for the past two years, building contingency plans for each scenario," Wilson acknowledged. "But you're right. This is probably the worst case scenario. Such an attack would quickly decimate the global population and throw the world back into the dark ages. Our detection technology is limited to telling us that something is going on but it isn't capable of telling us the source. Someone has to go through the portal to confront them and attempt to put a stop to it."

"Go through the portal to confront them?" Stauffer exclaimed. "But that would be a suicide mission. We don't know what to expect on the other side of the portal, but surely they must be armed to the teeth."

"Yes, Barton, that's about what I figure. But it's what I've been training for ever since I took this job."

"You've been training for?" Stauffer sputtered. "What are you talking about, Garner?"

"Sure, Barton, why do you think the old man put me in charge of Hole operations the second time around instead of you? He wanted someone with Special Ops experience and capabilities that could respond in just such a case. But I need your help."

"Help?"

"Yes, the whole contingency plan response system for such a scenario is under two-person control. General Goldwyn set it up that way," Wilson responded. "In his absence, I need you to help me to access a couple of two-person control mechanisms."

Wilson stood and motioned to Stauffer to stand and follow him. Gesturing to the rest of the group surrounding the table, he said, "The rest of you just sit tight for a moment. We'll be right back."

Wilson walked over to his desk and entered a code on his keyboard. He turned to Stauffer and said, "Your side of the two-person code is your father's name, all upper case letters."

Stauffer grimaced. As Wilson turned his head away from the keyboard, Stauffer quickly typed in G-O-L-D-W-Y-N. The shimmering outline of a portal appeared over against the wall.

"Where does this portal lead, Garner?" Stauffer asked.

"Actually, Barton, I really don't know. General Goldwyn never revealed that to me. Hang close."

Stauffer followed Wilson through the portal and found himself standing in a large enclosed vault area. On a table in front of him was a large back pack affixed to a metal pack frame. Wilson stepped forward and moved the back pack around so that Stauffer could see two alphanumeric keypads on the harness. "The keypad on the left is mine. The keypad on the right is yours."

Stauffer was intrigued but perplexed. "But I don't know what the code is, Garner."

"The old man told me that your code is the name of your quiet spot where you like to watch sunsets, no spaces between words, all upper case. Does that make sense to you, Bart?"

"Yes, it does, Garner. But just what is this back pack anyway.... high explosives.... C4....?"

"No, Barton, it's a man-pack nuclear weapon, a very advanced version of the old Davy Crockett, only much lighter with a much higher nuclear yield, and this one has been modified with a temporal transponder to send a signal back to the Hole just before it initiates."

"Nuclear yield.... temporal transponder?"

"Yes, Barton. It's going to take a nuclear yield to incinerate all of the vectors the bad guys have accumulated before they can set them loose on the world. If I can get in quick enough, I just might be able to stop them."

"But why a nuke?"

"Because we've got to ensure that we burn up all the contagions they've gathered and dismantle their temporal program completely at the same time. A nuke is the only approach that pretty much guarantees both outcomes."

"But why a backpack nuke? Why do you have to deliver the package? Why can't we just drop it through the portal with an automatic detonation switch?"

347

"It's got to be under human control. We don't know what's on the other side of the rogue portal. It may be necessary to abort the mission."

Stauffer was running out of arguments and changed the subject. "This is a nuclear weapon back pack? It must weigh two or three hundred pounds."

"Actually, it only weighs a little over a hundred pounds. Remember I told you I have been training for this mission for some time now. I work out carrying a 150-pound simulator backpack three times a week. I'm ready for this."

"A hundred pounds?.... What's the nuclear yield on a weapon that size?" Stauffer asked.

Wilson answered back with a smirk, "Now, if I told you that, Barton, I'd have to kill you."

Wilson swiveled the back pack around and positioned it on the edge of the table. He backed up to the table and, bending down slightly, slid his arms through the shoulder straps and brought the chest harness straps around in front of him, securing the buckles in place.

Stauffer was beginning to understand the big picture of this contingency plan. "But Garner, how will you get back through the portal before it detonates?"

"I don't think that I will be coming back through, Barton. That was never part of the plan."

"But...." Stauffer started to sputter again.

"Listen, my friend." Wilson turned and faced Stauffer, putting his hands on his shoulders. "We both know this is a suicide mission. I know that. You know that. I've known that all along. I.... want you to know that it's been a privilege working with you. Keep the place running. Good luck.... Now, let's get back to my office. My people have been setting up a horizontal portal that I can jump through to follow the plague corpse through the rogue portal as it opens up. Remember, I've only got a ten-second window. It wouldn't do to get sliced in half passing through the portal too late as it shuts off. We know what that's all about."

Wilson passed back through the shimmering outline of the portal on the vault wall with Stauffer on his heels. As they reentered Wilson's office, they found General Goldwyn standing at the conference table. Goldwyn turned to Wilson and spoke softly but sternly, "When you initiated the worst case scenario contingency plan, your people pulled me back here through an auxiliary portal. Dr. Campbell has just briefed me up on your analysis of the situation and I concur — it is the worse-case scenario. It looks like it's finally happened. Are you ready for this, son?"

"Yes, sir. Would you please make sure that my family is taken care of. And please make sure they know how much I love them."

"Yes, Garner, I will do that. Have you and Barton entered the codes?"

"Not yet, sir. I thought we would wait until right before the jump."

"Alright then," Goldwyn paused. "Let's get on with it. We don't know how much time we have." Steering the two men over to where Hole technicians had set up a horizontal time portal close to the office floor, General Goldwyn asked the lead technician, "Fred, is it all set to go? Have you set the time and place parameters precisely for when the plague corpse drops through the rogue portal?"

"Yes, sir. I set it so that Colonel Wilson will drop approximately three feet above the rogue portal one millisecond after the corpse disappears. With a five second leeway before the rogue portal shuts off, that should give him plenty of time to complete the jump and pass all the way through the portal."

Turning to Stauffer, General Goldwyn instructed. "Come here, Barton, and enter your code on the right strap keyboard. Garner, you enter yours on the left. As the two men entered their two-person codes, a red light appeared on the left shoulder strap indicating that the weapon was now armed and the temporal transponder activated. Goldwyn spoke softly to Wilson. "Okay, Garner, the ball is in your court. If you press the blue button, the device will detonate after a one-second delay. Unless you enter the abort code within ten seconds, the device will auto-detonate anyway. Either way, hopefully, the pack takes care of all the contagions they've gathered. Good luck to you, son."

"Yes, sir. Thank you, sir."

Garner Stuart Wilson IV turned and stepped up on the small platform set up adjacent to the horizontal portal. Turning back to the people gathered around the room, a big smile stretched across his face and he gave them a big thumbs-up sign. "Take care, all.

It's been a pleasure." Turning back to face the portal, he hunkered down a few inches and then leaped with both feet off the platform and out onto the center of the portal. As he dropped through the portal and disappeared, everyone in the room turned to face the wall monitor that had been synced to a temporal monitor. They watched as the plague corpse disappeared through the rogue portal and then watched as Colonel Wilson dropped down through the portal that opened just above it, passing on through the rogue portal right behind the corpse. A second passed and the rogue portal blinked off. The technician running the time portal and the temporal observation monitor in Wilson's office toggled their portal off as well.

General Goldwyn turned to Stauffer and said, "They should be receiving Garner's transponder signal right now. We should know something quickly." Goldwyn walked over to Wilson's desk and picked up the red classified phone handset and entered a number. He spoke in a quiet voice so that no one in the room but Stauffer could hear. "Phil, we've just initiated Contingency Plan Black Rain. You should be getting Colonel Wilson's location transponder signal right now. Set your monitors to check for nuclear detonation."

General Goldwyn paused for a few seconds and then turned back to speak to everyone in the room. "I just received word confirming a nuclear detonation in Kaechon, North Korea, about fifty miles north of Pyongyang. If Colonel Wilson got there in time, the detonation fried all of the contagions they had accumulated and all of their temporal technology as well. We'll know soon enough. But if it didn't eliminate the contagions, they will surely have unleashed a global pandemic that could dwarf the casualty figures of the Black Death plague of the 1300s. It may take a few days for it to travel around the world, but with today's transportation technologies, I suspect that it will spread much more quickly than that. Team chiefs, I want you to release all of your people to go home and gather up their families in their homes. Recommend that they hunker down there and no one leave their homes for at least a month or so. We'll initiate an all-clear notification when contamination danger is over."

Everyone rushed out of the room, but Stauffer stayed behind. General Goldwyn had picked up the red telephone and started to dial when he realized that Stauffer was still standing there in Wilson's office. "Is there something else, Barton?"

"No, sir. It just seems like there's something else that I ought to be doing."

"There is, Barton, General Goldwyn instructed. "I want you to go home now and gather your family together with you for the next month or so until the danger has passed. I need to call the President and the National Command Authority to alert them of the potential for a global pandemic. And I need to evacuate Garner's family."

Stauffer blurted out, "Sir, my family isn't at home. They're out in Los Angeles visiting family during the school break."

"Then call them and tell them to get on the next plane home. You need them here with you right now, not somewhere out in California."

"Yes, sir," Stauffer replied mechanically and turned and left the office on the double as General Goldwyn continued to dial on the red telephone.

\* \* \* \* \* \* \* \* \* \* \* \* \* \* \* \* \* \* \* \*

Stauffer hurried down to his office and made sure that everyone in the Crypt had received word to evacuate and go home. On his way down, he stopped by Hank Phillips' crystal and DNA research labs to ensure that they had the word as well. When he finally got to his office, he phoned his wife and gave her instructions to forget about their luggage and get the kids to the airport and take the quickest flight home.

As he was leaving his office heading for the elevator to depart for home, he ran into a small group of his team. They were essentially all alone in the world with no family and had decided that staying down in the Crypt was probably the best option for them. They could access and stockpile food supplies, and Maggie Martinez had already used a time portal to go back one day and make arrangements with a local wholesaler for a tractor trailer of food stuffs to be delivered to the Carlisle Barracks motor pool today. They had just received word that the truck was going through the post security check point, and they were on their way to the motor pool to get it offloaded and the trucker on his way so that they could begin moving the pallets of food and water down into the Crypt through a portal. Apparently, personnel from the Hole and the Repository were also making similar arrangements and everyone that didn't have a place to go seemed to be well provided for here.

Satisfied that he couldn't do anything more, Stauffer took leave of his friends and went topside and drove home. When he got there, Gwen called to tell him that they were at the LAX Airport about to board a flight for Harrisburg with only one brief stopover in Chicago. She and the kids would arrive that evening at the Harrisburg International Airport at 11:15 pm. Stauffer began to relax a little knowing that he would have his family home with him soon.

\* \* \* \* \* \* \* \* \* \* \* \* \* \* \* \* \* \* \* \*

Unfortunately, it wasn't soon enough. Apparently, the people operating the rogue temporal site in North Korea were set up for practically instantaneous dismemberment and distribution of the bodies they had recovered through multiple portals. They put the bodies through a large machine which shredded the bodies into small pieces and managed to send the offal through a large array of time portals rapid fire before Wilson's backpack nuke could terminate operations. They targeted airports, concerts, and major athletic events around the world where tens of thousands of travelers and spectators were gathered. Shredded pieces of the infected bodies literally rained down on the crowds from portals opened several thousand feet in the air above them. The crowds below were spattered with miniscule droplets of the offal containing virulent strains of the worst diseases that had ever confronted mankind, and which were soon spreading rapidly throughout the global population.

Gwen and the children got to O'Hare International Airport in Chicago following an uneventful four-hour flight. But when they switched planes at O'Hare for the flight to Harrisburg, a host of people who had attended a game at Soldier Field moved through the airport terminal and several boarded their flight for Harrisburg. Two of them were already sniffling and coughing, and by the time the plane had taxied down the runway and was in the air for the two-hour flight into Harrisburg, the entire plane was infected.... including the flight crew. An hour and a half into the flight, the entire cabin was hacking and coughing and several people had died in their seats from respiratory stoppages or were collapsed in the aisle.

The pilots, who were also ailing by that point, declared an in-flight emergency and requested emergency landing instructions for Pittsburgh from the air traffic controllers. As the aircraft made a broad circle around the city to align on the runway, the copilot lost consciousness. Just as the pilot brought the aircraft to the end of the runway and touched down for the landing, he too lost consciousness and the plane careened off the runway, tipped over onto its right wing, and cartwheeled down the median strip, ripping off the wings and breaking the fuselage into several pieces. Passengers and crew members were strewn all over the median and runways as the wing tanks exploded in flames. Gwen and the children were sitting in the forward section of the cabin and were instantly incinerated as the portion of the fuselage where they were sitting erupted in a wall of fire.

Stauffer had been monitoring the news on his computer and heard about the crash almost as it happened. He jumped in his car and raced back to Carlisle Barracks, and was soon running along a subterranean corridor in the Hole towards General Goldwyn's office.

As he arrived at the door, the door clicked open and General Goldwyn ushered him into his office.

"Sir....," Stauffer wheezed totally out of breath. "My family.... their plane.... it crashed in Pittsburgh.... they're...."

General Goldwyn grabbed Stauffer by the shoulders and shook him. "Barton, listen to me. I saw the crash on the TV and I've already implemented an intervention to save them."

"Stauffer's face lit up, his voice still quivering. "They're alive?"

"Yes, in a manner of speaking. They didn't perish in the crash at Pittsburgh. O'Hare was already rife with infection and so I had to get to them before the plane touched down in Chicago. Pulling them off the flight from LAX proved too difficult because Gwen and the kids were spread out over several rows, most of them in center seats and difficult to extricate through a portal. I decided to snatch them in the LAX terminal on their way down the gangway to board the plane. There was an elbow turn in the gangway itself and the people who were boarding behind them were stopped at the entry point trying to get their boarding passes to register on the bar code reader. I set up a portal just behind the group of passengers boarding in front of them, and Gwen and the kids all rushed right through it before they realized what was happening."

"Where are they then, sir? Where did you transport them?"

"Now that was the difficult part, Barton. I didn't know whether or not they were already infected so I couldn't bring them down here. I'm not even sure if you are infected after driving across town and coming in from outside."

"Sir," Stauffer's voice was cracking and insistent, "just where did you relocate them then?"

"I had to move them to a safe place where they could be checked out and treated if necessary," General Goldwyn explained carefully. "But there wasn't any such place available right then and so I moved them into another interdimensional plane where a potentially deadly infection just wouldn't matter."

"Wouldn't.... matter? What are you talking about, sir?" Stauffer was distraught and confused.

"Don't worry, Barton. Your family is safe.... alive and well.... and you will be with them before they know it. I moved Garner's family there as well. But for right now, I need to have you come over here and lie down in this reconstitution chamber. It will identify any potentially infectious contagions you might be carrying and eliminate them from your body."

Stauffer was still trying to come to grips with the safety of his family and wasn't concentrating and focused on what General Goldwyn was telling him. "Lie down in that box? Why, sir?"

"Barton, listen to me. You might be infected. We need to eliminate that possibility. Now, you're a good soldier who knows how to obey orders, and I'm ordering you to lie down in the reconstitution chamber so that I can take care of you."

Stauffer moved towards the imposing sarcophagus-shaped box that was positioned to the side of the room next to Goldwyn's bookshelves. As Stauffer sat down on the side of the chamber, General Goldwyn assisted him in swinging his legs up and into the cavity of the box. As Goldwyn was helping him get situated, Stauffer mumbled, "How does it work, sir?"

"You'll soon be asleep, Barton," Goldwyn responded, "and when you wake up, you'll feel better than you ever have in your life."

As General Goldwyn lowered the lid to the chamber, Stauffer managed to get out one last question before unconsciousness overwhelmed him, "Why....?"

As the chamber lid clicked into place closed there was an audible whirring sound as the air in the chamber was evacuated and replaced with a blue-colored gas. Goldwyn looked through the transparent plate on top of the chamber at the now slumbering Stauffer. "Sleep well, Barton. This may take awhile, lad."

# Chapter 32

Stauffer stirred in the tight enclosure of the reconstitution chamber and began to struggle as his claustrophobia quickly set in. He began pushing frantically with his arms and legs against the confining walls of the box. The lid on the chamber swung open automatically in response to his jostling around, and Stauffer groggily tried to swivel his body around and extend his legs down to the floor.

From across the room, he heard General Goldwyn's voice, "Go easy, Barton. You've been asleep for some time. It's going to take awhile to get strength back in your legs."

Stauffer turned his head in the direction of Goldwyn's voice. He could barely make him out across the room through blurry, leaden eyes. "How long.... how long have I been out?" His mouth was dry, his tongue was swollen, and he had difficulty forming his words.

"It's been over a month, Barton," General Goldwyn answered back. "It takes a while to recover from the smorgasbord of diseases that you were carrying inside you when you arrived here."

"What.... what.... do you mean?"

"It appears that the attackers were quite effective in gathering together every virulent strain of virus, bacteria, and nastiness that has afflicted mankind for the past five hundred years. The chamber detected and documented at least 37 separate species of pathogens and disease strains racking your body. It took quite awhile to flush that all out of your system."

Stauffer slowly processed what General Goldwyn was telling him and looked around behind him to both sides of the box he was sitting in. "What is this box anyway? It cures disease?"

Goldwyn laughed, "That and quite a few other things as well. It's Ancient technology developed long ago that kept us healthy before the Departure. But it was effective in cleansing your body of all the contagions and infectious diseases that were trying to kill you...., your friends too."

"My friends?" Stauffer asked. "What do you mean?"

Stauffer stood up slowly as he was talking, steadying himself by holding on to the side of the chamber. Looking around General Goldwyn's office, he saw two more chambers just like the one he had been in. "Who is in those boxes?"

"Take a look for yourself. Here, I'll help you," General Goldwyn said as he took Stauffer's arm and guided him to the other side of the room where the other two chambers were positioned.

Looking down through the transparent observation plates on the lids, Stauffer saw that the chambers contained the bodies of Bob Zazworsky and Bill Tipton, lying there still unconscious. "How long have they been out, sir?"

"Almost as long as you were. They arrived together back here at the Hole about two hours after you got here. I knew they were coming and had already prepositioned two additional chambers for them. They were on the verge of succumbing and almost didn't make it here. They've been asleep ever since. The readout from the chamber control panels says that they were exposed to an even broader variety of virulent strains of disease than you were. They might be out for quite a while longer."

Turning to face Stauffer, General Goldwyn asked, "How do you feel, Barton?"

Stauffer did a quick self-inventory. "Other than some stiffness in my legs and back, I feel pretty good. In fact, I've never felt more invigorated or alive. I...., I don't seem to need these bifocal glasses anymore to see clearly. I can see just fine without them.... even stuff up close. What did that box do to me?"

"Well, Barton," General Goldwyn responded tentatively, "it did a little more than just remove disease from your body and fix your vision. It also reworked the DNA in your cells to bring your body up to maximum efficiency. In the process, I believe that it's given you the full physical characteristics of an Ancient, including longevity and regeneration."

"Longevity?.... Do you mean that I'm going to live to be 900 years old now?"

"I believe so, Barton. But first, I need to run a blood test to check it out. Could we do that now? Won't take but a minute."

"Okay. That would be a good thing to know."

"Good. Put your arm here on the table." As he spoke, Goldwyn retrieved a small transparent ampoule from his desk.

He removed the cap exposing a needle point and turned it upside down over Stauffer's arm. "Now this may sting a bit but it will pass quickly."

Before Stauffer could reply, General Goldwyn brought the ampoule needle down sharply on Stauffer's arm. Stauffer felt a pin prick but the sensation disappeared immediately. "That was it? It must not have worked," he mused.

"Oh, it worked just fine, Barton. See?"

General Goldwyn held up the ampoule which was now completely filled with bright red blood. "This should be just enough for the test," he observed and walked back over to his desk where he had a small electronic apparatus set up. He lay the ampoule on an indentation on top of the device and swiveled a mechanical arm over the top. He secured the arm in place and pressed a button. "Shouldn't take but a minute," he assured Stauffer.

Stauffer looked down at his arm where the needle had impacted his skin but didn't see any puncture wound or even any redness. It was as if General Goldwyn hadn't drawn any blood. He started to ask him what was going on, but General Goldwyn interrupted as an almost imperceptible bell on the apparatus sounded. "See, no time at all."

Goldwyn leaned over the apparatus, peering at a readout screen, and then turned to Stauffer. "Just as I had hoped. Your DNA has been enhanced and the gene for longevity has been activated."

"900 years?" Stauffer asked petulantly.

"That's right, Barton, at least 900 more years. And, as you've already seen looking for the needle prick, it's also activated the gene for regeneration as well."

"Regeneration? What do you mean?"

"Well, Barton, can you imagine all of the bumps and scrapes your body could accrue in 900 years' time? You would be just a mass of scar tissue by then. Regeneration means that your body doesn't just heal from wounds, it regenerates new tissue altogether. That's why you can't find the entry point for the needle I just drew blood with. Your body healed the puncture hole completely, regenerating new tissue so that it's as if you were never wounded by the needle. Check it out. You shouldn't have your appendix scar anymore or the scar on your left leg where you nicked it with the hedge trimmers last summer."

Stauffer quickly checked them out as Goldwyn had suggested. He couldn't find those scars or any of a hundred smaller, imperceptible scars on his arms and legs that he had had before. Even better, he noted that a boil on his thigh had disappeared, the wart on his elbow was gone, and he didn't have any moles anywhere. The chamber had been pretty thorough in working him over and wiping him clean. His skin was smooth and pristine.

Stauffer was overwhelmed by this new information flooding his thought process. "Sir, I've read about regeneration before but it was always in the context of newts and geckoes that grow new tails when one breaks off. Are you telling me that if I were in an accident and cut off my arm, I would grow a new one back?"

"That's it, Barton," Goldwyn responded. "I'm working on my third right arm myself. I'm not particularly adept with a sword and I had to defend myself a couple of times in ancient days. When my attackers saw that I didn't really bleed and my arm they had just cut off had already started to heal and grow back, they just turned and fled. The story made its way into quite a few legends and fairy tales."

Stauffer was incredulous. "I find this all so difficult to believe, sir."

"Here," Goldwyn responded. "Let me give you a little demonstration and set your mind at ease." Goldwyn walked back over to his desk and picked up a knife that he used to open envelopes and returned to the conference table where Stauffer was sitting. He laid his hand with fingers spread out on the table and brought the knife down swiftly, cutting off the tip of his index finger. There should have been blood gushing from the wound all over the table but only a couple of drops emerged before the wound began to heal over and a new finger started to sprout from the stub. "See, Barton. It's practically instantaneous. It only takes a few hours or so to grow new fingers. The finger nails take a little longer but they come back too. It takes a couple of days to grow new arms and legs.... Regeneration.... it's a great gift and absolutely essential for someone who's going to live over nine hundred years."

As Stauffer sat there with his mouth open, watching General Goldwyn's finger regenerate, Goldwyn quickly brought the knife around and made a deep cut in Stauffer's left arm.

Startled, Stauffer instinctively brought his right hand up and cupped it over the wound to quell the blood. "Move your hand,

Barton," General Goldwyn instructed. "You are blocking the view of the demonstration."

Stauffer cautiously pulled his hand away just in time to see the edges of the gash in his arm knit together and then disappear entirely. "You see, Barton?" Goldwyn observed. "Most cuts and other wounds heal themselves in a matter of seconds.... minutes for deeper wounds."

Stauffer sat there at the table rubbing his arm, somewhat in disbelief. "That machine of yours really changed me. I'm not who I was anymore."

"Actually, Barton, you've not changed all that much. You've always had the genes for longevity and regeneration written into your DNA. It's just that they were never activated. The reconstitution chamber simply activated those genes so that they could do what nature intended."

"Did the.... reconstitution chamber.... change anything else?"

"As a matter of fact, Barton, it did. I programmed the chamber to rewrite your junk DNA, recording all of the revised histories that have been produced to date by the Repository and Crypt historians and stored on our intranet database. It also wrote the histories of the Ancients that was recorded on my own DNA. You are now a living Hall of Records. You may be the most important human being on the planet."

"I'm a living Hall of Records?"

"That's right, Barton. The entire history of mankind from the very beginning is now recorded on your DNA."

Stauffer was having a very difficult time connecting the dots on all this new information and didn't know what to say. Finally, he changed the topic and sputtered, "Have you programmed Bill's and Ski's chambers the same? Are they going to live for 900 years and be able to regenerate body parts too?"

"Unfortunately, Barton, that won't be the case. The chambers were designed to work on Ancient physiology. We've found that they don't work in the same way on modern humans. Bill and Ski are both products of our assisted-birth program from back in the late 40's and early 50's and the chambers do work for them, but only in a limited way."

Stauffer was surprised as General Goldwyn reminded him. "When you intervened for Bill and Ski to be born.... that made them Ancients too?"

"Yes, in a way. They're hybrid children of modern mothers and Ancient fathers. The sperm for their artificial insemination was provided by other members of my team, not by me. Unfortunately, when we ran follow-up blood work after they were born, we found that they didn't have the genes for longevity or regeneration to be able to activate them. You did."

"Am I the only one then?" Stauffer asked.

"Only one what?"

Stauffer carefully reworded his question. "Am I the only one of the assisted-birth children you worked on who has the longevity and regeneration genes?"

"Yes, it appears so. All of the others appear to be mostly normal modern humans, like Bob and Bill."

Stauffer filed all this information in the back of his mind and pressed on. "Sir, you said I'd been asleep for almost a month now. Where's my family? What happened to them? What's happening outside? Were they able to control the spread of the contagions or did they get completely out of control in a global pandemic?"

"Like I told you before you went into the reconstitution chamber, Gwen and your children are just fine. I've removed them to safety." Goldwyn's face grew solemn. "Unfortunately, Barton, the situation topside looks pretty grim. The contagions got out of control almost immediately, even much more than we feared. Because there were so many different contagions in the mix released in so many densely-populated places around the world, even if people had a natural immunity to one contagion, they would likely succumb to something else. It was the rare individual who had a natural immunity to everything and survived."

"That doesn't sound good, sir."

"Oh, it actually gets worse, Barton.... much worse."

"How's that, sir?"

"Just before we lost all communications, Dr. Campbell received an encrypted message from her old employers at the Jet Propulsion Laboratory in Pasadena. They had just discovered and were tracking a large near-earth orbit object that appeared on their screens the week previous to the contagion attack. The object apparently entered our solar system and flew by Jupiter on a course that would have taken it back out of the solar system. But Jupiter's gravity grabbed hold of it and it slingshotted around the gas giant and flew off on a collision course with Earth's orbit. Worse, Jupiter's gravity pull apparently shattered the object and created a dust fan trailing behind it over fifteen thousand miles wide. The object eventually passed close.... it was a near-miss, flying between the moon's orbit and the Earth. The object was immense, perhaps fifty miles across, and it affected the Earth's magnetic field and caused some unexpected activity in the Earth's plate tectonics. There was a great deal of movement in the Earth's crust throughout the world. Here in the United States, the effect was particularly strong in the New Madrid Seismic Zone in the Midwest, along the Cascadia Subduction Zone in the Pacific Northwest, and the San Andreas Fault along the California Coast. Combined together, they resulted in massive, magnitude 9+ earthquakes all across the country. The gravitational effect of the object also caused violent volcanic eruptions in the Ring of Fire surrounding the Pacific Rim, killing millions in the near vicinity of the erupting volcanoes and shooting dust and ashes high up into the stratosphere."

Stauffer was horrified as General Goldwyn explained all that had been happening. "Sir,.... I.... don't know what to say. That's a perfect storm of events. It couldn't get any worse than that."

"Actually, Barton, it can.... and it did. The dust cloud following the object completely enveloped the earth as it flew by and a large quantity of the dust floated down to the Earth's surface. Most of it fell into the oceans where there was an almost immediate response. Hundreds of millions of fish began dying and floating up on the beaches around the world. The guys at Jet Propulsion Lab don't know what caused it, but apparently, the dust harbored some kind of microscopic bacteria frozen in cryogenic suspension. When the frozen dust particles fell into our oceans, they warmed up and the bacteria activated and started killing off whole species of sea life. A scientist posted at one of JPL's research stations in the South Pacific captured a sample of the dust and put it under a microscope. Although it doesn't look exactly like Earth bacteria, it bears a strong resemblance. The researcher reported, just before he died, that the bacteria gave off a strange exotic odor like absinthe."

"Absinthe, sir.... the distilled spirit?"

"Yes, Barton. But absinthe is also known by another name.... Wormwood."

Stauffer was becoming more despondent by the minute as Goldwyn revealed each additional calamity for planet Earth. Finally, he summoned the courage to ask the key question. "Sir, what are the fatality figures? Give it to me straight."

"Yes, Barton, of course. The pandemic spread quickly to the far corners of the globe. Even isolated areas have been affected. No area was left unscathed, although the fatality figures vary greatly from region to region. Some cultures were wiped out altogether while others fared slightly better, but overall, it looks like there was a global survival rate of less than ten percent. In those areas affected directly by earthquakes, volcanic eruptions, and tsunamis, the survival rates are much lower."

"The Earth's global population before this all started was well over seven billion people," Stauffer exclaimed. "Are you saying that more than six billion people have died? How could the mortality rate have been so high?"

"That's a question that we are still trying to figure out. The survival percentage rate has been much.... much lower than it was in other eras for similar pandemics."

"We, sir? Who's we?"

"Well, Barton, while most of our staff left to gather up their families and sequester themselves in their homes, about a hundred of our team members working in the Hole, the Repository, and the Crypt, didn't have any family to go to and opted to remain here underground. The air systems are filtered down here and so far no airborne pathogens have been able to get in. The three organizations have all combined into one and are essentially living and working together down in the Repository. They've set up dormitories with sleeping cubicles in several of the empty vaults, and they seem to be doing just fine. Some of the men and women have paired off and become couples. Two of them have sent me formal requests that I marry them as the sole surviving legal authority. We'll take care of one of those wedding ceremonies early next week."

"Who's running the show down here, sir?" Stauffer asked.

"I've left Alice Duerden in charge overall in the Repository and asked Pete Pendleton to take over logistics, maintenance and operations support."

"Pete? I thought that he would have left to join his family."

"Pete and his wife were empty nesters, and their only son was killed in an automobile accident several years ago. Pete's wife was in the hospital recuperating from serious surgery a week before this all happened, and she actually passed away the night before the contagions were released. Pete had come down to the Crypt to clean up a few things, when we sounded the alarm, and he elected to just stay here. There was nothing he could do to help his wife.... she was already gone. Pete wandered around here numb for a couple of days, but he seems to be okay now."

Stauffer's mind was racing. "What about the rest of the staff who went home to join their families?"

"As near as we've been able to determine, only a few survived beyond the first three weeks. Even if they managed to establish an effective self-quarantine in their homes, the airborne pathogens eventually got to them."

"When are we going to be able to get the survivors back here to the Hole?" Stauffer asked anxiously.

"Doctor Gates tells me that we may have to wait quite awhile. Some of these infections may have become endemic and there could be sporadic future outbreaks for the next five to ten years. Doctor Gates has set up several vaults in a recently-opened section of the Hole that was just completed three months ago. The section was originally intended for other purposes, but Doctor Gates has converted it into decon infirmaries and is bringing back staff members and their families while they were still alive using the time portals, and putting them through a lengthy decon process and blood workup to make sure that they're clean before they can be reintegrated back into our population down here. He's already brought back a few dozen key staff and family members and put them through the process. It seems to be working. We'll have them stay put there for a couple of months until Doctor Gates clears them, and then we'll move them back into the general population."

"What about Ski's and Bill's families?"

"Ski told me months ago that his wife, Fran, had been diagnosed with pancreatic cancer a few months earlier and that she was going downhill fast. The plague infections just released her earlier from her mortal pain. I moved Bill's wife and daughter through a portal to another interdimensional plane to join Gwen and the kids and Garner's family members."

At General Goldwyn's mention of his own family, Stauffer returned to his own primary worry and concern. "Gwen.... the kids.... are you sure they're alright, sir?"

"They're just fine Barton. Like you, they're feeling better than they have in a long time."

"Where are they, General Goldwyn? Why can't you bring them here now?

"As I told you before, I had to remove them to another interdimensionality. Unfortunately, it's a one-way trip. You won't be able to rejoin them until you go there yourself."

"Can I go now, sir?"

"I'm afraid not, Barton. There's too much work for you to do here. I'm hoping that you are up for the challenge."

Stauffer let that thought pass for the moment and pressed Goldwyn further. "With all of the casualties topside, what has happened to world governments and economic systems?"

"With so many casualties, most government and economic systems have ceased to function altogether. Oh, we have a small surviving cell of the Federal Government's National Command Authority still trying to perform continuity of operations duties, but they don't really have a mandate or any power. Right now, the world topside is in a general state of chaos as the survivors are shuffling around trying to reorganize in some fashion."

"Is there something we can do to help out?" Stauffer asked.

General Goldwyn just shook his head. "No, Barton, the situation is way beyond our capability to influence the outcome. For now, we need to do what we can down here to wrap up Repository and Crypt operations, putting all of the histories into some semblance of final order and then see what happens next."

"Roger that, sir. If you don't mind sir, I'll go down to the Crypt and over to the Repository to check in on folks. Will you please call me when Bill and Ski are stirring?"

"That I can do, Barton."

\* \* \* \* \* \* \* \* \* \* \* \* \* \* \* \* \* \* \*

Stauffer went down to his office in the Crypt first. He worked his way through all of the offices, labs, and vaults, but finding no one, he left and took the moving sidewalk tunnel over to the Repository to see what Colonel Alice Duerden and Pete Pendleton had going on over there.

As he walked down the Repository's cavernous gallery, he found Colonel Duerden's office door slightly ajar. Colonel Duerden was hunched over some paperwork on her desk. Stauffer knocked lightly on the door frame and Colonel Duerden looked up. Her shoulders were slumped down and her face appeared haggard. When she saw Stauffer, she jumped to her feet and ran over and gave him a big bear hug.

"Barton, you're a sight for sore eyes," she exclaimed in sheer joy. "You've been away for so long I was beginning to think you would never get back here."

"It's good to be back. And you're a sight for sore eyes yourself, Alice. General Goldwyn tells me you've got everything under control down here. How's it going?"

"Oh, you have no idea, Barton. It's been tough.... real tough. So many people died. So much death and destruction topside.... the world on the surface is in chaos.... Civilization as we know it is totally upended...."

Colonel Duerden's voice started to trail off as if she were distracted by her own private ghosts. Stauffer attempted to bring her back on track. "What about Carlisle Barracks.... and Carlisle.... and Central PA in general?"

"It's pretty bad, Barton. Carlisle Barracks was closed, locked up tight, and put into moth balls.... Everyone has left. Carlisle and the surrounding area is a ghost town. Still lots of dead bodies lying around everywhere. It happened all so fast that there wasn't anyone left to bury the dead. Not much moving up there on the surface anymore."

Stauffer whistled under his breath. "How many folks do you have down here now?"

"Counting all of the folks who used to work in the Repository, the Hole, and the Crypt combined, we've got a little over a hundred."

"How are you accommodating and feeding so many people?"

"We vacated a dozen vaults and moved the artifacts stored in them over to the Waxahachie vaults. Then we brought in beds and furniture from furniture company warehouses shortly after the release but before the contagions had spread. We've set up a number of barracks-style dormitories and a food kitchen in some of the larger vaults. Our maintenance technicians jury-rigged a series of reverse osmosis filters and distillers for our water supply system to make sure no contagions get in. The waste water evacuation system wasn't an issue. It was originally designed with special valves to allow only one-direction water flow. Our waste water is being pumped into the Conodoguinet. Not a very elegant solution and certainly not very ecologically sound for the moment, but there's no one topside now for quite a distance to complain about it. We'll have to work on that as the contagions on the surface diminish and we can do ground work up there."

"What about electricity? What are we doing for power generation and light down here?"

"Well, Barton, that one is beyond me. When Pete and I queried General Goldwyn about power, he just smiled and assured us not to worry about it. He told us we should have an unbroken, almost unlimited access to power, just like we've always had. The light bulbs are a mystery to me too. I've been down here in the Hole and the Repository for going on six years now, and I've never seen anyone replace a light bulb. They're not typical incandescent bulbs, and they're not neon bulbs either. I don't know what they are, but they just don't ever seem to burn out."

"Hmmmn.... I'm going to need to talk with General Goldwyn about that one," Stauffer said. "But it sounds like you've got a workable solution going so far. Tell me, Alice," Stauffer said changing the subject, "how is everyone down here faring. What do you have everyone doing right now?"

Duerden's face broke out into a weary smile as she leaned back in her chair. "A few days after the Decimation, General Goldwyn had me stage a command briefing meeting for him in the Majestic to speak with all of the survivors down here. Not many of us.... We only took up the first six or seven rows. At the beginning of the meeting, General Goldwyn fielded a lot of questions, but once he had those out of the way, he laid out a strong rationale for why it was important that we continue our work down here, finishing up all of

the projects that we were currently working on, and even extending
the History Quest into the future, keeping track of humanity on the
surface beyond the Decimation and adding that to our historical
record. Without going into any detail, he assured us that at some time
in the future, that record would be invaluable and he urged us all to
stay focused on what we were doing."

"And did everyone buy into that?" Stauffer asked.

"Actually, yes. Pretty much so. and it was most welcome
counsel and advice. I found out real fast that we needed to keep on
truckin', performing our normal mission work routine. Keeping busy
down here seems to keep most folks' minds off the loss of family and
friends on the surface."

As Stauffer and Duerden were chatting, Dr. Gates stuck
his head in the doorway to the office. "Howdy, Barton. They told
me that you were back. Good seeing you again. Am I interrupting
something?"

"No problem, Doc. Come on in."

"Thanks. How are you feeling, Barton. Are you on top now?"

"Yeah, Doc," Stauffer replied. "I'm fine. Alice and I were just
talking about potential mental health issues of the folks down here. I
figure that we could have some real problems."

"Unfortunately, I think you're right," Dr. Gates responded.
"We've got a few folks down here who are still suffering from shock
with the loss of loved ones and disrupted lives. Some of our folks
here are pretty fragile right now with post-traumatic stress disorder,
bipolar disorder, and chronic depression. One of the Repository
cataloguers has withdrawn completely into herself into a catatonic
state and is non-responsive. I've got her interned in my dispensary
right now, and other members of the staff come by and sit by her
bedside to talk with her, trying to engage with her and encourage
her back to reality. It's a tough case.... an uphill battle. We're not even
sure if she's hearing their voices. As for the rest, outwardly, most
everyone else seems to be doing okay, although I suspect that many
are carrying a heavy burden and some may even be harboring deep
anger and resentment. It's tough being a survivor when everyone
else you care about has perished. We're going to have to watch that
closely."

"Any potential suicide risks?" Doc? Stauffer asked.

Dr. Gates considered the question for just a moment and then responded, "No, Barton, I don't really think so. I'll let you know immediately if I suspect that anyone has taken a turn for the worse."

"Keep me posted," Stauffer said. "Hey, Doc, what can you tell me about the near-orbit object that flew past Earth and dusted us off with a toxic cloud? What was it anyway? General Goldwyn told me that it killed off whole species of sea life."

"He's right, Barton. Before we lost all communications, I was able to find out that the dust cloud was infused with extremophiles."

"Extremophiles? I'm drawing a blank, Doc. What's that?"

"Extremophiles are organisms that thrive in extreme environments of pressure and temperature. Here on Earth, we have terrestrial extremophile bacteria and microbial life that thrive in the crushing pressure and high temperatures living near hydrothermal vents at the bottom of the deepest parts of the ocean. The extremophile bacteria in the dust cloud apparently were just the opposite. They had the capability to endure the vacuum and extreme cold temperature of space. As the dust cloud entered Earth's atmosphere, the bacteria warmed up and activated. For the most part, the bacteria dropped into the world's oceans where they proved highly toxic to many species of sea life. I've seen pictures of sea coasts around the world littered with millions of dead fish."

"Has it wiped out all life in the sea, Doc?"

"Now that's the strange part, Barton," Dr. Gates responded. "It appears that the alien bacteria evolved almost instantaneously after entering our seas, and appears to have become innocuous to terrestrial sea life. The initial large die-off has greatly upset the ecological balance of our oceans, but even now it appears to be rebounding. I decided to run some tests of my own. I cleared it with General Goldwyn and used a portal to bring a small sample of the bacteria here to a controlled access vault. I suited up in full hazmat gear and ran a series of tests on the bacteria in the lab I set up. I ran experiments with it, exposing some of the fish from my aquarium to the bacteria cultures. There was no reaction at all. I've had the fish isolated under observation now for 26 days. Nothing. The fish seem to be behaving absolutely normally, and the bacteria appear to me to be dying out. They're almost gone from the microcosm of the aquarium tank. I'm going to need to draw another sample from the ocean soon to compare with my earlier sample to see what's happening, but it appears that the threat from the dust cloud to terrestrial sea life has passed."

"Well that sounds promising," Stauffer commented.

"Yes it does." Dr. Gates glanced at his wristwatch. "I'm going to have to excuse myself. I've got a meeting in two minutes with one of the members of the staff. He's been having bad dreams and night sweats and he wanted to talk with me to see if I could help him. I've got to run. I'd like to meet with you later, Barton, to continue this discussion if that's alright."

"Sure thing, Doc. Take care. See you later."

Turning back to Colonel Duerden, Stauffer picked up the thread of the conversation from when they were interrupted. "Alice, I know that you're keeping close tabs on the Repository mission. Who is running the show for Hole and Crypt operations?"

"Jared Lincoln was working for you before in the Crypt but with Garner gone, General Goldwyn moved Jared over to assume responsibility over operations in the Hole. Because there's not much possibility of another temporal attack right now, Jared's team is pretty small. Maggie Martinez took over Crypt operations until your return. General Goldwyn told us that you would be back soon. At least ten of your team members elected to stay down here, and according to Maggie, they're making progress with advancing the Crypt mission. You'll have to ask her to fill you in on all that."

"Where would I find Maggie, Alice?" Stauffer asked. "I was just over there and the Crypt was deserted.... no one there."

"Oh, she and Jared are meeting with Pete Pendleton over in Pete's office to discuss a couple of logistics issues. I think the rest of your crew are down in one of the Repository vaults assisting with inventory and classification. Why don't you just barge in on Maggie and the rest. I'm sure they would all be happy to break up their meeting to welcome you back. Here, I'll go with you."

Together, Duerden and Stauffer left her office and walked across the gallery to the vault where Pete Pendleton had set up shop. They found Pendleton, Lincoln, and Martinez huddled around his work table discussing a large flow chart laid out in front of them. As Duerden and Stauffer entered, they jumped to their feet and crowded around Stauffer to greet him. After a few minutes of pleasantries, Stauffer turned to take his leave to go back to the Crypt. Addressing Pendleton, he said, "Pete, General Goldwyn has assigned you to take over logistics and maintenance for the entire place, and Jared, he assigned you to take over Hole operations. I hate to lose you both, but you've got more important jobs to do right now. Maggie, you're stuck with me. Could you please round up the rest of the Crypt team who are here and meet me in my office in about two hours? We need to review where we're at and what we're doing to move forward."

"Can do, Barton," Martinez responded enthusiastically. "We'll all be there shortly. Good to have you back!"

As Stauffer walked back down the gallery to the double doors to the moving walkway back to the Hole, he was psychologically deflated as he rehearsed in his mind all of the death and destruction that had occurred on the surface. He was greatly depressed about the fate of his own family. General Goldwyn had assured him that they were alive and well, but Stauffer had a tough time reconciling that with his sense of discomfort and foreboding of not being able to be with them right now.

Stauffer tried to imagine the dead bodies lying unburied in Carlisle on the surface above them, and he was overwhelmed by the thought of the other six billion plus people around the globe who had also perished in the calamities of the past month and were just as likely lying unburied in buildings and cars and out in the open.... everywhere. He tried to imagine without success how the survivors were coping with the stink of all the dead and decaying bodies. He tried to envision what people were doing around the world just to survive.... just to keep on living from day to day. Stauffer's brain was fast moving toward the panic mode. He was having an impossible time coping with the magnitude of death that had overcome the Earth.

As he raced along the walkway, Stauffer's mind ran through a dozen different contingency plans in his head that they could potentially execute using temporal technology to prevent the plague scenario altogether before it happened. There might even be something they could do about the wormwood object that had flown between the Earth and the orbit of the moon, swathing the planet with its deadly toxins. He thought back on their previous successes in space temporal operations. They had great success with moving asteroids and satellites out of their destructive trajectories before. Perhaps if they went back in time, there was something they could do again now.

The more he thought about it, the more overwrought and angrier he became. As Stauffer emerged into the Hole, he hurried right past the turn in the hallway that led to the elevator down to the Crypt and went back up the circular stairway, practically on the run, to go to General Goldwyn's office. When he got there, he put his hand on the ID hand pad mounted on the wall and began pounding on the massive door. General Goldwyn's voice came over the speaker. "You are back already, Barton? That didn't take long. Please come in. I expect that we have much to talk about."

The door lock sounded and the great door swung inward. Stauffer rushed in, hastily swinging the door shut behind him.

As he moved across the office he glanced at the reconstitution chambers where Zazworsky and Tipton lay. The lids to the chambers were still closed and he could see their faces through the viewing panels on top. Stauffer moved right up to the edge of General Goldwyn's desk and leaned over. "We've got to do something, sir," he announced in a raised, anxious voice.

"Do something?" General Goldwyn calmly replied. "What do you mean, Barton?"

"Sir, we've got to use the temporal technology and go back and prevent the plagues and pandemics." Stauffer's voice started to break and he slumped down into the chair at his side. His eyes welled up in tears and he had a hard time eking out the words. "Sir, we've got to prevent all of the death.... and destruction.... and relieve the suffering. We have it in our power.... we have the technology.... We've got to do something."

General Goldwyn came around his desk and pulled up a conference table chair and sat down beside Stauffer. Goldwyn placed his hand on Stauffer's shoulder as he sat there and sobbed uncontrollably. Stauffer wept for several more minutes before he was finally able to bring his pent-up emotions under control.

General Goldwyn sat there patiently, waiting for the right moment to speak. Finally, as Stauffer's sobbing diminished, he said softly, "You know, Barton, I expected that it wouldn't take you too long to find your way back here to my office. It is overwhelming to consider the catastrophe that has beset the world. While you were laid out in the reconstitution chamber, I began thinking through possible things we could do with the temporal technology to avert it all and move to an alternate time line. But Enoch communicated with me a profound reminder of what it was all about. These calamities have all been foretold for a very long time by prophets and priests and seers and soothsayers of many different religious persuasions. Down through the millennia, most of the world's great religions have forewarned about the end times or end of days when great calamities and misfortune would befall the earth. Well, it finally happened and Enoch advised me that we have to let it stand as is. We can't attempt to change it. Enoch tells me that it will ultimately be for the best as the end days play out."

"Do you mean, sir," Stauffer whispered between sobs, "that we have to stand by and do nothing?"

"Yes, Barton. I am afraid so. We are not going to be allowed to intervene with some kind of temporal fix to put us on another timeline. We are going to have to live with this one."

"Well then, sir, just what are we supposed to do?"

General Goldwyn smiled patiently, trying to assuage Stauffer's fears and anger. "Well, Barton, I suppose that we will just have to try to do the best we can for now."

# Chapter 33

Stauffer sat nervously at the head of his conference table as he awaited the arrival of the Crypt team. He had already lost Pete Pendleton to overall logistics and Jared Lincoln to Hole operations. Bob Zazworsky and Bill Tipton still lay prostrate in reconstitution chambers up in General Goldwyn's office. Beyond Maggie Martinez, he didn't really know how many of his primary team were left and able-bodied.

A knock on his door disturbed his thoughts. He stood as the door opened all the way and Martinez led a parade of staff members into his office. "I brought everyone, Barton,....primary team and support staff," Martinez announced as she took her seat at the table.

"Indeed you did, Maggie," Stauffer responded with a wide grin as he inspected his primary team that assembled around the table: Maggie Martinez, Miriam Campbell, Sanjay Singh, Sammy Woo, Ken Red Elk, Ginny Nguyen, Hank Phillips, and Max Manchester. Standing at the far end of the table was a small team of about twenty support staff: inventory and classification specialists, translators, linguists, and historians. Stauffer was relieved that there were so many left to continue supporting the Crypt mission. Under his breath he observed, "They just might be able to put a serious dent in the work remaining to finish up after all."

Looking toward the end of the table at the standing members of the support staff, he said in a loud, positive tone of voice, "Let's get started on this new organization with a new rule. If anyone sits, everyone sits. Let's get the folding chairs out of the next vault and get enough in here for everyone to have a seat around the table. We can all crowd in."

Stauffer led a few of the men out his office door and into the next vault over where they had previously stored a number of folding chairs. They each grabbed some chairs under their arms and returned to Stauffer's office and set them up next to the table with an additional row forming a second tier of seats. When they had all the chairs arranged and everyone was seated, Stauffer started speaking slowly, not knowing quite what to say next. "You all have been through a.... great deal of pain.... during this past month. I have no way of knowing how it has affected you individually, but allow me to express my sympathy and condolences for any losses you might have suffered." He paused as his eyes moistened with tears, unsure of how to go on. "These are perilous times for Planet Earth. General Goldwyn has briefed me on the general global mortality rates of the pandemic that has swept the world, and the earthquakes, volcanic eruptions, tsunamis, and extra-planetary dust that have all compounded the problems on the surface. It doesn't look pretty. The world that existed just a little over a month ago is no longer there, and we don't yet know how the survivors will coalesce topside into new societies to replace it. We have been blessed to have survived down here. According to Colonel Duerden, between the Hole, the Repository, and the Crypt, there are a little over a hundred of us working and living down here now. I've been away, and I just got back, and so I don't know all that you've been doing down here to get accustomed to our new living and working conditions. I hope to rectify that quickly. Meanwhile, I've been told by General Goldwyn that we can continue to live down here as long as necessary, and the temporal technology provides us the means to make that possible. I want you all to know how much I appreciate Maggie Martinez for keeping the team together and providing leadership in my absence. I'm going to ask Maggie that, for the present at least, she continue acting as my second in command. As you can see just looking around the table, we are missing some of our original team members. The bad news is that some of our team members have perished. The good news is that I think that we'll have Bill Tipton and Bob Zazworsky back here with us shortly, within a few days or so."

Stauffer looked around the room into everyone's faces. They reflected what he interpreted as a note of hope and optimism that he hadn't seen when they first entered his office. He concluded his briefing, "Colonel Duerden told me about the meeting in the Majestic where General Goldwyn explained to you why it was so important to complete our projects down here. I appreciate your commitment to making that happen. What I need all of you to do right now is provide me an assessment of where we are at on all ongoing project investigations and operations we're doing here in the Crypt. We need to know where we are, working with the Repository crew, on completing the History Quest. We're going to need to figure out how to organize to get as much done as we possibly can. Let's meet here again tomorrow at 0900. Could everyone please bring an assessment for your area and let's get an overall feel for the immensity of the task at hand. This meeting could take a couple of hours, but I do think that it will be well worth the investment of time."

* * * * * * * * * * * * * * * * * * * *

Following the assessment meeting the next morning, Stauffer headed back up to General Goldwyn's office to report and get his guidance for how he wanted them to proceed. As General Goldwyn buzzed him into his office, Stauffer found both Bob Zazworsky and Bill Tipton sitting at General Goldwyn's conference table. "Well," he said, trying to sound cheerful and nonchalant, "it's about time you two woke up. Are you ready to get back to work or are you still trying to get your sea legs after snoozing for the past month?"

"Hey, ease off, compadre," Zazworsky responded with a half-hearted grin. "If you had gotten here on time just a few minutes earlier, you could have massaged my feet and served me breakfast in bed."

"Good to see you, Barton," Tipton said groggily. "General Goldwyn was just explaining to us about the reconstitution chambers. Pretty neat technology. The darn thing eliminated the scars from my injuries I got way back in jump school when I got a Mae West when my chute didn't open right. And my skin is as smooth as a baby's bottom now."

"Me too," Zazworsky joined in. "I just discovered that it wiped my U.S. Army and Mother tattoos off my arms. I hardly recognize myself."

"Well, you're both looking pretty good. I'm glad that General Goldwyn was able to offer you such nice accommodations and help you get rid of all your warts and imperfections." Stauffer's voice became muted and strained. "Has General Goldwyn briefed you on all that has happened topside while we were in the reconstitution chambers?"

Both Zazworksy and Tipton shook their heads to the side. "Why Boss?" Zazworsky asked. "What's happened?"

"Well, we've got a lot to talk about, guys," Stauffer said. "The world on the surface is a very different place today, and we're going to have to learn how to deal with it and our new lives down here." Turning to General Goldwyn, Stauffer asked, "Sir, are you done with them for now?"

Goldwyn nodded and said, "Yes, I think these two are ready to return to duty and get back into the fray."

"Is General Goldwyn right, guys?" Stauffer asked. "Are you two really ready to get back to work?"

"Yes, sir!" they both responded in unison.

"Good, then here's what I want you to do," Stauffer said. "Go down to the Crypt and greet the team. Oh, and unless I miss my bet, I think that General Goldwyn would just as soon that you keep mum on the reconstitution chambers for now. Get an update on all that has transpired topside. And I want you to walk around the Repository and get a feel for how everyone down here is working through their losses. We can talk about it later today."

"What will I tell them when they realize that my tattoos have gone AWOL and that Bill's face looks like a baby's bottom now?" Zazworsky quipped.

"That's not what I said, Ski," Tipton countered with a gentle chop to Zazworsky's ribcage.

"Yeah, I know," Zazworsky replied, "but it makes for a better sound bite."

Zazworsky and Tipton exited the office, jostling each other, and closing the door behind them. Stauffer smiled, "Those two will be most helpful to keep the place cheerful in spite of all that's gone down."

General Goldwyn nodded and motioned for Stauffer to join him at the conference table. "So, how is it going so far, Barton? Have you got your modified team off and running yet?"

"Yes, sir. We had an assessment meeting this morning, identifying where we are with all of our ongoing projects and who we have left to do it all with. It's going to be slow going for awhile but I think that we'll be able to pull it off."

"That's good," General Goldwyn responded. "What help are you going to need from me?"

"Well, sir, not much for now. But there are a couple of questions that I'd like to run by you."

"Go right ahead, Barton. Question away."

"Yes, sir," Stauffer began. "Alice Duerden briefed me on the situation down in the Repository and the set up for water and air and such. But she was pretty vague about our power supply down here. She said that you had told her not to worry about that, and that we had an almost unlimited access to power, just like we always have. Would you like to fill me in on that, sir?"

"That one is pretty straightforward, but you can't share the answer with anyone, at least not just yet. I told you earlier that Nikola Tesla was part of my stay-behind team. Early in the last century, he came up with a whole series of interrelated inventions regarding power generation and transmission, only part of which were ever implemented on a mass scale. Now, electricity is not my area, and so I don't really understand everything about it. Tesla told me that he had come up with several different approaches for generating free energy. Some of his ideas had to do with different applications of photovoltaic cells and generating power from sunlight. But he also showed me diagrams for how you could harness power from lightning, the moon's gravitational pull, cosmic energy that enters Earth's atmosphere from space, and even from the Earth's own natural magnetic field."

"That all sounds pretty revolutionary!" Stauffer observed.

"It was, Barton. And the ideas were way ahead of their time. Because they sounded so out-of-the-box, Tesla had a difficult time obtaining patents for many of his ideas. He built several small-scale models to demonstrate their feasibility and ran them by me before he went forward again with his patent applications. When I saw them in action, I commissioned him to build two full-scale free-energy power generation systems that had the capability to draw power from several alternate sources — the sun, cosmic energy, the moon's gravitational pull, and the Earth's magnetic field. I gave him a rather large quantity of gold to finance the project and to use in the construction of the system components for longevity purposes. He came back to me a year later and demonstrated the two systems he had built. They weren't identical, but relied on different approaches to achieve the same result. I put the systems into storage during World War II, and brought them both here when we brought the Hole online."

"And that's what's been providing power for us down here from the beginning?" Stauffer asked querulously.

"Not quite, Barton," General Goldwyn responded. "Both systems were installed in a special section here in the Hole but they weren't activated initially. One would the primary power provider for the Hole, the Repository, and the Crypt, and the other is the backup system. Because of the system design, Tesla assured me that once put into use, the systems could probably generate abundant supplies of power for upwards of several thousand years. We had been working on external PPL-provided electricity ever since we first started operations down here in the Hole. But I switched the entire system over to Tesla's power generation equipment a couple of days after the Decimation began when the PPL power supply started to fail. The system seems to be working just fine, and I expect that it will continue to operate well for at least the next thousand years."

"Sir, what about the light bulbs?"

"Light bulbs, Barton? General Goldwyn asked. "What do you mean?"

"The light bulbs down here in the Hole, and the Repository, and the Crypt," Stauffer responded. "Alice pointed out to me that they never seem to burn out. She's right. I've never had to change a light bulb in all the time I've been down here."

"Alice is correct. The bulbs never do burn out. They are another invention of Tesla. The bulbs are not incandescent.... they are a form of gas tube lamp. They are designed to burn indefinitely because, like neon tubes, they don't have any kind of filament inside to burn out. I had a whole warehouse full of different shapes and sizes of the gas tube lamps manufactured to be used for our operations down here. Every light bulb used in the Hole, the Repository, and the Crypt, and even down at the Waxahachie vaults, are Tesla's gas tube lamps. Light should never be a problem down here."

Stauffer paused to consider Tesla's genius and ponder what other Ancient technologies might be at work down in the Hole.

General Goldwyn's voice prodded Stauffer back to the situation at hand. "Do you have any other questions, Barton?"

"Yes, sir. I have a whole laundry list that I wanted to run by you. For starters, why is it that you seemed to know so much about the Ancient city that now lies buried under that thick layer of broken shale in North Middleton? As we were working through recovery operations on that project, you seemed pretty familiar with everything."

"The short answer, Barton, is that the city was my birthplace and hometown. I lived there for a little over a hundred years before I left for Atlantis."

Stauffer was visibly surprised. "Well, sir, that explains a lot.... You told me earlier that there was a tomb and sarcophagus buried right below the block building on top of the step pyramid. Who's buried in that sarcophagus?"

Goldwyn responded quickly, "Methuselah...., Enoch's son and my nephew. He was a great man.... a little eccentric perhaps but really a great man. When Enoch told him of the plan to depart with Atlantis and that he wanted Methuselah and his son Lamech and families to stay behind to carry on the patriarchal lineage, Methuselah was at first a little resistant with the idea. But when Enoch promised him that by staying behind, he would live to be the oldest living mortal man in the history of the planet, his ego was assuaged, and he willingly accepted the assignment."

Goldwyn continued, "There were four Patriarchs who came before Enoch who were still alive at the time and they remained behind on Earth when Enoch departed with Atlantis — his father, Jared, his grandfather Mahalaleel, his great-grandfather, Cainan, and great-great-grandfather, Enos. Those four men all died later after Atlantis lifted off but well before the Flood, leaving just Methuselah, Lamech, and Noah. Noah was born four years after Enoch and Atlantis departed. Almost six hundred years later, Lamech, died. Methuselah died five years after that in the same year as the Flood itself, at the ripe old age of 969 years, not quite a millennium but setting the record for the longest-living man. Because of the perilous state of affairs among mankind at the time, I think that Enoch would have liked to go ahead with the Flood a little earlier, but he had to wait for Methuselah to outlive Enoch's father, Jared, who had lived upwards of 962 years. Enoch gave him a full seven years more so there wouldn't be any quibbling about the record holder later on."

"That doesn't track, sir. If the city and the step pyramid and block building were already buried under a mountain of broken shale at the time that Atlantis departed, how was Methuselah laid to rest in the sarcophagus in the tomb six hundred years later?"

"That was an easy proposition, Barton. As you have already noted, the tomb and sarcophagus were constructed in place hundreds of years earlier. We just opened up a portal into the tomb and laid the old patriarch out in his sarcophagus after his passing. It seemed like an elegant solution for protection against potential grave robbers."

"Quite a story, General Goldwyn," Stauffer sighed.

"Yes it is, Barton, which brings me to an important point. Enoch promised Methuselah that if he stayed while everyone else departed with Atlantis, he would have the honor of being the longest living man. Given all the jumps in and out of time I've made during the past five thousand plus years, I'm now over 967 actual years and my time on planet Earth is fast drawing to an end. I can't outlive Methuselah's distinction of longest living man. It was promised to him and the promise must be kept."

"General Goldwyn, are you telling me that you're going to leave us soon?"

"Yes, Barton, very soon now."

"But who will replace you to run this place? Is there another member of your stay-behind team who has more years left who can step in and take over?"

"That was never the plan, Barton. Most members of the stay-behind team are already gone. Smathers is the only man left, and I have him working one last special assignment and then he'll leave as well. When I depart, there won't be anyone else. And besides, Enoch and Atlantis will soon be returning to help with the reestablishment of order on the surface of the planet. They should be touching down anytime now. Enoch's scout airships have been preparing the way for years, and with the events of the past month, it can't be far off." General Goldwyn got a faraway look in his eyes and stopped talking for a moment and then turned back to face Stauffer. "No, Barton, I've been tracking and guiding your development through the years ever since you were born to prepare you to take over for me when the time arrived at last for me to go."

"Me, sir?" Stauffer sputtered.

"Yes, Barton, you are the only modern man left who has the active longevity gene and can stick around for an extended stay. You've got about a hundred folks down here under Carlisle Barracks to help you finish up the various missions and projects we're working on, but soon, they will all start leaving or dying off, and rather than marriage ceremonies, you're going to be presiding over what will seem like non-stop wakes, funerals and memorial services.... and then you'll be all alone. That's a challenge that Enoch didn't even ask of Methuselah."

"What do you mean, sir?"

"Barton, you began training for this job early in your military career, performing custodial duty at the nuclear warhead detachment. Remember how lonely and isolated you sometimes felt then? Well, it's about to begin again. You are about to become the custodian of the Hole, the Repository, and the Crypt, and everything else that's buried down here under the Barracks and over in Texas at the Waxahachie vaults.... the sole surviving custodian.... and I'm afraid that we're going to ask you to do it for a very long time."

"How long, sir?"

"Enoch hasn't told me that, Barton. He and his people will be living and working on the surface, but he has asked that we have a continuing custodial presence down here until we get close to the endgame."

"Endgame, sir? What's that? And why does he want a custodial presence down here? Can't we just put the whole facility in cosmoline and mothballs?"

"Let me answer your second question first, Barton. Every time in the past that we left a repository site unmanned and unattended, something almost always happened that degraded the site's longtime storage integrity. In a couple of cases, we lost an Ancient repository site and a library altogether when they were pilfered by looters. Having a vigilant custodian on site could have avoided some of those issues. But we also need to have you continue to monitor mankind's activities on the surface with the temporal technology to keep the history record you and your team compiled updated and current all the way to the end."

"The endgame, sir?"

"Yes, Barton. It was foretold long ago that there would be almost a thousand years of peace on the earth following great calamities, and then violence would erupt once again and consume it all in one final curtain call. Enoch assures me that you won't be required to stay here until the very end.... but almost. I'm going to provide diversions and things for you to do to keep your mind occupied, but it will get lonely. The years will seem to go by slowly.

Every so often, you'll need to take a rest in the reconstitution chamber to revitalize and refresh your body and mind, but more importantly, to update the history of the world on your DNA. You can set those sessions in the chamber for as long as you want, but I ask you to give it your best shot to stay the course awake the majority of the time."

"Are you going to give me warning before you go or are you just going to disappear one night?"

"Barton," Goldwyn answer back, "I could never do that to you. I'll get with you to say goodbye and give you some final guidance before I depart. Trust me."

* * * * * * * * * * * * * * * * * * * *

Stauffer met with Zazworsky and Tipton later that evening in his office. He asked Pete Pendleton to join them so that they could discuss some of the logistics issues that had occurred to him. "Bill...., Ski...., did you have someone brief you up on what happened while.... we were away?" Stauffer asked.

"Yes, Boss," Zazworsky answered. "Alice Duerden gave us a pretty thorough overview of what it looks like topside on the surface now. Not a very pretty picture."

"Yes, Bart," Tipton interjected. "It's surprising to me just how fast and how thoroughly the world came unraveled. What do you have planned to do with the temporal technology to go back and put things back the way they were?"

Stauffer hesitated. He hated the answer that he had to give them. "We're not going to be able to do that guys.... We can't go back and try to prevent the Decimation.... or anything.... General Goldwyn told me that we're going to pretty much have to leave it alone as is. The most we are going to be able to do is go back and pick up some of our staff and family members before they died and bring them down here to see if Doc Gates can nurse them back to health in his quarantine labs."

"That would go a long way towards improving everyone's spirits down here!" Tipton observed.

"What do you mean, Bill?" Stauffer asked. "What did it look like to you as you did a swing through the Repository?"

"Well, Barton," Tipton responded. "it's kind of hard to explain. Things look pretty calm on the surface and most folks seem to be going about their business like they always have. But I sensed a lot of tension and anger...., maybe even hostility, just barely contained beneath a thin veneer of civility,.... like a powder keg about to go off."

"Yeah, I sensed that too, Boss," Zazworsky added. "People are being polite to each other and all, but you get the distinct feeling that it wouldn't take much to set everyone at everyone else's throat. There's a little too much island fever going on down here. I saw the same thing when I had a brief assignment at Schofield Barracks in Hawaii. I would go down to the beach when I could break free to body surf and just lie in the sun. I was always striking up conversations with the beach bums, and when I told them how lucky they were to live in a paradise like that, many of them got angry and scoffed at me and told me how much they wanted to get off that rock and back to the mainland. A couple of them even tried to pick a fight."

"And you sense the same thing here, Ski?" Stauffer asked.

"Yeah, I think so. You know, we're pretty much safe and secure down here, but there's nowhere to go to just be alone to work your way through your feelings. We're going to have to set something up to help people lighten up some. If not, the whole place down here could get hostile pretty quick."

"That bad, Ski? These folks all know and like each other," Stauffer countered.

"I know, Barton," Tipton said. "But I think I agree with Ski's assessment. Yes, we've got it pretty good down here right now, but living and working elbow-to-elbow in such close quarters is going to wear pretty thin quickly. We need to be proactive on this one to keep the lid on it."

Stauffer turned to Pete Pendleton. "Pete, you've been down here under the new circumstances longer than anyone. What's your read on the situation?"

"Well, Barton, I think that Ski and Bill have nailed it. People are still doing their best to adjust, and they want to do well, but we need to find ways to help them through it all."

"Do you have any ideas how we can do that, Pete?" Stauffer probed.

"I did have a couple of ideas occur to me as Ski and Bill were talking. Would you give me that assignment as part of the logistics mission? Before my wife died, we went on a cruise around the Caribbean. After a couple of days, it could have gotten kind of dull and boring doing the same thing day after day. But the cruise director was incredibly creative and full of fun and she kept coming up with new activities to keep us all occupied and enjoying ourselves. I think that I could groove on that role down here.... the Repository Cruise Director."

Zazworsky and Tipton laughed and made jokes comparing Pete to Julie on *The Love Boat*, but Stauffer only had to think about the suggestion for a brief moment before he made a decision. "I like the idea, Pete. Done. You are now the Repository Cruise Director. Go for it."

* * * * * * * * * * * * * * * * * * * *

The next week, Stauffer attended the marriage ceremony officiated by General Goldwyn between Maggie Martinez and Ken Red Elk. It was a brief ceremony. The bride was radiant, dressed in a white Repository jump suit draped in long swaths of white silk salvaged from the New York City fire of 1835. The groom was dressed more simply in just a blue lab jumpsuit with a string bowtie made with dark blue ribbon.

After the ceremony and the banquet that followed, Bob Zazworsky and Pete Pendleton chauffeured them in one of the larger Repository golf carts down to the far end of the gallery to a makeshift honeymoon suite, a vault that had been decked out with luxurious furniture and fittings. The cart made a tremendous clatter as it traversed the long gallery as the tin cans that Max Manchester and Sammy Woo had tied on strings to the back of the cart bounced along the cement surface.

Zazworsky had personally gussied up the otherwise drab interior of the vault with specially selected golden artifacts from throughout the ages. Pendleton further dressed up the bridal suite with several ornate wooden tables bedecked with romantic lighted candles. As the friends ushered the bride and groom into the vault, they showed them all of the special touches that everyone had contributed to make it a truly special and memorable occasion, right down to the complimentary Hershey Kisses that had been positioned on the pillow bolster on the king-size bed. Stauffer wheeled a cart over to where the couple was standing and proudly presented them with a bottle of very expensive, chilled champagne and a silver tray with a plate of steak and French Fries, the bride's favorite food, accompanied by a small amphora of garum. Zazworsky lifted the lid on the cover to the tray to show the couple the food, and then, he and Pendleton beat a hasty retreat from the vault.

As they emerged into the gallery, they hung a long floor length drapery in front of the vault door with the words "Just Married." spray painted across the front. Then, they did their best impersonation of Bert the cop and Ernie the taxi driver, from the movie *It's a Wonderful Life*, serenading the newlyweds with their rendition of "I Love You Truly." When they were finished, they disconnected the strings of cans from the golf cart and quietly turned it around and made their way back to the crowd at the other end of the gallery who were still partying and whooping it up.

* * * * * * * * * * * * * * * * * * * *

"The wedding was quite a nice affair, Barton," General Goldwyn acknowledged. "I appreciate all of the work that you and your people put into it. I know that Maggie and Ken were appreciative. And everyone seemed to be having a good time at the wedding party after the ceremony. It was a good break for all of us."

"I agree, sir," Stauffer responded. "It did much to relieve tension and lighten up spirits down here. We were getting to be a pretty somber group. Everyone seems energized and more focused now."

Stauffer paused, waiting for General Goldwyn to say something. When he didn't, he continued hesitantly, "Sir, I don't have a great deal more to report this morning. Do you have something else for me?"

"Yes, Barton. I do. I asked Smathers to join us here to update us on Garash. He sent me an email saying that he had more to report. He should be here anytime now. Can you spare another few minutes until he gets here?"

"Sure thing, sir. While we're waiting, could I ask why you call him Smathers, rather than Colonel Smathers or by his first name? I don't even know what his first name is."

General Goldwyn laughed. "Smathers **is** his first name. Remember, he is an Ancient and in the day when he was born, people generally only had one name. I was an exception to that rule. Our father, Jared, named my older twin Enoch and me Kubal, but later on in life, he started referring to me as Kubal Golden One and the name stuck. When I integrated into the Army research team at Wright Field after the crash at Roswell, the name morphed into Cubby Goldwyn over time, and no one ever remembered what my real name was. It's just as well."

"But how could Smathers exist on Army records with just one name?"

"After I had been working at Wright-Patterson for a few years helping the Air Force reverse-engineer Ancient technology, I sent for Smathers and worked him into the black project where I was assigned. Because it was such a top secret operation, it was relatively easy to bring him on board surreptitiously, and I created a false personnel jacket that showed Smathers as his last name. I took a big marking pen and drew a heavy black line through the space for his first name, as if it was to be kept secret. Well, the ploy worked and Smathers has been on the Army payroll for over fifty years now moving in and out of various black projects with just one name...."

As General Goldwyn was speaking, the buzzer on his desk sounded, signaling Smathers' arrival. Goldwyn buzzed him in and the three men sat down at the end of the conference table.

"Tell us, Smathers," General Goldwyn asked, "just what do you have to report about our friend Garash?"

"Sir," Colonel Smathers retorted, "Garash was NOT our friend. In modern vernacular, the man was a sleazeball.... the worst of humankind.... well...., that's not entirely accurate."

"What do you mean?" General Goldwyn asked.

"Garash was not entirely human," Smathers stated matter-of-factly. "I followed his activities through the years and chanced on one occasion to see him remove his clothes to bathe. I know that I violated the Repository's rule about personal privacy by not backing away immediately, but just as I was about to toggle off, I discovered an astonishing thing.... Garash was not completely human. He was a hybrid, the result of early DNA and gene splicing experimentation conducted by a group of rogue scientists in the days before Atlantis departed. The group created all kinds of combinations of human and beast, the stuff of legend and mythology. Garash was apparently one of the milder mutant combinations...., part man on his upper extremities and part goat on his lower extremities."

"Garash was a satyr?" General Goldwyn asked quite astonished.

"Yes, sir. Some of the satyrs they created looked more goat than man, but Garash was mostly man, except for his goat legs, cloven hooves and tail. He escaped somehow from the compound where he was created, and he tried to integrate into society. He manufactured himself a set of prosthetic feet that looked so human-like that no one ever questioned him about them, and he always wore long robes and loose-fitting clothing to disguise his odd shape. Apparently his condition caused him a great deal of bitterness and anger. At one point in time, I watched him sit down on the ground and amputate his lower extremities with a laser cutting tool. It didn't work. His goat legs just regenerated and started to grow back. As Garash watched the blood stanch and his legs grow back from the stumps, he just sat there on the ground and cried like a baby. It only took a few days and he was up and walking around again. But that's why, when we first saw him much later procuring the giant skeletons at Lovelock, Nevada, he looked so odd in his ill-fitting suit. It was the best he could do to disguise the reality of his true physical makeup under his clothes."

"But what has Garash been up to during all the intervening years since Noah and his sons ran him off?" General Goldwyn asked. "After he did a temporal jump over the Flood years, what did he do on Earth? Were you able to relocate him to see what he was up to?"

"Yes, sir," Smathers responded. "As a matter of fact, I lucked onto it. Apparently, after he had been rejected by both Enoch and Noah, he became very resentful and bitter and focused on the death and destruction of the survivors of the Flood. When Garash emerged on the other side of the Deluge after the waters had receded, he immediately started sowing discord and unhappiness. He had a rough time getting anyone to pay any attention to him for quite awhile, but over time, he gained traction. He was successful in influencing some of the most bloodthirsty conquerors and tyrants the world has ever known.... and that influence was extensive throughout the centuries. Garash was the one who convinced the Chinese emperor Qin Shi Huang in 213 B.C. to burn all history books and bury Chinese scholars and intellectuals alive. He taught the Persians, Carthaginians, Macedonians, and Romans the gruesome art of crucifixion.... He convinced Vlad, Prince of Wallachia, to impale his victims on the ends of sharpened stakes.... He inspired the warlords and barbarians of the Dark Ages in endless wars and bloody conflict.... He travelled around Europe dressed in a long, black hooded robe spreading infectious diseases and the Black Plague...."

"Wait, Colonel Smathers," Stauffer interrupted. "Are you suggesting that Garash was the Grim Reaper.... the Angel of Death of the Middle Ages?"

"Absolutely right, Colonel Stauffer. Yes I am. That's exactly what I'm suggesting. And on that count alone, he was responsible for the deaths of over a hundred million people."

Stauffer sucked in his breath when he heard the unbelievable statistic.

Smathers continued, "Garash was behind the torture and excesses of the Spanish Inquisition.... He singlehandedly influenced the burning of the great library at Alexandria, not once but on several different occasions over the centuries.... He convinced the Mesoamericans that their gods required human sacrifice.... He convinced the Conquistadores to burn indigenous Americans alive who refused to convert to Catholicism.... He was behind the Salem witch trials.... He had a great deal to do with the butchery of the world wars and the Holocaust.... Garash was patently an evil being through and through. He was the epitome of evil.... He thrived on death and suffering." The otherwise calm and self-assured Smathers had worked himself up into a rage and practically shouted the last few sentences.

Unable to contain his curiosity, Stauffer spoke up interrupting, "Have you discovered how he moves around in time without the apparent use of portals?"

Smathers caught himself and lowered his voice. "I still don't know how he did it. Somehow he perfected a technology or technique for moving through time without the mechanics of the temporal portal technologies we depend on. But I discovered quite by accident that he could only move in one direction — forward in time — into the future. He couldn't move backward in time into the past. And whatever it was that he was doing to move through time, it didn't move or displace him in space. He always reappeared in exactly the same place at some point in the future. That's how I caught up with him. When Barnum's house detectives threw Garash out of the American Museum, I followed him down the street with the temporal monitor. He turned into an alleyway and promptly disappeared. I chanced to set the temporal monitor on fast forward and discovered that he reappeared in exactly the same spot three days later. He left the alleyway and made his way back to the smoldering ruins of the museum. Barnum and his people were working their way through the ashes and rubble to see what they could salvage. Garash stood off to the side across the street for hours, a great smile of satisfaction on his face, apparently relishing Barnum's pain and the loss of history the fire represented."

"How did Garash wangle a position as an agent for the Smithsonian?" Stauffer asked. "He was responsible for acquiring and sequestering trainloads of skeletons of giant antediluvian humans and other important artifacts in the warehouse subbasement of the Museum of Natural History. He started the stuff moving in that direction even before construction on the museum was completed. How did he manage it?"

"Garash was an opportunist," Smathers replied. "Funding from James Smithson's estate finally worked its way clear through British legal wickets in 1838, and the U.S. Congress passed legislation shortly thereafter in 1846 creating the Smithsonian Institution. Smithson himself apparently had a clear idea of what he wanted the institution to be — 'an establishment for the increase and diffusion of knowledge for the United States of America.' But as ideas for the Smithsonian began to take shape, it had to be put on the back burner because of the Civil War. In 1865, toward the end of the war, as energy for formalizing its mission and purpose grew, Garash got very busy. Not only did he set fire to Barnum's popular American Museum, he also started a blaze in the Smithsonian Institution Castle Building on the Mall in Washington, D.C., earlier that year on January 24, 1865, almost three months before the surrender at Appomattox."

"Garash burned the Smithsonian Castle too?" Stauffer was astonished at the audacity of the man.

"That's right, Colonel Stauffer," Smathers responded. "Along with a number of important pieces of colonial art, the fire destroyed most of Smithson's original letters and papers which defined the Institution's fundamental purpose. With those defining documents out of the way, Garash wormed his way into the confidence of the Institution's curators and convinced them that they needed to be afraid of popular science and all of the discoveries of mounds and skeletons of giant humans and curious artifacts that were turning up all over America at the time. Rather than becoming an institution that fostered the discovery of new ideas, he convinced them that these discoveries needed to be suppressed because they ran contrary to the theories of established science. He acquired a contract from the Smithsonian to roam around the country, seeking out what he convinced them were obvious archeological frauds and deceptions and shipping them back to Washington where they could be hidden out of sight to avoid confusing the accepted Eurocentric understanding of the ancient Americas."

"How could they be so short-sighted?" Stauffer lamented.

"Oh, but they were," Smathers answered. "Garash had them mesmerized with his spurious ideas and the curators totally bought into the deception. Consequently, they never made any attempt to examine any of the archeological treasures that Garash sent their way for storage in the subbasement warehouse of the Museum of Natural History. And when that space filled up with unopened, dust-covered crates, they funded the construction of several other warehouses around the Beltway, where they stored mountains of all the other artifacts that Garash and other Smithsonian agents could obtain that didn't jive with the accepted science of the day. The paradigm became impossible to break, and, in the process, Garash managed to obliterate most of the evidence of antediluvian occupation in the Americas."

"Smathers," General Goldwyn interrupted, "you have been referring to Garash in the past tense. What has happened? Is he dead?"

"Yes, sir," Smathers responded. "I was just getting to that. I was able to spot Garash several times during the past four or five decades. He had changed his modus operandi once again. He had gone beyond merely collecting antiquities and was now involved in inciting riots with violent, destructive crowds of angry people. He was always the instigator, the one who whipped the crowds into a frenzy. He was a ringleader of the race riots during the sixties in Watts and Detroit and elsewhere. He was behind the slaughter of countless Africans in Rwanda, Nigeria, Algeria and the Congo. He was an instigator of the Tiananmen Square massacre in China. I most recently picked up his trail in Iraq and Syria where he was working with ISIS forces, killing defenseless civilians and destroying ancient Sumerian antiquities and archaeological sites. He has been hard at work in the Gulf trying to erase the last archeological vestiges of one of the first great population centers to emerge following the Flood. He was the moving force behind the destruction of the Nergal Gate in the ancient city of Nineveh and the bulldozing of Nimrud. He was an evil, vindictive, destructive man.... er, half-man."

"Those are very recent occurrences," Stauffer interjected. "But is he really dead now?"

"Yes, Garash is now dead, and it didn't happen easily. During the last century I have been observing him, I watched him regenerate several body parts as they were severed during some of his more dangerous exploits. In fact, during one encounter when he was trying to steal an important artifact from a museum in Athens, I watched him take several bullets square in the chest when he was shot by a museum guard. Blood was spurting everywhere. He fell to the floor for a moment or two, and then he stood right back up again and ran out of the museum with the artifact still in his arms, leaving the shaken museum guard standing there terrified and speechless at what he had just witnessed."

"So how did he finally die if he could regenerate so easily?" Stauffer asked.

"It was a perfect storm for Garash. He was working with a small team of ISIS soldiers, all of them dressed in black robes and facemasks. They were carrying powder bags of explosives from the back of a truck and stacking them against the outside wall of an ancient church in Mosul."

"Wait," Stauffer interrupted. "If they were all wearing facemasks, how do you know it was Garash?"

"I watched him put on the mask right after eating a sandwich in the truck on the way to the church. The church was full of worshippers at prayer — men, women, and a few children. As Garash and the terrorists were offloading the explosives, a missile came flying in and hit the truck. It exploded on impact, and the bags of explosives that Garash was carrying in his arms blew up in his face in a secondary explosion. I watched the scene in super-slow motion as the explosive force ripped the mask off his face and Garash's body was torn to shreds. There were pieces of Garash lying everywhere all over the street. Some of the larger pieces vibrated momentarily and seemed to struggle to regenerate, but they finally ceased movement and settled down into a dark mass of burned flesh on the dusty road."

"I waited and watched the aftermath for over an hour. The parishioners emerged from the church at the sound of the explosion. Fortunately, only the terrorists were killed or injured by the missile impact. But the bottom line is, Garash is no more. They swept up the smoldering pieces of his body and deposited them in several large plastic trash bags and hauled them off to a land fill. He is dead at last."

General Goldwyn sat there pensively digesting Colonel Smathers' report. After a few moments, he let out a long sigh of relief and finally spoke. "Well then, Smathers, with Garash gone, that completes your assignment. You are now free to go. I extend to you your release from active duty. You can return to your family now. I want you to know that I have greatly appreciated your commitment and support during all these years, especially since the Great Decimation. Go in peace."

Goldwyn stood and embraced him as a look of immense relief passed over Smathers' face. Tears filled his ice-blue eyes. "Yes, sir. Thank you, sir. It has been a great privilege serving under your command."

Turning to face Stauffer, Smathers said, "Barton Stauffer, I want you to know that I have greatly admired your work from the beginning, and I have also considered it a great privilege to work alongside you on this mission."

Stauffer was at a loss for words. ".... Thank you, Colonel Smathers."

Turning back to face General Goldwyn, Smathers came to attention. "With your permission, sir, I'll be leaving now."

"Yes, of course, Smathers. Here, let me set it up."

General Goldwyn turned and leaned over the conference table. As Goldwyn's fingers skimmed over the wireless keyboard, the shimmering outline of a temporal portal appeared against the wall. Smathers walked around the table and faced the portal. He stood briefly at attention once again, then after nodding to General Goldwyn, he walked forward through the portal and was gone.

"Where did you send him, sir?" Stauffer asked.

"I sent him to a pre-arranged pick-up point for a rendezvous with one of Enoch's scout teams. He will be with his family before evening."

"Colonel Smathers has a family?" Stauffer asked.

"Yes, Barton. He has a beautiful wife and fifteen children, most of them grown now. He has been able to take leave and visit them periodically during our stay-behind mission, but it has been a long separation for them most of the time during this deployment. They will all be glad to be together again."

Stauffer sat there contemplating everything he had just experienced during the past hour, lost in thought, until General Goldwyn interrupted his reverie. "Did you have something else for me, Barton?"

Startled, Stauffer stood and turned to face General Goldwyn. "No, sir. I believe I have more than enough to think about for the present. With your leave, sir, I think I'll be getting back down to the Crypt."

# Chapter 34

*Carlisle Barracks, Pennsylvania, Friday, May 1, 2016, 4:45 p.m.*

Stauffer sat at his desk working on an analytical comparison between the ancient legends of Noah, Gilgamesh, Zoroaster, and the many other stories and mythologies of the Flood. The team had been very successful in running to ground many of these myths, and they had discovered that much of what was considered mythology and legend today was really based upon actual events that happened as the great Flood overwhelmed the world. Much of it had been greatly distorted in the retelling, but there it was — mankind trying to record and explain the great calamity that had upended their old world and how they attempted to survive in the new one that appeared as the waters of the Flood receded.

Stauffer paused to consider whether or not there were groups of survivors topside right then who were doing essentially the same thing — trying to record and register their perceptions of the calamities of the contagions and pandemics, the earthquakes, the volcanic eruptions, the tsunamis, and the poison dust that fell from the sky. He personally felt that it wasn't only possible but highly probable. But he surmised that a comparison between the different records from around the world might look like they all were describing very different events. From past experience, Stauffer knew that what you see depends very much on where you stand.

Stauffer's red telephone rang. He walked over to his desk and picked up the receiver and saw that it was General Goldwyn on the caller ID. "Yes, sir. Stauffer here."

"Barton, I'm glad that I caught you in your office. Could you come up to my office please. We have a couple of things we need to talk about."

"Be right there, sir," he replied as he hung up the receiver and headed for the door. When he arrived at General Goldwyn's office, the door was already ajar and Stauffer pushed it open as he knocked on the portal.

"Ah, Barton, you got here fast. Thank you. Please come in and say hello to Mabel."

Barton was genuinely surprised. He had never seen General Goldwyn's topside secretary anywhere but in her office in the sub-basement of Collins Hall where she used to inprocess all new arrivals into the Hole. He had supposed that she had perished in the aftermath of the global pandemics. "Hello, ma'am, er.... Mabel. It's good to see you."

"It is good to see you as well, Colonel Stauffer. You have done very well down here. I am pleased that Kubal Golden One found someone as talented as yourself to replace him as we depart."

Stauffer was now totally confused. He didn't understand at all what Mabel had just said. General Goldwyn saw Stauffer's confusion and spoke up. "Ah, Barton, I see that your impeccable logic is failing you. It's all really quite simple. Remember when I told you that I was piloting the craft that crash-landed at Roswell? Well, Mabel was my copilot.... She is also my wife. Please meet Mā-Bel in this new light."

"Mā-Bel,.... your wife?" Stauffer stammered.

General Goldwyn stepped forward and took Mā-Bel's hand in his own. "Yes, Barton. She has been here by my side for the greater part of this stay-behind assignment. She has been the best companion and helpmate that I could possibly have asked for." Goldwyn looked down at Mā-Bel and beamed as she looked up at him with loving eyes.

Stauffer looked back and forth between the two. "I never knew...." he acknowledged. "I never suspected.... It never occurred to me.... How have you been able to keep it a secret all this time?"

"It was actually quite simple, Barton," General Goldwyn explained. "Mā-Bel never entered Collins Hall through normal controlled entrances. In fact, she never even used the door to her own office. She had a temporal portal setup on the far wall of her office which allowed her to move back and forth between our apartment down here in the Hole."

"Apartment?.... Down here in the Hole? But where?"

"Right here, Barton." General Goldwyn walked over to the wall behind his desk. He pushed a button concealed on a bronze plaque and a hidden door opened up into a large chamber behind it. As it opened, the lights came up in the chamber illuminating a spacious well-furnished apartment.

Stauffer stuck his head through the door and quickly looked around. "Wow, it looks like it was taken from the pages of *Better Homes and Gardens*."

"Actually, Colonel Stauffer," Mā-Bel responded quickly, "it was in part. Kubal promised me that if we were going to live underground in the Hole for an extended period of time, I could decorate it any way that I desired. I leafed through a lot of magazines and we went through a lot of modern model homes to see what I liked and Kubal made it all come together."

"Well, Mā-Bel.... it's just beautiful. You've done a nice job." Stauffer turned to address General Goldwyn. "Sir, why are you revealing your secret just now, letting me know about Mā-Bel and your hidden apartment down here?"

"Because, Barton," Goldwyn responded, "it is now time for us to go. I am coming up on my 968th year and I promised Enoch to be out of here before my next birthday. We're showing you the apartment because I am turning responsibility for the whole operation down here over to you. Mā-Bel has been cleaning the apartment and it is ready for you to occupy."

"But when are you leaving?"

"In just a few minutes or so," General Goldwyn responded. "That will give me just enough time to brief you on the few things you absolutely will need to know for now." Turning to his wife, General Goldwyn suggested, "Mā-Bel, would you please go into the apartment for a few minutes and get together everything you want to take with you while I bring Barton up to speed?"

Mā-Bel nodded and retreated into the apartment and Goldwyn turned to Stauffer. He started to say something but Stauffer interrupted, "Sir, when are you going to say goodbye to everyone on the staff? Are we going to have a change of command ceremony? What do you have planned?"

"Nothing planned, Barton," Goldwyn responded. "This is one of those assumption of command situations. I've prepared the document and signed it and it's over on my desk. Make copies of it and circulate it among everyone down here. They all know you well and respect you and the transition should be relatively seamless and straightforward."

"But how will I know everything I'm supposed to do? I've always come to you for guidance."

"That part is easy, Barton," Goldwyn assured him. "You are well familiar with the ongoing projects that we are still working on down here and you are more than capable of managing them through to completion. You will be able to work out most of the issues you may encounter with rational thought without any assistance whatsoever. But, if you come up against something that has you totally stumped and you don't know which direction to turn, refer to the continuity file binder I left on my desk. It has answers for just about any question you might come up against down here." General Goldwyn motioned over to his desk and Stauffer's eyes followed in the direction of his outstretched finger. There on Goldwyn's desk was a stack of gold sheets bound together with a series of golden rings. Stauffer moved over to the desk and picked it up carefully. It was heavy, perhaps as much as fifty or sixty pounds.

"This weighs a bunch, sir," Stauffer commented.

"Yes, I tried to be comprehensive with all of the information you might need. It is a desk copy for sure, not a pocket reference. I hope that it answers most of your questions. But if that still does not do it for you, just think the issue out in your mind. Don't forget, you are telepathic. Someone on Enoch's high command staff will telepathically provide you guidance. Okay?"

"Yes, sir, I suppose so."

"Good, now the first thing you need to do after we are gone is to move your stuff into the office and the apartment here. I have already moved most of my personal belongings over into a small vault over at Waxahachie. I have left you my personal library and you can bring your own books up from your office and add to the collection. They will come in handy for keeping your mind alert after everyone else has gone. Oh, and I've left some blank wall space there for you to hang your 'I-Love-Me' wall. Make sure that you hang lots of pictures of your family. Better yet, you ought to use a portal to go over to your home in North Middleton before all this excitement began and gather up more of the family photos you've got hanging on the wall going up the staircase in your living room."

"Yes, sir," Stauffer responded. He was somewhat numbed with the realization that Goldwyn was about to leave and his thinking processes had switched over to automatic on overload.

"I've already told you that when you last laid down in the reconstitution chamber, it overwrote your DNA with the complete history of mankind compiled to date by Repository and Crypt historians. As you continue working on that project down here, you will need to occasionally go back and lie down in the chamber so that it can keep the record updated."

"How do I operate it, sir?"

"Don't worry about that. It is all automatic. Just lie down in the chamber and the overhead door will close automatically. You will go to sleep and the chamber door will open up again automatically when it has finished updating the files."

"And for what purpose do I need to keep my DNA files updated, sir? You've never explained that to me."

"At some point, Barton, someone is going to ask you to turn over the Book of Life and what they will really be asking for is the Hall of Records recorded on your DNA. You will know what to do when the time comes."

Stauffer was scrambling to get all of his questions answered before General Goldwyn's departure. "Sir, you said that Ski and Bill would have normal life spans like everyone else down here. That means that most everyone will be gone within thirty or forty years at most. How much longer beyond that will I need to remain here?"

"I thought that I had already laid that out for you. I know that this is more than a little daunting for you to understand but your life span is now upwards of 900 plus years. You may be required to be here for most of that time."

"All alone, sir? I'll go stark raving mad in the solitude."

"I've considered that, Barton. Once everyone is gone, I've prepared a little artificial intelligence program to interact with you to mitigate the loneliness. I think you might come to enjoy the experience. I've also set up a few automatic programs around the Repository that I think you might enjoy. After everyone is gone and the loneliness closes in on you, just say my name out loud and it will initiate the AI program."

As Mā-Bel emerged from the apartment with a white shawl wrapped around her shoulders, Goldwyn turned to her and said, "You look lovely, my dear. Are you ready to travel?"

"Yes, Kubal Golden One. I am."

"Good. Barton, I need you to go with us to see how this is done. It will only take just a minute."

Goldwyn walked over to his desk and typed in a word on the keyboard. "Did you see that, Barton? The codeword is simply H-O-M-E. When your time comes, just type in H-O-M-E and the portal will activate and take you on your journey back to your family." General Goldwyn reached across the desk and pulled a long white box toward him. Opening it, he pulled out a long-stemmed red rose and handed it to Mā-Bel with a huge smile on his face. "One last rose for you My Lady," he said lovingly and kissed her on the cheek. Nodding to Stauffer, he said, "Now, Barton, just follow us through the portal and you will see how this works."

General Goldwyn turned and faced the outline of the portal that had illuminated against the office wall next to Goldwyn's conference table, and, taking Mā-Bel by the hand, they walked confidently through the portal with Stauffer close behind.

They emerged onto an open flat plain strewn with enormous boulders fashioned into odd shapes. In front of them was a tall flat rock cliff with a large door-shaped portal carved into the face of the rock. Goldwyn led Mā-Bel over to the portal and reached into his pocket and pulled out the golden dodecahedron. Turning to Stauffer, he apologized, "I'm sorry, Barton, I borrowed this from your office earlier this morning without asking. Make sure you recover it and take it back with you. You will need it later on."

Stauffer wasn't sure exactly what Goldwyn meant but he held his peace.

Turning back to the carved stone portal, General Goldwyn said to Stauffer over his shoulder, "If you're having trouble breathing, remember, this is the Hayu Marca plateau in the Peruvian Andes near Puno. The altitude here is a little over 14,000 feet. Beautiful country, isn't it?" Goldwyn extended his hand with the golden dodecahedron and placed it carefully down in the small alcove in the center of the portal, orienting it in a precise way. "Watch closely how I placed the dodecahedron here in the alcove, Barton. Make certain that, when the time comes, you orient it in exactly the same way."

As General Goldwyn spoke, the rock facing of the portal began to fade away and a powerful blue light emanated from the opening. Turning his head around to face Stauffer, Goldwyn remarked in parting, "Barton, I guess this is it for now. I have treasured our time together and I want you to know that I have full trust and confidence in your ability to complete the mission. Take care. We will meet again."

Goldwyn smiled and, still holding Mā-Bel by the hand, led her into the blue light. As they disappeared from sight, the blue iridescence faded away quickly and Stauffer found himself standing alone there on the Hayu Marca plateau. He realized that the dodecahedron was still there in the alcove and he leaned over and carefully memorized exactly how it was oriented — which hole was on top and which hole was facing outward. Once he had a mental picture fixed in his mind, he retrieved it quickly, clutching it in his hand. He turned and looked around him. A few steps down the hill, he saw the shimmering outline of the portal that they had just come through from the Hole. He stepped down the rock-strewn path towards it, passed through, and found himself back in General Goldwyn's office.... his office now.

# Chapter 35

Time passed and the work down in the Repository and the Crypt advanced little by little. Stauffer sat in his office one afternoon assessing the progress they had made. He glanced across the room at the digital clock hanging above the doorway. *"TEMPUS FUGIT,"* — *"Time flees — Time's a-wastin."* Stauffer checked the calendar on his computer monitor screen — Friday, April 20, 2018. It was almost two years since General Goldwyn and Mā-Bel had departed.

General Goldwyn had been correct about his departure. When Stauffer gathered the staff together and announced that General Goldwyn had left and distributed the assumption of command order with Goldwyn's signature, most of the staff were disappointed they hadn't had an opportunity to say goodbye, but the order was readily accepted and supported by everyone. Stauffer asked Maggie Martinez to resume leadership over Crypt operations, and he moved from his office in the Crypt up into General Goldwyn's old office to provide oversight and coordination for all operations in the Hole, the Repository, and the Crypt.

Stauffer found that on most days, it was a good transition, although he felt somewhat marginalized by the additional layer of hierarchy that separated him from day-to-day operations. He set up weekly meetings with Alice Duerden, Jared Lincoln, and Maggie Martinez to keep close track of what was going on in each of the three areas. He also met frequently with Hank Phillips to monitor his team's progress on DNA and crystal storage research.

Work in the Repository moved along well enough. In the early days of Repository operations, the balance between the collectors and the historians was initially weighted heavily toward the collectors. Now, with the accumulation of so many scrolls, tablets, and artifacts in the vaults, most collectors reverted to their secondary historian role to assist in inventorying, classifying, translating, reading and interpreting what they found. They rarely conducted on-the-ground recovery missions anymore.

405

＊ ＊ ＊ ＊ ＊ ＊ ＊ ＊ ＊ ＊ ＊ ＊ ＊ ＊ ＊ ＊ ＊ ＊

Immediately following General Goldwyn's departure, Stauffer had monitored the surface for the return of Enoch and the city of Atlantis as Goldwyn had told him was soon to happen. Every time Stauffer had a spare moment, he would conduct random temporal surveys across the face of the Earth above to see where the enormous craft would set down. After about three weeks of intermittent searches, Stauffer chanced to come across the Antediluvian ship out in the American Midwest. It had already landed. He backtracked fast-time to see it actually landing, and then he forwarded real-time to see how the scene unfolded. He watched with fascination as the ship appeared in the sky escorted by thousands of smaller flying craft. The fleet flew in mass until the Atlantis ship separated from the rest and dropped down to the surface. As soon as it touched down and stopped movement, the rest of the fleet spread out across the face of the land around it and touched down as well. Because of the horrific earthquakes and extensive flooding that resulted from the shifting of the tectonic plates throughout the New Madrid Seismic Zone, and the pandemic which had all but wiped out the human population, what few survivors there were had all picked up stakes and moved away. The area where the Atlantis ship made landfall was entirely deserted. As Stauffer scanned the surface just prior to touchdown, there didn't appear to be any human beings or animals for hundreds of miles around.

Once he had observed touchdown of the Atlantis fleet, Stauffer sat through the remainder of the night at his temporal monitor observing the activities of Enoch's people as they disembarked from their aircraft. At one point, Stauffer thought that he saw Melek disembark from one of the larger scout ships, hand-in-hand with a lovely young woman, whom he assumed must be Ulla. Stauffer was fascinated as he observed the area surrounding the Atlantis ship take on the trapping of a great metropolis before his eyes.

And then suddenly, without warning, the screen went blank. Stauffer fiddled with the controls but couldn't bring up a picture. He tested the equipment by moving to a different area on the surface of the planet and a picture immediately came up. It definitely wasn't the temporal equipment. Stauffer assumed that General Goldwyn must have set some kind of automatic temporal block in place before he left so that they wouldn't be able to observe the return of Atlantis. Stauffer was greatly disappointed but turned his attention and the attention of his staff working in the Crypt to other matters tracking the activities of Earth's survivors as they struggled to establish a foothold in a hostile land.

\* \* \* \* \* \* \* \* \* \* \* \* \* \* \* \* \* \* \* \* \*

The Repository manuscript team worked with the techs to develop a hardware/software combination designed to scan scroll documents from one end to the other as one continuous image. Because the scrolls were in relatively good condition, they were simply placed on roller brackets which fed the scroll through the scanner from one end to the other. But even with technology to quickly scan entire scrolls at a time, the work of digitizing all of the scrolls they had acquired moved along slowly at best. Although they had processed over a million and a half scrolls already, Colonel Duerden reported that there were four additional vaults stacked high with uncatalogued and unexamined scrolls. They had their work cut out for them. Once processed and digitized, all of the scrolls were returned to storage in special vaults where the air was removed and replaced with an inert gas to inhibit aging of the papyrus, parchment, or paper. General Goldwyn had asserted before he departed that such protective storage should preserve the scrolls intact for many thousands of years.

Colonel Duerden estimated that it would take years, perhaps decades, to review all of the original source material, translate it, and place it all in an historical context. That represented a major work effort by itself, Stauffer reasoned. But the historians had already begun processing all of the fragments of information and historical insights they had already developed and weaving it all together into a more complete and accurate narrative of the history of mankind. As additional scrolls were translated and reviewed, the historians were sometimes forced to go back and edit their work. But, it was only a matter of time, Stauffer reasoned, before they had massaged it all into place and had taken their work as far as they would be able to go.

The historians working in the Repository patently had a tough task ahead of them, and Stauffer met frequently with Colonel Duerden and her historian team to discuss the philosophy of historiography and to share his own ideas of how to approach this final phase of preparing the history of mankind. Interpreting history requires choosing a focusing perspective, with reductionism at one extreme and holism at the other. Among the historians who were actively leading the research and revision of history, both perspectives prevailed with some historians focusing on the big picture while others were down in the weeds, self-absorbed in all of the detail.

Stauffer himself, leaned towards the holistic view and the big picture. He believed that all historical eras are connected to earlier periods of history that have gone before. From Stauffer's perspective, everything in the past was interrelated, interconnected and interdependent. He asserted that the tapestry of history could only be understood in its entirety. Small patchwork views could be misleading when considered without the connective tissue to adjacent blocks of history.

To complicate matters, the Repository historians had frequent disagreements about how to interpret particular historical events or periods. Some historians became so attached to one way of thinking that discussions between them occasionally became loud and rancorous, and Stauffer was frequently called upon to mediate differences and guide them toward some acceptable compromise. Stauffer enjoyed mediating these spats between historians. He considered conflicting viewpoints to be a healthy, natural dynamic that was to be expected and appreciated. Because of great differences in the interpretive values applied by historians, the lens through which history was observed and evaluated sometimes created interpretations of history that were entirely at odds with each other. Stauffer encouraged different perspectives, but he suggested that, when in doubt, disputing factions find ways to record the historical text that would reflect different possibilities for interpreting the past.

The historians working in the Crypt had a different set of challenges. Their work basically involved exploring and interpreting antediluvian times and finding ways of connecting it to the postdiluvial historical narrative being written up by the Repository historian team. The task of researching and writing the antediluvian historical narrative had to be accomplished with the assistance of very few original source documents. Although they hadn't been able to directly translate any of the scrolls and books and other written materials recovered from Melek's crate using the crystal sets, they had found much greater success with scrolls recovered from the blockhouse atop the step pyramid buried beneath Stauffer's home in North Middleton and from the other sites around the world which had been systematically buried by the Atlanteans. And so the Crypt historians ultimately had a modest collection of original source materials to draw from.

However, most of the historical narrative that the Crypt historian team was able to develop was based largely upon viewing the actual events in question through the temporal observation monitors. This was problematic because, much like the Repository historians, two members of the Crypt team could be looking at precisely the same images on their temporal monitors, and interpret what they saw in very different ways. Stauffer liked to remind them that reviewing temporal monitor screens to answer questions of action and activity was fairly easy and straightforward. But he cautioned them that questions of motive and motivation behind that historical activity was much more difficult to assess. In the end, linking the antediluvian historical narrative to the postdiluvian historical text was a challenging task at best, but made somewhat easier by the natural break created in the passage of history by the waters of the Flood.

\* \* \* \* \* \* \* \* \* \* \* \* \* \* \* \* \* \* \* \* \*

Although Bob Zazworsky had historian credentials, he mostly focused on preparing a comprehensive inventory of all the gold and treasure that they had accumulated and stored in the Repository, the Crypt, and the Waxahachie vaults. Before the Great Decimation, General Goldwyn had organized a special team to transfer all of the heavy golden bars from the deep cavern at Victorio Peak and the gold bars and other artifacts sequestered away in the storage vaults in the subbasement of the Pentagon to the vaults at Waxahachie. It was an extraordinary amount of gold and came close to completely filling up the available vaults that had been completed at Waxahachie. Only another two or three dozen vaults remained vacant.

Zazworsky had never entirely lost his excitement for treasure hunts. After the Decimation, Zazworsky convinced Stauffer to allow him to lead a team to recover cargo from several foundering ships during the Flood. It was a decision that almost cost Zazworsky his life. When planning recovery operations, Zazworsky always timed the interval between when the crew abandoned ship and when the vessel finally sank and planned the mission time accordingly. What he didn't take into account on the third such recovery mission was how the additional weight of the four members of the recovery team working inside the hold of the ship would cause it to sink much faster than they had originally timed without them onboard.

When the ship they were scavenging started to list and turn over on its side during recovery operations, Zazworsky's three teammates made it safely back through the portal, but Zazworsky was thrown off balance and became wedged between the side of the ship and a huge wooden chest that had dislodged and slid across the floor. He couldn't break free to get to the portal and water began to fill the hold around him. Maggie Martinez, who was serving as mission team chief, saw the danger on the temporal monitor back in the time lab and dispatched Ken Red Elk and Sammy Woo back through the portal to assist him. By this time, the water was up to their chests and rising rapidly. Working together, the three of them managed to push the heavy chest away from the wall and free Zazworsky. Meanwhile, Martinez had moved the position of the portal over next to the three men and as Zazworsky broke free, they pushed the chest on through the portal and followed after it back into the time lab. When they were all safely back in the lab, Martinez closed the portal. The water level in the lab by this time was about four feet deep. Martinez opened another small portal close to the floor in the vault which opened out into the antidiluvian world several meters above the surface of the sea. The small portal acted as a drain hole and the water in the lab rushed back out into the antediluvian sea. It still took them almost two hours to evacuate all of the water out of the lab and then towel down all of the surfaces.

When they finally had the water mess dried up and put the vault through a thorough hazmat clean up, Zazworsky turned his attention to the chest. It had a large hasp and locking device that he couldn't manipulate open, and so he just hit it several times with a large hammer until the hasp broke. When he opened the lid to the chest, he found that it was full of precious gems, gold jewelry, and several sophisticated nautical instruments. After it had all gone through decon, Zazworsky asked permission to store the chest and its contents in his office as a reminder of his narrow escape. He never asked approval to mount another recovery mission again after that. Zazworsky seemed to have been cured of his gold fever at last.

\* \* \* \* \* \* \* \* \* \* \* \* \* \* \* \* \* \* \* \* \*

About that time, Tipton approached Stauffer about conducting a special project. Prior to coming to Carlisle Barracks to work in the Hole, Tipton spent seven years working DOD black projects inside the Beltway and around the country. He had a pretty good idea of many of the top secret black projects that were underway before the Great Decimation, and he knew that most of them were being developed and conducted in deep underground research facilities similar to the Hole and Repository facilities at Carlisle Barracks. Tipton suggested to Stauffer that it might be a good idea to conduct a temporal monitor survey to see if any of the projects were still ongoing and whether any of the participants were still alive. Stauffer readily agreed but asked him whether or not, in this post-Decimation environment, with the government all but dissolved, it wasn't now possible for Tipton to share what some of the black projects were all about.

Tipton readily agreed and provided Stauffer a short time later with a computer-generated list. As Stauffer scanned down the page, he was astounded to see all of the amazing projects that the Government had been working on — micro-miniaturization of weapons systems, creation of super-soldiers through gene splicing, biological weapons systems defense, Mach 10 aircraft, satellite-mounted laser weapons, artificial intelligence systems, invisibility, alien technology reverse engineering, three-dimensional robotic self-replication, telepathic communication, super-high resolution satellite imagery, levitation, telekinesis, remote visioning, and Kirlian photography.

As Stauffer looked up from the list, he stared at Tipton with a look of astonishment. "We were working on all this? I would have never guessed."

Tipton simply shrugged and said, "I'll get back with you on what I find out."

\* \* \* \* \* \* \* \* \* \* \* \* \* \* \* \* \* \* \*

Stauffer was sitting in his office when the telephone rang. It was Bob Zazworsky. "Boss, Hank Phillips just had another heart attack. We've tried to make him comfortable in one of the dispensaries in the Repository. You had better get down here fast. Doc Gates says he may not have much time left."

Stauffer jumped up from his desk and hurried down the circular staircase to the crossover level and ran the full distance to the Repository. When he reached the double doors, Zazworsky was waiting there for him. "Follow me, Boss. He's right down the gallery here."

As Stauffer entered the dispensary vault, he saw Phillips lying out flat in a hospital bed, a number of intravenous tubes attached to his arms. Dr. Gates was standing by the side of the bed. As Stauffer approached, he asked him softly, "How's our patient doing, Doc?"

Gates turned to Stauffer and said, "He's resting now, Barton. I expect he'll be feeling better soon and be up and about in no time." Gates tried to make it sound cheery and upbeat, but the expression on his face belied his positive prognosis. It clearly didn't look good for Phillips.

Stauffer pulled up a chair to the side of Phillips' bed and asked, "How's it going Hank?"

Phillips slowly opened his eyes and turned his head to look at Stauffer. "Not so good this time around, Barton. I think that this may finally be it for me."

"That doesn't sound very optimistic, Hank."

"No reason for me to be particularly optimistic at this point, Barton," Phillips lamented. "I seem to be staring the grim reaper squarely in the eye, and I haven't completed any of my primary tasks down here. We don't have a viable crystal storage technology yet. Although we've had a limited success with our DNA storage experiments, we're not ready to roll it out yet. And I.... my.... greatest failure.... I never did locate the Hall of Records."

"Well, old friend," Stauffer consoled him, "I think that we can remedy at least part of that bucket list."

Turning to Zazworsky, Stauffer said, "Ski, would you please go and scrounge up a portable temporal monitor and control keyboard and bring it back in here for us to use for a moment?"

"Sure thing, Boss," Zazworsky responded and disappeared out the vault door. He was back in less than a minute, pushing a large flat screen temporal monitor on wheels. He had a small wireless keyboard tucked under his arm which he handed to Stauffer. "What do you have in mind, Boss?"

"Yes.... Barton," Phillips said faintly. "Just what do you have in mind?"

"Hank," Stauffer explained solemnly, "I was conducting survey scans on another matter and chanced upon this quite by accident. I hadn't had time to get back with you on it yet. I think you'll find it very enlightening."

As Stauffer fiddled with the keyboard controls, a picture came into focus on the flat screen which Stauffer repositioned so that Phillips could see it clearly. "That work for you, Hank?" he asked. "Can you see the screen okay?"

"I can see it just fine, Bart. What do you have for me to see that I haven't already seen before?" Phillips voice displayed a hint of defeatism.

"Well then," Stauffer answered back. "Just take a look at this."

Stauffer hit another key which initiated a video on the screen. It started with a panoramic view of the Giza Plateau and gradually panned around and centered on the Sphinx. As the camera angle pulled back and panned down the cliff in front of the Sphinx, Stauffer explained, "When you clear away all of the rubble in front of the temple on the cliff in front of the Sphinx, Hank, you get quite a different view from what we're used to seeing." The video continued panning downward until it reached the bottom of the cliff and revealed the tunnel opening. Stauffer worked the arrow keys on the keyboard and the temporal monitor zoomed in on the tunnel opening and down the staircase to the massive door at the end of the tunnel that opened into the cavern.

"I don't have a key for the door," Stauffer explained, "and so we'll just use the temporal monitor to jump over to the other side."

The screen went dark momentarily, and Stauffer adjusted the time interval to view the scene when Ham was laying the wooden box with the Book of the Fathers on the table in the center of the cavern. The light from the torches carried by Ham's servant illuminated the cavern and all the treasures stored within.

"What's this, Barton?" Phillips asked cautiously.

"Hank, this is the legendary Hall of Records buried deep under the Sphinx. That wooden box on the table holds the Book of the Fathers that came down from the time of Adam through the patriarchal lineage all the way to Noah's son, Ham."

Phillips sat up in bed and watched the screen as Ham removed the tattered book from its case and carefully unwrapped the shawl around it. As Ham lay the book on the table, Phillips sucked air into his lungs and exhaled loudly. "I know the face of that man. It's the face of the Sphinx.... Ham is the face of the Sphinx?"

"Yes Hank. When the sons of Noah left their father to make their own way in the new world following the Flood, Ham and his family traveled south to the Nile River Delta region and Ham set himself up as the first Pharaoh in a long line of pharaohic dynasties. He even had Enoch's face on the Sphinx, which had been damaged by the Flood, obliterated, and he had his stone artisans carve his own likeness in its place.... But this is it, Hank.... The Hall of Records.... You were right all along.... It was right under the paws of the Sphinx.... right where you said it would be. We just had to clear away the rubble from the face of the cliff to find the tunnel accessing the cavern. It's all right here."

Phillips leaned back on his pillow, smiling faintly, his energy all but depleted. "What else is there in the cavern, Barton?" he asked.

"Here, take a closer look, Hank."

Stauffer started to pan around the cavern, focusing on all of the scrolls, statues, and artifacts stored there. As he looked back at Phillips to check his reaction, he realized that Phillips' head was twisted off to the side and his eyes were glazed open. "Quick, Doc, get the paddles and resuscitate him."

"I'm sorry, Barton," Doctor Gates replied as he pulled the sheet up over Phillips' head, "but that runs counter to the desires of Hank's living will. He specifically asked **not** to be resuscitated, under any circumstances. But you gave him the greatest of all parting gifts, something that he has been longing to see the greater part of his last ten years working down here in the Hole and the Repository. I have a feeling Hank died a very happy man."

Stauffer stood there quietly at Phillips' bedside for some minutes contemplating the loss of his friend, and then he turned and left the dispensary vault and walked slowly back over to his office in the Hole.

＊＊＊＊＊＊＊＊＊＊＊＊＊＊＊＊＊＊＊＊

Stauffer asked Alice Duerden to host a meeting around her conference table in the Repository to hear an update from Max Manchester and Miriam Campbell on the progress with the Golden Rosetta Stone project.

Manchester stood slowly, in obvious pain in his lower back and knees, and leaned on a cane as he began speaking, "Alice.... Maggie.... Barton.... we've gathered together to update you all on our progress with the Repository's Rosetta Stone project."

"As a reminder, the original Rosetta Stone was inscribed on a granodiorite stele about 196 B.C. and recorded text in three very different languages — Ancient Egyptian hieroglyphs, Demotic script, and Ancient Greek. Because the stone displayed the same decree in each of the three languages, it assisted later scholars in translating Egyptian hieroglyphs, which up until then had proven almost impossible to decipher."

Miriam Campbell continued, "Our project was much more sophisticated than that. We were tasked with the proposition of building an enormous data base which would allow future researchers to cross-reference any language from any period of time in history and from any locale with any other language from any period of time from any locale. The number of permutations and combinations of different language comparisons is astronomical, and we realized that we could quickly become overwhelmed with the complexity of the whole thing. And so we did our best to reduce our own Rosetta Stone project to its simplest elements."

Manchester took a deep breath and continued the presentation. "We wanted to be able to print any language entry in the data base on just one page each, and so we decided to limit the data base to only eight elements or fields — Language Name, Time Frame, Geographical Locale, Alphabet Characters, Brief Pangram, Number Characters, Universal Text, and Specific Cultural Quote. The language name, time frame, and geographical region fields were merely for purposes of indexing the language. The alphabet characters field provided a place to display all of the characters of the alphabet employed by that language."

Pete Pendleton spoke up and interrupted, "But what's a pangram, Max? I don't think I've ever heard the term before."

"I'm glad you asked, Pete. A pangram is a short sentence that employs every letter of the given alphabet at least once. In the past, they were used by typesetters to display typeface glyphs or by calligraphers to display the fancy cursive lines of all the letters. The best known English pangram is 'The quick brown fox jumps over the lazy dog.' And if my German is up to snuff, a similar German pangram has been around for over two hundred years: '*Victor jagt zwölf Boxkämpfer quer über den großen Sylter Deich.*' The pangram field simply provides a short phrase employing all of the alphabet characters so that researchers can see how they were used and displayed in real sentences. The number characters field provides a space for graphically portraying how the numbers were written. It also provides an opportunity to reflect what base number system the particular culture used. The purpose of the universal text is obvious. Like the original Rosetta Stone, we needed to reflect a common text in all languages to provide a means of comparing one language with another. The specific cultural quote provides a field for the researcher to select a short text that reflects the zeitgeist or spirit of the age of that language and culture during that particular time period."

Dr. Campbell entered a few keystrokes on the wireless keyboard and a graphical image appeared on the flat screen monitor on the wall. She pointed at it and said, "This is an example of the page we prepared for 19th Century American English. The universal text we selected for displaying in all languages, as you can see, is the Preamble to the Charter of the United Nations, signed in San Francisco, June 26, 1945, by 50 of the original 51 member nations in the aftermath of World War II:

**WE THE PEOPLES OF THE UNITED NATIONS DETERMINED**
- to save succeeding generations from the scourge of war, which twice in our lifetime has brought untold sorrow to mankind, and
- to reaffirm faith in fundamental human rights, in the dignity and worth of the human person, in the equal rights of men and women and of nations large and small, and

- to establish conditions under which justice and respect for the obligations arising from treaties and other sources of international law can be maintained, and
- to promote social progress and better standards of life in larger freedom,

**AND FOR THESE ENDS**

- to practice tolerance and live together in peace with one another as good neighbours, and
- to unite our strength to maintain international peace and security, and
- to ensure, by the acceptance of principles and the institution of methods, that armed force shall not be used, save in the common interest, and
- to employ international machinery for the promotion of the economic and social advancement of all peoples,

**HAVE RESOLVED TO COMBINE OUR EFFORTS TO ACCOMPLISH THESE AIMS**

Accordingly, our respective Governments, through representatives assembled in the city of San Francisco, who have exhibited their full powers found to be in good and due form, have agreed to the present Charter of the United Nations and do hereby establish an international organization to be known as the United Nations.

Manchester continued, "The specific quote that we believe most appropriately reflects the zeitgeist of the United States during the 19ᵗʰ Century is Lincoln's Gettysburg Address:"

Four score and seven years ago our fathers brought forth on this continent, a new nation, conceived in Liberty, and dedicated to the proposition that all men are created equal. Now we are engaged in a great civil war, testing whether that nation, or any nation so conceived and so dedicated, can long endure. We are met on a great battle-field of that war. We have come to dedicate a portion of that field, as a final resting place for those who here gave their lives that that nation might live. It is altogether fitting and proper that we should do this.

But, in a larger sense, we can not dedicate -- we can not consecrate -- we can not hallow -- this ground. The brave men, living and dead, who struggled here, have consecrated it, far above our poor power to add or detract. The world will little note, nor long remember what we say here, but it can never forget what they did here. It is for us the living, rather, to be dedicated here to the unfinished work which they who fought here have thus far so nobly advanced. It is rather for us to be here dedicated to the great task remaining before us -- that from these honored dead we take increased devotion to that cause for which they gave the last full measure of devotion -- that we here highly resolve that these dead shall not have died in vain -- that this nation, under God, shall have a new birth of freedom -- and that government of the people, by the people, for the people, shall not perish from the earth.

Abraham Lincoln, November 19, 1863

Manchester and Campbell sat down and Bob Zazworsky continued the briefing with technical details on the engraving. "Now this page illustrates some important points about our Rosetta Stone volumes. We have had to manufacture oversized sheets of gold to accommodate lengthy text entries. The sheets themselves are sized to 10 inches by 14 inches rather than the standard American typewriter paper size of 8 ½ inches by 11 inches or some smaller book binding standard size. The sheets of gold are rolled out to a thickness of approximately .012 inches, about the thickness of 100 lb. cardstock. We tested it thoroughly and the sheets hold laser-engraved characters well and are sturdy enough for punching holes for binding with seven rings and, they appear to stand up well to continuous page turning."

Zazworsky continued, "I'm passing around a copy of the sheet that Max just showed us on the screen so that you can get a sensing for its weight and tactile strength. Each individual sheet doesn't weigh all that much by itself but when you put all of the twenty to twenty-five thousand sheets together that we anticipate using to complete the project, they weigh a considerable amount. Colonel Stauffer has authorized the removal of up to one thousand of the eighty-five pound gold bars from our vaults at Waxahachie to be melted down to produce the needed gold sheets for our Rosetta Stone volumes. The first several hundred pages alone are needed just for the table of contents, indices and cross-reference tables. As a side note, we'll be using even more gold sheets than that for the History Quest volumes of revised history when we get to it."

Dr. Campbell stood and picked up the thread of the presentation. "In addition to our own staff here in the Repository, we have had expert linguists, philologists, etymologists, ethnologists, cryptologists, historians, calligraphers, and graphic artists contracted to work on this project for some time, and we are beginning to get caught up now on all their input we received before the Great Decimation. Some of our experts early on worked out of special university labs around the country and in other parts of the world. Those who were working outside the Repository had no real knowledge of the project's ultimate purpose and were only peripherally aware of the specifics of their own assigned language groups. With all that effort, there will probably still be some gaps. Even with temporal technology, there may still remain some languages that are dead to us today, with no way for us to work out a translation, and we'll just have to accept that. We're still engraving some of the remaining work that was accomplished before the Great Decimation onto gold sheets. But I believe that for the most part, we're going to achieve our objective very soon."

Max Manchester broke back in again to complete the briefing. "Here is what our initial efforts have produced." On the wall monitor, a screen capture of a vault filled with floor to ceiling shelving appeared, with each shelf already stacked with individual golden volumes lying horizontally side-by-side. Manchester continued, "We estimate that we've probably completed about 95% of the project at this point. When we're finished with the final engraving work, we're going to have one very large vault with specially-built, high-density, extra-heavy-duty, storage shelves to accommodate all of the golden volumes we've produced. They will provide future generations of scholars — whoever that might be — easy access to the indices and individual pages for every language of every historical era, and for every geographic locale. It won't be perfect, but it will be a darned sight better than anything the world has ever seen before. Oh, and here's a fascinating finishing touch that Hank Phillips suggested just before he died." Manchester input another keystroke on the keyboard and the view into the golden Rosetta Stone vault zoomed back into the Repository gallery showing the vault door and then the walls to the sides of the vault. To the right side of the heavy vault door, a tall stone stele came into view.

"What's that?" Stauffer asked. "It looks kind of like the Rosetta Stone but it appears to be much larger."

"You're right, Barton. The Rosetta Stone that has come down to us is really only a fragment of the original. Scholars have always conjectured what was on the missing pieces of the stone. We decided to find out and lay the matter to rest. We mounted a temporal monitor search for the original Rosetta Stone when it was first engraved back in 196 B.C. It wasn't all that difficult finding it and then all we had to do was identify a time window when no one was directly watching the stone so that we could snatch it and make a casting."

"It turned out to be an easy proposition. It sat in the stone carver's shop for almost a month after it had been engraved before it was released to be positioned in a public temple. The carver stored it in a back room of his workshop and pretty much ignored it the entire time. We made the snatch and brought the original stone here to the Repository to make the casting. As soon as we had a good mold, we replaced the original stone right back where the stone cutter had stored it."

Pointing to the stele on the monitor, he continued, "This is an exact replica we made of the Rosetta Stone as it originally looked. It's fully fifteen inches taller than the Rosetta Stone fragment that wasn't discovered until over two thousand years later in 1799 by a French soldier posted at Fort Julien in the Nile Delta during the Napoleonic expedition to Egypt. He found the stone encased in a portion of a crumbling wall where it had been used as building construction material. In this case, dumb luck trumped sound research and scholarship. If that soldier hadn't noticed the inscriptions on the stone and reported it, we might never have discovered so early on the key to translating ancient Egyptian hieroglyphics.... Well, there you have it. Does anyone have any questions?"

As Manchester finished speaking, Stauffer and the other team members assembled in the room just sat there in silence staring at the wall monitor. Most had been aware of the ongoing project, but none were totally read in on the magnitude of the work involved and just how advanced the project really was. As the single sheet of gold with the entry for 19th Century American English made its way around the conference table, each of the team members held it, spellbound, slowly scanning the information engraved in the small concise font on the face of the page.

At last, as the meeting broke up and the staff started filing out of Colonel Duerden's office, Stauffer turned to Dr. Campbell and Max Manchester. "Great work, Miriam.... Max.... As you were briefing, I was reminded of a quote from Robert Louis Stevenson.... 'All speech, written or spoken, is a dead language, until it finds a willing and prepared hearer....' I hope that somewhere down the line, all of our efforts will pan out and fall into the hands of willing and prepared hearers. That would really make all this work effort worthwhile."

\* \* \* \* \* \* \* \* \* \* \* \* \* \* \* \* \* \* \*

"Yo, Bart. You got a minute?" Tipton said as he walked through the door to Stauffer's office.

"Sure Bill, what have you got?"

"I finally finished my survey of black projects that were ongoing at the beginning of the Decimation."

"So soon, Bill? What did you find? Did any of them make it through all of the contagions and pandemics?"

Tipton scowled, "Well, Barton, as near as I can tell, most of them survived for only a couple of weeks at best.... a few of them survived for several months or longer as they remained locked up below ground. But, after awhile, they all ran out of provisions or water or breathable air, and, when they broke the seal with the outside world, they were exposed to persistent airborne pathogens, and it appears that they have mostly all succumbed. There were only a few survivors among the personnel working on those projects, probably just those with a natural immunity or resistance. But I think that the projects themselves are now all pretty much non-op and defunct. Oh, there are still personnel working underground in the NORAD Operations Center deep beneath Cheyenne Mountain. That wasn't exactly a black project.... more of an active operational control center for NORAD. It appears that they had sufficient provisions to stay buttoned up for a considerable length of time, and personnel working there are still at it. I'm not too sure whom they might still be communicating with. It's practically impossible to track down radio communications with temporal monitors, but it appears that there are other pockets of Air Force and DOD operations out there that are still active. It possibly might be just a few nuclear submarines that were deployed at the moment of the Great Decimation. They have the capability to remain submerged for extended periods of time."

"Thanks, Bill," Stauffer replied. "I guess that that tells us that we need to stay hunkered down here for an appreciable while longer until the danger from the residual pathogens and airborne disease agents has passed. Who knows how long that will take?"

"Do you think we ought to set up some kind of monitoring program to determine when it is safe to walk freely on the surface again?" Tipton suggested.

"That's a good idea, Bill. Would you organize a team and set up a monitoring protocol. We need to determine how well humans, animals, and plant life topside are faring. At some point, the contagions and threat of infections will have subsided, and our folks down here will want to start returning to the surface. But we need to make sure that the plants and animals are safe as a food source before we venture out."

"Can do, Bart. I know a dozen people who would be excited to work on that action."

\* \* \* \* \* \* \* \* \* \* \* \* \* \* \* \* \* \* \*

Pete Pendleton launched into his new job title of Repository Cruise Director with almost a religious fervor. One of the first things he did was set up one of the larger vaults with smaller attached vaults as privacy rooms where staff members could go just to be alone. Pendleton kept a signup roster on the Repository intranet and the rooms were kept busy as people found it useful to retreat to the privacy rooms just to spend some time by themselves away from everyone else. Pendleton also set up one of the larger vaults as an exercise gym with top-of-the-line exercise equipment lifted from workout centers and exercise gyms from around the country. The gym turned out to be patronized pretty much around the clock by the staff and Pendleton ultimately had to set up a second exercise vault facility to accommodate the demand.

Pendleton was constantly setting up new recreational and entertainment activities to keep staff members active and engaged. He organized weekly movies at the Majestic showing old silent movies accompanied by Pendleton playing the theatre organ on Friday evenings and classic talkies on Saturday evenings. One of the Repository techies was an expert at copying digital files and was able to access the vaults at several of the Hollywood film distribution companies and compiled several thousand recent digital movies.

Many of the Repository survivors played musical instruments, and every Sunday afternoon, they gathered together in a bandstand set up in the middle of the Repository Gallery and played old-fashioned music from bygone eras for the enjoyment of all the staff members gathered together seated around on artificial turf eating picnic lunches and sipping lemonade.

Pete and his team snatched several portable basketball standards from the Carlisle Recreation Department storage shed that was used to store equipment for the Carlisle Annual Street Hoops

3-on-3 Basketball Tournament. Many of the women joined the men in rigorous basketball play each morning for their PT.

Most of the staff continued to retreat to the handicraft lab on a regular basis to work on their creative interests. Stauffer even staged a couple of contests to instill a sense of competition, and they set aside a special vault for all of the handicrafts and works of art that the members of the staff produced.

Pendleton was irrepressible in creating new and fun things for everyone to do to help them pass the time. One month, he set up an indoor ice skating rink for everyone to try their hand at ice skating and the following month, he set up a hundred meter slip-and-slide down the center of the Repository gallery. But the event that everyone seemed to enjoy the most was the zip-line that Pendleton rigged from a high tower at one end of the Repository gallery sloping down to near the floor at the other end of the gallery. He acquired a selection of adjustable harnesses and encouraged everyone to give it a try. The flyers moved at a fairly good clip on their pulleys down the length of the gallery with all of the staff lined up along both walls dousing them with high-powered squirt guns as they went. There was much shrieking and laughter and everyone thoroughly enjoyed themselves, letting their hair down and acting a little childish and out of character. It did a great deal to reduce the stress and island-fever from living in such close quarters for such an extended period of time underground.

\* \* \* \* \* \* \* \* \* \* \* \* \* \* \* \* \* \* \* \* \*

Through the passage of the next few years, the teams in the Repository, the Crypt, and the Hole kept hard at it, working on their tasks as a labor of love. They were committed to completing their individual and group projects. As General Goldwyn had predicted, several of the elderly members of the staff grew old and finally died. Funerals and memorial services became part of their routine and one of the primary place markers in the passage of time. Max Manchester was the senior statesman of the Crypt staff and he was one of the next team members to pass on, a victim of pneumonia. It was hard for Stauffer to lose his old friend and War College faculty teammate.

But as life ended, life also began. Many of the couples living down in the Repository had babies which added quickly to the resident population of children. Eventually, Stauffer had Pendleton move a couple of vaults of material over to the Waxahachie vaults to clear space, first for a nursery, and then, later on, for a school classroom.

Stauffer himself found it comforting to take a break from his normal activities from time to time, and take a shift in the nursery comforting infants, and as a teacher's helper in the classroom. The noise of babies crying and children playing noisily was reassuring to him that life was indeed continuing on the injured planet. Stauffer enjoyed working with the children and it helped him not to miss his own children quite so much. He became part of the classroom teaching team specializing in math and history. There was no shortage of experts on the staff and many other staff members also found it therapeutic to work in the nursery and the classroom and it was easy to find sufficient volunteers to keep both operations functioning well.

\* \* \* \* \* \* \* \* \* \* \* \* \* \* \* \* \* \* \* \* \*

Five more years passed. Following an afternoon of meetings with all of the team chiefs, Stauffer sat at his desk and sketched out all remaining tasks they needed to accomplish in each of the three areas. In the Repository, they had completed and digitally copied all of the remaining scrolls, metal books, and stelae. The historians were only one or two months away from completing their revised digital history of the world, the ultimate goal of General Goldwyn's History Quest.

The historians in the Crypt had done a magnificent job of connecting antediluvian history with the postdiluvian history narrative, and, although it wasn't exactly seamless, it really went a long way towards improving understanding of the complete spectrum of human experience on Earth throughout the past six thousand years.

The golden Rosetta Stone volumes had been finished for years, and the historians frequently referred to the digital copy posted on the intranet to resolve knotty translation issues. The one big project that hadn't yet been completed was the preparation of a golden archival copy of the revised golden History Quest volumes. They couldn't really get started on that until the historians had finally completed their compilation work digitally and stored it on the intranet data base.

\* \* \* \* \* \* \* \* \* \* \* \* \* \* \* \* \* \* \* \* \* \*

Colonel Bill Tipton sat at the head of the conference table leading the discussion with the members of the survey team he had organized years earlier to survey surface activity topside and residual pathogens since the Great Decimation. Tipton had organized the team from the remaining Crypt team members — Miriam Campbell, Pete Pendleton, Sammy Woo, Sanjay Singh, Ginny Nguyen, Ken Red Elk, Maggie Martinez, and Bob Zazworsky. Dr. Gates served as the medical advisor to the team. Tipton's estimate that the team members would enthusiastically embrace the new mission proved true. As the team members completed their portion of the temporal monitor survey scans and analysis of the Ancient world, they welcomed the opportunity to turn their attention to the present and survey the world topside in the aftermath of the Decimation.

Stauffer realized almost immediately that he needed to expand the scope of his original guidance to Bill Tipton. In addition to monitoring residual pathogens topside to determine when it would be safe to return to the surface again, the team could also serve an important History Quest purpose by running activity surveys topside to keep the historical record constantly updated beyond the upheaval of the Great Decimation.

"We've been monitoring the surface world now since the Great Decimation," Tipton began, "and I think that we need to acknowledge a couple of things for the record. First, although we continue to refer to the outcome from all of the disastrous events of the past several years —the earthquakes, shifts in the tectonic plates, volcanic eruptions, tsunamis, and pandemics that were unleashed on the world — as the 'Great Decimation,' we need to make certain that the historical record we're preparing reflects that the word "decimation" greatly understates the drastic reduction in the world population that resulted from those events. I've been crunching the numbers from the survey data you've been forwarding to me and trying to add up your regional population estimates, and I can't come up with a current total world population figure of more than about two hundred million people spread across the face of the globe. With a starting global population of more than 7.3 billion, that means that the survival rate in the human population wasn't ten percent.... it was closer to just short of three percent."

"I had no idea the numbers were that dismal," Martinez commented in a hushed voice. "I knew that what I was seeing in my regional area reflected population numbers well below the ten percent estimate, but I didn't know that it would be that low globally."

Dr. Campbell spoke up, "Bill, you tasked me to gather estimates from team members of arable land available globally today. Of the Earth's total 197 million square mile surface area, approximately 150 million square miles are underwater and only about 47 million square miles are still dry land. My estimate is that only about 5% of that land is arable, and not all of that is currently under cultivation. The remainder of the land surface has been swallowed up by forestation or desertification."

"I'd like to add to Miriam's analysis," Singh interjected. "From the perspective of today's human population topside, the Earth is relatively empty. However, the animal population appears to have been affected by the Decimation to a much lesser extent than the human population. There appears to be abundant animal life everywhere across the face of the world. There are great numbers of herbivores and carnivores in practically all regions of the world. There are great herds and flocks of formerly domesticated animals living wild in many parts of the world, and the human population topside is attempting to bring some of those formerly domesticated species back once again under human control."

"Based upon what team members have reported back to me," Zazworsky said, "it appears that most major cities and population centers were mostly abandoned following the.... Decimation.... and survivor groups of people gravitated to rural areas where they could engage in hunting or raising their own food. Most of the metropolitan centers have fallen into disuse and decay and are populated only by small human groups of scavengers and marauders."

"Although there are large groups of hunter-gatherers scattered across the face of the earth," Red Elk added, "it appears that the Earth has returned to the agrarian age with only a smattering of the remaining people engaged in industrial or pre-industrial activities. The majority of survivors on the surface appear to have adopted an agrarian lifestyle raising mostly traditional, domesticated crops — wheat, corn, rice, soybeans, potatoes, sweet potatoes, yams, cassava, sorghum, plantain and the like."

Tipton was taking notes as each member of the team reported their findings and observations. Looking up from his scratch pad, he remarked, "All this suggests to me that we are moving rapidly toward a time when we can once again return topside. But we know that the small percentage of the human population survived because they mostly had a natural immunity to all of the pathogens that killed off everyone else. Some of those pathogens may still be persistent on the surface. What we need to know is whether or not there is a lingering danger of infection from these pathogens were we to return to the surface. We don't necessarily have any natural immunities."

"Metaphorically speaking," Ken Red Elk offered, "we need a canary in the coal mine."

"A canary in the coal mine? What does that mean, Ken?" Nguyen asked.

"It refers to a practice that coal miners used a century ago of keeping a caged canary in a coal mine to alert miners of the potential danger from the build-up of deadly methane and carbon monoxide gases. Because canaries are very sensitive to those gases, as long as the canary lived, the mine was considered safe for the miners to continue working the underground coal veins. But if the canary died, the miners knew they needed to evacuate the mine quickly to escape the deadly gas build-up."

"I understand the principle," Nguyen responded, "but what could we possibly use for our 'canary'? I'm not quite sure of what or who that would be."

"We could always call for volunteers to return to the surface for short periods of time to see how they fare," suggested Pendleton. "I'm fairly certain that there are several members of the staff who would gladly volunteer to give it a try. Heck, I'd even volunteer for a turn on the surface. If I got sick, you could always bring me back quickly through a portal into a quarantined vault where Doc Gates could nurse me back to health."

"Yes, Pete," Dr. Gates responded. "But what if I couldn't nurse you back to full health, or worse, what if you died before we could even get you back here? It seems to me that the risk is much too great. I have a better suggestion. Why don't I simply run quarterly pathogen monitoring? I could sequester myself in an isolated, quarantined vault wearing hazmat protection, and bring in samples of air and water and animal and vegetable foodstuffs to discover what persistent pathogens they still might harbor."

"Could you pull those tests off, Doc," Tipton asked, "without significant risk to yourself?"

"I think so, Bill," Doctor Gates replied. "I'd like to give it a try."

\* \* \* \* \* \* \* \* \* \* \* \* \* \* \* \* \* \* \* \*

Stauffer gave approval for the plan and Dr. Gates began collecting specimens quarterly to monitor for lingering pathogens. His initial tests revealed small amounts of persistent germs, bacteria, and microbes that could prove problematic for human physiology lacking a natural immunity. Specimens were collected each quarter from different areas in the world and the results from the tests varied from place to place. Some isolated places in the world appeared to be safe for return to the surface but Dr. Gates suggested caution overall.

After five years of conducting the tests, Dr. Gates had a lab accident exposing him to the samples he had just collected. The seal on his hazmat suit broke, and he himself became literally the canary in the coal mine. In spite of his exposure, he completed the tests to see what pathogens they might still contain. Although the tests revealed trace amounts of potentially dangerous pathogens, after two months in isolation following exposure, Dr. Gates still hadn't suffered any negative effects at all. It appeared that it was now finally safe to return to the surface.

\* \* \* \* \* \* \* \* \* \* \* \* \* \* \* \* \* \* \* \*

And then came the day that Stauffer dreaded. A large group of the remaining staff approached Stauffer and related to him that, after twenty-plus years working underground in a troglodyte existence, and with all of their projects now completed, they were prepared to use the temporal portals to return to the surface and try their hand at survival in the new world that awaited above. They longed for a return to some kind of normalcy now that the immediate danger of infection from all of the contagions had passed. Several of them had scouted out an area in Southern Virginia where the weather was generally mild to where they would relocate en masse and establish a new community. They had already begun stocking up and prepositioning provisions they would need to reestablish themselves on the surface. Stauffer asked for a headcount of who would be departing and who would be staying. It turned out that only Stauffer, Bill Tipton, Bob Zazworsky and Pete Pendleton elected to remain. Stauffer was now 79; Tipton was 74; Zazworsky was pushing 81; and Pendleton was the kid in the crowd.... he was only 73.

On the appointed day, the four old friends stood to the side of a triple-wide portal as a long column of staff and family members lined up to pass through to a new life on the surface. As they slowly filed by, Stauffer, Tipton, Zazworsky and Pendleton shook hands with each of them, and embraced them, and cried with them, as they said their goodbyes. Stauffer noted that Jared Lincoln passed by them hand-in-hand with Miriam Campbell. Mrs. Lincoln had passed away several years earlier and Jared and Miriam had struck up a friendship in their loneliness. Some of the family groups that departed had three or four children who had all been born while living underground in the Repository. They had never seen the sun or the stars in the sky and they were all excited to at last be going outside.

And then, all too soon, the four friends stood there alone in the deathly stillness of the now-empty Repository gallery. Tipton flipped the toggle switch off on the control keyboard for the triple-wide, and the shimmering outline of the portal faded away. The four friends just stood there looking at each other.

Stauffer finally shrugged and broke the silence, "Well, guys, I think I know a place where I can get some iced-down sarsaparillas and root beers. What say you? Are you old codgers up for a little liquid refreshment?"

"Arghh, Boss," Zazworsky spoke up. "Don't we have any of the bottled spirits left that we picked up from the New York City fire? Sarsaparilla may be your favorite.... but it sure ain't mine! I'd rather drink camel spit."

\* \* \* \* \* \* \* \* \* \* \* \* \* \* \* \* \* \* \* \* \* \*

With all the rest of the staff now gone, it fell to the four friends to complete the work of engraving the golden history volumes, which framed the output from the History Quest, the revised histories that had been prepared through the years by the Repository and Crypt historians. The histories were all stored digitally on their computer servers, but the golden record volumes constituted the low-tech, long-term storage medium that General Goldwyn had envisioned. Had the staff remained, they could have completed the project within a couple of months. With just the four of them left to complete the task, it took longer.... much, much longer.

They cleared out several vaults next to the enormous vault with heavy-duty, high-density storage shelving that Hank Phillips had set aside for storing the golden volumes, and set up a workshop for printing the history on thin gold pages, and binding them into volumes held together with golden alloy rings.

Zazworsky assumed responsibility for the laser engraving of the gold pages. He had a separate storage vault stacked to the ceiling with cardboard boxes of sheets of gold, similar to the kind that were used for the Repository Rosetta Stone volumes. The heavy-duty laser engraver accepted a stack of gold blanks in a tray at one end and produced engraved sheets which flowed into the output tray at the other end. Zazworsky took several engraved sheets at a time and punched seven holes in them along the side with a titanium steel industrial punch. Then he placed the completed sheets in a stack on the end table where Tipton could retrieve them.

Zazworsky's favorite part of the process was sweeping up the golden punch-out holes into his hand and depositing them in a large brass bucket he placed to the side of the punch machine on the table. Over time, the bucket filled up with the golden punches and Zazworsky had to switch out the buckets for empty ones. But he never tired of running his fingers through the golden punches and seeing the reflected light sparkle on their miniature surfaces.

Tipton took the engraved plates and bound them by hand with golden rings into separate volumes. The rings looked similar to the stainless steel rings that they used to be able to buy at Staples before the Decimation, but these rings were made of a gold alloy they had manufactured right there in the Repository that were designed for strength and durability. As he picked up each small stack of punched gold sheets, Tipton checked them over to ensure they were in the right order and then bound them with the rings. When he had a volume completed, he handed it off to Stauffer, who placed it on a roll cart and moved it down to the vault with the heavy-duty, high density storage shelves for archiving. Stauffer's job was to make sure that each volume was shelved in the proper order. The volumes were stacked on their sides rather than vertically to avoid placing undue stress or pressure on the gold sheets, causing them to buckle. Each volume was archived by itself side-by-side with the next volume, on heavy duty shelves spaced close together, but nothing was stacked on top of any individual volume. Before Stauffer shelved each new volume, he set it on a reading table and turned the leaves, page by page, scanning them for continuity and engraving errors. Frequently, he became engrossed in reading the history recorded on the plates, and Stauffer was frankly the bottleneck in the whole process.

But, little by little, moving along at a measured pace, they slowly completed the project. As Stauffer, Zazworksy, and Tipton worked on the golden history record, Pendleton attended to the gargantuan task of keeping the underground facility systems operational. For a time, he even ran the machinery that produced the golden binding rings when their on-hand supply ran low.

Although Pendleton was the youngest of the four, he was the most vulnerable to the effects of age. Whenever Stauffer, Zazworsky and Tipton began to feel a little run-down, they could always retire to the reconstitution chambers to refresh their bodies. Because the chambers didn't work for normal, modern humans, Pendleton couldn't take advantage of the chambers' therapeutic action, and his body started to show the effects of advancing age long before the others. He began to slow down, and it was only with great effort that he moved around the Repository performing his maintenance and logistics functions.

And then, one morning, Pendleton couldn't get out of bed. His legs were too weak to support his weight. He knew that the end was very near for him, and so he asked the other three to help him up onto a gurney, and wheel him down to the other end of the Repository for one last visit to the Majestic and the great theatre organ. As the three friends wheeled Pendleton down the aisle to the stage and up the ramp to the organ, Pendleton took heart seeing the huge console light up in the center of the stage. He had them lift him onto the bench where he could steady himself in front of the console, and asked them if they would mind just leaving him there for awhile to play alone by himself. The three friends nodded in agreement and walked down the ramp off the stage and up the aisle to the entrance to the theater, where they stood outside in the gallery under the Majestic marquee and listened to him play. Pendleton was midway through a medley of Gershwin tunes when the music suddenly stopped in a deathly stillness. They rushed back into the theater and saw that Pendleton had fallen off to the side of the organ bench. When they reached him on the stage, Pendleton was already dead.

They took a casket from a local abandoned mortuary and dug the grave with a backhoe they brought in through a double-wide time portal. They buried Pendleton alongside his wife's grave in the old Carlisle Borough cemetery, just a few rows down from the gravesite for Molly Pitcher, the artillery heroine of the Revolutionary War. It was the first time that any of them had been topside on the surface since they had gone underground. It was exhilarating for a moment, but then it passed and as soon as they had accomplished a brief graveside service, Stauffer, Tipton, and Zazworsky retreated back through the portal to the Hole.

* * * * * * * * * * * * * * * * * * *

Recognizing that all of them were growing older, the three friends redoubled their efforts to complete the golden History Quest volumes. Gradually, over the next few years, the vault filled up, and finally, twenty-five years after they initiated the project, they completed the final volume, bringing the record up to date with all the historical detail they had gathered in the intervening years since the Decimation. The three friends placed that last volume of bound golden sheets onto Stauffer's wheeled cart, and together, they rolled it down the Repository to the vault where the golden volumes were stored. As they placed the final volume alongside the others, they let out a war whoop and slapped each other on the back. By Stauffer's count, they had produced a set of 1,345 golden volumes. By comparison, Robert's *The History of the World* was just one printed volume. Asimov's *Chronology of the World: The History of the World from the Big Bang to Modern Times*, was likewise just one thick volume. Will and Ariel Durant's *The Story of Civilization* was much more comprehensive at eleven volumes and Toynbee's *A Study of History* was twelve volumes. The encyclopedic *The Historians' History of the World,* published toward the beginning of the 20th century, was 25 volumes. Even accounting for the much greater thickness of the gold pages, this work effort output from the Repository and Crypt historians was extraordinary and without comparison in the annals of mankind. It was something they were very proud of. They had completed General Goldwyn's vision for a sweeping History Quest narrative. After a few minutes of exuberant self-congratulation standing there in the golden vault, Zazworsky turned to Stauffer and Tipton and exclaimed, "What are we going to do with our time now?"

\* \* \* \* \* \* \* \* \* \* \* \* \* \* \* \* \* \* \* \*

The question turned out to be a moot point and a non-issue. With the focus of their existence for the previous twenty-five years now behind them, Zazworsky and Tipton both died within the month. They had contracted a bronchial infection and even a couple of days in the reconstitution chambers didn't seem to help. Their bodies were just too old and lacked resilience. The infection didn't seem to affect Stauffer, but by the following morning, both Zazworsky and Tipton had weakened as the life drained out of them and they passed away quietly within a few hours of each other.

Stauffer had long anticipated this day, and he had planned out precisely what he was going to do. Using a time portal, he raided another local mortuary in the past on the day after the contagion attack and snatched two mahogany hardwood caskets on metal wheeled frames. He managed to lift each of his friend's bodies from their beds and leveraged them into the caskets. Once he had them positioned just right, he pushed the caskets out into the center of the cavernous Repository gallery and stood between them. Then, speaking loudly, as if the gallery was crowded with old friends, be delivered an heartfelt eulogy, recalling to mind all of the special memories they had shared together through the years. His voice resonated off the walls and the curved Repository ceiling as he spoke, and Stauffer forced himself to work through the flood of emotions that threatened to derail his prepared remarks.

When he was finished speaking, and satisfied that he had done right by his two friends, he retrieved the two golden recognition awards that General Goldwyn had presented to Tipton and Zazworsky long ago. Tipton's was a large piece of gold fashioned into the shape of a valentine heart. Across the face of the object was engraved the word, "HEART." Zazworsky's award was a small statuette in his own likeness, carrying a small Amish boy over his shoulder in a gunnysack to escape a fragment of the falling UARS satellite that threatened to snuff out the boy's life on the edge of a manure pit. Along the base of the statuette was engraved the word "COURAGE." Stauffer reverently laid his friends' award recognitions at their sides in the caskets, and then, as an afterthought, he retrieved a small leather pouch he had made in the craft shop, filled with golden punch-outs from the production of the golden history volumes, and laid it next to Zazworsky's folded hands in the casket. After a moment of silence and quiet contemplation, Stauffer reverently closed the lids.

"Goodbye, Bill.... Goodbye, Ski. The good news is that we completed our work.... The bad news is that I'm going to miss you two very much.... very.... very much indeed..... God speed."

Stauffer entered a few keystrokes on the control laptop for a double-wide portal he had prepositioned to the side of the caskets and the outline of a time portal illuminated in the middle of the gallery. Stauffer pushed each of the caskets through the portal, one after the other. On the other side, he deposited the caskets of his two friends in the block house building on the pinnacle of the step pyramid, buried deep beneath his old house on the hill in North Middleton. As he finished positioning the two caskets side by side in the center of the room where Pandora's urn had once stood, he raised his voice so that it echoed off the walls of the empty chamber, "Methuselah, I have brought you some company.... two of the finest men I have ever known.... Bob Zazworsky and Bill Tipton. I know that you will all get along well. Rest in peace my friends."

\* \* \* \* \* \* \* \* \* \* \* \* \* \* \* \* \* \* \* \*

When Stauffer returned to his office, he was depressed and in a very dark mood. According to General Goldwyn, his family was removed far off to another interdimensionality, and he had just laid his two best friends to rest in death. He had never felt such crushing, paralyzing loneliness before. He dropped into his chair behind his desk and laid his head down on his hands on the desktop. He tried to hold it back, but the tears flowed as his body released the pent-up emotion he was harboring within. The tears flowed freely, uncontrollably. He sat there for almost an hour trying to regain his composure and get his emotions in check. Just when he thought he had it about licked, another wave of melancholy and sadness overwhelmed him and his head sank back onto his hands. Finally, he raised up and sat back in his chair and cried out in despair, "General Goldwyn, why have you done this to me?"

The figure of General Goldwyn materialized in the center of the room. "Done what, Barton?"

"What?...." Stauffer sputtered. "General Goldwyn.... you left with Mā-Bel....How did you get back here?.... Why?...."

"Barton, Do you remember that I told you before I left that once you were alone, I would provide you with company to help you cope with the loneliness. I am a holographic projection. I spent a lot of time preparing this before I left. I am powered by a special artificial intelligence application, programmed to converse with you on practically any subject of your choosing. I look forward to discussing with you any of the books in my personal library. Oh, and I'll take you on in chess whenever you like."

"You sound just like General Goldwyn," Stauffer stammered as he regained composure.

"I ought to.... I recorded over forty thousand responses to potential questions you might ask. The rest of the time, the program's voice generator will take over, guided by the AI application, but it should be indistinguishable from my recorded voice.... So, tell me Barton, why did you summon me? Do you have a question? Are you lonely?"

Stauffer marveled at the likeness of General Goldwyn's holographic projection standing there in the center of the room. It looked solid and substantial. It was almost like having General Goldwyn there in the office with him again, just like old times.

"Yes.... Yes, sir.... Ski and Bill died this morning.... Everyone else died or left long ago. I'm pretty much alone here now.... You say.... you say that you are programmed to play chess?"

"Yes, Barton. I am. Would you like to play a game?"

Barton thought about it a moment. He wasn't sure how this was going to work out. Finally he uttered in a hesitant voice, "Yes, General Goldwyn. I would like that very much. It might take my mind off things for the moment..... But, I'm afraid I don't have a chess board."

"Oh, but we do. It's right over here on the conference table."

As the General Goldwyn hologram motioned to the conference table, the holographic image of a large wooden chessboard with ornately-carved, classical chess pieces appeared on the table.

"I know that you are well familiar with chess terminology, Barton," the Goldwyn hologram said. "All you have to do to move the pieces is announce your move out loud and I'll take care of the rest."

As Stauffer slowly stood and made his way over to the conference table to sit down, the Goldwyn hologram moved and took a seat opposite him at the end of the table. The image picked up a white and a black pawn in each hand and moved them around behind his back. When he brought his two hands back around, the pieces were hidden from view in his closed fists. "Go ahead, Barton. Pick a hand."

Stauffer started to reach over to point and then stopped himself. "Left hand, sir."

The Goldwyn image opened his hands, revealing the white pawn in his right hand and the black pawn in his left. "I am white. My move," Goldwyn said. "Pawn to King Four."

General Goldwyn's pawn moved forward two spaces on the chess board. Stauffer sat up in his chair, startled by Goldwyn's unexpected opening move. "Perhaps," he thought out loud, "being alone like this might not be quite so bad after all."

"I hope so, Barton....," the Goldwyn hologram responded sincerely.

# Chapter 36

Although he mostly lost track of time as the years passed, the calendar on his computer reminded him of important dates when he and his family had celebrated special times together — birthday parties, Christmas, Thanksgiving, school musicals, marching band performances, piano recitals, elementary and high school graduations, fishing trips, vacations at the sea shore, summer outings, and long, cross-country drives in the family van to visit family out west. It all brought back wonderful memories for Stauffer and sustained him in his loneliness.

Stauffer developed a regimen of alternating back and forth between work on updating the History Quest record and using his temporal monitor to look back on those special family times together. It was a little unsettling for Stauffer to watch his former self interacting with his family in those days, but it was reassuring and uplifting for him just to be able to be with them, if only virtually. He even frequently used the monitor to look in on his family when they went to a special movie at Thanksgiving, a long-standing Stauffer family tradition. He watched the Star Wars, and Indiana Jones, and Harry Potter and Lord of the Rings movies dozens of times with them. Sometimes, he even retrieved a bucket of buttered popcorn from a theater concession stand through a time portal at the end of the business day when the popcorn wouldn't be missed. He would sit there in his darkened office in his easy chair, watching the movie over the shoulders of his family in the row of seats in front of him on the temporal monitor flat screen on the wall. The smell of hot buttered popcorn added to the illusion and it was a comforting activity for him. Stauffer enjoyed those quiet moments revisiting his family. But there was always that dreadful moment of depression and despair he felt when he had to switch it off and return to the present in the Hole. Stauffer worried that the tantalizing proximity of his family.... so close and yet so far away.... was slowly driving him mad.

With the passage of time, reading became an obsessive pastime for Stauffer as he worked his way through General

Goldwyn's extensive personal library. He sat there in the easy chair in his office finishing a worn copy of Mark Twain's *A Connecticut Yankee in King Arthur's Court* he had been reading. He rubbed his eyes. It was three o'clock in the morning but Stauffer had ceased to pay attention to the clock and the outside difference between night and day. Down here in the Hole, it just didn't seem to matter. He sat back in his chair. as he closed the cover on the book. He experienced a deep feeling of satisfaction from completing another great read. He stood to take the book back to the bookshelf and make another selection, but then thought better of it. He decided to keep the book on his desk for his next conversation with General Goldwyn's hologram. The classic novel was about time travel and Stauffer wanted to inquire about how Twain came to explore that topic so effectively.

Rather than waiting, he called out, "General Goldwyn. I have a couple of questions for you."

Goldwyn's hologram response was immediate as it appeared in the center of the room. "What questions do you have, Barton?"

"Well, sir, I've been reading some of the books in your library by Samuel Clemens and I'm a bit puzzled...."

Goldwyn's Hologram responded quickly, "So, you finally got around to my Twain collection. Which books have you read so far?"

Stauffer sat back in his chair and started reviewing a mental list in his head, "Well, let's see,.... the standards,.... *Tom Sawyer, The Adventures of Huckleberry Finn,* and also *The Tragedy of Pudd'nhead Wilson, The Prince and the Pauper, The Diaries of Adam and Eve, Life on the Mississippi, Roughing It, The Mysterious Stranger,* and I just finished *A Connecticut Yankee in King Arthur's Court.*"

"That's a pretty good start on Twain. What do you think so far?"

"Well, I'm a little intrigued by Twain's use of time travel to develop his story line in *A Connecticut Yankee.* It doesn't read so much like a novel of an imaginary time and place as it does a newspaper reporter's column in a weekly news sheet of Twain's day. He sounds like an experienced time traveler reporting his adventures. Much like H.G. Wells in *The Time Machine.*"

"That's pretty perceptive, Barton. He did."

"Did what?"

"Samuel Clemens had a very good idea about time travel. He did it frequently. So did H.G. Wells."

"He what? They did?" Stauffer was sputtering. "How did that happen?"

"Actually, Barton, there has been a number of your fellow mortals who have been privy to time travel during their earthly sojourn: Moses,.... Confucius,.... Buddha,.... Plato,.... Aristotle,.... Galileo,.... da Vinci,.... Nostradamus,.... Newton,.... Marie Curie,.... Einstein,.... H.G. Wells,.... Jules Verne,.... Mark Twain,.... quite a few more than that throughout history."

"Hmm.... but why did all those people have access to time travel? I would have thought that you and your stay-behind team would have limited that throughout the ages. Why would you allow people mucking around through time?"

"Actually, in some cases, we introduced them to it and encouraged their time travel. In all cases, they were already brilliant thinkers. Time travel helped them to gain a more holistic view on the universe and to understand how everything connects together. In turn, they were able to share important ideas and insights with the rest of humanity. For some, what they learned travelling through time helped them to solidify their thinking. For others, it initially helped them but ultimately proved a curse as they learned things they could not share, and they had to write around matters of great importance without revealing them. That was Mark Twain.... it ultimately drove him to drink.... but it was only a short drive." The holographic Goldwyn chuckled at his own joke.

"Where did Mark Twain learn about time travel?"

"It happened early in life before he really began his writing career. You've read *Roughing It*. In 1861, shortly after the beginning of the Civil War, Twain joined his brother on a stagecoach journey out west to Nevada, where his brother had been appointed Secretary of the Nevada Territory. *Roughing It* is a hodgepodge of his adventures on that trip.... some true accounts, but mostly made-up anecdotes drawn from his overactive imagination. *Roughing It* was hard for Twain to write because he had to conceal the most important thing which happened to him on that six-year journey."

"And what would that be, sir?"

"Twain included accounts of his visit to Salt Lake City and meeting Brigham Young, gold and silver prospecting in Nevada and California, and even a journey to the Kingdom of Hawaii. But he neglected to inform his readers of a boat trip he took down the Colorado River through the Grand Canyon."

"When did he find time to do that? It's not mentioned anywhere in the book."

"I know. I told him that he must not include that in any of his books."

"You told him?.... You knew Mark Twain? How?....When?.... What?...." Stauffer had become agitated and began sputtering again.

"Be patient, Barton. I'll get to it. You have to remember that Samuel Clemens was first and foremost a riverboat captain on the Mississippi. When he saw the raging Colorado, he just had to have a try at navigating the river. He hired a small but sturdy craft owned by a man named Kincaid in Green River, Colorado, and together with the man's son, Garrick, they pushed down the river through the rapids of the great gorges and canyons until finally they reached the Grand Canyon. As they were traversing that section of the river, Twain spied the mouth of a cave high up on the canyon wall. He had Kincaid pull the boat over to the narrow shoreline and anchor it, and, while Kincaid and his son waited below, Twain began to scale the canyon wall. The climb was dangerous and he frequently slipped on the loose rocks, but he was driven on by memories of the massive Missouri caverns where he had played as a child in Hannibal. He thought that perhaps, this might be another enormous cavern like that."

"Was it? What did he find?"

"Oh yes, and much more. When he finally reached the mouth of the cave high on the canyon wall and entered in, he quickly realized that this wasn't a natural cavern. It appeared to be manmade. He picked up some dried brush and wrapped it around a stout stick and lit it on fire with his flint and steel. With this makeshift torch in hand, he made his way down a long passageway cut into the side of the cliff until it opened out into an enormous cavern inside the cliff.... only this one was much different than the one he knew in Hannibal. As far as the light from his torch would reveal, he could see that the cavern was full of statues, plaques, stelae, mummies, and what he assumed were artifacts from ancient cultures."

"What did he do then?" Stauffer asked.

"Well, from the perspective of Kincaid and his son down on the river bank, Clemens was gone for about two hours, and then they saw him making his way painstakingly down the face of the cliff to get back down to the river. When he finally approached the boat, Kincaid was surprised to see that Clemens' beard, mustache, and head of hair had grown a full two inches and had a most unkempt appearance. His clothes were threadbare and were beginning to show holes from much wear."

"His hair grew that much in just two hours? How is that possible?"

"Clemens was actually gone for over three months. As he explored the great cavern, he came upon a strange artifact, a machine made of finely worked metal and crystal. On the face of the device were small knobs and dials and Clemens started manipulating them to see if he could figure out what the machine's purpose was. The large crystal face lit up and revealed a picture of a lush meadow and stately trees along a wood line. To the side of the machine, the shimmering outline of a doorway appeared. Clemens was startled but he moved over to the strange shimmering apparition and tentatively stuck his hand between the edges of the outlined door. His hand disappeared as it passed through."

"The machine was a time portal?"

"Yes, one prepared by the Ancients millennia ago. Clemens jerked his hand back in fear and fell backwards onto the floor of the cavern. He lay there for several hours contemplating what had just happened and weighing his options. His torch had long since burned out and the only light in the cavern came from the crystal monitor screen and the shimmering outline of the portal. Finally, driven on by his insatiable curiosity, he stood up and cautiously approached the outline of the portal. Then mustering his courage, he rushed forward through the portal. The cavern disappeared behind him and he found himself standing under a tree at the side of the meadow he had seen on the crystal screen. He looked back and could see the outline of the portal in the air next to the tree. He walked back towards it and thrust his hand through the portal once again. It disappeared and Twain assumed that his hand was back in the cavern. Thus emboldened, he ventured out into the meadow to see what he could see. In the distance, he saw a castle rising out of the mists with a small village of huts clustered around it."

"Wait a minute. Stop. Are you telling me that Clemens.... Mark Twain.... was the Connecticut Yankee in King Arthur's Court?"

441

"Pretty much, Barton. Of course he embellished the story a great deal as only Mark Twain could. But that's where the idea for the story came. When he later passed back through the portal, he went over to the control panel and turned one of the knobs. The scene on the crystal panel changed and he saw a new view, another pastoral scene of sorts but this one was very different. He hurried back through the shimmering portal and found himself in a beautiful garden lush with flowers and fruits. He heard someone coming and so he hid himself behind a large tree. A lithe young woman appeared, walking down a path through the trees. She was totally naked, but she had modestly draped her long hair around her body so as not to become entangled in the branches of the thicket. As she passed by the place where he was hiding, he noticed a large snake hanging down from a branch of the tree. Incredibly, he realized that he was in the Garden of Eden and he couldn't help himself as he played out that scene of temptation in his mind that he had learned as a child in Sunday School class back in Hannibal. He couldn't see the woman's lips move but he clearly heard her responding to the snake's promptings that he himself scripted in his mind. As Eve reached for a large piece of fruit that hung low on one of the tree's branches, Clemens realized that he might be creating in his mind the dialogue for the snake that was tempting Eve, and he surreptitiously turned and fled back toward the portal and escaped the scene back into the cavern."

"That was where he got the idea for the *Diaries of Adam and Eve?*"

"Well, sort of. After that, he was afraid to reenter the Garden through the time portal and Clemens used the observation crystal monitor a great deal to track the dealings of Adam and Eve in the garden from the safer vantage point in the cavern. Over time, he learned how to manipulate the knobs to move the portal through time and space and he experimented with viewing and sometimes visiting many places in history that had always interested him."

"Was that where Mark Twain got all of his ideas for his novels.... observing history through the temporal observation.... crystal?"

"Well, certainly a good many of them.... the two volumes on *The Recollections of Joan of Arc.... Is Shakespeare Dead?.... A Connecticut Yankee in King Arthur's Court.... The Prince and the Pauper.* even portions of his visit to the Kingdom of Hawaii in *Roughing It.* He saw it all through the temporal observation crystal."

"You said something about restricting what Twain could include in his writings. What was that all about?"

"When Clemens activated the knobs on the time portal, it alerted me that someone had accessed the cavern and I immediately began close observation of what he was doing. I tried to avoid intervening in any way.... our Prime Directive...., but when I saw what he was seeing and experiencing with the technology, I had to do something. When Clemens emerged back in the cavern after his encounter with Eve and the snake, I was there waiting for him. For effect, I had dressed in a long white robe, similar to the kind I wore when I was much younger back in Atlantis. That got his attention. I think he might have thought that I was Diety Himself and he was fearful for his life."

"You threatened him?"

"Oh no, but I needed to get his attention and absolute commitment to secrecy about some matters. I told him he was forgiven for accessing sacred realms and instructed him that if he chose to write about what he saw, he had to disguise the source of his knowledge and he could never reveal the existence or location of the cavern."

"Did he keep his promise?"

"He pretty much avoided mention of time travel or the repository cavern in the Grand Canyon in his writings throughout the remainder of his life, but then he had a great hiccup towards the end. In later years, he became ill with a respiratory problem while on a world tour. He couldn't seem to shake it off, and so, when he returned to the United State, he traveled by train out west again and spent the cold winter months of 1896-1897 in the warmer, dryer climate of Tucson, Arizona. One night, Twain was nursing a bottle of whiskey at the hotel bar where he was staying when a young soldier came up and sat down beside him. The soldier was an enlisted cavalry trooper on leave from his post at Fort Grant, not far to the northeast from Tucson. The soldier introduced himself as Burroughs, Trooper Edgar Rice Burroughs."

"Edgar Rice Burroughs, the creator of Tarzan?" Stauffer was astounded at the connection.

"That's right, though Burroughs was just a young hapless soldier at the time. Well, Twain took an instant liking to young Burroughs and together they nursed that bottle of whiskey long into the night. The more Twain drank, the more his tongue loosened up and he spilled his story about time portals and the cavern in the Grand Canyon. For his part, Burroughs enjoyed the crusty old man's company. He wasn't much of a reader and he wasn't familiar with any of Mark Twain's literary successes. But he was fascinated by the yarn that Twain spun as he went on about stumbling upon the cavern in the Grand Canyon and looking into the ancient past and traveling to far-off lands through a mysterious portal."

"Ouch! He broke his promise for sure," Stauffer observed.

"That's right, he did." Goldwyn's hologram acknowledged. "When Twain realized through his drunken stupor that he had probably crossed over the line into things he shouldn't be talking about, he masterfully started injecting additional fanciful stuff and outright lies into his story to obfuscate the truth and cover his tracks to throw the young soldier off. He figured the more fantastic the lies, the better, and Twain told him some whoppers. He told him about exploring the jungles of Africa and meeting a wild man who lived in the trees who had been lost as a child and raised by the apes. And he told him about traveling to Mars and Venus and his wild adventures with the aliens there. For a zinger, Twain added in a lie about traveling to a land at the center of the hollow earth. Twain laid it on thick with his swollen tongue and slurred speech. Finally, when Twain figured that he had embellished the story sufficiently to make it impossible to distinguish truth from fiction, he made the trooper solemnly promise that he would never tell anyone about what he had told him until after he had passed on. He even made young Burroughs raise his right hand as he swore the oath. Then, satisfied that he had taken care of the issue, Twain excused himself and stumbled off to bed."

"Did that end it there?"

"No, Burroughs continued sitting there at the bar finishing off the bottle and reminiscing on Twain's stories in his mind. He retrieved a pad of hotel stationary from the front desk clerk and he spent the rest of the night writing down some of the wild tales that Twain had related, about the cave in the Grand Canyon where he was transported to Africa, and Mars, and Venus, and the center of

the hollow Earth. He particularly liked the part about the wild man
raised by apes in Africa, a character Twain had referred to as 'Tarzan.'
When Burroughs had written down everything he could remember,
he carefully folded the thick stack of paper and stuck it in his military
blouse pocket and made his way over to the livery stable at first light
to get his mount for the ride back to Fort Grant."

"What happened then?" Stauffer asked. He was clearly
engaged in the story now.

"Burroughs left military service shortly thereafter and
bounced around engaged in low-paying jobs for quite a few years.
Along the way, he became aware that the drunken old codger at the
Tucson hotel bar had been Mark Twain and he started reading some
of his stories. But he held true to his word never to tell anyone about
his conversation with the old man until after Twain had passed on.
Samuel Clemens was born on 3 November 1835, just two weeks after
Halley's comet's closest pass to earth that year, and Twain boasted
in later years that he would go out with the comet on its return visit.
That happened in 1910. Halley's Comet made its closest pass that
year on April 20, 1910. Twain died the next day."

"What did Burroughs do then?"

"When Burroughs read in the newspapers about the old
man's demise, he realized that he was now released from his oath.
He retrieved his notes on the hotel stationary that he kept guarded in
an old leather suitcase and began to sketch out stories and sell them
to pulp magazines. Eventually, he became an established author in
his own right and his novels of *Tarzan of the Apes, John Carter of Mars,*
and *Pellucidar,* a novel that took place in the hollow earth, established
him as one of the great fantasy writers of his day and made him a
great deal of money. Burroughs never thought of Twain's ranting in
the hotel bar that night as anything but the numbing effects of booze
and his overactive imagination. He visited the Grand Canyon later
in life, but he didn't attempt to do any exploring below the canyon's
rim. Little did he realize how close some of his novels came to the
reality of fact."

Stauffer stood up and walked over to the book shelves on the
wall and scanned the shelves with his eyes. Most of the books were
those he had inherited from General Goldwyn's personal library
and he now looked at their covers with different eyes. He recalled
that, in addition to complete collections of the works of Mark Twain

and Edgar Rice Burroughs on the shelves, Goldwyn also had the complete works of L. Frank Baum. Stauffer turned with a start and directed a whimsical question to the Goldwyn hologram. "You didn't by any chance have anything to do with Baum and the Wizard of Oz books, did you?"

"Ah, Barton, you are the suspicious one," the Goldwyn hologram laughed. "Well, I might have had a little something to do with a couple of the books in the Oz series. But there were other authors I helped along the way as well."

"There were others?" Stauffer was incredulous.

"Yes. I had several conversations with young Charles Dickens when he was struggling with writer's cramp trying to sketch out the storyline for *A Christmas Carol*. Dickens wanted to make a strong case in the novel for the plight of the poor but he wasn't quite sure how to go about it. At night, he would walk through the mean streets of London looking for inspiration and trying to consolidate his thoughts. I joined him one evening on one of his walks and we spent several hours together as I discussed with him temporal concepts of looking into the past and the future for the true meaning of life."

"*A Christmas Carol* is about temporal technology?"

"Essentially, Barton. Go back and read it. The ghosts of Christmas Past, Christmas Present, and Christmas Future, are temporal guides who lead Ebenezer Scrooge through a stark self-examination, looking through temporal portals of sorts. I actually steered Dickens into a deserted warehouse one night and had him sit down on a overturned barrel while I displayed a review of his own life on an oversized temporal monitor screen. It had quite an impact on him and it broke his writer's cramp. The novella, *A Christmas Carol* is one of his most successful works."

"Is that everyone?" Stauffer asked.

"Everyone what?" Goldwyn responded.

"Is that everyone that you helped write great works of literature?"

"Actually, no, Barton. There were several others. Through the millennia, I have had occasion to rub elbows with many great thinkers and literary giants, some of whom I made suggestions to along the way for a story that became well received. But, let me tell you about just one author, that you might not be familiar with, but one whose short story has had great influence on America during the past fifty years."

"Who would that be, sir?"

"His name was Phillip Van Doren Stern."

"I don't know that I've ever heard of him."

"You probably haven't, and you probably haven't even heard of the short story he published in 1945, toward the end of World War II. It was called 'The Greatest Gift.'"

"You're right, sir. I don't think I've ever heard of it."

"It's another story broaching on temporal technology, very reminiscent of Dickens' *A Christmas Carol*. I met Stern one day in 1939. He was working as an editor for Simon & Shuster and Alfred A. Knopf in those days. He was a capable researcher and author in his own right and he had published some impressive books on the Civil War that had brought him to my attention. I wanted to talk with him about one of his history books in particular and made an appointment to meet with him in New York City. It turned out that he was very busy that day but agreed to meet with me over lunch at a deli near Time Square."

"So what happened?"

"When I pointed out to him the potential misinterpretation of his research about a particular incident during a Civil War battle, he quickly acknowledged that I might be right and promised to address the case in a future piece on that battle that he was currently researching. And then, a strange thing happened. As we worked our way through a couple of Reuben sandwiches, Stern admitted that with all his writing and publishing success, he still felt inadequate. He felt like a failure. He expressed a desire to write and publish something that would be of greater, more immediate value to mankind. Stern was really down on himself. Well, I couldn't pass up on that one and I suggested to him that an easy way to prove out his own worth would be to consider how the world would be different without him in it, without his ever having been born. In other words, I suggested to him the idea of how the world would be on another time line, an alternate temporal reality, where he didn't exist. I suggested to him to describe what difference it would make in the lives of his family.... and the people he knew.... and even the people he didn't know."

"What did he do?"

"It was surprising, Barton. Stern stopped talking and stared off into space, totally distracted, for almost five minutes. As he was deeply engrossed in thought, considering the possibilities for what I had just suggested, an enormous smile swept across his face. He jumped to his feet, thanked me for a most enlightening luncheon experience, and practically ran out of the deli. He apparently wrote a short story based on my suggestion within a few days after that, but, because of the war effort, he was unable to get it published until the end of the war. It was finally published in *Good Housekeeping*, with the title, 'The Man Who Was Never Born.' The story eventually came to the attention of Hollywood and the film rights were purchased. It was finally developed by director Frank Capra into the great Christmas movie, *It's A Wonderful Life*."

"Wait a minute, sir. Are you suggesting to me that you're the inspiration for Clarence, George Bailey's guardian angel?"

"Well, perhaps in a manner of speaking, but you need to understand that I never suggested to Stern anything about bells ringing and angels getting their wings. That's an embellishment to the storyline that Capra came up with."

Stauffer was enthralled by Goldwyn's tie-in to all of these great authors and stories and he begged another question. "Please, sir, what other authors did you inspire. You seem to have been quite the muse."

"Yes, there were others, but let's save that conversation for another time."

"Okay, I get it.... I'll give it a rest for now," Stauffer responded. "But your story about Mark Twain has one big gaping hole in it. What happened to Kincaid, the boat captain, and his son, Garrick?"

"Ah, now that is an interesting turn of events. The older Kincaid died soon after that first river trip. Young Garrick was only 12 years old when he accompanied his father and Twain on the river. Now an orphan, he took on odd jobs as a river guide along the Colorado River. He spent as much time as he could trying to find the place on the river where they had pulled over to the beach and Twain had climbed up the steep canyon face to the cavern. In later years, when he was in his 50's, he still remembered quite clearly how Twain had looked so changed when he came back down to his father's boat from the cavern. In those later years, Kinkaid had fallen on hard times and was destitute, and he became obsessed with the wild idea that Twain had discovered gold high up on the canyon wall in the cavern. Kinkaid took all of his savings and purchased a small boat to travel back down the river to see if he could locate the spot where the cavern entrance was located."

"Did he finally find it after all those years?" Stauffer asked.

"Once he had his own boat, Kincaid disappeared for several months and then reappeared downriver in Yuma, Arizona, with a few small artifacts which he claimed he had recovered from the cavern. A front page story appeared in the *Phoenix Gazette*, one of the most prestigious Arizona newspapers of the day, dated April 5, 1909, reporting that one G. E. Kincaid had discovered a great cavern in the Grand Canyon full of hallways and chambers filled with strange objects made of gold, silver, and copper, several Egyptian mummies, oriental statues, and all kinds of hieroglyphic writings on clay fragments and the cave walls. The story excited a great deal of attention in Phoenix and an expedition back down the canyon was soon mounted, led by a man by the name of S. A. Jordan, supposedly under the auspices of the Smithsonian. I could tell you the story of what happened next but I've set up a prerecorded video file to play if you ever came to this point on my hologram feed. I think you'll find it interesting."

As the Goldwyn hologram spoke these words, the hologram faded out and the flat screen monitor above the conference table came to life. As the picture on the monitor came into focus, Stauffer saw a group of men in several large wooden boats working their way down the river with the steep cliff walls of the Grand Canyon rising above them. As the video on the monitor zoomed in on the scene, Stauffer was surprised to see Garash, the man in the ill-fitting suit. From all appearances, he was the leader of the expedition. Apparently, he was S. A. Jordan of the Smithsonian. The video tracked the expedition several miles down the river and then jumped to a new scene. The boats had beached along a narrow stretch of sand set against a steep cliff that rose precipitously high into the sky. The members of the expedition had loaded back packs with digging gear and ropes and were walking along a narrow ledge of rock that seemed to track up the face of the cliff.

The video followed their movement for several minutes and then cut away again. When it came back into focus, the group of climbers had gathered on a rock ledge in front of the broad opening into a cave set high on the canyon wall. The men pulled out flashlights and lanterns and began moving single file into the mouth of the cave. The video file followed at some distance behind the men, tracking the movement of their lights in the darkness of the narrow passageway. Suddenly, the cave opened up into a large cavern, and as the video file panned the interior of the cavern, Stauffer could see the men fan out across the cavern, examining the treasures spread out everywhere you looked. Stauffer looked for signs of the Ancient's temporal monitor and time portal but couldn't find it among all of the movement of lights and shadows in the cavern.

"Did they find the time portal?" Stauffer asked out loud.

"No," the voice of the Goldwyn hologram responded. "I had already removed it and several other critical items from the cavern years earlier, and I now have them stored in a much safer place."

"What did the expedition do with all of the artifacts they found in the cavern?" Stauffer asked.

"Just watch the monitor and see. They were pretty ingenious and determined to get it all out of there."

Stauffer turned and looked back at the monitor. The man in the ill-fitting suit, S. A. Jordan, stepped back out of the cave entrance and fired a flare gun high into the sky. The video capture split into two scenes, one of Jordan on the ledge and the other of a large group of men in wagons high on the canyon rim who were apparently tracking the progress of the expedition down on the river. As soon as they saw the flare, they started moving along the rim towards where the flare had appeared above the edge. After covering two or three miles, Jordan grew impatient down below and fired another flare.

This time, the group on the rim of the canyon was only a few hundred yards away and they quickly closed the gap, moving towards the edge of the rim. Two of the men jumped down from the wagon and pounded a large circus tent stake into the ground to which they tethered a long stretch of heavy rope. They took the rope over to the edge of the rim and tossed it over. The rope uncoiled as it fell and eventually passed by Jordan and continued another 100 feet past him down the canyon wall. The rope was long, at least 1500 feet. Jordan grasped hold of the rope and started pulling it back and forth to signal that he had it.

Meanwhile, the rest of the men in the party back up on the rim were busy pounding more circus tent stakes into the ground and jury-rigging a block and tackle pulley system with the boom tip of the arm extending out over the edge of the rim. When they had it all in place, they started lowering empty wooden crates over the side of the rim down to Jordan and his men below. They took the crates into the cave and brought them out a few moments later now laden with artifacts from the cavern. They reattached the filled crates to the ropes and the men on the rim began hauling up the treasures.

The men worked in teams around the clock for the next seven days hauling artifacts out of the cavern. As they filled a wagon up to capacity, it left the site and made its way over to the railhead at Flagstaff where they began filling an empty warehouse with the loaded crates. At the end of seven days, they had evacuated over 475 crates of various sizes from the cavern and moved them to the warehouse in Flagstaff. Then, a special freight train travelling from California stopped at the Flagstaff freight depot and they loaded all of the crates onto the train for the trip east. The video capture tracked the train's progress until it reached Washington, D.C., where the train was offloaded onto a long line of waiting freight wagons at the Baltimore and Potomac Railroad station at 6th and B Street.

The wagons made their way the short distance to the Smithsonian complex on the Mall where roustabouts began offloading the crates onto wheeled carts and moved them into the freight receiving area at the rear of the Museum of Natural History. The building was still under construction on the upper floors but the basement receiving area had just been completed. Stauffer wasn't surprised to see the crates deposited in the same subbasement storeroom where he had previously observed the crates with the giant skeletons from Humboldt Lake, Nevada, being dumped the following year. No attempt was made to open the crates and examine their contents. The man identified in the *Phoenix Gazette* as S.A. Jordan, the man in the ill-fitting suit, stood by observing as the crates were just unceremoniously stacked on the subbasement floor in a long row next to the thick foundation walls of the then new building. When the work was completed, Jordan walked back over to the stairs and slowly made his way up the steps.

"That's it? All of those artifacts just disappeared into the bowels of the Smithsonian never to be seen again?"

"Well, Barton," the Goldwyn hologram responded, "not quite.

After we had confirmed that no one to this day ever made an attempt to access any of the crates stored in the Smithsonian Museum of Natural History subbasement, I organized a special unit here in the Hole to begin recovery operations. There weren't any security systems set up down in the Smithsonian basement, so it made it a relatively easy operation to go in at night and open crates and transfer their contents to other crates and remove them through time portals to new lodgings in the Waxahachie outer ring. There was a lot of artifacts stored down there, and it took seven full-sized vaults at Waxahachie to relocate all of the material to safer storage facilities."

Stauffer was perplexed. "Did you have them just box it all up again and store it away without really looking at what we had?"

"No, not at all," the Goldwyn hologram replied. "I had the team set up an inventory and classification operation right there at the Waxahachie vaults, and they tried to make sense of what they found as they opened the crates for examination. Everything was weighed, measured and photographed from different angles. It was all classified and catalogued as best they could, although some of it was admittedly guesswork when they didn't really understand what the artifact was or where it came from. Some of the objects underwent other kinds of specialized examination procedures to determine age and chemical makeup. It was a difficult process since they had little information to go on about where the artifacts originated."

"So what did you do when you had emptied the Smithsonian's basement of their toys? Wouldn't they realize when they went down there that someone had been messing with the crates? Just the disturbances in the dust would be evidence of some tampering."

"That was the fun part of the operation. I put Bob Zazworsky in charge of returning the basement to its original configuration after the evacuation operation was completed."

"You had Ski working on another top secret project I didn't know about?"

"Yes, I'm sorry if that bothers you, but I wanted to keep the team working the recovery operation as small as possible. I wasn't quite ready for the existence of the cavern in the Grand Canyon and its contents to become general knowledge in the Hole and Repository or even down in the Crypt just yet. Zazworsky's team took hundreds of photos of the stacks of crates in their original configuration before the recovery team started its work. All of the crates were weighed before they emptied them, and then Bob and his team were responsible for filling them with replacement items that weighed exactly the same so that they would match the railroad bills of lading taped to the sides of the crates."

"What did Bob and his team fill the crates up with?"

"Ah, now that was why I put Bob in charge of the operation. He has a child-like genius for coming up with clever solutions to complex issues like that. His solution for this challenge was brilliant. Bob knew that New York and New Jersey ship a good portion of their garbage over the state line to Pennsylvania landfills. There's a constant convoy of the 18-wheeler garbage trucks moving from New York City to landfills here. Bob was always annoyed when he saw those trucks pass by him on the Interstate on their way to the Cumberland County landfill near Newburg, just west of Carlisle. Who knows what toxic waste they might hold? Well, Bob came up with a brilliant idea. He hired an empty local warehouse and, using the temporal technology, filled the warehouse full of garbage and junk as it was dumped by the trucks into the landfill. It passed through a huge projection portal his team had set up and directly into the warehouse without ever even entering the landfill. Then, he and his team filled the empty crates in the basement of the Smithsonian with handpicked New York City trash, turning it into, in Bob's own words, 'a giant midden heap.' When they were finished making the switch of treasures for trash and had all of the crates back in their original position, his team sprayed a fine coating of dust everywhere over the crates and the floor. When they were finished, unless you didn't know better, the subbasement and crates looked like they had been left untouched for years."

"What about all of the trash left over in the rented warehouse?"

"Oh, that was Bob's greatest accomplishment. He simply transported it all through the portals, load by load, back onto empty trucks returning to New York City, his gift to the Big Apple. When the warehouse was empty again, he hired a professional cleaning company to come in and scrub it down and the job was done."

"You said that the inventory and cataloguing team at Waxahachie made a complete inventory list with photos of all of the artifacts recovered. Where can I access that list? I would really like to see what they found."

"You can find the list on the classified intranet. The password access key is "grandcanyon." I think you'll enjoy looking it over. By the way, I had the recovery team set aside a representative collection of artifacts snatched from the Smithsonian. I've stored them in the room behind my desk."

"The room behind your desk?"

"Yes, I meant to tell you about it earlier. It is actually located right here next to the apartment. Go over to my bookshelves and push on the top of the Louis Pasteur bust. It will tilt backwards on a hinge. Say your name out loud, 'Barton Stauffer,' for the voice recognition system and the mechanism will unlock the door to the room."

Stauffer was almost trembling with anticipation as he approached the bookshelf where the Pasteur bust was positioned. He pushed gently on Pasteur's forehead and the bust tilted backward like the Goldwyn hologram had prompted and Stauffer calmly said his name, "Barton Stauffer."

Stauffer heard a clicking sound and the book shelf separated from the rest of the wall of book shelves and moved backwards into the array and then pivoted off to the right. As it swung to the side, lights came on illuminating an enormous, spacious room. Stauffer entered and looked around in amazement. He had always been perplexed that, unlike most military officers, General Goldwyn didn't have an I-Love-Me display on the walls of his office. But, like the Roman General Equitius, this appeared to be General Goldwyn's I-Love-Me room. Positioned around the room were hundreds of personal items and artifacts from various periods throughout history. Against the far wall, there was an unusual array of photos. As Stauffer approached them, he realized they were three dimensional holographic images. They appeared to be images of a much younger General Goldwyn surrounded by what he imagined must be family and friends. Stauffer stared at a picture of Goldwyn standing with Mā-Bel when they were just a young couple and three young boys.

One of the boys in the picture displayed a remarkable resemblance to his own boyhood pictures. Stauffer spoke out loud, wondering if the Goldwyn hologram program was set up to function in this inner sanctum. "Is this your family General Goldwyn?"

"Yes, that's Mā-Bel, and our three children-- Enochelam, Mikal, and Necho when they were young. As adults, they stayed on with Mā-Bel and me as part of the stay-behind team."

"You must miss the boys very much."

"Not exactly Barton. I'm with them now. Remember, this voice you're hearing is only a pre-recording that responds to selected key words and phrases. I'm not really here."

Stauffer was taken aback for a moment and, recovering from his confusion, responded, "No.... of course not.... you're not really here.... and I am here all alone in this stinking hole."

"Barton, I sense your anger. But it will all be over soon and you will be reunited with your family. The sensors we set in place around the globe before the catastrophes began tell me that the end conditions are just about right. Can you hang on for another year or two?"

Stauffer bit his lip and took a long pause before responding, "Yes, sir, I suppose I can. Another year or two will give me an opportunity to look over all your trophies here in your secret room and review all the files on the intranet associated with the Grand Canyon cavern repository. That should be about right. But then I think I need to be moseying along, pardner."

"Barton, get a grip on it.... you have lapsed into cowboy-speak again."

Stauffer stood there transfixed momentarily wondering how General Goldwyn had managed to anticipate so many different situations and scenarios to prepare such a comprehensive holographic response package. The AI built into it made it seem like he was really talking with General Goldwyn in the flesh and it was really easy for him to lose sight of that fact. Finally, Stauffer started moving again, wandering around the room examining the representative artifacts that Goldwyn had left him. He wondered if he would find another dodecahedron.

# Chapter 37

*Carlisle Barracks, Pennsylvania, Monday, September 2, 2886, 6:30 a.m.*

Stauffer sat there alone in his office. He was thoroughly bored. He had read through most of Goldwyn's immense personal library but he wasn't prepared just yet to start over. It had been many years.... centuries.... since Bill Tipton and Bob Zazworsky had passed away and he missed having someone to talk to. General Goldwyn's AI hologram was a great help, but it wasn't real.... a close facsimile simulation perhaps.... but still not the real deal.

On a whim, Stauffer wandered over to the conference table and initiated the temporal observation monitor to look back in on Noah. As the screen came into focus, he saw the ancient Patriarch lying back propped up on his cushions just where he last had seen him. Noah appeared to be asleep. His eyes were closed. Suddenly, his eyes opened and a smile crept across his wrinkled face.

*"Barton Stauffer, you are back."*

"Noah, it's good to see you again after all this time."

*"All this time?"* Noah's smile slowly morphed into a quizzical frown of not understanding. *"But you just went away a few hours ago. What do you mean by 'all this time?'"*

"I'm sorry, sir. For me, it's been many years. It's been a hard time. My other colleagues grew old and died and I've been quite alone for a long time now."

*"Is that why you came to look in on me? You are lonely? It was not just morbid curiosity to see how long the old man would actually live?"*

"No, not at all sir. The history that has come down to us through our Bible informs me just how long you lived.... Oh, I guess that I shouldn't have said that."

*"Do not worry about it Barton Stauffer. I already knew that you knew that. When I sensed that you knew, I immediately blocked it off myself. I don't think that it would do anyone much good to know the precise date of their demise, do you?"* Noah's eyes sparkled in fun as he thought the words.

"No, sir, I suppose not."

*"I am glad that you looked back in on me. There was something that I wanted to ask you about the last time we communicated."*

"What would that be, sir?"

"When I was eavesdropping in on you, I discovered that while you were searching the waters of the Great Flood for the Ark with your temporal equipment, that you threw up in a bucket. Can't handle being out on the water all that well, heh?"

"Actually, sir, not very well at all. Many years ago when my wife and I were first married, we went to Acapulco, a resort town on the west coast of Mexico, for a second honeymoon. While we were there, we went out on a glass-bottomed boat in Acapulco Bay."

"A glass-bottomed boat?"

"Yes, sir, the bottom of the boat had a huge heavy transparent glass window and you could see all the way down to the bottom of the bay. As I sat there on a bench leaning over and looking at all the fish swimming around and the plants swaying in the current at the bottom of the bay, I got dreadfully ill and had to run to the side of the boat to unload. Not a pleasant memory."

On the temporal monitor, Noah was laughing. "You don't know how bad it was inside the Ark. After we closed and sealed the door and windows, we had very little light and then when the waters backed up and set the Ark adrift, it was very frightening not being able to see where we were headed. A glass-bottomed boat would have been handy. With all the tossing and turning in the waves that overwhelmed the Ark, the boat rocked back and forth relentlessly. It never let up for five months. And there was something even worse."

"Worse, sir?"

"Yes, you know how when someone yawns, soon everyone is yawning. Well, it only took one person on the Ark to start throwing up and pretty soon everyone was heaving. The buckets were overflowing and it was hard to keep them from tipping over with all of the wave action. It was a mess. Even the animals were throwing up. It was weeks before the water was calm enough that we dared unseal and open a side window on the Ark and throw out all the vomit and manure we had accumulated. If you get sick just by sitting in a .... glass-bottomed boat,.... I don't think you would have fared very well with us on the Ark."

Noah was obvious pleased with his dubious one-upmanship on Stauffer and laughed again. "Would you like to do me one last favor, Barton Stauffer?"

"What's that, sir?"

"I learned when I was eavesdropping on you early on when you were monitoring me while we were building the Ark that you had spent some time deployed as a soldier and that you used to listen to music to ease your stress and tension and help you sleep at night."

*"Oh, you must mean the time I was deployed up on the Korean Demilitarized Zone commanding my artillery battalion. Yes, sir, I had to leave my family behind during the assignment and I didn't get to see them very much. I got very lonely then, and at night, I would put on a video tape of the movie Brigadoon, a musical production about a fabled city in Scotland that appears only one day in every century to avoid the evil influences of the world. I must have played that movie a hundred times going to sleep at night. I almost wore the tape out."*

*"Ah yes, I remember the story line now. As I recall, it had wonderful music."*

*"You can hear the music in my head? That can't be good. I can't carry a tune in a bucket."*

*"It isn't your singing that I would like to hear, it's the music itself. Actually, if you will just think about it, I get great reception and, er,..... high fidelity. That is the favor. Would you please think of.... Brigadoon.... and try to recall the movie from the very beginning. Remember, your mind is a perfect recording instrument and it is all stored up there. I can help you remember once you get us started."*

Stauffer was hesitant but replied, *"Yes, sir.... I'll give it my best shot.... Let's see, it all begins with the two American hunters lost in the Scottish highlands overnight and they see the hamlet of Brigadoon appear in the mist. You can hear the voices of a chorus singing in the background about Brigadoon as the camera zooms in...."*

Stauffer stopped thinking about his telepathic connection with Noah as the play and music exploded in his consciousness, only it was like experiencing it in super-fast motion as the scenes and music rushed by in a blur. And then, suddenly, it was all over. The whole movie had run in his head from start to finish in just a few minutes, leaving Stauffer totally out of breath and in a cold sweat. *"That was an.... interesting experience,"* he observed sarcastically. *"Did you really get anything out of it?"*

*"Oh yes, Barton Stauffer. That was wonderful. I really enjoyed it. I will be humming the tunes for days. I may even try my hand at dancing the old soft shoe."*

*"Sir?"*

*"Just making a witticism.... Apparently not a very good one.... You know, Barton Stauffer, that little village of Brigadoon reminds me very much of the city of Enoch in my own day. My grandfather, Methuselah, told me it was there one day and the next day it was gone. It was taken up just four years before*

*I was born. I never got to see it myself, but by the time I had reached manhood, I had heard the legends of the City hundreds of times and I have always longed to see it. My father told me that it was foretold that it would one day return again to Earth. Perhaps I will be able to go there yet."*

"*Sir?*"

"*Oh, Barton Stauffer, I have no illusions about my longevity from here on out. I think my life has pretty well run its course. It's been some 350 years since we disembarked from the Ark. My wife has since grown old and passed on. My family has grown and spread out over the face of the land and I don't get to see many of them very often. I have grandchildren and great grandchildren and great-great.... and so on.... and there are so many that I haven't even met. I am just a few years short of the age of my grandfather, Methuselah, when he passed on. He was the longest lived of all my forefathers. I don't think that I want to vie for that honor.... My time has come my friend.... I want.... to.... thank you .... I have enjoyed your company.... You came to mean a great deal...."*

Noah's telepathic connection cut off short in mid-sentence. Stauffer had been distracted, looking at the clock across the room, and when he realized that the old man had stopped transmitting, he turned back to face the screen. Noah's head had fallen to the side leaning back on his cushion. His eyes were open and in death the corners of his mouth were turned slightly upward in a gentle smile.

Stauffer was traumatized. He knew intellectually that the man had died millennia ago, and yet, to him it was as if it had just happened. He stood there in disbelief staring at the screen as one of Noah's servants entered the tent and found the old man dead. He went running out to fetch others and soon several more people came rushing into the tent. Stauffer walked over to the temporal monitor control panel and switched it off. "Yes, goodbye my friend. You came to mean a great deal to me as well."

# Chapter 38

Almost nine hundred years had passed since General Goldwyn had taken his departure and left Stauffer in charge. Stauffer calculated that he was in chronological years, over 940 years old. Stauffer had spent the past several days working down in the Repository engraving gold leaves and binding them with rings into volumes to update the golden History Quest collection. Like Zazworsky had done centuries earlier, Stauffer swept up the golden punch-outs into his hand and carefully transferred them into the brass bucket to the side of the press. He noted that it was almost full again. It would soon be time to start on a new bucket.

As he moved the new volumes down the gallery to the vault for storage, Stauffer contemplated all that he had accomplished during the past centuries. Although he was somewhat detached intellectually from what was happening on the surface, he dutifully kept up with the task of conducting temporal monitor surveys to track the activities of mankind during the past 800 plus years and recording his observations on the intranet history files. That was challenging for Stauffer. Engraving that updated history onto the gold sheets and preparing new volumes was even more challenging for him. The manual labor involved in moving the heavy volumes from the engraving lab to the storage vault was becoming more and more difficult for him. By the time he had positioned the last new volume in its place on the shelf in the vault, Stauffer was breathing hard. He picked up his walking stick and made his way back down the Repository gallery to the double doors to the long tunnel back to the Hole. The moving walkway had long been out of service and Stauffer had to walk the whole distance back. By the time he reached his office an hour later, he was worn out. He sat down at the conference table and called out, "General Goldwyn."

"Yes, Barton," the Goldwyn hologram responded. "What can I do for you?"

"I just wanted to report that I just finished up another three gold volumes for the History Quest vault. I don't know how good the historical narrative is. My heart just doesn't seem to be in it much anymore."

"I understand, Barton. Would you like to take a break now and maybe play a game of chess to relax?"

Stauffer reluctantly considered the offer. He was tired and would have preferred taking a nap, but he finally relented. "Yes, sir. That would be fine. Please set up the board."

Stauffer was soon engrossed in a chess game with the Goldwyn hologram. It was a good game and Stauffer thought that he might have a chance to at least go for the draw. But as he sat there, his breathing became labored and a searing pain shot through his chest. Stauffer gasped as the pain overwhelmed him, restricting his breathing. He sat there at the table, doubled over across from the Goldwyn hologram unable to move, with a contorted look of horror on his face. The AI program that ran the hologram didn't have a visual sensory input and wasn't aware of Stauffer's distress.

"Your move, Barton."

Stauffer couldn't speak. After a few minutes, the pain lessened and he managed to get out a few words in a halting, muffled voice. "General Goldwyn...., I think I'm having a heart attack or a stroke or something. I'm in a lot of pain. I may have overexerted working down in the Repository this morning preparing those last volumes.... this could be it.... I thought I was supposed to live over nine hundred years."

"No Barton, your DNA programming sets the parameters so that you could live that long, but it doesn't guarantee it. Some of the ancient Patriarchs barely made it to 900 years and Lamech only lived to be 777.

The Goldwyn hologram stopped speaking and then asked, "Are you still in pain, Barton? How badly does it hurt?"

"The worst of it seems to have passed for now. But I'm feeling pretty weak."

"Okay, here's what I want you to do. Stand up slowly if you can and make your way over to the reconstitution chamber and get in. Let's let the technology give you a good going over and fix you up."

Stauffer pulled his walking stick toward him and he slowly pulled himself up to his feet. He was still a little dizzy from the pain episode and he shuffled more than walked across the room to the chamber. As he sat down and leaned backwards swinging his legs upward into the chamber, another searing pain shot through his chest. He lay there in the enclosure of the chamber gasping for breath as the overhead door closed automatically. The skin on his face had already started to turn a slight bluish hue.

* * * * * * * * * * * * * * * * * * * *

The cover on the reconstitution chamber raised slowly as Stauffer regained consciousness. He lay there in the enclosed space for several minutes trying to reorient himself and collect his thoughts.

"How are you feeling now, Barton?"

Stauffer turned his head around in the direction of the Goldwyn hologram's voice. "How.... how long.... have I been out?"

"About a week, Barton. The chamber readout said that you had a heart attack and it immediately set about breaking up the blood clots to restore normal circulation. It took several days longer to remove the plaque buildup in your blood vessels and rebuild the damaged heart muscles and valves. But, according to the readout, you were pretty much good as new within about five days. But then you remained asleep for another two days more. The lid to the chamber never raises until the occupant regains consciousness and begins to stir. That just barely happened. Apparently, you needed the additional rest. Your strength and energy must have been pretty depleted."

"Yes. I think so. I was tuckered out.... But am I okay now? Am I fully healed?"

"Yes, I hope so.... The chamber readout says that you are back up to 100 percent.... Uh, Barton, I hate to bring it up so quickly, but we have a problem."

"We have a problem? What kind of problem?"

"We apparently have an intruder down in the Repository. I don't have any way to check it out, but the trip wire monitors we set in place were triggered this morning a couple of hours ago and you really need to go down and investigate it if you're feeling up to it."

"I can do that. I'm feeling just fine. I'll get moving on it.... Any idea of who or what it might be?"

"None whatsoever, Barton."

Stauffer stepped down from the chamber and started to move across the office toward the door.

"Wait, Barton. You need to be prepared for whatever you find down there. Go over to my desk and sit down. Open the middle drawer and reach up under the lip of the desk drawer on the inside and feel for a small lever."

Stauffer moved over to the desk and, as the Goldwyn hologram talked him through it, he felt for the lever. As he pushed it to the side, a flat metal box fell down into the drawer. Stauffer withdrew the box and placed it on the desk top. Opening the lid, he found General Goldwyn's M1911 45 caliber pistol with two loaded 7-round clips. He had forgotten all about it. General Goldwyn once told him that he had almost blown away the first Minibago with the pistol when it appeared unexpectedly out of nowhere on his conference table. Stauffer checked the clips.... hollow point bullets. General Goldwyn meant business.

Stauffer smiled confidently. He had a great deal of experience firing the M1911 and it felt comfortable in his hand. He pushed one of the clips up into the receiver and pulled back on the slide loading a round into the chamber. The pistol had been well oiled and greased before General Goldwyn had stowed it away and, although it felt a little greasy in his hands, the slide operated just fine. Dropping the other clip in the pocket of his jump suit, he started again out the door. He was still slightly weak from his experience of the previous week in the reconstitution chamber and he walked slowly down the long tunnel over to the Repository. As he neared the massive double doors leading into the gallery, he stopped to listen for sounds of the intruder. Off in the distance, he could hear someone or something milling around down the gallery in one of the vaults.

Stauffer slipped stealthily through the double doors and moved off to the right and began to advance cautiously down the gallery with his back to the wall. The lights hanging overhead from the roof of the gallery still provided dim illumination for the great hall, even after the passage of so many years. As Stauffer edged down the gallery, he could hear a sing-song voice muttering some kind of a chant. As he neared the open door to the craft vault, he heard the creaking of the heavy metal door to one of the large kilns as it was opened. He cautiously stuck his head around the corner of the vault door and looked in. Silhouetted in the dim light in the vault, he saw a figure dressed in a long, loose-fitting robe, loading two of the golden volumes of the History Quest into an electric kiln.

Stauffer held the pistol out in front of him and pointed it at the robed figure as he entered the vault. "Stop what you are doing and turn around. Keep your hands where I can see them."

The robed figure at the kiln slowly straightened up and turned and faced Stauffer. In the dim light of the vault he could just make out who it was.... Garash.... the satyr.... the man in the ill-fitting suit!

"Garash!" Stauffer exclaimed. "What are you doing here? I thought you were dead.... I.... I saw you die."

With a contemptuous sneer on his face, Garash turned to the side and slammed the kiln door shut, flipping the toggle switch igniting the kiln's electric furnace. Stauffer could see the temperature readout gauge quickly climb as the kiln heated up.

"Now isn't this a surprise?" Garash laughed disdainfully. "Just who are you and how do you know my name?"

"My name is Barton Stauffer and I am.... the custodian of this place.... and you are trespassing." Stauffer gripped the pistol tightly as he spoke, keeping the weapon aimed directly at Garash's center of mass.

"Barton Stauffer?" A look of distaste crossed Garash's face. "I have never heard that name before. I don't know you, do I?. You say you are the custodian of this facility?.... and you think you saw me die?"

"Yes, Garash. We have tracked your activities for thousands of years and I saw it all on a temporal monitor. I know who you are and what you are. And I watched you get blown to bits."

"But, how can that be my friend?" Garash scoffed. "As you can see, I am very much alive. You must have seen the demise of my doppelganger."

"Doppelganger?" I don't understand."

"Yes, my Doppelganger.... my clone."

"There was more than one of you?" Stauffer was shocked.

"If you've been watching me on your.... temporal monitors.... like you say, then you know that I am an Ancient and that I can regenerate when I am injured. Once, a very long time ago, I severed my lower body section and legs and they just grew back good as new. You might have witnessed that on your monitor.... But what you might have missed was what happened to my severed lower body section. It regenerated a new upper half of my body. By the time my legs had grown back, my lower body section had also regenerated a complete duplicate of me on top.... my doppelganger."

"Is that how you seemed to manage getting around so much in the past, stealing the history of mankind?"

"Actually, I was a little uncomfortable with the whole situation at first, having two of me, but after awhile, I realized that my new duplicate self allowed me to double my efforts in furthering my mission. I suppose that if I had done it enough times, I could have created a personal army of doppelgangers.... But I didn't. Two of me seemed quite enough."

"I haven't detected you for over 800 years now since the Great Decimation. What have you been doing all this time?"

Garash scowled and an evil smile crossed his face. "You mean when the race of man almost disappeared from the face of the Earth? Did you like that? That was one of my greatest accomplishments!.... my magnum opus.... it just doesn't get any better than that!"

"You had something to do with the dissemination of all the pandemics in the Great Decimation?" Stauffer was incredulous.

"Yes, of course. You don't think that that idiot North Korean psycho could have come up with such a delicious scheme all by himself, do you? I instructed him how to build up a temporal capability and then put it into his head how to use that capability to gather up dead bodies from past epidemics and spread new death and destruction around the globe. The plan went off like clockwork. But you surprised me with an immediate counterattack. I was barely able to temporally jump out of there when your man arrived with the atomic weapon strapped on his back."

"You saw Colonel Wilson jump through the portal following the plague corpse."

"Yes, Barton Stauffer. As soon as I saw him and the heavy pack he was carrying, I knew something bad was afoot, and I hightailed it out of there. I leaped forward two hundred years. It wouldn't do to make just a short jump and land back in the middle of a smoldering mess. When I rematerialized and found myself in the middle of an empty, desolate plain, I knew that there must have been some kind of atomic explosion and I started out on a long journey wandering around the globe, exploring the new world conditions. There weren't really many people left. My plan seemed to have been most effective. It almost wiped out humanity. As I travelled around, I stopped along the way helping groups of survivors to mount attacks on other groups, but I could never seem to get much response like I could before the.... what did you call it.... the Decimation? The people seemed content to just eke out a subsistence existence. They didn't seem much interested in competing for scarce resources of food and water or trying to subjugate their neighbors. I wasn't able to churn up much energy for new wars or conflicts anywhere."

"How did you find our site here?"

"Well, it was slow going but inevitable. After the sudden appearance of your man with the back-pack, I knew that there was a temporal facility somewhere in the world and it was probably associated with a storehouse of sorts full of memorabilia and artifacts that I needed to deal with. I am highly sensitive to temporal phenomena. I can almost see it. As I wandered around the Earth, I never encountered it anywhere else. But as I crossed back over to this continent and drew closer to the area above on the surface, I could sense the temporal energy in the air and I was drawn toward it like a magnet. When I finally reached the forest directly above us here, the impressions of temporal energy were very strong. As I wandered around on the surface exploring a glade, I accidentally stepped into a hole in the ground that was covered over with weeds and dead branches, and I fell down a long shaft onto the floor of a tunnel above this cavern. I caught my arm on a piece of metal in the fall and it ripped my arm off. I lay on the ground at the bottom of the shaft for several days as my arm regenerated and healed. When it had sufficiently recovered, I made my way down here and saw all of these vaults, and I knew immediately that this is where I needed to get started. There is a lot of demolition work to be done here, Barton Stauffer. It is going to take me awhile."

"You must be mad Garash. Why would you want to destroy all of our work? This repository represents the fruits of thousands of years of discovery and knowledge and learning."

"Mad, Barton Stauffer? Quite the contrary. I can't allow all of this evidence to endure. It would be devastating for future generations to find it. It must be destroyed."

Garash suddenly reached beneath his robe and before Stauffer could react, he rushed toward him and thrust a long bladed knife in his direction. Stauffer tried unsuccessfully to dodge it, and the knife sank up to the hilt in his left shoulder. Stauffer responded pulling the 45's trigger several times in rapid succession. He had been aiming at Garash's center of mass but the pistol quickly climbed and Stauffer pulled off several rounds pointed directly at Garash's head. The hollow point bullets struck Garash in the neck and face and his whole head exploded in a bloody mass as he was thrown backwards against the kiln. As his body crumpled to the floor of the vault, his arm caught on the safety release lever on the kiln door and it swung open, spilling out molten gold all over Garash's head and body and out onto the floor.

The smell of burning hair and flesh permeated the vault and made Stauffer nauseated. The molten gold glowed fiery yellow and red briefly, and then gradually began to cool. Stauffer stepped out into the gallery to clear his nostrils of the putrid stench. He reached up and jerked out the knife that was imbedded in his shoulder. The wound closed quickly with little bleeding and the pain subsided immediately. Stauffer wondered if that was the result of his body regenerating or the adrenalin rush that surged throughout his body masking the pain. As he stepped back into the doorway, he saw Garash's body move slightly, imperceptibly, under the golden shroud. Stauffer was astounded. It appeared that Garash was already starting to regenerate. Stauffer calculated that he only had a couple of hours before Garash would become completely mobile and a mortal threat to him once again. He had to think of some way to immobilize Garash permanently. Stauffer leaned against the wall of the gallery thinking through his options for stopping Garash. And then he had a moment of clarity and he knew precisely what he could do.

He moved quickly to the supply vault where they had stored cardboard boxes of blank gold sheets for compiling additional volumes of the golden History Quest. With great exertion, he loaded two boxes of gold blanks onto a rolling cart and pushed it back to the craft vault. The kiln had shut down automatically when Garash inadvertently opened the door. Stauffer struggled to position the boxes of gold sheets into the now mostly empty kiln interior and shut the door again. He flicked the toggle switch to relight the kiln and then, stepping around Garash's prostrate body, retreated back outside. He hurried down the gallery past a dozen vaults. He stopped before one of the locked vault doors and began spinning the combination dial. The tumblers clicked into place and the door swung open. It was the vault where the inventory specialists had been working on one of the last recovery missions on an Egyptian tomb. Inside, Stauffer spied what he was looking for. It was a massive, ornately-carved, stone sarcophagus. The sarcophagus was very heavy and, for ease of handling, the technicians had mounted it low to the ground on a wheeled cart and had installed a set of special modern mechanical hinges so that the heavy stone lid could be mechanically raised and lowered into place with minimal effort. Stauffer pulled the heavy sarcophagus out into the gallery and began slowly pushing it back down to the craft vault.

When he got the sarcophagus into the vault, he pulled a block and tackle hook on a moveable ceiling mount over to where Garash lay prostrate on the floor. Putting on a pair of heavy asbestos gloves that were used for working with the kiln, Stauffer wrapped the chain on the end of the block and tackle around Garash's body, now covered in a thick coating of congealed gold, still very hot to the touch, and lifted him up into the air. When he had the body high enough off the ground, he positioned the sarcophagus directly beneath the body, and then lowered it back down into the cavity of the ancient stone box.

Garash was beginning to regain consciousness and move around under his gilded coating. In a panic, Stauffer quickly turned his attention to the kiln. He checked the temperature gauge reading.... 2500 degrees. Stauffer knew that gold melts at around 1950 degrees. and the gold sheet blanks had now been in the kiln for almost half an hour. He hoped that that would be enough. He pushed the sarcophagus over against the side of the stand the kiln was mounted on. The bottom of the kiln door cleared the lip of the open sarcophagus by just a couple of inches. Garash started to stir and thrash about in the cavity of the sarcophagus. Suddenly, Garash reached out with his left arm that wasn't encased in gold and grabbed hold of Stauffer's leg. Caught off guard, Stauffer tried to move backwards to escape, but Garash held him fast in his desperate grasp. Stauffer grabbed the full clip from his jump suit pocket and reloaded the 45. Locking and loading a new round, Stauffer emptied the entire clip into Garash's head and body. Garash released his grip and

Stauffer lurched backwards. From the far side of the vault, Stauffer could see that some of Garash's outer skin layer had already begun to heal over from his burns from the molten gold. Stauffer paused for just a microsecond, and then moved back across the vault and hit the safety release on the kiln door. It opened once again, spilling a large flow of molten gold out into the sarcophagus, thoroughly covering Garash's body with another thick, viscous, incandescent coating. Garash, who had been struggling to sit up, fell back into the sarcophagus' interior and ceased moving.

The stench of burning flesh again filled the vault. Stauffer turned to the side and threw up on the craft table. He pulled an empty waste pail toward him and began puking uncontrollably. When his nausea had passed, he pulled himself erect leaning on the table and turned to face the sarcophagus again. He could make out Garash's form under the thick blanket of gold that was beginning to coalesce around his body. Stauffer considered for a moment the wretched existence of this tortured soul and then pushed the mechanical release button on the heavy sarcophagus lid. The lid quickly lowered into place on the pneumatic hinges, forming a tight seal with the cavity of the sarcophagus. Stauffer walked down the craft vault and retrieved a heavy iron sledgehammer. He pounded on the mechanical hinges and they broke off and fell to the floor. They couldn't be used now to leverage the heavy sarcophagus lid open again. Stauffer retrieved several lengths of heavy-duty, steel strapping material and sealed the lid down tightly on the sarcophagus.

Stauffer was reeling from the exertion. He was totally exhausted.... physically, mentally, and emotionally. He momentarily experienced a sense of horror as he realized that he had just encased a living being in a covering of molten gold, which would for most people be an instant, painful death...., but not for Garash. For Garash, it could become a living hell, as his body regenerated and renewed itself, but find that he was unable to escape from his sarcophagus prison. Stauffer tried to imagine if there were any possibility that Garash would be able to escape. There would always be that doubt and he felt a compelling need to get Garash out of the Repository in case he were eventually able to work his way free.

And then Stauffer had another blinding moment of clarity. He pushed the sarcophagus back through the vault door out into the center of the gallery where the double-wide time portal still stood which Stauffer had used so long ago to move Zazworsky's and Tipton's bodies to their final resting place. Stauffer spent a few minutes at the temporal observation screen exploring possibilities. Then, he input a few final key strokes on the portal keyboard control and the shimmering outline of the portal illuminated the gallery in a faint glow. Stauffer stepped back and pushed the heavy sarcophagus through the portal, and it disappeared into nothingness. Stauffer stepped back over to the laptop screen to confirm where the sarcophagus had landed. Satisfied that Garash was going to have a difficult time escaping his tomb, Stauffer toggled the temporal equipment off and limped back down the gallery to the double doors on the way back to his quarters.

When he finally reached his office an hour later, Stauffer was totally enervated. Still grasping tightly to his walking stick, he staggered across the office floor and collapsed into his easy chair next to the reading lamp. He sat there for several hours with his eyes squeezed tightly shut, breathing hard, and trying to think through his terrifying encounter with Garash. The sight of the charred skin pealed back on Garash's head and body haunted his memory. The stench of burning hair and flesh still permeated his nostrils and wouldn't go away. The wound in his shoulder had already completely regenerated but the dried blood and knife hole in his jump suit sleeve reminded him of Garash's savage attack. Small golden flecks on the sleeves of his jump suit provided ample physical evidence of his unorthodox "Midas-touch final solution" to deal with Garash permanently.

As he gradually regained composure, Stauffer slowly opened his eyes and spied the Goldwyn hologram standing frozen in place over next to the conference table where he had been standing when he alerted Stauffer about the intruder in the Repository.

"I'm back, General Goldwyn," Stauffer announced.

The hologram reactivated. "You've been to the Repository and back? What did you find? Who was the intruder?"

"It was Garash," Stauffer responded.

"Garash....?" The Goldwyn hologram paused as the AI program attempted to process the information. "That can't be possible, Barton. Smathers reported that he had personally witnessed Garash's death. He was totally dismembered in the rocket attack explosion."

"That's right, General Goldwyn. But that wasn't Garash. What Smathers apparently witnessed was the demise of Garash's doppelganger. Garash was still very much alive somewhere else."

"Garash had a doppelganger? There were two of him? How did that happen?"

"He told me that he regenerated a whole new body way back when he severed his lower body half. His legs and tail regenerated, but he claimed that his lower half also regenerated an entirely new body.... an unorthodox clone.... his doppelganger. I think that that was one of the reasons why it appeared that Garash was able to get around and cover so much ground so quickly doing so much damage. There were two of him at work."

"What was Garash doing in the Repository, Barton?"

"He was bent on destruction. When I got there, he was loading volumes of the golden History Quest collection into a kiln and was melting them down."

"What happened when you confronted him?"

"Well, he didn't seem all that alarmed to see me, but he attacked me with a knife and tried to stab me. I managed to squeeze off several 45 rounds into his chest and head and he collapsed backwards and fell against the kiln door as he dropped to the ground. The door opened, spilling molten gold all over him."

"Ouch! That had to hurt, but it wouldn't keep him down very long. Smathers told us that Garash regenerates very quickly. What did you do?"

"I loaded Garash's body into the cavity of an Egyptian stone sarcophagus from one of the vaults and filled it up the rest of the way with molten gold. I dropped the lid into place and secured it with steel straps. Then I manhandled it out into the gallery and pushed the sarcophagus through the double-wide portal in the gallery."

"Where did you send him, Barton? Sooner or later he will completely regenerate and he won't give up until he's broken free from the sarcophagus."

"That's about what I figured. I decided to send the sarcophagus to a place where it would be unlikely that Garash would be able to dislodge the lid and escape."

"And where would that be, Barton?"

"I dropped it into the construction site for Hoover Dam, when it was being built back in 1934."

"Hoover Dam? Garash is now buried in a stone sarcophagus inside the walls of Hoover Dam?"

"Yes, sir. I dropped the sarcophagus into one of the rectangular forms for the wet cement located precisely in the center of the construction between the dam walls. I timed it just right so the heavy stone sarcophagus quickly sank into the wet cement already poured into the form and then it was covered over almost immediately by the next bucket load. No one noticed the sarcophagus and it was soon covered over completely by several more construction buckets of wet cement. Garash now lies entombed in the middle of over six and a half million tons of cement. It's not likely that he's going to escape that anytime soon."

"I think you have him well under control, Barton. Well done.... Checkmate!"

# Chapter 39

Stauffer sat in his office at his desk. The air filtration system had ceased functioning effectively a few months back and dust gathered on horizontal surfaces everywhere in the room. Stauffer resisted trying to keep ahead of the dust with regular, perfunctory cleaning. After all, he rationalized, it wasn't like he was getting ready for company.

Stauffer leaned back in his chair and stretched, a yawn extended his mouth open for the longest time. Stauffer was weary with years. True to General Goldwyn's word, his body hadn't aged significantly with the passage of time, but his soul had. He had been really alone for over eight hundred years since the deaths of Zazworsky and Tipton. His only company had been the hologram of General Goldwyn discussing the books he read and playing chess and looking in on his family far in the distant past with the temporal observation portal.

He initially thought that conversing with a holographic image would be mechanical, dull, and uninteresting, but he quickly found that the artificial intelligence software that organized and ran the hologram was extraordinary. It didn't seem to matter whatever comment Stauffer might make about any of the books or authors, Goldwyn had anticipated the point and had recorded an appropriate rejoinder. Thus, through years of dialogue and discussion with the Goldwyn holographic surrogate, Stauffer had learned to appreciate the wisdom and depth of understanding of the great thinkers of the past and of the Old Man himself.

At first, following the Great Decimation, Stauffer and his team had used the temporal technology to carefully track the activities and fate of mankind on the surface and update the historical record of mankind as they went. But, through the years, Stauffer became more and more detached from what was happening topside in the real world. Although there were pockets of humanity repopulating on the surface around the world, there didn't appear to be another living human being within a hundred miles of Carlisle. He hadn't even looked in on the descendents of the Repository staff who had departed so long ago for the wilds of Southern Virginia in several months.

The entrances from the surface down to the Hole and the Repository had gradually filled up with rubble and dirt through the years and were no longer passable, but he could always have used the temporal technology to visit the surface, had he wanted to. He could have gone topside without fear of any interaction with another human being, but he simply had no desire to. The temporal monitors revealed that Carlisle and the rest of Central PA had been reclaimed by tall forests and woodland meadows. Nothing of human infrastructure remained visible. Downtown Carlisle, shopping centers, warehouses, schools, housing subdivisions, highways, and bridges had all been broken up and buried and reclaimed by the relentless pressures of weather and encroaching forestation.

Occasionally, Stauffer would set up the parameters of the temporal observation monitor to check on his house on Sheraton Drive perched on the top of the ridge overlooking the Cumberland Valley. The house was long gone. It had only lasted a little over a hundred years before it disappeared entirely in a heap of rubble that quickly took on the appearance of a small knoll covered by clumps of river birch and Japanese maple trees. Stauffer tried to imagine the antediluvian ruins buried deep beneath the crest of the hill under hundreds of feet of broken shale, where Methuselah, Tipton and Zazworsky now lay buried. Looking out over the Cumberland Valley, Stauffer had watched the last vestiges of civilization disappear one by one, with the giant warehouses arrayed along the intersection of the Pennsylvania Turnpike and Interstate 81, and the iron water towers that had served Carlisle, Carlisle Barracks, and satellite communities, finally succumbing and keeling over into heaps of rusted girders that soon dissolved into giant red mounds of rubble. Stauffer was amused at how quickly trees and shrubs had broken up the enormous Wal-Mart parking lot and turned it into a woodland meadow. Eventually, that whole part of Central Pennsylvania looked like virgin forestland and nothing was left as evidence of the communities of people that had lived and worked there long ago.

In his solitude, Stauffer lived well enough. He ate well, perhaps even better than he had before the Decimation. To preserve his zero footprint in the past, he used the time portals to scrounge food that high-end restaurants were throwing out at the end of the day. He never ceased to be amazed at the quantity and quality of food that was wasted in his generation. He kept a log of restaurants visited by date so that his excursions never overlapped on each other and he could select his cuisine from some of the world's finest restaurants of the past. To satisfy his need for fresh produce, Stauffer would occasionally visit his old vegetable garden before the Decimation and glean zucchini squash, bell peppers, tomatoes, and herbs.

To keep up his PT program, he would walk along the defunct moving sidewalk down to the Repository and back, sometimes making multiple trips to build up his heart rate. He set up one of the old time portal vaults with a tanning bed and he would occasionally catch a few rays under a sun lamp. In short, Stauffer had everything he needed to get by just fine.... Everything except people and human companionship. Stauffer was terminally lonely and desperate for another human to talk to.

But the world that he had known was long gone and he didn't really have much of a desire to see the new one that had taken its place. He was aware that there were growing groups of the world's remaining population that were living together in relative peace and even prospering under the new conditions following the Decimation. He was also painfully aware that there were isolated pockets of conflict and violence that never seemed to rise to the level of global unpleasantness and generally subsided into an uneasy equilibrium over time.

Time.... He certainly had a healthy inventory of time on his hands. At first, after Tipton and Zazworsky died, he ravenously worked his way through the first ten volumes of the *Great Books of the Western World* with the Goldwyn hologram to counter his consuming loneliness. Along about Volume Nine, he realized that at the rate he was moving, it wouldn't take long for him to finish up and, quickly, over time, he wouldn't have much left to talk about with the Goldwyn hologram.

And so, Stauffer began to divide his time, spending the greater portion of it reviewing the electronic files of the compiled histories that the historian teams had created in the Repository and the Crypt before they shut down operations. By and large, he was very impressed with how well they had done with the History Quest. From his perspective, it was an impressive work indeed. Although, granted that the language might not be quite as elegant as that of some of the great historians of the past, it was infinitely more accurate in its review and analysis of its subject matter. Stauffer considered with some satisfaction that they had gotten the history of mankind during the past six thousand years about right.

Occasionally, he would compare portions of their compiled history side by side with the works of some of his favorite historians — Thucydides, Flavius Josephus, Garcilaso de la Vega, William Prescott, Will and Ariel Durant, Edward Gibbon, and David McCullough — to see how well they had done with the limited original source material available to them by comparison with what the Repository and Crypt historians had to work with. In many places, these eminent historians had absolutely nailed it and their facility of expression with the language was, from Stauffer's perspective, a thing of beauty.

As time passed, Stauffer suffered through periods of self-doubt about how long he had been there and how much more time might be remaining. He kept track of time on the computer on his desk. Goldwyn had ordered the Repository and Hole computers specially made with components designed for long-term use.... exceptionally long-term use. Many of the electronic components were made of pure gold because they conducted electricity so well and they didn't corrode. And, by and large, they held up well through the years. Each time Stauffer arose from a sleep period, he would walk over to the computer and check the passage of time.... days.... weeks.... months.... years.... and finally centuries.

The years passed by slowly for Stauffer. He tried to keep busy monitoring surface activity and recording it on the digital history file, working from his computer at his desk in General Goldwyn's old office. Occasionally, when he had sufficient new material, he would walk over to the Repository, and use the old assembly line setup that they had employed centuries earlier to augment the golden History Quest record by engraving additional volumes for the record. When he had accumulated sufficient sheets, he would bind them with golden alloy rings and move the new volume over to the adjacent vault on a wheeled cart to position it with the rest of the golden volumes. After the incident with Garash in the Repository, Stauffer had to go back and re-engrave and bind the volumes that Garash had destroyed in the kiln. Every time Stauffer entered the vault holding a new golden History Quest volume, he experienced an intense feeling of personal satisfaction.

From time to time, Stauffer would retire to the reconstitution chamber for a rest to update the History Quest record on his DNA and to recharge his batteries. His sessions in the chamber were still set on automatic but he noted that they were taking longer and longer for the chamber to deal with the effects of the passing years on his body. When he emerged from the chamber, he always felt refreshed and reinvigorated, but he noted when he looked in the mirror that his body was indeed aging with the passing of time.

Stauffer developed a regimen of alternating back and forth between work on updating the History Quest record and using his temporal monitor to revisit his family. Looking in on them brought him great comfort but also a great deal of pain as it reminded him of how much he missed them. One of his favorite family interludes was when he had taken the whole family to New York City to see the Thanksgiving Day Parade. It had been an exciting day and the kids were enthralled by the huge balloons that the street handlers paraded down 42$^{nd}$ Street off Times Square where the Stauffer family had stood huddled against the chilly wind. After the parade was over and Santa's sleigh had passed by, Stauffer had herded everyone into a pizzeria and they lucked into getting an empty window seat where they could observe the bustling crowds walking up and down the sidewalk in front of the building. Stauffer always tracked the family with the temporal monitor throughout the entire parade and then followed them to the pizzeria. He positioned the monitor perspective so that it was as if he was standing outside on the sidewalk with his nose pressed up against the windowpane looking in on his family wolfing down thick slices of New York pizza. It was such a precious memory for him that for awhile, Stauffer used a screen capture image of the scene displayed on the flat screen monitor on the wall next to the conference table where he could see them anytime he wanted.

Occasionally, Stauffer used the temporal monitor to track the progress of deterioration of Carlisle Barracks and the topside area overlaying the Hole and the Repository. In its prime years, before the great Decimation, Carlisle Barracks was thickly covered by an almost infinite variety of stately deciduous and conifer trees. After there was no one left to tend the grounds, the trees had quickly claimed the installation real estate, the adjacent golf course, and the AHEC property. As Stauffer observed the rapid deterioration of the installation above him, he gradually despaired and stopped tracking the progress of the trees. At about the five hundred year mark, on a whim, Stauffer set up the parameters on the temporal monitor to look down on the Barracks from about a thousand feet to check out what it looked like from the air. As he had suspected, the entire installation had disappeared under thick vegetation growth.

However, he was astonished that there appeared to be a pattern of low-growth and no-growth in the otherwise thickly-forested area. The pattern had the appearance of a large X a hundred meters across. Stauffer quickly ran a backward scan on the X to check out the location of the crosshairs of the X. It turned out to be directly over the AHEC elevator shaft down into the Repository. The next time he was discussing a new book with the Goldwyn hologram, he ventured to ask about the X on the ground above them.

The response from the Goldwyn hologram surprised him. "Ah, Barton. You've discovered the sign post I left in place to help future generations of archeologists and explorers find the Repository. When the AHEC was built, I had the construction engineers position a number of solid state transmitters which emit a radio signal that discourages the growth of vegetation. The net effect should be to produce a design of non-growth in the vegetation that should be easily discernible from the air. If future generations redevelop the capability of flight and are paying attention, they ought to be able to see the X and take a look at what might be there. The walls of the elevator shaft going down into the Repository are over two feet thick so, although it may have partially filled up with rubble, the shaft ought to provide a direct route down to the Repository and the vaults. Once they crack the code of what's stored there, they also ought to be able to interpret the clues we've left there to find the auxiliary vaults at Waxahachie. I know that after awhile, you're not going to be monitoring the surface activity very much. The intrusion detection alarm system will alert you should anyone find their way down into the Repository or the Hole again. It will be up to you to decide whether to fade into the woodwork or to greet the interlopers and guide them through the vaults."

Stauffer pondered General Goldwyn's cryptic message. He hadn't given the matter much thought. What should he do if anyone found their way down into his subterranean refuge? Stauffer didn't really come to any immediate conclusion, and gradually, it migrated to the back burner of his mind where he didn't give it any additional thought at all.

# Chapter 40

Almost nine hundred years had passed since General Goldwyn had taken his departure and left Stauffer in charge. He had begun to self-identify with the ancient, grey knight left to guard the Holy Grail in the movie *Indiana Jones and the Last Crusade*. When Stauffer played the Goldwyn hologram a game of chess, he took to repeating in an affected way whenever Goldwyn made a particularly good move, "You have chosen well" or, on rare instances when he thought he detected a weak move and he calculated that he might have an opportunity for defeating the hologram, "You have chosen poorly."

Stauffer remembered Goldwyn's explanation that his reprogrammed DNA would give him a total life span of just under a thousand years. Stauffer walked over to his desk and reviewed the date on his computer clock, November 1, 2915. He observed with a grimace that it was his birthday. He pulled a yellow pad over to him and did the calculation. Today, he was 968 years old. His actual age startled him. He was in danger of overcoming Methuselah's longevity record. That just couldn't be. Finally, after so many years alone, Stauffer concluded that he had served his time and that he could rightfully step down from his duties as the Custodian of the Repository, the Hole, and the Crypt.

He walked over to the conference table and sat down. "General Goldwyn."

The holographic image of Goldwyn appeared in the center of the room. "Yes, Barton. What do you want?"

"Well, sir. today is my birthday and I'm now 968 years old. Don't you think that I need to be moving on before I encroach on Methuselah's record? Is there any important reason why I need to stay down here any longer? I think I'm about to the end of my tether and would really like to rejoin my family now."

The image of Goldwyn paused for a moment and then reactivated. "Barton, I just checked the chronographic parameters on the computer system. You are right. It is time for you to depart and rejoin your family. I would hate to have to face Methuselah one day if we allowed you to go over.... Are you prepared to travel?"

"Just like that? I am free to leave now? All I had to do is ask?" Stauffer was incredulous at the news.

"Well, your 968th birthday sealed the deal," the Goldwyn hologram agreed. "You simply can't stay any longer. It is time for you to leave.

"Well then, I should probably get spruced up a bit. It may take a couple of hours."

"That's fine, Barton. I'll be waiting right here for you."

The image froze and Stauffer walked out the door and down the stairs to the walkway over to the Repository one last time. He had gotten used to slowly walking the distance over to the entrance to the Repository. He had recovered his favorite walking stick from his house on the hill north of Carlisle shortly after the Decimation, and he sometimes used the staff to assist him when walking long distances in the underground tunnels. He had disengaged the locking mechanism on the doors many years earlier, and when he finally came up to the two massive double doors, he just pushed hard on both of them and walked on through into the cavernous gallery of the Repository.

After all these years, many of the lights had dimmed or no longer functioned altogether, but there was still sufficient light to illuminate the gallery all the way down to the far end where the marquee for the Majestic theater stuck out from the wall. Stauffer was comforted by the positive feelings and memories he felt whenever he was in the Repository. Some of the great moments of his professional life had unfolded here. Now, as he stared down the empty gallery for the last time, he got choked up. He walked a short distance down the gallery until he came to Vault B, the one Zazworsky had designated so long ago for the makeshift shower room for the men who worked in the Repository. He pushed open the vault door and entered. Two lone lights in the vault illuminated as he passed through the doorway. Stauffer walked directly to the far side of the vault where he disrobed next to the hazmat shower. He pushed on the red emergency knob that activated the water flow and it came rushing down over his body. It was cold, very cold, about 60 degrees, the same temperature as the underground aquifers in the area. Stauffer shivered and grabbed an aged bar of soap from the soap dish, lathering up as best he could in the cold water. After a few minutes, he rinsed off and toweled dry. He pulled down a Repository jumpsuit from the shelf on the wall and slipped it on. It had fared well in the passage of years and although the material was a little brittle from age, it seemed to work just fine. He sat down and slipped on his socks and shoes and then exited the vault.

He stood there for just a few moments in the vault doorway, looking to his right and left, and then finally decided to do one last grand tour of the Repository before he departed. He turned and started walking down the gallery toward the Majestic. As he passed the long rows of vault doors on both sides of the gallery, his mind rushed back to their early years of recovering artifacts from oblivion and wondered when, if ever, anyone would chance upon the Repository and discover the treasures of history stored here. As he passed the massive replica of the Puerta del Sol from Tiahuanaco that General Goldwyn had acquired from the Bolivian antiquarian authorities, Stauffer paused to admire the relief portrait of his old friend, Bob Zazworsky, immortalized in stone as the Andean American god, Viracocha. "You've never looked better, Ski," Stauffer observed as he stood erect at attention, supported by his walking stick, and saluted the image smartly.

When Stauffer got to the Majestic, he entered in, walking down the red, carpeted aisle about halfway to a row of seats in the middle of the theater auditorium. The aging carpet crumbled under his footsteps. Stauffer sat down and reminisced about all the great events they had staged down here in the Majestic. He looked up at the imposing theatre organ that Pete Pendleton's team had rescued from a grand old theater in Dresden just before it was destroyed by Allied carpet bombing of the city during World War II. Before he died, Pendleton had jury-rigged the great theatre organ with a self-playing mechanism, and for many years thereafter, Stauffer, Zazworsky, and Tipton had come down here to the theater from time to time to hear recorded concerts. After Zazworsky and Tipton had died, Stauffer still made an occasional trip to the Majestic for a private concert. But after a while, those trips had tapered off and Stauffer hadn't been to the Majestic in over two years. He wondered if the system was still operational. Stauffer repeated the mechanism's voice recognition password aloud in his best military command voice, "Play it again, Sam." And then, as an after-thought, he added, "A little traveling music, please."

The lights on the organ console came up, and he could hear the organ's blowers and tremulants slowly activate. Pete had worried that the leather components of the organ would eventually deteriorate and render the organ inoperable, but apparently, they had held up fairly well. Stauffer sat back in his seat and listened expectantly. And then, the organ began to play "Somewhere Over the Rainbow," from *The Wizard of Oz*, one of Stauffer's favorite movie musicals. He sat there entranced, lifted up by the majestic sounds that Pete had recorded for the self-playing mechanism. As the music came to a crescendo at the conclusion of the piece and shut off, Stauffer sat there in the stillness of the theater in contented satisfaction. "Thanks, Pete," he whispered. "That was a fitting swan song.... That was just fine...."

After several minutes, he slowly got to his feet, and, gripping his staff tightly, he walked back up the aisle and out into the gallery. He kept on walking without looking back, his eyes misting up in salty tears. It took him almost half an hour to walk back the full length of the gallery. He stopped and paused by the vault entrance to the staff offices where Bob Zazworsky had hung the ornate, carved wooden plaque from General Equitius' atheneum, *"Quis Custodiet Ipsos Custodes?"....* "Who Guards the Guardians?" Stauffer chuckled as he posed that familiar question and challenge in his mind one last time. "Who indeed?" he muttered to himself. Then, turning slowly, he continued on down the gallery to the double doors leading out to the walkway to the Hole. As he reached the doors, he looked up at the tattered pasteboard sign that Zazworsky had snatched from Barnum's American Museum and posted here above the doorway so long ago, "This Way to the Egress."

Stauffer chuckled again. Aloud, he said, "Yes, Ski, I think it's high time to find the egress."

It took him another full hour to slowly make his way along the long subterranean passageway back to the Hole and then up the two levels to where his office was located. He had left the massive door to the office ajar and entered without pausing. He walked across the office past the frozen holographic image of General Goldwyn and sat back down at the conference table.

"General Goldwyn, I think that I'm about ready."

"That's good, Barton," the Goldwyn hologram responded as it reactivated. "But there's one more thing that you need to do before you go."

"What's that, sir?"

"You need one more session in the reconstitution chamber to update the files on your DNA one last time. It won't take but a moment and then we'll have you on your way."

Stauffer sighed and responded petulantly, "Yes, sir, I guess I can do that."

Stauffer walked across the room to the imposing chamber. As he stretched his legs out into the box and laid his head back on the head rest, the overhead door automatically closed down as it had countless times before. Stauffer was immediately asleep. As the lid opened at the end of the DNA update session, he slowly came back to full consciousness and swung his legs around to stand up.

"Well, my friend, are you about ready to return home?"

The voice took Stauffer by surprise. It wasn't the voice of the Goldwyn hologram. It was someone else. Stauffer looked across the room through bleary, unfocused eyes. As his eyes began to refocus, he made out the indistinct image of a large man, dressed in a white robe, standing next to the frozen Goldwyn hologram.

"Who are you?" Stauffer demanded. "How did you get in here?"

"I guess I should introduce myself, Barton Stauffer.... I am Enoch, Kubal Golden One's older twin brother."

"You are Enoch....? You're General Goldwyn's brother?" As his vision cleared, Stauffer recognized the Patriarch's wizened face. He looked much like his image on the temporal observation monitor when Stauffer first saw him as a much younger man when he scanned the build-up of Atlantis. Only now, his face was lined with deep wrinkles, and he could tell that Enoch had advanced greatly in years. He now saw the close resemblance between General Goldwyn and Enoch, although Enoch was a giant of a man. As he looked up at him across the room, Stauffer judged that Enoch was probably close to eight and a half feet tall.

"How is it that General Goldwyn had to move on to avoid overtaking Methuselah's longevity record and you are still around?" Stauffer asked. "Aren't you in danger of messing up Methuselah's record?"

"Oh no, not quite yet my friend. While my brother led the stay-behind team through thousands of years of Earth's history, I did a great deal of leapfrogging into the future using our temporal technology, leaving Kubal Golden One pretty much in charge so that I would have sufficient life line left beyond the Catastrophes and the Great Decimation to lead my people back home here to Earth. And I have even been doing a great deal of leapfrogging through time since we returned to be able to stay on until the endgame."

"Back here to Earth?.... Yes, I saw the Atlantis ship set down.... out in the Midwest on the temporal monitor a year or so after the Decimation. I think I even saw Melek disembark with his bride, Ulla. But after that, General Goldwyn apparently had set an automatic temporal block in place and I couldn't observe anything more."

"Actually, I set the block in place myself, Barton Stauffer. You still had a great deal of work organizing the efforts of your intrepid time explorers and historians, preparing your revised history and vaults of artifacts,.... your Hall of Records and the History Quest,.... and I did not want you to be distracted by what was going on with the return and reestablishment of Atlantis."

"But I have so many questions, sir. Where have you been all this time?.... Why did you come back?.... How are you intermixing with the surviving humans up there on the surface?"

Enoch held up his hand and laughed. "Wait, Barton Stauffer. Kubal Golden One warned me that for every fact you get, it generates a thousand additional questions. You will get answers to all your questions in due time. For now, we will just hold those questions in abeyance. Agreed?"

"But why.... why are you here, sir?"

"I am here for the best of reasons, Barton Stauffer. Like my brother was fond of doing, I have been keeping track of your efforts for all these years since I returned with my people. I have kept a careful temporal monitor on you to track your actual age, and an alarm sounded for me this morning that you had communicated with my brother's hologram to remind him of your 968th birthday and to state your desire to leave now. You have been doing admirable custodial work down here, but I concur.... It is finally time for you to move on. Is that satisfactory for you, Barton Stauffer?"

"Yes sir. I was just getting ready to go."

"That is well. I will leave you to say your final goodbyes here. Did Kubal Golden One show you how to rejoin your family?"

"Yes, sir. He even allowed me to accompany him and Mā-Bel when they departed to see how it was done."

"Then there is just one thing left to do...."

Enoch had been standing slightly bent over with age but he slowly stood erect, almost at attention, now towering over Stauffer. In a formal, command voice, Enoch directed, "Barton Stauffer, after a long and respectable assignment as sole custodian of these precincts, I, Enoch, son of Jared, relieve you of your responsibilities. Would you please step forward and turn over to me your Hall of Records at this time as a sign of the transfer of responsibility."

Stauffer stood there dumbfounded not knowing quite what to do. "I'm not too sure how I'm supposed to do that, sir," he said in a muffled voice.

"Oh, my friend, it is quite simple. Please step forward and pull back the right sleeve on your jumpsuit."

Puzzled, Stauffer did as Enoch directed. As he pulled back his sleeve, Enoch drew a blade from under his robe and quickly slashed across Stauffer's wrist, making a long deep cut which began to spurt blood. Then, quickly drawing the blade across his own right wrist, Enoch placed his bleeding wrist over Stauffer's.

Stauffer was in shock. He hadn't expected that. Enoch looked deeply into Stauffer's eyes and said, "In ancient America, Barton Stauffer, we would now be considered blood brothers. I am very proud to honor that distinction, my friend."

Letting loose of Stauffer's forearm the two men turned their arms upward to examine their wrists. The blood had stopped flowing and the wounds had almost totally regenerated.

"Sir, what was that all about?" Stauffer managed to sputter.

"I think that it ought to be obvious, Barton Stauffer. We just exchanged a portion of blood between us and with it, I gained the Hall of Records stored on your DNA. You just updated the record in the reconstitution chamber and now I have your blood flowing through my veins. It will only take an hour or two before the whole record stored on your DNA will be transferred and recorded on my own DNA."

"But didn't your people keep their own record, even after Atlantis departed?"

"That we did, Barton Stauffer," Enoch acknowledged. "I am looking forward to reviewing how closely your record of humanity matches our own. I have much to learn from it."

"By the way, Barton Stauffer," Enoch added. "You were right."

"Right, sir?" Stauffer asked. "Right about what?"

"The evolution of language. While you have been down here maintaining custody of the history of mankind, the languages of mankind have been rapidly evolving on the surface. They don't speak any languages today that you would recognize or understand. I have several linguists on my staff and they tell me that there have been no less than 1350 new, distinct languages that have appeared around the planet since the Decimation. One of the first tasks my people will have after you depart will be to update your excellent golden Rosetta Stone volumes. Without an addendum update, there wouldn't be anyone on the surface who could read and make sense of your historical record."

A benevolent smile crossed Enoch's face as he continued speaking, "And now, my friend, I seem to be holding you back from moving on and rejoining your family. Would you please extend my best to Kubal Golden One and Mā-Bel as well? I hope that we have opportunity to visit again soon." Looking over at Stauffer's desktop, he added, "Oh, and I have made arrangements for you to take it with you."

"Take it with me, sir?.... Take what with me?"

"Your bronze dodecahedron. I know how much it has come to mean to you, and.... after all.... it is symbolic of the true nature of the cosmos.... Goodbye, my friend."

Enoch wheeled about smartly and walked back across the room toward the far wall and disappeared through a portal outline that Stauffer hadn't noticed earlier. He was left there standing alone in the office once again. He stood there unmoving for several minutes, contemplating what had just transpired. Still somewhat in disbelief, he walked over to the desk and typed H-O-M-E on the keyboard, the password that General Goldwyn had given him long ago to use when it was time to leave. It was an easy password to remember. "Dorothy was absolutely right," Stauffer muttered aloud thoughtfully as he pondered finally rejoining his family. "There is no place like home."

The shimmering outline of the portal appeared to the side of the conference table wall. Stauffer looked around the office which had been his sanctuary.... and prison.... for so long. He turned to face the Goldwyn holographic image that was still standing there frozen near his desk.

"Well, goodbye, General Goldwyn.... Kubal Golden One," Stauffer reflected out loud. "I have enjoyed the pleasure of your company, and I look forward to seeing you again on the other side."

The Goldwyn hologram reset and came back to life. "Leaving now? Good. You have done well here, Barton. You ought to know that there is a small expedition of men and women up on the surface making their way towards the **X**, and I suspect that it won't be long before they find their way down here. I think that you ought to know that most of them appear to be descendents of staff members from the Repository, the Crypt, and the Hole, that emigrated to Virginia so long ago and left you, Bill, Ski, and Pete to finish up the engraving of golden History Quest volumes. They made their way here to Carlisle on foot, guided by the traditions of their forefathers that there is a labyrinth of tunnels and vaults buried deep beneath the ground. They just arrived at the **X** and have begun clearing away the debris that blocks access to the old elevator shaft down into the Repository. Are you sure that you wouldn't like to wait them out and greet them?"

Surprised by the sudden change of events, Stauffer thought about the offer for just a moment. But looking back at his family photos on his I-Love-Me wall, he responded, "No, sir, I think I'll just leave the place here for them to rediscover. I've already transferred responsibility for the Hall of Records over to Enoch and I definitely don't want to get on Methuselah's bad side. I don't think they need me here running interference at this point."

"I understand Barton. Do you mind if I ask you one last question before you leave?"

Stauffer was startled at the unexpected request. "Yes, sir, sure.... What do you want to know?"

"What have you learned from this experience?"

"Sir?"

"What have you learned, Barton? You were at the heart of all the work assembling the unabridged history of mankind, and after everyone left or died, you had another eight hundred and fifty years to review that history and think about it.... What did you learn from the experience? What is the most important take-away? I would be interested in hearing your perspective."

Stauffer paused to consider the Goldwyn hologram's question. There was so much that he had learned through it all. What was the most important thing he had learned? After a few moments he responded slowly, "Well, sir, I suppose that it's the insight that the only constant throughout history has been change. The societies of mankind and the earth itself have always been in a constant state of flux. Throughout Earth's history.... at least the parts that we had an opportunity to observe and survey...., there has never been anything close to a state of historical equilibrium. Everything was always changing.... adjusting.... evolving.... self-organizing. Change is what keeps the Earth alive as an ecosystem. At one time early on before everyone left, I thought that we were in a pleasant equilibrium because change on Earth occurred so slowly. But everything is incrementally changing — plate tectonics are constantly adjusting the relationship between the continents; global climate change results in ice ages, forestation, and desertification; rivers are formed and then disappear again; mountains are raised high into the air and continental land masses sink back into the sea. The Earth topside today bears little resemblance to the Earth I knew in my earlier lifetime, and that in turn bore little resemblance to the Earth of earlier eras and epochs."

"Is that all, Barton?"

"No, sir. Mankind changes too. During the periods of time we monitored, I observed man at his very worst.... and at his very best. As a race, we have the capacity for horrendous acts of violence, rapacity, and depravity.... and we also have the capacity for great love, kindness, and compassion..... They have seemed to balance out through the millennia. Through it all, mankind has proven pretty resilient. We managed to make adjustments over time.... and survived.... at some points in the historical record.... we have even prospered and flourished. Down through the ages, there have been many who have tried to dominate and enslave.... driven by hate, selfishness, and ruthlessness.... but in the end, I suppose that the greater force.... perhaps mankind's greatest virtues.... have been love...., and self-sacrifice...., and service to others."

The Goldwyn hologram smiled. "That's not a bad start, Barton. Those are profound insights. I'm looking forward to sitting down with you in person very soon and debriefing you. I would like to hear more about your thoughts on the matter. I'll see you soon on the other side." The holographic image of Goldwyn abruptly froze again and then faded away, leaving Stauffer standing there alone once again in the solitude of the office.

Stauffer looked up at the shimmering outline of the portal next to the wall and then turned and walked over to the bookcase on the opposite wall. He ran his fingers lovingly over the covers of the books shelved there. The books had become his devoted friends and companions throughout the years. The covers on the books were in a sad state of repair. Most of them had started to fall apart. The pages of many of them now crumbled at his touch. He surveyed the titles on the spines of the books. He had read all of them, some of them many times over, and he paused a brief moment as if to say goodbye. Then he turned and walked over to his desk and sat down one last time. He picked up the jar of blue ringwoodite crystals and turned it over in his hands. The crystals cascaded over each other, producing a million shards of sparkling blue light reflected from the ceiling lights high above his desk. He set the jar back down on the corner of the desk and picked up the small glass display case with the two golden nuggets that Zazworsky had picked up at Tiahuanaco that had fallen from the sky as Manco Capac and Mama Ocllo had passed by overhead. He reflected back on his visit to Cuzco with General Goldwyn and the alcove set in the vault wall deep beneath the ancient city that contained hundreds of thousands of such nuggets, the sweat of the Sun. Stauffer smiled and set the display case back down. He picked up the golden dodecahedron in his right hand and the bronze dodecahedron in the other and held them out in front of him. For him, they held the key to the mysteries of the universe. He stood and turned them over in his hands one last time, and then slipped each into the cargo pockets of his jumpsuit.

Pushing his chair back, he stood to face his I-Love-Me wall where all of his professional memorabilia hung, the plaques and certificates and pictures and mementos that served as reminders of all the assignments he had had during his military career. He walked over and looked closely at an 8x10 photo of his old staff in the Crypt. They were all dressed in period costumes at a staff Halloween party held long ago. He smiled as he recalled a thousand interactions with them and how much he had come to rely on them during their adventures in the ancient past.

Stauffer had recovered family pictures, framed 8x10s, from his old home in North Middleton and hung photos of his wife, Gwen, and the five Cs: Cameron, Crystal, Colin, Carlee, and Corbie, in a special grouping on the wall. The photos were all faded and yellow with age now, and some had started to crumble on the edges. It reminded Stauffer again of how much time had passed. He missed them all so much! He had stared at their pictures every day of his interment here in the Hole, sometimes for hours on end. Now, at last, he was leaving to join them, and he felt a profound sense of urgency in moving on.

After a few minutes of deep contemplation, Stauffer girded himself up for what might lie ahead. With a look of resolve and determination on his face, he turned his back on the desk and the book shelves and his I-Love-Me wall and moved over to face the outline of the portal. He picked up his staff that was leaning against the conference table. He surprised himself by singing a little tune, "Happy Birthday to me, Happy Birthday to me...." and stepped through the portal.

Stauffer found himself standing back on the high Peruvian *altiplano* near Lake Titicaca, looking across about twenty meters of rough, uneven terrain at the stone cliff of Hayu Marca. The sun was to his rear and it shown over his shoulder at an angle that clearly outlined the Puerta de Hayu Marca carved into the face of the cliff. Stauffer looked around at the rock formations that dotted the landscape for a brief moment. For him, this was one of the most fascinating places on the planet.

He started moving methodically toward the stone portal, picking his way through the rocks and rubble, using his staff to maintain his balance on the uneven ground. He stopped just a few feet from the face of the solid stone portal cut in the cliff. He looked down at the small indented alcove carved into the face of the portal and then pulled the golden dodecahedron from his jumpsuit pocket. He stood there, almost in a moment of indecision, and then carefully, expectantly, he placed the dodecahedron on the thin ledge of the alcove cut into the stone portal, orienting it precisely as it had been oriented by General Goldwyn so many years ago. Then he stepped back and waited.

There was an almost imperceptible whirring sound and the surface of the stone door became translucent, emanating a soft blue, radiant energy. Stauffer stood there transfixed by the light, uncertain of what to do next. As he stared at the portal, he was startled to see General Goldwyn moving through the gateway toward him. Goldwyn was dressed in a long white robe wrapped around him and girded at his waist with a blue sash. He seemed much younger looking than he remembered him. Goldwyn stepped forward and embraced Stauffer with a hearty *abrazo*. "It's about time you showed up here, Barton. I was beginning to wonder if you would ever get here."

"Really, sir?"

"No, Barton. I'm sorry, but I exaggerated and I was being a little sarcastic. It actually seems like I've only been here a few short moments and here you are coming through the portal right on my tail."

"A few short moments, sir? It's been almost 900 years by my count."

"That may be true for you, Barton, but time works in a different way on the other side of the portal. It's kind of hard to explain. Ah, I know.... Do you remember the old adage that 'time is what keeps everything from happening all at once'? Well, on the other side of the portal, it's pretty much.... timeless. Time, as the fourth dimension, functions in a different way and from a different perspective in the dimensional reality there. It takes a little while getting used to...." Goldwyn paused thoughtfully and then laughed. "Actually, Barton, it doesn't take any time at all."

Goldwyn was chatting lightheartedly, obviously glad to see Stauffer again. But his demeanor changed, and he became more somber and serious. "900 years! Was it hard for you, Barton? Was my AI hologram helpful to work your way through the loneliness of the passage of time? I was worried that I hadn't done enough to prep you for it and buoy you up through the long years."

"Yes, sir, you did well. It has been an extraordinary experience. I was lonely.... painfully lonely, for much of the time. I have missed Gwen and the kids most of all. But conversations with your hologram helped immensely."

"I can understand that, Barton. A devoted family man passing nine hundred years without his family can be a most painful experience. I know.... I passed through that separation experience part of the time myself early in my deployment on the stay-behind team. But I can imagine that the reunion with your family will be joyous for you. But, remember, from their perspective, it has only been a short moment since they arrived on the other side. It is you who has had to suffer through the passage of time."

"They're all waiting for me on the other side of the portal.... Gwen and the Five Cs?"

"Yes, Barton. I asked them to wait there at the portal until I could escort you through. Are you ready for that next big step?"

Stauffer suddenly had a look of panic on his face. "But I've gotten so old.... They may not recognize me.... They may not want anything to do with this old man!"

"I wouldn't worry about that at all, Barton," Goldwyn chuckled. "That will all sort itself out as you pass through the portal. It is a.... rejuvenating experience."

Stauffer looked deeply into General Goldwyn's eyes and replied earnestly, "Well then, yes, sir,.... I believe I am ready to go."

General Goldwyn beamed and took Stauffer by the arm. "Good, then, Barton Stauffer, let's get a move on." Goldwyn guided him up to the portal and, together, the two men passed through. As they disappeared into the blue light, it immediately began to diminish until all that was left was the solid stone door cut into the face of the cliff with the golden dodecahedron resting in the small alcove in the center of the portal.

The iridescent outline of another time portal opened up almost immediately in the rocky field directly in front of the stone door and Capac, the shopkeeper from the Cuzco Plaza de Armas, stepped out and picked up the golden dodecahedron in his right hand. Turning to face the portal behind him, he tossed the dodecahedron gently into the air and caught it again, and then, with a smile and look of satisfaction on his bronzed, weathered face, he stepped back through the portal and disappeared, leaving the Hayu Marca plateau once again in splendid solitude.

# Epilogue

*An Alternate Interdimensionality, Timeless.*

Barton Stauffer reclined on a blanket laid out on an immense expanse of manicured grass next to his beloved wife, Gwen. True to Goldwyn's word, Gwen and the Five Cs had been waiting for him directly on the other side of the portal and it had been a glorious reunion. For Gwen and the children, it had seemed like just moments earlier that General Goldwyn had transported them from the airliner jet way where they were loading the plane at LAX and transported them here to this place. After they passed through the portal, Gwen found a handwritten note on the ground from General Goldwyn telling her that he would be along shortly to explain to them what had just happened to them. As they stood there, several other groups of people appeared through portals arrayed around the field. Almost immediately, General Goldwyn and his wife Mā-Bel appeared as they came through another portal that opened up on the field just a few meters away from Gwen and the children.

After they got introductions out of the way, Goldwyn excused himself, saying that he would get Stauffer and that he would be right back. He reentered the portal that he had just come through and within seconds, he came back leading a much bewildered Stauffer.

Gwen was at first alarmed to see how greatly her husband had aged. When he came through the portal with General Goldwyn, he appeared to be a very old man. When Stauffer told her that, for him, it had been almost nine hundred years since he had last seen her, she wept openly as they collapsed together in a firm embrace. But as they stood there, the years seemed to melt away and, within moments, Stauffer's features morphed into a much younger version of himself in the prime of life. For his part, Stauffer hadn't felt so good, so complete, so fulfilled in years.

Goldwyn had been right about time. It didn't seem to play out here as it did on the other side of the portal in their previous life. On the other side, time's arrow flowed forward in just one direction and demarcated life's events in linear, sequential fashion. Here, as General Goldwyn had tried to explain, everything seemed to happen all at once. Time, as the fourth dimension, didn't really seem to have the same application here in this strange and delightful place.

And so, Stauffer settled in, reacquainting himself with his family. It was a wonderful reunion. All the years of loneliness crumbled away and were lost in a distant reality that no longer seemed relevant.

And then, General Goldwyn walked up to where Stauffer and Gwen lay on the grass conversing. "Barton, I'm sorry to interrupt but I've just received a telepathic impression that we need to go back to the other side to consult with Enoch. Something has happened."

"Go back, sir? But I just got here."

"I know it seems that way, but we've really got to go back. We simply can't converse with Enoch from here. The difference in time perspective creates too great of a disconnect."

Turning to Gwen, Goldwyn said apologetically, "I'll have him back here with you before you know it, Gwen."

Gwen smiled and gave Stauffer a gentle push. "Sounds like you've got some business to attend to, Barton. Don't be long."

Stauffer got to his feet and asked Goldwyn, "How do we go back? I thought that you said that coming here was essentially a one-way trip?"

"It usually is. Enoch has apparently received a special dispensation for us go back for the moment."

"Do you know what it's all about?"

"I don't have any idea, Barton. At this point, all I have is the impression that we need to step through the portal to consult with Enoch."

"What portal, sir?"

As Stauffer spoke, the shimmering outline of a portal appeared to the side of them, surrounding an iridescent panel of soft blue light. "Here's our ride," General Goldwyn observed. "We better be moving, Barton."

Goldwyn stepped through the portal with Stauffer right behind him. As they emerged on the other side, they found themselves once again on the Hayu Marca Plateau. Down the hill on the rock-strewn path below them stood Capac, the last in the long line of custodians of the Inca royal lineage. Capac hadn't appeared to age. He looked almost exactly the same as he had when Stauffer had first met him in the Cuzco Plaza de Armas shop, except that Capac had now tied a long piece of torn white cloth around his head. There appeared to be flecks of red on the cloth. Stauffer observed that it looked a lot like blood stains.

As the blue portal faded away, Goldwyn turned and retrieved the golden dodecahedron from the alcove and walked down the hill. He greeted Capac with a warm *abrazo*. "Capac, it's good to see you again, my friend." Goldwyn paused and then asked awkwardly, "How much time has passed since we last brought Colonel Stauffer through the portal?"

"Over sixty years, Kubal Golden one. Much has happened. The world is in a bad way."

"Is that why Enoch summoned us?"

"I would imagine so, my friend. Enoch communicated to me to come and open the portal and then leave you two here by yourselves to converse with him alone. Summon me with your mind when you are ready to go back, and I will return with the key."

Goldwyn transferred the dodecahedron to Capac's outstretched hand. As Capac picked his way back down the hill, he passed through the outline of the portal and disappeared. As he was lost to view, another much larger portal appeared off to the side and Enoch came striding through almost immediately. Goldwyn stepped forward to greet his brother and took Enoch's outstretched hand in his own. "I appreciate your coming back, Brother. I have need of your services."

Goldwyn looked perplexed. "I can't imagine what could be going on here that requires our help."

"Let me sum it up in one word.... Garash."

"Garash?" Goldwyn questioned. "Barton took care of him before he left. Garash is entombed in a crust of solid gold, encased in a stone sarcophagus, buried in millions of tons of reinforced concrete. It's a pretty secure prison. How can he be a problem now for you?"

"Yes, I've reviewed the history files." Nodding to Stauffer, Enoch continued, "Barton Stauffer, you did admirable work on that mission. You put Garash away for almost a thousand years."

"But," Stauffer interrupted, "are you implying that Garash has escaped?"

"Unfortunately, I am. You entombed Garash's sarcophagus in the great cement dam back almost a thousand years ago. The dam held up well during all the intervening centuries. But, after a thousand years of neglect with no one maintaining it, the structure began to suffer the effects of old age as weathering and minor movements of the earth began to open up cracks in the great structure. Then, thirty years ago, a major earthquake in the area, split the dam wide open revealing its interior structure. As luck would have it, the schism created in the cement opened up right to where the sarcophagus was entombed and it broke free. It tumbled down the face of the great dam, breaking open into small pieces at the bottom of the canyon on the rocks below. Garash's body was thrown free, and the golden casting that covered his body was shattered and fell away. Garash lay there at the bottom of the canyon for several days recovering his strength as his body regenerated, and then he got to his feet and made his way out of the canyon."

"Why didn't you eliminate him right there before he could cause any trouble?" Stauffer interjected.

"We didn't discover that he had escaped until almost a year later," Enoch said, "when we detected his influence in raising high levels of unrest among populations of people in several parts of the globe. That creature has an evil streak in him. He has become the leader of the Resistance."

"The Resistance?" Goldwyn asked.

"Yes, Brother." Enoch responded. "After we returned with Atlantis, we enjoyed a relatively peaceful world for over nine hundred years. But since Garash's escape, the world's population has divided into two camps, the forces for good and the forces for the Dark Side."

"The Dark Side?" Stauffer said with a smirk. "Isn't that *Star Wars* jargon?"

"Yes it is, Barton Stauffer. It was a storyline that we carefully planted with the George Lucas writing team to provide the people of earth with a mental construct for understanding the true nature of the cosmos. There are essentially just two sides of things in the multiverse.... the good side, which Lucas referred to as 'the Force', and the evil side, which he labeled 'the Dark Side.' Lucas got it pretty much right in his movies. In actuality, throughout the cosmos, on a hundred million different planets, it has played out pretty much the same. Sentient beings have tended to gravitate toward one or the other of these two camps. But you can't have both. It may be surprising to you but, over time, it proves out that there isn't a lot of gray area between the two extremes. There is a natural field attractor that tugs you toward one or the other. In the end, there is no middle ground."

Goldwyn spoke up, "Are you saying, Enoch, that all of the surviving peoples of Earth are dividing into warring camps and are preparing to go to battle?"

"Not exactly, Kubal Golden One. They have been engaged in bloody, armed conflict for some time.... almost 30 years now on a global scale. The survivors of those conflicts are beginning to gather together for what appears will be one great final battle."

Stauffer had been busy internalizing all of the new information and was trying unsuccessfully to make sense of it all. "What is it, sir, that you need us to do? Why have you summoned us here today?"

"Well, Barton Stauffer, I believe that the outcome of the final battle is certain.... the forces of the Dark Side will be soundly defeated. However, I am less certain about Garash. He is a slippery creature and just as likely to escape and live to foment more hatred, death, and unhappiness another day. I would like you to help us deal with Garash and put him out of commission once and for all."

"What could I possibly do?" Stauffer asked.

"I have sent many brave men against Garash already. He has slain some and wounded others. But at the first indication that he is at a fighting disadvantage, he simply uses his temporal capability to jump out of there to escape. Garash knows you. You are the only man who has ever engaged Garash directly in hand-to-hand combat and come out the winner. You are the one who entombed him in a block of gold in the stone sarcophagus and put him away in the cement dam for almost a thousand years. It stands to reason that he has a profound hatred for you. When he sees you coming at him on the battlefield, we believe he won't use his temporal capability to flee. On the contrary, I believe that he will rush toward you with a fierce vengeance. His hatred for you will blind him to the danger."

Stauffer tried to follow Enoch's logic trail, but he still didn't quite understand his intent. "You want to use me as.... a decoy....

in the battle to distract Garash so that you can kill him before he temporally jumps?"

"Not quite, Barton Stauffer," Enoch responded. "I want you to confront Garash in direct combat and, if the opportunity somehow presents itself, kill him outright. But as a minimum, we need you to distract him long enough so that my scout teams can move in and kill him. The ongoing wars are a thing of this generation of humankind, and it isn't really incumbent upon us to intervene. But Garash **is** a product of my generation, and we must accept accountability for him and responsibility for putting him away. And so, simply stated, Barton Stauffer, understand that we need your assistance to get the job done."

Goldwyn stood off to the side listening intently to the conversation between Enoch and Stauffer, shifting from one foot to the other in obvious discomfort with the direction the conversation had turned.

"Kill Garash?" Stauffer exclaimed. "Just what do you want me to do to play into that?"

"I don't know what to tell you, Barton Stauffer. Based on the records I've read about your previous ingenious plans of attack in the past, I expect that you'll come up with an effective plan for dealing with Garash."

Goldwyn broke into the conversation, "Enoch, my brother, you can't expect Barton to confront Garash all by himself. That might end up being a suicide mission."

Enoch responded, "You are right Kubal Golden One. We would not leave Barton Stauffer to face Garash alone." Turning to Stauffer, he continued, "Here are two members of my primary staff who will act as your seconds and liaison support. They will have telepathic communication with all of my back-up forces."

Enoch turned his head in the direction of his portal and two figures emerged, Smathers and Melek. They were both dressed in simple white robes and each had a white scarf tied around his forehead. They both approached Stauffer and saluted. Smathers commented, "Colonel Stauffer, it is a pleasure to work this mission under your command."

Melek said, "Barton Stauffer, it is very good to see you again. I owe you much!" Melek was obviously overjoyed to see Stauffer and he smiled broadly.

Enoch continued, "I am offering all of the support you might require, but you have the lead here, Barton Stauffer. How do you want to do this?"

As Stauffer realized that Enoch was entirely serious, he paused to consider his options. "Would you give me a moment to think about this, sir?"

"Take all the time you need, Barton Stauffer. But not too much time. We really need to get back to the battle at hand."

"Roger that, sir.... A couple of questions, sir.... Have you tried to track Garash as he makes his temporal jumps? Is he still just moving forward in time, and does he still remain in the same place when he reappears?"

"Yes to both questions," Smathers interjected. "On the battlefield, he generally makes short leaps of only a couple of hours each, but that has proven sufficient thus far to remove him from harm's way. What do you have in mind, Barton Stauffer?"

"Well, if he only makes jumps of a couple hours or so and he doesn't change positions, then why don't we just allow him to jump, but when he reappears, we'll have set a trap in place to immobilize him so that we can dispatch him once and for all."

"A trap?" Enoch questioned. "What kind of trap, Barton Stauffer?"

"I'm not sure yet, sir. There are a number of possibilities. We need something that will temporarily immobilize him.... Wait....sir...., do you still have Nicola Tesla on your staff?"

"Tesla? Why yes, I believe so. He has been leapfrogging through time like most of my staff since he returned from his assignment on the stay-behind team. But he has almost run through his life line. He doesn't have much time left."

"I won't need him for much time. Could you get him here fast, sir? I need to ask him a couple of questions."

Enoch nodded to Smathers, who stepped back through the portal and disappeared. Almost instantaneously, he reappeared with another man following right behind him. Smathers stepped up to Stauffer, gesturing to the other man, and said, "Barton Stauffer, please meet Tesla."

Tesla extended his hand and shook Stauffer's energetically. "I am pleased to meet you at last, Barton Stauffer. I have heard many good things about you. How can I help?"

Although Stauffer was in awe of being in the presence of the great scientist, he got right to the point. "It is good for me to meet you, sir. I need to know if it is possible to use an electrical or magnetic field in some way to attenuate temporal energy."

"Yes, Barton Stauffer. That should be possible. In fact, most of our temporal technology has special circuitry installed to eliminate the effects of stray static electricity or magnetic anomalies. After Kubal Golden One's aircraft crashed near Roswell, I personally investigated what might have gone wrong and it turned out to be a defective circuit. The magnetic anomalies out there in the desert near Roswell disrupted the temporal controls and brought the craft down."

"Okay. Got it. That leads to the next question. Do you think you could build some kind of a large, sturdy, steel or iron cage, maybe fifteen or twenty feet on a side, top and bottom, with the capacity to generate such a field and attenuate temporal energy in the same way? What we're going to try to do is to trap Garash in the cage so that he can't jump temporally out of it."

"I'm sure that I can do it.... but it will take some time."

"We don't have any time from what Enoch tells me. We'll need to do a temporal compression. What I want you to do is go back into the past and build the cage. When you have it ready, put it into position to move to the battlefield at the time and place I tell you. I need the cage ready to go in about five minutes. Can you do that, sir?"

Tesla smiled as he considered the time compression element that Stauffer was suggesting. "Yes, Barton Stauffer. It will be ready to go."

"Good. Colonel Smathers will work as our liaison and provide you the temporal coordinates for when and where to move the cage. Make sure that you can remotely initiate the cage's field and turn it on and off at your command. I suggest you get to work, sir."

Tesla nodded and turned and quickly disappeared through the portal at his back.

"Okay, Barton," Goldwyn said. "You've got the trap. How are you going to bait it?"

"Oh, sir, I think that's obvious. I'm going to need to be the bait." Turning back to Enoch, he asked, "Do you suppose, sir that it would be possible for someone on your staff to return to my old office and retrieve the 45 caliber pistol in my desk drawer? There are extra boxes of bullets there in the drawer as well. I'll need both clips filled with seven cartridges each."

Melek responded without being asked, "Sir, I will do that gladly. Melek turned and practically ran through the portal. He returned after just seconds, carrying the pistol and the clips in his enormous hands. Are these what you wanted, Barton Stauffer? You don't know how hard it was to load those tiny cartridges in the clips. My fingers are way too big."

Stauffer laughed and accepted the pistol and clips from Melek, slapping him on the back. "You are a good man, Melek. Thank you."

Turning back to face Enoch and General Goldwyn, Stauffer continued, "Okay, so here's my plan. I'll go to that area of the battlefield where Garash is operating. I'll need to wear some kind of body armor. I'll keep the 45 out of sight under my robe. When I see Garash, I will yell at him from across the field and challenge him to battle. If he hates me as much as you seem to think, he will take the bait. As Garash closes ground with me, I'll pull out the 45 and make as if to fire at him. If necessary, I'll pull off a couple of rounds at his extremities to let him know his life is in peril. If he feels at all threatened, he'll make the jump. That's when we need to have Smathers work with Tesla to position the cage in the exact place on the battlefield where Garash jumps from. When he reappears, he will be inside of the cage. At that point, Tesla needs to flip the toggle switch to turn on the juice and attenuate any temporal energy that Garash could generate to jump again. That should keep him confined in the cage."

Enoch was fascinated by the simplicity of Stauffer's plan. "How do you propose to dispense with Garash once we have him confined in the cage?"

"I haven't gotten that far yet, sir," Stauffer answered. "I hoped that you might have an idea. We know from past experience with Garash's doppelganger that it's possible to blow him up into pieces so small that he can't regenerate. Do you have another idea that might work?"

Enoch responded, "We have been considering about the same thing, except that we couldn't figure out how to get Garash to hold still long enough while we did it. In fact, we tried it once, but

Garash simply jumped microseconds in front of the explosive blast that would have done him in. I think you just might have found the final solution here."

"With Garash contained," Stauffer asked, "how do you think we can blow him up while still limiting collateral damage to the good guys out there in the near vicinity on the battlefield?"

Enoch responded, "I think we could put three scout aircraft up into the air over the battlefield and when Garash appears in the cage, they can triangulate in on him, hitting him simultaneously from three different directions with high energy beams. There should be more than sufficient power to rip him to shreds, and the triangulation should keep the blast focused and contained."

"That should do the job. Let's do it, sir," Stauffer said. "When do you want to get started?"

"I think we have almost all of the elements of the plan in place," Enoch responded. "Smathers just messaged me that Tesla has the cage ready. The three scout aircraft have already scrambled and they are already in position in the air over the battlefield. And I just got the latest Intel update of where Garash is located. I think we are good to go."

Melek had disappeared again but reappeared back through the portal carrying the same Kevlar vest that had protected Garner Wilson so many years earlier during the Flight 2666 interdiction mission. "Here, Barton Stauffer, I remembered where you had this stored down in the Repository. I believe it is still.... serviceable. You are going to need it to protect yourself on the battlefield."

"Once again, Melek, I am in your debt," Stauffer said. "Thank you."

Melek beamed at being able to help out. As Stauffer slipped into the Kevlar vest, Enoch stepped forward and drew a long white scarf from his robe pocket. He wrapped the scarf around Stauffer's head and tied it in a firm knot on the side. "You are going to need this on the battlefield, Barton Stauffer."

Enoch looked at Goldwyn and then back at Stauffer. "I think we are ready to launch."

\* \* \* \* \* \* \* \* \* \* \* \* \* \* \* \* \* \* \* \*

Stauffer looked around him where he had materialized on the battlefield. He was surprised to see that most of the combatants in the near vicinity on both sides were armed with swords and spears and shields....low tech weaponry. As he scanned the close-in battle lines, he saw heaps of bloody bodies piled up on top of one another. Everywhere he turned, he saw more stacked-up piles of bodies. The mortality rate on this battlefield was exceedingly high.

There wasn't any evidence of automatic weapons, tanks, artillery, or high performance aircraft that he had been used to seeing on the modern battlefield during his own lifetime. What surprised him most was the nature of the combatants themselves. This wasn't a battle between warring factions of warriors, protecting their wives and families who were well back of the forward lines. Their wives and children all stood together with the men right there on the battlefield, all massed together. Their bodies made up the heaps of carnage piled everywhere in equal numbers with the men. This was indeed a final war of attrition. Stauffer didn't detect any discernible uniforms. Each side distinguished itself simply with a scarf tied high around their heads. The warriors for good wore a white scarf and the Dark Side warriors wore a black scarf.

Smathers had selected a position on the battlefield that was relatively free from active combat operations, but there was heavy fighting on both flanks less than three hundred meters away. Stauffer walked forward several hundred steps until he stood on the crest of a small knoll from which he could survey the entire battlefield close by. He scanned the horizon for a glimpse of Garash but didn't see him immediately. And then, Stauffer spied him standing on the edge of a small group of black-scarved soldiers, waving his arms and pointing in the direction of another group of combatants wearing white scarves.

With his target located, Stauffer girded himself for the confrontation ahead and ran down the other side of the knoll across the battlefield in the direction of Garash, yelling at the top of his lungs. He had run several hundred meters before Garash detected his voice among the clamor and tumult of the battlefield and turned to gaze in Stauffer's direction. When he recognized who it was, Garash stepped away from the protection of the group of soldiers he was with and started moving in Stauffer's direction. After a few tentative steps, Garash started running as well. He had shed his boots and was running on his goat hooves. It surprised Stauffer how fast he was able to move toward him. Stauffer withdrew his 45 from his robe pocket and began waving it so Garash could see that he had it. Garash ignored the threat and continued racing directly toward him.

When Stauffer realized that Garash would not be deterred, he began squeezing off rounds in Garash's direction aiming at his arms and legs. Two of the first four rounds were direct hits in Garash's legs, but it didn't seem to slow him down significantly. Stauffer could see where the bullets hit, but the wounds seemed to close almost instantaneously. Now, Garash and Stauffer were separated by just thirty meters and closing very fast. Stauffer was beginning to panic. The plan called for him to convince Garash to make a temporal jump, and it didn't appear that Garash had any intention of doing so. Stauffer raised the 45 higher and pointed at Garash's center of mass. He squeezed off the remaining three rounds in the clip rapid fire. All three were direct hits in his chest, but Garash didn't seem to be affected by them. As he reached Stauffer, he grabbed him by his gun arm and jerked hard, pulling it out of his shoulder socket. Stauffer dropped to the ground and lay there at Garash's feet writhing in pain. Smathers appeared through a portal twenty meters to Garash's left front and pointed a shoulder-mounted grenade launcher in his direction. With Stauffer lying on the ground, Smathers thought that he had a clear shot that might force Garash to jump. As he pulled the trigger, Garash reached down with one hand, scooped Stauffer up, and held him close in to his own body with his arm wrapped around Stauffer's neck. As the grenade rapidly closed in on Garash and Stauffer in a short, looping trajectory, Garash finally jumped temporally and disappeared from view, taking Stauffer with him. The grenade exploded harmlessly in the void.

Smathers telepathically messaged Enoch immediately. "He's jumped, but he managed to take Barton Stauffer with him. I've sent the coordinates to Tesla to drop the cage into place, but when Garash rematerializes inside the cage, he'll have Colonel Stauffer still with him. How do you want to proceed? Colonel Stauffer is at grave risk if we continue with our original plan."

Goldwyn interrupted the telepathic transmission. "Smathers, is Barton still armed?"

"No, sir. After he emptied the clip into Garash, he dropped the weapon when Garash dislocated his shoulder."

"Smathers, I know that you are an expert with hand-held weapons. Are you armed?"

"No, sir. I am not."

"Then we're going to have to improvise. I want you to temporally transport into the cage where Garash and Stauffer are going to rematerialize and find Stauffer's 45. We're going to send you another full clip. I want you to position yourself so that you can empty the full clip into Garash without hitting Colonel Stauffer. Understand?"

"Yes, sir. What then?"

"We're going to send you a full clip of hollow point bullets. I think that the first clip was filled with full metal jacket ball ammunition, and the bullets just went right through Garash without doing much damage. He regenerated practically immediately. The hollow points should do significant damage and put him down on the ground long enough for you to move Colonel Stauffer off to the side. We'll turn off the Tesla grid on the cage and bring you through a portal to get you both out of there. Then, we'll reactivate the cage and send in the scout aircraft with the energy beam weapons to finish the job on Garash. Understand?"

"Yes, sir. Do we have any idea how far into the future Garash might have jumped?"

Enoch broke in. "No, Smathers. We do not. You are just going to have to hunker down and remain vigilant. I've got five members of my team monitoring the area. We'll send you a telepathic notification as soon as we detect anything."

Goldwyn added, "You are going to need to be outside Garash's range of vision when he first appears so that you can pull off a couple of rounds before he detects you and can maneuver to respond. Once he discovers that he can't temporally jump, there's no telling what he will do. Once Colonel Stauffer is clear, put as many rounds as you can into Garash's head. That should stop him for a moment."

\* \* \* \* \* \* \* \* \* \* \* \* \* \* \* \* \* \* \* \* \*

Smathers carefully scouted the terrain where he had seen Garash disappear with Stauffer in tow. He found a pool of blood on the ground, probably Stauffer's, from where Garash had ripped his arm part way off. The 45 pistol was laying on the ground nearby. Once he had determined the location where Garash would rematerialize, he tried to visualize exactly where Garash had been looking as he disappeared. He moved to a location where Garash wouldn't immediately see him when he rematerialized and where he would have a clean shot without endangering Stauffer. He received a telepathic impression from Goldwyn that a new clip was on the way, and he saw the clip in a plastic bag materialize on the ground in front of him. Smathers pulled the clip from the bag and inserted it into the pistol. He pulled back on the slide and locked a round in the chamber. He smiled grimly. He had just seven opportunities to bring Garash down. He hoped that it would be enough.

* * * * * * * * * * * * * * * * * * * *

Smathers hunkered down and waited. He hoped that Garash would make just a short jump and rematerialize within the next few hours. One hour passed. Two hours. Then three. After almost four hours, the sun was beginning to go down and it was starting to get dark. The noise of the great battle tapered off as the stars began to appear in the sky. Smathers assumed that the combatants had moved to bivouac positions to rest up to continue the battle the next morning. After so many hours on his feet, Smathers felt the effects of insufficient rest. His eyelids drooped. Then, he got a strong telepathic impression from Enoch to be alert. With a start, he opened his eyes fully and saw the silhouette of Garash against the skyline reemerge onto the battlefield. Almost immediately, Smathers saw the iron cage appear around them. Garash dropped Stauffer to the ground and attempted to make a temporal jump. Nothing. Tesla had done his work well. Garash wasn't going anywhere.

Smathers pulled back the hammer and fired three quick rounds into Garash's back and side. The hollow points literally ripped off both of Garash's arms. Smathers fired two additional rounds into Garash's upper chest and neck, doing much additional damage. Garash was now enraged and swiveled around, charging Smathers. He jumped into the air and knocked the 45 from his hand and continued stomping Smathers with his cloven hooves. With Garash's attention focused entirely on Smathers, Stauffer crawled slowly across the broken terrain, moving in the direction of his 45 just a few feet away on the ground. When he finally reached it, he wrapped the fingers of his good left hand tightly around the pistol grip and pointed upward, pulling off a quick two-round burst into the underside of Garash's chin, completely blowing away the top of his head. Garash reeled backward and crumbled to the ground. Stauffer dropped the 45 and crawled to his knees. He grasped the bleeding, unconscious Smathers with his good left hand and lifted him up. When they were both somewhat upright, Stauffer hobbled over to the side of the cage, trying to put distance between them and Garash. When he was about ten feet away, he sent a telepathic message to Goldwyn, "Beam us up, Scotty."

A portal appeared immediately to their side and Melek rushed through into the iron cage to assist Stauffer and Smathers getting back through the portal. As soon as the portal closed, three of Enoch's scout aircraft appeared in the night sky over the battle field and focused high energy beams on Garash's prostrate body. The combined effect of the energy beams caused a tremendous explosion and left the ground surrounding the area in a molten mass of vitrified rock. Garash was completely disintegrated in the blast.

\* \* \* \* \* \* \* \* \* \* \* \* \* \* \* \* \* \* \* \*

"Well, how are you feeling, Barton Stauffer?" Enoch asked. "You've suffered quite a bit of trauma."

Stauffer looked up from the reconstitution chamber where he lay and smiled weakly. He reached up with his left hand and rubbed his right shoulder. It felt whole and fully functional. Stauffer moved to sit up and swing his legs over to the side of the chamber to stand up. "I seem to be good as new, sir. How long have I been out?"

"About three days, my friend."

"My plan.... did my plan work.... did we terminate Garash? Is he gone?"

"Yes, Barton Stauffer. You did away with Garash. He will trouble the world no more."

"What about the final battle? Is it still raging on?"

"Now that's the interesting part, Barton Stauffer. As soon as Garash was destroyed, most of the forces wearing the black scarves shed them on the ground during the night and surrendered themselves to the white forces at the break of dawn. Apparently, Garash had some kind of hypnotic power over them. Once he was out of the way, they came to their senses. The great wars of the End

Times are fast drawing to a close. You have saved a lot of people a great deal of pain and heartache."

"Where is General Goldwyn?" Stauffer asked in a panic, looking around. "Did he go back without me?"

"Not at all, Barton," Goldwyn spoke up behind him. "I'm right here. I've just been waiting for you to get back on your feet so that we could make the trek back home together. Do you feel well enough to travel?"

"Let me try standing up and see." Stauffer stood and attempted to walk across the room. He was still a little groggy and swayed slightly from side to side.

General Goldwyn laughed. "Well, I don't think you could pass the drug-alcohol field sobriety test by the side of the highway, but I'll bet that our friends here can help me get you to the portal to get you back home."

"Friends? Where, sir?"

As he spoke, Smathers and Melek stepped forward and greeted Stauffer.

"Hello Colonel Stauffer," Smathers said. "I understand I owe you my life. I thank you and my family thanks you. You are a most valued friend and ally."

"Hello Barton Stauffer," Melek interrupted. I am glad you are now awake. I brought you some ice cream and pizza to cheer you up."

\* \* \* \* \* \* \* \* \* \* \* \* \* \* \* \* \* \*

A portal opened up on the Hayu Marca plateau, and Enoch, Goldwyn, and Stauffer, stepped out onto the rock-strewn slope adjacent to the massive stone Puerta cut into the face of the cliff. Off to the side, the shimmering outline of a smaller portal appeared, and Capac emerged onto the plateau. He was still wearing the torn white sheet around his head. He stepped forward and handed the golden dodecahedron solemnly to Goldwyn and then stepped back to exit through the portal he had just come through.

"Wait, Capac," Enoch said. "Thank you for bringing the portal key. Please tell your people that the Travail is now past and you can remove your white scarves. Tell them to be happy and rejoice, for good has triumphed in the end.... Tell them that they are loved."

A broad smile crossed Capac's weathered, taciturn face. He nodded and stepped back through his portal and disappeared.

Enoch turned to Goldwyn and Stauffer. "And so my brothers, we part company once again. Barton Stauffer, I can see why Kubal Golden One valued and esteemed your contribution so much during all the years he worked with you. I, too, would like to express my profound esteem for your assistance in dealing with Garash. You demonstrated great courage and resourcefulness, and mankind is in your debt. Thank you."

Enoch took Stauffer's hand in his enormous grip and shook it. Enoch nodded to Goldwyn with a smile and then turned and walked back through the portal through which they had just arrived. As Enoch passed through, the outline of the portal dimmed and then vanished altogether.

"Well, Barton," Goldwyn commented, "seems like only just a moment ago we were standing here."

"Yes, sir. Just how much time has actually passed?"

"Almost a full week. We surely packed a lot of activity into that short amount of time," Goldwyn laughed. And then he became quite solemn and serious. "Barton, are you sure that your arm and shoulder are completely healed? It wouldn't do to have you go back grimacing in pain to greet Gwen."

"Won't passing back through the stone portal pretty much fix up anything left that needs fixing, sir?"

"That it will, lad.... that it will."

Goldwyn took the golden dodecahedron he had received from Capac and positioned it in the alcove and stepped back. The stone portal was engulfed in a soft blue light and Stauffer and Goldwyn stepped forward. As they entered into the light, they were met by Gwen and Mā-Bel with welcoming embraces. As they passed on through the portal, the blue light diminished and then went out altogether.

At the same moment, Capac reappeared through the portal at the bottom of the hill. He stepped gingerly up the path to the portal and retrieved the dodecahedron. Turning to the side, he carefully removed his white scarf headband and hung it on a outcropping on the cliff to the side of the stone portal. Then, smiling, he walked back down the path to the shimmering outline of his own portal and disappeared, leaving the plateau in eternal, peaceful silence.

Printed in the United States
By Bookmasters